MAKING MONSTERS

BERONIKA KERES

IMMORTAL
WOODS BOOKS

www.beronikakeres.com

Cover design by www.trifbookdesign.com

ISBN 978-1-7390443-2-9 (paperback)
ISBN 978-1-7390443-3-6 (hardcover)
ISBN 978-1-7390443-1-2 (ebook)

CONTENT WARNING

The Cracked Coffins series is a dark fantasy thriller series that explores the horrors of abusive relationships with a vampiric twist. This series is not a dark romance with a HEA, but a story of survival.

Making Monsters contains heavy subject matters and dark themes readers may find uncomfortable or triggering. Elements include, but are not limited to:

- **Violence:** Graphic violence, torture, gore, kidnapping, captivity, and confinement.

- **Abuse:** Domestic violence & abuse (emotional, physical, mental), reproductive coercion, and repeated sexual assault & rape.

- **Other Mature Content:** Morbid sexual content, and strong depictions of trauma & mental illness (PTSD, dissociation, grief, suicidal ideation).

Though much of the above content appears in previous books, the nature of the plot in *Making Monsters*, novel length, and the culmination of certain arcs, may make the content have a heavier emotional impact. Please keep this in mind before moving forward and remember your mental health matters.

Visit www.beronikakeres.com for detailed information and a full list of series triggers.

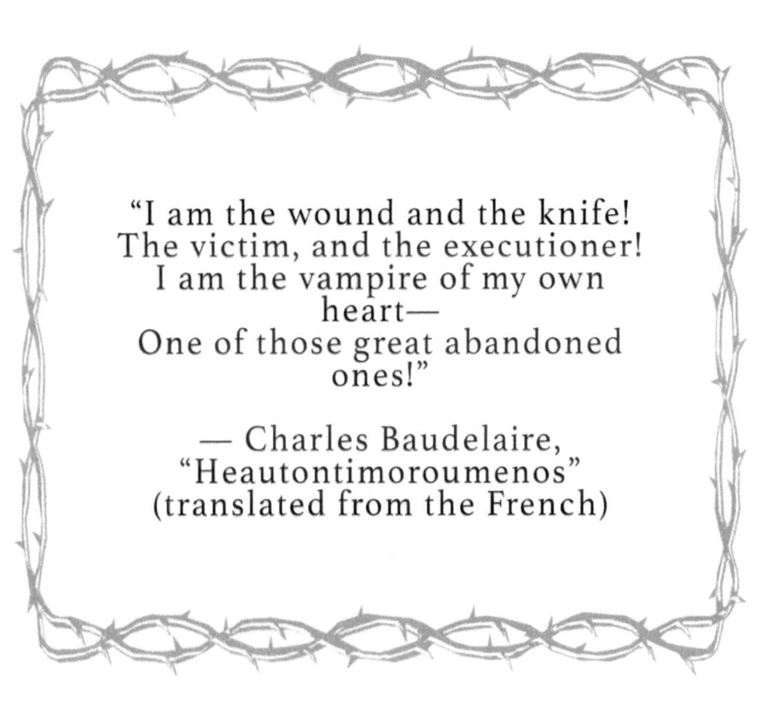

"I am the wound and the knife!
The victim, and the executioner!
I am the vampire of my own
heart—
One of those great abandoned
ones!"

— Charles Baudelaire,
"Heautontimoroumenos"
(translated from the French)

I

A golden death glows on the horizon. Through my tear-muddled gaze, the trees blur past the car window, our tires screaming down the snow-glazed highway. Mere minutes have passed since Viorel's veil over *The Castle that Never Was* fell, allowing Denendrius to escape with me before it sealed the castle off from the world again.

I remain curled up in the backseat of the car Denendrius forced me into during his escape, my hands clamped over my mouth in a poor attempt to hold back the wave of grief-induced nausea and stifle the sobs shaking my body.

Adelia's panic-shrill voice pierces from the passenger seat as Denendrius wrenches the car left and slams the brakes. I throw my palms against the back of his seat to stop myself from rolling onto the floor. He boots the driver's door open and disappears.

"Hurry!" she begs. "We have seven minutes until we burn to death!"

Before I'm fully seated, Denendrius—bare chest streaked

with crimson and still looking monstrous from the power of Viorel's blood he stole from my veins—is dragging his father, Adelius, over the snow-covered ditch to the trunk. A branch lodged in his chest has made his immortal body comatose. I blink at the sound of the trunk slamming, and suddenly Denendrius is in the driver's seat, foot on the gas before the door even clicks shut.

I sit with my knees to my chest on the backseat, watching the sun wake, its long arms slowly stretching across the sky as if feeling around the Earth for us. Denendrius and Adelia argue in Latin, his voice furious, hers frantic, as he pushes the car to its limits. The engine growls in protest, the frame shuddering like it's going to spill its metal guts onto the highway. I nearly hope we don't make it somewhere safe in time. It would hurt less to die in the sunlight than to endure the darkness Denendrius has thrust my soul back into. If my newborn daughter, Aeliana, weren't at the castle with Viorel—if she didn't exist, and if I didn't have his love to live for—I'd beg the sun to wake faster.

To be unlucky enough to have so much to live for now . . .

The car slows as a dirt road appears between the trees, and the tires launch us toward it as Denendrius cranks the wheel. The tense seconds sting like tiny needles as we race through them. I'm both relieved and distraught when a small farmhouse comes into view. The dirt road widens into a circular patch—a makeshift driveway—with a beaten truck and car parked.

"Get her inside! I'll grab him," Denendrius orders, cutting the engine and vanishing the moment the driver's door swings open.

I push open the door—Denendrius didn't have time to set the child lock on *both* rear doors—and clamber out, with Adelia close behind. I barely round the car before Denendrius bounds up the farmhouse's sagging steps, Adelius slung over his shoulder. He sends the front door flying open with a single kick. I drag my grief-weighted body forward and stumble through the doorway. Denendrius clutches a dead man, crimson droplets from his messy feeding dripping into the steaming cup of coffee on the kitchen table.

I'm so caught in the horrible reality of Denendrius's chaos that I don't notice a woman enter the room until he's latched onto her throat. The door slams shut behind me with a jarring *bang,* and I flinch.

What are the odds I'll survive long enough to return to the castle? His fury, his violence—they're nothing compared to his thirst. Can I survive that after nearly a year of his starvation in the dungeon?

From the window to my right, a weak streak of sunlight cuts the room in half. It slices across Denendrius, sending him reeling against a tall cupboard. The force splinters the cupboard door, but his fangs remain buried in his victim. In a blink, Adelia yanks the heavy curtains shut, plunging the room into darkness.

"What now, *frater*?" Adelia asks, her voice trembling as she tucks her tangled, long brown hair behind her ear with a shaky hand. Though her scarlet eyes hint at her hunger, there's no sign of my blood's power left on her face as she stares down at Adelius. She inches closer to his comatose body beside the table where Denendrius dropped him, and I wonder if she burned through the last of it dragging him from the castle, forcing him through the veil in time.

After several tense seconds, Denendrius drops the pallid corpse in a heap on the floor and straightens from his slump against the cupboard. His bloodied tongue darts across his soaked lips before he heaves out a breath and says, "We'll hide here through the day and leave at sunset. Huarsar will send men as soon as night falls. This will be their first stop."

It's not soon enough.

I clear my throat and swipe at my tear-streaked cheeks with trembling hands. "Do you think Viorel has men who can walk in the sun? If he stopped torturing you with sunlight in Sirmium once you began building immunity, do you think he used that to his advantage?"

Denendrius stares at me, unblinking, crimson from burst veins flooding his eyes. The swollen veins beneath them send a chill through me, like I'm back outside in the snow. How long before my blood's effects wear off? Will the stolen blood from his victims dilute it?

"I don't know," he says finally.

"You can walk in the sunlight like Alaire and Edmond?" Adelia's voice rises, shaky with disbelief. "No one at the castle had heard of such a thing until they arrived."

Denendrius's upper lip curls in a snarl, as if he's still furious at them for taking me from school a year ago to lure him, even though he killed them for it. "I *could*. Before being turned human undid it all."

Adelia takes a shaky breath. "Where will we go?"

My knee buckles, and Denendrius appears at my side. The cold of his bloody touch on my biceps twists the nausea in my gut into sharp cramps. He pulls out a chair from the table with his foot, and I collapse into it.

"We'll discuss it when we're on the road again," he says tersely. "Start searching for money and valuables."

She pads off toward a dark hallway on the other side of the kitchen. My tears return as I think of how painfully close, yet unbearably far, I am from the castle. Only miles separate us, but it could take months or years to reach it.

A sob rips through my center, and I'm lucky to be sitting as I hunch over at the mercy of my emotions.

I can't fathom *years*.

My only chance of escaping Denendrius is as an immortal.

Even then, unless that seer was right about my becoming a powerful vampire, escaping him will prove painful.

When I get home, if my body survives, will there be anything left of me? And if my daughter is still alive, if she has grown up without me all this time, will she even remember who I am?

"Marianna . . ." Denendrius's monotone voice pulls my gaze upward. His lips part like he wants to say something, but from the blankness in his eyes, I'm not sure what it could be. He closes his mouth and looks off across the kitchen to a dark and sunken living room.

He stands still as stone, unblinking, and lost in the chaos of his own mind. His long, medium-brown curls hang past his collarbones and frame his emotionless face, tangled with drying blood.

My sobs nearly drown out the sound of Adelia rummaging through rooms.

When he speaks again, he doesn't look at me or even blink. His voice is so faint I only know he's speaking because his lips move. "I love you."

I squeeze my eyes shut, knowing what I knew the moment I saw him upstairs in my castle bedroom, hidden by Adelia in the wardrobe. Pretending is my only chance of survival. If I have any hope of escaping Denendrius, I must act as I did when I was his blood slave.

I have to choke out, "I love you too."

And he has to believe it.

"We're free now." His voice is so monotone I can't tell if there's more meaning to his words. Is he trying to reassure me? Himself? Or suggesting I should be happy we're free and have no reason to cry?

Perhaps not the latter, as he looks no less tormented than he did in the depths of Viorel's dungeon.

"I know, but I'm upset about Aeliana," I explain with a staggered sob. I don't want him to think I'm crying for any other reason. "Viorel has her."

"She could be dead." There's no emotion in his voice to tell me how he truly feels about that fact. He wanted us to have a child so badly but admitted he would prefer her dead than in Viorel's hands.

She could be. Viorel may have gotten enough energy to put the veil back up, but there's no way for me to know if he made it somewhere safe with her. "I know."

He finally looks at me, but his blistering red eyes are empty. "We should hope she is. The alternative is a lifetime serving Huarsar."

This time, I don't dare defend Viorel against the intentional disrespect of him refusing to use his new identity.

Denendrius's bloodied chest lifts with a deep breath. "There was nothing I could do."

Nodding has more tears spilling over my lashes. "I know," I squeak, the fresh memory replaying of how he tried to mark Aeliana but couldn't since Viorel's blood mark is permanent. I'm grateful Viorel healed me in time to intervene with Denendrius trying to kill her in retaliation.

I stiffen when Denendrius appears beside me. He bites into his wrist. I don't have time to push his arm away or turn my face before he's pressing the wound against my lips. It's good I don't, because I wouldn't have the instinct to refuse his blood if I truly loved him. Tears blur my sight as I drink him up, the flavor of his blood still sparking euphoria as it did when I was marked to him, yet there's no sense of connection now.

When he pulls his wrist away, I don't feel unplugged from him as I once had. It's likely I could have pulled away from the flow of his blood on my own.

I brace myself for the fury he showed upon realizing he couldn't overwrite Viorel's mark on Aeliana, but he's as unemotional as before.

"His mark is permanent." I lick the blood from my lips and hate how it has lessened the weakness in my body.

"I assumed as much, considering the scent of his blood affects yours as strangely as it did Aeliana's . . ." Slowly, he backs toward the middle of the kitchen, coughing and cringing with the pain of thirst. He clears his throat. "Still, you need my blood for strength."

If it weren't for Viorel's blood coursing through me and the spare moments he spent healing me, I probably wouldn't be conscious—especially after Adelia attacked me and stole my blood for both herself and Denendrius. The slit throat and stomach wound Denendrius gave me to draw Viorel out once we exited the tunnel—and the severe bite he inflicted to gain the upper hand again—didn't help either, despite Viorel healing me.

Adelia returns to the room with stacks of money in her hands. "I found ten thousand RON. They didn't have any nice jewelry, though."

Denendrius nods and throws his hand toward their father. "Let's deal with him."

"Should we tie him up or something?" Adelia asks.

"No." Denendrius squats down and looks up at her. "Where's he going to run? Outside?"

She takes a steadying breath and gives him a nervous nod. "He's a coward, though," Adelia warns. "I wouldn't put it past him to burn us all to death."

"I know he is." Denendrius wraps his hand around the branch serving as a stake. "He's my father too, unfortunately."

Denendrius stands, yanking the stake free from Adelius's chest. He tosses it aside as Adelius comes to with a flail of panic and a hacking cough that sends bloody spittle past his lips. When his eyes settle on Denendrius, who towers above him, he tries to scramble out from under him before Denendrius stomps his foot into his chest.

"Fuck!" he roars as he tries to pry Denendrius's foot off his sternum.

"Have a dinner party to attend, hm?" Denendrius says flatly.

Adelius's eyes dart across the room, from me to Adelia and back to Denendrius.

"*Filius . . .*" Adelius pleads.

Denendrius takes his foot off his chest and strolls to the knife block. "Son, is it now? Hm?"

Adelius scrambles upright as Denendrius pulls a cleaver from the block and slowly rotates.

Denendrius crosses the room so fast that by the time he brings the cleaver down on Adelius's fingers, blood has already sprayed across several floor tiles. My delayed gasp escapes me.

Adelius roars in pain and launches himself backward against the cupboard, holding his fingerless hand as he sits on the floor. Five severed fingers lie in splotches of dark blood.

"You touch my sister—" Denendrius snatches a finger off the floor without hesitation. He holds his father's head against the cupboard with one hand and forces his jaw open with the other, shoving the severed finger inside. "*You touch her—*"

Adelius gags and writhes as Denendrius forces it down his throat, his frantic blows against Denendrius's chest ignored. Denendrius grabs another finger off the floor—his middle finger—once the index is down his throat, and forces it down too.

Aghast and unblinking, I watch as Denendrius force-feeds his father the rest of his fingers.

Tears streak Adelius's bloodied face as he gasps for breath.

Denendrius grips the cleaver in his slick, bloodied hand, raising it to the side of Adelius's head.

"*Filius*, please," he begs, crimson eyes desperate.

Denendrius leans in close. "I'm not your son, remember? Isn't that what you've always told me—everyone?"

He grips Adelius's ear, his pained bellow making my ears ring as he slices it off.

Blood gushes down the side of Adelius's head. I wonder if he can even hear Denendrius through the stream of blood and his own pained, guttural groans.

Denendrius snarls, *"I could hear what you did to her."*

Then, he goes for the second ear.

"Every time I tried to stop you—" He lifts the cleaver above Adelius's arm and brings it down on his wrist, separating his hand from his forearm. *"You beat me."*

He stares at his father, whose eyes are wide with pain, tears streaking the splashes of blood on his face. Adelius is pathetic, his lip trembling as he begs the man he refused to call his son until now for mercy.

Denendrius, furious eyes still locked on his father, moves the cleaver to his other hand and lifts it above Adelius's hand. It hangs in the air as he grits his teeth, his words spilling out with fury. "I got bigger than you, stronger than you. I learned to fight, and you still didn't stop. Like a coward, you'd wait until I wasn't home."

He parts his father's hand from his body; his arms now limp at his sides while he shudders and groans in agony in a slowly growing pool of blood.

Still squatting, Denendrius shifts back until Adelius's feet are at his sides.

"You ran." Denendrius laughs, the sound hollow and cold. "I didn't even know you were alive, and you spent your eternity running from me, didn't you? Always hiding, making sure I never knew. Feared me so much you locked yourself away in a castle."

Denendrius's face twists with fury as he hacks off Adelius's foot, and hardly a second passes before he severs the other.

"When *I* ran, you beat me harder!" Denendrius bellows, his voice so loud my head pounds.

"I thank the gods each day you're not my biological son," Adelius chokes out. "Your mother defied them by bringing you home. You were meant to die, but she interfered. I am not surprised you became a fucking barbarian! I gave you a place in my home, let you call me your father, and this is how you repay me? I should have dealt with the political and social consequences of telling my wife to put you back on the street."

Denendrius spits, "You were never a father. You didn't teach me a thing. When I was too young to know better, I tried to be a man like you. I had to study you because you never spoke to me like my friends' fathers did. Do you remember finding me and Verna in my room? You pulled me off her and pushed me out the door. Then you sent me into the city with a pocket full of money and scolded me—told me I don't get to practice being a man with *your* slaves. I was thirteen. Do you remember what I told you when I came home in the middle of the night?"

Adelius's eyes dart away, his jaw working as if he wants to speak but knows it'll only make things worse.

Denendrius grips Adelius's jaw and forces him to meet his eyes. "I told you the owner kicked me out. My first time there, he dragged me away from the girls before I could dress, tossed me half-naked onto the street, and told me not to return until I could control myself. The other men saw. Teased me. Do you remember what you said?"

A pit forms in my stomach as I recall how Adelius admitted to sending Denendrius to a brothel with money after catching him being rough with his slaves.

Adelius squeezes his eyes shut, but Denendrius's grip tightens until they snap open.

"You told me the girls probably just didn't like me. That I wasn't man enough for them. You handed me more money, sent me to a different brothel the next night, and told me to do my best to make them like me. That was the best you could do as a father." Denendrius's lip twitches with disdain. "The whores taught me more about being a man than you ever did."

Adelius gives up on holding his tongue, knowing he's going to die anyway, and grinds out from between his fangs, "You weren't worth the effort to teach. That brothel owner would have done me a favor if he'd kicked you to death."

Hate hardens my face as I stare at Adelius. The image of Denendrius behaving violently enough to be thrown out of a brothel makes me want to shred Adelius. He practically orchestrated Denendrius's failure, knowing his son's only frame of reference for intimacy was watching his own mother get assaulted over the years. Worse, when he should have told him not to be rough with the sex workers, he instead *fucking encouraged* him to play nice, so they'd like him. My god, did he take that advice to heart. He was so nice, I even agreed to date him.

Denendrius is a blur as he rises to his feet. He stalks back over to the knife block and sets the cleaver on the counter before pulling a chef's knife out. Returning to his father, he shifts his gaze to Adelia—who remains frozen, aghast, with unblinking eyes—and says, "I want you to kill him."

She trembles, wrapping her arms around herself as he holds the knife handle out to her. "I-I can't," she squeaks.

"Cut his heart out," Denendrius urges, his brow furrowed over his monstrous, begging eyes. "*You* deserve his death. He's hurt you worse than me."

Adelia bites down on her trembling lip but inches closer to him.

"Take it," I say, a little selfishly since I'd cut his heart out myself. For everything he did to Denendrius, to how he pushed the first domino that collided into mine, I want him to suffer. "He deserves it."

Her scarlet gaze flicks between Denendrius and me, our pressure enough to make her reach out with a shaky hand and curl it around the knife. But she hesitates once it's in her hand, staring at the blade like it wants to cut her.

Denendrius grips her wrist and yanks her down to her knees in Adelius's blood beside him.

"Kill him," he urges.

"I've never done something like this before." Tears drip down her cheeks, falling into the growing pool of blood. Her entire body trembles, arms wrapped around herself like she's trying to hold herself together.

"Do you remember what he did to you?" Denendrius leans close to her, their shoulders pressed together. He speaks softly into her ear. "Do you remember when we were human? How you'd run to me in the middle of the night after it happened? Do you remember how I'd break the door when I'd hear you two together?"

Adelia flinches at his words, like they're a blade in her own body. Her eyes widen like she remembers, glistening with tears, but she doesn't speak.

"How we'd fight, and you'd beg us to stop? How you'd beg him to stop hitting me? What about the nights you would spend in my room, curled up between the wall and me, hoping it would be enough to keep Father away? Do you remember how your mind would wander off, and I would hold you, terrified by your glazed over eyes?"

Her breathing comes in uneven, shallow bursts, like she's trying to hold back sobs. "That's why that happens? It's his fault? He told me it's because a Child of Stars corrupted my transformation—"

I grit my teeth, hatred boiling inside me as I watch her fit the shattered pieces of her past together. All those centuries of confusion, and Adelius let her believe she was broken from something beyond their control. By something that had *nothing* to do with him.

"He's a liar," Denendrius seethes.

She aims the blade at Adelius's heart, though there's still so much space between the tip and his flesh. Her body trembles as she sobs.

"I remember," she cries, her wild eyes locked on Adelius's. "You told me I didn't have a brother. I remember how you hurt me. I remember being so little I would hide from you in the wooden chest in his room." Her brow furrows with the memory, tears streaming down her cheeks. "There were holes in the side—sloppy, like he made them so I could breathe. He'd sit on the lid while you searched the house, calling my name."

Adelius rocks his head back and forth, a mumbled plea bubbling up from his lips. "Adelia, my sweet daughter, don't let him turn you into a monster like him . . . You know I would never hurt you. He's planting false memories in your delicate mind. You know—"

"Shut up!" she shrieks, slashing the knife through the air at him but still not making contact. "I remember, you liar! I remember!"

"Do you remember the bruises?" Denendrius whispers to her. "The scratches? The way I would tend to them because you were too scared to tell Mother, even though she already knew. Even though you knew he was hurting her too. Do you remember when you were so little, and I was still too small to win a fight against him? How we'd whisper beneath the dark of my blanket about all the ways we might kill him as we listened to our mother cry . . . but we were too scared to act on any of those ideas."

She shakes with sobs now, her shoulders hunched, tears splattering into Adelius's cold blood.

"We can kill him now," Denendrius murmurs, pressing his lips to her temple. "I'll help you. We'll do it together, like we once talked about."

She nods rapidly, and Denendrius wraps his bloodied hand around hers. Her hand relaxes beneath his grip, and she gasps for breath as Denendrius takes his time bringing the blade forward, as if he wants Adelia to soak in every moment leading up to their father's death. When the blade contacts his bare flesh, Denendrius leans his weight into it, and she gasps, her mouth wide, as it cuts into him. Adelius gags and fails to shove Denendrius away with his stump of an arm as Denendrius twists the knife in his chest, the crunch of bones under the force echoing through the room.

My heart pounds as I watch the blood drizzle down his already-soaked flesh, feeding the pool.

"Can you feel your heart straining around the blade?" Denendrius growls at Adelius.

His eyes roll back, and his mouth stretches wide. His ribs break under Denendrius's strength, the *crunch* jolting my heart. From where I sit, I have a perfect line of sight to watch as Denendrius and Adelia abandon the blade.

"Reach in and tear it out," Denendrius directs her in a soft voice.

Her hand shakes as she locks eyes with Adelius, then slips her hand into the bloodied, fleshy crevice in his chest. Her eyes widen, and she yanks his heart out so swiftly it's as if she couldn't bear the feeling of his life.

Adelius stares at his own heart in her hand before slackening against the cupboard and floor.

Her chest is stiff and breathless as she stares at the pink-and-crimson mound of muscle gripped in her palm and fingers. My heart beats in my ears as I await her response, but she's frozen.

Denendrius places a soft kiss on her temple and murmurs something in Latin. It sounds like he's proud of her.

She sucks in a shuddering breath, and her fingers loosen, splaying back from the heart like flower petals opening.

Adelius's heart rolls from her palm and lands with a squelch in the blood on the floor.

"I want him off me," she wails, her shrill voice cracking.

Adelia disappears down the hallway, her bloody handprints on the wall and footprints the only indication of her direction before a door shuts and a shower turns on.

II

Denendrius rises to his feet, his crimson gaze locked on Adelius. He stands that way while Adelia showers, her sobs and frantic scrubbing loud enough to be heard from where I sit.

"I killed him too swiftly." Denendrius shifts his feet, as if contemplating a step back, and the thick blood ripples around them. "It was much too quick."

I chew on my lip in thought before answering. "I don't think there's enough time in the universe to give him the punishment he deserves."

"You're right, but I should have done more."

A knot forms in my throat. "I'm not sure she could handle more, Den."

His head bobs with a single nod.

We fall into silence, staring at Adelius's body. From Denendrius's stiff posture and the bitter knot tightening in my stomach, it's clear neither of us feels the way we might have hoped after his death.

He's dead, but it doesn't seem to make a difference. The

damage remains, embodied in the man soaked in his blood before him.

I'm just glad I got to see him die. It's the only good thing to come from this day.

I don't notice that Adelia has turned off the shower until her teary voice calls my name from the hall.

When I stand and cross the kitchen, there's not enough left in me to care about the cold blood sticking to my feet and trailing behind me down the hall.

"What's up, Glitch?" I ask, finding her with her head poking out of the bathroom.

I can't tell the difference between the water from the shower and her tears. "I need a towel and something to wear."

My eyes flit around the hall until I spot a narrow wooden door at the other end. I trudge over and find a towel for her body and hair. I don't have the energy to find her something to wear, and I'm sure she can manage rooting through the woman's drawers herself, so I return to the kitchen and flop back down in my chair.

Denendrius remains where I last saw him.

"I suppose this is better than nothing at all. I thought I killed him—left him choking to death in his own blood when I was a newborn. Though that would have been a better outcome," he says.

"Do you feel any better with him dead?" I whisper.

"I don't feel anything at all." After a few beats, he rotates to face me. "Why did you call my sister *Glitch*?"

My heart stutters, his face so serious despite how his expression hasn't changed.

"It's a nickname," I explain carefully. "That's what she enjoys being called . . . said *Glitch* makes her feel like a cute robot with wires crossed."

He scowls. "I don't like it. It's disparaging, and you shouldn't entertain her self-hate."

I swallow hard and nod once, knowing defending Adelia won't keep me alive. "Okay."

Denendrius sighs. "You should shower before we leave tonight."

My heart spasms. Will he expect to join me?

His gaze flits around the room. "I'll figure out where to move Adelius while you clean up."

My breath whooshes out of me with relief.

The shower doesn't provide the refuge from Denendrius I had hoped for. Though he remains in the other room, the bathroom walls may as well be papier mâché between us. I cry quietly as I scrub, crimson swirling down my body in long tendrils, like vines trailing down my legs and to the rusty drain.

It's impossible to convince myself to get out, but when a cold burst of water sprays against me, I freeze. It's like someone disconnected the hot water. I shiver under the icy drops as they pelt me, but the fact I've used all the hot water before Denendrius has showered is more chilling than the temperature.

I practically tiptoe back to the kitchen after dressing in the dated clothes Adelia found for me, stepping on dry spots on the floor to avoid the bloodstains as I reach the table.

Denendrius and Adelia sit at the table in silence, staring off in different directions. She looks *hurt* in a way that's different from the pain of dealing with their father, and her gaze away from Denendrius seems almost purposeful. Did he scold her about her nickname too?

I cringe as I say, "I think I used the last of the hot water, Den. I'm sorry."

He lifts his face to me. "That's fine."

I swallow. "Still, sorry. I know you like hot showers."

"I'm going to skip showering," he mumbles.

Slumping back into my chair, I join their tense silence, half my mind left behind in the castle woods. I twist my gold ouroboros bracelet around my wrist to give my hands something to do, my thumb pressing against one of the snake's ruby eyes with each rotation. I hope Denendrius doesn't make a thing out of me continuing to wear it since he can remember now that he took it off Tatiana's wrist when he murdered her after escaping Sirmium, even if he gave it to me when he was human and likely couldn't remember.

When the repetitive motion draws his eyes to my wrist, I formulate an excuse—how I want to wear it since it was a valuable gift from him, to cover the truth that I've continued to wear it to honor Tatiana. Despite never knowing her, she was special to Viorel, and he told me they designed and crafted the bracelet together. It deserves to be more than a cursed artifact, her horrific death the last memory of her planted on it.

Denendrius's eyes narrow as he tilts his ear toward the ceiling.

"Is that a plane?" Adelia asks, sparing him a glance.

The room blurs as Denendrius grabs me, my vision straightening when we're suddenly in the kitchen's corner. He puts his index finger over his mouth, his head tilted as if listening.

Thirty seconds later, the low grumble of the plane joins the sound of my blood pumping in my ears. I hold my breath, my body stiff against Denendrius's side. How low are they flying for him to be this worried? Is Viorel having someone sweep the area for signs of us? My heart thumps with glee. It would be so easy for him to find us. There's only so far we could have gone before sunrise, and few places we could have taken shelter from it. I think of the car out front and the fresh tracks in the snow it would have made over the dirt path. Mine and Denendrius's bare footprints, and Adelia's shoe prints. He'd have to suspect the three of us are together, since she helped him escape, and he must know how it happened now.

Another thirty seconds pass. When the sound of the plane

has long since faded from my ears, Denendrius straightens and unravels his cold arm from me.

"That was a military plane." There's no sign of worry in his eerily even tone, though his eyes are narrow and calculating.

"Do you think they know we're here?" Adelia's eyes widen.

"Yes," Denendrius and I say in sync, and he lists all the signs I thought of that would give us away.

She gnaws on the corner of her lip. "What does that mean, *frater*?"

"They have a human flying the plane," he concludes before twisting into the living room—Adelia and I following—and snatching the TV remote off an old wooden dinner tray.

He turns the TV on.

The television light floods the room, and I'm confronted by a Romanian emergency news broadcast and *my face*. Denendrius stiffens beside me. His photo—a clear still from an old home video I brought to the castle—appears beside one of Adelia I've never seen. Our names are attached to our images, though they're calling twenty-seven-year-old Denendrius "Charles." My brow furrows in confusion, and I reel, dropping onto the couch. My mind whirs as Denendrius stares and slowly lowers himself onto the couch beside me, his attention locked on the urgent, rapid-fire Romanian from the news broadcaster. An international number occupies the bottom of the screen, along with a reward of thirty-two million RON.

"They're *already* broadcasting a reward for my capture?" Denendrius shakes his head slowly. "That's like ten million American dollars. I'm going to have bounty hunters and wealth-hungry immortals on me like flies, which I suspect is the point."

"What's she saying?" I utter, my breath thin and tight against my ribs.

He's speechless for a few long beats until he says, "I'm wanted internationally for terrorism, the deaths of foreign political figures, serial rape and mass murder, and kidnappings. They're saying I kidnapped you and Adelia, that I'm armed, and extremely dangerous."

My throat dries, my heart pounding like a headache in my temples.

"You killed political figures?" Is he really so stupid to draw that sort of attention to himself?

He finally blinks. "No. Not unless you're bending the truth to insinuate *clan leaders* to every vampire watching."

Just as he finishes, the image of a wealthy-looking Romanian family—a pair of blond-haired parents with their adult children and several relatives—appears on screen. It's followed by early morning footage of a mansion being ravaged by flames and several burning blurs obscuring bodies on the front lawn.

Denendrius's breath catches.

"What?" I demand, exchanging a quick, bewildered glance with Adelia, who appears just as clueless as I am.

"That's one of Romania's most influential political families —the Argeşti clan. They're the second most powerful in the immortal world. Still ants compared to Huarsar, but they've used this family as human puppets for over a thousand years … And now they're saying I massacred them."

Understanding seizes me, and it hits me how far Viorel's reach into the world is despite him never leaving the castle. How could I have ever doubted the extent of his influence?

"This is Viorel's doing," I whisper, a flicker of hope sparking in my chest as tears well in my eyes. If he could orchestrate this so quickly, maybe he's already planning something else.

It's only been *hours*, and he got Denendrius on an international list? The timing of this clan's death can't be coincidental either.

"Could they have been killed by vampires you released from the dungeon?" Adelia asks.

"No," Denendrius snaps, his upper lip twitching as he stands. He paces as he rants. "He's killing two birds with one stone. After I escaped his fortress in Sirmium and it fell to opportunists, this clan slowly began gaining power, while Huarsar hid or *sulked* for centuries." He pauses and shakes his head. "I always wondered why he'd rebuild in Romania, of all places. But clearly, he was forcing them into his shadow and waiting for the right moment to crush them." He plants his feet, the muscle in his jaw tensing as he grits his teeth. "Now he's eliminated the largest threat to his power while he's at his weakest—and pinned it on *me*. Figures he'd make his move now . . ." His bitter laugh cuts through the air, cold and dark. "Especially after I crippled his castle. If there was ever a time to strike him and repeat history, it's now."

"But . . . won't people realize that Viorel's behind it?" Adelia presses, her voice uncertain. "I mean, why would you go after them so soon after escaping the castle?"

"No," Denendrius snaps, his patience frayed. "It's going to appear as if I've just torn up the vampire king's domain for a second time, then went straight to the second most powerful clan to terrorize them too. Everyone believes I was killing powerful clans a few centuries ago for kicks, when I was really looking for the cure and needed powerful vampires to test it on. It'll be assumed I'm on the same path again. He even burned their home, just like I often did."

"Oh . . ." Her voice trembles with dawning fear. She glances at me, as if she seeks confirmation that this is truly as disastrous for her and her brother as it seems.

But as Denendrius's words sink in, hope flares in my chest. Viorel might be winning, but seeing Denendrius rattled feels like a different kind of victory.

He heaves out a breath and drops beside me again.

"What else are they saying?" I bite my cheek.

Denendrius's hands curl into fists on his knees. "They're

monitoring harbors, ports, and airports—no doubt he'll have men at private ones as well—to find us. Random traffic stops too. They're saying neighboring countries are cooperating in the search."

Denendrius flips the channel, only to find the same news report airing there too. "Huarsar obviously has men in governments, so there won't be a vampire on the planet who doesn't know who we are. Once this dies down in a few decades, I'm sure he'll invent another crime to stir things up again."

"What do we do?" I know Denendrius won't surrender because of this—Viorel must know that too—but now he's cornered. He can't just slip into the night with me and disappear. If our faces are on every television in Romania—possibly the world—he's not even safe stopping for gas. All it takes is one human to spot him. One call, and I'm sure it'll reach a vampire eager to send bounty hunters after us. And if a vampire spots us?

"We'll get out of here. It'll just be a little more complicated."

I swallow a knot. "What do you think his orders are?"

Would Viorel risk keeping him in his dungeon again? He'd have to be stupid.

"I'm going to take a wild guess and say the order is to kill me on sight."

My heart skips. "Why do you think that?"

Denendrius pulls in a deep breath and slowly exhales. "He's put my capture in the hands of humans now too. If he's sending human governments after me, he knows I'll fight back and likely get riddled with bullets. Enough bullets in my skull and I'm comatose until someone picks them out of me. Sending humans after me risks exposing vampires to the world. He'll probably try to mitigate that by giving kill orders to vampires so they can take me down quickly without risking another escape again or my exposure to humans."

He's missing the most obvious reason. *He took me.* If Viorel loves me as much as he acts—and clearly he must, if he's willing to risk exposing vampires to the world by manipulating government agencies to get me back as quickly as possible— then he'll want Denendrius dead and his skull fashioned into a trophy.

Adelia finally speaks, her tone restrained by guilt or uncertainty. "They're saying you kidnapped me too. Is that what Viorel thinks?"

"No," Denendrius snaps. "Don't be so naive. Saying I kidnapped two girls adds more urgency than just one. He wants to recover you, same as Marianna, but while he locks her up, you'll be the one filling my place in the dungeon."

White rims her eyes, and I'm sure she'd pale if she wasn't so already. "H-he'll l-lock me in the dungeon?" she chokes out.

He tilts his head at her. "*Of course he will*, Adelia. You let me out. You caused the deaths of hundreds—maybe thousands— of vampires in the castle. Your actions led to his blood slave being taken from him."

She shakes and hugs herself tighter. "But it's not my fault. I didn't know you were going to let everyone out of their cells . . . I didn't know so many people were going to die."

Denendrius sighs. "It's your fault. All of it. *You let me out.* You used his blood—*Marianna's blood*—to overpower the guards and set me free. He's luring you into a false sense of security, pretending you're a victim, when you betrayed him in the worst possible way."

Tears spill over her lower lashes, and though I have a fleeting thought that Denendrius is being cruel by blaming her, he's not wrong. This is all her fault. Sure, he's responsible for emptying the dungeon and those deaths, but none of it would have been possible without her.

"I didn't know the castle would fall apart," she cries, her voice cracking with desperation. "I just wanted my brother back. The one who used to hide me in his room and comfort me after Father would hurt me. I wanted you to kill him for me. I wanted Marianna to be free from the castle. She was trapped! I didn't know so many people would die. I love Viorel—I didn't do this to hurt him."

"How else did you expect me to escape the veil?" he asks, tilting his head.

"I thought we'd just be able to go through it with her blood. I thought maybe that's how you escaped the first time—"

Denendrius shakes his head. "I got lucky the first time. I threatened a guard who was already abandoning Huarsar during the chaos, and he barely resisted when he let me through the veil. This time, I needed to force his hand. I needed him so weak he'd lower the veil to preserve himself."

She sobs, clutching herself tighter, as if wishing for another pair of arms to wrap around her and offer comfort. But I hope she feels as lost as I do now, grieves the loss of her home, and bears the guilt of knowing *it's all her fault*. Denendrius didn't make her do this. No one forced her to betray the king and her best friend. I don't know what she was thinking, but I hope she sees how wrong she was.

He stands, his steady hands raised as he moves toward her. "You are *the best sister* a brother could ask for, Adelia. It may be your fault, but I am proud of you. Without your help, it might have taken me centuries to escape. You may not have remembered me or looked for me for all these centuries we were apart, but you came through for me as soon as you could."

As Denendrius wraps his arms around her, she drops her head and sobs into his chest. "He hates me now, doesn't he?" she wails.

Shushing her softly, he rocks her side to side and smooths her long brown hair down her back. "Yes. He'll torture you if he captures you."

Adelia chokes out, "But I loved him for so many centuries."

"Yet you betrayed him," Denendrius murmurs, his tone void of sympathy.

"But I'm only fifteen. Viorel doesn't torture teenage prisoners. He just leaves them in their cells."

"Then you'll probably be the first," Denendrius says flatly.

I flinch at the image of Adelia in Denendrius's cell—bled, bloody, and beaten. Tortured like the men Viorel used his surgeon's tools and ancient torture equipment on. My stomach roils, partly because I don't think such violence matches the part she played, but also because I don't think Denendrius is wrong.

Viorel grips his grudges for centuries, and he's merciless to those who hurt him personally. He burned fifty-four vampires, including Mitchell, at the stake. Some for their *thoughts of betrayal,* and others for active intent. Yet she thinks she's above physical punishment for betrayals she's actualized? I don't want to know what Viorel would do to her. Mitchell tried and failed to breach the steel door to the basement to kill me while pregnant and dethrone him, and that was enough for Viorel to mutilate and hang him from the iron chandelier in the grand room for two weeks before flaying him and killing him. Despite the blame I cast on her, I don't think she deserves the full extent of the horror he's capable of inflicting. I don't think she even fully understood the consequences of her plan, or if she thought *any of it* through.

Denendrius pulls away from Adelia and places a soft kiss on her forehead. "I need you to go to Italy," Denendrius murmurs, his tone soft and brotherly. "I bought a villa for Marianna and me, so you're going to live with us now. You'll be safe there, but I need you to go ahead of us. Viorel will assume you're with us, so it's safest if you hide at the villa and wait. It'll be harder to find you if you stay hidden in one place."

"But I'm scared. I want to stay with you." She wraps her

arms around his waist, clinging to him. Her voice rises an octave. "What if I forget things? What if I get lost?"

"I need you to be brave." He wraps his arm around her shoulders, holding her tight. "We have a better chance of getting caught as a group of four once Sergei joins us. Besides, other clans are looking for me, with their own agendas beyond Huarsar. If they capture you, you'll only face harm alongside me."

"But I'll be all alone in Italy," she whispers, her voice thick with tears. "I hardly know anything about this new world. What if my brain glitches out? I don't trust myself."

"I know. You'll need to hypnotize a friend and have her guide you. Make sure she does whatever it takes to keep you hidden and safe at home."

She draws away from him, wiping her eyes. "*Okay*. How long will you be?"

He shrugs. "I have some things to wrap up in America. As soon as I'm done, we'll join you."

"Can you estimate?" she pleads. "A few weeks? Months?"

Denendrius swiftly straightens. "That's a big truck turning down the road . . ." He scowls at the covered window, like he's tempted to peek outside.

My heart drums, my knees weak with relief. Could this be Viorel sending men to save me? Could he have figured out a way to help me during the day?

"What do we do?" Adelia asks, panic lacing her voice.

"Kill them." The iciness of his command sends goosebumps skittering across my skin. "Unless you want to be dragged back to the castle."

She swiftly shakes her head and pulls a boning knife from the knife block.

The ground trembles as the truck rumbles down the driveway. The room blurs as Denendrius's arm wraps around me. A moment later, we're standing in the overturned master bedroom Adelia searched.

I yelp as he brings my wrist to his mouth and tears into my vein. My head swims as he drinks, the faded veins in his face now as swollen as before. He pulls away after a few moments, gasping for breath, his eyes wide like he's taken a hit of some dangerously potent drug. He makes a strangled noise and clears his throat, as if fighting the urge to sink his fangs back into me and drain me dry.

"Stay put, sweetheart," Denendrius says, his voice tight with thirst, as he pushes me into the wooden wardrobe nearby and shuts the doors to plunge me into darkness. "Everything will be fine. I love you."

"Love you," I choke out, slumping against the back of the wardrobe and pulling my legs up to my chest.

My breath whooshes in and out of me; the darkness clings to me, filled with the touch of hanging fabric and cold metal hangers. Something heavy drags along the floor, and the wardrobe wobbles slightly as he pushes a piece of furniture— the large wooden dresser by the door, if I had to guess—against the wardrobe doors. It won't stop Viorel's men from rescuing me, but it'll give Denendrius a few extra milliseconds if they try. From my experience, those few milliseconds are all he needs to turn a fight in his favor.

"How can they get in?" Adelia questions from the other room, doubt clear in her voice. "Won't they burn?"

Denendrius's muffled voice comes from the other room. "You think they plan to walk in the front door?"

The rumbling grows dangerously close to the house, and something heavy is ripped off the wall in the bathroom. A sparkle of light fills the hairline gap at the top of the doors, and I suspect Denendrius opened the curtain in the bedroom to put sunlight between me and whoever comes to my rescue.

A deafening thud against an exterior wall widens my eyes,

and with the groan of rolling metal, glass shatters before heavy boots hit the floor. I hold my breath, straining to distinguish the slow steps moving through the kitchen—some heading toward the hall, others in the opposite direction.

A boot crunches on something just outside the door, and a split second later, the solid thud of the door slamming against a body is followed by gunfire tearing through the silence.

An unfamiliar man's voice shouts an order in Romanian, followed by a roar of pain and a scrambling thud—flailing?—against the floor as Denendrius curses in Latin, as if he's been hit.

I try to piece an image together. Denendrius must have been hiding behind the door, slamming it into whoever came through to catch them off guard and gain the upper hand.

Boots thud against the floor toward us but stop abruptly as Denendrius grunts in pain. Something heavy—a person?—slams into a wall. A guttural scream of pain echoes, followed by a rapid shot and the sound of something shattering. I realize Denendrius must have been using the mirror from the bathroom, as the scent of burned flesh seeps into the wardrobe.

Denendrius snarls in Romanian before the sliver of light in the gap vanishes, followed by a sickening, wet crunch that makes me flinch.

I try to wrangle my rapid breaths, waiting for the dresser to move and the doors to open, hoping it's not Denendrius on the other side.

As much as I wish for rescue, there is little hope within me.

"I got one, *frater!*" Adelia screams from across the house with glee before her excitement turns into a yelp, followed by splintering wood and rapid fire that makes her cry out.

"*Adelia!*" Denendrius's war cry echoes, accompanied by the sound of flesh slamming repeatedly against something metal and hollow.

Frantic, a soldier shouts orders from the opposite corner of the house, his voice moving rapidly until it's drowned out by shifting glass and the hollow thuds of scrambling on metal. An electronic radio crackles, and he repeats a frantic plea before his message turns to gurgling and cracking bones.

Silence.

My heart slams against my ribs while I wait for any sign that the fight isn't over. Is there still a chance I might get to go home?

The crunch of glass and Denendrius's stiff Latin question from the other room leaves me slack with defeat.

Adelia's quiet, pained cry and blubbering Latin catch my attention, but all I feel for her is bitterness. How could someone so ancient be so fucking naive? What did she think was going to happen when she released one of the world's most violent and unhinged vampires?

The thick smell of burning flesh chokes me, and I gag, coughing violently.

III

Denendrius stands soaked in blood, bullet wounds peppering his arm and abdomen. His eyes are so monstrously wide and wild I can't help but press myself against the wardrobe.

"It's safe now," he says limply.

I take a shuddery breath as I step out of the wardrobe with trembling legs. A man—or what's left of one—lies sprawled across the wreckage of the room. Blood soaks his torn black tactical gear, the long barrel of his automatic gun—magazine missing—shoved through his midsection. His head's at an unnatural angle, and every part of exposed flesh is charred. Shards of mirror litter the doorway and hall. A shoulder-height dent mars the door, its wood splintered inward.

Denendrius turns around and drops to one knee. "There's a lot of glass. I'll carry you to the living room."

My hands slide on his blood-slicked shoulders, but I lock my legs around his torso. He stands, his body shifting beneath me, making it harder to hang on with my dread-weakened limbs. I cough against the acrid stench in the air, fighting the nausea churning in my gut.

Still, I hang on with Denendrius's help as he steps over the dead man and into the hall, where another lies half-burned and slumped against the wall, his gun broken in half beside him.

My breath swells in my constricted throat as the kitchen comes into view.

There's a large vehicle pressed against the exterior kitchen wall, the shattered kitchen window exposing its open interior. A vampire in tactical gear lies slumped against the back of the driver's seat, death-gripping a radio. There's a gaping hole in his chest, his torn black vest soaked with blood. His wide, black eyes stare at me, and I swear the panic in them remains.

Was he calling for backup? Did he realize he was on a suicide mission? I wonder if he wanted to be extracted. But if it was Viorel behind the order, leaving without fighting Denendrius to the death would have been suicide too.

With *my blood*—Viorel's power—in Denendrius's system, they didn't stand a fucking chance against him.

My eyes narrow at the interior of the vehicle. Where a windshield should be is a set of computer screens displaying a camera feed of the outside. Sunlight sparkles off the snow like silver glitter. The dashboard is a chaotic mess of wires and buttons, and the only seats are for the driver and passenger.

Another man lies face down on the kitchen floor, one arm twisted unnaturally behind his back, his head hanging by a few sinews from his neck. Denendrius steps over him, his bare feet crunching against the glass as he carries me past the over-turned kitchen table and into the living room, where Adelia is curled up in a bloody ball on a worn leather recliner. I can't tell if it's exhaustion or shame weighing her down.

There's a dead vampire splayed on his back across a

collapsed wooden coffee table, Adelia's knife buried in his throat, a gaping hole in his chest where his heart was.

She mumbles an apology as Denendrius passes her and stands in front of the couch. He slides me off his back, and I thud into the soft cushions, my bloodied hands leaving prints on the beige upholstery as I adjust myself.

He spits clipped Latin at her before adding, "You never call out and give your position away . . ."

She swallows and hangs her head. "I'm sorry . . . I just got excited that I was able to surprise and kill him."

"You need more practice fighting."

She nods sheepishly, her shoulder sagging. "I don't have much."

Denendrius sighs and sinks onto the couch next to me, staring blankly at the muted TV. After a moment, he stares down at his bullet-ridden torso and arm.

"How bad does that hurt?" I mumble, trying to sound like a sympathetic fiancée, though the words catch awkwardly in my throat.

He grunts, pushing his fingers into the torn flesh of his torso, the sound wet as he digs out a wooden bullet. "Would hurt a lot worse without your blood."

I study the effect on his face as he digs bullets out of himself —the broken blood vessels in his eyes, the swollen red veins spider webbing beneath them. When his monstrous gaze snaps up to mine, I can barely suppress a flinch.

"Does his blood hurt you?" I ask to disguise my fear. "From your eyes . . . it looks like it hurts."

Denendrius scowls as he plucks a bullet from his waist and flicks it at the dead vampire. "The opposite. Makes me feel stronger than Mars."

I gulp, the weight of his words settling uncomfortably in my chest.

"What should we do now?" Adelia asks, the brown splotch in one crimson iris standing out as she meets my gaze.

"Getting out of Romania will be the hardest part," Denendrius says. "Huarsar is going to use everything he has to stop us from getting over the border."

I hope it's enough to stop us.

"We could use that vehicle," Adelia suggests, her eyes fixed on her bloodied hands, her voice small but steady. "Then we could travel during the day."

"It's a military vehicle," Denendrius says. "It's been assigned, and its drivers had orders. No doubt there are planes still flying around. We're not the only vampires that escaped. He's going to want to wrangle every escaped vampire that found refuge from the sun before they can commit mass murder and endanger the existence of our kind. If that vehicle goes off course, he's going to know about it."

"It probably has a tracker on it," I add, stealing an opportunity to feign support. "Tech like that? There's no way they'd risk losing it. If they were *smart*, they'd put it on the outside, where you'd need to risk sun exposure to disable it."

Denendrius nods absently beside me. "The sun should be down soon. Both of you, get ready to run to the car the moment it's safe," he says, then rises to tear through drawers and cabinets.

"What are you looking for?" I get to my feet and carefully navigate the chaotic floor before sitting back at the table.

"Can we help?" Adelia adds.

He grumbles something under his breath, yanking a drawer open until it catches with a jolt. He digs through the packed drawer until he pulls out a small flashlight, which he tosses to me underhand without warning. I catch it with a thud in my palms and tuck it into my pocket. Denendrius rakes his fingers through the junk drawer, his eyes flicking over the items until he plucks something round and black with a stretchy band from the mess. It looks like something meant to loop onto a jacket's zipper.

"What's that?" I question, craning my neck to peer over his arm.

"A compass." He turns it in his hand as if testing its balance, then shoves it into the pocket of his jeans. "It'll be good in case I can't see the stars tonight." He continues rustling through the mess. "Marianna, find a bag and fill it with snacks, drinks, and toilet paper. We're not stopping at any gas stations."

My face scrunches, heat rising in my cheeks at the thought of him pulling over for me to piss in the woods. "Seriously? I have to piss on the side of the road?"

"Yeah, sorry. If it's any consolation, people have been doing it for centuries. You think there were constant pit stops when we were traveling by horse and carriage?" He shrugs. "At least you can bring toilet paper."

For some stupid reason, that does make me feel better. Maybe because it means they're used to it, and I won't feel as humiliated.

I grunt, planting my hand on the table to push myself to my feet. I find a worn beige tote hanging with the jackets behind the door and move through the kitchen, grabbing anything that looks appetizing from the cupboard and stuffing it into the bag. A small collection of sodas and fizzy water sits in the lower cupboard with the bakeware; I add a few rolls of toilet paper to the tote with them.

"What can I do?" Adelia asks, glancing thoughtfully around.

"Both of you, look around for maps or anything that tells us where we are. I'm searching for valuables."

"But I already—" Adelia frowns, scowling at me in annoyance.

I try to console her, saying, "He robs places all the time. He'll know the best hiding spots."

A handful of minutes later, Adelia and I have papers scattered around the living room, half of them soaking up blood. Denendrius hollers from the master bedroom that he's found heirloom jewelry. Adelia's scowl returns, and she rifles through the papers and books with more intensity, like she needs to prove herself to him.

Denendrius calls out that he's found bank receipts and business cards from a town that must be nearby judging by how frequently they appear.

"I generally know where we are," he says as he returns to the kitchen, "but my knowledge of Romania is a little outdated, so we still need maps."

"How outdated?" I rise from a pile of half-bloody papers and steady myself against the ache in my legs.

"Well, I've avoided Romania ever since I heard the castle was here . . . nine-hundred years ago." He gives us a tight-lipped smile that doesn't quite reach his eyes. "So definitely before most of the modern towns and roads. I know basic things, and I've specifically studied the coast to avoid it."

Adelia sighs. "I wish I could be more help. I've lived in Romania since the castle opened its doors to us in the beginning and have never even known where we are. Even on scheduled trips, the guards ensured we couldn't familiarize ourselves with its exact location."

"Don't worry, girls," he says with an attempt at a soft smile. "I'll get us out of here. Just trust me."

Unfortunately, I *do* trust his abilities to get us out undetected. He spent over fifteen hundred years evading capture.

Denendrius tells us the sun will be up in a few minutes and warns me to use the bathroom, since we won't stop until the car demands it.

"Should be safe any moment now . . ." Denendrius presses himself against the wall and yanks the curtain aside in one swift motion. No sunlight spills into the room, not even the faintest glow. "Okay, time to go," Denendrius declares.

He appears at the door, tearing it open as we follow him close behind. His gaze swings from side to side, as if vampires have already teleported here in the dark. He hisses at us to race to the car. I nearly trip over my feet as they hit the frosty ground, the evening chill swirling loose snow around us as we dart to the car. Adelia has the passenger door open for me before I'm even halfway there. I scramble into the seat, desperate to escape the frozen ground. She shuts the door for me, the cold air briefly seeping in before she climbs into the back.

My eyes flit around the dark outside, cottony gray clouds stretched thin across the navy-blue sky, glinting with silver. They glide across the sky, shadows shifting over the hills and slopes of the farm as they pass over the moon, hidden from my sight. I search the shadows for Denendrius but can't find him.

Instead, I spot a mass of muddy fur from a German Shepherd as it struggles to crawl out from a pile of old wood, rusty metal, and broken-down farm equipment only a handful of yards away. Scrapped barbed wire tangles its leg and throat. I can't help my frown, knowing its owners are dead in the farmhouse behind us and how, if it can't get itself free, it might die.

Adelia sighs behind me and whispers, "Think Denendrius would protest if I helped it?"

"Probably." I swallow a knot.

A couple minutes later, Denendrius appears behind the car and opens the trunk. After filling the gas tank with a jerry can, he lifts three medium-sized gas cans and a second jerry can into the trunk. He coils a tube around his arm, shoves it into the back, and carefully lowers the trunk hatch. The dog glances silently toward us—like it's too strangled to bark—as if it wants our help.

Denendrius opens the driver's door but pauses as he stands

behind it to stare at the struggling dog. It writhes more frantically in the rubbish pile now, clanging and whimpering: begging for help. I think he's enjoying the sight, waiting to see how long it takes to kill itself, and I can't help but remember Adelius's account of Denendrius strangling his dog out of jealousy when he was ten.

He disappears from beside the car, suddenly dragging the yelping and writhing German Shepard from the junk pile.

He slams the dog against the ground—Adelia gasps sharply behind me—and grabs its snapping snout. It writhes harder, its body and fur shifting unnaturally until I'm gaping at the sight of a man beneath Denendrius. Denendrius punches into his chest, his heart coming out in his tight grip.

"Shapeshifter," Adelia hisses.

My jaw hangs, dumbfounded as Denendrius returns, wipes the blood on his jeans, and climbs into the driver's seat, the sharp reek of gasoline trailing in with him.

"How'd you know he was a shapeshifter?" I ask him.

"There's no buildup of dog smell here, no sign of food, bowls, pet ownership . . . and even if he was sleeping all day hiding scared in that pile of junk, he sure acted calm for a dog trying to escape until he saw *me* staring at him."

He drops a roll of duct tape in my lap, flicks a few buttons on the left of the steering wheel, and starts the car.

"Shit, you're right," I agree.

Denendrius nods. "He's one of the vampires I released from the dungeon. But he undoubtedly heard everything we said while we were in there all day."

"Whew," Adelia says. "Good catch, *frater*."

He cracks the door, spits on the ground, and carefully pulls it closed with a soft click. Scowling, he smacks his lips and looks at me sideways as he shifts the car into drive. "Want a kiss?"

I frown. "Did you use your mouth to help siphon the gas?"

The corner of his lip quirks, though the humor doesn't reach his eyes. "Didn't want to waste time looking for a pump."

"Gross," I retort. I settle deeper into my seat, comforted by the thought that the stench of gasoline will keep him from kissing me during the drive. "What's the duct tape for?"

He instructs me to cover the interior lights on the dashboard with duct tape as he drives forward. I bite off chunks of tape, nervously gnawing at my cheek as I make it harder for anyone to spot the car in the dark. He warns Adelia and me not to open any windows, explaining that it'll leave a trail of my scent behind, and that if we talk at any point, we need to whisper.

"What if there are shapeshifters pretending to be other people?" I question, hoping to inject extra paranoia into him in case it makes him slip up.

He chuckles and shakes his head. "No, I've never heard of vampires reliably shapeshifting to look like another human. It's much harder, and there's far more to it if you want to get it right. But it's something I've heard of some *ancient* vampires being able to do briefly. Animal shapeshifting is a simple enough of an ability from what I know, though."

I blow out my breath.

"Where are we going?" Adelia asks.

"South," is all Denendrius says as he hooks the compass on the volume knob for the radio.

IV

As soon as the tires hit the highway, Denendrius gradually presses the gas pedal. I squint at the speedometer through the dark. The only light comes from glimpses of moonlight filtering through the windows, and I watch as the needle slowly rises.

Soon, we're a bullet in the night, the engine's hum blending with the rush of wind. The trees are black masses whipping past us on either side of the winding road. At first, I scour the dark for signs or buildings, hoping that one day I might return and find my way home as a vampire. But we're moving too fast, and any structures or signs blur into the forest and mountains. The minutes pass in silence, and soon the lack of conversation and the endless dark void beyond the window let exhaustion creep in. The gradual curves and long stretches of the road are soothing despite the dread pounding through my body. With every mile, the distance between me and everyone I love grows. My body has been through so much with no rest, and now it begs for a break.

I permit my heavy lids to close, if only to escape the stark reality of my life for a while. The hum of the engine surrounds me. It, along with the slow thud of my heart in my ears, lulls me to sleep.

When I wake, the car is still, and Denendrius is missing from the driver's seat.

"He's filling up," Adelia whispers from behind me.

"How long was I sleeping?"

"About five hours."

I rub my eyes as Denendrius climbs back into the passenger seat, closes the door, and starts the car.

"Where are we going?" I yawn, my jaw stretching wide at the end of my sentence.

His voice comes so low I strain to hear. "We're going to catch a ship from the Port of Constanța. There should be a route to America. If we're lucky, we can sneak onto a transatlantic route. At worst, we'll have to hop from port to port."

"Why not a plane?" Adelia asks, leaning her head between the front seats. I wonder if they've spoken at all while I was asleep, or if they merely sat in tense silence. "We could go to Italy and then you and Marianna could continue to America."

Denendrius gives her a firm shake of his head. "No. You can't sneak on and off a plane at will like you can on a ship. We'd need a private flight, and I don't know where any private hangars are, so we'd waste time looking. Plus, Huarsar is bound to have men patrolling every hangar and port he can, and we'll get cornered on a plane and discovered before takeoff. At least we can leap into the ocean if needed."

"Got it." Adelia leans back in her seat.

"Besides, if I accidentally drink the pilot, we're going to fall out of the sky. I don't know how to fly. At least if the ship's captain dies, we'll still be afloat," he says.

Adelia makes a noise of concern from the backseat, her voice tentative. "Should we stop somewhere to feed first?"

"Don't have time," he mumbles as he applies pressure to the gas.

I close my eyes, begging sleep to whisk me away again. For the last few hours, sleep was merciful, granting me nothing but darkness as we moved through it.

A dark abyss seems so cozy right now.

Denendrius nudges me. "You need to eat and drink something. We're making good time at this speed."

I groan, too drained to argue.

Paper ruffles behind me, and I squint into the backseat through the dark. Adelia has a massive map stretched out between her hands. "We're approaching Bucharest soon. There should be some side roads up ahead."

"Got it." Denendrius adjusts in his seat and glances at me sideways. He eases off the gas and gently presses the brake.

"What's wrong?" I whisper. "Didn't we just stop?"

"A vampire just darted across the road," he mutters.

"One of Viorel's men?" I question, though I doubt he would slow if he thought that.

"Another escaped prisoner." His eyes narrow, studying the forest surrounding us.

My brows lift, but a few moments later, he slams on the gas. I jerk against my seatbelt as it locks.

I nibble on wafer crackers and sip peach-infused sparkling water as Denendrius avoids the busy roads near Bucharest by taking a slight detour around the city. My head rests against the cool window as I stare up at the sky, the faint glow of the city against the distant clouds holding my attention while I snack. It's tasteless on my tongue. The bubbles in my drink make me wiggle my nose as I gulp it back. These roads are bumpier, and my heart rattles in my chest as Denendrius speeds down them just as fast as he did on the smooth highways. At least he's quick to dodge the worst bumps and potholes.

Eventually, the trees thin, and I stare across wide expanses of fields, scattered farmhouse lights dotting the bare lands. The darkness feels thicker in the long stretches between farms, with no trees casting shadows to break it up. With the way the car moves over the ground so swiftly, and the relentless night, there are moments when it feels like we're floating.

Denendrius curses under his breath as we race toward another yellow dot of light ahead.

"What?" Adelia whispers from behind us.

"I'm so thirsty, and I can hear their heartbeats in my head from miles away. It's making me want to sink my teeth into Marianna."

I lean away from him, pressing myself into the door. The silence in the car becomes as heavy as the night until I say, "Maybe we should take a quick stop."

Do I want Denendrius to go murder an entire family? No. But selfishly, I'm desperate for those few extra minutes. They might allow Viorel's men more time to prepare at the port or catch up to us if they've been gaining on us in the shadows all along.

"She's right," Adelia says. "You need to quench as much thirst as you can before we're on the ship. You'll be surrounded by the crew."

"What about you?" Denendrius asks her.

Her voice is quiet. "I'm starving, but I know you're thirstier than me."

He sighs and slows the car as the post with the light comes into view now that we're not moving so fast.

"You need to drink too—"

"There's not enough at this farm for both of us," she argues, her voice dry with thirst.

"We'll stop at a few." Denendrius slows the car to a crawl and turns onto the gravel road leading up to a small farmhouse. "Hopefully, we'll be on a ship hiding before anyone wakes up, finds the dead families, and reports them."

"Sounds like a plan," she agrees.

My brow furrows as he parks at the start of the long driveway. He turns to me, and low, says, "I have to stop here so I don't wake the dog. Don't get out of the car. I'll take care of it and be back in ten seconds."

Adelia's voice wavers, her eyes wide. "You're not going to kill the dog, are you?"

He turns his head to look back at her. "It'll wake everyone, and I don't want the free-roaming mutts from the nearby farms showing up and causing a scene. Huarsar's men are going to be watching for any signs of disturbance."

She frowns and hangs her head, but nods.

"Can I take a pee break while we're here?" I ask, partly because I know I'll need to soon, and partly to buy myself a few more minutes.

He purses his lips. "Yeah, that's a good idea, actually. Your scent won't linger outside as long if you go inside."

I heave out a breath. Perhaps it's better to piss outside, then.

"I'll give you a piggyback in and out so you don't touch anything but the bathroom. Your scent will be a lot weaker this way," Denendrius says as he pops the driver's door open. "Adelia, stay here and keep watch. The next farm is yours."

With that, he's gone.

My heart hammers against my chest as I strain to hear the faint yelp of a dog, but the night remains silent. I'm not sure ten seconds have even passed when Denendrius opens the passenger door and kneels for me to crawl onto his back.

I hook my arms around his neck and waist. In a flash, we're at the front door of a white farmhouse that's in much better condition than the last one. Denendrius twists the knob, metal grinding as it fails. With a firm shove of his shoulder, the door flies open, and he catches it before it can hit anything.

The inside of the house is nearly as quiet as the outside,

except for the ticking of a clock somewhere in the dark and the hum of appliances.

My heart beats so hard I'm sure Denendrius can feel it hammering against his back as he carries me through the shadows. The faint glow of a nightlight in the hall makes the glass picture frames shine, but I can't make out the faces of the families, just their general poses.

Faceless.

It's a painful observation. They're nobody in this dark world Denendrius and I creep through. In my world, they exist only to prolong our escape, and in his, they're simply food. I'll never know their purpose in their own world.

Denendrius turns into a small bathroom with another nightlight and lifts the toilet seat with his foot. When he squats down for me, I step carefully onto the balls of my feet, the cold floor making my toes curl.

So low I barely hear him, he whispers, "Quietly. I'll come back for you. Wait here."

I press my lips together and give him a nod, cringing as he leaves the room.

The night remains silent as he feeds. The only signs of death are his thirsty gasps echoing through the house and the faint *drip, drip, drip* of blood hitting the floor in the room above my head as I pee.

My heart doesn't stir at the knowledge of their deaths. My breaths remain as shallow and tired as they were before our world collided with theirs.

I'm numb with death now. Perhaps I'll never see it the same again.

Though, how could I?

How could the deaths of strangers move me after losing so many people I cared about? After I've stepped through the blood and entrails of vampires who have been my friends and cared for me? It's a waste to cry over people I don't know. I already ache so horribly for those I did.

Perhaps being with so many vampires has fully desensitized me, stripping away what little empathy remained after my days growing up in Venganza Roja stole most of it. After all, you can only step over so many drained bodies going about your day before they become just another obstacle, like the folded over corner of a rug.

Denendrius appears in the bathroom, and when my gaze meets his blistering red eyes, I realize I'm still on the toilet.

"You okay? Did you fall asleep?" he asks.

I swallow a knot and wipe as he leaves, whispering something about grabbing valuables before I finish up. He's back before I finish washing my hands, pulling wads of cash from a pink pleather wallet and stuffing them into his pocket. A black backpack with a fuzzy heart keychain dangles from the zipper, and there's pink and silver glitter writing—Romanian—in a few places.

"There were older daughters. I grabbed some outfits for you and Adelia," he whispers. "Get you both out of that old hag's clothes."

"Okay."

Hands dry, he piggy backs me through the house again, snagging a pair of black boots that look vaguely my size on our way out the door.

With my scent, the bodies, and the personal items we've taken, it'll be obvious to any of Viorel's men that we were here. I know Denendrius must recognize this too. The fact that he's willing to risk it, even when he's so desperate to stay undetected, makes my palms sweat as I consider the true odds of Viorel's men finding us.

The farmhouse was an obvious choice. We were bound to a specific radius, thanks to the sun.

But now? Fuck, for all Viorel knows, we could be *anywhere*

in Romania. He has no way of knowing which direction we're headed, or how.

We stop on the side of the road near another farm with new vehicles in the driveway and fancier equipment. Denendrius instructs Adelia to bring him any cellphones she finds while she's inside. I try on the leather boots while Adelia has her fill, and she returns five minutes later, smiling, black-eyed, with a thin, shiny gold chain around her neck. She hands two cellphones to Denendrius—a flip phone and one with a full keyboard—and he opens them both to inspect before dropping the flip phone in his lap to focus on the other.

He takes off down the road, splitting his attention between the phone as he furiously types, and the road that flies beneath our wheels.

"What are you doing?" Adelia whispers over his shoulder, having a better visual of the screen than I do.

His voice comes low. "Ensuring you're safe in Italy. I'll explain on the ship."

When he's done mere minutes later, he crushes both phones and SIMs beyond recognition in his hands and whips them into two separate fields as we fly by.

We barrel through the night, beyond midnight.

After a few more wafers, I use the sporadic light from passing windows to organize the clothes in the backpack smelling of vanilla body spray, making room for my snacks and drinks.

"How are we going to get on the ship?" Adelia asks from the backseat.

"I'll park near the port. You both will stay hidden in the car. The place will be swarming with human security—and likely Huarsar's men—so I'll have to be sneaky. I'll figure out which ship we need and when, then come back for you two. We'll sneak on and hide. Once we're in open waters, I'll take control of the crew and captain."

"Sounds like a good plan," Adelia says.

I can't help but inject a bit of doubt into the conversation. "What if there are no suitable routes?"

"Then we'll leave Romania. Keep driving, find somewhere to hide during the day. There are other ports in other countries. We just need to get out, and things will be easier. Most of his efforts will be concentrated in Romania and the surrounding countries for a while. If we can stay hidden for a few days, he won't know where to shift his focus."

We fall back into silence as Denendrius drives. Occasionally, I hear planes in the distance, though the sound of them doesn't seem to draw Denendrius's attention. I hold on to hope that someone will spot us, despite how we rip through the shadows like a ghost.

But my hopes dwindle further when Adelia asks, "Do you think they have fewer men searching for us because of all the other escaped vampires?"

A metal band tightens around my chest. How many others escaped? Is Viorel prioritizing them to eliminate the threat before they wreak havoc and expose our secret? Is that why he's using human governments to track me down—or would he have done so regardless?

"I don't know," Denendrius admits. "It's hard to say how many escaped when the veil came down. How many outran the sunlight and found shelter like we did? Either way, there will be fewer men coming from the castle. I killed every guard I could, and plenty were already dead."

I bury my face in my hands.

V

Denendrius returns, the urgency in his voice spiking my heart rate as he scrambles into the driver's seat and hits the gas. "We have to go *now*. The ship we needed disembarked almost twenty minutes ago. It left hours late because of increased security checks. There won't be another transatlantic for a week. We can't wait that long."

"Then what are we going to do?" Adelia stares at him wide-eyed as the car hurtles down the road.

"We're going to intercept it before it gets too far from shore for Marianna to survive in the water," he says.

I gape at him, the speed of the car pressing me into my seat. "What do you mean, *intercept* it? Please tell me we're not fucking swimming to the ship."

"If I can't find a boat fast enough, then yeah, we're swimming to the ship," Denendrius says.

My jaw lowers, and I stare out the window at the stretch of sea in the distance. "How the fuck are we going to do that?" The panic is high in my voice.

Viorel was teaching me to swim in his fantasy worlds, but I'm not *swim-in-the-Black Sea-to-a-ship* good.

He heaves out a breath. "It'll be a bit of a swim—probably two to three nautical miles from shore—depending on where we intercept. You'd be on my back."

"It's going to be pretty cold for her," Adelia says. "Like . . . *hypothermia* cold."

"She could survive the swim," Denendrius snaps. "Especially with Huarsar's blood in her. If she didn't get *frostbite* when we were running from the castle *barefoot* through the snowy forest in *February*, she won't die of hypothermia!"

She shrinks away, yet argues quietly, "But snow isn't the same as water—"

"Adelia, she's clearly not feeling the temperature like a normal human should, which isn't all that surprising since apparently she can't survive *the sun or garlic* now. The alternative is not making it out of Romania before we all get captured. She'll end up back with Huarsar. This is our best opportunity, and I'm done arguing about it."

Adelia presses her lips firmly together, and I hope he's fucking right. Fleeing the castle was mostly a blur of panic and pain. I barely felt the bite of the snow beneath my feet or the sharp chill when my focus was on Viorel, who was fighting while holding our newborn as I bled out.

That, and I hadn't exactly gone outside this winter until Denendrius forced me to. The absurd heat of that mild summer day, when the sun maimed me—and later, the garlic— was much harder to ignore.

"I have some ideas of where to find boats, so that'll only be a last resort," Denendrius reassures us.

Soon, we're barreling out of town and onto a highway flanked by beach and lake, until the beach disappears and only the endless water on our left remains. Denendrius glances toward the open waters ahead, the distant, blinking lights of a ship moving through the choppy waves.

When we slip back into the cover of buildings, Denendrius darts through residential roads and along beaches. He jumps out of the car intermittently, running up and down the edges of backyards, searching for signs of small boats. His frustration intensifies as he rants about boats and the urgent need for rope and a grappling hook, or anything that could serve as one. He rages about how all the equipment and small boats are likely locked inside, and he doesn't have time to search building after building while the ship slips farther out to sea.

I'm not sure how much time we have left, and his rising anger only fuels my anxiety. I don't want to be on that ship, but if he's going to force me, I'd rather get there by boat than end up swimming.

When he returns at some point with a muddy length of rebar, I can't help but cower in the passenger seat like he plans on using it as a weapon. He stands outside the driver's door in the alley we idle in. The sight of him so easily bending the rebar into a crude grappling hook—one end twisted tight into a loop, the other bent open into a sharp hook—doesn't settle my growing unease. I've always known of his strength, but seeing it so blatant . . . No wonder he was bled and starved when Viorel kept him in the dungeon.

"There, that'll work better than a store-bought grappling hook. Now I just need rope." He passes the makeshift tool to me, and we continue our search.

He doesn't believe the crew will see us, or even think to look, if we're in a small dinghy, especially with the waves crashing around us. After all, who the fuck would be crazy enough—never mind, strong and fast enough in these currents —to row out and board a container ship at sea?

The buildings and houses become sparse, and Denendrius

turns left toward the ocean when the road ahead opens into fields. Soon, we're speeding along a bare gravel road, the tires crunching over dry grass, dirt, and rocks. He pulls a hard right around a corner, and I get a closer look at the giant ship glowing orange in the distance. We race alongside the ocean, the cargo ship with its massive containers and towering hull silhouetted against the starry horizon. He rolls to a rough stop that has me grunting against the seatbelt as it locks.

We're just off center from where the ship floats in the waves now.

"Stay here," Denendrius says. "There are a couple of boats down there. Hopefully, they're not full of holes like the ones at the last beach."

Adelia and I sit in tense silence, my eyes locked on Denendrius's silhouette as it materializes from the shadows along the ocean's edge. It looks like a mermaid's tail, the sandy shape tapering off toward the water, jagged rocks glinting like scales in the dark. A shadowy building sits back from the rocky shore, with a few trucks parked alongside it.

"I've got a boat ready, and found rope in the shed," he says as he pulls the door open and swiftly spins to drop to his knee so I can clamber on his back.

In a blink, we're standing on the shore, the dark water sipping at the edge of the sand. A battered metal dinghy bobs in the water, the ocean's pull straining against the frayed rope that keeps it tethered to the shore.

"No paddles," I whisper, my anxiety prickling as Denendrius holds the boat steady for me to climb in.

I step carefully into the center of the dinghy, the waves rocking it just enough to threaten my balance. I stumble forward, clutching the frigid edges to steady myself.

"You're okay, sweetheart. Sit at the bottom," he says. "I can't promise you won't get hit with waves, so hang on to something. I'll push while we swim."

My brows lift. "You're going to push the boat all the way to the ship?"

He pulls the line off the shore and tosses it into the boat, where it lands in a heap with the rebar hook that now has a fancy knot and a long length of rope attached to it.

"Easy peasy at this distance," he reassures me as he pushes the boat into the water. "I've swum across the entire Black Sea before. May as well be a kiddie pool."

Yeah, easy when you can't drown, have immortal energy, and could easily fight off—or snack on—sharks.

I grip the edges of the metal boat as Denendrius creeps into the water, the black waves rippling around us as his bare torso cuts through them. Adelia wades into the sea beside him, slicing through the waves with the grace and precision of a seasoned diver, keeping a steady pace ahead of us. The biting wind makes me shiver, though it's considerably less cold out here than it was up in the mountains. There's not even any snow on the shore.

Denendrius swims, his powerful kicks propelling us through the lively waves. He grips the edge to guide us along.

I don't stay dry for long. Despite Denendrius's best efforts, waves crash over the little dinghy the farther we get from shore. The sharp cold cuts the breath out of me, silencing the shriek of shock I'd otherwise let out. The foamy swells tilt me at dangerous angles, and I have to grip the sides until the boat becomes level, my heart racing with the danger of slipping into the sea.

As we near the ship, a massive wave crashes into the dinghy and spills inside, making the edge of the boat I furiously grip indistinguishable from the water's surface. Before Denendrius can stop me from sinking, the natural swells of the sea collide with the ship's wake, and a towering wall of water knocks my world out of focus.

Frigid water engulfs me, rushing into my mouth and

burning my nose as it blinds me. I fight to reclaim the air the current ripped from my lungs, but the salt sears my throat, sharp and choking. I can't tell up from down, and my outstretched arms and kicking legs never break the surface. Something—fuck, the ropes—is tangled around my legs.

My heart leaps when an arm circles my midsection and my head breaks the surface. The water is so cold I can't feel Denendrius's frigid skin. I cling to him as I sputter and gasp for air, and he wrestles the flipped, sinking dinghy upright. Icy water pours out in torrents. He curses Neptune for shifting the waves like it was to personally spite him.

It feels like forever before we reach the ship's stern, the massive vessel looming so high I have to crane my neck to see it. The propeller wash churns the water into chaos, rocking the dinghy violently. Adelia steadies us as Denendrius climbs in beside me, keeping us from being tossed overboard.

He wicks water away from his face and spits saltwater back into the sea. Pulling in a heavy breath, he grabs a long length of rope with the rebar hook attached.

I watch, shivering and clutching myself, as he maneuvers the rope in a calculated loop along the bottom of the dinghy. He picks up the hook and shifts his hand to grip the rope just below so it's dangling in his hand.

"Get low and cover your head!" he yells, eyes narrowing with focus as he swings the hook, his voice barely cutting through the chaos of the water.

I scramble to the other side of the dinghy and hunker down, lifting my arms and watching him between them as he builds momentum with his swings, his balance trained and perfect despite the waves. In a blink, the hook leaves his hand, and the rope quickly ascends into the shadows above. The hook must have caught on something solid, probably the rail, because the rope doesn't fall back down. He gives it a rough yank, and it goes taut.

He looks down at me. *"I'm going to climb up and drop the service ladder for you and Adelia!"*

I gulp, my *"okay"* lost in the roar of the ship's engines.

On tiptoe, he reaches up as far as he can and grasps the rope in both hands, pulling his knees up to the rope and swiftly disappearing, leaving only the rope swaying in the wind.

VI

I gasp for breath as we hit the metal deck, my soaked clothes clinging to me while icy winds whip around my body. I shiver violently, limbs trembling and teeth chattering.

Denendrius swiftly pulls the dinghy up, stashing it beside metal equipment and ropes that my waterlogged, blurry eyes can't make out. He propels me forward in quick bursts through narrow corridors and up steep stairwells, keeping us clear of open deck spaces. Everything around us is a smear of red metal.

I try to clench my jaw to stop my teeth from chattering and drawing attention, but I doubt any of the crew can hear us over the noise of the ship and the howling wind. He moves again, and we settle into a small room with a well-crafted wooden bed beneath a narrow window.

"Adelia, get her warmed up. I'm going to take control of the crew." The order rushes out of Denendrius before he vanishes.

Adelia strips me. I try to help, but my stiff fingers refuse to uncurl, making it impossible as she pulls off my jeans. When I force my arms up so she can slip off my shirt, my frozen joints resist every move. I don't care that I'm standing exposed, shivering and soaked to the bone—it's better than Denendrius stripping me naked—if it means I'll get warm faster.

In a blink, she disappears and returns with a white towel from the bathroom a few feet away, carefully drying my body as if pieces of me might break off in icy chunks. My shivering continues, my whole body shaking so violently my muscles ache. Once I'm dry, she pulls back the blanket from the bed and tells me to get in.

She doesn't have to ask twice. I move to the bed as quickly as my weak body allows and curl into a trembling ball on the blue sheets. The salty scent of my skin mingles with the sharp, clean smell of industrial laundry detergent. I barely feel the blanket as she pulls it over me.

"Don't move," she whispers. "I'm going to sneak out and find a couple more blankets."

After a few heavy thumps of my heart, she's back with a stack of blankets. She lays them on me, and I pull them over my head, my breath filling the dark space as I shudder, naked against the mattress.

Her weight presses down on the edge of the bed. "Once Denendrius is back, I'll find the kitchen and make you something warm to drink."

I can't stop my teeth from chattering long enough to say anything. My thoughts remain sluggish, my mind wrapped in a fog that lifts as warmth seeps into my bones.

"The ship's ours," Denendrius says, and I peek out from beneath the blanket. He stands in the center of the small room with a crooked smile.

Adelia heaves out a dramatic breath of relief. "Wonderful, *frater.*"

"We can all move around freely. The crew knows we're here and that I'm in charge. I've hypnotized them to forget about our existence for communications and port checks. That way, they won't seem like they're hiding anything. They won't cause us any issues." He gives her a long look. "Don't eat the crew."

She scowls. "But what if I get thirsty?"

"They'll be shorthanded if we kill any of them, and we need them to operate the ship if we want to reach our destinations. I'll ask the captain to show me around, but with so many moving parts on ships like these, I can't comfortably sail it alone."

"Can I at least drink from them?" she asks.

"Yeah," he relents. "Just don't leave them too weak."

I couldn't give a fuck about any of it. "C-can I-I h-have—"

"Warm drink, right." Adelia stands and vanishes.

Denendrius and I share a long stare, his face no longer showing signs of my blood's power. He heaves out a breath and lazily crosses the room, stripping off his soaked jeans.

"I'll have to find us dry clothes," he mumbles as his jeans hit the floor with a wet, heavy thud.

When he reaches for his boxers, I pull the blanket over my face, my warming breath bouncing back against my icy skin as it hits the fabric.

He grunts as his weight sinks onto the bed beside me. "How are you doing, sweetheart?" The softness in his voice makes my heart jolt.

I stutter, "C-cold as f-fuck."

"The shivering is good," he says evenly. "Your body is trying to warm itself. You should be in worse shape right now too, so I was right."

As if this isn't bad enough.

"I'll find you something to wear until your clothes dry. Sorry to say, it'll probably be clothes from men on board," he adds.

An intense shiver rips through me before they seem to settle a notch. "W-whatever."

Clothing is the last thing on my mind when I'm on a ship bound for America, drifting through the Black fucking Sea with *Denendrius.*

He releases a long exhale. "We should be in the clear now. Taking the dinghy was probably a better choice than sneaking aboard at port. It was hard enough for me to slip past so many guards—a good number of them immortal—never mind all three of us. They were conducting extensive checks on both cargo and ships. I doubt we could've slipped aboard without someone catching your scent."

"Here's tea, Marianna. I'll hold it for a bit to cool it down faster," Adelia says.

"Give it to me." He holds his hand up. "Get yourself and Marianna something dry to wear."

"Where?" she asks. "How do we know what's in each cargo container?"

I can practically picture the annoyance on his face. "No, Adelia. You'll have to rummage through the men's drawers. See if you can find some shirts and sweatpants. She needs another layer close to her skin."

"Right," she says. "Okay, be right back."

Denendrius sighs. "It's nice to have you both back."

I keep shuddering, but my teeth click together a little less now.

"Thanks for finding her," Denendrius murmurs, his hand pressing against my arm through the blanket. The blanket is thick enough that I can only feel the weight of his touch. "You have no idea how grateful I am, sweetheart. You're such a smart girl, figuring out who she was when she didn't even know herself. And it means a lot to me that you two became best friends before you even knew who she really was."

Tears brim in my eyes, the sharp sting of betrayal still cutting deep. Had I never figured out who she was, would I still be with Viorel? Would she have remembered on her own? Perhaps this was inevitable.

It figures that the moment everything was finally right in my life, everything that could go wrong would.

Am I destined for tragedy, or do I just keep finding ways to collide with it? I ponder, shivering beneath the blanket, my hot tears warming my face. Was there anything I could've done to avoid this?

"I know you're furious with me right now for taking you away from Aeliana," Denendrius says. "You're a wonderful mother, sweetheart, willing to endure his abuse just to stay close to our daughter."

Grief pushes words to the edge of my tongue, but I hold them back. I'll only make things worse if I meet him with resistance. It's better to stay quiet.

After what feels like a few minutes of stagnant silence, with only the faint hum of the ship and the murmur of bodies moving and talking on board, Denendrius says softly, "Want to see if your tea has cooled enough to drink?"

I peel the blanket back from my face with a shaky hand and find him still sitting on the edge of the bed, now with my towel wrapped around his waist. A minty scent permeates the air. He holds a white mug, the kind that reminds me of coffee in old diners. Weak tendrils of steam rise from the pale green surface.

His blistering red eyes carry a distant look as he turns with the cup. "Careful," he says, moving it toward me. "I don't know if it'll burn you. It still feels like a fire in my hands."

I pull the blanket tight around my body and slip an arm out. The cold air sharpens the goosebumps on my skin as I reach for the cup.

"I'll hold it," he says.

Slowly, I poke my finger into the tea. The liquid is hot, though it doesn't cause me pain. I wonder if my body temperature affects how it feels and whether I'll still burn my tongue, but I shift forward anyway as Denendrius lifts the edge of the thick rim to my lips.

Mint drowns my senses as I take a sip, steam curling into my nose. I don't mind the flavor when it comes with heavy, lingering warmth. It spreads through my mouth, trailing down my throat and into my stomach. I shiver at the sensation of it moving through me, but it helps.

"It's good," I whisper before hastily wrapping the blankets tighter around myself as they start to slip, unwilling to give him a glimpse of anything more. I lean against the wall and touch the mug at Denendrius's request. The heat is manageable, so I cradle the warm drink in my hands and stare down at the deck below, taking long sips.

White, foamy waves frame the sides of the ship, the deck below covered in neat stacks of colorful shipping containers and soft orange lights. The containers take up most of the surface, though narrow paths run between sections.

We don't talk as I sip, not sharing a single glance until I'm halfway through my drink, when Denendrius stands and says he'll make me another. It's ready by the time I finish my first, and this one tastes more like honey than mint as I gulp it down.

When the tea has done its job of thawing me, all I'm left with is a deep ache in my muscles and bones, along with a pounding skull. My jaw and teeth ache from all the shivering, but it's a good excuse for my clipped responses as Denendrius checks on my health.

Halfway through my second cup of tea, my need to pee springs up. I scowl and hold it, refusing to uncover myself. From the way he coughs and clears his throat like the smell of me strangles him, he doesn't seem in the condition to pull anything. Even though he moves to the desk chair like he can't bear to be near me, I don't want to risk stirring his desire.

Thankfully, Adelia returns, pouting, with a small armful of clothes.

"At least some men here are cute," she mutters, "but I hate the thought of wearing random men's clothes."

"I couldn't care less," I retort limply as she brings the stack over.

She's still soaking wet and reeking like the sea, though I suppose her clothes aren't as uncomfortable on her immortal body as they were on mine. "I guess, but you can still smell them on the fabric, even though they've been washed."

My nose wrinkles. "What kind of smell?"

She sighs, dropping the stack and motioning for me to go through it. "Nothing unhygienic, but their natural scents still linger . . . and there's a faint hint of machine oil."

"Whatever," I mumble, setting my tea on the wooden nightstand beside a lamp before rooting through the pile. Maybe wearing another man's clothes will help turn Denendrius off.

The sizes are all medium and large, but there's a pair of sweatpants with a drawstring that'll work. Equipped with those and a faded T-shirt from an eighties rock band, I slip back under the covers and wriggle into them.

When I come out, Denendrius is gone, and Adelia slips out of the bathroom wearing a copy of the same clothes, though her shirt features a different rock band.

"Where'd he go?" she asks.

I shrug. "Probably to find clothes."

She wanders over and drops onto the edge of the bed with a sigh. "I'm scared to be in Italy by myself."

A sneer crosses my face, and I'm thankful I'm sitting behind her, where she can't see it. How can she expect me to comfort her when I'm terrified about every facet of my life?

"Denendrius seems to have a plan. I'm sure you'll be fine." There's no comfort in my voice, but she doesn't seem to notice.

She shrugs. "I don't get why you guys have to go to America."

"Denendrius has unfinished business there." I swallow a

knot, my mind circling around the fact that he visited a fertility clinic in Bellevue right before he turned back into a vampire. He hadn't fully disclosed his intentions and claimed he only wanted to make sure he was fertile, but I see it for what it is now. He planned on turning back and wanted to ensure he'd still be able to have biological children.

The reality of that weasels its way through the agony of grief and the panic manifesting from my current situation.

How long will he wait before trying to get me pregnant again . . . *and how the fuck can I get out of it?*

"Like what?" she whispers, staring down at her lap, picking at her chipped nail polish.

"I don't know," I half-lie. I'm sure he wants to gather his belongings to send them to Italy and meet with Sergei, but who knows what else he might have to do now?

She sighs. "We just found each other. What if something happens to you two? I'd be all alone."

Something happening to Denendrius is the best-case scenario. Though I can't quite bring myself to be okay with the fact that Viorel will probably torture her if he gets his hands on her, I don't think she deserves to run around free either. I place much of the blame on Denendrius for what she's done, and for who he was to her while they were human.

"We'll be fine," I say.

I don't want to understand why she's done this to me, but her twisted point of view still forms in my mind. Maybe it wouldn't if we hadn't been best friends before her betrayal. It's hard not to see why she chose to jailbreak the person who always tried to protect her from their father while they were human. Perhaps she thought the dungeon wasn't punishment enough—a sentiment I once shared about Denendrius's imprisonment—and wanted the man who once protected her to fulfill that freedom fantasy they shared long ago.

Perhaps she couldn't wrap her head around the reality that

the big brother who tried to keep her safe is also the embodiment of evil. I suppose she's never witnessed such truths first-hand—or can't recall them—beyond bloody gladiator fights.

Does she hold resentment toward Viorel too? After all, she lived under his care with her father for centuries, and no one did anything about the abuse she suffered. I don't believe Viorel knew, considering he hardly left his chambers, and Adelius actively concealed who he was and avoided him. But does she think he knew and simply ignored it? Or perhaps his refusal to let her see her brother again, and how terse he was about the mere idea, trimmed some of her loyalty away. Does she blame Viorel for imprisoning her brother in Sirmium, as he does?

I suppose her reasons don't matter as much as the result of her actions.

Still, I wonder if she sees it now. If she can fathom the gap between the brother in her memories and the one who emptied the dungeon and destroyed the castle. I know it wasn't what she intended; she thought we could simply slip away through the veil with a bit of my marked blood.

Does she regret it now, or were all those deaths worth it to her?

"I'm sorry you lost Aeliana." Her voice is low and teary. "I thought Denendrius could get her out."

I drop my gaze to my lap and fight back a thousand words.

"Do you hate me?" she whispers, her voice heavy with pain.

I squeeze my eyes shut, my aching muscles tensing. "No," I lie, knowing I'll have to feign friendship with her to stay in Denendrius's good graces. "But I'm angry, Adelia."

A sharp sob slips out before she chokes it back. "I didn't intend for things to go the way they did. I had a different plan."

"What was it?" Maybe I'm looking for a reason to understand her.

Maybe if I can blame everything on Denendrius and see

Adelia as another one of his victims, the bitter sea I'm flailing in will become shallow enough for me to find footing. The thought crosses my mind that perhaps I can use her against him. After all, it's unlikely she fully understands what her brother has done. Would her feelings for him twist if she discovered he's hurt girls far worse than her father hurt her?

"I only wanted to get him out. I was going to ask him to kill our father right there in his cell while I tried to hold off the guards with the strength of Viorel's blood. Then, I was going to come back for you. I knew how you felt about things, but I thought you seemed so sad about never seeing beyond the castle that you'd choose to leave, anyway. I thought we'd be able to get Aeliana and slip out of the veil. I know you and Denendrius have butted heads, but your attitude toward him completely changed when Viorel marked you. Blood slavery and marks can be complicated, and Ainsley used to tell us in the nursery that the truth is always somewhere in between."

Her naivety is painful. It's clear she spent centuries detached from the real world. That, combined with a brain frozen at fifteen and compounded by trauma, is a recipe for disaster.

Perhaps I shouldn't have shied away from telling her the details of Denendrius's abuse toward me. I didn't want to talk about it, especially after discovering their relationship, but the consequence was a vague story she could fill with assumptions.

My nose burns with the threat of tears, and I wrinkle and wiggle it to force them back.

She draws in a shuddery breath. "My father and mother fought a lot," she whispers. "Yet they stayed together. I think they must have come to love each other during their marriage, despite it being arranged. They never divorced, and I had friends whose parents divorced for many reasons. Surely, what made you so angry at him couldn't have been so bad that you can't fix it? I know he loves you."

I merely hang my head. It's all I can do to combat her naivety. How does she reconcile all of this? Does she really not know how bad Denendrius is beyond his escape from Sirmium and the killing of clan leaders? Were they tight-lipped because Denendrius was too horrible to think about, or because they didn't know enough to gossip?

Denendrius returns in an unfamiliar pair of blue jeans and a black T-shirt. He hovers in the doorway, staring at me. "You need food."

There's no space for food with all the grief filling my body, even though it's been two nights since I've had a proper meal. "I guess I'll try to eat something."

I'm going to need all the energy I can get just to put up with him.

He gives me a single nod. "I'll find something, then we should sleep. The sun's about to come up."

"I'm just going to head to bed," Adelia whispers, rising to her feet. "I took the room next door."

"Sleep well," Denendrius says as he stands aside for her to pass.

I barely catch her small voice as she mumbles, "We'll see."

VII

My eyes are heavy with exhaustion, though my mind is wide awake. Denendrius tells me he'll return shortly, so I take the time to remove the tacks from a few posters of the Rocky Mountains on the walls and use them to hold the thick curtains in place.

Denendrius returns with a steaming bowl of chili. My stomach opens up after the first few bites, and I scarf it down in a matter of minutes, then chug a glass of water. He brings me more before sitting in the metal chair at the wooden desk fixed to the left wall. Staring across the room, he's unblinking and lost in thought.

My chewing slows after a few minutes, the tension in my chest making it hard to swallow. "I'm not sure whether to ask if you're okay."

He doesn't move, though his head twitches ever so slightly toward me, like he heard me but can't escape whatever thoughts have ensnared him.

I study his stiff posture as I spoon chili into my mouth.

"I keep thinking about Aeliana," he says finally.

Her name cinches my stomach shut, and I force down a mouthful of chili that feels like a stone all the way to my stomach. "What about her?" I set the bowl on the nightstand and gnaw at my lip.

"I failed her," he says on an exhale. "I spent too much time staring at her beautiful face and missed my chance to kill her. Now she's going to be trapped there and suffering for the rest of her life."

"Don't beat yourself up over not being able to kill your own daughter," I say, though calling her *his* makes the chili churn in my gut. "It's not natural for a father to do that. Of course you hesitated."

He hangs his head. "You should eat more," he whispers. "You haven't eaten much lately. Did he starve you?"

"No," I admit.

Denendrius nods. "I suppose he wouldn't, given the circumstances."

My hands shake as I take my bowl back and cradle it in my lap, stirring the beans and chunks of meat while I stare into it. Occasionally, I take a small bite, and it sticks on the way down, waiting for my stomach to open.

Eventually, I finish the bowl and set it on the nightstand. Denendrius hasn't moved the entire time, rigid and silent in his chair.

"You're all the way over there?" I wonder aloud. He's only a couple of meters away, but it's surprising he's not sitting next to me.

"I'm thirsty," he mumbles. "You smell good. If I didn't have so many centuries of control in similar circumstances, I'd have emptied you by now."

"Oh."

Slowly, he stands and turns toward me. He pauses, seeming

to ponder something, before sighing and coming to bed. "I miss you."

My heart launches into the base of my throat. I should have known he'd take my question as an invitation to join me.

He clears his throat as he draws the blanket back and crawls in.

"Mm, it's so nice and warm under here." His frail smile flickers as he settles on the edge of the bed, resting his head on the pillow. His hand finds my leg under the blanket, and he gently wraps it around the back of my knee. "Come here, sweetheart."

His touch dries my throat, and I silently pray he's too thirsty to risk intimacy.

I tremble as I lower myself onto the pillow beside him. He turns on his side to face me.

"You're so beautiful," he whispers. "I missed your face."

I swallow. "I missed yours."

His ruby eyes sparkle as he looks me over, his hand emerging from beneath the blanket to stroke the side of my face. I can't stop the tears welling in my eyes at his cold touch. My mind barely drifts back to that human man in Bellevue—I think of his brutality instead.

"What's wrong?" he murmurs, his chilly breath wafting against my face. "Why are you crying, sweetheart?"

He gently brushes my tears away with his thumb, the salt in the air mingling with the bitter taste of grief on my tongue. The faint creak of the ship fills the silence between us. The feeling —no, the reality—of being trapped is inescapable. I feel like I'm drowning beneath his touch, and there's nothing but a vast sea waiting if I try to run.

Each breath feels like it disturbs a collection of razor blades in my chest, dozens of tiny slices tearing through my lungs with every inhale and exhale.

"I'm so sad," I choke out. It's not a lie, though the reason for it will have to be. "It really fucking hurts."

"I know," he murmurs, his throat bobbing with a hard swallow. "I know, sweetheart."

I try to bite back a strangled wail, but it falls out of me, my vision of him a blur of brown hair and golden lamplight.

"It's okay to cry." The mattress shifts as he scoots closer and pulls me tight against his chest, my head resting over his silent heart. "I'm here now."

My sobs spill out. I shake in his arms, enveloped by the stark reality of his touch and the pain it brings. It would feel better to cry alone, even if he strokes my hair and whispers how proud he is of me, telling me I'm such a strong girl.

"We're together now," he whispers, his chilly breath brushing against the top of my head. "Huarsar will never touch you again, I promise. You're so brave for surviving him. I know he was having his way with you. You could have killed yourself, but you stayed alive for me."

I don't bother talking, not that I can with my sobs.

"I missed holding you." His lips brush my forehead like he's scared to kiss me. It's still enough to make me whimper. "You have no idea how much I missed you. I'm never letting you go again."

Eventually, I choke back my tears and shove the pain pulsing through my limbs into some dark, shallow crevice inside me.

"I love you," he murmurs.

My voice is hoarse. "I love you too, Den."

"We should sleep," he suggests. "At least try. It's dawn."

Exhaustion overtakes me, and I fall asleep. I dream of the night Denendrius escaped—how the floors were slick with the blood of vampires and humans, how bodies draped over furniture and littered the floor of the grand room. Denendrius tearing out Rayonne's heart in front of me replays in my mind, and I wake to the sound of crying, which I quickly identify as my own.

"Are you okay, sweetheart?" Denendrius's voice sounds distant enough that my brow furrows in confusion.

I twist the knob on the lamp, its dim yellow glow seeping through the aged shade and illuminating the room. Denendrius leans against the wall, seated in front of the door. His blistering red eyes are locked on me, fangs on display.

"Are you?" I pull the blanket tighter around me.

My heart pounds harder, and he licks his lips.

"I'm thirsty," he chokes out. "Just . . . stay over there. I don't want to hurt you."

"Why don't you feed on a crew member?" I suggest, my voice flat. I've dealt with enough shit the past few days. It's someone else's turn.

"I'm worried I'll drain the entire crew. I don't want us stranded in the middle of the Black Sea." He hugs his arms around himself, pressing his back into the wall.

"Why not ask Adelia to help? She could pull you off before it's too late."

His eyes wander over me, and he licks his lips. "I want you . . ." Desire clings to every word. "I miss the taste of you. I don't want salty sailors, just my sweet girl."

My heart thrashes in my chest, my eyes widening as I turn to stone.

He wets his lips again and stands like I'm a doe ready to run. "I have an idea," he says, reaching into his pocket and producing a folding knife. The click of the blade flicking open jolts me in bed. "I'll cut you instead of biting, so it's easier to pull myself away."

Slowly, I shake my head as he inches toward me. "I-I don't know. What if you lose control?"

"I'll give you the knife, and if I don't release you on ten, stab me."

I gulp, leaning away as he carefully crawls onto the bed, practically panting, his breath coming in shallow gasps as he shifts toward me.

"Just a bit," he chokes out, his crimson gaze locked on my throat before jumping to my wrist. "I'll take your wrist. There's a first aid kit in the bathroom. I'll clean you up after . . ."

"I-I don't know, Den . . ."

A pained grunt rumbles in the back of his throat, and I go limp with fear—my body too terrified to show even a morsel of resistance—as he pulls my hand from the blanket, turning my arm over in his grip. He gasps for breath, each swallow looking painfully labored as he traces a finger along the vein in my wrist before settling the sharp edge of the blade against my skin.

I hiss in pain as the blade parts my flesh, the flood of red instantaneous. He drops the knife into my lap, rushing the wound to his lips and lapping up my blood. I snatch the knife and begin counting to ten, my grip tight on the rough handle as I watch him swallow long gulps of my blood, my pounding heart speeding the spill along. The veins beneath his closed eyes swell in furious shades of blue and red, just like when I first saw him after he escaped with my blood in his system.

Ten.

I give him a gentle shove, not wanting to resort to the knife right away in case he flips out. "Okay, enough."

His grip tightens on my forearm, his eyes squeezing shut more firmly before he shifts his mouth. The sharp pinch of his fangs makes me gasp in pain.

"Denendrius!" I bring the knife down into his thigh, but he doesn't react. My thoughts flurry as I yank the knife out and drive it into his abdomen. He keeps drinking, more desperate now, his grip tightening, reddening my skin with the pressure.

The room spins, and I feel lightheaded—either from panic or blood loss. I press my palm against the rough wallpaper to steady myself, my eyes snapping to the window when my finger brushes the bottom edge of the curtain.

With a thoughtless jolt, I grab a fistful of the heavy fabric and shove it aside, ripping the tacks from the wall.

Pain lances through my head as weak sunlight flashes across Denendrius's torso and face. The sizzle of his flesh accompanies his pained howl as his head snaps back, and the curtain falls back into place.

He disappears. Squeezing my eyes shut, I force the tacks back into the wall with trembling fingers. Pained gasps echo from the bathroom, followed by a frustrated groan.

"*Ugh*, I'm sorry," Denendrius grovels, his voice strained. "Sweetheart, *I'm sorry.*"

"Are you okay?" I press the heel of my hand into my forehead, pain pounding behind my eyes with every throb of my heart.

"*Yeah* . . . No—Adelia!" Denendrius hollers, then gasps for breath, a quiet, agonized whine slipping out. "*Adelia.*"

I can't help but think of the last time I tried to see the sun—when Carol and I took that day trip into the castle garden—and how the afternoon light left my flesh bloodied and my vision ruined. I'm lucky that, despite Viorel's blood in my system, the weak dawn light didn't leave me like before.

The door opens and shuts, though I don't glimpse her enter.

"I'm so thirsty," he whines. "It hurts."

"I know," she consoles from the bathroom. "I'm sorry I didn't come faster. I wasn't sure if I heard someone shout or if I was dreaming."

"It's okay, but I need you to stay here," he begs. "I want to drain her."

She doesn't hesitate as she says, "Okay, sure."

He reappears with her from the bathroom, red-stained teeth bared in pain as he fumbles with the first aid kit, trying to lick blood from his fingers and face as he opens it. He's healed already, the fury of my blood in his system only faint on his face now.

Denendrius delegates wrapping my cut wrist up to her as he curls on his side against the door. Adelia tosses him a blanket, and he sprawls out on it, pulling the corner of the beige fabric over his face like he's trying to filter the scent of laundry instead of me.

She sighs and sets the first aid kit aside once my wrist is wrapped. "Can I bunk with you?"

I scoot against the wall, making space for her in the double bed. As upset as I am with her, I'm not about to complain about using her as a shield against a thirsty, blood-deprived vampire.

Rolling over, I bury my head deeper into the pillow like I can smother the ache jack hammering behind my eyes. I fight for sleep, but Adelia's eventual cool and even breaths against the back of my head are only one additional factor keeping me awake. The idea of Adelia between Denendrius and me is nice . . . yet she's still half his size and is unlikely to protect me if he really loses it.

Knowing Denendrius is awake doesn't help me fall asleep, either. Each low grumble or thirsty grunt as he shifts around on the floor only has me more aware.

I focus on the hum of the ship to distract myself from the slow-fading pain. Though once it eases off, I notice the lingering sting of the incisions in my wrist.

It could have been worse, I suppose.

My eyes pop open at Adelia's low whimper, and I release a long sigh. Her muffled squeak has me rolling over to wake her from her nightmare, since her whimpering won't make falling asleep any easier.

She stares half-lidded in the low light, unblinking and unaware, her lips pressed tight together.

Frowning, I lift my hand to her shoulder and gently shake her. A whimper catches in the back of her throat.

"Adelia," I call, my even volume making Denendrius sit upright and lift his chin to peer at us.

He moves to his hands and knees, skittering to the edge of the bed. His breath is half-held as he asks, "Has her mind run away?"

"I think they call this dissociation these days," I whisper, unable to hide the tense edge to my flat voice as he kneels at the bedside. I wish my pounding heart would shut up before it draws his attention.

His crimson eyes dart between Adelia and me as he scoops her off the bed and appears against the door with her rigid body. He sits on the rumpled blanket, Adelia in his lap with her head on his chest. She's so small in his grip, his large hands stroking through the long strands of her hair. With her being close to my size, I imagine I look similar in his arms. He whispers Latin to her, his lips brushing her pale forehead.

Sitting upright, I rub my sore eyes. "Did she have memory issues when she was human?"

Denendrius's gaze shifts back to me, and he shakes his head. "No, but she . . . *dissociated* . . . frequently. Disorientation was normal when she came to her senses—not knowing where she was at first or what happened—but never an issue with her memories as a whole."

I sigh, my shoulders rolling forward as I ponder them and twist my fingers in the blanket in my lap. "Maybe it's both the abuse and her transformation being interfered with. At the castle, she'd forget what she was doing in the middle of things, couldn't remember much of her human years, and sometimes temporarily forgot things without dissociating first. She'd forget who I was occasionally, where she lived, or what was happening . . ."

Denendrius tilts his head back against the door, his frown deepening as his grip on her tightens. "It's not unlikely another vampire was drawn to what I left behind." He grunts with pain as he swallows deeply. "There were thirty-seven dead bodies strewn about . . ." His gaze shifts past me, like I might see the memory in his gaze. He looks down at Adelia. "Thirty-five, I suppose. Anyway, if a Child of Stars tried to draw my venom out, failed, and left theirs in her too, who knows? It's not as if anyone is studying vampire transformations. All I know for sure is that the transformation has a severe impact on our memory systems, so it would make sense if it messed with it."

Adelia's tiny whimper snatches both of our attention. Denendrius rocks as he closes his eyes and leans his cheek atop her head. He hums a soft tune as he continues to stroke her hair, a Latin word slipping out between the warm notes.

My throat tightens as I watch them.

This is Adelia's Denendrius. This is the man she wanted free from the dungeon.

I reach for my hate of her, but it slips further away, leaving tears to sting my eyes. My heart shudders, beating out of rhythm.

Denendrius gazes up at me, a sweetness in his weak smile that only makes the pain worse. "Thanks for sharing me with Adelia without complaint, sweetheart."

I press my lips firm, my chin trembling. Emotion clogs my throat as I fight to hold brewing tears back. A single nod has one gliding down my cheek.

"She needs her big brother," Denendrius explains, like he thinks it would be logical for me to argue but wants to provide me with another perspective.

"You're a good brother," I choke out as I wipe the tear, my words sounding true only because nothing's proven them false —yet.

He strokes his fingers down her arm. "I've taken care of her like this since she was so little. Sometimes I'd find her on my bed, staring at the wall. Other times on her own, with her tunica rumpled, and I knew something had happened. Sometimes I'd find her standing around with a doll in her hand. The littlest things would send her mind scrambling. A door slamming too loud, the front door opening, Father's sudden voice. He'd hug or kiss her passing by and I'd have to walk after her mind to catch it." He bites the edge of his lip in thought but says nothing more.

Fearing the end of our conversation and not wanting to sleep while she's still unresponsive and unable to protect my throat, I nudge the conversation awake. "Your mother never helped Adelia?"

Denendrius shrugs. "The slaves oversaw childcare more than her. I loved my mother—she truly loved me, and she did the best she could—but her own abuse had her running away in different ways. I was the only one who could lend comfort to Adelia. It was not the slaves' duties either to notice the harm our father inflicted on us."

All that care for his own sister's trauma and abuse, and yet how many girls did *he* go on to rape and murder? How many siblings no longer have their own sister because of him?

"Why did you lie about your transformation and how your family died?" I re-compare his stories. The lie he told as a vampire: that he stalked and killed a woman, and her husband turned him in revenge; that he went home and tried to share the gift of vampirism with his mother and sisters but failed. Versus the truth: he tried to help Mariana's mother when her husband's behavior was terrifying her, and Marianus accidentally turned him after he got too close and triggered a violent reaction, then left him for dead in a patch of woods outside Rome. "It's clear you loved them. So why did you frame it like you didn't?"

"I had to tell you something eventually, didn't I? You wanted to know about my family. It couldn't be the truth. I hated to think about it, and it made me appear weak and vulnerable."

I shake my head. "The truth didn't make you appear weak, Denendrius. It humanized you."

Denendrius sucks his teeth. *"Yeah,"* he says pointedly, like I've nailed down the exact issue.

I chew the inside of my lip before exhaling a deep breath. "You never mentioned you were adopted, either. You compared your appearance to your sisters and mother. Gave the impression you were biologically related."

He straightens his head to meet my gaze evenly. His voice is measured as he says, "I recounted how we looked alike. I didn't lie."

I rub my thumb against the bandage on my wrist, a faint, damp red creeping through the soft white. "You knew I was going to be adopted by Vianna and Kenneth before they were murdered, but you still never brought it up. Why? We could have related to one another."

Denendrius hums in thought for a long moment, his unblinking, claret eyes pondering me. "I watched you closely, and I knew you better than anyone. Would you have wanted to relate to me—much less love me—knowing my mother was likely a slave or a prostitute? You hated yourself. I knew it was partly because you never knew your father, and because your mother was a prostitute."

My brow furrows as I try to untangle his meaning. "You thought I couldn't love you because your past was too similar to mine?"

"Yes," he says simply. "You wanted normal, and I was already abnormal enough without a big thing like that."

I sigh. I want to tell him it wouldn't have mattered because I hated his fucking guts by then anyway. Instead, I say, "I think it would have brought us closer. You didn't seem too worried about telling me once you were human."

"When I turned human, I didn't have enough immortal memories at first to know you. I couldn't even remember spending centuries trying to bury my own painful ones." He gives me a faint smile. "But hey, it can still bring us closer."

I quirk a brow, my eyelids heavy.

He licks his lips, then says, "Did you ever wonder about your father?" He looks like he's going to add more but presses his lips into a line and leaves his question unaltered.

Despite knowing he was probably about to bring up his theory—that I was a child vampire, and that Viorel hypnotized me into believing I wasn't after discovering something—I'm glad he has the situational awareness to not mention it right now.

I drop my gaze to my lap and tangle my fingers together. Though I don't want to have a heart-to-heart with him—not when I'd rather tear his out and toss it into the ocean—I say, "Yes. I liked to think my biological father made a one-time mistake with my mother. That he wasn't one of the men who frequented that rundown house. That he wasn't one of the ones who wandered into my room too." I sniffle. "I always hoped he was someone smart. Maybe someone hurting, who had a lapse in judgment once, and slept with my mother in his car or at some hotel."

Denendrius doesn't react to my words, which makes me think *he's* still convinced I had a completely different, immortal set of parents, and that my musings are meaningless.

"What about you?" I ask.

"Sometimes," he starts, a dull look in his eyes, "I don't think my life would've been better, even if I'd known the truth. I was exposed. It probably wouldn't have changed anything." He shrugs faintly. "I suppose it doesn't really matter if my mother was a slave or a prostitute. If I was conceived by rape, by sale, or by some secret love. I was unwanted, or they were too poor to keep and love me. I wouldn't have minded being poor and loved, though." He exhales softly. "But at least my adoptive mother loved me in her way. And I grew up rich."

I pick at my nails, not sure what to say except, "Yeah. I suppose."

He gives me a shadowy, weak smile. "At least one day you'll get to know for sure who your real parents were when you were a child vampire."

My sigh leaks out of me, and I lie back down. Not wanting to argue about it, I merely echo, "I suppose."

VIII

According to Denendrius, the ship is due to make port in New York State in approximately twenty days. Adelia will disembark near Italy in seven, as we pass by. He explains he sent an email with coded language to Sergei from a burner account, using the phone Adelia took from the farmhouse. Sergei will already know Denendrius escaped—either from the news broadcast or word spreading through the vampire community—so he'll be expecting communication. Since Sergei always checks his email through an obscured IP, we don't have to worry about the message being traced to him or a real location.

Denendrius doesn't want Adelia becoming a liability once she leaves the ship, so Sergei should be waiting on shore to bring her to the villa and set her up with a smart, hypnotized familiar to take on tasks for her while she stays hidden. After that, Denendrius expects Sergei to be back in America waiting for us.

I spend the first three days of this doomed voyage to hell rotting in bed, only getting up to use the washroom or to cry in the shower instead of between the sheets. I fall in and out of sleep, Denendrius the only anchor tethering me to time as it passes. He gives me space through the night, alternating his time between Adelia and the crew, then slipping into the dark room to implore me to eat. We talk little beyond his soft, comforting words, which do nothing to ease my grief as he strokes my hair or back.

At first, I ponder his avoidance. Does he not want to deal with my tears? Does he simply want to drink me dry? Is he upset that I refuse to leave the room to tour the ship and is giving me the silent treatment, hoping I'll beg for his attention?

But then, on the third night, after hours of uncontrollable sobs, I hear him in the hall with Adelia.

"Let her rest, Adelia," Denendrius whispers. "She's grieving something worse than her baby's death. She has to cope with the fact Aeliana is captive and in for a life of suffering. Mother lost babies between adopting me and having you, so I know how this works. Give her time."

"But I don't think Viorel would hurt Aeliana—"

"You don't know what he's capable of. I do, and now Marianna does too. She's dealing with that trauma. He would rape and torture her."

"Marianna never told me he hurt her," she argues, but there's confusion in her voice rather than anger.

"He made her his blood slave," Denendrius explains. "He'd hypnotize her, likely so she couldn't tell anyone about her suffering. I saw the signs myself."

"The signs?"

"Come on," he whispers. "Let's talk where we won't disturb her."

My heart pounds. Part of me wants to scramble out of bed and intercept their conversation. Will Adelia believe everything he tells her? Will he be able to gaslight her out of believing her own memories of Viorel and me?

When Denendrius returns later to refresh my water and comb his fingers through my hair, I have to stop myself from asking what they talked about. I want to press him on the supposed signs of my hypnotism he claimed to see, but I know there aren't any, and it's just a product of his delusions.

Though he falls asleep at my side each sunrise, I spot him curled up near the door every day when nightmares wake me. I'm thankful for his thirst and how it keeps us apart, even if I know he'll soon feel comfortable enough to be as close to me as he once was. As close as I used to despise.

On our fourth night, I wake with nervous energy coursing through me so thickly it nearly forces me out of bed. With it comes an emptiness begging to be filled. I'm not hungry, but I pace the room, thinking about stuffing it with food anyway.

With Denendrius already awake somewhere, I slip out of the cabin and wander in search of the kitchen. The smell of bread hits me, and I follow the bright lights down the corridor, my bare feet sticking to the cold floor as my fingers trail along the cool metal handrail.

I push through the doors, the scent growing stronger, accompanied by the faint sound of Romanian conversation. I step through another door into a brightly lit room, the glare of stainless steel momentarily overwhelming before the intricacies of the kitchen come into focus.

A couple of men halt at my entrance, their heads snapping up, eyes widening slightly at the sight of me.

"Hungry?" asks a tanned, skinny, middle-aged man with slicked-back black hair, his Romanian accent thick.

I nod and straighten up, scanning the food spread across the stainless-steel counters. My eyes drift past greens, spices, and meat, along with scattered prep tools, before settling on the fresh bread at the back.

"I want bread." My mouth waters. "Please."

He grins and says something to his workmate, a bigger,

younger man, who grabs a plate off the counter and carries it to the bread.

"We're cooking stew. You could wait in the mess hall, and I'll bring it to you if you'd like," the skinny chef says.

Shaking my head, I lick my lips as I step deeper into the room, assessing the spread of food. "I don't want to go out there," I say, as the muffled sound of men gathering for dinner rises behind the far kitchen door. "I'll eat here."

"Ah, okay," he says, his posture stiffening behind the large pot on the stove.

I wander to the fridge and crack it open. It's packed and neatly organized, but the sheer volume overwhelms me, and I shut it again.

"Here," says the larger man, his unfamiliar Romanian voice snapping my attention toward him.

He angles a chair against a clear spot on the steel counter, then slides my plate of bread onto it. I sit and tear off fluffy chunks, lost in thought, my gaze fixed on a ring of light reflecting off the metal.

I jolt when the skinny chef sets a steaming bowl of stew in front of me a few minutes later.

"Sorry," I mumble. "Thanks."

"*Hey,*" he says, his tone drawn out and friendly. "You okay? You cry a lot."

"I'm okay," I lie, tearing another chunk of bread with stiff fingers. Am I really that loud?

His serious eyes flick over my face, and he gives me a slow nod—more of a head bob than anything. "Okay. You are welcome to take food whenever, okay? Help yourself."

I grab the silver spoon jutting from my stew, just to give my hands something to do. "Okay."

He cracks a smile, but his eyes glisten with pity. "I'm Cristian. What's your name?"

I lift my blank face toward him and stare for too many

seconds, unsure what to say. I can't decide if using my real name would upset Denendrius more than avoiding it.

"Ah, it's okay," he says, brushing the question off with a wave of his hand.

Picking at my food, I linger for over an hour, devouring seconds and grazing on chopped veggies. It's nice to be in their presence as they cook, a welcome change from seeing only Denendrius and Adelia these past few days. I wonder what they think of our situation. Did Denendrius fabricate some story about why we boarded, or was he only concerned with our general safety?

When I'm done with supper, I pace the cabin corridors, lost in thought, as I trail my fingers along the metal bars. The gentle hum of the ship's engines reverberates through the walls, and I move on my tiptoes as if daring powerful waves to rock the boat, forcing me to grasp the bars for safety.

I don't know what to do with myself, but I know with certainty that I don't want to go down to the deck or below, where I'm sure Denendrius is. The cabin it is.

Stifled sobs catch my attention as I wander down the hall, growing fainter as I near Adelia's room and falling silent when my steps falter before it.

I close my eyes and pull in a steadying breath. There shouldn't be an ounce of concern in me after what she did, but I relent. "Glitch? Can I come in?"

Holding my breath, I listen for her response. *Nothing.*

I could walk away. It's not like she didn't hear me. But I know a best friend who doesn't hate her would try harder. "Glitch?"

"Don't call me that," she squeaks out between staggered breaths.

Fucking Denendrius. I grit my teeth and roll my eyes, inhaling slowly through my nose. "Can I come in, Adelia?"

"Okay," she blubbers from somewhere deep in the room.

I frown as I open the door and find her sitting in bed, back against the wall, tears streaking her cheeks.

"I thought you liked being called Glitch." My weighted steps carry me to her.

She lifts her shoulders to her ears and drops them hard. "Denendrius told me at the farmhouse that he doesn't want me to use it. That it's mean, and Alaire and Edmond were bullying me by calling me that."

I didn't misread their silence at the kitchen table after my shower, then.

Fury licks at my throat, a dozen nasty words for Denendrius begging to tear free. I swallow hard. "You said they were nice to you. That the nickname helped you feel better about how your mind worked. That it made you feel unique."

Her nose wrinkles, and tears stream thick down her cheeks. "Denendrius is my big brother. He knows what's best for me, Marianna."

I study her tight mouth and furrowed brow and sigh.

"What's wrong?" My voice is so limp I worry it doesn't sound genuine enough.

She wipes her eyes with the back of her hand. "I keep thinking about Rayonne."

My teeth snag the inside of my cheek as I stare down at the blankets, the memory of her heart in Denendrius's hand tightening like his fist around my own.

"About how he killed her?"

"Yes," she squeaks. "I don't understand why he'd do that. She was our friend."

"Rayonne was unfinished business," I explain. "She escaped when he killed her clan, husband, and son. When he was human, he believed she was trying to come between us."

"Rayonne was trying to hand him over to Viorel," she whispers.

"Yeah."

"But she was our *friend*," she sobs.

She's not the first friend Denendrius has killed. I can't help but picture Jenna lying in that alleyway again with her wrists slit because he hypnotized her into taking her own life.

"I didn't mean for things to happen this way," she sobs, desperation creeping into her voice. "I just wanted Denendrius to help me kill our father so we could all be free out in the world together. I didn't mean for anyone to die. Maybe a few guards if they refused to let us go, but not our friends."

She keeps explaining, as if her regrets could change anything.

Tears well in my eyes again, and I sink onto the edge of the bed. Are Carol and Derek still alive? I never saw them amidst all the madness.

Adelia crawls to my side, and I sling an arm around her, my limbs as heavy as the weight in my chest. Her guilt seeps into my borrowed T-shirt as she cries into my shoulder.

"I thought my *glitching* would stop if Denendrius and I

killed our father," she confesses. "Like his death would flip a switch in my head, making all my episodes disappear." She buries her face deeper into my shirt. "The only real change between him being dead and Viorel locking him up is that now I know for sure he can't hurt me. But in my heart and mind, I still feel the same."

My throat tightens, my grip hardening on her. "Viorel never would've let him out, Adelia."

"It wasn't enough," she whispers, her voice thick with pain. "The dungeon . . . it just wasn't enough. He was across the castle, and he was still too close to me."

I swallow the urge to tell her I understand. She'd have to know I'm talking about Denendrius. So instead, I say, "That makes sense."

She pulls in a deep breath. "I remember how the episodes started whenever I knew my father wanted something." She gulps for breath. "When he would—he would—he—" Her quick breaths rush in and out. "He would come near me, and the way he touched my leg or breathed . . . I would just disappear inside my head. It started happening more frequently when I was a vampire, even when he wasn't an immediate threat. Sometimes, just thinking about it would fling my mind out of reach. I suppose having a vivid, perfect memory isn't always a gift."

I'm unsure what to do but hold her harder, knowing my grip won't hurt her.

"He started waiting until I'd dissociate or forget things, then hurt me."

"You never told anyone?" I ask, my voice free of judgment.

"No," she whispers. "For centuries, he was all I had, and I was scared I wouldn't be able to take care of myself with how my brain works. I was afraid to be on my own. At the castle, I don't really know why I helped him hide it. Maybe I was afraid he'd kill me if I told, or maybe I just didn't want everyone in the castle to know. If they knew, I might have been ashamed and wanted to leave, and I wouldn't have known how to do that. The world was changing so fast, and it seemed so scary to figure it out myself."

I gnaw on my lip. "You have Denendrius and me now. We'll keep you safe."

She takes my hand, and my fingers stiffen. "I just hope I don't feel like this forever."

I swallow. "One day, everything with your father will feel like a smaller, shorter part of your life. You've made it nearly two thousand years already. What's a few thousand more?"

"I'm so thankful to have such a good best friend and brother." She exhales a shuddery sigh. "Why did you and Denendrius fight so much, anyway? What happened?"

"Do you really want to know?" I fight the urge to pull my hand away. "You might wish you hadn't asked."

Her grip tightens, and her voice slips out soft. "I'm sure I can handle it, Marianna. You can tell me. I'm here for you."

With a swiftness that likely isn't long enough, I assess the risk. How loyal is Adelia to Denendrius? Despite her naive, misguided reasons for helping him escape and letting him take me from the castle, would she do *anything* for him? Would she overlook the most abhorrent truths simply because he's her brother? Does her gratitude for how he cared for her when they were human give him ultimate power over her? Or does our friendship—the fact that I uncovered who she truly is and helped her escape her father—balance her loyalties?

I test the ice instead of darting straight onto it. "Can you hear him right now?" I whisper.

She shakes her head against my shoulder. "I haven't been able to for a bit. He must still be across the ship."

I draw in a deep breath. "Okay."

Adelia listens in silence as I start from the beginning. I tell her how I was in the process of being adopted when I was five, and how my adoptive parents took me to Enchanted Land. I wandered off—got lost—and met Denendrius there. She holds her breath as I tell her how he took me for twelve days before my homesickness convinced him to return me. How he had planned to give me to his friend Sergei to raise, so he could return when I was a teenager.

"Didn't your family miss you?" Her voice is so quiet I nearly speak over her.

"They did. The FBI was looking for me."

She says nothing more, so I continue. I tell her how, despite going back to my adoptive parents, immortal bounty hunters had already seen Denendrius and me together before he returned me. After I was back with them, they asked him to trade his life for all of ours. He gambled on the assumption that they would keep me alive because of their rules against killing children. Though they did, they still killed my adoptive parents, and I was sent back to my birth mother after she and Red Revenge bribed a judge.

It feels like recounting another life as I tell her how my mother kept me locked in my room for years and sold me, until Denendrius came back when I was nine and discovered what I'd been going through. He beat her, called the police, and I was placed back in foster care.

I briefly recount my foster care woes, my heroin addiction, and the gang violence. I tell her how I met Denendrius at the mall on my seventeenth birthday—what I thought was the first time—how he took me out to dinner and a movie that evening, and how we had our second date the next day on a boat on the lake.

"But when he took me home, he didn't even ask for my address. It scared the shit out of me, realizing this man I thought I didn't know had been stalking me."

"That's a reasonable response," Adelia says, to my surprise. "Did everything get cleared up after he explained how you two really knew each other?"

"He never did," I whisper. "He told me he had his reasons for waiting so long to tell me the truth, but by then, he had already taken me to his apartment, where he wanted me to stay as his girlfriend."

She lifts her head off my shoulder and looks at me, confusion easy to read in her eyes. "Well . . ." She doesn't finish her thought, just bites her bottom lip as she waits for me to continue.

"I was scared out of my mind, you know? I thought he was a stranger and didn't understand what he had in mind for us. I fought him, and he got frustrated and hauled me out to the woods."

It's subtle, but she leans away from me slightly when she asks, "What'd he do?"

It takes me a moment to convince the words to leave my mouth, a ripple of fear spreading through me at the thought that Denendrius might be outside listening. But since Adelia has given no sign that he is, I say, "He stabbed me. *A lot.* He was . . ." I take a deep breath, my heart seizing at the memory of that day. "He intended to kill me, but he realized how much he loved me, and healed me instead."

Adelia's gaze drops to her lap. "Is that why you have so many scars?"

"Yes," I whisper, knowing she must have seen them while we were dressing.

"*Oh.*"

My throat tightens as I continue. "He was very . . . *angry* when we were first together. We were both really angry. Sharing each other's feelings through his mark probably made it worse."

Sadness hangs on the corners of her lips. "How angry was he?" she asks, like she knows there's more.

"Our relationship was pretty violent in the beginning," I admit. Though I don't put the blame on him, she should know it was one-sided from the mere fact he has immortal strength. "I wasn't ready to be intimate, and he was *extremely* impatient."

Adelia wraps her arms around me and returns her head to my shoulder.

"We were in hell, Adelia," I admit. "We acted like we hated each other while he insisted we were in love."

I tell her all this in a way that simply states the truth, appointing no blame. I attach no emotion to my words, lest she form her own conclusions about my feelings for Denendrius and take her observations to him.

"Is that all true?" she chokes out when I finish.

Tears cling to my lower lashes. "Why would I lie?"

Adelia starts to cry.

So many times during our conversation, I wanted to tell her about the tapes—about the number of girls he's raped and killed. That he's worse than her father. Yet I can't get the words past my lips. Maybe I'm afraid to tell her, or maybe I don't want to share the pain of knowing with her. She already regrets the chaos of freeing him, and despite the knife of betrayal burrowed so deep in my back that my heart thumps against its sharp tip, part of me wants to protect her from the full weight of her mistake.

In the end, knowing what a monster her brother is won't change anything. He's shipping her off to Italy, and I want someone alive who might be on my side when we get there. I don't trust her to handle insurmountable guilt when she's scared and alone.

"We can still love him, right?" she asks. My brow furrows, and I can't help but wonder how much weight she gives my thoughts and opinions over her own. It seemed like she was trying to prove herself to me—to show how strong she was—by pushing against her father once I stood so boldly in her defense.

Maybe she expects me to say yes, but I can't shake the feeling that she's asking for permission.

Regardless, there's only one answer. "Of course."

"Even if he was violent with you, you two made up, right? You loved each other when he was human, and love conquers all."

Except, it's not love he wishes to conquer me with.

"Have you ever been in love, Adelia?" I bite my lip, wondering if she's even capable of understanding.

She was only fifteen when she died, shaped by Roman values, clearly unmarried, and kept under her father's thumb for nearly two thousand years. She must have no concept of a healthy, modern relationship.

"Perhaps once," she murmurs. "There was a boy I really liked when I was human. He was the son of another landowner—one of my father's friends. He had dimples and short, cropped brown hair. We kissed a few times and would go on walks, peruse the forum, and sit together to watch the gladiators. We thought our parents might arrange a marriage for us."

"Did they?" I wonder. Did she die engaged?

A sob escapes her, and she chokes it back. "He joined the legion, and Father said it was for the best. Father never thought any boy was good enough for me. I thought he would've kept me unmarried forever if he could."

It's likely, since he made it hard for her to have friends.

She moves her lips to my ear and whispers so low I have to hold my breath to hear. *"He's coming."*

I go rigid as Denendrius enters the room, my tongue too knotted to speak.

"Hi," Adelia whispers.

Denendrius just stares at me. "Are you telling her how I used to beat you?"

My wide gaze plummets to the floor, my heart thumping so hard it feels like it might give out. "I—I was just filling her in on what happened before the castle."

"It's true," Denendrius says, his voice monotone. "I'd break her bones and knock her unconscious. She'd holler and cuss, and I'd choke her."

Adelia gasps, tightening her grip on me.

"We fed on one another's anger when we were bound by blood. We made everything more complicated than it needed to be, and I resorted to the violence I had always met others with. I haven't hurt her on purpose since before I received the cure for vampirism. It helped us, stripping all our anger away and allowing us to be happy. I will never intentionally hurt her again."

"Do you promise?" Adelia asks, her voice barely above a whisper.

Denendrius moves across the room with deliberate slowness, his eyes trained on me as he kneels. His gaze, silky and red like cut rubies, locks onto mine. He scoops up my limp hand and rests it on my lap. A sourness churns in my stomach, and my palm sweats in his.

"As I vowed before Sergei turned me back, I'll remain as I was when I was human. We'll share the same love. We'll be happy." He squeezes my hand. "I promise."

Adelia reaches out, resting her hand on his shoulder. The corner of his lip lifts as he turns to kiss her hand before his gaze settles back on me.

"We're going to be one big family, Marianna. You, me, Adelia, Sergei—and all our children. When we return to Italy, we're leaving all this pain behind us. All this grief. We're starting fresh, and we'll finally be happy."

I want to scream that I was happy. I had my fresh start at the castle. I had a big family—Viorel and Laurentius to share my heart with, a baby, my Aunt Carol, and Derek.

Best friends. Rayonne—dead now. And Adelia, who might as well be, giggling beside me in relief, her fresh tears still pattering against my T-shirt.

I'm alone in my nightmare.

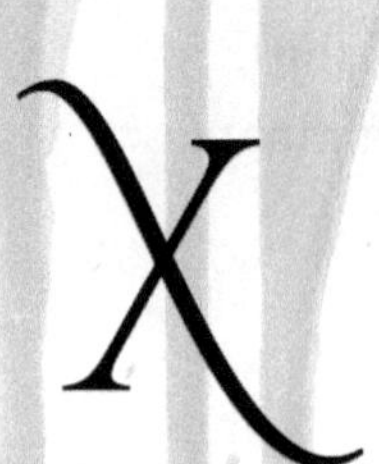

I spend the rest of the night watching movies with Adelia in the lounge—rather, my mind drifts as I stare unfocused at the screen. Denendrius checks in periodically, though only for a few minutes. As our worries about his control compound, she opts to find him.

I return to my cabin and crawl into bed early.

Hours later, Denendrius joins me, his cold, iron-tinged breath wafting over my face as he nuzzles into his pillow, his starry eyes locked onto mine. He pulls the blanket up to our shoulders, a soft smile tugging at his lips.

"I love you," he murmurs.

"I love you too." My voice is low, and I fear its lack of passion.

He lifts a hand to my face, my muscles twitching beneath his touch as his fingers trail across my cheekbone.

"I missed you so much, sweetheart," he says, his words saturated with a longing that makes my heart scramble. "I've been wanting you *so horribly* since we were reunited, but I feared my thirst was too strong."

Every muscle in my body screams, my flesh burning at the thought of his bare body on mine. My mouth is a desert, dry as if filled with sand. I go stiff as he shifts forward and presses his lips to mine. His wet lips glide over my dry ones, and I force my eyes shut since his already are.

When his hand drifts to my waist, my muscles strain beneath my skin, desperate to push him away. But it's useless to try—to think I can do or say anything that might make him stop. I know I have to keep pretending to love him, just as I did when I was his blood slave, if I ever want him to turn me.

"You're so tense." His lips ghost over mine.

"I worry," I lie. I don't tell him my body is screaming beneath his touch. "Are you sure you have enough control?"

He presses his lips firmly to mine before pulling away. "We'll only know if we try."

I can't breathe as he tugs my pants down, sliding my lacy panties past my thighs. He tosses them aside, but I don't hear them land through the ringing in my ears. Darkness pounds at the edges of my vision, my wide eyes locked on the ceiling as his wet fingers slip between my legs. The ringing in my ears shifts into a frantic buzzing, spreading across my skin like a thousand tiny crickets skittering over me. The darkness swallows half my vision, and Denendrius's voice barely reaches me when he asks what's wrong.

Both his hands cradle my face, their cold touch coaxing a thin tendril of breath past my lips and into my tight, resisting lungs.

"What's wrong, sweetheart?" he whispers. "Why are you panicking? I thought we worked past your fears when I was human."

A strangled noise escapes my throat as my eyes meet his. They're soft, but I still can't draw enough air to speak.

He sighs, leaning back on his elbow, his other hand stroking my cheek.

Darkness descends over his gaze, burning with hate. "It's Huarsar, isn't it?" he accuses, though I know the bite of his anger isn't directed at me.

Tears sting my eyes. I try to blink them away, but they spill down my cheeks instead.

"He's hurt you so badly that a simple touch sends your body into full-blown panic."

I nod, the motion sending more tears cascading down my cheeks. If only he knew that it's his touch making my body want to shut down.

"How often did he rape you?" Denendrius demands, his voice raw. "Hm?"

I manage a breath, a wet screen blurring his furious face. When I try to force out a lie that will satisfy him, a strangled noise twists free.

He exhales against my face, something in the simple sound making him seem so lost.

"Was he rough?" Denendrius asks, his voice lower, as if he doesn't want to hear his own question.

More disjointed sounds slip from my lips as I fight for a response.

"Okay." He sighs. "I'm sorry. I'm sure my questions don't help, but they've been driving me crazy for months. The guards used to tease me, saying they could hear you screaming for him to stop—that it went on for hours."

I squeeze my eyes shut, the mere idea like a needle in my chest. I tell myself it wasn't Viorel's idea to send the guards with such vile taunts to torture Denendrius, but that they came up with them themselves.

Viorel's touch was always kind. Commanding and guiding, but never harsh. He took control, but it never felt like he controlled *me*. Despite the blood he spilled, I never felt harmed. Every touch, rough or soft, was always given with love.

I think of him, my mind looping around the scent of rose perfume he sometimes wore in his hair. His soft lips on mine, the music of his voice whispering in my ear, his chest pressing against me, his body pushing mine into the bed. We were always connected, perfectly in sync, thanks to his ability to read my thoughts.

With him, I felt safe.

The memory steadies my breath, easing the tingling that ripples across my skin.

"That's it, sweetheart," Denendrius coos. "You're safe now."

Slowly, I lift my lids, forcing words to come together. "It was worse than when I was a child," I lie, knowing he was the one who helped me overcome my panic attacks around intimacy caused by my childhood trauma. But now, the story I feed him must be darker if I want to earn enough patience and sympathy to survive.

His crimson eyes roam my face before he nods.

"I . . . I don't know if I'm ready," I choke out. "The last time he—" I suck in a breath, the lie so bitter it tastes like betrayal. "It was the night you escaped. I'm still a little . . . *sore*, even though he wasn't as cruel as usual."

The image my lie conjures clenches my stomach. It's so far from reality that I feel exposed, like Denendrius might see right through it. Perhaps I fear Adelia—who may still think highly of Viorel unless Denendrius successfully warped her thoughts—overhearing and pressing me on it later.

Still, my words aren't enough to quell Denendrius's hunger. His hand trails down my chest, curving over my hip bone before gliding to my thigh.

"I'll be gentle, then," he whispers. "I'll make you feel better and erase the sensation of him. Just like when I was human."

I tense, my breaths turning shallow as his hand slips

between my thighs again. My mind scrambles for distraction, but the room beyond Denendrius is too dark to focus on, and thoughts of Viorel only make panic bite at my extremities. So I focus on breathing—deep inhales, slow exhales—pushing the panic away as he moves his hand.

His swift fingers coax pleasure from my gut, the unwelcome sensation sending my heart into a frantic drumbeat, my eyes flying wide. The muscles in my arms and legs flex beneath my clammy skin, my uncompromised nerves begging me to swat him away or squeeze his hand still. But I know stopping him is dangerous. It's just one more thing I'll have to force myself to endure until I'm strong enough to sever the ropes binding us.

"That feels good?" Denendrius murmurs, his lips hovering before pressing to mine.

I ache to tell him no, but the pleasure intensifies, and a moan slips out before I can stop it. Tears sting my eyes.

Guilt coils around my limbs, tightening with every response Denendrius wrings from me. It seeps through my skin, cinching tight around my bones as he crawls on top of me.

I tell myself it's not my fault. I can't help that he spent weeks mastering my body while I was his blood slave. My thoughts aren't connected to my nerve endings. I read it once, buried in a dusty psychology book about trauma from the back of the castle library. But facts don't still my shuddering heart, nor do they console me while my own body betrays me.

I hate him. I know I hate him. So how can I recoil at his mere presence, yet tremble beneath him when he's as close as physically possible?

Maybe it's the remnants of his blood mark, tangled with the simple mechanics of physiology. Viorel's blood may have stripped Denendrius's mark, but did it erase the damage it left behind?

Denendrius moves faster, and a sharp jolt of pain splits

through my core like lightning, wrenching a cry from my throat.

"Sorry," he gasps, moaning. But I see the trigger go off in his eyes, and he comes undone on top of me.

I stay still beneath him as his staggered breaths even out, blinking back tears, restless for the moment he pulls away. When he finally does, muttering another apology—claiming he didn't mean to hurt me—I draw my legs together against the ache and let out a shuddering breath. I can't stop the tears that slip free, trailing hot down my face, only partially from the physical ache.

Denendrius wipes them away, then pulls the blanket over me. "It's hard, having this strength." He rests his head on the pillow beside me. "I have centuries of practice. I'll get it under control again soon, once I've mastered this thirst."

Master his thirst? Since when has he ever been capable of that? I recall his bottomless stomach, carved deep from three hundred and twelve years of cycling deprivation. He even had a taste for vampire blood.

I swallow my tears and roll away from him. He sighs with satisfaction behind me, curling his body around mine and nestling his face in my hair as he breathes me in. I don't dare let a single whimper slip past my lips. Instead, I choke out an excuse about the bathroom and carefully ease out of bed, limping across the small room before shutting the door behind me.

I clap a hand over my mouth, sobs silent against my palm. Tears spill down my cheeks, slipping over my fingers as I hug myself and press into the wall.

Betrayal coils through me, so tight it crushes the air from my lungs, my heart aching against it. I know it's not my fault—Denendrius manipulated my body against my will—but it still feels like I've betrayed Viorel and Laurentius. What Denendrius forced from my body was nothing like what Viorel and I shared, yet it guts me to know Viorel must have felt it through our mark. Does he think I enjoyed it? Is he back at the castle cursing my name, believing I'm letting Denendrius do this to me?

Shame is a hot blade twisting in my gut, so sharp it sears down my legs.

I can only hope that the feeling rocking through me now is enough of an explanation for him. I have to believe he's smart enough to connect the two. He must feel the agony, the violent swing of emotion the moment I came down. Still, part of me fears what he's thinking. Will he hold this against me when I return? I shove the thought away, telling myself Viorel isn't that kind of man—that I've just spent too much time with Denendrius, and he's clouding everything.

"Are you okay?" Denendrius's voice drifts through the door, his concern jolting me from my spiral.

It's impossible to hide the sobs trapped behind my clenched teeth when I unlatch my jaw to choke out, *"I don't know."*

"You don't sound okay, sweetheart . . ." The warmth in his voice only makes the sharp ache running through my legs worse. "Did I hurt you so badly?"

A hiccup catches in my throat as I swallow a sob. *"I don't know."* My legs finally give out, and I sink to the floor.

I hang my head as the door slides open, my hair falling like a curtain between us. Through the long strands of my sandy brown hair, I see him squat, arms crossing over his knees.

"What's wrong, hm?" he coos. "I don't smell blood. Maybe I just scared you more than anything?"

With my forehead pressed against my knees, I close my eyes and wrap my arms around my legs. *"Maybe."*

"Did it bring back bad memories? Make you think of his abuse?" he whispers, his soft touch on my bare leg wrenching a sob from me.

But I cling to his excuse, nodding before he has a chance to consider any other reason for my distress. The last thing I need is for him to suspect it has anything to do with him.

"You're safe now, sweetheart. I promise." He takes my limp hand, prying my arm away from my legs. "He'll never touch you again. I'd kill us both before I let that happen."

"*Okay,*" I sob, and for good measure, whisper, "*I love you, Den.*"

He strokes his thumb over the back of my hand. "I love you too, sweetheart. Let me carry you back to bed."

I sniffle, lifting my head to wipe my tears. "Please."

As he scoops me into his arms, I rest my head against his shoulder, wondering where the fuck this man was when we first started dating. Perhaps if I had been the crying mess I've slowly devolved into, he would have met my fears with more understanding. If I'd sobbed into the phone instead of meeting his stalking with fury, would he have treated me like a mewling kitten, the way he does now, instead of an aggressive dog snarling at him?

Maybe it's for the best that he beat the fight out of me. Pretending would be harder if the gaping hole in my chest still held snarling beasts instead of the sorrow that drowned them.

I close my eyes as he lays me on the bed, then crawls in after me. He presses soft kisses to my lips, salty with tears, as he tucks me in and whispers goodnight.

I don't know how long I lie there, staring into the darkness, begging for sleep to grant me a reprieve from reality. Denendrius doesn't sleep either. I can tell by the way he breathes, shifting ever so slightly—like he's trying not to disturb me.

Eventually, I can't take the silence anymore. "What else did the guards say about me being down there with Viorel?"

He clears his throat, the thirst razor-sharp in the sound. "They said that, at first, he kept you in a cell. That you slept on the cold floor until he discovered you were pregnant."

I don't bother telling him that, despite being in a cell, I had a bed, a dresser, and no bars. And it was only until Viorel marked me. It's no use when I know Denendrius saw the bars in place when we went to Viorel's chamber to find Aeliana.

"Did you know I was allowed upstairs sometimes? That I had a bedroom I shared with Rayonne, and eventually, Adelia?" I ask, wondering how his reality reconciles with that.

"Yes," he whispers. "I heard he was close with that priest, Laurentius. That he took a liking to you after seeing you with Huarsar. They said he let you upstairs to indulge some fantasy that you were Laurentius's girlfriend. That he's psychotic. That most of the clan felt uneasy around him."

I chew my lip, unsure what to say.

"I heard of him before he went to the castle."

My brow furrows. I should dismiss everything Denendrius says as a lie, but I ask, "About the priest?"

He nods. "Not much, but I traveled enough to notice patterns—similar stories repeating over the years. He was stirring trouble with his cult. He'd infiltrate Catholic churches, preaching the Bible, then slip in his own ideas. People weren't well-traveled back then, nor could they easily seek information. So many couldn't even read. He'd draw in curious parishioners, leading them deeper into his doctrine outside of sermons. Somehow, he sought vampires to fold into his flock, pairing them with humans as familiars. Most of these were villages or small towns. The head priests would catch wind of it, and things would explode in his face. He did this town after town, using vampires to *save* souls from God—I guess he thought the Church had it all wrong—until a girl accused him of rape and devil worship. I stopped hearing about him after a while, but it's no surprise he fled to the castle."

He repeats much of what Laurentius told me, yet somehow makes it sound *far more* nefarious.

I don't bother telling him the girl who accused him did so, supposedly, to salvage her reputation after her family discovered their affair—or that she drowned herself in the baptismal pool and he was blamed for murder. Laurentius may have strange ideas to some, but he's never seemed like someone who could be capable of abuse like that. I had to *convince* him to kiss me.

Denendrius sighs. "I never had a problem with him—thought his take on religion made more sense, even if I hated *all of it*—until he went after you."

I close my eyes, focus on my breathing, and wait for the conversation to end.

"Was he as cruel as Huarsar?" Denendrius asks.

"No," I whisper. "He was kind. He defended me when other vampires were cruel because of my connection to you."

He's quiet for a beat—too quiet—not even a breath leaving him, so I lift my heavy lids to take in his smooth expression.

"Hm. Well, better than the alternative, I suppose." He sighs. "Perhaps he truly thought you could be his girlfriend. I was told he was fraught with delusion, that he thought angels were talking to him and had a chosen one complex."

I drop my gaze from Denendrius, Laurentius's sweet face vivid in my mind. My heart aches for him, and I can't fathom what he's going through right now if he's still alive.

If he's still alive.

Tears well up again, and I squeeze my eyes shut. How can I still have more to shed?

At least with Viorel's mark alive in me and his ability to manipulate the news, I know he made it back to the castle safely. But the last time I saw Laurentius was when Denendrius forced his rosary down his throat. What if I never again feel the comforting embrace of his soft arms? Never get to thread my fingers through his overgrown brown hair just to better see the light in his maroon gaze?

Laurentius and Viorel are two pieces of my heart, and I

don't know if it will ever beat properly again if one of them is missing.

"I'm sorry for bringing him up," Denendrius whispers, brushing his cold fingers over my puffy cheeks. Despite how his touch knots my stomach, the coolness of his hand soothes my flushed skin. I'd still prefer a cold rag, since at least it's not attached to him. "I've been sitting with these thoughts for months. I used to wait for you, even if it was just to hurt me. I preferred your cruelty over not seeing you at all."

"I'm sorry for that," I lie.

"It's okay," Denendrius coos. "You did what you had to. I understand. Knowing you were in that position hurt more than anything you ever did to me."

I squeeze my eyes shut even tighter, pale colors flaring behind my lids. "We should sleep."

"Yes." Denendrius heaves out a long and cold breath against my face. "Sometimes, I fear that if I close my eyes, I'll wake up back in the dungeon. Do you feel that way?"

If only I could tell him that every night I close my eyes and pray to wake up in the castle.

"Yes," I lie, wondering if I'll set a record for the most lies told by the end of this.

XI

I dream of Aeliana—of never making it home to see her again, and of how she grows up without me. Yet I see her vividly, as if I already have. Her medium-brown hair—so much like Denendrius's—falls in thick, loose curls down her back. Her eyes mimic mine, her face so much like mine that there's no doubt it's her. At the castle, she sleeps in the room Viorel gave me, in the same four-poster bed, and keeps her clothes in the same wardrobe.

She sits at Viorel's puzzle table with him, working on something colorful and more suitable for a human, nestled between the wooden pieces of his own puzzle. Her voice is muffled, as though I'm hearing it through water, as she vents about Laurentius not returning her affections. I can't see Viorel through the glow of candlelight—even in my dream, I yearn so desperately to see his crimson gaze and long, shiny brown hair framing his pale face—as he tells her she must give up on the idea. Laurentius helped him raise her, will never see her that way, and was in love with *me*. He tells her it's only been eighteen years since I died, and that Laurentius will need an eternity to grieve what happened.

Her voice is as clear as crystal when she asks, *"Have they found him yet? I want to find a partner on the other side of the veil. Don't forget, you promised I can travel once they find him."*

Viorel's response is so vivid it jolts me, as though he's truly here. "No, Aeliana. We still don't know where he went. That hasn't changed since he killed her."

"I hate him," she growls, her fury and hatred born from mine. *"I love the castle, Tata, but I hate being trapped here. It's all his fault I've never left."*

Viorel sighs, despondent. *"You're more like your mama than you know."*

My heart throbs, the grief so sharp that I wake to the sound of my own sobs filling my ears. I'm upright in bed, hunched over as my wails have Denendrius's hands stroking my back and thigh.

"What's wrong, sweetheart?" Denendrius murmurs from where he's propped on his elbow beside me, his kiss singeing my arm. "Nightmares?"

My breaths carry sobs in and out of me, clinging to them so firmly that I can't get any words out. I nod instead, my tangled hair a fluttering curtain between us.

I stay stiff as Denendrius sits, wrapping his legs around me and pulling me against his bare chest. My head feels like a weight I can't bear on my own, so I let it drop onto his chest and cry in his arms as they wrap around me. He pulls the blanket over me, tucking an edge between my shoulder and his chest to hold it in place as he strokes my back.

"I love you," he whispers.

I'm merely a host to my emotions, without even enough control to echo the words back. Instead, he hums softly in my ear and sways ever so slightly, pressing kisses against the top of my head from time to time.

Eventually, I wear myself out, and the dream loses some of its brightness as my consciousness lingers. Still, her face remains clear in my mind.

"What did you dream about?" Denendrius murmurs when my sobs have subsided, but my staggered breaths remain.

"I never saw her again." I choke on a few breaths and leave out the part where it's because he killed me. "But in my dream, she was my age."

Denendrius squeezes me tighter, his breath heavy beneath my head. Then he holds it so long that my lungs would ache, and his breath shudders when he releases it.

Though I know it was just a dream, I fear it as Viorel sometimes fears his own when he's unable to fully distinguish them from his visions. I can't bear the thought of my dream becoming reality. Vision or not, I know it's not an impossible outcome of this journey Denendrius and I are on. The threat of him killing me has always been present, like a third wheel I can't get rid of.

"When can you turn me?" I whisper, desperate for the immortality that could set me free. "I don't want to be marked by him anymore, Den."

He hums in thought as he runs his hand through the back of my hair. "I know. I want to sever his connection to you as well, but we have to build our family first."

Terror zaps my heart, dread so thick it suffocates any other emotion. I may have an out, though. "Any baby I have will be marked by Viorel," I say, my voice laced with tears, making me sound as upset over that fact as he believes I should be.

"I know. When I couldn't remove her mark, I realized we'd have to adapt our plans a bit."

My heart pounds in my temples. "How?"

"You remember how I went to the fertility clinic before Sergei turned me back, right?"

I nod against his chest.

"On top of giving a sperm sample to check if I was fertile, they froze some for later." He says it like it's a little surprise I hadn't already figured out. How else would I have interpreted his words when he assured me we would still have a family in the future, knowing he visited the clinic? "We can still have biological children."

"But his mark . . ."

"Mm. You're not going to be happy with this, but I know you'd rather have this option than not at all. We can take your eggs and do IVF. I'll give you the final say in the woman who will carry for us."

"A surrogate?" I breathe, trying to wrap my mind around the idea.

"Yes. But," he starts, like he's ready to place a cherry on top of the dessert of his idea, "since you won't be carrying them, I can turn you as soon as I have the control to bite you without drinking from you."

My brow furrows, a strange concoction of panic and relief swirling inside me. I could be a vampire *so soon*. I won't be forced to carry more children he's given DNA to . . . but they'll still exist. The idea of bringing siblings home for Aeliana is tantalizing, but I don't want Denendrius to be the one to create them. Besides, I'm not sure how having children would impact my escape. How could I possibly choose between Aeliana and the other babies made from both of us? No matter what, I'll be abandoning someone.

Would I flee to my firstborn and Viorel, or would I suffer through a life with Denendrius so that any future ones he forces into the world aren't left alone with him?

I hate that I already suspect it would be the latter—because if Aeliana is alive, at least she's safe with Viorel.

Regardless, I can't accept either outcome. If we have more children—*if*, as if there's even a question to his plans—I would have to find a way to bring them with me.

My plan will have to include killing Denendrius.

Fresh tears slip down my cheeks beneath the impending, crushing weight of my future. Death, undoubtedly, would be easier. If I had nothing to live for . . . well, I wouldn't insist on living at all.

Denendrius sucks his teeth in pity and strokes his fingers against my back. "I know you'd much rather carry our children," he coos. "I could hardly see that you were pregnant with Aeliana, but the sound of her life inside you . . . I wish you could carry them too."

I wipe my cheeks with the heel of my hand, and a question flickers through me, budding with hope. Maybe we won't be able to use my eggs at all. "But even with my eggs, won't they be marked? They're from me."

"I've never heard of vampires attempting this exact method to bypass a mark, but I've been pondering it from every angle. Logically, no. A human must have pure vampire blood introduced into their system to be marked. When Viorel marked you and Aeliana, she was only a whisper of life—too new to be anything but an extension of you. Just a few weeks developed. No heartbeat, no blood of her own, no soul or essence. Only what you gave her—material already influenced by his mark. She would have become her own person, but with his influence baked in from the start, drawn from your body as she formed. There wouldn't have been transference. She would've just existed beneath his power from the moment the gods allowed a soul to take root in that mark-formed little body."

He's quiet for a long moment, as if grappling with the extent of loss shaped by these conditions. Then he exhales. "He couldn't mark a human just because you gave them your blood or an organ. So why would an unfertilized egg carry his mark? The mark exists inside you. It strengthens your body, makes your mind more reliant. It's rooted in your essence. That's why only death—or, usually, a vampire overwriting it—can break it.

It will remain in your blood, no matter how much I drink from you."

I can't think of a logical counterpoint, so I sit in silence, absorbing the new complexity of returning home.

"Think about how wonderful it would be," he continues. "We could still build a biological family, even as immortals. How many vampires get to do that? We could potentially have multiple little families throughout eternity, spacing out their births. We could have them all at once, or we could raise a few before turning them—enjoy immortality with them for a while —then start again. And when we run out, we could still have cycles of families by adopting. Think about how many children we would have to love us. Eventually, they would all catch up to one another in age."

"I thought you wanted to turn them into vampire children so they wouldn't be old enough to stop loving us."

Denendrius sighs. "I've thought about that more since discovering you were pregnant. I want to see them grow up, to see how they look and who they become. We could turn them as teenagers or young adults, so they'd be old enough to help expand our family. I'm sure they'll still love us, and we won't spend eternity wrangling immortal children."

"I don't know much about IVF. How many children could we have?" I muse.

My mind spins with ideas, veering away from Denendrius's onto a path of my own.

Denendrius's voice carries a shade of happiness. "I've always wanted a big family. If you don't have to carry them, we could probably have a dozen or more, spread out over a century or two. We shouldn't have more than a handful at a time, so we can share our love evenly before they've grown. A surrogate may not be ideal, but it means you don't have to settle for having only one or two children yourself just so you can turn while you're still youthful. We'll start with one baby until you've mastered your thirst. How about this—to make up for it, you can mark the surrogate? You'll get to experience the pregnancy through her. It's not the same as mothering your own, but it's a worthy price to pay for immortality."

My mind seizes the sudden opportunity in front of me. Before Romania, I always thought I'd want a family of my own someday. Though the specifics of the dream were vague, and I was nowhere near ready to shape them, I still wanted the normalcy of a husband and kids. Part of my reason for having Aeliana—despite Denendrius's involvement in her creation—was the belief that she would be my only chance at some semblance of that dream.

"How long?" The question rushes out of me, a mishmash of desperation and dull excitement.

"IVF will take some time, but as soon as I'm ready and they've retrieved enough eggs from you, I'll turn you. I can use hypnotism to speed things along and bypass some health protocols since I'll be turning you afterward anyway, but retrieval will still take about a month. By then, I'll probably have enough control. We'll have everything shipped to a clinic in Italy before we go and then find a surrogate."

My heart pounds as I grip onto his words.

This could be one more thing to cling to desperately. One iota of benefit to salvage from this nightmare. I could have more biological children, an idea I never would have been capable of forming in the castle. Viorel and I could use my eggs—perhaps even Laurentius, if he's interested in being a father. Though I know neither of them can have biological children, maybe Viorel would like the idea of choosing a donor to have more with me, especially if he was willing to accept Aeliana as his own, even though she's biologically Denendrius's.

If I time things right, could I attempt to escape before Denendrius uses my eggs?

"Do you think you can keep fighting his mark for another two months, sweetheart?" he murmurs. "I know it'll be hard."

"Yes," I breathe.

I tremble with anticipation. I can pretend for another two months. Two months feels so soon compared to no tangible timeline at all. I don't know how long it will take me to return to Romania, but at least the time leading up to then will be spent as a vampire. With immortal strength and speed, an opportunity to escape will present itself eventually. And if I keep playing this game, Denendrius will eventually relax—settle into the peace of his delusion—and let his guard down. Hell, maybe he'd be so relaxed in bed that I could simply drive a stake into his heart with such speed he'd have no time to react.

Denendrius exhales a long breath, his arms loosening around me. "I know we were both happy with adopting children, but I'm overjoyed that we can have our own too."

"Me too," I lie.

XII

The next few days pass with my eyes a little drier. I grip Denendrius's words that I could be a vampire in two months. The idea gives time shape, making it feel a little less endless as I move through it.

I let Denendrius show me around the ship, my eyes drifting over machines and equipment in the engine room that I'm only partially present to acknowledge. He talks endlessly, his excitement palpable while describing things I can't find a place for in my mind.

The chef, Cristian, brings me supper at night and prepares a midnight meal at the end of each shift, since my routine is backward. Questions linger in the eyes of every crew member who glimpses me, but they never ask.

Most of my nights are spent preparing Adelia for the modern world. She knows so little that we end up on a dozen tangents just to clarify our original points.

Denendrius insists there's no reason Sergei wouldn't be on shore waiting for her—no way his capture in Bellevue could have compromised Sergei's position. Viorel gave no indication to either of us that they even knew where to start looking for Sergei. Denendrius told him to run, then went back to our house in Bellevue to face Viorel's men alone.

He urges Adelia to relax, assuring her that Sergei will make sure she has a properly prepared familiar before being left alone. But just in case Sergei doesn't show, Denendrius walks her through a backup plan—how to identify a reliable familiar on her own and get to the villa safely.

When she begins to spiral about the possibility of going with the wrong vampire, he gives her a clearer mental image of Sergei and arms her with details to verify his identity.

I tell her it's probably best to let her friend do most of the talking in public until she learns. I warn her not to rely on what she's read in books or seen in movies, as they're usually inaccurate representations of the real world—though not always completely wrong. She's so insecure about the entire thing—explaining that she's never had to think about plans before since she always followed her father's lead blindly—that Denendrius and I lay everything out for her step by step, even the obvious.

Denendrius warns her about modern-world safety measures: how she should assume there are cameras everywhere—sometimes even in someone's home or pocket, in or on cars and in alleys. They can see in the dark, and destroying them won't erase what's already been recorded. Always act as if someone is watching; more often than not, someone is, even if they don't realize it, and they might remember you later.

My own future as a vampire simmers at the back of my mind as we give her advice. There won't be anyone to help me navigate the world once I'm turned. With the autonomy vampirism would grant me, I wouldn't be surprised if Denendrius did everything short of literally leashing me when we step outside . . . if he even allows me outside at all.

Though I don't settle her nerves, she seems more excited to experience the modern world. Despite her restrained enthusiasm, she once again suggests that she remain with us. I'd love to help her convince Denendrius to let her stay, but I need to be on his side. Since her request mainly stems from the risk of her mind putting her in danger, Denendrius takes a Sharpie and writes critical information about reaching shore in Latin on her arm.

Soon, we near the coast of Italy, standing on the gangway with red metal walls behind us, beams and rails offering some safety from the churning sea below.

"Are you sure I can't come to America too?" Adelia asks for the dozenth time, staring across the water at a landmass too blurry for my human eyes to appreciate.

"It's safer for us to split up," Denendrius reminds her. "Huarsar will expect you to be with us."

"I'm scared," she admits, drawing in a deep breath. "I've never been alone like this."

"I'm confident Sergei will be waiting," Denendrius insists. "You'll be fine, even if he isn't."

She nods and takes another deep breath.

I gnaw at my cheek, fighting the urge to grab her arm and hold her back. With her here, pretending with him would be easier. Her presence might even help keep his behavior in check.

"I'll be okay," she says, though I can tell she's trying to convince herself. "How long until you come home?"

"Only a few weeks. We'll be as quick as we can and fly back," Denendrius assures her.

"I haven't been back to Rome since we died," she whispers, an ache in her voice.

"Me neither." Denendrius heaves a breath, as if considering how he might feel when he's as close as she is to arriving.

Adelia turns, her brow furrowing. "You mean you haven't been to the villa?"

My brows lift in surprise. I assumed he had, but that wouldn't make sense because he told me he hasn't been back either.

"No," he admits. "I've seen photos and videos, and Sergei has gone on my behalf, but I haven't set foot near Rome since."

"It's going to be weird," she breathes. "Seeing how different everything is. Everything we knew is in ruins now." She pauses, lost in thought for a moment before shifting her gaze across the sea, purposefully avoiding his face as she asks, "Do you think any part of our home is still standing? Recognizable?"

"I hope not," he says, his tone dull. "It's for the best if most of it is in ruins."

She bites her lip and nods. Tears well in her black eyes before she leaps forward, throwing her arms around me. "I'll miss you," she says, squeezing out the words. "I can't wait for you to come home and be turned."

I wrap my arms around her and give her the kind of relentless bear hug a best friend would. "Miss you too," I say, and in a way, I mean it.

I already miss our friendship . . . or at least what we had before she did *this*.

She pulls away and steps up to Denendrius, burying her face in his chest as they share a tight embrace. He whispers something soothing in Latin before they separate, then leans down and gives her a swift peck on the lips. A smile tugs at her lips as he pulls away, though my eyes fly wide. She turns back to the ocean, exhaling an anxious sound.

"Okay, love you guys," Adelia says, climbing onto the railing and balancing. She leans forward, lifts her arms above her head, and leaps. She's so graceful I don't even hear her slip into the water, but I catch a glimpse of her a few yards away, a streak of moonlight gliding with her as she swims.

I sigh and turn away from the rail, now alone with Denendrius.

I can't help the judgmental arch of my brow as I cross my arms and meet his gaze. "You and your sister kiss on the lips?"

He snickers, a grin spreading across his face. "Oh, sweetheart, please don't tell me you're jealous of my sister."

I roll my eyes. "No, I've just never seen brother and sister kiss on the mouth before."

Denendrius's laugh only intensifies. "You're silly, sweetheart. In Rome, closed-mouth kisses were common between friends and family."

"All right." I relent, knowing better than to make a thing of it.

He slides closer, his smile so wide I almost think he's happy until I see the emptiness in his eyes.

Hooking his hand beneath my jaw, he tilts my head back and slowly closes the gap between our lips as he murmurs, *"I'll show you how I'd never kiss my sister."*

I inhale sharply as his lips crash against mine, his tongue darting into my mouth. His other hand fists my hair, gripping my head to his before sliding down my back and pulling me flush against him.

"Do you think the crew would mind if I had you right here?" he says, his words heavy with lust.

"On the cold, grimy metal?"

He groans against my lips. "It'd be much more romantic on my ship."

Yeah, I'm sure every girl he forced back to his cabin on his pirate ship thought it was *oh-so-romantic* too.

It's not long before we reach the Atlantic Ocean, and Denendrius's mood dramatically relaxes for the same reasons that have my muscles winding tighter. With so much open ocean stretching as far as I can see, I know the chances of Viorel's men tracking us down dwindle with each mile. My only realistic hope now is to make port in America and get captured while trying to leave the ship.

Still, I stare across the endless waves, watching the glistening water for a fleet of ships ready to ambush us.

None ever comes, and over the next couple of weeks, time moves like the waves—sometimes so gentle I glide through them, other times pushing and pulling at me as though I'll never move forward.

We play board and card games with the crew occasionally in the lounge, though Denendrius quickly grows bored of constantly winning at skill-based games, and the luck-based ones are too repetitive to hold his interest. He resorts to hypnotizing the crew for fear-driven, high-risk activities, but they don't hold his attention for long because he knows he can't kill any of them.

He has more fun taking me—naked—to enjoy in various places around the ship.

First-person shooters and fighting games provide a minor outlet for my stewing, bitter emotions, but when Denendrius plays with me, it almost completely negates any therapeutic effect. For a man who claims he only played arcade games in the eighties, he sure knows how to kick my fucking ass. It's all in his quick reflexes—sometimes so fast the game itself can't keep up—and his sharp mind, so I don't take it personally, despite how the constant losses make me want to beat him with the controller.

I give my full attention to the movies Denendrius picks, losing myself in the stories and pretending, for a while, that my life isn't my own. It's an easy escape. There are times when something reminds me of everything I'm losing, and the movie ceases to exist beyond the grief torpedoing through my mind.

But more frequently than not, the days push and pull at me, trying to pull me under as I gasp for breath. I flail through them like I'm drowning. I suppose I really am. I gulp down breaths when I can, but each time, a bit of water floods into my lungs. My chest has this ache that doesn't seem to go away. Some days are so bad I can't get out of bed, and my food looks like garbage in the bowl.

Thankfully, Denendrius is understanding and pins my mood on my being a grieving mother. I don't dare tell him about all the other people I miss so horribly too. I let him assume I'm hurting, that my trauma is an anchor keeping me in place against the current.

Some nights, I can't help but stare out the little window, my gaze rocking with the dark waves, hypnotized by their rhythm. I search the shadows for ships, for islands—*anything*. There's nothing but water.

When the monotony of my room becomes unbearable—Denendrius off somewhere with the crew, often leaving me alone for hours—I walk the long stretch of gangway to the bow, where the wind whips at me, sending my hair swirling in a tangled mess I don't have the energy to fix.

The bright red paint of the ship's bow is like daggers in my eyes, and I weave through the machinery and ropes, which remind me of giant spools of thread, to climb a little ladder attached to a small, bar-enclosed platform big enough for me to sit and look over the bulwarks. The crew leaves me alone, though I doubt I'm supposed to be here.

I focus on the rhythmic crash of waves against one another and the ship. Breathing in the scent of saltwater as we cut through it, I wish I could reach out, splash the cold water against my face, and shock myself awake from this nightmare.

Something about the ship's movement through the water, the sensation of it, soothes me. The way the water dances is strangely familiar. I stay there for hours, daring a glimpse of the sun . . . until Denendrius inevitably finds me and coaxes me back into the darkness of our cabin.

I want to wear the ocean like a blanket, to be wrapped up in it so completely there's no hope of untangling myself. It would be so easy to fall over the edge. Could I drown before anyone noticed I'd gone overboard? Sink so deep among the fish and sharks that my lungs would be too full of salt to save me, no matter how swiftly he swam me to the surface?

Or, with the containers stacked so high and plentiful behind me, I fantasize about a wave so strong and violent that it crashes against the side of the ship, toppling them over to crush me. Denendrius may be strong and quick, but I doubt he could navigate them in time to save me.

Lost at sea is a much more romantic idea.

One night, as a violent storm seizes the ship, I curl up against the cabin window, watching waves churn and lightning slash across the dark sky. The ship rolls side to side, excitement and panic pounding through my heart.

I struggle to keep my balance in bed as items slide back and forth across the floor, others flung from tables and shelves in the surrounding cabins. Waves spill so thickly over the metal containers that I can't distinguish them from the rest of the ocean. The storm feels inescapable. Once I come to terms with the fact we're going to fare the weather, the roaring sky and relentless rain against the metal of the ship have me feeling wistful.

Denendrius returns before dawn, soaked to the bone, his dripping hair hanging loose and his eyes alight with excitement. He strips and climbs into bed beside me, eager to watch the storm's fury.

"These are my favorite days at sea. Now imagine the thrill of facing this in a ship with sails," he says.

We steal a few extra minutes past sunrise, since the rolling black clouds blot out the horizon, and appreciate the way light fractures the sky as the sea pitches us back and forth.

XIII

On our eighteenth night aboard, Denendrius appears with the chilly wind on the forecastle deck, stepping up beside me where I sit on the small, barred platform against the bulwark's edge. Bare-chested and barefoot, he wears only jeans. There's a faded streak of black grease smeared across his chest, his fingers stained with it.

"She's beautiful, isn't she?" he murmurs, the breeze sending loose curls fluttering against his face. The smell of diesel wafts off him and fills my nose.

"What?" I whisper as I pull the thick, oversized coat tighter around me—the one Cristian gave me when he saw me wandering around shivering. I realize what he means the moment the word leaves my lips.

"The sea. It's much more beautiful with immortal sight, but you seem to appreciate it. The way the moonlight glistens on the curves of the water, the sound of the ship cutting through it, the crisp smell . . ." He pulls in a deep breath and looks down at me with a wistful smile.

"Do you miss it?" I hug my knees and rest my chin on them, safety bars digging into my back. "Being captain of your own ship? You seem so preoccupied with the crew."

"I do," he admits, his smile fading. "It's always nice being back on open waters, but ships have changed so quickly since *Neptune's Curse* sailed. I miss how simple they were, how quiet. Everything on this ship makes noise. Even the way it cuts through the water—the metal instead of wood—sounds different." He sighs and straightens, clasping the safety bar beside my head. "Still, it's interesting. It keeps my mind busy despite the thirst, and there's so much more to learn."

"They must appreciate your help," I tease. "Considering a couple of crew members have gone missing."

He smirks. "Want to stand on the gunwale? I'll hold you so you don't fall. We can have a little *Titanic* moment."

Since my safety barely matters to me right now, I rise and descend the metal stairs to join him on deck.

He lifts me by my hips, and I plant my boots on the damp metal of the bulwark's flat top—the gunwale, as he called it—as the wind presses against me. He leans his head against my back and begins to hum Celine Dion's "My Heart Will Go On," the tone rife with sarcasm. The crisp salt air wafts against me, and danger is only a slip away into the dark water below. Yet, an unusual calm settles over me, and I can't help the laugh that escapes.

Denendrius stops humming to chuckle.

"*Titanic?*" I tease. "How about *Dracula*? You know, the chapter about the *Demeter*?"

The volume of his barking laugh has me flinching in surprise, and his grip tightens. I giggle at my joke.

"I won't drink them all," he claims, a smile in his voice. "This ship's too big to run on my own."

His arm unwinds from my midsection, and for a heart-pounding fraction of a second, I'm standing unsecured before he's suddenly sitting at my side. He carefully helps me ease onto the ledge, then curls his arm around my waist. The gunwale is no more than a foot wide, leaving my thighs dangling over the void of the sea below. The danger—though I know Denendrius won't let me fall—is exhilarating. For the first time in weeks, I feel something close to alive.

"They don't notice a couple crew members missing?"

He feigns cluelessness. "I'm sorry, who? No one's missing. We've been undercrewed the whole time."

I purse my lips. "It'll be nice when I can hypnotize people," I say, ensuring to slip in mentions of my future as a vampire to keep it fresh in his mind.

"Ah yes, I can see it now. The children will never argue about cleaning their rooms." He chuckles.

I bite the corner of my lip and swing my legs a little. All the scattered pieces of information I have about his life as a pirate fail to come together to create a clear picture. "Why did you decide to become a pirate?"

"I wanted a fresh experience. I'd always enjoyed being at sea on the ships I traveled on, but I wanted one of my own."

"I heard you raided villages," I say.

He smirks. "Yeah, sometimes. Robbing and killing was a good cover for feeding, and there were always valuables, little treasures worth taking."

"Do you have buried treasure lying around?" I tease, quirking a brow at him.

He makes a tickled noise, his smirk softening as he nods. "Not necessarily buried . . . but hidden. You have to, with how long I've been around. I've got a few artifacts museums have been after, and it's fun keeping them lost."

I'm cautious with my next question, my body rigid as I pose it. "I remember when you were human, you mentioned a Child of Stars, who you took the last name Sovetta from as your own. Called him your big brother and said he died by getting a cannonball through his chest? Was he on *Neptune's Curse* with you?"

"Yes. We spent most of our time together. He died when the Spanish crew Mateo was part of sank my ship. He might have survived if he'd been better fed—we were on our way to port—or if he hadn't been distracted tending to other injuries. But they got him. Right in the heart." Denendrius's eyes narrow on the water, as if there's something suddenly more interesting about it. "What about him?" His voice is so stiff with reservation, my next question practically reverberates off the steel walls he's built around himself.

Sweat coats my palms, and I wipe my hands down my thighs and rest them on my knees. "In your letter to yourself, for if you took the cure, you wrote he helped you through the darkest time in your life. That he stopped you from killing yourself . . ." I place my hand on his thigh, and the muscle clenches beneath my touch. "He sounded like such an important part of your life, and yet I barely know anything about him or that part of your past. Can you tell me more?"

The lively waves and my nervous heart are the only sounds between us. Too many seconds pass with him staring off across the water, and I conclude I'm not getting an answer.

I sigh and lean my head against his bare shoulder, inhaling the scent of oil and diesel coating him. I force myself to be comforting in hopes he'll fill my curiosity on this increasingly dull journey and fall deeper into the delusion that I love him and he can trust me. My focus moves to the water, following the reflection of glittering stars as they ripple from wave to wave. I trail my fingers up and down his thigh.

My heart jolts when he finally speaks. "Sovetta found me in an Egyptian bath house. It was a week after I escaped Sirmium, and I uncontrollably drank everyone there. The water was tinged red, bodies floating. I slit my wrists, my throat, and thighs. The stench of blood drew him in, and he found me halfway through the process of cutting my heart out. He talked me out of it. He could read my thoughts and related to me in more ways than I could ever say aloud."

I tuck my arm between our bodies to wrap it around his back, planting a kiss on his arm before nestling my head back against it.

"Why did you take Sovetta's name?" I wonder, hoping my affection has primed him to offer more answers. "I remember your letter saying your Roman family names didn't matter anymore."

He nods vacantly. "Father was legally obligated to have his family names written with mine, but he refused to give them to me in any ways more than that. Denendrius was my cognomen, and he let Mother give it to me just so she had something to call me. Socially, he made sure nobody called me anything else. It was an old, adapted name from my mother's family's close friend, and it had lost meaning. He was the last in his lineage. They were good people, she told me."

He pulls in a chesty breath, his ribs expanding against my grip on him, and slowly releases it. "Sovetta was my friend's only name. He was the last of what remained of his culture. He came from a tropical island—now long at the bottom of the ocean—that a clan of Children of Stars turned into a carefully curated cattle pen. Before the vampires enslaved them, his ancestor was named Sovetta. He didn't know what it meant, as they lost their language, but every descendant born from her was given the same name so the vampires could track the maternal lines. His keeper had grown fond of him and turned him. Sovetta was all he had left of his family and culture, so he kept it. He was like a brother to me, so I took it as my family name too."

"What happened to the island?" I frown, unsurprised that a clan of vampires would resort to such a thing at least once in the past. "To the clan and people?"

"Five hundred years before I was born human, a small fleet of ships—another clan—stumbled across the island and observed what was happening there. Their leader disapproved of what they had done to the people and culture, becoming so enraged that the volcano on their small island erupted and the ground shook beneath them. He had his fleet circle the island, and they killed every immortal there. Sovetta thinks he escaped because his keeper kept him a secret. She wasn't supposed to turn any of the humans, and not enough time had passed since his immortal birth for him to be detected. He was the only Child of Stars there who had been made from their food, and while the others attacked the fleet, he fled."

He's silent for a few rapid beats of my heart, and I think I'll have to prompt him for more until he says, "Sovetta remembered watching the ocean swallow the land, the way the lava sizzled and spat when it hit the water. The humans died so swiftly during the disaster that he couldn't find his mother or siblings, not that he could have helped them through the ocean, anyway. He didn't know what else to do but follow the fleet. There was no other land around. He told me how their clan leader stood on deck and watched the ocean swallow his home. Sovetta snuck onto his ship as a stowaway until they stopped in what is now Italy."

I lift my head off Denendrius's shoulder, my brow furrowing. I'm conflicted about where my mind leads. "The clan leader sounds powerful if he caused a natural disaster. Who was he?"

Denendrius turns his head and locks eyes with me. "Sovetta said he looked more monstrous than the other vampires. He had long, straight, dark brown hair, and crimson eyes. He showed his fangs like it was an intentional, constant warning, and moved with a group of black-eyed vampires at his side. Sovetta heard my thoughts when he found me and recognized him in them."

I swallow a knot, my eyes dropping from Denendrius's. *"Viorel."*

A memory resurfaces, Viorel's fury when he first drank from me and tasted my pregnancy. It remains the most enraged I've ever seen him, so much so that the candles burned so hot I felt the fire in the air and observed the wax dripping down the walls . . . I can only imagine how his fury could have unsettled a nearby volcano, especially if he wasn't using most of his energy back then to keep the massive, magical force field that is the veil over the castle.

"Sovetta hated Huarsar too. They hated being slaves, being kept like cattle, but *he* wiped them out." He sighs. "Our bond started from that same hatred and hurt, from how we both escaped him."

My eyes flit over the ocean as suspicion fills me, like I'm trying to hide its presence from Denendrius. I don't believe for a moment that Sovetta managed to hide on a ship from Viorel. It's more likely Viorel purposefully turned a blind eye. He would have heard Sovetta's thoughts and what he went through. Considering Viorel was taken from his own lost culture to be turned by his maker during his mission to create a superior breed of vampires, he probably sympathized with Sovetta and intentionally let him live.

I swallow the rest of my questions surrounding Sovetta and study the thin clouds gliding across the glowing moon as I ponder. If my memory is correct, it was 1887 when Denendrius wrote that letter to himself to help him if he took the cure. If he was a pirate in the Golden Age of Piracy, that means there were less than two hundred years between Sovetta dying and Denendrius finding the cure after violently hunting it down, leaving at least three hundred immortals dead.

Was Sovetta dying his trigger? After centuries of his best friend keeping him together, did losing Sovetta drive him to want to end his life as a vampire again, though by different means?

Denendrius heaves out a sigh. "I miss my ship. I keep waiting for it to be uncovered by historians, perhaps pieces of it put on display, but they haven't yet. It's sunk in the middle of the Indian Ocean." He sounds dramatically grumpy when he adds, "I had to swim all the way to Madagascar, and did you know shark blood tastes horrible?"

I oblige his clear desire to tell me more about his ship. "What was your crew like?"

"Criminals, mostly," he says. "Sometimes during raids, we'd spring fit men from prison if they agreed to serve us."

For the next couple hours, I let him fill my ears with dark stories of adventure and details about his ship. His voice carries a rush of excitement, his descriptions so vivid it's as if he can see his memories on the water like it's a projection screen.

I'm yawning by the time our conversation comes to a natural close, a thin, wet fog slowly spreading around the ship like a cloud wanting to envelop me for sleep.

"Can you hear the sea animals?" I rub my eyes, yet to glimpse signs of anything as the night passes.

"Yes." He points across me to my left, somewhere in the distance amongst the thickening fog and waves that I can't quite place. "There's a whale and her calf over there, a few meters below the surface."

I squint, trying to see a burst of air on the shimmering surface in case they come up, but there's nothing. "Anything else?"

He grunts. "There's plenty of life, Marianna. It may not look like much from here, but it can get noisy below the water. It's muted, unless you're swimming around in it. They're much easier to hear when you're not on a thousand feet of metal."

We settle in a silence filled with churning water and the noise of the ship. I look up at him in question when he stiffens against my side and tightens his arm around me. His crimson eyes dart over the water, widening, then narrowing as he sets his jaw and crushes me against his side.

"What is it?" I squeeze out.

His voice comes through low and guarded. "You've heard of mermaids, yes?"

I stare at him through slitted eyes. "What about them? I thought they were a myth. Besides, didn't you say no other mythical creatures exist?"

Denendrius's gaze flickers over the water, intense focus shifting between the waves. "In Rome, they were sirens. Half-bird women who lured men with song. I have never encountered such things. At first, I thought perhaps I was glimpsing Nereids—daughters of Nereus, the Sea God. But Nereids aren't part fish as I've seen and don't resemble the girls I—" He cuts himself off and clears his throat.

The hair stands up on the back of my neck and my heart pounds. "They're real?"

His nod is slight. "They're the girls buried at sea, those who were once on ships. It's why sirens were thought to lure sailors."

Denendrius's past with girls on *Neptune's Curse* comes to mind, though it wasn't a topic he dared tread near tonight. I think of one girl he kept on his ship, when Mateo and his crew sank it and rescued the girl Denendrius kept prisoner in his quarters. She threw herself overboard during the night.

How many girls did Denendrius bury at sea?

"Do you see them?" I ask, a bit of horror laced in my words.

Denendrius's gaze flickers toward me, then back to the waves. "Don't you?"

I merely gawk, until he frowns at the water, and with a dark blur, we're standing back on deck.

"We should go to bed. It's nearly sunrise." His hand presses firm against my back. "Besides . . ." He hesitates, his crimson eyes flicking once more to the water. "I don't want them to see you."

Or is it that he doesn't want me to see them? He must be aware I know he's killed and buried girls at sea. Would he accuse me of being jealous, as he did when I discovered his videoed crimes against other girls?

"Why not?" I suspect there are no dead girls turned sirens flicking their tails through the sea, and this is merely another instance of him seeing dead girls, like when he believed there were ghosts in the apartment. I don't hear their songs, at least.

He grins down at me as he takes each of my hands in his and sways us backward toward the gangway.

I gaze out at the water, scouring for flicking tails of emerald or amethyst, for long brown hair shining wet with the silver of the waves under the moonlight.

"Sweetheart . . ." The smooth honey of his voice pulls my attention back to him. His smile is bright. "Do you know you're my favorite person in the entire world? Through all of time, *you're* my favorite. My girl." He draws me closer, releasing my hands to wrap his arms around me and sway. *"My sweetest girl."*

XIV

I wake with a gasp at the feeling of eyes on me, spinning over in bed to try peeling back the darkness for whoever stands there. I fumble for the lamp switch, and when my sweaty fingers finally twist it, my breath catches.

Denendrius stands in the middle of the room, his eyes blazing crimson, a waterfall of red spilling from his mouth. It flows thickly from his jaw, down his bare chest, staining his jeans.

"*Jesus Christ*, Denendrius! You scared the shit out of me." I heave out a breath. Strangely, seeing him dazed and covered in blood is more of a relief than my first fear that someone from the crew had slipped into my room to watch me sleep.

With Denendrius, I have my tricks to manage him. But with a different man?

His voice is flat. "I killed the crew."

Rubbing sleep from my eyes, I sit upright to take him in. "What do you mean?" I ask, careful to keep my voice even. "The *entire* crew?"

Surely, I must have misunderstood. He must be joking, just as I did the previous night.

But he only says, "Yes. The entire crew."

I notice the silence and glance at the wall-mounted clock. It's barely seven. There are no footsteps, no late sounds of the crew moving about the ship this evening.

"Are you okay?" I dare ask, my eyes drifting down to his crimson-stained feet and the bloody footprints trailing across the thin carpet toward him.

For him to spill so much blood must mean he succumbed to his thirst and lost control.

"Oh." He merely stares at me, and I quirk a brow and lean away. "We need to abandon ship."

My eyes widen. "*What?* We're in the middle of the ocean …"

"We could reach the shore in the dinghy by sunrise."

My jaw lowers, and I shake my head like I can clear the scene before me. Am I dreaming?

"The fucking *dinghy*, Den?" My voice is shrill. "Why don't we take the lifeboat?"

He stares at me like I'm stupid, his brow quirked. "You mean the big neon-orange lifeboat with GPS, the one specifically designed to ensure its passengers are rescued? You want to take that?"

"Goddamn it," I snarl. I would like to take that, actually, but for the exact reasons he doesn't.

"Dinghy," he reiterates. "I brought it aboard for a reason. Just in case."

"Can't we take the ship closer?"

He licks the blood off his lips and shudders. "No. Eventually, they'll radio us, and if the captain doesn't answer, it'll raise an alarm. We can't make port, or we'll be discovered."

"You killed the *captain* too?" I heard him, but I want to be wrong.

"There's nobody left but us. I tossed everyone overboard when I was finished."

My jaw hangs dumbly.

He drags a hand down his chest, leaving a dark smear of blood in its wake. "We need to leave before we get too close to shore. Either way, they'll know it was us if a ghost ship drifts in and any vampires sent to inspect catch your scent. But if we go now, we'll reach land before the ship, and we need every second we can get to cover ground before they figure it out."

"Why the fuck did you kill the crew?" I snap, a shiver running through me at the memory of that short, miserable trip in the dinghy. "Now I have to be in a dinghy all night? Fuck, man. *Fuck.*"

His expression remains blank. "You'll be fine, I promise. We're lucky the water's calm tonight, and we're even a little ahead of schedule. Gather your bag."

I throw off my blanket, adrenaline forcing wakefulness into my body. "You couldn't have picked off a few? It had to be *everyone*?"

Denendrius blinks, his lips twitching as he makes a few stilted sounds before saying, "I was thirsty and got blood drunk."

My feet hit the floor, and I pause. "You what? Blood drunk?"

He licks his bloodied lips again and gives me a wobbly nod to go with his vacant stare. "Yeah, I couldn't stop."

"I—" I exhale sharply. "But you're okay now?"

"Yeah," he says flatly, his eyes twitching in sync with the beat of my rapid heart. "Go ahead, pack up. I'll get things ready."

I gulp, standing as I snatch my backpack. "You don't seem okay."

"Everything's way too loud and smelly right now. It's a little much. It's been so long since I last indulged . . ." He turns slowly—painfully, deliberately—and stumbles sideways, reaching for the wall. His arm goes straight through.

I gape at him. *"Dude."*

In a blink, he rights himself, cursing in Latin under his breath. "I didn't mean to do that."

"Maybe we should wait a bit—"

He shakes his head so fast it blurs. "No. I could really use a swim to burn off all this energy. Feels great, but I also kind of want to peel my skin off. I'm buzzing."

I'm going to fucking drown out there.

He swings his head toward the bathroom, staring at the shower as his hand drifts to his crotch, rubbing himself over his jeans. "I think I'm going to take a hot shower first." He shudders. "I would make love to you, but I'd most definitely kill you by accident."

Or, I might go drown myself.

"Have fun . . . ?"

He's noisy as he moves to the bathroom, and I do my best to push what he's doing to the back of my mind as I dress in layers and a heavy jacket before moving around the room to gather my belongings. I have no idea when I'll eat next, so I head to the kitchen and cram as many snacks and drinks as I can into my bag. I grab a blanket and wrap it around myself in hopes of making the journey more bearable.

Once I'm packed, I follow his bloody footprints around the ship, heading to the bridge first. There's blood splatter across the windows and electronics, a pool of it in front of the helm. Moving back down the ship toward the stern, blood slicks the red metal of the gangway, glistening in the moonlight. I step around long smears of blood left by dragged bodies.

I make my way to the dinghy at the stern, where Denendrius left it, and sit beside it on the cold metal to wait.

"You're down here already?" he asks as he returns in the same bloodstained jeans I last saw him in. His half-assed rinse has only cleared some of the blood, leaving long streaks where the water cut through the red on his chest.

I mash my lips together and nod. "Thought I'd wait."

He smirks and lowers the service ladder, then grabs the rope from the boat, tying it to the railing before swiftly lowering it into the water. "All right. I'll go down and get it straightened out."

A handful of minutes later, I'm back in the dinghy, gripping the blanket tightly around myself as he pushes the boat away from the crewless ship.

"Remember that joke I made about the *Demeter*?" I yell over the rush of waves as he swims, pulling the boat forward.

"What about it?"

Scowling up at the dimly lit ship, gritting my teeth against the hours of waves ahead, I snap, "You weren't supposed to take it seriously."

He laughs, the sound half choked by water. He spits it out. "Yeah, well, wouldn't be the first time."

I roll my eyes. "How many ghost ships are your fault?"

"Too lazy to count." He slows the dinghy, syncing it with a wave before it can splash over me. "You know how hard it was to cross the Atlantic back then? Months at sea, a single crew to ration? Eventually, you snap—or decide it's more productive to drink them dry and use the extra energy to swim to shore."

"Yeah, I guess that makes sense," I mutter begrudgingly as his powerful kicks drive us forward again.

I watch the waves for hours, my mind drifting as Denendrius steers us toward shore. He says we'll need to take a slight detour to avoid the port, so he veers off course toward land farther down the coast, still near New York State.

Halfway through the journey, Denendrius's head pops out of the water as he drifts alongside the boat, crossing his arms on the edge while treading water.

"What?" I ask, shivering, soaked from a rogue wave that I wasn't lucky enough to be swept away and drowned by.

"I can't stop thinking about you," he says with a grin, the water settling around us. "I really want you."

I swallow hard. "Den, we're in the middle of the ocean."

His grin turns goofy, and he nods. "Yeah," he breathes, batting his lashes at me. "Under the stars, rocking on the water. That would be so romantic."

Another shiver rips through me. "I'm actually *f-freezing*."

He purses his lips and reaches out to run his hand over my soaked body. "Hm."

"Can we keep going?" I plead, hugging the soaked blanket tighter around myself, like that'll do anything besides hide my body from him.

He sighs heavily and licks his lips, pondering me.

I consider my options: let him have sex with me in the middle of the ocean on a cold, wet metal boat, or offer something just as appealing—maybe even more in my favor . . .

"How fast can you get me to shore without drowning me or flipping the boat? If you hurry, you could have me on the beach before sunrise. Now *that* would be romantic."

At least the night will pass faster this way, and I'll probably ache less since he'll burn off some of that energy swimming.

Denendrius hums and bites his lip. "Yeah, that's a much better idea."

I huddle in the bottom of the dinghy as the boat glides across the ocean with his swift strokes. Still, it takes so long. I search for constellations I've never learned to recognize and try to mentally prepare for shore. Occasional waves slap me or crash over my lap, forcing me to shake off the jolt and start all over again.

But I don't think I could ever fully prepare for him. It doesn't seem like I've had enough time before he's racing the dinghy onto shore, pulling me out, and sprawling me on the wet sand. I gasp for breath as he lies on top of me and paws my soaked clothes.

"Den," I gasp as I shiver against the icy sand, "slow down."

He stiffens, steadying his rapid breath. "You're okay." He shudders. "I'm okay."

I swallow hard and wrap my stiff arms around his neck, my breath ripped away as his mouth crashes against mine.

"Oh, I love you." He gasps as he yanks the belt from his pants and whips it aside into the dark. *"I can't believe how much I love you."*

"I love you," I manage between his frantic kisses.

"You're so *perfect*," he practically purrs. He undoes his wet jeans and wrestles them off with a few quick kicks of his legs. His lips crush mine. "So pretty. So warm. You're so soft."

I lean my head back to catch a breath before he can steal it again, my heart thrashing as I struggle to breathe beneath his weight. "Slow, please. *Please.*"

He flicks his tongue against my upper lip, and I stiffen as it darts into my mouth before he retracts it, nipping my lips hard enough to draw a bead of blood.

"I really want to shake you," he whines, pulling my legs—muscles sore from shivering—apart as he kneels between them, his hands finding my shoulders. He grips them, the pressure pulsing in his fingers before he trails them down, clutching both of my biceps.

My eyes widen under my furrowed brow. "P-please don't fucking do that. Why the hell would you want to?"

With an exhale, he slips his hands off me. "I don't know, but I won't."

Instead, he runs his hands up and down my body, like my skin fascinates him more than usual.

Despite his frenetic motions on top of me, he manages not to hurt me. I shiver beneath him the entire time, which he misinterprets as pleasure.

Thank fuck he doesn't last as long as usual, and I'm too cold for my body to betray me this time.

After we redress, he helps me climb onto his back. The next thing I know, we're standing at the door of a house in some random neighborhood as Denendrius hammers on it.

As he sets me on my feet, I ask, "Where are we—"

A sleepy-eyed man yanks the door open. "It's four a.m.—"

"Hey there, I'm Anthony. Welcome me in like an old friend and let me use your phone. Everything is normal right now," Denendrius says smoothly.

With his blue eyes locked on Denendrius's, he nods and steps aside. "Yeah, of course, buddy."

I follow Denendrius into the dark house, the furniture and décor obscured by shadows. We don't have to go far; a cordless phone sits on the entryway table. Denendrius shakes moisture and sand from his hands before plucking the phone from its base and pressing a handful of green-lit buttons. He exhales deeply, crossing one arm under his elbow as he lifts the phone to his ear.

The man studies me as he flicks on the entryway light. "Hi, I'm Cooper. You are . . . ?"

"His fiancée," I clarify as I wrap my arms around my trembling body. "Jane."

Cooper gives me a warm smile, straightening his messy mop of red hair before adjusting the tie of his bathrobe. "You guys are wet and sandy."

I nod, glancing at Denendrius as he grumbles and ends a failed call. He dials again, glancing over his shoulder—past Cooper—toward the hall. A few moments later, a girl with cherry-red hair yawns and appears behind Cooper.

"Cooper?" she asks, glancing between Denendrius and me.

Cooper catches her yawn and gestures to Denendrius. "This is my friend, Anthony, and his fiancée, Jane."

Denendrius's eyes skim the room for information before

settling on the girl. He half-smiles. "We went to Stanford together. You must be Leslie."

She nods and releases a breath. "Oh, yeah. Cooper never told me about you."

"We just recently reconnected." Denendrius's smile is so warm that the underlying danger of it makes my heart skip.

Leslie rubs her eyes, yawning again. "Why are you two soaked?"

I hear the phone line connect, and Denendrius shoots me a purposeful glance, silently passing them to me to handle as he begins a conversation in Russian. It must be Sergei.

My laugh is forced, exhaustion bleeding into it. "We got a little drunk and went down to the beach . . . fell asleep and got absolutely wrecked by waves."

She smirks and elbows Cooper. "We've been there." Looking back to me, she adds, "In warmer months, usually."

Denendrius pauses, turning the phone away from his mouth to meet Leslie's gaze. "She could use some dry clothes, and all hers need to go in the washing machine." He returns to his conversation, his tone more serious now.

Leslie waves a hand dismissively. "I have some stuff that's too small that would probably fit you, Jane. It's been sitting in my closet, waiting for the thrift shop. But let's get you rinsed first."

"Sorry to wake you so early," I say, following her down the hall and dripping onto her nice hardwood floor. The bathroom is small and pink, with a green cartoon starfish on the shower curtain and matching towels and bath mat.

"I had to wake up in fifteen minutes for my opening shift at the diner, anyway." She grabs a pink towel from under the sink and hands it to me before backing out of the room. "Be right back with clothes."

Fifteen minutes later, I'm warm in a pair of name-brand jeans and a fuzzy sweater. She hands me a fuzzy pair of socks from her drawer, and I go commando. Denendrius remains in the entryway, deep in conversation, but he lifts his gaze to acknowledge me.

"Are you heading out right away?" She flips on lights as she walks through the living room to the kitchen on the other side.

I spot Cooper's Stanford diploma on the wall now, and the photo of her and Cooper tucked half behind another with *"Leslie and Cooper 4ever"* engraved on the border, on the other side of the living room.

Since I have a good idea of what Denendrius and Sergei are discussing, I say, "He's just trying to get us a ride. Our friend was at the beach drinking with us too and left us there."

"Jerk," she teases with a grin.

My laugh is flat. "Yeah."

"Well, I'm about to start breakfast if you want some."

I agree, and since I can't shake the twinge of guilt for breaking into her home—I'm not completely sure she's going to live—I follow her into the kitchen, which shines with chrome appliances and white cabinets.

Cooper stands at the coffee machine as a pot brews. He asks if we want any, but I decline and accept a block of cheese and a grater while she cracks eggs for omelets. She asks if Anthony wants breakfast, and I tell her he will, knowing I'll get to eat his share when he rejects it.

Denendrius hangs up the phone, and I watch the doorway as he steps in from the living room, leaving a trail of water behind him. Leslie shoots Cooper a look I take to mean she wants him to deal with the man dripping all over their kitchen. Cooper merely sizes Denendrius up, like he already knows he has no clothes to offer this six-foot-four man when he's probably not even six-feet tall himself.

Neither of them protests as he drags a wooden chair from the kitchen table and drops into it.

"What's the plan?" I ask, half a block of cheese grated. I steal little mouthfuls every few passes over the metal.

He sighs, his eyes nearly black—a maroon easily mistaken for deep brown—as he watches me from across the room. "Sergei's in Lorimer. He can be here tonight. He was on shore waiting for Adelia, and she's safe at the villa with a familiar now," he says.

I don't realize how worried I've been about Adelia until some of the tension in my chest releases.

Cooper tries to interject with friendly questions, but Denendrius pauses to hypnotize them both—making them ignore our conversations, forget we exist the moment they walk out the door for work, and tell no one about us before they leave. He tells me we have to let them live, since missing persons this close to where a ghost ship will appear would give us away.

"Do you think it's safe for us to stay here all day?" I hand the cheese to Leslie, who stands at the stove.

"Yes. The ship is likely still miles from shore. There's no way for them to trace our path through the ocean, so they'd have to walk the coast for clues . . . which the tide will have already washed away. You were on my back beyond the tide's reach, so there will be no trace of you except what lingers in the air, and that will fade soon. Essentially, we're in the clear."

My heart sinks, but I say, "That's a relief."

When Leslie and Cooper leave for work and I've finished my two helpings of omelets, Denendrius secures their bedroom window and strips the bed, replacing the sheets and adding a fresh blanket. I crash almost immediately once my head hits the pillow, the soft warmth of the sheets and comforter blissful after the cold of the Atlantic. After so many weeks at sea, it's strange not to feel the ship rocking gently below me. The stillness jolts me awake in confusion until I remember where I am.

Denendrius lies beside me, but every time I stir, his eyes are open.

At some point, he nudges me—harder each time—until I gasp in surprise and wake.

"What's wrong?" I slur, drunk with sleep.

"I'm going to touch you," he whispers, slipping his hand between my thighs as I freeze.

His other arm shifts at my side, working himself, as his fingers graze over my underwear.

"What . . .?" I blink hard, shifting against the mattress. My brain lags behind my body, sleep pressing on me like a thick fog. "How are you still in the mood?"

He grunts. "Just am."

My stomach knots, and something prickly and acidic slithers under my skin, curling in my gut with the nausea of exhaustion.

"I'm sore, Den. Tired." I swallow against my dry throat. "Why'd you wake me up?" My voice is whiny, but I don't care, despite knowing the words are a waste of energy.

"You told me when I was human that you don't like being touched in your sleep, that you couldn't tell it was me and you'd wake up scared. So I woke you first, so you'd know. You can sleep. I won't get on you."

I squeeze my eyes shut, doubtful that I can, and nearly wishing he didn't wake me for some miniscule chance I might have been lucky enough to sleep through it. I hover in semi-consciousness as he works on himself beside me, his other hand between my legs as the blanket shifts and his breaths stagger, and drift off as soon as he's done.

I hope this doesn't become an everyday thing like when he was human. I'm not sure how much of his cravings I'll be able to endure, but I know better than to hope.

"Did you sleep?" I ask hours later when the sound of Cooper returning from his nine-to-five wakes me.

Instructed not to enter their room upon returning home—along with a dozen other rules Denendrius hypnotized them to obey—we're left alone.

"No." He sighs, rolling over to face me. "There are hundreds of heartbeats nearby, and I can't get them out of my head."

"Thirsty?"

Half-lidded, he nods.

I hate that I offer him my wrist, but it's what a good fiancée would do.

"Thank you, sweetheart, but after all those men on board, I'd be worse than blood drunk the moment I drank from you."

I'm not about to argue, so I just roll over and try to sleep.

Sergei throws his arms around Denendrius the moment he steps onto the sidewalk. Denendrius freezes under his grip for a beat before wrenching free, shoving Sergei back, and holding his arm out to keep him at a distance.

"Don't grab me like that," Denendrius snaps. "You know I hate it."

"It's a hug!" Sergei grins, rolling his black eyes. "Oh, come on. I missed you! Thought you were going to rot in that dungeon forever."

Denendrius rolls his shoulders like he's trying to loosen them as he motions to the car. "I missed you too, Sergei. Now get us out of here."

Sergei runs a hand over his blond buzz cut, his combat boots crunching on the gritty asphalt as he turns toward the car. "You need to loosen up, friend. I know you Roman fucks used to kiss each other on the mouth no matter man or woman. You still too good for hugs now?"

Denendrius stops short of the rear passenger door, hand

frozen and gripping the handle as he gives Sergei a long stare over the top of the car. "I will *literally* kill you if you ever kiss me."

Sergei laughs, opening the driver's door. "Not interested in kissing you, friend. I only tease."

Denendrius shakes his head, popping the door open and waving me in. I settle into the back seat as he moves to the front.

"The plan?" Sergei asks, cranking the car into drive.

"We need a hotel in Lorimer. Two beds. You're staying with us."

Sergei nods, and I keep quiet, watching the roads smear past as they talk in Russian. Every so often, I hear my name and Huarsar's, and Denendrius mentions Adelia too. I don't care much about what they're talking about—Denendrius is probably feeding him his twisted version of events—until he mentions Aeliana, tearing me from my thoughts.

Sergei gasps. "No fucking kidding, eh?" He glances at me in the rearview mirror. "A little baby? Wow. Where is she?"

"Yeah, don't get excited," Denendrius mutters. "Huarsar has her."

"How are we getting her back?" Sergei questions with a dark tinge of concern, like he worries Denendrius has a crazy and futile plan to do exactly that.

Denendrius heaves out a breath. "We're not. We can't."

I tune them out as he explains why.

It's strange seeing Lorimer's lights in the distance as we tear down the highway toward the city. I thought I'd never see it again, and when once that idea was scary, I now find I don't want to at all.

Thankfully, Sergei takes us to a middling hotel on the outskirts of the rich north. I have so little experience leaving the city—especially from this side—that I don't even recognize the buildings and streets around me.

Denendrius and I wait in the car while Sergei goes inside to secure a room. When he returns, we follow him to a room with an exterior door. Denendrius is relieved he doesn't have to go past the counter or risk drawing attention to the fact he's half-naked and shoeless.

"I need new clothes," Denendrius mutters as we step inside.

The faint scent of cigarettes—so foul now that I haven't smoked in a year—mingles with cleaner in the air.

I take in the beige walls and gray carpet with a sigh, passing the bathroom on my left to toss my bag onto the green-and-gray blanket of the first queen bed.

"Next one," Denendrius instructs as he glances around the room. "I want Sergei between us and the door."

"Happy to be your shield," Sergei mutters.

"You're such a good friend," Denendrius teases, shooting him a wry smile over his shoulder. "Mind taking a quick trip into the city to grab me something to wear?"

Sergei lifts his chin. "Hm. I see how it is. Immortal shield *and* errand boy."

Denendrius smirks. "And don't forget—you're my personal pilot."

Nodding with a grin, Sergei gives Denendrius a rough pat on the shoulder. Denendrius flies out from beneath his touch, spinning around to face him with a fury-twisted expression and balled fists at his sides.

Sergei lifts his palms in surrender as he chuckles and backs toward the door. "Touchy, okay."

Denendrius shakes his head to himself as the hotel door clicks shut, then rolls his shoulders and exhales sharply.

"You okay?" I ask carefully, torn between sitting on the bed to stay out of his way and stepping closer to comfort him.

But since I'm trying to prove I love him, I lace my fingers together and step toward him. He lifts a hand to stop me, his gaze flicking toward the bathroom.

"Just—" He gestures for me to back up, and I slowly retreat to the bed and sit.

"Is that new with him?" I inquire. "All the hugs and back pats?"

"No," he admits. "I just . . ." He sighs. "I'm going to take a shower. Watch TV or something. Stay in the room."

"Okay," I mumble, my concerned gaze locked on him until he shuts the bathroom door behind him.

My brows lift in surprise that he didn't rope me into being naked with him again. It's concerning, but I'm thankful.

I chew the inside of my lip, stealing a glance at the bathroom as the shower turns on, then grab the remote. I scroll through the channel guide, my thumb pressing the stiff button until the sight of my name in a show description has me turning to stone.

It's an episode of *Crime Nightly*—a true crime show—and they're fucking interviewing *Sarah*. My heart launches itself into the base of my throat, my body hot and slick with sweat as I mute the TV so Denendrius can't hear and select the show.

My eyes trail over the subtitles, the black bars and white words perfectly synced.

Against a dark screen, a middle-aged reporter with shoulder-length blond hair says, *"As of recording, it's been nine months since the disappearance of seventeen-year-old New York State teen Marianna Shay Cortez, and authorities fear the case is going cold. With a rocky past of drugs and criminal behavior, it seemed like a cut-and-dry runaway case—but her friends say they know exactly what happened to her."*

My stomach lurches when they cut to Sarah sitting on a beige couch in a dim room with the reporter, her long blond hair cut into a bob, her eyes bloodshot despite the makeup they caked on her.

Hands folded in her lap, the reporter asks, *"When news*

broke that she was missing again, what did you tell the police when you walked into the station with your father?"

"That Marianna's boyfriend kidnapped her," Sarah states.

"What made you come to that conclusion?" the reporter asks, eyes attentive.

"I found her puking and sobbing in the bathroom. She was beaten up and had a ring on her finger," Sarah says. *"She knew something bad was going to happen to her."*

"Here—minutes after their conversation—Marianna is seen running off school property."

A video plays: the over a year-old black and white security camera footage of me running down the sidewalk and across the street before cutting back to the interview.

"Why do you think she knew this would happen?" the reporter asks Sarah.

Sarah swallows visibly, her shaking hands clenching in her lap. *"She planned to leave him and get a restraining order. She knew he killed my friend CJ—a guy who liked her. If Charles could do that to him, what could he do to her?"*

Charles. The thoroughness of his damage control sends a headache pulsing through my temples.

The screen flashes and CJ's school picture appears on a red background. His shaggy blond hair is a little shorter than I remember, but the hoop in his lip is the same. *"CJ Bennett, loved by peers and faculty, was a straight-A student who dreamed of becoming a guitarist. Unfortunately, his life came to a brutal end at a house party. He was found the next morning, beaten to death."*

My chest aches as his picture vanishes. For some reason, I expect them to bring up Jenna. But no one will ever know the truth about her. Is that better? If there's an afterlife, does Jenna know Denendrius hypnotized her to kill herself, or does she still think it was her choice?

The picture changes, snapping my attention back. *"But that's not all, right? You, yourself, were victimized by Charles. It's very brave of you to join us tonight when he's still out there."*

There's distance in Sarah's eyes. She takes a deep breath and says, *"After he assaulted me, he told me if I said anything to anyone, he'd kill me—that he's done it to countless other girls already. But I knew Marianna was in trouble, and I promised her that if anything happened, I'd tell. I know she would do the same for me."*

Tears line my eyes, and I wish I could hug her. Wish I could tell her how much it means that she'd go on national television for shitty little me. That she'd tell everyone what happened to her just so people would know I didn't die as some street thug or drug fiend. I'd tell her I wish it hadn't taken both our lives being ruined to get over our pettiness.

I turn off the TV and stare at my reflection, lost in thought and unable to bring myself to finish the episode. It's hard to wrap my head around the fact that Sarah is somewhere in the city—that she and I still exist in the same world. The same lifetime. Everything that happened feels like a distant memory.

But it was just last year.

I stare into space, listening to the rush of water in the bathroom, too numb to cry as thoughts of Viorel, Aeliana, Laurentius, and everyone else I love back home crowd my mind.

I swear I hear muffled sobbing a couple of times, but I brush it off. Probably someone next door.

When I check the clock, an hour has passed since Denendrius started the shower. I sigh. A caring fiancée would check on him, so that's what I do.

The heat is suffocating when I slip into the bathroom, the steam so thick I can swat at it. Through the steamed-up shower door, I search for his tall form but find only a shadowy shape huddled near the floor. I crack open the shower door and find Denendrius curled up on the tile. Water pummels him, cranked as hot as it will go.

"You okay . . .?" The question dies in my throat as I notice the open switchblade near the drain, pink-tinged water swirling around it.

"I don't feel good," he whispers.

"Are you thirsty?"

He shudders under the water, hugging himself. "I feel nauseous."

"I didn't think vampires could get sick."

"I can't."

It's psychological, then. "What's bothering you?"

He rubs the white, crimson-stained washcloth over his face. "I can't stop thinking about the dungeon."

I force some sympathy into my voice. "What about it?"

Denendrius spreads the washcloth over his face. "I don't want to talk about it."

"Okay." I hover for a few moments, then step back toward the door.

"Please don't leave me alone," Denendrius whispers.

I stifle my sigh before it escapes too loudly and lean back against the counter. The heavy heat makes me dizzy, the damp air blurring the line between sweat and condensation on my skin.

"I can't feel the water anymore." His voice is so low I almost miss it.

"You should come out," I suggest.

I cross my arms over my stomach as he shifts onto his hands and knees, then pushes himself upright, twisting the tap before staring blankly at me.

"Is there anything I can do to help?" I ask, rubbing my arms as he pushes the glass door open.

I'm willing to give him some blood to get him out of this tense mood—maybe then I won't feel so on edge thinking about what he might do.

"Yeah," he breathes, crossing the small bathroom and

clutching my hips with soaked hands, spinning me around roughly.

"Oh—" My heart leaps as I plant my hands on the damp countertop. "I meant—"

He grips the nape of my neck and pushes me forward against the counter's edge. I don't resist as he bends me over, pressing my chest onto the slick surface. Dizziness sways through me as he shimmies my pants and underwear down to my knees. He grabs a hand towel and wipes steam off the mirror, his dull maroon eyes locking onto mine in the reflection.

I freeze as he touches me, moisture soaking through my top as I stay still. I let my eyes unfocus until he becomes a foggy blur, my body stiff with anticipation for him to start. Instead, his grunts and agitated mutters fill my ears as he works on himself.

"Stand up," he orders, voice low.

When I try, I barely lift myself off the counter before his grip on my neck tightens, guiding me back down. My face scrunches in confusion.

"Sorry." He grunts. "Now."

I manage to straighten a little more this time before he shoves me down—just rough enough to jolt my heart.

"Den . . ." My voice wavers with confused panic.

I yelp as he slaps my ass, my eyes flying wide, half his hand catching my lower back. I rear up against his grip on the nape of my neck, but there's nowhere to go. He shoves me harder against the counter. When his hand caresses my stinging flesh, I jerk away, my hips digging into the counter.

I gasp for breath, heart drumming so ferociously it pulses in my temples. *"Den—"*

"Shh . . ."

Squeezing my eyes shut, I grit my teeth and brace for his hand to strike again. But it never does. I remain frozen under his grip, his other hand absent from my body as he focuses on himself. Minutes stretch on, my panic simmering as I wait.

"How's your stomach?" he asks after I squirm, his tone so flat it dries my throat. "Be honest."

It aches, but only because of *this*. "Hurts a bit," I admit.

"I bet you're tired too."

I consider my response. "Y-yeah, I guess."

His grip on my neck loosens before slipping away. "You should go to bed," he whispers. "I don't want you to be sick."

Despite him no longer holding me down, I remain sprawled against the counter. "A-are you sure?" I ask, as if this is some strange trick.

"Yeah, sweetheart. Go ahead," he murmurs. "I'll join you soon."

The shower door opens, followed by the rush of water. I swallow a knot in my throat and force myself to straighten, tugging my clothes back into place.

It's not until I change into a dry shirt and crawl into bed that I realize he used the two reasons he'd let me avoid intimacy when he was human, like a get-out-of-jail-free card for himself.

Part of me suspects he had trouble getting himself ready . . . but that's never happened before. And I don't want to think about what that could mean, either.

I don't realize I've fallen asleep until Denendrius's cold flesh shocks me awake. He pushes his body against my side, lifting my arm off the mattress so he can slip beneath it and rest his head on my shoulder.

"You're going to crush me," I tease limply.

He drapes his arm over me and buries his face in my neck. *"I just want cuddles."*

I swallow thickly, my dry throat tightening as worry pulses through me. He's never backed out of intimacy before, and the implications unsettle me. At least with him here on my shoulder, I can tell myself it has nothing to do with me.

"Can you run your warm fingers along my back?" he asks softly.

"Okay."

He hums contentedly as I trail my fingers along his spine, tracing swirls and patterns over his cold skin.

"I love you," he says into my neck, his cold sigh wafting against me.

"I love you too."

"I'm sorry." He inhales deeply, his breath catching in his lungs before shuddering out in a slow exhale.

"For what?" I whisper.

He doesn't respond.

Soon, Sergei returns, dropping a suitcase onto the carpet with a thud that makes Denendrius groan.

"Why are you two in bed already?" Sergei teases. "We've still got two hours of night left."

Denendrius grunts, then straightens against the headboard. His blistering red eyes make my heart stutter, and Sergei clicks his tongue in disapproval as his shoulders drop.

"You weren't this thirsty when I left," Sergei says, his tone accusatory.

I think of the blade and the blood in the bathroom. How much did Denendrius bleed himself? And why?

"What did you bring?" Denendrius asks flatly.

Sergei motions to the suitcase. "Some of your stuff I cleaned up after you were taken—sunglasses, jacket, clothes, phone."

"Thanks," Denendrius mutters. Then, after a beat, he adds, "What happened to the house in Bellevue?"

"Had to hypnotize the cops to get your shit out. Neighbors heard fighting and screaming, saw black vans leaving, and thought the mafia or someone had abducted you two. So they called the police."

"Where's my Mustang?"

Sergei gives him a long stare. "I put it in storage, since you're emotionally attached to the damn thing."

"I want it."

Sergei's brows lift. "You want to drive it? The cops are looking for that exact make and model."

Denendrius crosses his arms, leaning his head back against the wall before grunting. Sergei stares, baffled, waiting for a response that never comes.

I take the opportunity to shift the conversation. Gazing up at Denendrius, I rest my hand on his knee. "When can we go to the fertility clinic?" I ask, eager to visit the doctor if it speeds up my path to immortality.

Denendrius rests his hand on mine. "I'll call around later this afternoon, see if I can convince a doctor to see us tonight. If not, we'll have to track down some home addresses."

They go over logistics before Sergei crawls into bed, bidding us goodnight.

Denendrius is restless, nudging me as he tosses and turns, groaning in moments of half-wakefulness. A thump jolts me awake. I roll over to find Denendrius hunched on the floor between the bed and the wall, his head tilted back against the nightstand.

"Are you okay?" I whisper into the dark, crawling toward his side of the bed.

"Don't come near me or I'm going to rip your throat out."

I slide back to my side of the bed, carefully eyeing him.

Denendrius groans. "Sergei . . . *Sergei.*"

His eyes remain closed as he speaks. "What? The sun's still out."

"I need to hunt."

"Are you joking? It's nine-thirty in the fucking morning."

His chest lifts and plummets like he's struggling to breathe. "I'm thirsty."

"You'll be fine."

"I need to feed. I need to get out of the city," Denendrius whines.

"No, you need to stay in the city if you want to relearn self-control."

He laces his fingers over his head and groans. "This hotel is going to be a graveyard soon."

"The sunlight will stop you from leaving. Go the fuck back to bed," Sergei growls.

"It hurts to sleep next to Marianna."

"You seem fine on the floor, then."

"I'm not kidding," Denendrius says, his voice pitching higher as he gasps for breath, the sound ragged—like he's choking. *"I need to kill someone."*

"I can help you feed from Marianna—"

"No."

"I'll pull you off her—"

"Oh yeah? Because you did such a great job controlling me in Bellevue?" Denendrius snaps.

Sergei lets out a loud, exaggerated groan as he sits. "I'll call someone to the room. It'll have to be a hooker—only damn people willing to walk into a hotel room without being met at the door."

"I don't care. I'd drink a drug-addicted bum at this point," Denendrius says, his desperation so unlike him that I seriously consider gluing myself to Sergei's side. He didn't even want me to smoke *cigarettes*, never mind the pills and heroin he fought to get out of my bloodstream.

An hour later, a drained blond lies on the floor at the foot of our bed, her glossy hair tangled across her face. Sergei booked her for the whole day, giving us time to get out before anyone comes looking.

She's not enough for Denendrius. He crawls up from the foot of the bed, sinking his fangs into my throat for only a few beats before Sergei yanks him off.

Denendrius pants for breath, his monstrous eyes blazing as he paces the small room.

"What the fuck is wrong with him?" Sergei demands, incredulous, his worry-filled eyes studying me for answers.

"Viorel's mark makes my blood powerful," I explain, pressing a rag against the bite marks on my throat.

An hour of restless pacing later, and Sergei snaps, "Go lie down, fucking crackhead. Good thing I found your aviators. You're going to need them."

XVI

A middle-aged doctor, his brown hair peppered with gray, unlocks the door of the fertility clinic for Denendrius and me while Sergei waits in the car. Denendrius convinced him to stay late with the promise of paying an increased fee and a sympathy trick. He told him I suffer from a sunlight allergy and can't be in the sun without pain. He claimed every other clinic he's called could not accommodate us—though this was actually the first clinic he called—and it's beginning to feel like discrimination.

"Good evening, Maria and Anthony," Dr. Sampson greets as we step into the shadowy clinic, the dim after-hours lighting making our appointment feel almost illicit.

Denendrius and I return the sentiment, following him to his office. The warm beige walls seem inviting, bathed in the soft gold glow of a lamp on his desk. At his request, we each take a seat in one of the brown leather chairs.

He hooks his aviators onto the neck of his shirt—Denendrius's face no longer so affected by my blood that he needs them. As he explains what we want, he subtly hypnotizes Dr. Sampson, guiding the conversation through logistics until the doctor's initial hesitation fades, and he agrees to work with us.

I remain silent for most of the conversation, only offering information when needed.

Dr. Sampson stares at me when I tell him I gave birth on January 15th. His brow furrows. "You had a baby two months ago?"

I glance at Denendrius for help, unsure what the issue is. But he's just as lost, tilting his head as he asks, "Why is that a problem?"

Dr. Sampson sighs, his chair squeaking as he leans back. "You're postpartum, which means your body is still full of hormones. A blood test can determine your levels, and we can adjust treatment accordingly, but it could increase your risk of complications, such as ovarian hyper-stimulation syndrome—OHSS—and other hormonal imbalances. And because you're postpartum, there's a slightly elevated risk of blood clots or hormone-related complications."

My heart thuds harder, but the golden carrot of immortality dangling in front of me is far more tempting than my safety. Anything that happens to my human body will vanish with vampirism.

"I'll take the risk." The words spill from me before I can second-guess them.

"How fast can you run a blood test?" Denendrius asks.

"Typically, it takes—"

Denendrius shakes his head. "That's not what I asked. If a blood sample was rushed to a lab tonight and analyzed immediately, how long would it take?"

"A few hours," Dr. Sampson says.

The corner of Denendrius's lips lift. "Perfect. How many

eggs can you expect to retrieve from her after ten to fourteen days of treatment?"

"We can expect to retrieve ten to fifteen, but only a portion will fertilize and develop into viable embryos. Of those, even fewer typically result in live births . . ." Dr. Sampson says, his tone growing more careful as Denendrius crosses his arms at the number. "Does that concern you?"

Denendrius's leg bounces. "Yeah, I want a big family, and that won't suffice if only some result in live births."

"Oh, well, this doesn't have to be a one-time thing, Anthony. You and Maria are welcome to return for multiple treatments as you expand your family—"

Denendrius's swift shake of his head sweeps the rest of Dr. Sampson's sentence away. "No, I need better results the first time." He leans forward, locking eyes with the doctor. "Tell me —medically—what you can do to increase that count."

I bite the inside of my lip as Dr. Sampson blinks a couple of times, then exhales heavily. "Well, we could increase the hormone dose and potentially retrieve double the amount. But we need to find a balance, right? We don't want to retrieve more at the cost of quality, which could lead to poor results, anyway."

Relaxing his forearms on the arms of the chair, Denendrius says, "Okay, let's try that."

"Right, but while plausible, that would be an aggressive treatment," Dr. Sampson warns. "It could cause long-term health issues for her, and in the short term, the side effects could be more extreme."

"Like what?" A sharp twinge of worry flickers through my erratic heartbeat.

"With a regular treatment, you may already experience mood swings, minor cramping, and bloating. A higher-than-recommended dose of hormones could exacerbate that."

"But it's at most fourteen days for the hormone treatment," Denendrius counters.

"Well, she'll need a few days to heal after retrieval, but yes, the short-term side effects would eventually subside. Still, the risk of long-term complications makes me hesitant," Dr. Sampson says, disapproval etched deep into his expression.

Denendrius smiles. "How much money would it take to convince you?"

Dr. Sampson leans back in his chair, shaking his head. "Sir, I'm a doctor. The health of my patients is . . ."

Denendrius pulls wads of cash from my bag, stacking them on the desk as he furrows his brow and squints at the doctor. "You were saying?"

Dr. Sampson holds his breath, leaning forward to glance over the money and exhale. "That's a considerable amount of cash."

"Yeah, it's interesting, isn't it? How quickly you so-called moral professionals reconsider with a bit of pocket change."

He gulps, hesitating before reaching out to touch the money, as if unsure it's real. "That's an . . . aggressive amount of money."

"I've been called aggressive before," Denendrius says with a smirk.

His eyes flick to me, then back to Denendrius. His voice wavers. "If she consents—"

"She does," Denendrius says simply.

His eyes dart to me.

"I consent." The words spill from me, a mix of anxiety and excitement tightening my chest. "I want this."

The sooner I get through this, the closer I am to immortality—and to getting home. I push aside the thought of having more children with Denendrius and instead focus on the possibility of using my eggs to build a bigger family in Romania.

Dr. Sampson's lip quirks with delight as he glances over the money again. "Well, if you two want this so badly . . ." He exhales in reluctant acceptance. "I'm sure some other doctor would agree, so why not me? Right?"

Denendrius laughs. *"Right."*

Soon, I'm led to a medical room, where a nurse with dark circles under her eyes draws my blood. Denendrius steps outside and arranges for Sergei to transport it to and from the lab with requisition forms once they're ready shortly—he'll need to hypnotize some techs into dropping everything to analyze my sample—while I wait alone in the medical room with the nurse and Dr. Sampson. She whispers something to him, and he quietly tells her she can go home.

He rests against a counter as she leaves the room, an anxiety surrounding her that has me adjusting in the medical chair.

"You're clean?" he asks.

I don't have to ask what he means, knowing the nurse would have clocked the faded signs of my past heroin addiction when she drew my blood.

"Yes," I confirm as Denendrius returns and stands beside me.

"Well over a year now," Denendrius adds as he leans against the side of my chair. "So, now what?"

"We'll do a quick transvaginal ultrasound to assess the health of your uterus and ovaries, as well as check your base-line follicle count." Dr. Sampson pulls a pair of teal medical gloves from a drawer before coming to the rolling cart with a computer and plastic wands.

"What does transvaginal mean?" I demand, my anxiety crisp.

He takes a wand from the cart, my heart pulsing as he explains how it'll be quick and painless, and inserted vaginally so they can get a clear picture.

I'm already trying to clamber out of my seat through my narrow vision before he can finish explaining fully, my body tingling with panic as Denendrius's firm grip holds me in place, my *no's* tumbling weakly from my lips before I ask if he can convince Dr. Sampson that it's unnecessary.

They talk through the buzzing in my ears. Dr. Sampson asks if I'm okay, if I need a few minutes first, while Denendrius tries to soothe me and convince me how important it is. Dr. Sampson steps out for a minute to give us space, telling Denendrius to call for him when I'm ready.

Denendrius's tender voice is no help as he positions me back in the chair, telling me it's all okay as I explain not wanting the doctor to see me half-naked. How I don't want that big plastic thing inside me. He presses his bloodied wrist to my lips, and the detached euphoria stabilizes me some, makes the world slow back down.

I wipe my eyes and lick his blood clean from my lips as Denendrius strips my pants and underwear before covering me with the provided white blanket that's supposed to give me some illusion of privacy. He positions my stiff, heavy legs for me.

He calls Dr. Sampson back, then pulls a chair up beside mine and links our fingers together, murmuring, "I'm here with you, sweetheart. You're safe, I promise. Close your eyes, if you'd like, and I'll take care of everything."

For once, I willingly oblige him. I squeeze my eyes shut, turn my head, and feel the cool shoulder of his leather jacket as the door creaks open.

"Hey, Maria, how are you doing now?" Dr. Sampson asks, his voice moving closer until it's right near my legs.

"She's okay. We can go ahead," Denendrius says, and I nod in agreement.

I squeeze Denendrius's hand so tightly he'd be crying out if he were human, but it's the only way I manage to stay present as Dr. Sampson talks me through preparation and adjusts the sheet. I'm stone, so tense it hurts as the cold air wafts against my bare skin.

A heavy silence settles in the room, and I press my head closer against Denendrius's shoulder as Dr. Sampson clears his throat in discomfort. I know he's seeing years of scarring, the evidence of my childhood abuse and Denendrius's.

"What's wrong?" Denendrius demands.

"Oh, nothing." Dr. Sampson clears his throat again. "Hey, Maria, have you watched any good shows lately—"

"Dr. Sampson," Denendrius snaps.

He sighs quietly.

There's no distraction capable of stopping my terror from choking me, though. My heart thuds so hard I'm dizzy, and I tremble with anxiety as I feel the gel-covered wand find its place. A pitiful noise rises in my throat.

"Good girl," Denendrius murmurs, kissing the side of my head.

"That's the worst of it, Maria," Dr. Sampson says. "Just a few more minutes."

He's quiet, the sound of buttons and keys making me furrow my brow.

"What does all that show?" Denendrius asks, like he's watching the ultrasound screen.

Dr. Sampson's voice is even as he says, "We'll go over it all once we're done in a few minutes."

My heart rate spikes. Has he seen something bad and doesn't want to tell me yet?

Denendrius says nothing more, and the moment the plastic wand leaves my body and Dr. Sampson says we're done, I'm scrambling upright looking for my clothes. He tells us to meet him back in his office, and I stand on the cold floor, shaking while I allow Denendrius to wipe me clean and help me back into my clothes. I ruefully accept more blood before we regroup in the doctor's office.

Dr. Sampson turns away from his computer screen as we sit down, eyeing us over carefully as he folds his hands on his desk like he's not sure what else to do with them.

"All right," Denendrius urges.

Nodding, Dr. Sampson carefully says, "You did well back there, Maria, but there were a few significant things that stood out to me on your ultrasound."

My throat tightens.

"I noted some significant internal scarring," he continues. "Most of it appears old, likely from childhood or early adolescence. But there were also signs of newer healing interrupting older scar patterns, which is unusual. This level of scarring isn't something I typically see in patients your age unless there's a history of trauma. I'm not trying to push, but from a medical standpoint, it's important I understand any past trauma or injuries you've experienced—"

I can't feel the leather chair against my body anymore, and the soft lights become a little brighter.

"It's not relevant," Denendrius says, his tone final.

Dr. Sampson exhales as he slowly leans back in his chair. His lips purse as he looks between Denendrius and me.

"I'm safe now," I manage to tell him.

"Okay," he says gently. "I'm not trying to press, but medically, it's important I understand any relevant history so we can create an appropriate plan—especially since your ultrasound also showed smaller ovaries and a slightly lower follicle count than expected for someone your age. It could be linked to delayed puberty or an underlying hormonal condition. Have you ever been diagnosed with anything like that?"

Well, I'm nearly nineteen now, considering Viorel discovered I'm actually a year older than my mother told the government.

I swallow and half-shrug as Denendrius scowls beside me. "I've never had my period before."

Dr. Sampson's brow furrows, and he gives me a long, assessing look. "Okay, go on."

Sighing, I spin Viorel's theory that Denendrius's healing resolved a pituitary tumor into fact, hoping it satisfies Dr. Sampson. "I think I started puberty normally, but a pituitary tumor must have developed and disrupted things before I could finish. I never got my period, but after the tumor was treated, everything sort of resumed because I got pregnant right after." I recall Laurentius explaining how ovulation happens before a first period, and add, "I still haven't had my period since giving birth."

"That's not uncommon. Were you lactating?" he asks.

I lower my head a bit and shake it. "No. I still wasn't quite developed enough for that, I guess. My boobs didn't really change during pregnancy either."

I'm relieved when he nods along like it makes sense and twists to type details into his computer. When he asks for medical specifics, I shoot Denendrius a look and he subtly hypnotizes Dr. Sampson to move past the full facts.

Before Dr. Sampson can speak again, Denendrius cuts in. "How will that affect egg retrieval? Will we get fewer eggs?"

Dr. Sampson twists to fully address Denendrius, his tone tight with controlled concern. "*Possibly.* Since she has smaller ovaries and a slightly lower baseline follicle count, I wouldn't expect as high of an estimate as I gave earlier."

"*Estimate,*" Denendrius presses.

Dr. Sampson hesitates and draws in an even breath. "Maybe eight to ten eggs maximum with a moderate stimulation protocol—"

"We already agreed on an aggressive treatment," Denendrius reminds him.

After clearing his throat, Dr. Sampson continues with, "Of course, but then we're still only looking at approximately up to twelve."

Denendrius merely stares coldly at him, jaw clenched tight. The look isn't enough to kill Dr. Sampson, though he does glance at me like he's checking to see if I have something more to say before slowly turning back to his computer to resume typing.

When he fills out my requisition form, Denendrius tells the doctor he wants my ancestry DNA analyzed as well. I don't bother arguing about it. Though I know it's going to return showing my mother's roots in Mexico, and likely that my father is white, I am a little curious about the exact details.

My stomach growls loudly just as Dr. Sampson makes a noise that suggests he's nearly finished entering information. As if it reminds him, he glances up and tells me to make sure I drink plenty of fluids and eat properly.

Denendrius's small smile puts me at ease, and I feel comfortable asking for food since we have time to wait. He has Dr. Sampson order pizza to the clinic as he grabs the blood sample and completed paperwork to rush them out to Sergei, who's waiting to run them straight to the lab. The doctor obliges, happy to get a meal since our appointment disrupted his supper. He and I share a pepperoni pizza—the nurse having gone home—while Denendrius quizzes him on everything related to the process and surrogacy.

I ponder as I eat, the warning about avoiding strenuous activities bringing a sneaky question to my greasy lips. "We can still have sex, right?" The question makes me squirm in my seat, and I hate the way it feels on my tongue. I only ask in hopes Dr. Sampson will disagree, giving me a break from Denendrius's constant urges.

Dr. Sampson swallows a bite of pizza and dabs his mouth with a napkin before answering. "I recommend refraining from penetrative intercourse during the hormonal treatment and for a short while after retrieval. Once your ovaries respond, they'll enlarge significantly, like the size of small apricots. Any sudden movement or pressure could cause ovarian torsion, which can cause a medical emergency."

Relief flutters in my chest, but Denendrius's dark stare clamps down on it. "So we just have to be careful," Denendrius argues. "Cut back to once a day instead of multiple."

Dr. Sampson chokes on his bite of pizza, coughing as he struggles to swallow. He clears his throat with a long sip of water. "Multiple times a day?" he echoes, still recovering. "I should be more clear. I recommend zero penetrative intercourse until I clear her after the procedure."

Denendrius merely stares at him. "Hm."

Dr. Sampson chuckles. "I'd like to know your secret. How do you manage intimacy multiple times a day with a newborn?"

"We lost her," Denendrius says flatly, and Dr. Sampson's chewing slows.

"I'm sorry for your loss," he says, glancing between us with poorly concealed pity. "Have you two received grief counseling? You understand this treatment won't alleviate any feelings from your loss or replace your child, correct?"

"I don't need grief counseling," Denendrius snaps. "We're fine. We just want a big family and don't have time to waste."

Dr. Sampson gives him a tense smile. "Understood. But I want to make sure you're clear that there should be no intercourse or any other strenuous activity."

I open my mouth to respond, but Denendrius interjects. "I don't think that's a reasonable ask."

My heart thrashes behind my ribs as I sink into the cool leather of the chair.

"Like we said," Dr. Sampson challenges, "it's only fourteen days for hormones, plus another for retrieval, and a few for recovery. I'm asking you to abstain for her health and the success of the treatment."

I fumble for the right words, trying to find a compromise that will satisfy Denendrius without jeopardizing my treatment. But my tongue feels heavy behind my teeth, and all that falls out is, "We're just used to two or three times a day, so it's a drastic change to our routine."

Dr. Sampson's brow furrows as he studies Denendrius and grabs another slice of pizza, the shared meal and odd intimacy of the after-hours setting loosening the usual barrier between patient and professional. His tone turns more casual as he adds, "It can be difficult, but most of our male patients manage to abstain for a short time. Changing an excessive routine may be frustrating, but it's necessary for her health." He glances between us, then adds casually, "Out of curiosity—how often do you think most couples engage in sexual activity?"

Denendrius double-takes at the question, squinting. "What? I'm not having this conversation with you. This isn't why we're here."

Dr. Sampson tilts his head side to side as he chews. "Okay, well, while you may just have a high libido, I'd encourage you to reflect on why abstaining for a couple of weeks is such a serious point of contention for you. Also, consider how the hormones will affect Maria—her mood, her energy, her comfort—and how that will impact your dynamic as a couple. As long as you understand, I strongly advise against any activities that could jeopardize her well-being."

We fall into silence until Dr. Sampson has the results of my bloodwork. He glances between the papers and me as they rest on his desk.

"You said you had a baby two months ago?" he asks, his brow quirking in disbelief.

"Yeah, why?" I lean forward in my chair, but I can't make out anything on his papers.

"Your full hormone panel came back perfect. Typically, two months postpartum, we'd expect elevated levels of certain hormones, like prolactin or residual hCG. But yours are completely normalized, as if you hadn't been pregnant *at all* recently."

"That's good, isn't it?" Denendrius says.

"I suppose," Dr. Sampson says, though there's hesitation in his voice I can't place. Does he think I'm lying? That something else is going on? "I haven't seen anything like this before."

I know Viorel's blood is the reason for my good health and balanced hormones—and perhaps his healing, too, since he had to use his abilities after I nearly bled out from a full placental abruption before delivery. I wonder if evidence of that shows up in my results, but Dr. Sampson doesn't say anything to suggest it has.

My heart pounds as I follow Dr. Sampson back to the medical room for my first hormone injection, Denendrius at my side. The sight of the needles makes my palms sweat, and my mind circles around the memory of sticking heroin-filled ones in my arms and the feeling it'd bring. I hold my breath as he pushes the needle into my abdomen. Afterward, he shows me—Denendrius watching intently—how to give myself an injection each day and tells me I'll need to come in every few days for checkups.

I ask Denendrius to handle the injections for me, the thought of a needle back in my hand making anxiety slither through my veins like thick oil. Thankfully, he agrees.

My heart flutters crookedly, a tickle in my throat with each quick pulse as I follow Denendrius back out to the car. I do my best to convince myself this is a good thing—that it benefits me more than Denendrius—and that it'll be easy peasy. Just an injection every day and a quick procedure at the end. My reward? Immortality.

"Why'd you give him so much money on top of hypnotizing him?" I ask as we slide back into the car.

Denendrius chuckles as he starts the car, Sergei greeting us from the passenger seat. "You'll find money can be even more hypnotizing. It has a wider reach than hypnotism and covers things I might not think of. Money makes people *think carefully*."

"Which lot did you store the Mustang in?" Denendrius asks as he turns a corner.

Sergei scoffs. "You actually want it?"

Denendrius shoots him a look, as if he's ridiculous. "Of course."

Sergei rattles off the location, and Denendrius immediately veers right.

"You will get caught driving it," Sergei warns as he clicks his tongue in disapproval.

Denendrius grunts. "They'd have to assume I'd be stupid enough to drive it, considering how much time they've spent keeping an eye out for it."

"I agree," Sergei quips. "*Moron*."

Denendrius smirks, glancing at Sergei from the corner of his eye. "They don't think I'm stupid—especially since Huarsar has made me internationally wanted. Stupid people don't evade capture for this long. They'll assume I ditched the Mustang after Marianna and I left and won't consider otherwise. Really, the smartest thing would be to hide in plain sight with it."

"Many words to say you simply miss your car," Sergei teases.

Denendrius chuckles. "I'm not wrong, though."

"Eh ..." Sergei shrugs. "We'll see."

"It makes sense," I agree, though I'm willing to get behind any idea that might fuck Denendrius over.

Sergei mutters something grumpy in Russian, earning a smirk and an eye roll from Denendrius.

Thirty minutes later, Denendrius and I wait outside a car storage lot, watching as the Mustang's yellow lights flash through the windows. Sergei rolls out of the lot, the timed gate shutting behind him as he pulls up to the curb.

As Sergei steps out of the Mustang to move around to the passenger seat, Denendrius and I abandon the car and dart across the desolate road through spotlights of yellow streetlamps. He pushes the driver's seat forward for me, and my heart beats erratically, snagged on my ribs, as I crawl into the backseat.

Goosebumps litter my flesh at the familiar leather smell. The last time Denendrius and I sat in here was while we were living in Bellevue. I wonder if the books and random accessories I found at the bookstore and forgot to bring in that last night of shopping remain back there. Part of me doesn't want to know, like keeping the trunk shut will force that part of my past to remain feeling like an intensely vivid dream.

Denendrius exhales a pleased sigh from the driver's seat, pushing it back for more legroom. He tells Sergei he'll need him to arrange for it to be shipped to Italy. I can't fathom what's so special about this car—probably burdened with far too many miles by now—to justify moving it across the ocean.

I curl up against the back seat, staring out the small window at the smear of shadowy buildings passing by, the streetlamps casting a rhythmic dance of light and dark.

"What are we doing?" I ask finally, as Denendrius continues making calculated turns down residential streets, scanning the driveways of particular houses.

"I have a list of addresses where I've seen Mustangs with the same make, model, and color. I want to swap plates with one of them. Not perfect, but it's better to be linked to a real owner with a matching Mustang than the expired fakes currently on it."

Denendrius navigates to another neighborhood, maintaining his speed as he passes a matching Mustang parked in the driveway of a sleeping house. He swings into the alley and returns barely a minute later, the plates already swapped.

"Where now?" Sergei asks as Denendrius shifts the car back into drive.

Denendrius clears his throat, the sound dry and hoarse. "Quick stop, then I need to get out of the city for a bit before I go on a rampage."

XVII

We pull into the parking lot of a twenty-four-hour department store, the bright lights blinding as we park beneath them in the middle of the lot. A sharp chill moves through the air, and I shiver inside my hoodie.

"Are you sure you should go inside?" I ask as Denendrius pops the car door open.

"I'll manage."

Sergei claps Denendrius on the back, but Denendrius grits his teeth and twists away. "I'm here to make sure he doesn't tear apart the customers."

Oh yeah, because Sergei did such a great fucking job controlling Denendrius when he turned him back. It's not like he escaped, slaughtered multiple families, and torched their houses—*definitely* didn't draw attention to us or get Denendrius captured.

The sarcastic words roll around on my tongue, but I bite them back.

Denendrius takes my hand as we cross the parking lot, our shoes crunching through the fresh layer of snow on the asphalt. Nearing the edge of the parking lot, Denendrius lifts the hood of my hoodie, pulling it over my head.

"Don't look at anyone. Don't look at the cameras," he warns under his breath.

I'm absolutely looking at every fucking camera I can get away with.

As we approach the store, the automatic doors slide open, making me flinch. I grip Denendrius's hand as he heads toward the carts.

My face on a missing kids bulletin board catches my attention, displayed above the long line of carts. Beside me, Denendrius bitches about needing a coin for the cart while Sergei digs through his pockets.

It's an old poster, likely from around the time Denendrius and I fled to Bellevue. The corners curl, and the ink has faded from months of sun exposure through the large glass windows and doors. My school picture dominates the page, my identifying details listed below. A blurry security camera photo of Denendrius in my school hallway sits beside it, along with a grainy image of his Mustang—making it look like a vague black car—parked across the street from the school. If I hadn't seen his face in person, I might not even recognize him.

I feel like I exist in a different reality than everyone else. It's surreal. I'm just another passerby looking at myself. How ironic would it be if I were found in front of my own missing poster? That would make for a noteworthy headline.

One day, the date on my poster will be years old, just like the others. Some curious passerby will glance at it while waiting for a friend to finish shopping or a cab to arrive and think, *Whatever happened to Marianna?* Then they'll probably never wonder again. Most people probably already assume I'm dead.

And from looking at my face among the dozens of other missing person posters that plague the board, I already know what their thoughts will be. Marianna Shay Cortez became a tragic story, just like all the other kids. She became as cold as the cases sitting in a box in the back of a police station.

"Come on," Denendrius grumbles when he catches what has my attention.

I swallow hard and tear my gaze from the board. "Can I push the cart?" I ask, needing something to steady myself so I don't collapse.

"Yeah." He steps aside but stays close as I rest my arms on the handle.

The fluorescent lights sting my eyes as another set of sliding doors open for us. My heart stumbles in my chest as my gaze flickers across the massive store—rows of shelves and dozens of people moving between them, despite the late hour, making it flutter even faster. The hum of shoppers fills the air, underscored by the faint murmur of a radio station that's too low to make out the song. My head pounds as we pass the entrance displays, the thick energy in the air drying my throat and throwing off my balance.

It's been almost a year since I've been in public like this.

Denendrius releases a strangled cough beside me and groans something at Sergei before slipping his mirrored aviators over his eyes.

"It's so loud," he complains.

I wonder if he's drowning in the same overwhelm as I am.

"Where the hell is the camping section?" Denendrius clears his throat, and I can practically hear the pain in it. "Did they move everything?"

Sergei merely chuckles and says something to him in Russian.

We weave through aisles toward the back of the store, my legs barely keeping up with Denendrius's frantic pace. I can tell he's holding back, stopping suddenly whenever he gets too far ahead.

Denendrius grabs the end of the cart and turns us down an aisle before squatting down to inspect the butane space heaters. His eyes swiftly scan over the details on a few boxes before he sets one in the cart. He snatches a handful of one-pound butane tanks off the shelf further down, then grunts as he grabs the end of the cart again and guides us forward.

"Are we going camping or something?" I whisper, leaning my full weight on the cart.

"Or something," Denendrius mumbles as he adjusts his leather jacket.

We move through the aisles, Denendrius loading the cart with supplies—matches, a few knives, a battery-powered lamp—before mumbling something to Sergei about the housewares department.

As we pass shelves of baby clothes on the way, Denendrius studies my reaction when my steps slow. I can't help but scrutinize the tiny outfits, my thoughts circling Aeliana. I come to a slow stop, and Denendrius pauses silently beside me as I lift a heavy arm to touch a flowery dress with a matching headband. It would likely fit her in a couple of months.

I bite back my tears and force myself to pull my hand away. Who knows when I'll see her again, or if she'll be too big for it by then? Without a word, Denendrius unhooks the hanger from the rack and places it in the cart.

He leans close to my ear, wrapping an arm around my waist as he clears the thirst from his throat again. "I'll buy it for our next daughter."

Emotion strangles me, so I merely nod and look away from the rows of clothes. Thankfully, Denendrius steers us into the next aisle, then another lined with bedding.

He grabs a plastic-wrapped full sheet set—plain dark green—and tells me to pick a blanket I like.

The patterns blur together, just another detail my brain can't process. I run my fingers over the shelf of blankets, the colors a smear in my vision, until they land on soft sherpa. I pull it from the shelf, the black-and-white sherpa blanket practically begging me to rip off its cardboard packaging, wrap myself inside, and collapse onto the floor.

My leg buckles as I turn toward the cart, and I all but drop the blanket on top of everything.

"You'll need something warmer too," Denendrius says, grabbing a queen-size comforter off the shelf and placing it in the undercarriage.

Next, he grabs the two most expensive down pillows on the shelf and throws them at the cart. They'll both land, but I reach out for one as if it might not. I use catching it as an excuse to hug it tight to my body.

"What else?" Sergei asks.

Denendrius's voice cracks as he forces out a handful of words. He coughs, clearing his throat. I don't miss the flash of his fangs as his lips barely pull back with a noisy inhale. "Food and electronics. She needs a jacket too."

I hug the soft pillow between myself and the cart as Denendrius guides it forward. The wheel rattles as we turn a corner, and both of us complain in unison at the sudden sharp noise.

We grab batteries and a radio in electronics before doubling back for food. Denendrius gives me free rein over anything non-perishable, but my appetite escapes me, and nothing looks appealing.

Lost in thought, I scowl at the shelves of snacks when he halts in the middle of the aisle. I slam into his side with the cart. The metal rattles on impact, and he stiffens, his jaw setting. Slowly, he turns to stare at me, like he's deciding whether I did it on purpose.

My heart seizes, then pounds so hard I go dizzy. I grip the cart to stay upright, panic building in my chest.

"I'm sorry," I squeak. "I-I wasn't expecting you to stop so fast. I didn't mean to, I swear."

I don't realize there's another person in the aisle until he looks over, staring at me like he's trying to piece together why I'd react so strongly to accidentally hitting my partner with a cart. But he doesn't know that a year ago, Denendrius probably would have smacked me right here in the aisle for it.

Denendrius notices the man assessing the situation too and slowly maneuvers around the cart toward me. He wraps his arms around me in a tight hug. "It's fine," he whispers. "I'm sorry you're so upset over something that was clearly an accident. Love you, sweetheart."

Relaxing in his arms, I sense no trickery in his words. "I love you too."

I wrap my arms around Denendrius's midsection, but over his shoulder, I see the man watching us with pity—like he believes it was someone else who used to make me suffer for little mistakes, and this man is the good one, helping me heal.

I can only assume he never saw my missing poster on the bulletin board.

We pull apart, and Denendrius helps me pick some snacks before leading me to the deli aisle. He grabs a couple of sandwiches for me and some non-perishable pre-made dinners.

On the way to the front of the store, Denendrius tosses a black winter coat into the cart as we pass the limited selection. Sergei sends Denendrius and me back to the car while he checks out—probably so security doesn't have too much time to notice us waiting in the long line—so we step into the crisp night and climb back into the car.

"That sucked," I admit, melting into the backseat. A sharp ache lingers in my abdomen where the needle poked. "There was way too much going on in there, and now my head hurts."

Denendrius leans back in the passenger seat and heaves out a breath. "I had a couple close calls."

Sergei returns twenty minutes later. He piles the trunk full of supplies and then we head out of the city.

I nibble at an all-meat-and-cheese sandwich, sipping from a bottle of apple juice as the highway blurs beneath the tires. Soft snowflakes dot the windshield, the occasional one catching the headlights with a brief shimmer. Staring at the trees, I feel invisible to everyone in the world except for two very bad men.

As we speed past a Vermont sign leaving New York State, my chewing slows. Swallowing, I glance between Denendrius and Sergei—who sit in silence—and ask, "We're going to Vermont?"

Denendrius sits rigid, hands clenched on his thighs, eyes closed, head tilted back against the headrest. "Yep," he says, clipped. He takes a shallow breath, holding it, his chest unnervingly still.

I'm not sure what other answer I expected. Perhaps something more specific.

At some point, Denendrius cracks the window open, making me scowl as I shift behind Sergei, out of reach of the sharp early-spring wind. After thirty minutes, his back straightens as he leans toward the window while breathing through his mouth.

"I smell a hitchhiker." Denendrius's eyes flare vivid red, hunger rasping through his hoarse throat.

Sergei speeds up. "I'll stop."

Denendrius twists sideways and grabs the door frame. "Pick me up instead."

Before Sergei can object, Denendrius climbs out the window so fast I don't even see where he goes.

Fifteen minutes later, we approach a tall figure on the side of the road and slow to a stop. The headlights illuminate Denendrius's bloodied face like a stage spotlight. We're the only ones on this highway who would stop for such a sight instead of hitting the gas.

"Satisfied?" Sergei asks as Denendrius pulls the passenger door open and climbs back in.

Denendrius licks his bloodied fingers clean. "Never."

"Just give me another route to the house when we get close. That old dirt path will be overgrown by now and snowed-in."

Eventually, Denendrius points to a small clearing between the trees off the side of the road. It's nothing but a sheet of white, and my brow furrows until the crunch of gravel beneath the tires gives the road away. The snow isn't as deep as the banks in the trees surrounding it, so I consider how it's likely used occasionally.

Sergei kills the headlights, and Denendrius cringes every time the car bottoms out or scrapes against chunks of ice. He teases him about retrieving the Mustang, but Denendrius's teeth are clenched too tight to respond.

After twenty minutes of winding through sparse trees on the gravel road, the Mustang stops beside a tangle of bushes and bare branches. The road stretches forward into the dark.

Denendrius climbs out and flips the seat forward for me to crawl through. I nearly collapse when I set my boots on the ground, fawn legs wobbling. If only I could convince Denendrius to go back into the city.

Holding my breath, I let Denendrius lift me into his arms. After a few long moments of darkness, we stand before a familiar sight, bathed in moonlight and buried in snow. The decrepit house he had brought me to *months* ago—to show me a captured Child of Stars—still stands.

Sergei appears ahead of us, a few bags gripped in one hand and a white comforter in its package.

I gnaw my bottom lip as Denendrius trudges through the snow toward the house. He shoves the dilapidated door open, a gust of snow blowing inside through the gap. After he sets me down, he shakes the snow from his legs and guides me through the darkness of the main floor. I see much better than last time, easily avoiding the holes and weak spots in the floor on my own. Moonlight filters through holes in the roof, casting a faint glow over the crumbling fireplace and abandoned antique furniture.

At the top of the stairs, Sergei hands me a battery-operated lamp. I study the half-collapsed steps, searching for a safe way down. Denendrius grips my waist and lifts me effortlessly over the sketchy steps as he descends.

"We'll stay in here," Denendrius says as he pulls me through the doorway of a long room carved from the earth.

Sergei slides a sheet of wood aside, revealing another small room carved into the dirt. Without a word, he disappears inside, handing a few bags off to Denendrius first.

I stare at the white mattress in the corner, across from the doorway, chewing the inside of my cheek. It's stained—though the dim light makes it impossible to tell what the wet-shaped shadows are—and likely full of frozen spiders, despite looking only a few years old.

I can't help but voice my concern. "There's a mattress here?"

"I own this place," Denendrius says, pulling a sheet set from the bag. "So I hide here from time to time."

My brows lift in surprise. "You're kinda shit at upkeep," I tease.

He gives me a half-chuckle and a smirk. "It's amazing what a few decades can do to a house when you're gone."

"When did you live here?" I wonder.

He tucks the bottom sheet around the corner of the mattress as he says, "I had it built in the thirties."

"Wow. How many homes do you have?" I hug myself and shiver, then spot the winter jacket in one of the bags and move to put it on.

"Hm." His eyes narrow as he pauses, studying me thoughtfully while I tear off the tags and slip my arms into the plush sleeves. "I'd have to check on a few, but somewhere around seven, including our villa in Italy."

Our age discrepancy stands stark between us. His centuries of life experience is something I could never dream of catching up to.

Once the bed is set up, Denendrius settles onto it, the corner of his lip quirking up. "I got something for you off the hitchhiker."

I cock a brow as he leans back, slipping a hand into his pocket. He produces a beaten metal cigarette case and gently tosses it toward me. My brow furrows as I catch it, but as I flip it open, a grin tugs at my lips. Inside are a few joints.

Denendrius's smile is so sweet it might crush my heart if I didn't know better. "Hopefully, it helps with how the hormones might make you feel."

I lower myself onto the bed beside him, pressing a hand to my abdomen. "I swear I'm already a little bloated. Maybe it's in my head."

He plucks a joint from the case in my hands, pulls a lighter from his pocket, and flicks it to life before lighting the joint for me. "Here . . ."

Taking it from him, I pull in a long breath and hold it in my lungs until I can't anymore. Wisps of smoke curl past my lips as I slowly exhale. The weed isn't as good as what I got from Xavier at the castle—a Christmas present I was surprised Viorel allowed—but any weed is good enough to dull the pain of being near Denendrius.

"What are we supposed to do out here?" I grumble, sprawling onto my back. My eyes settle on the circular ring of lamplight cast on the ceiling's floorboards. They've likely been repaired to block out the sun, like the sheet of plywood I suspect is covering a window on the wall to our right.

"We could listen to the radio," he starts. He sprawls out at my side and places his hand on my thigh to massage his fingers into it. "We could make love."

A coughing fit slams into me, and I pound my fist against my chest as I lurch upright, hacking out my lungs. Smoke bursts around me in sharp clouds.

"Careful," Denendrius teases, like I merely breathed wrong.

I chug the last of my apple juice and force myself to breathe. "The doctor said we shouldn't."

I don't know why I bother reminding him when it's clear he never intended to follow those instructions.

"There's not as much risk in the first few days," he argues, his voice so smooth it doesn't match the rot of his coercion.

He lets me finish my joint, at least, but I don't have the ammunition to poke enough holes in his argument to hold him off.

By the end, frustration—the desperate need to shove him away but knowing I can't—coils in my chest like a centipede, a hundred legs skittering against my heart, fangs sinking into muscle, injecting a poison that weakens me. I likely won't be able to tell if it's the hormone injections or him that leaves me so sore and exhausted.

I regret the haze of weed clinging to my consciousness, heightening every sensation, making my nerves more sensitive. I hate how it calms my body, how it makes it easier for him to pull a reaction from my lips as heat swells inside me. My anxious thoughts drag, scattered and sluggish. Panic is a hand around my throat that neither tightens nor lets go. Everything takes longer to be over.

When Denendrius rolls off me, I don't move. The effects of the weed have thinned, but either that or my psyche has left me unable to move.

"I bet you're tired," he murmurs, drawing the chilled blanket over my body with a satisfied sigh. "We were going for over two hours. It's long past sunrise."

Thin tears well in my eyes. Perhaps it wasn't the weed that made it feel so long.

Denendrius snuggles up at my side. "I love you."

My lips form the words, but no sound comes out. Thankfully, he notices, and the corner of his mouth quirks up. He presses a stinging kiss to my lips, then reaches across me to switch off the lamp, plunging us into darkness.

XVIII

His body entwines with mine again at the first sign of my wakefulness, the air still warm from the heater—its tank swapped during the day when I started shivering. Reality is crisp again, and thankfully he only takes half as long as before. My body is too sore to betray me this time, my emotions ping-ponging between the anger I bite back and tears I rapidly blink away. A fullness lingers in my lower abdomen, separate from him; bloating that makes me feel heavier, though it's not yet visible on my body.

When he's done, he cleans me up, presses a kiss to my forehead, then crawls off the bed to turn the lamp and butane heater back on with a fresh tank. He retrieves a bottle of water and a pre-filled hormone injection from my backpack.

I squeeze my eyes shut as he approaches with the needle, unwilling to watch it pierce my skin. My heart races at how near it is, and the sharp pinch in my abdomen stings like the memory of needles that once pierced my veins. I can't help the tears that spill from the corner of my eyes or the shaky inhale of breath. An old, dormant need twitches from the dark, thankfully never fully rousing, left without the rush my body expects but doesn't receive.

"It's that hard?" Denendrius murmurs, brushing a soft kiss against my cheek.

I wipe my eyes with the back of my hand, gritting my teeth as I nod. Another kiss presses against my other cheek.

"It wasn't so bad before Dr. Sampson brought the needles out," I admit, pulling in a deep breath in an attempt to calm myself.

"I won't let you relapse," he promises me.

"*Thanks,*" I choke out, and for once, the word is genuine. With his control, relapse is damn near impossible.

I suppose that's one thing to be grateful for. A human captor—or a mortal, abusive boyfriend as insane as him—would likely fuel my addiction to keep me controlled. As impossible as Denendrius makes escape seem, at least he doesn't have something like heroin to make me cast aside my will or safety for another dose.

"Of course, sweetheart." He presses a kiss between my furrowed brows, and against my will, they relax. "I understand how intense cravings can be. I'll do whatever I can to help."

I hate how I know his words are true, perhaps because they stand in such contrast to what kind of person he is.

He sprawls beside me, marking the flesh of my stomach and chest with silky kisses. I think he's going to try for round two, but he sighs and flops onto his back, his content hum filling my ears as he rests his hand on my upper thigh.

"Den?" I squeeze my eyes shut as the inquiry swells on my tongue. "Can we have an honest talk?"

I dare peek at him from the corner of my eye. His chest rises with a held breath, but doesn't fall as he says, "About?"

"I love you, and I'm glad your libido never leaves me aching for more. And I hate what the doctor said too . . . but I'm scared. What if ignoring his advice hurts me, and I can't be a mom?"

I allow my tears to escape, born of built-up stress from his relentless desire and fear of his potential response.

"We're being careful," he says, and I'm relieved his words aren't laced with anger.

I wrinkle my nose, sniffing. "I'm not supposed to walk upstairs too fast or twist the wrong way. And even though you're trying to be careful, it still shakes me up."

He exhales a heavy sigh, and I carefully check his expression. His face is blank, his gaze locked on the ceiling.

"It's harder to enjoy when I'm scared something might go wrong and that I wouldn't be able to have babies with you. I just don't understand why we can't follow his instructions. He's a doctor. You can still have BJs . . ."

I despise myself for offering, but I know he won't agree to anything less.

"It'll be . . ." He draws in a noisy breath. "Really hard."

A flicker of fury curls in my chest, but my tears smother it before it can catch. "Hard, but worth it. We'll get to have cute little babies together."

A faint smile curls the corner of his lips—then vanishes. "You help me feel better. I crave the feeling all the time. If I don't get it, I feel sick. On edge, like I can't breathe properly, like there's this giant weight on my chest. It becomes all I can think about."

I ponder his words for a moment. "That's how I felt about heroin."

He doesn't say anything.

"I know we did it a lot in Bellevue, but this feels . . . different. *More.* It's just scary with the risk, you know?"

Denendrius's voice drops low. "I was imprisoned for months. So yeah, I need relief. I just want to feel better. You make me feel better."

I roll onto my side to see him clearer, but his eyes stay fixed on the ceiling.

I swallow a knot. "I'm glad I make you feel better," I lie. "But can we please hold off for at least half the days when it's most risky? I don't want to believe you'd rather I feel sick than you. I don't want you to feel bad, but I'm also terrified. And I feel worse knowing that not waiting a couple of weeks might mean I never get babies . . . especially with the higher hormone dose making things riskier . . ."

He thinks for a long moment, each silent second stretching my anxiety tighter. When he props himself up on his elbow and stares down at me, my heartbeat swells, strangling my breath.

"You think I care more about making love than having babies?" His expression stays smooth, maroon eyes flicking over my face.

My instinct tells me to nod, so I do.

Denendrius pouts slightly, brushing the back of his hand against my cheek. "I'm sorry I gave you that impression. It's not true." His breath wafts against my face as he exhales slowly. "Okay. We'll take a break after your next appointment in a couple of days. I can figure out how to handle that. I don't want you to think I don't care about you, or your chance of being a mother. I know how important having babies is to you."

I nearly cry in relief. "Really? Thank you."

He smiles softly, his eyes glittering as he bites his bottom lip before saying, "I guess you'll be suffering along with me, having to abstain more than I do."

I pick at my container of gummy bears at the end of the bed. Denendrius is slumped against the wall, eyes closed. If not for the steady rocking of his foot, I'd think he was asleep. Well into the night and desperately aching for some sort of distraction,

I've made a game of decapitating my gummy bears and pairing their heads and bodies in clashing colors.

With no more gummy bears left to Frankenstein, I scoop them off the blanket and drop them back into the container. I let out a loud, deliberate sigh. Exhaustion grips me like another layer of clothing, heavier than the jacket and long-sleeve I have on. A headache pulses in my temples, my gut heavy with bloating.

"What's wrong?" Denendrius asks.

"I am bored," I enunciate dramatically.

He jerks upright, eyes snapping open and alert.

"What's wrong?" I pop a gummy bear into my mouth, grinding it between my teeth.

"I heard a rifle fire."

I snap the lid onto my container, the crinkling plastic loud in the empty space. "What does that mean for us?"

He flashes a fanged grin. "It means dinner for me and whatever coyote he's hunting."

Denendrius presses a kiss to my lips—then he's gone.

Sergei calls after him, and I sigh, now left alone with nothing but my candy to occupy myself.

I'm stone when Denendrius comes in with a rifle a handful of minutes later, a tickled grin on his red-stained lips. He tosses a camouflage bag down and sprawls onto the mattress beside me. Flat on his back, he rests the rifle's butt against his shoulder and aims at the ceiling. "Sergei is up there," he whispers. "Should I scare him?"

I gnaw on my cheek, pulling my hands into my sleeves. "Uh . . . What if he has PTSD from fighting the Germans in World War Two?"

Without missing a beat, Denendrius says, "He does. That's why it would be funny."

My lips pinch as Sergei appears in the doorway.

"If it wasn't funny last time, it wouldn't be funny this time," he retorts.

Denendrius smiles and chants something in German. Sergei flicks a hand at him in annoyance and walks away with a grunt.

I purse my lips and decide I probably don't want to know what he said.

Denendrius sighs, setting the gun down on the dirt floor beside him before snatching up the bag and digging through it. He pulls out a box of ammunition, rope, and various other hunting supplies, like protein bars that I eye suspiciously when he hands them to me.

Denendrius studies the box of bullets before calling Sergei back in. They exchange a few words in Russian before Denendrius tosses him the box of ammunition and the rifle.

"What's he doing?" I ask as Sergei leaves.

"I'm having him make wooden bullets in case any of Huarsar's men decide to show up." Denendrius lies back down, folding his arms behind his head. "Might get lucky with some headshots if we catch them creeping up on us. But we're deep in the woods and far from the car, so I doubt anyone will stumble upon us."

"Ah." I pull another joint from the metal case, rolling it between my fingers before placing it between my lips and lighting up. "Are we coming back here after my appointment the night after tomorrow?"

"Yeah. Sergei's hitting a blood bank for me tomorrow night, but we'll spend the night of your appointment around people. We'll get a motel room so we can all shower. An entire city of heartbeats is so much harder to tune out than a handful of men on a ship."

After a quick trip to the outhouse out back, I nibble on snacks and sip another bottle of apple juice, wishing I'd asked Denendrius to grab some books or a rechargeable DVD player.

At least he distracts me with conversation—debatably better than silence—and we manage to catch a radio show.

By sunrise, my abdomen aches, and I toss and turn, groaning. I'm warmer than usual and can't shake the anxiety that grips me like a phantom trying to convince me there's doom just around the corner. My head throbs, each beat of my heart a radiating pulse of pain. My muscles ache, but I'm not sure if it's from the hormones or the effort Denendrius previously exerted on my body. The weed doesn't help, but despite my restlessness, I'm thankful for it, because instead of crawling on top of me, Denendrius opts for a gentle massage that surprisingly helps.

XIX

After an uneventful checkup with Dr. Sampson, who gave me some non-narcotic painkillers before we left, we return to a middling motel on the outskirts of east side Lorimer.

I step out of the steamy bathroom, the clinic's touch scrubbed from my skin, and find Denendrius blocking my path, a mischievous smile playing at his lips.

"I have a surprise for you." His glittering eyes trap mine. "Get rid of the towel."

My throat dries as my heartbeat quickens. I don't question him, just unclench my fist from the damp fabric and let it fall. He nudges it aside with his foot.

I hug my stomach, biting my bottom lip as his eyes sweep up and down my body, a blissful smile tugging at his lips.

"Okay . . ." His voice drips like honey. "Close your eyes."

"W-why?" I stammer.

"Trust me," he insists.

But the glimmer in his eyes is soft—sweet rather than

lustful—so I take a deep breath and let my lids flutter closed. I brace for his touch but something soft brushes my shin.

"Lift your foot," he murmurs.

I obey, only realizing as he guides my leg through a fabric hole that he's dressing me in new underwear. Soft velvet glides up my legs, fitting perfectly as he pulls them into place.

"New underwear?"

"*Shh*. Lift your arms," he orders softly.

Swallowing, I squeeze my eyes shut tighter and lift my hands above my head. Silk brushes against my palms, sliding over me, two thin straps settling on my shoulders as the flowy fabric cascades to my ankles.

"Can I look now?"

He tsks. "Not yet, sweetheart."

I sigh, relieved when he takes it as playful and chuckles.

"Keep your eyes closed," he warns, his cadence pulling me back to Bellevue.

"Okay," I breathe.

He runs a brush through my hair, and the moment he gathers strands, I know what he's doing.

"You're braiding my hair?" I whisper, my eyelids slick with tears. "You used to do that when you were human."

"You loved it."

I choke back the emotion and nod ever so slightly so I don't mess it up. "I looked pretty like that."

"You always look pretty," he coos, pressing a kiss to my bare shoulder.

He twists the braids and pins them at the back of my head, and I sniffle.

"Are you sad?" he whispers, his fingers trailing from my hair down my bare back, stopping at the fabric on my hips.

"I don't know." I wipe stray tears away with the back of my hand.

"Don't open your eyes," he says softly. "Not yet."

"When?" I ask, my heart pounding with sharp, anxious beats.

"Soon."

I flinch as a length of silk brushes over my eyes. He ties it at the back of my head, then slips flats onto my feet.

"Give me a moment, sweetheart," he says, voice trailing behind me.

There's rustling like he's changing his clothes.

"All ready," he says.

He laces his fingers through mine and gives me a gentle pull forward. I follow his lead.

"Where are we going?" I reach my free hand up, worried I might bump into a wall or door.

He chuckles. "You'll see. Relax, I won't let you walk into anything."

He guides me down the hall to the elevator, his arm securing around my waist as we descend. Heat rises to my cheeks when we reach reception, and someone nearby coos an *awww* as Denendrius leads me past. The doors slide open, and a gust of cold air snakes through my dress, sending a shiver through me.

After a few steps, he guides me onto the warm leather of a car seat. When he sits beside me and pulls the door closed, I ask, "You're not driving?"

"We have a driver tonight."

I raise a brow. "A driver? Fancy."

My heartbeat stutters, a seed of dread lodging deep in my gut as he holds my hands in my lap, occasionally tilting my chin for long and deep, lingering kisses. Time blurs until the car slows to a stop, the driver shifting gears before wishing us a good evening.

Denendrius leads me out of the car, the biting wind slipping through the gaps in my dress as he pulls me forward. A man greets us, tells us to enjoy our night, and a door creaks open. I'm pulled into warmth, the sudden change in temperature making me shiver.

"Where are we going?" I ask again, but the only answer is the ding of another elevator.

Denendrius chuckles softly beside me as he pulls me into the elevator, the metal door sliding shut with a heavy thud. He untangles our fingers only to slip his arm around my shoulders, pulling me close. As the elevator lurches upward, I lean into him to steady myself. I wait, quickly growing impatient when it seems to go on forever. It makes no other stops, and we must be at the top of a skyscraper by the time it shudders to a halt and dings as the door opens.

Soft, muffled piano notes drift to my ears as Denendrius entwines our fingers and guides me forward. The sound swells, the keys crisp, rich, and too perfect to be anything but a real piano. A knot tightens in my throat as a door creaks open, then softly clicks shut behind us.

The overpowering aroma of roses circles me, the air unevenly heated at my hip as he walks me forward.

I let out a strained laugh. "What's going on, Den?"

He releases my hand, and I freeze, lifting my hands slightly but unwilling to take a single step in the unfamiliar space.

Footsteps click toward me, the air shifting against my arm as they stop directly behind me.

Denendrius's hand finds mine again as I nearly turn.

I stiffen as fingers brush the back of my head, gingerly loosening the silk knot before slowly drawing the fabric from my eyes.

My heart palpitates as a cold shudder moves through my center. Sweat wets my trembling hands.

"Marianna," Denendrius begins, kneeling on a bed of rose petals before me, a red velvet ring box cracked open in his hand. "Will you marry me and spend the rest of eternity with me?"

I gape at the diamond ring nestled in the box. It's nearly identical to the first one he gave me—a domed white diamond set in a silver band.

My lips part as I take him in. His brown hair tumbles over his shoulders in curls and waves, cascading over the black silk of his dress shirt. With his bright smile and warm, glittering eyes gazing up at me with adoration, he looks so sweet. So painfully beautiful.

The corner of his lip lifts into a crooked smile. "Marianna?"

I swallow against my tight throat and give him a rapid nod as I force out, *"Yes."*

It's the only answer he'll allow.

Denendrius's grin grows, and he gently releases my hand to remove the ring from the box. I can't breathe as his gaze snags mine and the ring slides down my finger. The light catches the diamond and the tinier ones in the band, casting rainbows over my hand as I tilt it.

He rises smoothly, pulling me into a tender kiss. Tears sting behind my lashes and pool in the corners of my eyes.

"I love you," he murmurs against my lips, lingering before pulling away.

"I love you too," I choke out, my gaze skittering away when he tries to catch it again.

Instead, I scan the room, focusing on steadying my breaths so the tingling panic in my fingers doesn't overtake my entire body.

We stand in the center of an expensive restaurant, each table overflowing with white candles and bundles of red and white roses. Hundreds of candles flicker, their glow dancing with the crystal chandelier overhead, draping the room in soft, shifting light. Across the restaurant, there's a table set for two—the only set table—against one of many floor to ceiling windows that give a panoramic view of the outside beyond the reflection of candlelight.

Aside from the staff gathered near the kitchen on the far left, the man seated at a glossy grand piano, and the girl behind me, we're the only ones here.

"Wow," I whisper, taking in the room.

I wipe my eyes and finally look down at myself. The toes of my black flats peek out from beneath the flowy crimson silk of the dress hugging my torso and falling at my hips. It's a simple thing that glistens in the candlelight.

"Should we sit?" Denendrius murmurs, placing his hand on the small of my back.

I swallow and nod, my weak legs carrying me across the room. The candles flicker as I pass, their flames shuddering and licking at the air in the window's reflection as we near the table by the glass.

Denendrius pulls out a white upholstered chair for me, but I'm too enthralled by the view outside to sit.

The city sprawls below us, the dark sky speckled with silver above the countless glowing buildings and towering skyscrapers. It's like gazing at a living map, the roads below reduced to delicate threads of light. Colors blur along the streets, a rainbow of twinkles—of bustling lives—calling my attention as I study the millions below. It stretches so far that the edge dissolves into the horizon.

It reminds me of sitting in the castle turret with Laurentius, gazing over the endless forest.

A pang of homesickness ricochets through my chest, though it pales against the loss—the loneliness—of overlooking Lorimer.

There was a time when this city was the worst thing to happen to me. When drugs and gangs were the biggest dangers. When alleyways and long nights were the darkest paths I could find myself on.

It was only a year ago when I couldn't recall vampires.

I unfocus my eyes until I'm faced with my reflection—a girl

who no longer belongs in the world she overlooks. Who hardly has a place in the world at all. I stare down at the roads again, at the city that feels foreign despite never changing, and think of the friends still down there, somewhere in another life. Is the ghost of this girl with them?

"Entranced?" Denendrius's smooth voice pulls me back to him. "You've never seen the city like this, have you?"

"I didn't realize there was a restaurant up here," I whisper, thinking of one of Lorimer's tallest buildings, standing at the heart of the wealthier downtown district. On holidays, it lights up with festive colors that can be seen from miles away.

He motions to the drawn back chair and I finally sit, my gaze turning back to the city as I look past the reflection. White flecks dance past the window as they fall, so far to go before hitting the ground that there's no way to guess where the wind will have them land.

"What do you think?" Denendrius asks as he sits across from me.

Do I tell him it aches? That every muscle in my body strains under the weight of grief? "It's beautiful."

I never loved Lorimer. It was both a trap I couldn't escape and the wealth of a dream forever out of reach. But it's where I was born, where I struggled to grow up, in a neighborhood so far and forgotten in the distance—so unimportant to the city built against it—that I can't even see it from here. I crumbled with that neighborhood.

I can't quite place why it hurts so bad. It has something to do with Denendrius . . . but mostly, it has something to do with me.

I exhale a shuddering breath, goosebumps pricking my bare arms as I straighten in my chair to face him.

With his soft smile and warm eyes, he shows no sign he notices my pain. Does he understand this indescribable feeling? The ache of looking at a place once so familiar—be it friend or enemy—only to see ghosts and memories draped over a stranger?

Perhaps he does when he sees Italy . . . or any place that once carved itself into his memory.

"What are you thinking?" he asks.

I wet my dry lips and pull in a chest-lifting breath before slowly blowing it past my lips. "Seeing the city like this . . ."

His chin dips with quiet sympathy as he offers a soft smile. "I thought you'd like to see it one last time before we go home. We likely won't return for decades, but this memory will remain whole in your mind—even when the city changes beyond recognition."

A single tear slips down my cheek before I can stop it. He reaches under the table, his fingers curling around mine. I bite down on my bottom lip.

"I remember Rome in fragments—roads, buildings, the amphitheater, the fields . . ." His thumb moves in slow circles over the back of my hand. "It would have been nice to see it from above, as the gods did. By the time I saw it again— running—three hundred and twelve years later, it had changed so much that I feared looking back, terrified to see the truth: that every trace of the world I had known was gone."

I sniff as another tear darts down my cheek. I wipe my eyes with my free hand and stare back out at the city, memorizing the way the busy streets wind and twist. So many roads I've traveled, just *here,* in this place. I can't even imagine what it will look like in centuries . . . Will there even be graves left of my friends for me to visit?

"The feeling doesn't go away," he admits. "Sometimes it's awe, sometimes it's grief. Even the shores change. You can see where the waves have worn them down, how time carves the land bit by bit. And you stand there, remembering each time you returned and noticed the same erosion. Your memories are so sharp you can flip through them like pages in a photo book.

Sometimes you marvel at the progress, at how far things have come. Other times, it's barren land, and even the spirits have moved on."

Is this why Viorel never leaves the castle? Is every step too heavy with grief to bear? Does he feel like the entire world has left him behind? At least Denendrius has the ruins—fragments of a past that still exist—to remind him he belongs somewhere. But what does Viorel have? Is he the only thing left unchanged, a constant adrift in a world of shifting tides?

"How do you do it?" I ask, letting the city blur in my peripheral. The glow of candles around the roses forms a warm barrier between it and me.

He shrugs. "You think you'll grow accustomed to it, but you never do. What changes it is sharing it with someone. Then you're not the only one carrying those memories. You're not alone with them. The past becomes something that binds you together." His voice lowers, a murmur now. "I want that."

I swallow the knot in my throat as he squeezes my hand. My thoughts drift to Viorel. He's truly alone. Even with the clan, he has no real connection to anyone. The longing to go back to him swells inside me, almost too much to bear. I want to be his other half, to share the weight of the memories the next millennia will bring. I want to hold his hand as time leaves us behind, to unshackle the chains tightening around his wrists and ankles with every passing moment, so we can race through eternity together. Like water and wind, I want to be unchanging for him.

And though Laurentius only has a thousand years of loneliness compared to Viorel, I don't want him to suffer a single one more. He may not bar himself in a subbasement like Viorel, but he's invisible—ostracized from the clan for his unorthodox beliefs. I want to be that comforting crystal voice in his ear to counterbalance the mumblings of rogue demons and the proclamations of angels, offering ears always open to catch whatever thoughts escape him. I want to be the unwavering, never changing being in his world of warping, waking illusions.

I want to be *so much* for them. As much as they've been for me.

I squeeze Denendrius's hand beneath the table. "I do too."

And he's going to give it to me. One day, Denendrius will be nothing more than a dark place I once visited, a shadow that no longer exists.

A surge of happiness ripples through me, and I grin up at Denendrius. It won't be much longer now until he turns me . . . then I can run home.

"Are you hungry?" he asks before beckoning a waitress over.

"Starving." I tighten my grip on his hand, and he responds with a squeeze.

A girl with pearl earrings beneath her wavy chin-length hair approaches with a single menu. She sets it in front of me as Denendrius requests water and an expensive bottle of wine. She gives him a polite nod before walking away.

I quirk a brow in question, and he says, "I hypnotized the entire staff."

"Ah, that works." I chuckle and look down at the menu, my eyes trailing over the expensive dishes.

"You only have so many meals left," he teases softly. "Will you try something new? Or go with a favorite?"

I tap the index finger of my free hand on my choice, the diamond glittering on my hand as it catches the light. "I'll get the elk."

A cub needs her meat if she's to grow strong enough to gut her prey.

"Good choice," Denendrius approves.

I study the room, the piano chords fluttering in my ears as I take in the roses and dripping candles.

"You went all out," I say.

The waitress approaches, setting a glass of water on the

table before pouring me a glass of wine. Denendrius gives her my order before she leaves us again.

"Do you like it?" He lifts a hopeful brow.

"It's a dream." *For any other girl. With any other man.*

"I'm glad you think so. I didn't think my first proposal was enough, and since you needed a new ring, I seized the opportunity to do it again."

I wonder if the previous ring Denendrius gave me is still sitting in the bottom of Viorel's bedside drawer, or if he disposed of it soon after tossing it there.

I offer a small, careful smile. "Definitely more romantic than the cemetery."

He snickers. "I thought it was romantic, proposing—promising—eternal life in the face of the alternative. In a place that would never serve another purpose for you."

"Poetic," I tease.

He merely grins, releasing my hand as he leans back in his chair, drinking in the sight of me. "You're so beautiful, Marianna."

I feign bashfulness, tilting my head just slightly, peering at him through my lashes.

"Will I be more beautiful when you turn me?" I pick up my glass of red wine and take a slow sip, letting its bitterness coat my tongue before I swallow. Deliberately, I lick the wine from my lip. His chest rises with a deep inhale, the sound audible in the quiet space between us.

"Impossible. I can't picture you more beautiful than you are now . . ."

"How much longer?" I ask, excitement threading through my impatience.

"A few weeks," he says. "Once we're finished up in Lorimer."

"What else is there left for us to do?" I take another long sip of wine.

"Nothing exciting enough to discuss over our engagement dinner," he muses.

When my dinner arrives, I eat slowly and deliberately, as if willing my brain to cling to the taste of every morsel. Will I miss this when I'm a vampire? Will the memory of food serve me, or will it all pale against the taste of blood? If drinking human blood as a vampire is as addictive and consuming as drinking vampire blood as a human, then maybe this is all wasted effort. Regardless, it prolongs the night a bit, as I know Denendrius is going to want more … *romance* … than just this.

Later, as we return to the motel, the painkillers wear off and let the full force of my side effects crash back over me. I resent the pain, but it saves me. It turns me into a teary, mewling kitten. I admit, I lean into the suffering, wading in the pool of pity he stands in. My tears benefit both of us, really. He runs me a warm bath, massaging my scalp as he murmurs about what an exemplary mother I'll be. How my willingness to suffer for our family only proves what a devoted wife and mother I am. How proud he is of me for enduring even more pain when I've already suffered so much with *Huarsar*.

He dotes on me all night, brushing my hair, and smoothing lotion into my aching muscles. And in the end, he only asks for my hand to satisfy him—and even then, I don't need to lend my tired mind to the task, as he does all the work.

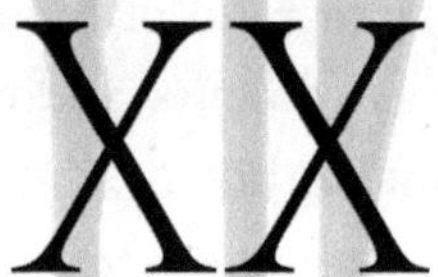

We return to Vermont the next night. Sergei drops a cooler full of blood near the bed, which he acquired during our proposal dinner the night before. Denendrius doesn't waste time digging in, slurping through three blood bags as Sergei prepares nose-stinging garlic water in a spray bottle.

"I'm glad I took my share already," Sergei grumbles as he reapplies the garlic solution around the boarded-up window and our door to keep Children of Stars out.

Denendrius doesn't acknowledge him, merely tearing into a fourth bag as Sergei sighs and leaves to secure the rest of the crumbling house.

I lie quietly in bed, painkillers and discomfort battling for control of my body as I scrutinize Denendrius. There's no control over how he drinks, his bloody fingers already moving toward a fresh bag as he drains the last of his current one.

"I'm surprised you're drinking those cold," I say in an attempt to break up the sharp silence.

He merely continues gulping them back until there's a pile of eighteen on the dirt floor beside him.

"How do they taste?" I lick my lips, wondering how the different humans and their compositions impact the flavor. He finally looks up at me and gives me a crimson grin.

"Impatient to turn and find out?" He quirks a brow at me.

I purse my lips and prop myself up on my elbow. "Curious, I guess. At least I only have a few weeks to wait—"

He's quick across the space, and I jolt against the mattress as his finger smears blood across my lips. He's practically giggling as he lifts the blood bag back to his slick, blood-stained lips, sucking crimson through the tube. His lips stay curled in amusement, his hungry eyes locking onto mine.

I'm unsure whether it would be wiser to lick the blood from my lips or wipe them with the back of my hand. It doesn't matter though, as Denendrius drops the empty bag and crawls toward me with his eyes focused on my mouth. His cold, iron-tinged breath fans against my face before he slowly and deliberately drags the tip of his tongue across my lips.

"*Mm . . .*" He hums against my lips before slipping his tongue inside, flooding my mouth with the tang of blood.

I press my palms against his bare chest as he repositions his body above mine, his labored breath pulsing against my clammy skin. "Den . . . You're blood drunk again, aren't you?"

"Only a *tiny* bit." Denendrius tugs the blanket away, the rush of cold air making my hormone-wracked stomach twist with nausea. His freezing hand grazes the flesh of my stomach and chest as he pushes my shirt off.

"We shouldn't—"

He closes his eyes and silences me with his mouth. I loop my arms around his neck, turning my face away just enough to make him believe I'm not denying him.

He kisses my throat as I say, "I don't feel good. We're not

going to make love, right? You said we would stop after my appointment."

His lusting grunt sends a fearful quiver through me. "We *are* stopping after your appointment, sweetheart. Once more, to tide me over, and then we'll wait."

Of course he would wield semantics to get what he wants.

"I'll be so gentle," he whispers. "You'll feel better."

My eyes pin the pile of empty blood bags on the floor. I doubt it's near the amount he drank while slaughtering the ship's crew, but that doesn't reassure me.

I recall when we were first together, how I got out of kissing him by warning him I might puke from all the garlic I consumed in an attempt to deter him. It worked then . . .

"I know," I begin, forcing a weak cough before adding, "I'm just really nauseous . . . I don't want to puke on you."

His claret eyes sparkle. "You're so thoughtful, sweetheart. But I wouldn't worry. If you puke, you puke. It's easy clean-up down here." He winks. "And trust me, nothing grosses me out."

Clean-up . . . Was that what really worried him back then? When I first threatened to puke on him, we were in his car. Was it about keeping the interior spotless?

The vague memory surfaces of overdosing in his car when he was abducting me to bring me to his apartment. He slammed on the brakes and held me over the street to puke, instead of in the passenger seat.

A weight settles over me, sinking me deeper into the mattress. "That makes me less worried." It's the only appropriate response.

Denendrius doesn't take long to get on with it. I'm caught in the violent swing of warring emotions—wanting to sob, wanting to bite his head off, wanting it all to end. I don't notice my breasts are sore until he grips them, and the ache pushes me over the edge.

His labored breath pulses against my ear as he thrusts and

rubs me between my pleasure-shaking legs. I bite my lip as a knot of pleasure coils in my core, threatening to snap and unravel. I force myself to think of anything else—the howling wind, the distant caws of night birds—anything but the way he makes my body betray me.

"Oh, you like that," he murmurs, his honeyed voice sending a jolt through me, even as it curdles my stomach.

Still, I bite back a moan, gasping as heat blooms between my thighs. His presence, his touch. It's too consuming to fight, too overwhelming to let me escape into my thoughts.

I'm desperate to tell him to stop. My pleas pile on my tongue, but I know uttering them could be futile and dangerous.

"Come for me," he murmurs, his voice thick with longing. "I know you want to."

My denial squeaks out, fragile and hoarse, the flood of hormones making it harder to swallow the agony of him. *"I don't."* A sob wrenches free, my breath hitching so hard my ribs pull away from his chest. A gag claws up my throat, my stomach clenching so hard I'm convinced for a terrifying moment I'll vomit. *"I don't want to anymore. Please stop."*

Denendrius crushes his mouth against mine—no pause, no hesitation—as he continues on.

I shove my hands against his cold chest, my lips tingling against his as he muffles my sobs.

He pulls his lips from mine a bit, his breath wafting against my mouth. "Silly girl, playing games. *I like games.* Your mouth lies, but your body doesn't. I can feel how close you are."

The backs of my eyes burn. I turn my head and dare choke out, "That's not how bodies work. Just because my body responds, doesn't mean I like it. I'm not in the mood tonight. I want to puke. I'm so tired, Den. *I'm so tired.*" I inhale a shuddery breath. "I can't control it."

He stiffens and stills on top of me, his heavy breath turning shallow. "What?" he asks, an edge to his flat voice that has me sure he's about to respond to my words with violence.

My tears are instant, and I protectively curl my arms over my head and bring my knees to my chest as he moves away from me.

As his weight lifts from the bed, I roll over and spot him halfway across the room, pulling up his jeans as he sinks to the dirt floor, pushing the blood bags aside. His eyes are hollow, empty.

"Is that true?" His voice is quieter now, distant. "That a body can respond without enjoying it?"

I can practically see the rush of thoughts in his eyes. Is he rethinking some rapes he's committed? Wondering how many of those girls weren't lying when their bodies might have betrayed them while they kept begging him to stop?

Wiping my eyes with the back of my trembling hand, I nod.

"How do you know?" he demands, a challenge flaring in his eyes.

I swallow thickly, clearing my throat. "There were a lot of science and psychology books in the castle library. I read a lot."

His lips twitch with a budding question, but it takes a moment to break free. "Is it the same for men? Can a man get hard and come, even if he doesn't want to?"

A wave of unease crashes through me. "Yes."

He stares at the dirt between us like he wants to lie beneath it. "What if a man was forced into a girl's role and touched by another man? He wouldn't get hard and come unless he secretly liked being submissive, right?"

My heart slams against my ribs, and though his misogyny has fury rising in me, I force it down. "That doesn't matter . . ." I swallow hard, my skin turning cold again. "Your body can respond to stimuli without your control. Like being tickled. That doesn't mean you like it or want it."

The look in his eyes . . . Tormented. Hopeless. It's the same one he wore in the dungeon when I carved *BITCH* into his stomach.

My heart stutters at the memory. Viorel taunted him and called him a dungeon bitch, made him hallucinate a man that had Denendrius quivering in his restraints.

"What did those guards do to you in Sirmium?" I rasp, knowing Viorel allowed them free rein over prisoners—anything short of killing them.

Denendrius turns his face away from me.

Tears flood my eyes, spilling hot down my cheeks as the realization hits. "Oh."

How didn't I see it before? Maybe I didn't want to. Maybe I was afraid to.

But I should have known.

I learned from Derek just how prevalent sexual violence was in ancient Rome. How consent wasn't a matter of morality, but hierarchy. A master could do whatever he wanted to his subordinate. It's why the issue with Denendrius trying to practice on his father's slaves was with Denendrius not owning them, potentially hurting his property, *not* because it was wrong to them.

It's why Denendrius *joked* when he was human that it was my duty as his wife to sleep with him. The reason he told me while we were in Romania that a man can't steal what has already been given to him.

Since Denendrius was already being tortured for three hundred and twelve years in unimaginable ways, why would they have drawn the line at *this*?

I know, even from my time in juvie, that in modern prisons, with laws and oversight, this kind of abuse is common. Where he was, there were *explicitly* no rules.

Part of me wants to accuse him of lying, for using this as a ploy for my sympathy. To divert my suffering back to him. But I think about the probabilities, and I know deep down it's likely impossible that he wasn't violated—at any point—over three centuries.

He says nothing, drawing his legs up and wrapping his arms loosely around his shins. His eyes stay fixed on the dark shadows swallowing the room.

"You were raped," I choke out. And all this time, he thought his body's response meant he secretly wanted it? Is that what they told him, over and over, for three hundred and twelve years?

Denendrius flinches.

"You were raped in Romania too, weren't you?" I rasp, the words scraping up my throat. The memory slams into me, the unfamiliar cologne clinging to his skin when Artair threw me into the oubliette with him.

He rubs the back of his neck, head tilting away as his gaze drifts to the darkness over his shoulder.

Reality does something dangerous to me. It shifts. Its edges blur, and suddenly, I'm lost in a dark forest of twisting confusion and questions. But then, a mark on a tree catches my eye. A red flag. I follow it, tracing it back to the next, and the next, until I find myself standing in a clearing of truth.

The abuse Denendrius suffered in Sirmium wasn't the first flag planted before he wandered into the deep—before he became the monster he is today, the monster he's embraced since escaping with Viorel's human niece, Tatiana, and raping her to death on the bank of the Sava River. The ouroboros bracelet she wore—stolen from her corpse, gifted to me by Denendrius when he was human—still hangs on my wrist.

That first flag—planted in uncertainty—wasn't entirely his fault. His father modeled abuse with his mother, teaching him that sex was force and violence. What else did he know?

Perhaps, when he was young, he had no other perspective to tell him it was wrong to *practice* on the slaves. How could he have known the lessons his father sent him to the brothel with would get him thrown out, naked, onto the street? And when he went home, his father certainly didn't clarify what went wrong. No one could have known for certain that more would follow.

But the flags are planted a bit more firmly after that. If Adelius's words rang true, Denendrius behaved when he was spending his father's money at brothels. When it was his own? Well, he admitted to me about paying extra for what he wanted. Adelius claims he only choked the girls enough to scare them, not harm them, but that the brothel owner feared he'd eventually strangle a girl to death.

Even when he was briefly human in Lorimer, I knew he was *off* before I succumbed to his mark. He was entitled, pushy, and far too comfortable trying to initiate sex with me, despite knowing he'd raped me when he was a vampire. Even the horrific tape I showed him of his own crime—one of eighty-two he helped me destroy—wasn't enough to make him reconsider.

Sure, he was never violent or physically forceful the way he once was. But then again, neither was he until now, despite the way every word he speaks drips with disregard for me. Back then, I couldn't understand his Latin to know for sure what all he was saying. Our language barrier lulled me into a false sense of security, and his mortal state made him vulnerable in ways he has never been as a vampire.

Maybe the worst of his violence started after Sirmium, with the rape and murder of Tatiana. With his vampirism, lack of control, and rage. That same *entitlement* is etched into every crime he's ever committed—not that he sees them as crimes.

I can't bring myself to believe he deserved what happened to him in Sirmium. For all I know, he wasn't thrown into that dungeon to pay for the same kind of abuse he suffered. He was caged for losing control—for panicking as a confused, terrified newborn, and for the two weeks of mayhem when he was killing indiscriminately: letting victims flee, leaving bodies in the open to be discovered, torching villages in a desperate attempt to be noticed by his own kind and helped. Neither Viorel or Denendrius has detailed the specifics of those two weeks to me. It would be so much easier to judge if I knew the scale and specifics of his mayhem.

And sure, Viorel reading his thoughts—how he briefly entertained staging an accident to kill Marianus so he could take Marciana as his own wife—didn't help his case. Then again, neither did Marianus telling Viorel's men he was dangerous.

Swallowing a jagged lump of truth, a sharp stroke scrapes down my chest with the reality that Viorel—*my Viorel*—allowed it, and that I don't know if it can be justified. But Viorel is as cruel as he is generous, carrying over twelve thousand years of archaic beliefs that only recent years have dared to challenge. There wouldn't have been anything out of the ordinary about his prison system back then, vampirism aside. And I've seen both sides of him myself. I try to shake the idea that Denendrius could potentially be right about how Viorel first threw him in the dungeon to sweep the problem away, but it imbeds itself in my brain like a sour little seed. Still, no matter if it's true, it doesn't change how Denendrius was still not quite right as a human. Viorel claims something dark was already dormant inside him.

And yet, I can't help but follow Denendrius's trail of wonder. How different could things have been if someone had guided him through being a newborn instead of damning him to the dungeon?

Maybe he could have been a vampire who was off, but not wrong enough to be a monster. Or maybe Viorel—with all his years, visions, and wisdom—knew *exactly* what Denendrius was capable of becoming and didn't want to take any chances.

It's likely the power of vampirism could have gotten to

Denendrius's head anyway and led him down a similar path, even without all the prison abuse.

I may be a victim who would never hurt anyone the same, but I didn't have my mind bent for three centuries or grow up with a father who normalized rape.

"It's not your fault," I whisper, trying to catch his eyes. "What they did to you—it wasn't your fault. You couldn't control it."

He looks up at me through his lashes, a wet sheen over his eyes.

With slow, measured breaths, I crawl off the bed and toward him.

"It's okay, Den," I murmur as I reach his side and lean my head against his shoulder. I don't care that I'm sitting naked in the dirt. Stabilizing him for my safety is more important. "You couldn't control it."

A ragged sound escapes his throat, and he rests his head on top of mine. "Do you still love me? It would make sense if you didn't."

I wrap my arms around his midsection, and the weight of my empathy makes the lie come easier. "Yes. I still love you."

"Do you still think I'm a man?"

I frown, holding him tighter. "Of course. How could I ever see you as anything else?"

"I tried to fight them at first, but they kept me weak." His voice shakes, growing anger beneath his words. "I told them I was a patrician, a gladiator, a fierce fighter like Mars . . ." He grits his teeth. "*They laughed.* Asked me where my money was now, how many wars I won. They spat blood on the floor and told me to lick it up. How I had no honor, no dignity, anyway, after voluntarily stepping into the arena like a common slave or criminal. *How dare I liken myself to a god when I was so eager to be Rome's slave?*" His muscles ripple with fury, with pain. "I told them Rome *loved me.* They loved that I was a gladiator. But they taunted me, and said Rome only loved me as much as the prostitutes were loved. That I was *just* an entertainer."

I can't help the sadness in my voice. "I'm so sorry, Den."

"They told me since I wanted to be a slave so badly when I was human, they'd make me one."

Squeezing my eyes closed, my tears wet his flesh.

"Sometimes, I agreed to it." He chokes on a breath, his voice warping as he whispers, "They'd chain me down and starve me for months, bring victims and drain them in front of me. Every time they'd spit blood on the floor, I'd cut myself on the metal restraints just to lick it up. If I wanted even a sip, they made me beg—made me ask for it like a girl. Sometimes they'd come as a group, or by themselves."

I fight the disgust tightening my throat, forcing my expression to stay neutral as tears spill past my lashes.

"It was survival, Den," I murmur. "You never wanted it. You were just starving. It's not your fault."

He shifts downward, resting his head in my lap. Cold tears spill onto my thighs. I choke back my own and run my fingers through his hair. He's nearly human again in my lap, nearly that Roman man that tricked my mind into loving him. That's the man I choose to comfort. Not the man who was abused and went on to abuse others in the exact same way.

I whisper comforting words to the man in the cell, who probably didn't do enough wrong to justify being there in the first place, in hopes of healing a little part of him that drives the man that terrifies me today.

That man . . . I hate him a little more. He's suffered what I've suffered, carries wounds that mirror mine—yet he chooses to pass them on. Does he think he can bleed it out that way?

I've read the statistics. How trauma can warp a person so deeply they grow into the shape of their abuser. But trauma isn't destiny. It can help explain, but it never excuses. I think it's called repetition compulsion. Identification with the aggressor.

It's what I've read in Viorel's psychology books. Still, as a victim myself, I just can't comprehend hurting so badly you'd want to brutalize someone else the same way.

How can he be this? How can he behave like his abusers and not be disgusted to see them in himself? Can he even fathom the connection? Or in his delusional mind, is what happened to him wholly different from what he does, because he's enacting his perceived right as a dominant man, and not a *submissive girl*?

"I hated it," he cries. "Sometimes it felt good, and I *hated* it."

"Your body just reacts to stimuli, Den," I reassure him softly. "That's all."

"I've never said it out loud before," he whispers, his breath ghosting over my bare skin. "Don't tell. *Please.*"

I rake my fingers through his soft hair. "Your secret is safe with me."

A quiet groan of agony rolls out of him. "Maybe I shouldn't have told you, but since we're trying to be honest with one another now, I needed to know if you could still love me after hearing my darkest secrets."

"I love you no matter what, Den. I *see you* now. You can tell me anything." The words slip out so easily, so smoothly, that I don't fully process the weight—the potential disaster they invite—until it's too late.

He lifts a hand toward his face, and for a moment, I think he's going to wipe his tears. But he doesn't stop.

His fingers keep moving down . . . *lower* . . . until they stroke between my legs.

My muscles lock, my fingers frozen in strands of his hair.

"You're so good at making me feel better," he murmurs, exhaling a cold sigh against my skin as his fingers push inside me. "You want to help me feel better, right? Just this last time, and I promise we'll wait until after your procedure."

I let out a strangled, *"Mhm."*

Of course, a brief heart-to-heart won't unravel centuries of his twisted mind, because he either doesn't see what he's doing to me, *or doesn't care.*

Denendrius straightens, his teary, pained eyes locking onto mine as he takes my arm and gently guides me back to the mattress. Tears streak my cheeks as he lays me down, tugs his pants off again, and climbs over me. I gasp as he begins just rough enough to send my heart trembling with fear.

He moans, leaning forward to kiss the tears from my cheeks. *"This makes me feel so much better."*

XXI

Each night of my treatment leaves exhaustion stacking higher. My emotions swing like a pendulum, shifting more frequently as the hormone injections continue. Holding everything in to keep up appearances with Denendrius is exhausting. I'm irritated more often than not, and even the most benign questions demand careful thought before I answer.

My fury burns in my throat, bringing tears to my eyes throughout the day. My sleeves are always damp from wiping my eyes.

Nothing has really changed, except Denendrius expects less from me sexually. It's a relief, but it doesn't make the days any easier.

My tits are sore, my head pounds, and I'm too bloated to get comfortable in bed. I toss, turn, and switch between layers of clothes, but nothing helps. Nausea rolls in and out of me throughout the days. I don't know how much Viorel's blood helps me, but I wonder if I'd be worse off without it. I'm practically high on weed the whole time, which helps a bit physically, but the anxiety still clings, raking its nails down my ribs, trying to steal my breath.

The gentle, cold massages Denendrius offers are begrudgingly soothing, and I oblige each offer of his blood since it takes the edge off my suffering.

Denendrius tries to console me with talk of babies and motherhood, but all it does is have me in tears missing Aeliana. I engage in his brainstorming for names and nursery set ups, knowing the excitement and calm it brings him makes it easier for him to deal with the occasional grouchy tone and clipped responses I don't manage to catch fast enough.

We visit Dr. Sampson every three days for a checkup, staying at the old house in Vermont for two nights and a hotel for each day and night of my appointment. Dr. Sampson says my side effects are normal given the level of hormones I'm on, and that regardless of them, I'm still safe enough to continue the treatment.

I ache for it to be over, reminding myself this is just a fraction of the pain I'll endure to become immortal. The world outside doesn't stop for my suffering, though. Denendrius's face keeps circulating in the international media, his crimes flashing across hotel TV screens like a countdown to disaster.

The ship we abandoned at sea makes American news, but it doesn't gain as much public attention as our case and isn't linked to us yet. But Viorel must know. How could he not? Maybe he's keeping it quiet on purpose, waiting to use it against Denendrius later. Or maybe he doesn't want everyone knowing my last location while he tries to find us first.

Adelia, who habitually checks in with Denendrius on his encrypted phone, says our faces are circulating on Italian news channels as well. She mentions a string of reported animal attacks that swept through the Romanian countryside in the days following the veil's lapse, along with a rash of violent murders—bodies torn apart and left in the open—spotted across several nearby countries.

One report she mentions comes from Hungary, where a man was attacked in an alleyway behind a nightclub after discovering a woman seemingly *cannibalizing* another in the shadows where he'd intended to piss. The victim was found dead at the scene, her neck torn open. The man, however, survived with only a broken arm, a broken nose, and a concussion, as the attacker fled.

Adelia says he was interviewed from the hospital, where he claimed government agents came to question him about the woman. The police dismissed the encounter, suggesting he was simply confused from the head injury.

I suspect she's trying to bait Denendrius into reacting to the horrific fallout of releasing all the prisoners when she brings up a new viral news story out of a small town in Serbia. Security footage shows a man bludgeoning orphanage staff and kidnapping all the children in the dead of night. None of them spoke as they calmly followed him out, which has Adelia convinced he's a Darkling who hypnotized them. Authorities had no leads until someone checking their trail cam a few days later caught him walking toward a notoriously dangerous cave system—with all the children.

She forwards the leaked video to us from the cave rescue team led deep by dogs. The audible terror and grief—the whining dogs, the broken voices of the cavers—as they found that vampire's nest is seared into my ears. They could only describe the dead, neck-torn children as having been cannibalized. To make matters worse, they found hundreds of small skeletal remains—centuries old—and an unknown language scrawled across the walls surrounding the pile of decrepit clothing he must sleep on . . . *when he's home.*

Yet the story doesn't move Denendrius the way it does me. He glances at the footage of the man with the children and simply confirms that he released him from the dungeon, offering nothing more.

What was once an old folk tale—reduced to legend after Viorel locked the monster away—has now returned home.

"Hey, Dr. Sampson," I greet as Denendrius and I enter the quiet fertility clinic.

"Good evening," he responds with a practiced grin, far too chipper for someone being forced to perform aggressive fertility treatments after hours. We follow as he moves through the clinic to his office, the cold shadows making me wrap my weak arms around myself. "How are you feeling, Maria? Ready for retrieval?"

"Nervous," I admit, twisting my fingers together in front of me.

"Everything will go smoothly." Dr. Sampson gives me a sympathetic smile. "But I wanted to discuss your blood work again before we proceed with retrieval. We have your ancestry results as requested, but there's more to discuss."

Despite having a pretty good idea what the results will be, my palms sweat and my heart stutters. My legs wobble as we follow into the dim office.

"Have a seat," Dr. Sampson says as he lowers himself into his chair while Denendrius and I sit across from him. "So, the initial labs presented some anomalies during genetic testing that we took the liberty of having further investigated."

Denendrius stiffens beside me, a warning in his voice as he says, "That doesn't sound legal, Dr. Sampson . . . and well beyond the scope of what I asked you to do."

Dr. Sampson's grin falters. He spreads his hands on his desk. "This isn't exactly legal either."

"What was so abnormal?" I demand, wanting to know the

worst before Denendrius can start a catastrophic argument with the man who still has to perform a medical procedure on me.

His smile returns as he looks at me and draws in a breath. "They found some irregularities that they couldn't ignore, which—long story short—led to a series of discoveries by the local university performing advanced genetic testing—"

Denendrius leans forward toward the desk. *"Excuse me?"*

Dr. Sampson lifts a hand to ask for patience. "I'll explain it as simply as it was explained to me. Essentially, they found two distinct DNA sequences in your blood. One is interacting with fragmented portions of your own, which suggests you had some kind of stress or alteration at a cellular level. But the foreign DNA is particularly unusual because—hear me out, I know how this sounds—it's not entirely *Homo sapiens*."

I feel the heat drain from my face. "What do you mean?" I ask, a tremble in my voice. What are the chances a blood test has just exposed the existence of vampires?

"The foreign sequences are definitely hominin, meaning they belong to a human or a close relative. But they also contain unknown markers—ones that don't match Neanderthal, Denisovan, or any other archaic human species we've identified. That's why the geneticists are baffled. Normally, if someone had two sets of DNA, we'd assume it was chimerism —like from absorbing a twin in the womb. But that clearly isn't the case here."

I stare at him. "But they're *human* genes?"

He nods. "Yes, they're abnormal and don't behave quite how we'd expect, but at their core, they're human. Maybe even from a species we haven't discovered yet."

My thoughts flurry with a mix of confusion and excitement. They found Viorel's DNA interacting with mine? What could it mean about his past if he's only partially *Homo sapiens*? Who could his people have been then, for there to be no evidence of them left behind, or yet discovered? He looks so much like modern people, despite the way vampirism has changed him.

I ache to be with him, to tell him I found a significant—though still mysterious—bit of information about who he is. Could him having DNA from another human species explain the way vampirism affects him—and, in turn, me? He had told me when he was recounting his past that none of the other human species he encountered had ever survived the transformation. What made him so special? So powerful? Did he have unusual power, even as a human? He had said his maker told him he was a divine leader revered by his people . . .

"You mentioned fragmented DNA?" Denendrius chimes in.

"Yes," he verifies, nodding at Denendrius before addressing me. "In your own DNA, we found sequences that appear to be disrupted or fragmented. These fragments are not what we typically see in a healthy individual's DNA and suggest that your DNA has been through some form of severe stress or alteration at a cellular level. This is also strange, because aside from that, you are incredibly healthy."

"Hm. I wonder what would cause DNA fragments like that," Denendrius says sardonically while shooting me a glance to match his smirk.

I scowl at Denendrius, and in Spanish, so hopefully the doctor doesn't understand, I snap, "It's his blood fragmenting it, obviously. *Not* a sign I was anything but human as a child."

Denendrius merely smirks at me. "Uh-huh. We'll see." Turning back to the doctor, he adds, "And what about her ancestry?"

Dr. Sampson clears his throat. "See, her ancestry is perplexing as well." His eyes shift to me. "What was your working belief about it, Maria? Considering Charles requested, but you didn't protest . . ."

My hands shake in my lap, my thoughts a mess. My mouth feels like cotton. "Nothing super specific, but my mom was from Mexico. She had darker features than me, so I always assumed my biological father was white or European. All I know is I have Latino ancestry."

His lips purse as he bobs his head from side to side. "According to testing, Maria, your ancestry doesn't descend from modern Latin America, but more so the opposite. Your genetics match the far ancestors of some modern Latin Americans, including some Mexicans, of course. The term Latina would technically be far too modern for you. Which is all"—he pulls in a deep breath—"scientifically insane, frankly."

I merely stare at him in stunned, wide-eyed silence.

Denendrius exhales disbelief and leans forward. "Which all means what, specifically?"

Dr. Sampson blows out a long breath and addresses me, saying, "Going purely off your genetic results, as impossible as they should be, both your maternal and paternal lines create a perfect genetic snapshot of someone from the Iberian Peninsula between 150 B.C. and A.D. 150. The snapshot includes ancestral markers common to broader Mediterranean populations, including distinct genetic ties to ancient North African groups. It's a perfect snapshot, as if you've time traveled from there."

Denendrius's astonished grin is blinding in my peripheral, and the moment he turns to me, I snap at him, my Spanish low and harsh as I snarl, "Is this what you wanted? To fake my ancestry just to make me doubt myself? To make me think I was a child vampire?"

The warning in his tight Spanish response snuffs my flame. "Don't cause a scene here. We'll talk about this later."

I scowl and cross my arms, hurt twisting my stomach.

From the tense smile on Dr. Sampson's lips as his gaze flicks between us, he didn't understand a word. But as his eyes settle solely on me, his tone softens as he says, "Just so we're clear, Maria, this genetic profile doesn't change who you are.

Your connection to Latino culture is the same as before. What-ever that looked like for you—speaking Spanish, anything more—is far more *you* than this strangeness of your DNA." He chuckles a bit then adds, "I know it might not help you feel better coming from a white man, but you can call yourself Latina. The only difference now is that you know your genealogy is a little more complicated than you hoped. But really, implausible ancient genes aside, you're one of billions who doesn't fit neatly into a modern racial box, and that's okay."

Some of the tension in my chest loosens, and I manage a nod. At least he's being kind about the lies Denendrius must have hypnotized him to tell me. "Okay."

His soft smile persists. "I was wondering, Maria, if I could have your consent for the scientists who currently have your blood to move out in the open with their studies, since there are admittedly ethical concerns with how they came into possession of it when only a simple genetic test was requested. We don't have to identify you at all, if you prefer anonymity too."

My heart throbs at the base of my throat, an excited jitter moving through my core at the idea that scientists could unlock ancient secrets about Viorel. If I could come back with the potential of giving him more children who are made of me, as well as a missing piece of the puzzle of who and what he was before being taken, it would be wonderful. I open my mouth to agree—

"She doesn't consent," Denendrius says smoothly, his gaze locking onto Dr. Sampson's. "And before we leave, you're going to give me all the names you have so I can handle this overstep."

My shoulders drop in disappointment, but . . . perhaps it's for the best. If they keep digging, they might find more than just a lost human species. I wouldn't want them stumbling onto biological proof of vampires, or Denendrius taking another opportunity to fabricate my past anymore than he has.

"Understood." Dr. Sampson blinks as Denendrius rests back against the chair and glances at the clock above the office door. "Let's get you prepped for retrieval."

I suck in a deep breath, my body aching from the treatment and the excitement to finally get it over with.

Following the nurse and Dr. Sampson, I change into a medical gown, the fabric thin and stiff against my skin. The medical room is sterile and cold, the scent of disinfectant clinging to the air. The dimness of the rest of the clinic beyond the room—the knowledge that we're doing this off the record—has me feeling vulnerable and at risk. Like we're not with a *real* doctor, but someone hired to work for a criminal organization.

We had a doctor like that on the payroll when I was in Venganza Roja. I saw him a few times—mostly when I was too scared to bring up a minor issue with whichever foster parent I had at the time. This feels the same. The dim clinic, the off-the-record silence, the way my nerves tighten like I'm waiting for something to go wrong. It reminds me too much of sneaking into that Southside clinic after dark with Julio.

At least this man doesn't do sketchy arrangements like this as his bread and butter. It's odd, but knowing Denendrius is only a few feet away assures me no one else will take advantage of my unconscious state.

With a deep breath, I lie back on the medical bed's crisp sheet, the overhead light glaring against my tired eyes. The nurse murmurs something about my vitals as she presses cool electrodes against my skin.

The IV pricks into my vein, a slow burn spreading up my arm as the anesthesia works its way through my veins. My eyelids grow unbearably heavy, my awareness slipping as if I'm sinking into warm water.

The next thing I know, I'm in an unfamiliar room, and I

don't even remember falling unconscious. The light is softer. Something beeps. My limbs feel weighted, my head stuffed with cotton. My blink is lethargic, my eyes struggling to focus as Dr. Sampson speaks. His voice is distant, words floating above me as if I'm hearing them underwater.

"Thirteen eggs." The words drift into my cloudy haze.

Denendrius responds before I can process it, his voice smooth with satisfaction. "That'll have to do, I suppose."

I try to respond, but my tongue is thick and knotted, my body dead weight. Denendrius thanks Dr. Sampson for both of us, his voice clear where mine is nonexistent.

Thirteen eggs. A strange mix of relief and unease settles in my chest. I remind myself this is what I wanted. *This is good for me too.* This brings me one step closer to my freedom. To my immortality.

XXII

I lie in the bed of another motel, the bitter taste of CBD chocolate Sergei tracked down for me a layer on my tongue. It dulls the ache in my abdomen a bit and makes the bed softer beneath my body.

Denendrius strokes his fingers through my hair, tears streaking my cheeks as I watch the TV on the dresser across from the bed. They're emotionless tears, like my body is trying to rid itself of the built-up hormones coursing through me.

"How do you feel?" Denendrius murmurs, wiping tears off my cheek with his thumb as he rests upright against the head-board above me.

"Fine," I mumble, sniffling.

"Are you sad, sweetheart? I know what we found out about you must feel overwhelming."

"No," I admit as I adjust my head against the soft pillow. Why would I be upset when I know it's an absurd lie? "I just keep swinging back and forth with emotions."

He bites into his wrist and presses the crimson wound

against my lips. I lap him up willingly, the sweet taste of his blood washing away the chocolate in my mouth and doing more for my body than the CBD ever could. He lets me drink until my stomach is more bloated than my abdomen, and it's nice to be able to pull away on my own accord since his blood isn't hooked through my freewill like a barbed fishhook.

I lick the crimson off my lips. "Does this mean you can turn me faster?"

He plays with my hair, curling strands around his fingers. "It'll still be a *little* longer, sweetheart. We're only in the first week of April, so I have a few more weeks before we hit that two-month mark I promised. I don't have enough control yet, especially with how strong your blood is. It's like a drug, so it'll be much harder for me to resist drinking it."

I push my bottom lip out. "I really don't want to be marked to Viorel anymore. Could Sergei do it?"

He hooks his finger beneath my chin and tilts my head back so I'm looking up at his softly scowling face. "I want to be the one to turn you. You're *mine*."

Swallowing, I say, "I know. I want you to turn me, too. I'm just desperate to be immortal with you rather than linked to Viorel."

Tracing his finger along my jawline, he says, "I understand. It won't be much longer, I promise. I've been handling my thirst easier these past few days."

"That's good." I exhale wistfully through my slightly parted lips, focusing on the sound of the shower stream in the bathroom across the room, where Sergei sings quietly in Russian. I can't help the quirk of my lip as I listen to him, wondering what the cheery-sounding song is about.

"Think I can convince Uncle Sergei to sing to our babies?" Denendrius's low chuckle makes my smile deepen.

I don't think about babies made of Denendrius and me in Sergei's muscled arms, though. I imagine what his own children might have looked like—blond and fair-skinned, perhaps —in his soft, human grip. What was Sergei like as a human? A devoted family man, going off how he described the great lengths he has used hypnotism to remain in the lives of all his descendants. Who is he today, despite Denendrius? Despite his hard appearance, an aura of genuine care and kindness envelops him. One that I think is to his own detriment, especially with his ride or die attitude with Denendrius.

"What are you thinking about?" Denendrius murmurs in my ear, his soft lips grazing the curve.

"Huh?" I blink the images of Sergei with a human family away. "Oh. I was pondering Sergei. Him and his family."

"Ah. He has a nice family. I've met many of them. We've got our competition cut out for us."

I lick my dry lips and force my eyes to focus back on the TV.

"Do you know what I'm thinking about?" Denendrius murmurs.

I squeeze my eyes closed. *Please don't be sex.* "What?"

"What your family might have been like when you were a little vampire child." He strokes the side of my face. "Hm? What are your thoughts?"

Annoyance pulses through my chest, my jaw straining from my grit teeth. I squeeze my eyes closed too tightly. It's like a colorful kaleidoscope behind my lids.

Denendrius chuckles. "Even with fragmented DNA and ancient Iberian ancestry, you can't believe, hm?" Denendrius says, and I can picture the coy fucking smile on his stupid fucking face. "You really don't believe you were a child vampire, even with medical and scientific evidence? The argument that Huarsar didn't hypnotize you is weaker every day."

"That's hardly evidence," I growl. "Viorel's blood is just fucking with my DNA, and they clearly messed up my ancestry."

"Uh-huh." He chuckles, the sound so condescending I fight

the urge to sit and rake my fingernails across his smug face. "His DNA is interacting with your fragmented ones, which just *happens* to be making you suffer from garlic and sun exposure for some unknown reason. And the geneticists just *accidentally* linked you to ancient Iberia. I'm no scientist, but even I know they can't just accidentally click the wrong button on a computer for that one."

"Really," I affirm, twisting away from him so roughly it sends a pang through me that's so sharp the room shifts on its axis. I hold my breath until it subsides, then say, "Alaire and Edmond had boxes and boxes of information about child vampires, and he picked through all of them. There was nothing about me, and I'm glad. He told me about a few child vampires and I'm grateful to not have gone through what they did."

Denendrius wraps his hand around my shoulder and gives me a tug to say he wants me to roll back over. "What did he tell you about them?"

I roll my eyes behind my closed lids and carefully rotate onto my back to gaze at him. "Well, the saddest child vampire he told me about was a Darkling girl who was nearly two thousand years old. She and her parents were caught by Alaire and Edmond when she was playing in a park one night. I guess he let them live because they willingly gave her up. She was a little girl and obsessed with having a normal life because of what she saw on TV about the modern world. She wanted to be like all the other kids—eat treats, ride the school bus—and was going nuts because she couldn't. Apparently, her parents would have to restrain her or give into letting her watch TV to soothe her. They must have really loved her because they handed her over to give her a chance to grow up. Viorel said she was going to be adopted from what Alaire and Edmond wrote, but she grew up with a fucked up life, though I guess she was lucky to not have the health issues the other vampire children did. Sounds like she made it to adulthood, but they died before they could take any other notes on her."

Denendrius straightens, unblinking, lips parted in disbelief as he stares at me with a deeply furrowed brow. "Did you not hear a word out of your mouth?"

I scowl. "What?"

"He was talking about *you*, Marianna. *You.*"

Pushing out a breath, I roll my eyes so hard in frustration that there's a twinge of soreness behind them. "I wasn't—"

"Just shut up a second," he says, tone far too delicate for how serious I know the demand is. "The fact he could tell you *all* that and you can't see how he's talking about you just proves he hypnotized you into believing you weren't a child vampire despite all the other signs." A sour smile shapes his lips. "And I finally get why. *You have living parents. Immortal parents.* Well, they were alive less than two decades ago, and I bet he knows whether they still are right now."

An acidic burn weighs heavily in my stomach. How can Denendrius be so delusional? Viorel *would never.* Viorel is capable of cruelty to the darkest degree, but I can't imagine he would keep a truth like that from me, especially for no good reason.

"Bullshit," I spit, some of that acid spraying out with my words.

He shakes his head, disgust drawing the corner of his lip back. "If your parents loved you enough to give you up for a chance at a human life, I bet Viorel knows they would love you enough to get their grown-up daughter back now that she's involved in our world again . . . if you knew about one another."

Shifting my hand to his thigh, I press my fingers into his skin. "He wasn't talking about me . . ." I plead for him to understand, fearing a violent tirade about Viorel.

Instead, his eyes soften as they wander over me. "Wow . . ." he breathes and moves his cold hand to cup the side of my face. "That means you could be potentially near my age, perhaps older, since I'm only 1,951 years old now. Almost two thousand years old and ancient Iberian, from *Hispania*. A Roman province. So close by modern standards, yet so far by ancient ones. But over the past two thousand years? I could have run into your parents at some point and have been none the wiser."

"I was never a child vampire," I whisper, not understanding why he wants it to be true so badly.

"You're obsessed with being a normal human, Marianna," Denendrius accuses softly, a pitying sheen over his eyes as he rubs his thumb over my cheek. "I never understood the look in your eyes when you watched other teenage girls on TV until now. It was intense jealousy and longing. You spent so much time in Bellevue watching teen sitcoms and dramas, making comments about their lives. You wanted to go back to school so badly and make normal friends. Hell, I remember you crying in the apartment when you were watching a show when I was first a human again, before you slapped the hell out of me and had a breakdown. No wonder you wanted me to stay human . . . No wonder you were so resistant to the idea of being in a world of vampires. You wanted a normal human life, just like you did when you were a vampire child."

My eyes brim with tears, and I choke out, "I wanted to be normal so bad because I never had that. I was born to a drug addict and was abused my whole life. The *only thing* different that Viorel found out about me was that I'm a year older because she told the government I was younger, hoping she wouldn't be in as much trouble—"

His swift headshake silences me. "I don't know how you ended up with Bonnie, but think about what Viorel told you and your own life. She was about to be adopted last Alaire and Edmond knew. But that didn't happen, and she grew up miserable? *Come on,* Marianna, who does that sound like? You were going to be adopted before Vianna and Kenneth were killed. You grew up miserable . . . *She's you.*"

I merely stare at him in defeat. Why does he want my life to be more complicated than it already is? Why does he want that nightmare for me?

He frowns as he takes in my expression. "Even though he hypnotized you, it would make sense if your subconscious is full of fear over the idea of having a completely different history and culture."

I rock my head back and forth against the pillow in protest, but it doesn't stop him from talking.

"You have to admit, sweetheart, that even if you were biologically related to Bonnie, she was too high to submerge you in the culture beyond her Latino gang . . ." He squints at me, pondering for a long moment. "Hm . . . You know . . . if you were five or six when she somehow got a hold of you, that doesn't leave much time to learn Spanish. And you are *fluent*. You were just as fluent when we met in Enchanted Land, and at that point, you would have only been human for a year or two. Yet you spoke it as if you learned it in tandem with English."

I fight the urge to plug my ears with my fingers so his delusion can't weasel its way in.

He gives me a soft smile, his eyes sparkling. "Maybe there's a bit of truth helping that hypnotism cling so tightly, hm? If I were Alaire and Edmond and wanted to integrate a newly turned human child into a *normal* world, but with enough familiarity that her subconscious would be comfortable enough to do it, I'd probably keep her on the same continent. Not the same country she was used to—don't want those repressed memories rushing back if it can be avoided—but maybe somewhere close to the normal she's seen on TV, but with the comforts of what she spent a lot of her vampire child life around." A smile ghosts over his lips. "Like, maybe, *Lorimer*, a normal American city with a large Latino population."

"No," I blubber, refusing to entertain the idea.

Denendrius sighs. "What happened to her?"

I swallow a knot. "Viorel couldn't say. They died before they could write anything else about her."

"Because *I killed them* before they could leave that warehouse with her," Denendrius retorts, tone so firm no argument I could come up with would shake these misguided ideas of his.

Tears barrel down my temples, soaking my hair. Still, I plead. "It's not true."

"I'm sorry," he murmurs, smoothing my hair against the side of my head. "I'm sorry you traveled through so much time, and that you didn't have the normal life you were promised, that you can't remember why it tortured you so. I'll turn you soon, sweetheart. I'll help you find your parents, and hopefully, there are enough good memories from those two thousand years to make up for your time as a human. At least one good thing has come from it. You were able to grow up. I'm sure they had to keep you hidden when you were an immortal child. At least now, you can spend your eternity as an adult instead of a never-changing child. And won't it be a relief to have parents who love you so much? Maybe our children could have grandparents. We could finally have some semblance of a family."

A sob bubbles out of me, and I turn my face and bury it in his hip as he strokes my hair. Frustration leaks from my eyes, and it's like a dozen pricks in my chest to know I'm not her. A tiny part of me is still disappointed I wasn't immortal despite the overall relief, because while she lived as a child vampire for over two thousand years and had a life clouded in dark, unimaginable mystery, she at least had parents who loved her, while I didn't. It was nice, for a moment, to think I might not have been born to a meth addicted prostitute who let men molest me.

XXIII

We stay in the same motel for the next few days while I recover, Denendrius's blood helping to speed up the process. I spend most nights tucked at his side watching pay-per-view movies while wondering how long we're going to have to stay in Lorimer, and what else Denendrius might have to wrap up before we leave. Both my eggs and his sample are set to be transported to a clinic in Italy for us.

The sound of Denendrius's keys wakes me, and I rub my eyes and glance at the digital clock on the nightstand between Sergei's bed—who is fast asleep—and ours. It must be just after sunset.

"Where are you going?" I whisper-shout as Sergei rouses a handful of feet away from me and stares up at Denendrius expectantly.

Denendrius adjusts his leather jacket on his shoulders. "I'll be back in a couple hours. I've got something to take care of quickly."

Sergei props himself up on his elbow, the ugly teal blanket falling down to reveal the wrinkled, white tank top he wears. "Sneaking off?"

Denendrius flicks the desk lamp on, the yellow glow dim enough it doesn't burn my sleepy eyes. "You two were resting." He points at the notepad on the desk, pretty handwriting in black ink scrawled on the branded paper. "I left a note."

Sergei sits upright, head swaying in disapproval. "Can you handle your thirst alone?"

With a long stare, Denendrius says, "I haven't had a real chance to test myself in the city without you babysitting me. I'm sure I'll be fine."

Grunting, Sergei lays back down. "Call if you need me."

Denendrius's eyes flicker to me and soften, and he rushes back to my side to kiss me deeply. "Be right back."

"Okay, love you." My muscles loosen, thankful for the break from being so tense around him.

"Love you too, sweetheart."

When Denendrius leaves, Sergei sighs and grumbles something in Russian before turning to look at me. "Movie?"

I pull the blanket tight around myself and nestle into my cool pillow. "Okay."

He puts on a comedy adventure. Despite the break from Denendrius, I can't quite relax enough to laugh as he does. When my stomach demands dinner, Sergei orders me delivery and sniff-tests my meal for traces of garlic before I devour my gourmet burger.

"How are you feeling?" Sergei asks once I'm halfway through my burger, and I lift my eyes to the TV upon realizing I've been staring down into the takeout box the entire time.

I swallow a chunk of greasy burger and bun, washing it down with icy soda when it catches. "I don't know."

The movie pauses, and I brace myself for conversation.

"Do you remain upset at me for turning Denendrius back?" There's something so soft and fatherly about the way he asks, but there's a guilty underscore that has me wondering if he desperately seeks my reassurance that he made the right call considering all that happened as a result.

My gaze sinks back to my burger, my tightening grip on the buns squeezing more grease onto my fingers. "I don't know," I admit.

As long as Denendrius follows through with turning me and I escape, then it's for the best he was turned back. But otherwise . . . Well, it might have been better—*easier*—if I had blissful blood slave ignorance instead of having to act my way through this.

I ponder if Sergei believes my act. I doubt it. Despite being Denendrius's best friend and creation, he's far more level-headed. Perhaps he sees it and knows it's better to let me play along. All he cares about is keeping Denendrius happy, and would Denendrius believe him anyway when I'm doing such a good job meeting his expectations? It's likely Denendrius would only turn on him if he called me out.

Still, I know better than to let my show slip in Sergei's presence, even when I set my burger down and say, "I don't understand why you turned him back if you're worried about your family's safety."

I think of the large extended family he told me about while Denendrius was human, how because of being turned, he could see them grow up, how hypnotism let him safely be a part of their lives with their memories of him only existing in his presence.

"I have a lot of family, Marianna, and I cannot be in more than one place at a time despite inhuman speed. At the end of the day, it does not matter if he is human or vampire."

"You really think he'd hurt them if you didn't oblige his

every whim?" I ask, knowing he would but wanting Sergei to say it aloud.

He tip-toes around his answer. "Denendrius's anger is a force to be reckoned with, and once he gets an idea in his head . . . good luck getting it out."

I read between the lines, understanding Sergei is balancing on his own tightrope. Does he think Denendrius would have gone after them, even as a human? I suppose it's easy to imagine Denendrius retaliating if Sergei had refused to turn him back. Though the easiest solution would have been for Sergei to just kill him.

"You seem scared of him," I say, and my observation receives a chuckle that has me looking at him.

Sergei smirks. "Who is not scared of him? There are times he scares himself."

"You never thought of killing him?" I quirk a brow. "You don't hate him, knowing he'd kill your family without a second thought if he decided it's justified?"

"Denendrius gave me so much with this immortal gift," he says. "I owe him *everything*. He's like a little brother to me. I could never stay mad at him, no matter his actions. People don't have to share the same ideas to care about each other."

"You don't think he's taken too much from you?" I counter, unable to wrap my mind around his thought process.

"Who in this world does not take from others?" he argues with a light smile. "None of us are innocent. Surely, I have done enough damage to countless other families by drinking blood."

I don't like his equalization, the insinuation that all our wrong doings are equal. Surely he can't lump drinking blood to survive and serial rape and murder together.

"Did you beat your wife?" I find myself asking.

"No," he says simply, not even flinching at my question.

"Your children?"

"Never. I was too soft as a father."

"What would you have done if someone had hurt them?" I wonder. "You had two children, right? One daughter?"

His lips form a taut line.

"What if someone had hurt her?" I whisper.

Sergei picks the remote back up and stares at the TV as he points it. He purses his lips like he's debating whether to end our conversation.

My heart thumps. "Would you have treated me like your own daughter had Denendrius brought me home for you to raise for him?"

I don't miss the way he swallows, or the guilt shining in his black eyes as he lowers the hand holding the remote to the bed. He doesn't say yes but doesn't say no either. His words are purposefully chosen when he utters, "I would have taken good care of you."

Part of me appreciates the unwillingness to lie, to claim he'd treat me like a daughter when a good father wouldn't raise a girl and let their friend groom her until he deems her ripe enough to tear off a vine.

"Is that why you convinced him to give me back?" I ask, responding to his unspoken words.

He doesn't reply, just plays the movie.

After a long minute of thinking he's done with the conversation and worrying I've said too much to oppose Denendrius and betray my game, he says, "I was glad he returned you. But hindsight is twenty-twenty, and ignorance is truly bliss."

"I would have been happier with you raising me." It's a simple fact of Denendrius's blood mark and an unfortunate truth that helps me appear on Denendrius's side. I would have been in an even deeper state of delusion than I had been in Bellevue. And despite my love for everyone back home, I would have had one pain growing up—Denendrius—instead of so many more. I'd probably even be a vampire by now, the soft silk sheet of ignorance torn away to uncover the rotten foundation I had been standing on all along. Yet, at least I would be immortal to deal with it.

Sergei offers a small smile. "A comfort I always tell myself ... Everything happens for a reason."

I can't agree. It seems like a lot of things have been happening for no good reason at all.

I'm lost in thought as my unfocused eyes rest on the TV. Even without Denendrius here, I can't help how my thoughts loop around him. How he lives in my mind. What's he doing out there? I glance at the clock. The fact he's been gone for just over two hours makes me gnaw my cheek.

Eventually, the door beeps with the acceptance of the room card, and I glance at the clock. He's thirty minutes late.

As the door opens, a flash of confusion crosses Sergei's face and he darts to the end of the bed toward the door, only to land in a groaning and twitching heap on the carpet, his eyes rolled back as tremors ripple through his limbs. I'm stone with shock, my brain unable to process the sight in front of me before a person moves in a blur to Sergei and stills with a stake in her hand that punctures Sergei's chest and renders him comatose.

The vampire woman stands, her silky black hair swaying around her stomach as she straightens her lanky body to meet my gaze with her tense onyx eyes. Knowing she couldn't have subdued Sergei with that ability, my eyes dart behind her, where a male form remains in the doorway, peering in with focused blue eyes beneath his shaggy blond hair.

"I'm Nira. Will you accept rescue and come willingly, Marianna?" she asks.

I gawk at her. "That really fucking depends now, doesn't it?"

She gives me a single, understanding nod. "I'm not stupid enough to harm you."

"Where's Denendrius?" I demand.

"I don't know."

"Do you have a line of connection to Viorel?" I question, wondering if she's smart enough to give me back.

"No," she admits. "Not yet."

I don't dare verbalize any sign of hope as I stand, lest Denendrius be nearby to overhear. "Denendrius will be looking for me," I warn her.

"That's the plan."

XXIV

With Nira behind the wheel of her maroon van, I sit comfortably in the passenger seat. Sergei is in the back with the Child of Stars. We're silent the entire ride out of the city, though from the glances Nira shoots at me as we turn onto various side roads, I imagine she has much to say.

After thirty minutes of driving, she turns onto a gravel road between two tight rows of thick trees. We approach a tall wrought-iron gate that slides open, allowing us passage to a massive but dimly lit mansion standing tall with white pillars. Had this been a year ago, I would have gazed at it with amazement, but the grandness of the castle has dulled my perception.

She pulls up near the entrance where a man stands with a long gun I can't quite make out, in the shadows near a pillar. My heart drums at the base of my throat, my limbs heavy when I climb out and follow her inside. A mix of onyx and colored eyes flicker toward me as we enter from where a handful of vampires are moving around upstairs beyond the second story railing.

"Come," she starts, motioning for me to follow her like I'm a friend she hasn't seen in a long time. "I want you to meet someone."

We move across the sitting room, a crystal chandelier hanging above our heads in the vaulted ceiling. I avoid the large fur pelts that several brown leather couches and chaises are situated around, keeping my shoes on the dark hardwood that extends through a long hall with many white doors.

Nira knocks on the last one before opening it to reveal a massive room. The white and soft pink of the walls and decor fill my senses first, and after a few moments I realize I'm standing in a little girl's room.

Its occupant looks up from her round bed and pushes the pink canopy net out of the way with a doll-filled, inhumanly pale hand. "Hi, Mama," she says with a smile, her shiny black eyes moving over Nira and me.

My feet root to the floor, my heart pounding in my ears at the sight of the vampire child who is probably no older than eight.

"Hi, baby." Her voice softens as she steps into the room, then glances over her shoulder at me with a nervous smile. "You have experience with the immortal children at the castle, right? This is Madelaine."

I swallow against my dry throat and clear it before forcing out, "A bit, but they had caretakers."

Viorel also doesn't allow them to exist beyond the castle ...

Madelaine grins up at me, her big eyes and long eyelashes so sweet. "Hi, Marianna."

My heart skips. "Hey."

I can't help but turn to Nira as Madelaine leaps off her bed and moves to a wooden dollhouse across the room, concern a metal band around my heart. "You know the laws, right?"

I don't mean to sound like a narc, but surely she has to

know the consequences of having an immortal child. Yet she wants to involve Viorel, somehow?

She swallows and nods before her careful gaze locks with mine. "I know of the prophecy rumored," she says. "How you are to be a powerful vampire. His queen. I was hoping I could get in touch with Viorel and explain my situation before we're found out, and that the return of Denendrius and you will grant us his favor."

Nira wants to use Denendrius and me as leverage to ensure she can keep her immortal child? I can imagine how furious Viorel would be to hear conditions placed on my return, on top of how she's committed a crime. I imagine he'd play along at first until I'm safe, then rain hell on her for her audacity.

But since I really want to go home, I don't dare express my opinion of her plan aloud. Perhaps I'm selfish for knowing what the outcome could be for her, and not warning her, but I find I can't care at this point. I'm not in a position to look out for anyone but myself. As it is, the belief I'll actually leave this mansion with anyone but Denendrius is so flimsy that it may as well be intangible.

"He could make an exception." Despite my gut telling me otherwise, I'm not a seer to say for sure. "But he would heavily consider the circumstances of her creation..."

Nira nods. "I suspected he might." She pulls in a long breath before slowly releasing it. "Madelaine was terminal when I turned her. My wife worked in a pediatric hospital, and after a legal battle, Madelaine was under government care for her cancer treatments. Her family, Jehovah's Witnesses, refused to allow treatment. She made my wife so happy, and I knew losing Madelaine would destroy her. We fought so hard to give her a chance at life. When her prognosis became terminal, I couldn't bear to see her suffer or let her die without experiencing a real childhood." Nira licks her lips and blinks away a wet film from the admiring gaze she rests on Madelaine. "Plus, I couldn't stand the thought of her never getting to have a proper childhood between the indoctrination and the cancer. No birthdays, no holidays. It was so unfair."

"I'm sure Viorel would be sympathetic." Even so, I'm not confident she wouldn't be punished. Though Madelaine looks happy in her room, I can't help the twang over the thought of her being taken from Nira and put with the rest of the immortal children in the castle. Sure, it's safer for both vampires and humans if immortal children aren't beyond the walls of the castle, but she looks so calm and peaceful as she plays with her dolls.

"She's a wonderful child," Nira says, trying to build her case, as if she believes I have any say in what happens around the castle and beyond. How many vampires have heard that one seer's prophecy and now believe I hold some power even in my human state? Some children who came from beyond the castle—bringing the seer's predictions with them—seemed to think I did.

I nod. "I'm sure she is, but . . . you know."

Nira nibbles her bottom lip. "She's only been immortal for four years, but she's very well behaved. She's gentle with humans and animals and has never harmed anyone. When she drinks from humans, it's only ever from willing donors. She's thrilled with her immortal state; I know the common concerns surrounding that. She's merely thankful to be alive after being so afraid to die."

I glance over my shoulder, half expecting Denendrius to be there already, but the hallway is still empty. Without a blood bond between us, it'll be harder for him to find me. He doesn't have that instinctual pull to guide him.

"What's your plan to capture Denendrius and get in contact with Viorel?" I cross my arms over my chest and pull in a deep breath, knowing I won't like what she has to say.

"I'll tell him where you are, and we'll be ready to subdue

him when he arrives. We'll call the hotline that's been on international news, and surely it'll get us connected to Viorel. Everyone knows he's behind the alert."

I shake my head in dissatisfaction, thinking of how many vampires it took to get him under control when he was a newborn again in Bellevue. They had to have multiple Darkling men restrain and bleed him before locking him in a steel coffin soaked with garlic.

Nira looks up, her head tilting like she hears something. "The Russian's phone is ringing."

My heart tosses itself against my ribcage, my legs weak as I follow her upstairs to a dim home library in the center of the house. The smell of burning wood fills my senses from a stone fireplace nestled between ceiling-high dark-stained bookshelves that line the walls.

Sergei is sprawled out on the floor on the carpet near the fireplace with weak flames, the stake still protruding from his chest. A demanding ringtone blares from his pocket.

She flashes across the room. I want to tell her not to answer it, that she doesn't understand how she needs a better plan first, but she has the phone against her ear before I can form a single word. At least there wasn't enough hope in me in the first place, that the rush of disappointment isn't jarring.

"Yes," she says evenly, "I have her." There's a pause. "Yes. We want you—"

Her swallow is visible, and I shake my head, mouthing at her to hang up so she can at least hear what I have to say, but she gives Denendrius directions to the mansion before he hangs up on her.

"We've been planning for days," she assures me, though either the nervousness in her eyes is too strong to disguise, or she doesn't try to hide it.

I heave out a breath and drop into a soft blue chaise. *They're all going to fucking die.*

"What's your Darkling to Children of Stars ratio?" I question, sure I saw more colored eyes than black upon arriving.

She takes a few tentative steps closer but stops and wrings her hands together in front of herself. "Myself, and three other Darklings. There are seven Children of Stars, some with abilities. We have a security system with cameras around the premises and weapons. They will act the moment they see him."

Slowly, I let my eyes fall closed, not even sure what advice I could offer her. My mind loops through all the times Denendrius has overcome attacks. Most recently, he took down a team of highly trained Darklings at the farmhouse after we escaped, and she thinks her little clan is enough to stop him?

Will Denendrius kill the vampire child too?

"He's unpredictable," I warn her.

She nods like she believes she has a grasp on what I truly mean, yet her child remains in the house when she should be *anywhere* but here, which means she greatly underestimates what she's in for. "We have several backup plans."

"Are you the clan leader?" I ask her.

"Yes."

"How old are you?" The question is loaded with meaning, and the tense line her lips form as she thinks tells me she picked up on it.

"I've been immortal for a couple of decades and have heard whisperings about him through that time."

Not enough, clearly. "Surrender, before he's even here."

She scoffs as she leans away from me and crosses her arms over her chest. "It's almost as if you don't want to go home with the way you speak."

I consider how Denendrius could be in earshot when I form my rebuttal. "I know him. What he's capable of. Unless you can get him with the element of surprise and the brute force of a large team of Darklings, he will outmaneuver you. He was a damn gladiator when he was human, and he's been evading capture for most of his existence. Any plan you can come up with, he's likely already thought up a hundred ways around it."

"Yet he was caught," she argues.

"A team of the king's *trained Darklings* nabbed him after he woke from being a newborn, while he was frantic and unprepared. We're currently sitting here while he uses however much of the night he wishes to figure out how to get in and out of here. You probably think you have an advantage by drawing him to your turf, where you're familiar with everything, but you're wrong."

Her eyes narrow. "We have our tricks."

"So does he," I snap. "How do you think he escaped the castle?"

Nira's mouth opens and closes as she realizes she doesn't know at all. Does anyone know how Adelia and Denendrius did it? I imagine Viorel would want to cover up how it was his blood that made it all possible, so what's the story then?

"What would you have us do?" There's a stroke of panic in the demand, and I know I haven't done well for the overall morale of every vampire that can overhear.

I look over my shoulder at the large and heavy dark blue drape over the window, then back to her as I make a writing motion with my hand.

Her brows stitch together, but she retrieves a pen and turns to a fresh page in a notebook before handing them to me.

Surrender. Let him take me and his friend, and if he lets you live, call the hotline until you're connected with someone who can relay a message to Viorel. He will send his own men. Tell him we're in Lorimer for a short while and have been staying in motels and an abandoned house somewhere in the Vermont woods. He's driving his Mustang with swapped plates, but that may change. He plans on bringing us to Rome, Italy soon.

I hand her the notebook and pen, and her eyes sweep over the page once to collect the message in her quick mind before she tears the page out and tosses it in the fire. She returns the pen and notebook to its home and gives me a solemn look with pinched lips that tells me she has no intention of backing down.

The hours pass, the house quiet with tense anticipation as the clan patrols the property waiting. But with each minute, I know their chances of capturing him decrease. All they're doing is giving him time to plan and stake out the property. He could have been here most of the time, simply watching and waiting for the perfect entry.

There's not a single flicker of surprise coursing through me when Denendrius inevitably appears in the room between us and the door with his hands behind his back and a wicked smile on his lips. Nira gasps in surprise, her eyes widening as she grabs my arm and yanks me off the chair like she's preparing to play tug of war with him.

"How the fuck did you get in here?" she demands.

His dark eyes lock on her. "I escaped the castle dungeon, and you think your handful of poorly trained clan members are going to catch me? Your ratio of men to doors and windows is skewed."

Her chest heaves, her lips parting to speak before Denendrius interrupts.

"Pick a hand." His smile deepens.

"What—?"

"Pick a hand!" he roars, the sound alerting several vampires who come rushing to a wide-eyed stop in the doorway behind him. Like a collection of statues, they stare at Denendrius's back.

"L-left . . ."

He chuckles as he pulls his left hand out from behind his back, and she recoils with a gasp. My jaw lowers.

Denendrius grips a dark green, segmented grenade—the kind that makes me think of World War Two—in his fist. I can't tell if the pin is missing or not with the way he holds it.

"What the fuck is in your right hand?" she asks in horror.

A deep laugh bubbles out of Denendrius as he shows his other hand. "What do you know? It's another grenade!" Though this one is more modern looking, black and cylindrical, with MK3 in yellow and partially covered by his hand.

"You think this is fucking funny?" she snarls, her fingernails digging into the flesh of my arm.

Denendrius's laugh continues. "Yeah, I do. So why don't you unstake my friend there and let go of Marianna?"

"Or what?" she challenges. "You're really going to use those?"

"Yes," Denendrius says simply. "Then when your walls have holes in them, and you're all picking shrapnel out of yourselves, whoever survives gets to scramble for protection from the sun since it will be up soon. And even if you manage to escape with the child down there *who has no human heartbeat*, I'll have already told every vampire I can think of about the crime you committed, and the king will come down on you so hard you'll wish I had shoved both these grenades right down your throat."

She gapes at him. "No. You killed their last clan leader, Atilla, so don't think you're getting out of here alive no matter what you do."

Denendrius shakes the grenades in his fists like they're maracas, and she stiffens. "Are you the one with at least two grenades? I don't think you're in a position to be making demands."

"At least?" one man, frozen in the doorway, asks.

Denendrius grins. "If you force me to release one, you'll

know how many more explosives I've got. Might have one that's piped-shaped too."

My eyes scale his body from his flat jean pockets to his zipped-up leather jacket, which doesn't hang quite as loose as it usually does.

"You don't understand. Their grudge against you is only second to my agenda. I need you both for immunity. For my daughter downstairs." There's too much bravery in her voice for her own good.

Denendrius clicks his tongue. "You think that'll work? That the king will let you use his blood slave as leverage for your demands? He would oblige your exchange, and I reckon he'd still wipe you out for daring to bargain with him."

Her upper lip twitches in disdain, the frustration at the truth of his words in her narrow eyes. She stares at him for a long moment, defeat growing in her gaze as her shoulders lower under its weight.

"I propose an exchange," she says carefully.

He lifts the hand grenades again, darkness smothering out any traces of humor in his eyes. "You do what I ask, or shove grenades in the bodies of the weaker vampires here."

Eye twitching, she pulls in a deep breath before her words rush out of her. "If you retrieve my wife from a clan leader named Sebastian Salias, I'll give them back to you. He blackmailed and kidnapped her, told her if we try to retrieve her, he'll turn us in."

Denendrius waves his grenade-filled hand at her as he tilts his head. "You know where Sebastian Salias is?"

With a hard swallow, she gives him a slow nod. "You know him?"

Denendrius lifts his chin a bit, his hands lowering to grip the grenades at his hips. "He's a bounty hunter who's been trying to claim a reward on me from another clan for thirty years. He's an annoyance, and I imagine he'll be looking for me again now."

Nira's grip loosens on my arm, yet she doesn't let go. "Do you agree, then? You get to kill Sebastian and have Marianna and your friend back, and you'll retrieve my wife"—she puts a finger up, fire in her eyes as she clarifies—"*alive* for me."

"Really, Nira?" one man shouts, Denendrius's body blocking sight of him as he positions himself between them and Nira. "You'll just let him go? Despite our wishes?"

Nira steps sideways—though Denendrius moves between them again and tightens his eyes on her like he thinks she'll try to run for the door—and says, "I haven't forgotten he killed Atilla, but she's been dead decades, and my wife is still alive. If anyone can kill Sebastian and get her back, it's this bastard. I trust he'll still get his, even if we let him go."

Denendrius smirks like the idea of him being captured a third time is asinine. "Deal, then?"

She draws in a deep breath. "Fine. We leave *now.*"

"Unstake my friend first. You—and you alone—are coming with us to retrieve your wife."

XXV

I sit next to Sergei in the back of Nira's van, Denendrius gripping a grenade—the pin still in place—in the passenger seat. The silent, tense air in the van is so thick I can only manage heavy, shallow breaths as we drive down the highway toward New York City. Since there isn't enough night left to make it all the way there, we pull over to crash at a motel in some village.

There's only a single queen bed available in their last room, but I'm the only one who sleeps, anyway. With the TV playing low, and my head on a pillow on Denendrius's lap as I lay sideways with Sergei sprawled out across the end of the bed, I come in and out of sleep all day.

Sergei's low, periodic conversation with Nira remains at the edges of my unconsciousness, though I usually can't make out what they're talking about. The few times I do, they're talking about kids and family. From the TV light, my moments of lucidity are half filled with Denendrius's expression of displeasure as he glances between Sergei and Nira, as if he doesn't like the fact they are becoming friendly but isn't sure if it's worth the effort to vocalize his issue.

I'm still half asleep when twilight returns. Denendrius carries me to the van himself as if my walking would waste too much time. At least the lack of movement allows me to fall back asleep when he places me on the seat next to Sergei, whose shoulder I lean my head against during my sleep. I expect Denendrius to be upset when I wake and realize how I'm positioned, but he seems unfazed and merely asks if I want to use his leather jacket as a blanket. I oblige, and he scoops grenades and a pipe bomb out of the interior pockets before twisting around to sprawl it over me.

I wake with a small gasp, startled by the stillness. We're idling in front of a modest white house, a streetlight casting soft bands of yellow across my lap. I rub my eyes and glance over at Denendrius, his face lit by the glow of his phone, his expression tense and focused.

"What are we doing?" I whisper, peering through the windows at the unfamiliar, dark street.

"We'll be right back." Denendrius turns his phone screen off and looks over his shoulder at me. "I need my jacket, sweetheart."

I yawn and hand it to him, goosebumps littering my skin from the chill. Denendrius notices and flips the heat on before shoving his arms in his jacket, slipping some grenades in interior pockets, much to Sergei's protests. He tells me he loves me before he and Sergei dip out of the van and vanish together.

"Where's the clan's house?" Though I know it's not logical that we would be parked in front of it, I study the shadowy homes for signs of Denendrius's arrival.

"A couple blocks over," Nira whispers over her shoulder. "Just close enough for us to hear them without them being able to smell you from the door opening."

The night offers me nothing in the silence, though from the

tense glances Nira shoots me in the rearview mirror, I suspect she can hear enough to get the gist of what's happening and is assessing what I can hear too.

"Did they get in?" I whisper, so low I can barely hear myself.

Nira nods and grips the steering wheel like she's using it to keep her rigid body in place.

"*Shit—*" she hisses, and a cool gust of wind tugs at me as the van door briefly opens.

I fling my wide gaze to Nira's empty seat, my hope soaring like a bird with weakened wings. My heart pulses in my head as I study the shadows and streaks of light for signs of them returning, hoping Denendrius might not be amongst them. If something were to happen to Denendrius, what would Sergei do with me? Would he simply release me, not caring enough about what I do? Would he turn me? Or would he remain loyal to Denendrius, even in death, that he would kill me to fulfill Denendrius's desire for us to be together in death?

My pondering is irrelevant though, as ten minutes later, flashes of shadows dart across the road, and the van's sliding door opens beside me as Nira pulls in a bloody and gagged red-headed woman who pitifully thrashes and scratches at her into the back of the van behind me. The van peels away, Denendrius behind the wheel with Sergei mumbling relieved Russian in the passenger seat.

I twist away from the bloodied men in the front seat, my stare pinned on Nira and the girl who thrashes and grit-teeth sobs in the prison Nira's made with her arms and legs around her. Nira tries to force the girl's jaw open with her bloody fingers, her other wrist leaking crimson as she tries to press the fang wounds to her tight lips to erase Sebastian's mark with her own.

"*Lacy, please,*" Nira begs, tears leaking from her maroon eyes and streaking down her cheeks. Her voice cracks. "It's Nira, babe. It's me."

"Might have to knock her out," Denendrius suggests casually as the car swerves around a corner, making me grip the back of the seat.

Lacy continues to resist, her teeth clamped and bared until she notices the fang marks on Nira's wrist heal. She screams for Sebastian, begs for him to save her, which has Nira hunching over her in a sob.

My ears ring from Lacy's volume, and my heart thrashes more wildly at the sight of her persistence. I'm cold to my core, knowing I must have appeared this way to Viorel when I was Denendrius's blood slave. Sure, I didn't know Viorel and likely still wouldn't have been ecstatic about being marked regardless of my blood slavery, but I must have appeared as feral as this woman. The fact that her mark to Sebastian is so strong she thinks her own wife—who she was taken from—is the genuine threat to her . . .

"You need to shut her up," Denendrius warns. The vehicle slows to a normal speed, though he continues to weave through streets. "I don't think we're being followed, but her voice is going to act as a beacon if any of the clan is looking for us."

Nira continues to beg Lacy to drink her blood until Denendrius is pulling over and clambering past me over the back seat to where they lie in a tangled heap. She begs Denendrius to back off, her pleading hand in his chest too weak for his strength as he wrangles Lacy away from her in a fuzzy blur that straightens with Denendrius's legs around Lacy's hips holding her legs down, and his arm around her throat in a choke hold. Lacy gasps for air with wide, wild eyes as he applies pressure, her bare feet kicking at the thin, scratchy carpet of the van as she tries to pry his arm away.

"Mark her," Denendrius demands through Nira's horror.

Nira rushes her bleeding wrist to Lacy's lips. She slams them closed tight. Denendrius shakes his head in annoyance and tightens his grip, her pale skin reddening as she tries to inhale through her nose until Nira pinches it closed. She flails harder as the lungs in her still chest beg for air. Nira begs Lacy to cooperate, Denendrius mumbling in her ear that he will choke her unconscious if she doesn't. When she slackens and her eyelids flutter, her biological instincts overrule her blood mark enough that she gasps for a breath. She's too oxygen deprived to close her lips when Nira presses the oozing fang marks to her pale lips.

I'm unsure if it's the lack of oxygen, or Nira's blood, but Lacy stills with sleep. Denendrius unravels himself from her and Nira scoops her up into her arms as she holds her tight and practices calming breaths.

"She'll be okay," I assure her, Denendrius sighing as he climbs back to the driver's seat. I want to tell her how I felt when Viorel stripped Denendrius's mark from me, but all I add is, "I promise."

Nira nods and wipes her eyes as they settle on Denendrius, who drives again. "Thank you."

His focus remains forward as he utters, "I didn't do this for you. I have a lot going on, and this benefitted me more than blowing up your clan to get Marianna and Sergei back. Being able to kill that annoyance, Sebastian, was a bonus."

She swallows, the corner of her lip twitching. "Whatever you want to tell yourself. You could have ditched after beheading Sebastian, instead of fighting three more Children of Stars and nearly getting staked to get to Lacy. So thank you. I appreciate it."

"I got your wife back to you, alive and unscathed. It just means you're indebted to me." Denendrius sets his jaw.

Nira's nod is slight. "I suppose it does."

"You're not going to tell anyone we interacted, that you even know where we are. Tell your clan to bury their idea of avenging Atilla. Her death wasn't personal, anyway. Got it?" Denendrius orders.

Her eyes lift and hold mine, and I know she's thinking of the note I gave her as I do. Does she still plan on trying to contact Viorel in hopes of gaining his favor, or does she believe Denendrius's warning of it being futile?

I can't tell when she drops her gaze to Lacy and says, "Got it."

Leaning back against the passenger door of the Mustang, Denendrius's lap beneath my crossed legs and his arm around my waist, I say, "That was weirdly . . . anticlimactic. You didn't even kill anyone in Nira's clan. Or throw a single grenade."

Denendrius grunts. "I listened for a while before coming in. They have many active connections to other clans. Someone would notice if they were eliminated, and likely know it was me since I killed Atilla. Grenades are fun, but we don't need any extra attention on ourselves right now."

"They will undoubtedly tell the other clans you are here . . ." Sergei says from behind the wheel.

"Yeah," Denendrius agrees. "But Nira will try her best to silence whoever she can, considering the little crime she's trying to keep hidden."

Sergei sighs. "We should go to Italy now."

"I'm still waiting to wrap something up."

"What?" Sergei and I say at the same time, and my brows lift as I shift sideways to look at him better. The fact Sergei doesn't know either has me biting my cheek.

"Hmm . . ." Denendrius loops his other arm around me too and entwines his fingers, something mischievous in his voice when he says. "You'll see."

I scowl at the beams of headlights gliding across the dark highway.

When we finally get back to the house in Vermont, I sprawl

out on the mattress since exhaustion won't allow any other position. Denendrius twists a new butane canister into the heater before giving all the grenades to Sergei to deal with before shedding his leather jacket and joining me.

He strokes the knuckle of his index finger across my cheek, and a wave of panic pulls my steady feet out from beneath me and sweeps me away. My heart pounds in my chest, and I rapidly blink away a sudden onslaught of tears, knowing my brief break from intimacy is about to be over. Though my hormones haven't quite steadied, my body isn't aching enough for him to accept any resistance.

"Is there anything you'd like to do before we leave America?" His soft onyx eyes hold mine, his calm breath gusting against my face.

"I don't know." I close my eyes so I don't have to look at him. "I just want to go to Italy and see our villa. I miss Adelia, and I want to start having babies. I want you to turn me."

"Mm." His chuckle is gentle. "Are you sure there isn't anything you want to do before that? We likely won't return to America for a century. We'll be busy raising our family."

"I'm sure," I affirm. "There's nothing more important to me right now than being immortal and starting forever with you."

His lips brush against my cheek. "You're the sweetest, Marianna. Give me a few more weeks, and I'm sure I'll be ready to turn you."

My heart thumps ferociously in my chest, strong with the hope his words bring. A few more weeks and I'll finally be able to put together a tangible plan to get home.

Tears well in my eyes again, the emotional waves relentless. I can't get my feet back beneath me to stand up out of them as they pummel me. I think of Viorel's face and Laurentius's. Of Aeliana's. How will they look at me when I return? Will Aeliana even recognize me?

His hand strokes over my body, and I press my teeth into my

bottom lip and wrinkle my nose as I squeeze my eyes closed. When his hand leaves my body, the sound of rummaging has my lids lifting. Denendrius digs around in the hunter's bag that remains nearby against the dirt wall. He pulls out a bundle of yellow rope and unwinds it. There's about six feet of length when it's undone, and he takes his knife and slices the rope in half.

He moves toward me with one half, a playful smile curling his lips. "Give me your hands."

My heart beats so hard in my dry throat I nearly choke on it, and I can't stop my face from morphing into a look of terror. I want to ask him *why*.

Denendrius's face softens, and he runs his hand up and down my thigh, the rope gripped in the other. "I won't hurt you, sweetheart. I'll tie it loose."

I can't speak past my heart in my throat or my rapid breaths, my limbs too weak to protest as he takes my limp hands into his lap and wraps the coarse and scratchy rope around my wrists. He uses a complicated knot I've never seen before to bind them with my fingers curled against one another and the heels of my hands pressed together. There's no room in the rope for my hands to move, and though it's not tight enough to hurt, I don't want to know what tight means to him if this is supposed to be loose.

Lifting my bound hands in both of his, he exhales a cold, lustrous sigh against my fingers as he brings them to his lips for a kiss.

I wish I could see Denendrius's desire for this sort of submission as innocent play since I know it's not uncommon in regular couples, but I know he's bound the hands of girls as they cried and begged for their freedom before inevitably ending up strangled and buried in an unmarked grave.

My head pounds with the buildup of tears, but I swallow them back. The question of *why* continues to ping-pong around my skull like a bullet ricocheting. Why does he need to bind my hands like one of his victims when he believes I'm his fiancée? When he's supposed to love me? Did he tie up his past girlfriends, and if he did, did they see it as innocent play in their ignorance of what he is?

He wraps one hand around mine and presses them to his chest. Then he leans forward, slipping his lips between mine and knotting the other hand in my hair.

I manage to kiss him back, my lips quivering against his as they move delicately against mine. He leans into me, forcing me backward until I'm nearly lying down. His hand slips from my hair to my back, easing me gently onto the mattress while he holds himself above me.

When he pulls my pants and underwear off, my shirt hiked to my pits since my tied hands make it impossible to remove, I can't help but hold my breath. He ducks under my arms before he starts on me, my bound wrists looped around the back of his neck as he roughly rubs his hand over my body and hungrily kisses me.

His thirsty eyes lock with mine, the desire so strong his heavy breaths rush between his elongating fangs. I'm tense, but I angle my head back for him as his mouth descends toward me. He bites into the top of my shoulder, the pain of his fangs bottoming out—snuffing out my breath and scattering blackness and silver stars across my vision. He's so deep in my shoulder he cuts into my flesh with the rest of his teeth like he wants to tear a bite from me. Dark blots my vision like ink stains, obscuring the full sight of his bloody mouth as he draws away from me, the feel of my hot blood dripping against my face from his lips and panting breath.

Eventually, he stretches my arms out above my head, one hand overlapping the rope and my wrists to hold me firmly to the mattress while he plants the other near my waist.

I feel like a doll, not a hint of pleasure combating the thick numbness that coats me. I'm dead silent, expressionless as I study the pleasure in the monstrous high of Viorel's blood in his scarlet eyes and the way his body moves like I'm merely an observer.

He smiles—his teeth coated in crimson—at some point, and says, "You don't have to be so quiet, sweetheart. Don't worry about Sergei hearing us."

I can't muster up the energy to unstick my dry lips, so I merely nod. Yet despite my continued silence, he doesn't seem to mind. At least I'm granted the little things through this horridness, like not having to perform for him, not having to pretend like I'm having the time of my life. It's a relief that my neutrality doesn't faze him . . . but then again, neither would sobbing and screaming.

When he rolls off me and lies beside me, I don't move. My body aches, mainly from the wounds from each of his teeth, my shoulders from my arms being pinned above my head for so long, and the skin of my wrists from the coarse rope rubbing.

"I love you," he whispers, skating his fingers down the middle of my torso as he sighs.

"I love you too," I whisper. "So much."

I struggle against the rope around my wrist as he pulls the blanket over us, testing his knot, but knowing I'm unlikely to even loosen it. He watches me for a long second—clearly enjoying the struggle—before propping himself up on his elbow and deciding to help.

"See, that wasn't so bad." His voice comes low and satisfied as he frees my hands, soft red lines left on my flesh that he trains his fingers over before bringing them to his lips to kiss.

I'm unsure what to say, merely thankful he didn't attempt more than binding me tonight. But I fear he'll push more from here, that he'll work on me until he can get away with choking and hitting me. Would I let him if he wanted to? I suppose I would have to accept it without complaint if I wish to survive long enough to get home.

"Tired?" he asks as he stretches out beside me on his back, bending one arm between his head and the pillow. "The sun is still down, but I could sleep after all that excitement."

I chew the inside of my lip and nod, pulling myself up against his side to rest my head on his chest.

The primal urge to flee tries to take control of me, my emotions tossing me back and forth like the icy waves of a hurricane. Fighting it—lying here, trying to use my rational mind to subdue it—is a losing battle.

I have to get out of here. Before he seeks my tears. Before he looks at them through the screen of his camcorder. I know I should wait it out . . . he's promised to turn me in a few weeks . . . but being near him makes me want to rip all my skin off and my mind is shrieking over every logical thought that begs for my attention.

Focusing on his breath and the lines his fingers draw on my bare arm, I wait for my opportunity. When his breaths are even and his hand slides to a stop, my eyes lock with the rifle mere inches from him, where he's kept it each night we've slept here. I can't shoot him here, not with Sergei sleeping in the next room.

When I'm certain Denendrius is asleep, I gingerly lift my weight from his body and move to my hands and knees. My heart pounds, my throat dry as I crawl backward to the edge of the mattress. I'd likely take less care moving around a bomb. Then again, a bomb can't activate from the sound of my heartbeat and breath, from the scent of me moving across the dirt floor to slip into my boots before moving toward the keyring that may as well make as much noise as one.

Teeth gritted, with a frozen grimace carved across my face, I lift the keys slowly, clenching them in my fist to muffle their jingle. I can't lie about sneaking off for a bathroom trip now, especially not when I also reach for the rifle and slip the strap over my shoulder. Then I dig into his jacket pocket just long enough to grab the phone and glance at the screen before I fully commit. I have a measly hour to get somewhere safe before the sun comes up.

My eyes adjust to the darkness as I sneak into the shadows of the hallway, the shape of Sergei asleep on a blanket on the floor of the half-collapsed second room. Moving closer to him and the stairs, the faint beat of music filters out of his room from his earbuds.

I refresh my lungs before holding my breath as I climb the stairs and move across the decrepit floor, putting the weight of a feather on each foot until I'm outside in the snow.

The cool morning air welcomes me, and I pray I can at least make it to the car before Denendrius discovers me missing or sunlight creeps over the horizon. I just have to get to the nearest town's police department, and they'll know who I am. I'm sure they'll bring me straight to whichever vampire in the surrounding states Viorel has instructed to retrieve me. I wouldn't be surprised if there are immortal police on the forces he keeps in contact with.

I search what little of the horizon I can see through the maze of trees for signs of the upcoming day. If I run out of moonlight, at least I can pull over and hide in the trunk and use the time to look up that hotline number. I'd search for it now, but I don't want to risk speaking or slowing down.

Freckles of stars shine above the thick trees as I speed-walk as fast as the deep snow allows, torn between the urge to run and the fear of slowing down to avoid detection from noise. I'm unsure exactly how far they can hear. Are my movements background noise to them, just as any wildlife would be . . . or are their brains made to distinguish any human movement amongst it?

I fight through the trees as they thicken, pushing through tangled branches and thin saplings as snow fills my boots.

Fuck, I'm not even sure I'm going in the right direction. I can't imagine Denendrius ran through this. Yet, once I've beaten my way through, I'm standing on the snow-covered dirt road much sooner than expected.

My heart leaps at the sight of the Mustang parked to the left. I'm aghast at my luck. This must be Viorel's mark working, subconsciously having me make the right directional choices to help lead me back to him.

I sprint toward the car, just a few feet away, when a sharp crack of branches behind me stops me cold. It's coming from the trees. Instinctively, I know what kind of animal followed me. I spin, press the butt of the rifle against my shoulder, and fire toward the sound.

With a bang that jolts my heart and shoulder, Denendrius appears at the forest's edge, clutching the right side of his chest and staring, stunned, at the blood on his hand. Through the shadows and moonlight, I feel the cold of his eyes as they shift to the stare of a man with his sights set on an enemy.

I move backward, hand shaking as I reload. I aim for his heart and pull the trigger, dropping the emptied rifle and pulling the keys from my pocket before I risk the time it would take to see if he's been hit.

The headlights flash as I unlock the door. My heartbeat deafens me, adrenaline making shakes roll through my body as I tear the door open and scramble into the driver's seat. I pull the door closed and lock it at the same time I jam the key in the ignition. Sitting on the edge of the seat so my feet can reach the pedals, I crank the car into drive.

The driver's window explodes, a glass storm raining down on me as my foot slams the gas pedal. My breaths strangle me, my heart lodged in my throat as his furious shouts deafen me while he reaches in the vehicle to wrangle me. My frantic babbling is incoherent as I fight to get the car moving. It jerks forward, halting after a few feet when Denendrius cranks the emergency brake.

When his hands are occupied with a fistful of my clothing, I get the emergency brake off and slam my foot on the gas again. A flash of silver in the cup holder catches my attention. Half blind with panic, I snatch it, heart leaping. It's the hunting knife from the glove compartment. I intercept his hand with the blade when he reaches for the keys, then slam my foot down on the gas. The car jerks forward as he roars in fury, yanking his hand back.

"*Marianna!*" he hollers, forcing the car door open.

With fistfuls of my clothing, he jerks me back, my foot slipping away from the gas pedal. It happens so fast that I don't register that he's got me in a choke hold on the ground to stop me from struggling until I see the end of the car has rolled a few meters away.

Denendrius throws me off him, and I grunt as I hit the snowy dirt. I lie there, trying to catch my breath as he dips into the driver's seat and stops the car. I'm dizzy when I try to stand as he steps out of the car and slams the door.

He disappears from the vehicle and knocks me back onto the ground.

"I'm sorry!" I blurt, no other ideas for apologies making it to my tongue.

Denendrius takes a fistful of my hair at the back of my head, his other hand around my jaw. He leans over and lifts my face to his. "*Shut up.*"

I spew apologies and beg for mercy as he throws me over his shoulder. The house appears moments later. He carries me inside as I kick and thrash, throwing me onto the dirt floor by the bed.

I'm too late to lift my arms in front of my face. His fist connects with my cheek, the force laying me out breathless against the dirt. Denendrius stands over me, my body pinned between his legs, leaving me nowhere to roll away.

"Who are you running to?" he bellows as his fist slams into my ribs. I cover my face with my arms and try to curl into a ball, but he kicks at me to open my body up for his violence. "Running back to a tyrant who kept you locked up? Who probably hypnotized you into having our baby just so he could have another thing to torture me with?" His knuckles hit my sternum, and any remaining trace of air leaves my lungs. He wrangles my arms away from my head, the red bruising practically instant on my forearms beneath his ruthless grip. His burning gaze holds mine. "You fought any semblance of direction I tried to give you, but you *dropped to your knees happily for his ruling fist.*"

Another blow lands in my abdomen, and stars explode across my sight. I fight for breath as he drops to his knees, straddling me. I gag as his hands circle my throat and cut off my air. He snarls furiously at me while tightening his grip and rattling me against the dirt.

My fingernails tear uselessly at his hands, and I have enough vision to see Sergei appear behind Denendrius with his forearm across his chest as he throws himself backward. Denendrius loses his balance and releases me as he falls with him, but their position changes before they hit the ground, with Denendrius kneeling over Sergei as he holds him against the ground by his throat while bloodying the knuckles of his other hand against the side of his face. He screams Russian at him, so loud spit sprays against Sergei's bloodied face.

Beyond his basic instinct to tense beneath Denendrius's beating, he doesn't fight back. He takes each punch and rib-crunching stomp to his chest as Denendrius moves to his feet.

I manage to suck a noisy breath back into my spasming lungs, my next exhale releasing a terrified sob-scream as I shift, wobbly, to my hands and knees a moment before he turns his attention back to me.

With him standing still, I can properly assess the damage I've done. His chest is soaked in blood, one bullet wound in the center of his sternum, the second—fuck, I wish I hadn't taken a second shot now—below his left collarbone.

Oh, I'm fucking done for.

"Please," I wail.

He licks the blood off his knuckles, the black of his eyes leaving me cold as he stalks out of the room with purpose.

Sergei sputters and coughs, half-laughing and mumbling something in Russian as his face slowly heals. He heaves out a breath as he sits, taking a moment to gather himself before he chuckles and rises to his feet.

"You feel better now?" Sergei asks as he faces the dark hall. "Got it all out without beating her to death or breaking her neck. Now I won't have to listen to you grovel with regret. You're welcome."

Metal rattles in the hall. There's something familiar about the mundane sound in this context that makes the hair stand up on the back of my neck.

Panic cinches my chest. "No, Denendrius, please—"

He returns with his fingers hooked through the top of a metal dog cage. It's big enough to hold a large dog, and I recall glimpsing it the last time he brought me here to show me a Child of Stars he had trapped. This time, I get a better look at it. It's a solid metal kennel, not the flimsy collapsible kind. The black steel bars are thick, with a removable plastic tray beneath the metal base with thin slats.

Denendrius shakes as he screams at me, the metal door rattling in its frame as he holds the cage in his grip. *"You like being locked up and constricted so much? Fine! I'll give you what you want!"*

"No!" I squeeze out as a shot of adrenaline has me scrambling past Sergei—who merely stands aloof with his arms crossed, watching us—and to the corner of the mattress against the wall. "Denendrius, no!"

"*Yes*, Marianna! This is what you need. If his blood mark is too strong for you to find the sense yourself, *I'll give it to you.* Help you remember what it feels like to be locked up since he's romanced you *out of your mind* and tricked you into thinking *the bars he has around you are rose vines!*" His chest lifts as he inhales a deep breath to spew, "You were just taken from me, and you want to risk it again? Next time you won't be so lucky! Nira would have sent you back to Huarsar the first moment she could. Do you understand you could have been hours away from his men taking you and returning you to a monster to be repeatedly raped again?"

I curl into the corner of the bed on my pillow, my body aching as I sob. I cover my face with my hands. My head pounds, my thoughts refusing to come together like a puzzle with mismatched pieces. I shouldn't have run. Why am I so stupid? Now, how the fuck do I backtrack out of this?

As he scowls and shakes his head, Denendrius pulls the cage against his side of the bed. He takes his keyring from the pocket of his bloodied jeans and squats down to unlock a heavy lock. As he opens the cage door, my heart tosses itself against the back of my ribs and my eyes well with tears.

I can't help but think about why he has a stained mattress *and* a girl-sized dog cage in this abandoned house.

Slow and stiff, he turns his head to the side. His sharp eyes snag mine, and he snarls, "*Come here.*"

"I won't run again," I promise with a squeak. "I'll do anything you want, Denendrius, anything, I swear."

I'll tie the rope around my wrists so he can have fun with me if it means I stay out of the cage. I'd rather have a few hours of rope than *this.*

"Then come here and crawl into this cage," he commands. "That's what I want."

I shake my head, my bloody hair swaying. "Anything but that."

He bares his fangs at me and rattles the cage. *"Nothing but this."*

Terror has me locked in place. I gape at him, wide-eyed, my chest heaving with noisy, desperate breaths.

His hand shoots across the mattress as he jolts forward, capturing my ankle in his steel grip and forcing a yelp from me. I squeak, failing to twist out of his grip as he drags me across the mattress and into his lap. Pleas tumble off my tongue as he wraps his hand around my throat and extends his arms so I'm lying half back on the mattress.

"Two choices. You crawl into this cage yourself, or I choke you, and you go in unconscious. Choose."

I gulp, the action making my throat strain against his tense hold.

"I love you—"

He slaps me so hard my ears ring and blackness blots out half my sight of him.

"Okay," I surrender, my voice sounding so quiet through the noise in my ears.

He releases me, and I feel around, half-blind and rapidly blinking to convince the other half of my sight to trickle in faster. My palm finds the cold metal of the cage's opening.

My breath whooshes in and out of me as I lift my knee through the hole and set it on the hard metal. Bringing my other knee in, my toes are against the metal wall, my nose mere inches from the back.

I twist around and sit, leaning back against the bars, less than an inch between my toes and the doorway. The door groans as he shuts it, and I battle the ache to kick out at him and spit every insult I can think of. It won't help, so I cross my arms and pull my knees up.

"Good girl," he murmurs, relief softening his face.

I suppose I should be thankful the cage is big enough to move around in, and that I can even sit and extend my legs. Did he opt for this size, or were his choices limited? However, from the thickness of the metal, the larger sizes are probably better made to suit stronger dogs. Which means I'm not breaking out of this cage. Especially not since he hooks the lock back on the door.

"You know I love you too, Marianna," he whispers as he clicks the lock closed. "I'm doing this because I love you."

Tears well in my eyes, a sharp pain radiating through my chest.

"I can't lose you again, sweetheart." Solemn, he shakes his head.

Blinking my tears away, I say, "How long do I have to be in here?"

He shrugs as he sits on the edge of the mattress and rubs his hands over his blood-soaked chest. "You can have bathroom breaks, but we'll see."

Sergei clears his throat. "Should we deal with the bullets?"

Denendrius heaves out a breath and lies back. "Yeah, cut them out of me."

Sergei approaches the bed as he retrieves a switchblade from his pocket. "I wasn't a military medic. Too bad, hm?" he teases as he opens the knife and lowers himself to Denendrius's side.

His scowl and clenched jaw are the only signs Denendrius feels any pain as Sergei prods at the bullet wound in his chest with his knife and fingers. He fishes out a long cartridge meant for dangerous animals.

Suitable.

I grit my teeth, the bloody taste in my mouth bitter knowing the pain radiating in my face, head, and torso must be worse than both shooting him and having the bullets cut out.

With the bullets out, Denendrius heals before my eyes. He tells Sergei he's going back to sleep, then turns the lamp off, pulls the blanket over himself, and rolls away from me.

"I can't sleep in here." A shiver rolls through me, though I can't tell if it's from temperature or stress.

He grunts. "Sure you can."

I lift the hood of my sweater, leaning my head against the bars and trying not to think about how much I want to stretch out.

Hours must pass until the soreness from my butt on the metal and my back against the bars becomes unbearable. My bladder demands to be emptied, and I go back and forth between whether I should wake Denendrius for a drink of water or wait until sunset.

The longer I'm in here, the more I can't help my low whine and tears or the hiccups that come with crying so hard I can barely breathe.

Denendrius sleeps soundly through my sobbing like it soothes him.

When I finally stop, I whisper, *"Please, can I come out, Denendrius? I want to cuddle you while I sleep."*

"Nope," Denendrius mumbles, his voice thick with sleep. "But hang on to that want. Let it settle in you until it's stronger than Viorel's mark."

I wipe tears from my eyes with the heel of my hand, my back aching for relief.

"But I want you to make love to me," I counter. "You can tie me up again."

For the first time, and even though the words taste foul like rot on my tongue, I give dirty talk a try. Nothing too obscene, but I whisper what I want his body to do with mine—

He rolls over so fast that I know I've fucked up before his twisted expression even registers in the shadows of my sight.

Denendrius smacks the side of the cage with his palm, his lips curled back in disgust as he shakes with fury. "Never open that sweet mouth of yours to sound like a whore again. Do you understand me? I don't want a whore."

"Okay," I squeak. "I'm sorry."

He sighs and runs his hands down the metal, then turns the lamp back on. "Why did you run from me, sweetheart? I don't understand. Everything was fine."

I turn my face toward the ground, unable to meet his eyes as I say, "I don't know. I couldn't help it. In my heart, in my mind, I didn't want to, but I couldn't shake the feeling that I had to run away. It felt so urgent."

He exhales a long breath. "It's his mark."

My voice cracks when I say, "I'm trying to fight it, I promise."

"I know," he whispers. "But we've been doing so well. We haven't fought once since we escaped."

My breath comes rapidly. *"I know,"* I bawl, uncontrollable tears spilling down my cheeks. "I've been so much happier with you again. I'm so sorry for running, Den. For shooting you. I didn't feel in control of myself. I—"

"I know, sweetheart. He's pulling your strings from Romania. I understand." He frowns and studies my swollen face. "I'm sorry for hitting you. I didn't mean to . . . You just made me so angry. You ran away, and you shot me. You got what you deserved, but I'm still sorry. I was too angry at first to think clearly about how it was his mark responsible."

My voice shakes. "I know, Den. We can make up if you let me out," I beg.

He runs his fingers down the side of the cage again, the tips of them thumping from one bar to another. "You want to make me happy?"

"Yes," I breathe, shifting forward and hooking my fingers through the bars near his.

The corner of his lips lift in a crooked smile, his eyes shiny with desire in the low light. When he straightens on his knees and unbuttons his jeans, I shift to mine to prepare for him to unlock the cage and bring me on the bed.

He tsks playfully and wiggles his fingers through the bars at me as he shifts closer. "There's enough space through the bars."

Dread has my muscles aching two-fold, my body begging to lie down and stretch out as I sit with my legs folded at my sides like he instructs. He leans his body against the side of the cage and plays with my hair through the top while I do everything he demands. By the time it's over, my muscles and flesh are shrieking at me, the imprints from the bars red enough that I know they'll stick around for a while.

I'm numb as I slip back into my clothes, my body aching with each movement. Bruises shadow my ribs from where he hit me, my face still sore to the touch. When I lean back against the bars, the pressure makes me woozy. I pull my knees up and wrap my arms around them as I stare at the dirt floor beyond the cage door.

"What time is it?" I whisper, unable to bring myself to look at Denendrius as he moves in my peripheral vision.

The sound of his pants zipping up has me hugging myself tighter, and I lay my head on my knees. I swallow against my thick throat and debate asking for a bottle of water as I lick my chapped lips.

"Just after sunset."

Sergei shouts a question at Denendrius from the other room, making me turn my head on my knees to see where he is in the hall's darkness. A shadow shifts around by the stairs, then comes closer until he's standing in the mouth of the room.

Denendrius responds in Russian, and I feel his icy stare as goosebumps litter my flesh.

"We're going hunting." There's no emotion in Denendrius's voice. "You need some proper food too."

I exhale a trembling breath and lift my head. I stretch my legs as far as they will go, pushing my feet against the end of the cage while I wait for him to shift to the lock so I can get out and stretch my body.

But he doesn't move.

"Where are we going?" I sit up and brush my fingers through my tangled hair to straighten it.

"*You're* not going anywhere," Denendrius clarifies with a cold, contemptuous curl of his upper lip.

Panic squeezes my heart, and I shift upright onto my knees. "What do you mean—"

"You can wait for me there. It'll do you some good to sit alone with your thoughts for a while, without any distractions."

My mouth stretches in wide horror, like it might be easier to pull in fleeting breaths that way. The room spins as I leap to the cage door and wrap my hands around the bars while he stands and squats in front of it.

"You—" I gasp for breath. "You can't leave me in here!"

"It'll only be for a handful of hours," Denendrius promises. "You can use the time to think about what's *really* important to you, so you don't end up in there again."

I yank on the bars to no avail, like some trapped animal, the motion only intensifying the ache in my muscles. "Denendrius, no—"

My heart leaps as he pulls the keys out of his pocket and reaches for the lock. He pauses with it in his hand, his empty black gaze holding mine. "I'll let you out for a quick bathroom break, but you're going back in."

My chest heaves with strained breaths, and the click of the lock opening has my muscles tightening. I shake with anticipation as the door squeals open and then practically collapse on the dirt floor as I scramble out of it.

Denendrius pulls me to my feet by my arm, the relief from being able to stand like a weight off me. I'm wobbly as he helps me into my boots before pulling me along upstairs and outside.

The quick trip to the old outhouse—that's far more maintained than the house—has me shivering, my teeth rattling as he brings me back into the weak warmth of the basement room.

When I step out of my boots, I twist against his unyielding grip. *"Please!"*

He drags me back to the cage, and I yelp when he squats down and pulls me to my knees beside him.

"It's just a few hours," he reminds me as he pulls the metal door open.

I lean back away from the cage—away from him—but his grip only tightens.

"I want to go with you," I choke out, trying to pry his hand off my forearm. "I promise I won't run. I'll behave!"

He merely stares toward the cage with his lips mashed together as he times his breaths.

"What if something happens when you're gone?" I argue, my continued attempts to pull from his stiff and unwavering grip futile. "What if someone finds me here and takes me?"

His stare continues, his grip intensifying and making me gasp in pain. "It's only a few hours. There's a better chance of someone seeing us in the city."

I give up on my fight with a gasp, landing on my sore rear. "What if something happens to you?"

His stiff head turns to me, his expression unreadable. "We'll be back in a few hours," he repeats tersely. "Now get in."

With a rough yank on my arm, I yelp with the sharp pain in my shoulder as I collapse over his lap.

Tears well in my eyes, and I grit my teeth in fury as I crawl back into the cage. My body burns with each furious thump of my heart as I twist and lean back against the metal bars.

Denendrius pulls the sherpa blanket off the bed and stuffs it in the cage with me, followed by a fresh bottle of water and a sleeve of toaster pastries before he screws a new butane tank into the heater and sets it to low.

"You can manage a few hours," Denendrius says as he closes the door and locks it. His heavy gaze holds mine. "A few hours in a cage is nothing. At least you know you'll be let out."

I turn my hate-twisted face into my shoulder, glowering toward the bed.

"I'll leave the lamp and heater on for you, and bring you back something hot to eat." Denendrius sighs as he stands. "I love you, Marianna."

"I love you too," I grind out.

When Denendrius leaves the room with Sergei, their steps creaking up the stairs, my frantic gaze follows. But there's nothing but darkness between us now.

A few achingly long moments pass where all I can hear is my heartbeat thudding.

"Don't leave me in here!" I roar, slamming my palm against the bars. "Denendrius! *Denendrius!* You bastard, don't leave me in here!"

I let out a furious scream, throwing my head back as I kick the bars with everything I have. I don't stop until the ache in my soles becomes too much to bear. Then I collapse, curling into a ball on my side, sobbing uncontrollably.

XXVII

I mumble expletives to myself and curse Denendrius as I lie on the hard metal of the cage floor, my head resting on the mountain of blanket at the end of the cage. Fury tears up and down my chest, so hot and twisted it has tears streaking my cheeks.

"You're going to fucking pay for this one day," I snarl to the empty air, biting back the urge to beat my fists against the bars until I've bloodied my knuckles.

My ranting ends when I cough against my dry throat, and I jerk upright and snatch the water bottle with the reminder of my thirst. I twist it open and let the glorious water splash over my tongue as I choke it down. I force myself to stop when it's half empty, leaning back against the side of the cage as I cap it and pant. Saving the rest to sip over the next few hours, I rest it in the cage's corner, then take the blanket and tuck the edge through the top row of bars at the back of the cage to make them softer to lean against.

"Absolute bastard," I mutter to myself as I rest against the blanket. The protection it provides is minimal, but it's better than nothing. I groan and lean my head back.

I just had to shoot the fucker.

I close my eyes and force myself to take deep breaths. It's only a few hours. My mother trapped me in my bedroom for longer ... for *months ... years ...* I can handle a few hours in a cage.

The minutes drag on, and I don't know how much time passes. I could guess an hour, but perhaps it's only been twenty minutes. My stomach gurgles from not eating all day and however much of the night has passed, so I pick at my toaster pastries as frustration gathers in my chest like a leaky faucet, each second a drip that makes me want to yank my hair as I complain loudly with, "*Oh my fucking god. Would you just get back already?*"

I beat myself up over my stupid misstep of succumbing to my impulse to flee when I really should have known better. Running from Denendrius *has never* worked before. He gets what he wants, I suppose, as I sit here mumbling to myself about how idiotic I am. Unless one of Viorel's men finds us, there's no getting away from Denendrius while I'm still human.

The rope previously around my wrists is a lot more comfortable than the metal under my butt and feet, than having to sit just right so my spine balances between two bars. Though the cage is big enough for a large dog, it's still so restrictive. I shift between my options in a desperate attempt at comfort. I lie down curled in a ball on my side, sit upright with my legs straight or bent, or on my back with them crossed flat against the bars. Lining the cage floor with the blanket provides as little comfort as covering the bars with it.

Only a few more hours ...

I groan and crave lying down so desperately that I nearly attempt to push my legs through the bars and onto the mattress that's so close I can put my hand through the bars and feel how soft it is. It fucking taunts me. But there's not enough space to get my whole foot through, and it'll only be more uncomfortable if I get stuck. Despite the cage's conditions, the hours would probably be more manageable if Denendrius hadn't beaten me and fucked me twice.

He better bring me back some good fucking food . . .

My stomach gurgles again as I finish my toaster pastries, the sugary carbs having practically no effect on my hunger. I finish my water since my dry mouth begs for it and my time in here must be nearly up.

I plot while I wait, pre-planning how I should react to whatever situation Denendrius might throw at me. I rehearse conversations, compiling a list of what I definitely shouldn't say, while coming to the nauseating truth that I will not win this by passively acting. Returning his affections and following obediently won't be enough. If I'm going to convince him, I need to pretend to be on his side so hard that I terrify myself.

I squeeze my eyes closed, not wanting to know what lengths I might have to go to as a vampire to convince him we belong together until I'm strong enough to escape.

The heater clicks off, and I stare at it in disbelief for a long moment before I shake a trickle of anxiety away. Knowing it lasts three to six hours, and that it was on low, Denendrius will probably be back soon to switch the butane tank.

It's fine.

I hug my hoodie tight to myself, not completely sure how long it will be before the cold creeps into the room. I should have asked for my winter coat, but Denendrius will be back before the heat dissipates, anyway.

Time continues on, and soon I've chewed my lip bloody in contemplation as I listen carefully for signs he's returned. I search the quiet air for their faraway conversation, for shoes crunching in the snow, or steps creaking on the old floor overhead. My exhaustion deepens, so I lean my head on my arms and wish I could fall asleep, but I know it will evade me in my current position.

Birds chip outside, a loud chorus beyond the wooden board.

It's an awful sound, their dawn song.

The sound makes me feel like I'm falling, and I grip the sides of the cage as I gasp for breath and try to fight off the imbalance of disorienting panic.

It's morning.

"*Denendrius!*" I scream, terror ripping up my throat. "Please tell me you're back! Denendrius!"

Only the birds respond, their song louder now as they move around and disturb the bushes outside.

"No . . ." I shake my head. "No, no, it can't be morning already."

Birds must start singing before the sun comes up, right? There must be at least some dark left that would give Denendrius time to slip inside. It's a close call, but he'll make it.

"He'll make it," I assure myself.

I practice deep breaths, a bit of relief passing through me knowing that Denendrius will be back soon. He said he'd be a few hours. As long as he's back before sunrise—and well, why the fuck wouldn't he be?—there's no harm. At least I know the time where he walks back into the room is mere minutes.

In a few minutes, he'll return with a hot meal for me. He'll let me out of the cage, and I'll tell him how right he is and how I'm completely straightened out now. I'll get some more water and a bathroom break.

Just a few more minutes.

Shifting in discomfort against the bars, I listen to the birds wake up, how they rustle in the trees and sing and squawk at one another. But then I hear squirrels chattering and darting through the snow, hear the birds respond by taking flight. The air warms.

The sun's up now, isn't it?

My heart drops into my stomach, and I'm not sure whether to cry or scream. I stare through the dim room as I listen to the sounds of day and grapple with the fact that Denendrius isn't back yet.

I'm sure there's a reasonable explanation, and he'll be back the moment the sun goes down. Maybe he tried to cut it too close to the sun and realized his mistake. Maybe they had car troubles and are now both smashed into the trunk together on the side of the road. I know Denendrius wouldn't leave me here alone all day on purpose. He'll be back tonight. But that's . . . *a whole day away.*

A strangled sob leaves me, and I can't get a single breath in. I grip the sides of the cage, my clawed fingers hooked on the bars as I try to drag in air and merely choke. My body shakes, the panicked spasms only making my sore limbs and muscles scream in agony. When I finally wrangle a breath in, it enters me shaky and strangled. I curl into a ball on my side and squeeze my eyes closed. Tingles overcome me, like little bugs nipping and skittering over every square inch of my flesh. I hyperventilate until I'm dizzy and my eyelids flutter with the threat of fainting. When I can finally steady my breaths, exhaustion grips me as tightly as my wounds and aches.

I flop over on my other side and lift my weak hands to my cheeks to rub the numbness out of them. I spot the case of plastic water bottles by the wall, and tears instantly rise to my eyes.

I'm unsure how much time passed in my panic, but my thirst screams at me now. My mouth is cottony, and as I lick my dry lips, my bladder creeps forward and demands my attention. Sitting, I wipe my eyes and lean back against the blanket covered bars, my spine begging to be stretched out. My stomach rumbles as I heave out a shuddering breath and lean the side of my head against the bars.

My bladder eventually hollers for my attention, its demands to be emptied only more prominent the more I try to ignore them. But with no option to get out and use the outhouse, I hold it. I hold it until my only option is to piss myself or pee through the cage's floor gaps into the plastic tray below. I suppose that's why it's there . . . so caged dogs aren't lying in their piss.

Shame is a hot knife in my gut—enough to stave off my hunger—when I opt to pull my pants down and pee into the tray below. The choice makes tears streak my cheeks, and I'm not sure how long I spend crying about it. I'd be no less embarrassed if I had an accident, but the thought of Denendrius and Sergei returning to see I've relieved myself like a dog has sobs searing my chest.

I use one of my socks to wipe what didn't quite make it through the small gap perfectly, and poke it out of the cage—still in reach—in case I dare need to relieve myself again. Then, I sprawl the blanket over the bottom of the cage again and curl up on my side.

If it's daytime, I should try to sleep. Maybe it'll help time pass faster. I push out a long breath, the smell of urine right below me as I firmly shut my eyes.

Despite my exhaustion, sleep is nowhere near. My mind races.

What is Denendrius doing right now? Is he trapped inside somewhere, worried about the fact I have no water and no food? Nowhere to use the bathroom? Or has he done this on purpose? Has he stayed the day somewhere else to make me squirm and panic? To make me plead with the universe to bring him back so I can be let out?

My eyes pop open with a thought that has a shiver rolling through me.

What if something happened to him? What if . . . *he can't come back*? What if he was captured or killed? Could Viorel's men have him and are currently trying to torture my where-abouts out of him? My chest cinches with the thought, because I know he'd rather me die in here than let Viorel have me. He'd think it more humane for me to starve and freeze to death.

But that will not happen. I can't let myself think that's going to happen. My aches, hunger, and shame are merely propelling my mind to the worst imaginable scenario. I force myself to take even breaths. Denendrius will be back soon. I shove away the panic trying to nestle itself in my chest again, because *there's no reason to be scared.*

"Denendrius will be back soon," I whisper to myself, just to hear something other than birds and squirrels in the whistling air.

I talk myself into numbness as time drags on, trying to keep the reminder at the front of my mind that as soon as night falls, Denendrius will be back. I can't figure out how much time passes, but I try not to think about the case of water just out of reach, or how I swear I can feel the temperature dropping.

At some point, my soft sobs draw me into a semi-lucid sleep. One where every ache and tingling limb keeps me partially aware. It's no break for my mind, because although I'm not deep enough to dream, I can't control my disjointed or racing thoughts. My bladder pulls me the rest of the way awake, an icy shiver ripping through me and making the urge stronger.

I wick tears from my eyes as I relieve myself again. Something shifts in the tray as it fills with more urine. A single long, dark brown hair floats—just a little too dark to be mine, and much too long to be his.

I give my head a rough shake. No, it's probably one of Denendrius's, and the shadows are just distorting it in the low light.

While I tell myself that makes sense, I curl back into a ball after cleaning up.

Cold creeps around me, and soon I'm shivering in my hoodie, with my breath billowing weakly around me.

"Fuck!" I gasp, each shiver making me cringe in pain as the movement exacerbates my soreness.

The birds stop singing, and the quiet of night makes me sob.

"It's okay," I tell myself, my voice a few octaves too high. My throat is raw and dry from thirst and sobbing. "If it's night now, that means Denendrius will be back right away."

He'll put a new tank in the heater and fill me up with warm food. It might be cold, but it's early April cold, not December cold.

I groan, agonized tears springing up in my eyes when my teeth chatter. With trembling hands, I tuck my hair into my hoodie so it doesn't fall between the cracks and into my urine when I wrap myself in the blanket and lie back down on the cold metal of the cage. I spend what must be hours shivering and sobbing, begging my brain to allow me to succumb to my exhaustion so I can escape this fucking cage for just a little while.

But soon the birds are twittering again, and the squirrels are starting their morning routine. *It's the worst sound in the world.* The hair stands up on the back of my neck and my sweaty arms are covered in goosebumps. My stomach feels full of lye and the pain in my chest has me emotionally breathless before a new shade of desperate panic has adrenaline pounding through me.

"No!" I wail as I gasp for breath and wrap my hands around the cage door to give it a weak rattle. "No! *God, fuck, no!"*

Why isn't Denendrius back yet?

I rattle the door in the cage. "Open!" I scream. "Fucking open! *Please!"*

I can't spend one more minute in here. *I can't.*

"Come on!" I scream as I give up on rattling the cage door

and begin beating it with my feet. *"Open, you bitch! Fucking open!"*

It doesn't open, of course.

I grip the bars at my sides and release a furious shriek into the air, my arms shaking.

"Denendrius!" I scream at the top of my lungs, my thirst making my voice crack. "Denendrius, let me out!"

The floor creaks somewhere near the front of the house.

XXVIII

Denendrius's voice echoes from upstairs. *"Marianna!"*

Relief floods me, adrenaline shooting through me as I collapse back against the cage and sob. "Oh, thank God. I was worried something happened to you. What happened?" I'm so thankful he's back that I'm not even angry he left for so long. My heart thumps as I watch the dark beyond the doorway, waiting for him to appear. Too many seconds pass without his presence. "Denendrius?"

There's no answer, no creak of the floorboards over my head to signal that anyone is there.

Tears prick my eyes, and I shrink back tightly against the bars. *"Denendrius?"* I squeak. *"Sergei?"*

He doesn't respond, and too much time passes for me to reasonably believe he was ever here.

But then, why did I hear him?

I lower my head and bite my trembling lip, eyes wide and darting around as a chill creeps up my back that only awakens my cold shivers.

"Denendrius?" I whisper, half my shivers now from fear.

The lamplight weakens and withdraws from me.

"Don't you fucking dare die," I cry, tears streaking my cold cheeks. "Please don't die."

I watch the lamp and will it to return to full brightness, to cast out some of the new shadows of the room.

In my peripheral, something moves in the dark beyond the bedroom opening. I turn rigid, my head so stiff my neck hurts. Every nerve in my body screams danger.

"D-Denendrius?" I choke out, a tear darting from the corner of my eye that I'm too frozen to sweep away. "S-S-Sergei?"

Something shifts in the dark again, and I can't breathe. If it's not Denendrius or Sergei, then who is it?

Reality screams the answer to me. What could possibly be in the hall, skulking around in the dark, and unable to pass through the protective shield of garlic around the dirt doorway?

The floor creaks directly above my head and a strangled, guttural groan crawls out of me.

There are Children of Stars here.

Did they hear me screaming? Catch my scent or the sound of my beating heart? With how quiet the woods are, anything could have heard me.

"Who are you?" My demand sounds so weak with the shake of my voice. "What do you want?"

I can only pray that they're not here to hurt me, though from the way they creep around in silence . . . those odds aren't great.

The lamp flickers and I plead with it to stay on. Something shifts in the shadows again and my heart thumps so hard I can feel it in my throat.

What if they have abilities? Do they work through the garlic shield, or will it protect me?

Somebody whispers something upstairs, and I shrink harder against the cage.

"Hello?" I call. There's no way to hide that I'm here, even if I were to keep quiet.

I gasp, and my heart stops for a moment when the lamp dies and plunges me into darkness. It's possible the batteries ran out after being on constantly, or maybe the lamp is just a cheap piece of shit . . . but what if one of the Children of Stars had an ability capable of turning it off?

My eyes rake at the darkness, the pitch black so thick I can't distinguish a single shape. I will my eyes to soak up bits of light from . . . *somewhere.* But with the boarded-up window and the gaps filled to keep out sunlight, I'm screwed.

Stifling my rapid breaths, I try to listen past my drumming heart and the blood pumping in my ears for creaks in the floor or more whispers.

I swear I hear someone call my name.

"Hello?" I call again, my gaze flitting around uselessly in the void.

I remind myself that if it's night, Denendrius still has a chance of making it back. I might not have to sit in the dark, shivering and trying to make enough spit to wet my dry tongue and throat for much longer.

He has to come back. He knows as a human I can only live so long without food and water, and the birds have already sung for morning twice . . .

The light flickers, and I hold my breath, waiting for it to come back. I will it to work, begging for any bit of light it's capable of offering.

"Come on," I whisper. *"Come on."*

I nearly give up being able to see again when it turns back on, the yellow light so low it barely counts as a glow. Barely glows inches against the dirt, but at least it gives my eyes enough input to adjust to the dark.

My stomach shoots a pang through my center, and I cough and squeeze my arms around my abdomen to try to shut it up.

My dry eyes burn with exhaustion, my center of balance failing every few minutes to leave me feeling like I'm falling through the ground. My lips are so dry that licking them is useless. I smack my lips, my mouth so cottony with thirst that I try to lick the tears that run past my lips.

Squeezing my eyes closed, the world tilts for a while, and I think I fall asleep. When I wake, I'm stiff like I haven't moved in hours, but I no longer know if it's day or night. With how exhausted I've been, there's no way of guessing how long I was out.

I let my head flop to the side, trying to make out the bed next to me in case there's some chance Denendrius returned and cruelly laid down instead of letting me out.

"Denendrius?"

Something shifts, and for a lightning moment, I feel relief.

"I love you. C-can I come out?"

But dread circles me, my mouth gaping with airless panic as a *short* black figure stands from the bed and walks across the front of the cage before disappearing into the shadows on my left. My mind whirls, my sense of balance completely lost in the dark void.

Sobbing, I lean my forehead on my knees as I quiver. The floor creaks above me, something wooden snapping in a different part of the house and making me yelp. Hushed whispers travel from my left and in front of the cage again. Someone gasps for air, but it could just be me.

I squeeze my eyes closed and beg my brain for unconsciousness, and everything tilts for a disorienting moment. There's a gnawing sensation in my head that sleep will only bring more danger. That anything can get me when I'm unaware of it creeping closer.

Don't sleep.

Don't sleep.

Don't sleep—

"Please," I cry.

Something shuffles in the dirt. There's a twang against the metal at my feet, and I feel the little door shift against the lock and vibrate the cage.

Don't look.

Don't look.

Don't look.

Hot breath on my face.

"Marianna?"

I grit my teeth and feel like I'm spinning.

Tiny, choked crying is only inches away from me.

I cover my face with my hands, refusing to look.

Can't make me look.

If it's not Children of Stars . . . I don't want to think about what else it could be.

Ghosts. I've never seen one before, but Denendrius believes they're real. If anywhere is haunted, it's the abandoned house he's owned for decades with the girl-sized dog cage in it. I don't want to think about how many people he might have killed on this property. I probably can't fathom it.

How many girls were in this cage before me? He killed some of them in this house, didn't he?

Are they here with me now? Calling to me as I sit starving and freezing, waiting for me to die and join them?

Will I join them?

"Look at me," Denendrius says, his voice ringing like crystal right in front of me.

My head snaps up, my heart clenching.

Denendrius is nowhere to be found. Instead, a girl sits curled up in the corner against the cage door in nothing but pink underwear and a cropped spaghetti strap top. Dirt stains her legs, bruises in various stages of healing blossoming across parts of her body. Her long, dark brown hair is greasy and stringy as it falls down her splotchy-blue back. Her fingers—nails torn—are hooked in the bars of the door.

I can't tell if it's her that reeks like sweat and piss, or if it's me and the tray below us.

A weak light surrounds us, and though I search the room for it, I can't figure out where it's coming from. The lamp shines no more.

My lips tremble against each other as I grapple with her presence. I force myself away from her, pushing myself harder against the bars to not touch her, but even then, there's so little air between her body and mine.

"Think he'll let us out?" she whispers, unhooking her fingers and trailing them down the bars.

"Who are you?" I choke out as a violent shiver rips through me and I cringe at the agony it brings.

She leans her head against the bars, her dirty hair obscuring her face.

"Marissa," she whispers with a sniffle. "What's your name?"

"M-Marianna." My tremors practically shake the syllables out of me.

"Oh . . ." She sniffles again, then lifts her weak and bruised arm to wipe her eyes. "I'm sorry."

"Y-you're s-s-o-orry?"

"Yeah," she whispers. "He'll keep you a lot longer than me. He'll be done with me soon. He said so."

"W-who?" I ask, though I'm sure I already know.

"Charles," she whispers.

My heart thuds crookedly as I try to convince myself I'm dreaming. But the girl looks so real in front of me, the bars still so vivid and ice cold in my tight and trembling grip that there's no space in my mind for logic.

"I'm back." Denendrius's voice has my head whipping to the side.

He walks into the room, his leather jacket unzipped and his

mirrored aviators hooked on the neck of his forest green T-shirt.

"Denendrius!" I shout, though the volume is as weak as I am. "You're back."

He comes to the cage, and she ducks her head. Trembles work through her battered body, little noises of terror emitting from her as Denendrius takes the keys from his pocket and squats in front of the door. Excitement pounds inside me as he unlocks the door. What little saliva my mouth can make sticks to my tongue as I think of water and food.

He opens the door and reaches in to brush his hand down her biceps. She shudders and pulls herself tighter against the corner of the cage. He doesn't look at me.

"Come on out," he murmurs, something sinister in his coal-black eyes as he watches her meek form crawl out of the cage.

I scramble forward to follow, but he shuts the cage door. Still, he doesn't put the lock on as he tucks the keys back into his pocket. I push against the door, but it doesn't budge.

"Denendrius," I plead. "I want out too, *please*."

Denendrius lifts his sandaled foot and presses it against the side of her ribs. "Go on," he murmurs as he gives her a gentle push toward the mattress a few inches away.

Marissa trembles as she crawls onto our disheveled blanket, sniffles and choked back cries escaping her.

When Denendrius reaches above the cage for something, I look up. The camcorder rests above my head, pointed toward the bed. Horror chokes me as he turns it on, the whirring of tape making the room spin.

I think I should close my eyes and turn away, but I can't blink, can't move from my frozen horror as I watch him peel his leather jacket and shirt off before crawling after her.

I fight for my voice, for my rubbery tongue to work.

"Denendrius!" I shout, but he doesn't look back at me. "Denendrius, don't!"

She reaches the center of the bed. He pushes her over, and she collapses onto her back, limbs splaying out uselessly. A twisted grin curls his lips as he crawls over her, his hand shaping around one of her knees to separate it from the other.

"Leave her alone!" I scream, my voice as weak as my body. Still, I force myself to my hands and knees, sitting sideways in the cage like it'll make any difference. "Denendrius, don't! Come use me instead."

I reach through the bars toward him, pressing my shoulder against the metal like I have any chance of reaching him and pulling him away from her. Straining toward him, I plead for him to ignore her and take me.

"What about me?" I cry, my eyes still so dry. I feign jealousy, hoping it's enough to get his attention as it has before. "Not fair! Why don't you make love to me instead? You know I love you more. Use me instead, Denendrius, please."

But my efforts are useless, and soon I'm twisting away and curling my shivering body up against the farthest corner I can get from them. I cover my ears and squeeze my eyes shut as she screams and fights while he assaults her. I mumble my pleas for him to stop, not enough air in my lungs to be much louder. I'm not sure he can hear me over the sounds she makes, anyway.

I flinch when her scream sharply cuts off, and the sound of her death rattle gives me flashes of cold, each wet gurgle making me clench my jaw and hold my palms tighter to my ears. I'm not sure why I peek; to make sure it's really happening beside me and that I'm not hearing things.

But there she lies, eyes and mouth wide as her last breaths fight to move past the coarse yellow rope that Denendrius has knotted around her throat, both ends in his tense hand as hers wrap—*pleading*—around his wrist. He leans over Marissa with his face shadowing hers as they lock eyes.

I whip my head away from the sight. My weakness is unignorable then, my head so heavy I can barely lift it back up as it slumps.

As I hear her loose arms thud back against the mattress with her silence, and he mutters something to himself, I dare another look.

Marissa stares wide-eyed and is lifelessly still on the mattress, her face a shade of red that creeps into the whites of her eyes. Her mouth remains open like she's still begging for air. Denendrius strokes her hair out of her face, whispering words to her that I can't quite hear. He sighs as he stands and fixes his pants.

"Denendrius?" I dare ask as he slips his shirt and leather jacket back on. It takes so much effort to get the weak words out, but I whisper, "Denendrius, can I come out to be with you now?"

He ignores me, no sign he even knows I'm in the cage, as he strolls out of the room.

XXIX

"Marissa?" I whisper, a wide emptiness inside me. I shift my head to see if she's really there.

But there she lies, as dead as moments before. Her brown eyes stare at me, and I fight the urge to look away. My head burns with the threat of tears, but this time none make it to my eyes. Pulling in a shuddery breath, I shift my slowly unraveling body to the other side of the cage. I move my limp hand to the bars and lift it through. I lean sideways, reaching across the bed, and just barely rest my hand against hers.

She's frigid. Cold like she's been lying there for hours when I think it's only been a minute since she died. *Since he strangled her.* Her skin's so cold that it hurts, and I whisper an apology as I withdraw my comfort to the blanket . . . but it's just as cold and hurts just as much. Pulling my arm back into the cage is draining. I lift my hand to my cheek and can barely feel my skin. It's like rubber. Like it's someone else's skin.

Frostbite?

The word rockets through me with a surge of blind panic

that twists my thoughts into a tangled mess. Could I be getting frostbite down here? In April? That's stupid . . . But I guess if it's cold enough for snow to remain on the ground outside . . .

"Marianna?" Marissa whispers.

A surprised breath leaves me. I'd probably jerk in response if my body had the energy.

"How long have you been in there?" she asks.

I tremble as I keep my gaze forward, not wanting to see how she speaks. Was she playing dead? Or will I look over to find a corpse as her disembodied voice continues talking to me?

My brow furrows as I wrack my brain, the hours before now muddled and dark. *Too long*, is all I know.

"I don't know." My voice comes out weak, barely a whisper. I try to lick my lips, but they're so dry that my tongue gets stuck to them for a moment. "I'm so thirsty."

My hunger is gone, replaced with a deep and sharp ache writhing through my abdomen.

"I'm here with you," she says.

Her attempts to comfort me have sorrow widening inside me. She's the one who's dead.

Though, I guess I might be soon too.

No. I can't let myself think that. I'm not going to die here.

"Denendrius is going to come back for me," I tell her, though I can't hear a morsel of hope in my fading voice. "When he does—" I cough against my dry throat and groan. "He's going to turn me into a vampire. I'm going to kill him for what he did. I'll make sure he gets what's coming to him."

"You'll do that for us?" Awe fills her voice.

Us. My thoughts are empty for a long moment as that single word rolls around to find meaning. Then, I understand she's not talking about just her and me.

"Yeah," I promise. A promise means I have to get out of here. The universe won't let me break such an important promise, right?

The light flickers. There's a white flash that has me squinting and wanting to rub my eyes, but I don't have the strength to lift my arms. They're too stiff to even try.

"When did you die?" I whisper, wanting to make sure she's still here with me and that I'm not alone again.

"2005," she says. "I was seventeen. What year is it now?"

I wrack my brain, the passage of time around this moment feeling blurred and mangled. A contemplative noise of confusion comes out with a breath.

"It's 2009," I mumble finally, the year popping out from the mess of incoherent reality around me.

"It's been so long, huh?" Marissa sighs. "You can't tell how much time passes when you're dead. Y'know?"

My heart flutters, the feel of it in my throat making me cough. If it weren't for its reminder that I'm alive, I might think she's trying to tell me something.

"Do you know where he buried you?" I mumble. I don't know why I ask, maybe so I can scare the shit out of myself more by thinking there are bodies nearby . . . or maybe because I already know there are.

"Here," she says.

"Where, here?"

I stiffen as movement in my peripheral vision captures my attention. From the corner of my eye, she sits and leans closer to me. I flinch when the tips of her fingers brush the dirty hair by my ear and carry on across my cheek.

"I'm right here, Marianna. Right beside you."

"In this room?" I choke out.

She rests her forehead against the side of the cage. "I think he ran out of space in the woods to keep us."

Us.

How many girls are buried here?

If he returns to find me dead, will he bury me here with them? At least I wouldn't be alone.

It's so terrifying being alone.

"I'm tired, and I hurt so bad I wish I could just sleep," I tell her, numbness climbing up my arms. They're like two weights pulling down on my shoulders. "I don't know why I can't sleep."

"You're scared. I used to be too. But it's okay to go to sleep, Marianna," she reassures me. "It'll help you forget the cage for a while. I'll wake you up if anything happens."

I shift my head to look at her, and she looks *alive* again. Dirty and bruised, but alive. She's also on the bed, and I'm not.

"How'd you get out of the cage?" I ask, the confusion drawing my brows together.

"He let me out." Her eyes study my face, and the sight of her blurs as I struggle to focus on her soft features. "He'll let you out soon too. In the end, he always comes back and always lets us out."

I blink hard and try to get her face to steady, but it's like the dim light is pointed directly at my eyes, obscuring her clarity.

"Can you let me out?"

The light twists when she shakes her head. "Only he has the key. I'll sit with you, though."

"Please," I whisper. "Keep the light on. Maybe you could pass me some water?"

"You'll get water soon," she assures me. "Just hang on until he's back. Go to sleep."

I close my eyes, managing a single full breath when her warm hand wraps around mine.

"Just focus on breathing," she murmurs. "In and out."

I do what she says, though my chest aches with each one.

She whispers something to me, but I'm deaf with sleep. I focus on the feel of her warm hand in mine and breathing around the pain as the cage fades.

"Marianna!"

A questioning grunt rolls out of me, my lids too heavy to lift. Sleep presses me into the cage.

"Come on! You have to wake up!" The urgency and the familiarity of the voice have me jolting awake.

Denendrius is crouched in front of the cage, his blistering red eyes looking over me desperately as he fumbles with his keys to swiftly get them out of his pocket.

"You're not real," I accuse, no power behind my voice as intended. "You're not real."

"I'm real this time, Marianna," he promises. "I'm so sorry you've been stuck in here."

I sob tearlessly in relief as he unlocks the cage and pulls my trembling and weak body out.

"Oh fuck, I thought you were never coming back," I wail as he scoops me up in his arms. "I thought I was losing my mind. I swore I heard you come back already, but then you never came down and the day came again—"

He cradles me in his arms as he stands. "We have to go," he says, the urgency in his voice sending a fresh stroke of panic through me. "I barely had enough time to come back and get you, but I couldn't leave you here."

"What happened?" I cry, wrapping my arms around his neck and leaning my heavy head on his shoulder. As much as I hate him, his presence is a comfort compared to the nightmare of the cage.

"Sergei is dead," he says tersely as he rushes out of the room. "There was a group of bounty hunters after us, but I think I lost them for a bit. I kept trying to double back for you the night I left, but I couldn't lose them. We had to hide out until nightfall, but they were right on our tail again. We need to get to the car now."

The room blurs, and we pause outside the house, Denendrius carefully looking around the woods before racing into them with blinding speed. We stop in front of the Mustang, and Denendrius yanks open the passenger door and sets me on the seat. He disappears, and I expect him to reappear with the driver's door opening.

Instead, he lies in the middle of the snowy dirt road, moonlight cast across him and a wooden stake in his chest.

Terror strangles me, and I don't have time to scream as the passenger door rips open and a pair of cold arms scoop me up. I writhe uselessly against a Darkling man's strength, unwilling to stop fighting until I know if I'm being rescued or captured.

"Let me go!" I shriek. "Please!" I stare at Denendrius's limp form as the man carries me past him, screaming his name, begging him to wake up and help me, despite knowing it's no use.

The forest and dirt road blur, my vision narrowing to the sight of a black van idling on the side of the highway. A white man with a shaved head pulls the trunk open and shoves Denendrius in the back as my kidnapper tries to swing me into the vehicle. I fight against his grip, his foreign shouts only making my panic intensify.

Still, despite my struggles, he gets me in the van with him. I scream at the top of my lungs and curse at him until his pale face and coal-black eyes fill my sight. He shouts something at me in another language, the sound so harsh and his fury so violent that venom sprays against my face. I call him every name I can think of and threaten him with the king's vengeance.

He responds with a swift fist to the side of my head that knocks my world out of reach.

When I come to, I gasp, my eyes flitting around in the dark. I lift my head off something cold and metal, the pain in my head dull compared to the agony pulsing through my whole body with each breath.

Where did they put me?

I stretch my hands out, trying to figure out if I'm still in the van or in a room now . . .

Metal bars stop my arms from extending, and I reel so hard that I fall backward against them.

"What the fuck?" I scream, my fingers curling around the metal bars of the cage. *"What the fuck!"*

I keel over and sob, my eyes dry despite the emotion tearing through my chest and making me heave with nausea.

What happened? *I was out.*

"A dream," I tell myself as I force my breaths to even out. "You had a vivid fucking dream, that's all. You didn't get punched, you whacked your head against the bars in your sleep. You're just scared he won't come back."

I feel a little silly talking to myself, but after who knows how many hours without conversation or noise, it's nice to hear something, even if it's my own voice.

I suppose being in the cage is better than Denendrius being staked and Darklings taking us who knows where. Somewhere that's probably worse than where I am right now.

At least in the cage, Denendrius still has a chance of returning. I'd rather he be the one to pull me out of this cage.

A flash of light darts through the black room again when I blink.

"Marianna, wake up!" a small voice demands with a bit of panic.

My weak lids lift, and there's no energy left in me to deal with the confusion. Marissa's soft and warm hand is still around mine. I roll my head to the side to take in her face.

Tears coat her brown eyes, her smile quivering as she looks at me. "I'm sorry," she breathes. "You were having a really bad dream. I thought maybe I should wake you."

My head pounds, a tight band cinched around it. "How long was I sleeping?" I ask, though now I can't tell if I'm really awake or asleep.

She shrugs, and her smile steadies a bit. "It's hard to tell how much time passes down here."

"Thanks for sitting with me." I swallow against my stark-dry throat.

The birds sing their dawn song, or maybe it's midday now, and I've been unconscious for hours. My head throbs, but somehow, I'm grateful for the noise. Their chirping grows so loud, it feels like they're either screaming or perched right here in the room with me. I feel like I'm spinning, the sound doubling, tripling, and overlapping into a cacophony that has my heart beating so erratically that I gasp for breath and clamp my hand over my chest.

When I can finally breathe again, they're shallow breaths. I try to reassure myself aloud, but I can't get my tongue to move. How many days have I been down here now? How many days without food or water? I know humans can survive three days without water before succumbing . . . Am I nearing that? Am I going to die?

Warm breaths whoosh against the side of my face.

"Marissa?" I mumble, barely audible.

The light disappears, and the night takes its chance and grips me so tightly that I can't shake it off.

"Please don't leave me," I beg, my voice so quiet it's practically all breath.

I can't decipher how time twists as the cold pushes itself against me. It presses me into the cage where I sit, and no matter how hard I strain against it, I can't move. My rear aches, my skin feeling like it's being pulled so tight the metal might break through to the bone. The blanket is like a sheet of ice around me. The cold grips me so tightly, imbeds itself in my flesh and bones, that there's no space left to shiver. I'm so weak my body has given up on trying to shake it away.

It might not be such a bad idea . . . giving up. I should know I don't have much time left. Viorel's blood will only prolong death a little longer, not eternally.

Besides, after all this, I probably won't have the energy to pretend with Denendrius anymore.

If I let go, I wouldn't be alone anymore. Viorel and Aeliana will be fine without me. He says he loves me, but he doesn't really *need* me. And if Laurentius is still alive, I know Viorel will take care of him too.

Right now, all I'm doing is causing Viorel pain. He can feel everything I'm going through, and there's nothing he can do about it.

If I let go, I'll just be doing him a favor. He wouldn't have to worry about me anymore. He could let go too.

But I think about Aeliana, about her cinnamon eyes and the warm cheeks on either side of her satisfied little smile after a bottle of milk or soft cuddles. How she looks like an angel against the silk of Viorel's chest. So beautiful.

The birds sing, their song shifting in and out of time, overlapping with the hours or days.

I think I close my eyes, but I haven't been able to tell for a while if they're open or closed. The dark persists relentlessly, no matter which.

Maybe it's better this way. Maybe I might be so lucky to die here. It's cold, and I'm alone, but the company of villains is no better. If Denendrius can't return to me because he's dead, then I can come to terms with that. I tell myself I'm lucky to be here, in a cage, where nobody can torture me in revenge for Denendrius's actions. It's a blessing to starve to death when the alternative might be unimaginably more horrific.

A line of sunlight appears around the edge of the wooden board, shining like gold against the dirt wall. The music of the birds swells, and with the board cracked, I can understand their conversation. Their chirps take meaning, and they talk about the sun and how warm it is on their feathers, how sweet the air is outside.

I can smell it then, past the stale dirt and damp air. I breathe in the crisp cold of early April as it wafts against me and pulls, like it's beckoning me. I can't get a breath in with its force, but then it slips inside my lungs and reaches out to draw more of itself into me. It breathes for me, tells me to stop trying and it'll do all the work for me.

"Let go," an unfamiliar man whispers, his voice so low it feels hollow. *"It's okay to let go."*

The birds chirp louder as the sound carries to me through the wind. Hundreds of birds sing, their overlapping songs and conversations becoming indistinguishable from one another. Until it becomes a racket that loses all meaning. They may as well be screaming in panic with all that noise.

I try to plead with them to stop, but my jaw won't move, and my tongue is paralyzed. The wind works its way in and out of me, so cold and crisp I can practically taste the moisture of the incoming spring. I'm so weak, it's nice to have the breathing done for me.

A painful twang ricochets through me, from my chest to the deepest part of my abdomen. The wind pulls more of itself into me and the pang comes again. It stretches my lungs, pulls more of itself inside them with no thought to if there's space.

My heart beats a warning at me, drumming so hard for my attention that I can feel it in my skull.

"Breathe," someone whispers. *"Push it out. You have to breathe. Don't let it strangle you."*

The stretching pain in my chest intensifies, like the wind heard the warning and is trying to get in quicker. As the board is pulled back into place behind the wind, the streak of sunlight vanishes.

The cacophony of birds picks up volume, their panic clear to me now as they squawk and shriek. They were trying to warn me all along.

It dawns on me that *something* heard me from the woods and crept out to follow the smell of death.

Rogue demons. Laurentius spoke of them, how there were angels who regretted falling with Lucifer and preyed on others. He thought they were creeping out of the woods and were coming after him . . .

"Breathe," the softer voice demands. "You know what will happen if you don't breathe."

I fight to pull a breath in, but my lungs are already so full that there's no space. I try to lift my hand to bat at my mouth, to get it away from me, but it pushes harder against my body. The bars practically meld themselves into my spine and shoulder blades. I try to push against them, try to exhale the cold entity.

If I don't, I'm doomed. Laurentius told me what happens to marked humans when they die. With their blood tainted by a vampire's, Heaven won't accept them, and turning into a vampire is the only way to be safe with Lucifer in Hell. He created them so we could escape God's fury.

Even if Viorel has marked me, I've been drinking Denendrius's blood. And he may not have been able to overwrite Viorel's mark, but Denendrius's evil, dirty blood is still inside me.

Laurentius said Viorel would take me home with him when he dies . . . but what if a demon drags me there first?

I will my body to work and my lungs to squeeze out the intruder until I'm breathing on my own again.

I can't die yet, if it means I'll be apart from Viorel and Laurentius for eternity. If my tainted blood makes me a toy for the rogue demons, and if Denendrius has spat in Lucifer's hand with how he's demonstrated his use of free will, I don't want to be there without protection for him to find me when he inevitably dies.

I manage a full breath, a shallow and stale inhale and exhale. The shriek of the birds settles some, though they don't return to their peaceful singing.

A deep laugh echoes through the room, and nausea comes with the sharp edge of doom. When something grips the cage and shakes it, my limbs are too stiff with ice to respond. I fall against the side of the cage. The metal presses into the side of my head and the pounding in my skull intensifies. I beg my body to adjust, a pinching pain spreading in the fleshy part of my hip.

The cage rattles again, so hard that my arms jerk in

response against the hard bottom and I can't breathe as my heart seizes in my chest. My gasping, guttural breaths fill my ears as the demon shakes the cage. And when that's not enough, he reaches in and rattles me too. I can hear my strangled breaths, pain behind my eyes as they strain against being rolled back.

I beg for him to stop, for the demon to let go of me. But he throttles me, drags me across the side of the cage so slowly I can feel each bar press into my stone-stiff body as I collapse in a shuddering and twisted heap on my side. The acrid smell of old urine fills my nose through the slats, and when the demon reaches into me like he can pull my life out by force, I lose all control of my body as he searches. Warmth spreads between my legs and soaks my pants.

The demon laughs at me as he withdraws from inside me, unable to find what he sought. He wrenches the cage once more before it settles back against the dirt and my body falls slack where he shook me.

"I'll sit here and wait," he teases, his voice surrounding me from every part of the room. He cackles. *"I have an eternity to wait."*

His dark shape disrupts the black void of the room as he moves through it, something like gray light faintly shuddering around his edges and giving me brief glimpses of what looks like a human figure.

He paces, each shift through the dark to the beat of my heavy heart.

"I won't have to wait much longer."

My eyes follow him back and forth through the dark, the activity of birds outside so disorienting that my mind shrieks in agony. I think of pressing my palms over my ears, but I can't move them from where they lie limply on the metal. From the bend in my arms, they must be somewhere near my face.

The shape of him moves closer, the faint glow warping

around him. The contrast burns my eyes. His cold breath beats against my face, but I can't hear his voice past the sound outside.

"*Shut up!*" he bellows as he twists away from me.

Silence descends upon us so fast my ears ring.

Finally, peace and quiet. Some of the weight shifts off my head. With the glow pulsing around him with every small movement, I catch my slow blinks. Each one creates the illusion of the light shuddering and withdrawing from him.

"Don't sleep," he orders, the clarity of his voice jarring what's left of my mind. "You'll die faster if you stay awake. I need you to die before he gets back."

I blink at him, my body not giving me a choice in the matter. My lids close, and I can't tell how much time has passed when I open them, but the demon still stands there in the dark. Though I can't make out his face, his eyes are locked on me.

"I've been waiting for him to bring someone back." He laughs, the sound twisted and hollow. "Of all the girls he's brought back here, I couldn't take *a single one*. I could tease them, but in the end, their souls were too pure for me to hold. But you . . ." A breath of delight leaves him. "With your tainted blood . . . with everything you've done in your life . . ." His voice comes directly from the other side of the cage, and I close my eyes against the sulfuric smell of his breath. "*You're mine.*"

Sorrow writhes in my chest, filling the gaps of what's left between every shade of pain.

"*Of all the girls he's brought here, you're the only one that truly deserves to be caged.*" He clicks his tongue at me. "See, the Lord made you this way, Marianna. Your story is almost as old as mine. Some humans—*you*—are written to experience nothing but pain and sorrow. You can't control the evil that happens to you no easier than the evil you enact. Do you know *why*?"

Even if I could unhinge my jaw, I wouldn't have an answer.

"*We're hungry,*" he growls. "The Lord wrote this eternal

hunger for suffering into us, and he feeds us with souls like yours to keep us from crawling out of the pit he cast us into and back to Heaven's gates. You, Marianna, have no other purpose in this realm. Your life was a losing battle. You were never meant to be happy. Your blood was tainted as a mere child to ensure we understood we'd receive you. Denendrius, a man with a story written with the same ink as your own, and this cage, is exactly what *you deserve*."

I shut my dry eyes, knowing they'd be brimming with tears if I weren't so dehydrated. A sob rolls around in my chest, but I can't give it a big enough breath to slip out. Everything he says is true. I've known it all along.

"So go ahead and give up, Marianna. There's nothing to fight for. If you survive, there's only worse to come . . ." There's a smile in his voice. "Do yourself a kindness and get it over with."

Just when I thought life was finally turning around for me, that I was getting some sort of happy ending, the worst happened. I had Carol and Derek at the castle with me, Rayonne too. I loved two men, and they loved me back. The vampire king took me as his own, accepted a baby Denendrius half made as his own child. Viorel was even starting to loosen restrictions on me, was going to take a huge step for himself and go on a horse ride and picnic with me in the woods.

Now?

Now he'll probably never leave the castle again. I'd be impressed if he manages to step outside his chambers. I worked so hard to convince him he was safe, that he didn't have to hide from danger all the time, that he needed to enjoy life . . . and the one day he gets the courage to step outside his comfort zone, his worst nightmare comes true.

My life was finally good, and it almost immediately unraveled.

The demon's right, but what can I do?

Giving permission for my lids to close, they shield me from the sight of the demon's pulsing form.

His voice, faint now, tries to coax me awake to no avail. I think of Viorel to block his frustrations out. The memories of Viorel are like stones in my pockets. They pull me down to the depths of sleep.

Just as I rest along the bottom, Marissa's soft voice reaches down to me. It's so muffled, like my head is really underwater.

"I'm here with you, Marianna. It's safe to sleep."

The water's a little warmer then. I feel her stroking my cheek, shooing some of the cold that presses down on me.

I exist somewhere below the surface, somehow feeling both asleep and awake. Time passes without clueing me in, my thoughts so disjointed I can't get them to take shape until something tickling my nostril has me jarring with confusion. My gasp causes movement to scurry down my face, tiny feet pressing into my neck until a weight rests like a lump on my shoulder.

A single squeak has me accessing energy I swore no longer existed in my body, and though my movement is slow, I manage to inch myself up so I'm no longer slouched. Until I feel the bars burrowing back in my spine. The weight drops to my lap and writhes until four little pressure points are against my aching guts.

Marissa giggles. "It's okay, Marianna. It's just a mouse. She's curious about you."

I can barely get the sound out. "Ge..." I huff. "Off..."

"Hey!" Marissa shouts with excitement, the volume of her voice making my heart skip. "Why don't we name her?"

Rabies. Has this girl never heard of rabies?

She giggles again. "It's rare for mice to have rabies."

That settles my heart a bit, and her laughter fades. I don't know how it happens, how the time bends and warps in a way that has her conversing with me one moment, and nowhere to be found the next while I feel like no time, and all the time, has passed.

"Marissa?" I whisper, so weak my lips don't move.

I stare into the dark, or maybe my eyes are closed, as I attempt to judge how much time has passed since I uttered her name. It could have been yesterday, for all I know.

Another voice calls to me instead, something so familiar about it that my senses wake.

A dozen candles illuminate the dirt room, and Viorel's satin voice caresses my ears as velvet fills my blurry vision in the dim light.

"My love . . ." The pain in his voice sends a sharp ache through me. "My darling . . . What has he done to you? How long have you been in there?"

Viorel? I blink at him, at the man I'm sure isn't real.

He shifts in the dim light and appears crouched beyond the cage, his pretty fingers hooking in the bars as he stares at me with watery crimson eyes.

A shiver rips through me. *He's not real.*

"I'm real," he whispers. "I've been toiling to master the ability that allowed our first encounter. That night, I was semi-lucid as I slept and had been thinking of Tatiana and wondering what might have happened to her bracelet. You were wearing it. The connection happens through our dreams. Neither of us is conscious right now."

I don't recall falling asleep.

Even in my dreams, I can't escape this cage.

"Your pain . . ." Viorel chokes out, his clawed hand on his chest. "It makes me feel like I'm *dying*. I haven't slept properly in *weeks*. Bodies litter the floor." Tears streak his cheeks, pain straining his voice when he says, "I need you, Marianna. Aeliana needs you. Please, where are you? I'll send someone to save you."

Vermont, I think at him, too weak to speak.

He closes his claret eyes for a moment. "Where in Vermont?"

I don't know. An old, abandoned house in the woods. Denendrius owned it decades ago.

"Vermont is nearly eighty percent forest," he chokes out, his tone begging for more. "How are my men supposed to find you before you perish?"

I stare blankly at him.

"Where's Denendrius?" Viorel asks, desperate eyes boring into mine.

I don't know. He's been gone for days. He said I would only be locked in here for a few hours.

"Something must have happened to him," Viorel says. "He wouldn't leave *you* here to die. It doesn't fit his behavior."

I'd nod if I had strength.

Viorel wipes his cheeks with the back of his hand. "You've been in agony. I can feel it. It burns my soul."

I manage a blink, and my thoughts circle around Aeliana. *Aeliana is alive?*

"Yes, she's perfectly fine, darling. Here, I'll sit with you as long as I can. But I don't know how long I can stay; this is the first time I've done this on purpose. I still don't quite understand it."

Viorel moves beside the cage and sits proper with a straight back and crossed legs. He hooks his fingers in the cage near mine, though I can't feel his flesh when he touches the side of my hand.

"I love you, Marianna," he murmurs.

I love you.

"I'll find a way to bring you home. I'm sorry this has happened. I stretched myself to my limits to keep the veil up. It slipped before I could stop it, and I couldn't get it back up until I resorted to draining another vampire. By then, it was too late. He was so strong with my blood in his system."

It's not your fault.

"It's my fault for not catching the poison spreading through Adelia. Of all those capable of betraying me, I never suspected her." He leans his head against the cage. "Nevertheless, she'll pay. Her and her bastard brother will pay in ways they cannot imagine."

Can you take me to the ocean? I ask, desperate to get out of this cage one way or another. I ache for the happiness that ocean reality used to bring me back at the castle. We'd lie there holding hands, looking as though we were simply asleep to anyone who might come upon us.

"I suppose I can try. I've never tried to conjure my fantasy worlds while dreaming before."

I see him slip his hand into the cage and hold mine. I wish I could feel him.

The sight of pink sand, foamy sea water, and vast blue skies flickers over the room like a mirage. A rush of waves and squawking birds pulse in and out of my ears as the image shudders a few more times.

"It's not working," Viorel whispers. "I'm sorry, darling."

Viorel and I sit in silence, wrapped up in one another's presence, until the faint sound of Aeliana's hungry cries fills the air, and Viorel vanishes from beside me like she woke him.

My eyes burn, and I wish I could cry. I'm alone again, but I remind myself he wasn't real to begin with.

Marissa returns some time later, reaching through the bars to stroke my limp limbs and hum to me. I can't speak anymore, can't even tell dreams from reality. But she's there at my side as I slowly die, whispering to me, telling me none of the things I see and hear are real. I ache to ask her to come back in the cage and hold me with her warm arms, maybe let me lean against her to relieve myself from the pain of the metal now that agony grips every inch of my flesh and bones, but I know it's not fair to ask her to sit in here with me.

When a black void shifts toward the doorway like it's alive, Marissa vanishes from my side.

Has Denendrius finally returned? There's nothing left in me for relief or excitement. I'm completely hollow now, my hunger having eaten away at whatever it could get its teeth around.

A man's voice swirls in the room, the familiarity seeping through the thick and suffocating dark like smoke through a crack.

"How the fuck are we supposed to get her out of there with the garlic?" a painfully familiar voice hisses.

What's left of my mind grips to the sound, turning over the familiar accent and trying to discern the identity of its owner.

There's another familiar man's voice, so *so* far away. *"We'll have to get one of the familiars to drag her out."*

"Fuck."

The void swallows them, extending to me. It's so thick even Marissa's soft voice can't reach me.

 XXXII

I'm an ocean tide licking at the shore of consciousness and reality before drawing back into the dark depths of the water.

In with the patter of stony water droplets on my aching body. Spray paint on tile fills my pin-prick vision, brown and pink-tinged water swirling around a pair of bare and bruised legs that are so close to me that they have to be mine. The only recognizable sensation in my body is *pain,* and my consciousness withdraws before I have a chance to become more than a host in my flesh.

"Love, I can finish cleaning her up if you need a break. Go get a drink," a familiar voice I can't quite place says from the shore.

The crying—*the bone-deep sobbing*—sails to me, and I can feel the ripples it makes. *"Won't matter. I'll still be able to feel her from the bar."*

Water rushes in my ears, and I'm stranded at sea alone until the tide stretches enough to carry me to more shallow water.

"I knew he was fucked, but look at what he's done to her. She's

got sores from being in there, and she's bruised like he's beat her and raw like he's been fucking raping her—"

"Try to breathe, Ziggy. Maxine is on her way back from the drugstore."

I'm pulled back out to sea, sucked into a wave that feels as dark as the dirt basement and smells like rot rather than salt. I crash so hard against the sea that I become human enough to remember I need to breathe, to feel the ache in my burning lungs and experience a strike of panic at why I can't fill them.

The rot twists to a skunky smell, and for a split second I'm back in the dirt basement and Denendrius is lighting up a joint for me. I sense my breaths while I wait for him to pass it to me.

But he doesn't, and instead a thick plume of weed and soft breath and flesh on my mouth clings to my every bit of awareness.

A soft voice brings the memory of Ziggy's face into my mind. *"Light it. I'll shotgun another."*

"She's going to be high as fuck."

"All considering, Lance, I fucking hope so."

My chest burns with the feel of lips and weed-fused, cold breath. It's strange how I can feel his lips, but not my own.

I crash so hard on the shore of consciousness that the ache in my body registers in my brain faster than my vision through my heavy, half-lidded eyes. I don't have the energy to moan in pain or move as much as a finger as my placement registers in my waking mind . . . though I'm only fifty percent sure that the chest moving with the black band T-shirt at the tip of my nose is real. The smell of weed and patchouli circles me, and from what I can feel through the ache embedded in my muscles, so does a cold arm.

Ziggy. I have the mind to understand it was him standing in the doorway of that basement bedroom with Lance, and piece together enough to know they must have brought me back to Estrella de Sangre to clean me up. I can't see over Ziggy, but can shift my eyes enough to take in the light blue sheet we're half laying on, and a beige comforter half over my face and on his shoulder, with a pattern so worn I can't tell what it used to be.

I can't produce much for thoughts in my slow brain as I lie with Ziggy for what must be quick-moving hours where I slip in and out of sleep. The cool wall against my back is soothing until it moves and I'm thrown into a twist of confusion that only settles when I remember Lance's existence again and put the idea together that I must be between the two of them in their bed.

Lance's arm drapes around me, the scent of leather and roses filling my nose. He casts a steady, smooth calm that envelops me as I lie still. Hardly a thought bumps around in my mind.

"You're awake," Lance whispers, the softness of his voice only making me feel more cottony.

I still can't find the effort to move my mouth, to move much of anything but my chest with shallow breaths. When his bitten wrist approaches my face, I find I have no thoughts about it. There's no desire within me to move when he tucks the bleeding wounds between my lips. My swallows are automatic, and the peace surrounding me fills my extremities. I'm floating on the bed.

"How do you feel?" he asks as he pulls his wrist away.

There's an ache at the edge of the calm surrounding me. The more I think of it, the more it takes my acknowledgement as an invitation. A quiet, pained noise slips past my numb lips.

Ziggy rouses in front of me, his arm sliding up from the depth of the blanket over us.

"She's been awake for a couple minutes this time," Lance whispers.

Ziggy's hand comes up beneath my jaw. There's no resistance when he lifts my chin, so I'm looking up at him.

"Hey, love, how are you?" he murmurs. His concerned, blistering red eyes dart across my face. Black eyeliner is smudged around his eyes, a faint black line down his cheekbone where a tear must have fallen. I have the thought to reach up and wipe it, but my hands don't respond.

"She seems weak still," Lance says.

Ziggy releases me and rolls onto his back, covering his eyes with the back of his forearm. He releases a tired groan. "I'm tapped out. I need to go feed."

Lance grunts. "Likewise."

My thoughts are a smear of incoherent pictures and words. Exhaustion creeps back into me, making my body feel heavier against the mattress. When they continue their conversation, it's mush in my ears like it's coming from a dream. I let my eyes fall closed, and when I open them again, I don't know how much time has passed.

Ziggy is stretched out on the bed beside me on top of the blanket, one arm behind his head while the other rests with his hand on his stomach as he stretches an elastic between his fingers. I'm higher in the bed, the edge of a pillow between Ziggy and my line of sight. Lance is still behind me, but his arm twitches against my back in time with the faint click of cell phone buttons.

"How was it, Emry?" Ziggy asks, his eyes trained ahead.

I shift my gaze down as a guy enters through a concrete doorway at the end of the room across from the foot of the bed, pushing a dark-green, sticker-covered door closed behind him. His blue-eyed gaze flicks to me and back to Ziggy as he shrugs out of a beaten backpack and rests it against a dresser covered in marker-graffiti that looks like it was found on the side of a road.

He exhales a long breath and runs his fingers through his short, dirty-blond hair. "A lot tougher than the assignments. I'm crossing my fingers that I passed."

"Which exam?" Lance asks from behind me.

"Biology. I've got calculus tomorrow."

Ziggy grins. "Shit, I'm sure you did fine."

Emry settles his unsure gaze back on me, his tooth scraping against the hoop in his lip. "Who's she? She looks sick."

Ziggy glances at me, then gives me a tired smile when his eyes connect with mine. He abandons the elastic on his stomach and puts his hand over the blanket on my hip.

"This is Marianna." He gives my hip a gentle pat, but I can't feel it through my numbness. "She's not sick, don't worry."

"Is she a new familiar?" Emry fidgets with his lip ring again.

Something in his tone makes me feel like I'm intruding.

"You'll have to share us with her for a bit. Unfortunately, I don't think I'll be able to keep her for very long," Ziggy says.

Emry cracks a bit of a smile. "That's fine, either way. Cool." He shifts toward the bed a few feet, then ducks down to look at me better. "Hey, Marianna."

I merely blink at him, unable to make my tongue move. An itch starts in my nose, and all I can do is twitch in response.

"She high?" he asks as he straightens and glances around the top of the messy dresser. He locates a lighter, then a half-empty pack of cigarettes under a broken CD case.

"Not so much anymore," Lance mumbles before straightening and saying, "Have you heard from Stacey today? She's upset but won't answer my texts or calls."

Emry places a cigarette between his lips as he shakes his head. He furrows his brow as he lights it and exhales white. "No, I slept until my exam and came straight here after. I think she had one today too, though. She was talking about how if she fails, her parents are going to make her self-fund her tuition."

Lance sighs and something—probably his phone—snaps shut. "I'll find her this evening and make sure she's okay."

"Her parents are fucking crazy," Ziggy mutters.

Emry shifts over and sits down on the edge of the bed

facing Ziggy. He balances his cigarette between his lips as he slides the sleeve of his black hoodie up and holds his scarred wrist out to Ziggy. "You look pretty thirsty. Sorry we've been so busy the past few days."

Ziggy sits as he takes Emry's wrist and brings it to his lips. He cuts into his pale flesh with his fangs, his hand tight around his forearm as he drinks. After a few long moments where Emry shifts, Ziggy groans and pulls his fangs out of his vein, releasing a pained gasp of breath.

"Pretty thirsty?" Emry asks as he takes a long drag from his cigarette and exhales a plume of smoke into the air.

Ziggy pushes the overgrown black hair from his unstyled mohawk out of his face, the front streak of bleach blond falling back with it. He flops back onto the pillow beside me. "I'll be fine."

Emry inhales another long drag as he contemplates Ziggy, fiddling with his lip ring again as he pushes out another gust of smoke.

"Can I share?" he asks.

Ziggy sighs. "I'm sorry, love. I've been giving everything I've got to Marianna here. It's taken a lot just to get her conscious."

He nods in understanding but looks to Lance in question.

"Same story here," Lance says. "We'll make it up to you, all right?"

He nods and gives them a sheepish smile. "It's okay, I get it. I'd offer more blood if I didn't need the energy for my exam tomorrow." He takes one final drag from his cigarette, then reaches across to the ashtray on the dresser to stub it out.

"You two are up early. Going back to bed? I was going to sneak in for a nap, to be honest," Emry admits with a chuckle.

Ziggy jerks his head toward me. "She needed help getting up for a wee, and I felt you come down. Stacey's stress woke Lance up a few hours ago."

I don't remember getting up to use the washroom, though I don't remember getting to Estrella de Sangre either.

"I had to piss so bad during my exam I almost didn't make it out of there in time," Emry says with a chuckle. "Fuck, I hope I passed."

Ziggy cackles. "God, do I not miss taking exams. I used to be so scared of failing that I'd have stress shits."

Lance laughs behind me, the sound traveling through his body and shaking mine.

Their smiles . . . their laughter . . .

I can't help the faint, emotionless smile that twitches across my lips.

Fuck, when was the last time I heard someone genuinely laugh over something mundane? It's been so long. Since the castle, I think.

"Well," Ziggy starts, hooking his arm around me and pulling my body against his side. "Crawl in."

Lance shifts over so I'm wedged between them, and Emry crawls over us and collapses on the mattress next to Lance, groaning about how fucking tired he is after studying so many late nights.

Lance pulls the blanket back over the four of us, making sure there's enough to go around.

Despite Ziggy and Lance's cold bodies, I feel so warm between them. So safe. Sunshine radiates from both of them, and it's so nice to have the softness of their bodies, the mattress, and the comforter, when I was pressed up against cold metal for so many days.

An ache of discomfort nestles into my spine, and Ziggy must sense it, as he's quick to adjust my body next to his. I'm pliable in his hands as he curls me up at his side, and when he stretches my limp arm across himself, I see how bruised my flesh is, how pale and skinny I am. My nails are torn, with lines of blood around my cuticles. Cuts cover my hands and fingers, and I faintly remember trying to beat the cage apart. My bracelet is missing from my wrist, but I don't remember it falling off.

When he fixes my legs and shoves a bit of blanket between my knees, a sharp ache radiates up my thighs that forces a low whimper from me.

"I'm sorry, love," he whispers. "We'll look at them again when we wake up."

Look at what? The question swirls around in my mind as he pulls my head onto his shoulder, his arm wrapped around me. I ponder what might be wrong with me, what that cage did to my body for however long I was in there . . .

Wait, how long was I in there? How long have I been here?

What happened to Denendrius?

My heart thumps against my ribcage with a few quick beats before a calm force—either Ziggy or Lance's calming ability— settles it and my thoughts.

"You're safe," Ziggy whispers to me, the cold of his breath tickling the top of my head.

A gentle hand rubs circles on my back, each loop making my eyes heavier and heavier. "Nobody's going to hurt you when you're with us, okay?" Lance murmurs from behind me.

"I can kick ass too," Emry mumbles, voice distant with sleep.

A low chuckle rumbles in Ziggy's chest.

"Here," Ziggy whispers as he brings his tanned wrist off the mattress and bites into it.

I'm unsure if I should drink, what with being Viorel's and Ziggy being so thirsty, but the desperation of my battered body isn't strong enough to disagree. Besides, it sounds like they've been sharing blood with me for a while now.

I let the taste of Ziggy's blood splash over my tongue and fill me with serene calm.

XXXIII

When I wake, I manage to lift my weak hands to rub my eyes. I can't feel Lance behind me, and Emry's bag is no longer propped against the dresser. Ziggy remains where I last recall, with his shoulder under my head and his protective arm wrapped around me.

There's a small surge of life in me, of awareness, that makes me test my voice. "Ziggy?" I croak.

He jerks awake beside me. "Hey, love."

But pain comes with that awareness. I'm conscious enough to feel how tight it grips me. It's embedded in my muscles and burns between my legs. It squeezes my every breath, and pounds along with each beat of my heart. Tears well in my eyes, and a groan slips past my lips.

"Shit." He carefully maneuvers me off him, each soft touch feeling so harsh to my bruised bones. He grabs a bottle of drugstore painkillers off the nightstand and shakes a few into his palm before grabbing a crinkled bottle of water off the nightstand. "Here, take these."

I struggle to lift my hand to take them, never mind lift my head to swallow water. So he shifts my head under his arm and slips them past my lips with a few sips of water, like giving me pills is routine.

The medicine scrapes down my sore throat. So sore I can hear myself screaming in my head again.

"You're talking at least," he notes. "You moved on your own."

"I feel awful," I cry, wetness welling in my eyes.

"Yeah . . . well . . ." He sighs. "Lance will be back in a bit. Hopefully full of more blood to share too."

I want to ask him where he went, but the insides of my thighs and my rear hurt so bad I end up asking about that instead.

"You've got pressure sores and a pretty bad rash from sitting in there in soiled clothes," he says. He looks sheepish as he carefully pulls the blanket back and says, "We need to put more cream on you now."

An embarrassed nausea creeps over me.

Ziggy relaxes and meets my eyes. "Hey, don't feel embarrassed. It's not your fault. What the fuck were you supposed to do? It's not like you could have unlocked the cage yourself to go to the washroom."

"Still," I whisper, "I'm sorry."

He smiles crookedly at me. "I've passed out in my own piss and vomit while drunk when I was human . . . more times than I'd like to admit. At least you had a good excuse."

I sigh and look down at myself. I'm clothed in an unfamiliar T-shirt, and a pair of loose boxers with cartoon characters from an adult comedy TV show.

"I know," he starts, like he's worried I'm going to react poorly to the reality he's seen me naked. "But we had to clean and dress you."

"Thanks," I whisper, lifting my eyes to his. "For taking care of me."

He bops my nose with his index finger, his black nail polish severely chipped. "Don't mention it. That's what friends are for. Just know, I'm keeping you for a while."

"Okay." I give him a small smile, and pain radiates across my face. I'd much rather be with Ziggy until I can get home to Viorel than with anyone else.

He stands and disappears into a little room to the right, coming back with a plastic pharmacy bag. He crawls back onto the bed and pulls out bandages, tubes, and Q-tips.

"Time to play doctor," he says with a quirked lip.

"I could try," I offer, though I'm not sure I can convince my arms to move enough to reach the stinging pain pulsing in my butt cheeks.

"I don't mind. I've already been doing it for the past couple days."

I gulp down an embarrassed lump as he rolls me onto my side and maneuvers behind me. As he shimmies the boxers off my hips, he says, "One time, my friend drank so much tequila that she shit herself after she fell down the stairs." I stiffen and wince at the feel of a wet Q-tip against a tender part of my flesh. "I was nearly too drunk to stand, but myself and another mate carried her to the bathroom and cleaned her up. Her girlfriends were fucking ruthless and thankfully didn't see it happen, or they would have bullied her for the rest of secondary school. It was concerning we were able to get her in the bathroom alone without them noticing, considering we were too drunk to be quiet."

When he rolls me onto my back, I wince in pain.

"I've got to get in between your legs. I'm sorry," he says. "I'd give you a mirror to do it yourself, but you absolutely do not want this shit in you or you'll have two problems."

"It's okay," I whisper, closing my eyes as he gingerly pulls just one of my legs out of the boxers. "You can't violate me any more than Denendrius has."

He clears his throat. "Yeah, I see that. I'm sorry, love."

I squeeze my eyes closed tighter, wetness springing up between my lashes.

"One time," he starts as he touches me with another wet Q-tip, "I was drunk—again, I know—and I lost my balance at a club urinal and pissed all over myself." I stiffen when he wipes another Q-tip between my legs. "As if that wasn't bad enough, my best mate was beside me. I pissed all over him too."

I can't help the strangled laugh that creeps up my throat at the thought.

"You probably think it can't get any more embarrassing than that, huh?" he says with a pained laugh. "But I zipped my nuts in my zipper moments later and cried my eyes out while he helped me get them out."

Another laugh bubbles out of me, a few tears leaking from the corners of my eyes with it.

When another Q-tip strokes a friction sore between my legs from Denendrius, I can't help the squeak that pushes past my lips.

"I bled all over the cab when he took me to A&E, and the nurses were all giggling ladies. I puked all over the one who had to stitch me up."

I manage to relax against the bed, my muscles loosening as he comes in with a few more Q-tips and some bandages.

"All done, love," he says as he pulls the boxers back up and splays the blanket back over me. "Are you okay?"

I sniffle, a relentless stream of tears escaping the corners of my eyes and running down my temples. "Mhm."

He wipes my tears with the edge of the bedsheet.

"Were your nuts okay after that?" I manage to utter in a weak effort to feel more human and less numb.

His face lights up as he leans his head back and laughs. "Yeah, but it bloody hurt like hell for weeks."

I want to thank him for trying to help me feel better about my embarrassment, but he offers me his wrist again before the words make it to my tongue.

"Want some proper food?" he asks as he wipes blood from the corner of my mouth with his thumb and licks it.

"No," I whisper. Despite being so desperate for food in the cage, my stomach is too full of their blood to consider it. Though, it's possible I've gotten so far past starvation that my body has given up on sending me hunger cues.

"Okay, but you'll have to try eating a few bites of something soon."

"How did you know I was in there?" I whisper, the movement of my jaw causing some of my hair to slip across my cheek.

Ziggy runs his finger across my cheek, collecting the loose hair and tucking it behind my ear. "We got a call from Viorel. He told us you were in the basement of an abandoned house somewhere in the Vermont forest . . . *in a fucking cage* . . . and had been for days. Told us to go search for you." He mashes his lips together and swallows. "Unfortunately, there's a hell of a lot of forests in Vermont. King's orders, so we spent a couple of nights searching off dirt roads and the highway while he had someone looking by air. No luck . . . until I got an SOS from your phone number with exact coordinates stating to help you before you die."

A knot of dread forms in my throat, but it's nice to know Viorel's appearance was real. "It wasn't really my phone. It was Denendrius's . . ."

He nods. "He must be in shit to be desperate enough to ask us to help you."

"None of Viorel's people are the ones who have him?" Anxiety is a fist in my gut.

"No."

The conflicted concern of his down-turned lips and furrowed brow mimics my feelings. Who has Denendrius? And what are the chances of him escaping and coming back for me before Viorel's men can bring me home? Sergei must be caught in the same situation, if he's not dead, for Denendrius to ask Ziggy and Lance to help me before sending him.

"Do you know how long you were in there?" He flattens his lips into a pitying line.

I blink. My eyes are so dry I'd rub them if I could muster the energy to move my arm. "I don't know. The days were blurring, even before he put me in there. I tried to run away while he was asleep." I wrack my brain. "Wednesday, maybe? Or Thursday?"

Ziggy's lips part as he tries to fight the horror twisting his face, and his voice shakes as he says, "Fuck. It was Friday when we pulled you out, and we got Denendrius's text on Wednesday when we had already been searching. So . . . at least a week."

A week?

It somehow feels both longer and shorter than I thought it had been while I was in there.

"How did I not die?" My brow furrows, the movement causing pain to radiate across my scalp. "I thought humans couldn't survive without water for over three days."

He shrugs. "You had an empty bottle in there with you, but I'm unsure of when you emptied it."

I sigh. "I really can't remember now."

"Either way," he starts. "You wouldn't have lasted much longer. It's taken Lance and me giving our blood to you for the past couple of days just to bring you to this point. Viorel said to do whatever it takes to help you, so hopefully he's not too pissed at the blood sharing. It hasn't removed his odd mark, so no doubt he knows and would have called to order us to stop if it were a problem."

My heart leaps as it dawns on me they've been in touch.

That he has a guard's number from our monthly calls while I was in the castle. "Can we call him now?"

Ziggy bites the corner of his lip but nods as he fishes his flip phone from his pocket. My heart pulses in my throat as he dials, and I hold my breath. The ringing seems to go on forever. I sink deeper into the mattress when it doesn't connect.

He pats my hand and helps me sit upright. "It's Mateo's phone, and he's been quite busy, from what I've heard. I'm sure he'll call back soon."

Disappointment weighs on the corners of my lips, and I heave out a breath. "Yeah."

Wetness fills Ziggy's heavy gaze as he studies my face. "I talked to Mateo a bit . . . He said Rayonne died, but they couldn't be sure who killed her . . ."

I drop my eyes to my lap, my legs thinner than I recall. The image of Rayonne opening the wardrobe Adelia hid me in, only for Denendrius to punch through her chest from behind with her heart in his hand, obscures my sight. "Denendrius did."

He pulls in a choked breath before clearing his throat. "I suspected."

In our silence, I can tell neither one of us knows what to say. I lift my eyes to study the room, trying to fill my mind with something other than the memory of her death. I scrutinize the various piles of worn clothes—likely belonging to both Lance and Ziggy, and their familiars—and the organized mess of fast-food recycling between the dresser and door.

Stickers, graffiti, and taped-up images from CD cases, magazine cutouts, and posters form a chaotic collage across the concrete walls. The metal posts of their four-post bed stand bare and useless, reaching toward a ceiling coated in a thinner patchwork of images. Beside the bedroom door, across from the foot of the bed, mismatched shelves sag under the weight of papers and various items I can't make out with my tired eyes. CD stands overflow with discs and tapes, a few precariously balanced on top. I look over my shoulder at the wall behind me. It's covered in overflowing clothing racks—most of the garments black with rare hints of color, and the faded green couch beside it looks unbelievably comfy despite the ash stains spotting the fabric.

With pain in my neck, I straighten my head and look toward the bathroom past the nightstand I can't recall using. The weakness in my body has me searching the nightstand for more weed.

"Who's this?" I ask, carefully picking up the plastic frame from his nightstand as it catches my attention instead. A girl with soft brown eyes surrounded by thick and dark makeup stares up from the glossy paper, half her teased dark brown hair so long. Her black lips are quirked in a smile. The way she's posed on the rungs of an emergency escape ladder, her platform boots hooked on the metal, makes me think it's a professional photo. She must be somewhere in her twenties. "She's pretty."

"My daughter," Ziggy says, an ache in his voice.

I stare at him, then back at the photograph as I recall him over sharing when we first met about how his then-girlfriend sabotaged her birth control and got pregnant. He didn't want a baby, and his family tried to force him to get clean and marry the girl. "Wow. I see it now. She's—"

"Older than me?" Ziggy finishes. He clears his throat. "It's strange. She's twenty-two now. Three years older than me, though technically I should be forty-one now."

I press my teeth into my bottom lip as I stare at her. "Do you ever see her?"

Ziggy shakes his head. "No, we've never met. She moves around but hasn't left the UK. She's the lead singer in a Gothic rock band—here, I'll play her CD." He moves swiftly across the room and takes a case from the rack, blinking back tears as he opens it and pops it into the beaten CD player on his dresser. He hits play.

He clears his throat and crosses his arms as we listen to the CD spinning before a girl's haunting voice fills the room, laced with melancholy and backed by the sound of distorted guitars and the rhythm of percussion.

"I buy all her albums," Ziggy says. "Did you know I wanted to be a rock star too?" A pained smile crosses his lips.

"She doesn't know you and still grew up like you."

He nods and clears emotion from his throat. "The consensus back home is that I killed myself, but they haven't found my body yet. I can't blame everyone for thinking so. I said a lot of shit the night I overdosed and died." He heaves out a breath. "She wrote a song about me—it hurts to listen to—about wishing she knew me. It's about depression and drugs. I guess she knows what her mother did too, and they don't talk."

I rest my head on his shoulder in an attempt to comfort him.

"Have you ever thought about meeting her? Bringing her into this world?" I ask.

He gives his head a swift shake. "I don't know. I just . . . She's so happy with her life, you know? I don't want to disrupt that. The thought feels so selfish. And even if I tried to meet her— pretended to be someone else—she knows what I look like. She has one of my photographs in an album booklet with the date I went missing . . . a kind of tribute. She'd recognize me."

"That makes sense," I whisper.

He sighs. "I send her money when I can, but she doesn't know it's from me. I first sent a letter with it, from some non-existent friend of mine who got rich in America. I wrote about myself, told her that her dad would be proper proud of her if he were still alive to see her. That he *wanted* kids one day but just wasn't doing too well at the time. I didn't want her to feel abandoned and unwanted."

"That's really sweet, Ziggy."

He reaches across the dresser and turns the stereo off, staring at us in the mirror. "Yeah," he whispers. "I met her once, when she was a newborn. I went over to my ex-girlfriend's house with what little money I had and gave it to her. She let me hold her for five minutes, and I remember thinking she was the most precious, beautiful thing I had ever seen. My ex tried to convince me to get back together, but I refused. She said I wasn't allowed to see her again, and well, I wasn't really in a position to fight her. What with being irresponsible, on coke, and living on friends' couches, and both our families against me for not marrying her . . . It was hopeless. I hadn't wanted to be a father, and it sucked my ex forced her to have me as one. I snorted enough coke to kill a bull that night. I'd be irreparably dead if Lance hadn't found me having a heart attack on that club's bathroom floor."

"I'm sorry," I whisper, circling my arms around him.

He inhales deeply, his chest lifting my arm. "Yeah, it's shit. But that's life, I guess."

"What's her name?" I ask, squinting at the CD case with only a band name visible.

He's quiet for a long beat before he whispers, "Jade."

"I have a daughter too," I murmur, the thought of her sending a sharp pain through my chest. "Aeliana. She's at the castle."

Ziggy stares at me in the mirror and his eyes widen. "A *daughter?*"

I nod. "Patricia's vision wasn't completely wrong."

"Fuck," he whispers. "Denendrius's, then?"

I shrug. "Viorel has taken her as his own. We're raising her together."

He wraps his arm around me and squeezes me close. "I guess it'd be selfish of me to keep you then."

I gasp and flinch away in surprise as Ziggy's ringtone blares.

He curses an apology under his breath as he retrieves the phone from his pocket.

"Viorel?" I cry as the line connects.

"It's so nice to hear you, Marianna," Viorel says, the cadence of his voice filling me with warmth. There's distance in the audio like he's on speaker and Mateo or another guard is holding it close for him to speak.

Tears flood my eyes, relief and the frantic need to be with him ripping through me. I want him to tell me his men are outside, that I'm moments away from Mateo putting me in a van to bring me home.

"Is Aeliana okay?" I choke out, still not fully convinced Viorel's visit wasn't a hallucination.

"Of course," Viorel says softly. "Listen . . ."

I hold my breath, leaning closer to the phone as I strain to hear any sign of Aeliana past Viorel's rousing words.

Her soft coos widen my eyes, and I'm weak with relief. *I miss her.*

"She misses you," Viorel says. "She thinks about you all day, but she'll have you back soon."

I let myself fall back, palms planting on the blanket to keep my weak body upright. "And Laurentius?"

"Laurentius is all right." The lie is sharp in the forced softness of Viorel's tone.

"What happened to Laurentius?" I bite down on my bottom lip, eyes locked on the animated icon of a cell phone on Ziggy's screen.

"I'm keeping him downstairs with me. It was that or the ward, but I can't bear to leave him alone in there. Laurentius is sick and mad with grief, Marianna," Viorel explains with a sigh. "He barricaded himself in his room after you were taken. He wouldn't feed, and the others heard him talking to himself day and night. Last time Mateo forced himself in, Laurentius had cut himself open again and was writing on the floor with his blood and pleading with something in the corner. With me, he at least obeys my orders to feed."

"Can I talk to him?" Desperation clings to my plea.

"He's sleeping now, for the first time in a week. It's best to let him rest. He's hardly coherent, so it's unwise until he can see you standing before him."

My chest aches, a cracked chasm in my center full of heartache and the desperate need to run down the castle hall and hold him. "Tell him I love him."

"I will," Viorel assures me.

He sounds like he's going to continue before I ask, "What about Carol and Derek? Did they make it?"

The pause has pressure building in my head and tears brimming in my eyes.

"Derek is alive," Viorel begins, tone restrained. "He's keeping Carol company in the ward until she's ready to return upstairs. She was attacked during the chaos of that night, and Derek turned her. She's fraught with worry for you and having a difficult time processing both her new existence and the trauma."

Tears streak my cheeks. I'm unsure what to say.

"Fuck," Ziggy hisses, exhaling loudly as he tips his head back to stare at the ceiling.

I want to tell Viorel all the ways Denendrius has hurt me, give him the reality to go with the horrific feeling he's likely been suffering with through his mark on me. I want him to hold me close and tell me Denendrius will never hurt me again. How he'll kill him.

"I want to come home," I cry, the words rushing out like I only have moments before Denendrius appears. The phone is a blurry black blob beyond my tears. I pull in a throaty breath, my arms shaking as I use them to keep me sitting. "Please have someone get me."

"There have been some issues since Denendrius escaped,"

Viorel says carefully. "I cannot simply send whomever to retrieve you, Marianna. Ziggy, you must keep her safe for me in the meantime. I'm sending Mateo with trusted men directly from the castle. They should arrive within two days."

"*Two days?*" I squeak. "What if Denendrius comes back by then? He sent coordinates to Ziggy and Lance to find me, so he'll know I'm here at Estrella de Sangre."

"He's not currently the sole risk, darling. Denendrius has essentially started a clan war. Men I thought I could trust have turned their backs on me in favor of powerful clans offering allegiances. There is no sum of money grand enough I can offer to some, and it's much easier to buy favors with the promise of resolved grudges."

"What are you saying?" I press. "People are turning on you?"

"When Denendrius was creating chaos looking for the cure, many clans he eliminated or clan leaders he kidnapped and murdered have clans or allegiances that persist today, with new leaders who knew those fallen. Under any other circumstance, they'd do as I wish, but they want Denendrius for themselves and do not care what my wishes are. I have moles in certain large clans, and some have feigned cooperation with my men, only for them to speak of using you to lure Denendrius. I cannot risk sending you with those who've sworn themselves to me, only to discover I've placed my trust in the wrong hands."

My lids fall closed, my flicker of hope snuffed out.

"Your brush with Nira alone has exposed the depth of this issue," Viorel adds.

My eyes snap open. A stroke of dread writhes in my gut, my thoughts spinning around the worst possibilities.

Thankfully, Viorel continues, saying, "Nira called the hotline immediately after Denendrius left with you, and laid the issue bare once transferred to my men. She admitted her vampire child crime but was desperate for help beyond such issues." He sighs. "Nira feared death should she return after negotiating with Denendrius. Her clan wanted Denendrius dead for the very issues surrounding this clan war, and she states they were already resistant to the idea of her involving me. I had men escort her back to her clan . . . and her fears were not illogical. They attempted to attack her and my men and had to be eliminated."

My quiet gasp echoes through the phone.

"But the team secured Madelaine, Nira, and Lacy, and they are at the castle now. I've walked through Nira's thoughts, and she is no threat, merely desperate. She knew relaying information about her interaction with you was vital, even if it endangered her. Regardless, I can't imagine her and her clan would have successfully neutralized Denendrius. Sebastian Selias was a known, morally compromised bounty hunter who has refused to cooperate with my men in the past, despite his desire to kill Denendrius, so no qualms with that turn of events, either."

"Even though she created a vampire child? I thought for sure her trying to use my safety for leverage would enrage you." I bite my cheek.

Viorel sighs. "Hearing her thoughts . . . *plea* is a more defining word than leverage. She was fully aware it could lead to her death, but the risk was worth it to her, as she assumed I would still grant Madelaine safety. With this current climate, and the castle's needs, there is a greater benefit to keeping her family here than strictly upholding the promise of death for such actions."

His careful wording spikes my anxiety. "The castle's needs?" I echo, thinking of the carnage I witnessed during Denendrius's escape.

There's a beat of loaded silence before Viorel, voice tinged with despair, says, "We lost many of the vampire children and their caregivers. Ainsley is overwhelmed with the traumatized survivors, and many of the vampires in general population are ill-equipped—intellectually and now emotionally—to help. Nira and her familiar fill a much-needed gap and benefit the castle's ecosystem far more than strict punishment for her crime ever would. Plus, Madelaine is a fresh, happy face helping the children recover."

Knowing Ainsley survived, and that Nira's family is safe, helps balance the grief of the castle's destruction. It's one less weight pressing on my chest.

"To my original point . . . Ziggy is your friend, so I am more comfortable trusting him with your safety."

"But he's a Child of Stars . . ." I frown at Ziggy. "No offense, but objectively, you're just not as strong as a Darkling."

He heaves out a breath. "Yes, well, there's many of us here."

My heart pounds in my ears, the room spinning. "Maybe we should hide somewhere else from Denendrius."

Viorel says, "I've instructed Ziggy to remain put. You're safer there, despite Denendrius knowing your location. I heard some hours ago a German clan captured him, and there are tense negotiations occurring that should give my men enough time to retrieve you."

There's so much hopelessness coating my body that it deflects any semblance of ambition for my rescue.

"Thank you again, Ziggy," Viorel says softly. "I understand the risk to your clan with her there, but it means much to me that you will defend her with your life."

Ziggy merely nods and looks off toward the wall, and I wonder what past conversations they've had while I was unconscious. "What else am I supposed to do, anyway? I can't let her die, and I won't give her back to him."

I mouth my apologies to Ziggy as he turns his teary eyes to mine. He mouths that it's not my fault and brushes tears from my cheeks.

My heart leaps when a low battery warning flashes across

Ziggy's screen. Panic tightens like a collar around my throat as my tired eyes dart around the room for a cord. Ziggy scrambles off the bed and quickly scans the mess, apologizing to Viorel that the line might die. He dashes out of the room, grumbling that one of the familiars must have taken or moved the cord again.

"I love you, Viorel," I tell him, furiously brushing tears from my cheeks.

Ziggy yells in the hall, the urgency of his tone making my heart drum like the dying phone equals catastrophe. *"Who has a fucking phone cord? Somebody fix the bloody signal receiver thing, please! The duct tape is peeling off the wall again, and phone calls are quite important right now!"*

"I love you too, Marianna. For eternity."

I clench the phone in my weak hand, as if I can hold his voice inside it just a moment longer. "For eternity."

The phone chirps again, and the low battery warning flashes.

"Lance and I have been giving her our blood," Ziggy blurts as he rushes in, like it's a crime he has to confess before his thoughts of punishment spiral out of control.

Phone cord in hand, he drops to his hands and knees, straightening the long extension cord snaking out from beneath the bed. He plugs in the dirty white cord—kinked, brittle, and looking like it was barely saved from a puddle of dried blood.

Viorel chuckles. "I know. I can feel it. Perhaps I should be as upset as you believe I would be, but I am merely thankful you're doing all in your power to keep her alive. If that's what it takes, so be it." He pauses. "Though I will have your head should you drink from her."

"I wouldn't dare," Ziggy mutters, lips twisted in a grimace as he jams the cord into the phone.

Nothing. The screen dims. No sign of charging.

Ziggy hisses through his teeth and rips the cord free. He inspects the end, sees the dried blood, then growls in frustration before whipping it across the room. It hits the wall with a dull thud and drops behind the disorganized stacks of CDs.

"God damn it. Sorry," he mumbles.

He collapses beside me just as Viorel says, "I hope you'll give me the honor of meeting you and your husband one day. And know you always have a home here."

The tickled smile in Viorel's voice is almost enough to bring my own, but it's not enough to stop me from feeling lost at sea. I drape my arm over Ziggy and hold on to him like he's my life raft.

"Of course. Thank you," he says as he wraps his arm around me and rests his head against the side of mine. The feeling of one of Ziggy's cold tears landing on my cheekbone has me flinching.

The phone beeps in warning again. The screen goes black.

Viorel must be able to hear it through the line, because he says, "I'll see you soon, darling."

I squeeze my eyes shut, wanting so badly to believe it but terrified of giving myself permission to. "I'll see you soon—"

The phone's powering-off tune plays.

I sob into Ziggy's T-shirt.

"Fuck's sake," Ziggy mutters. "I've been meaning to charge it."

Wiping the back of my eyes, I know I would have fought to keep the line connected until it died anyway, even if that meant hours.

I can't help the feeling that this was the last time I'll ever hear Viorel's voice again.

XXXIV

"Ziggy, I need you to commit a murder," a girl with black hair, purple streaks, and half a dozen facial piercings hollers as she flies into the room with Lance behind her, who holds a plastic shopping bag.

"I'm always open to murder, Stacey," Ziggy says breezily from beside me on the bed. "Who?"

"Nate," she snarls as she scrambles onto the end of the bed and plunks down at our feet.

"He cheated on her," Lance divulges as he travels toward me, his eyes no longer blistering red, but a warm blue now. He pauses as he passes Lance to press a deep kiss to his lips.

"He cheated on me," she echoes with a snarl.

Ziggy lifts a finger in the air. "I understand the reason, but I don't believe it's actually moral to kill someone for cheating—"

Stacey slaps his leg with such force that it would have sent a human reeling in pain. There's no sign he even felt her hand connect.

"But!" he interjects, straightening with a grin. "He can take a mysterious plunge down some stairs where he happens to break every bone in his body."

She gives him a wicked grin. "Do it."

"Tell him when you found out," Lance says as he joins us on the bed while rolling up his sleeves and crossing his legs beside me. He bites into his wrist, and I take his offering without complaint, the conversation holding my attention as I lap his calming blood up. It's like it's full of Xanax.

"Literally five fucking minutes before I walked into my midterm," she seethes. "I got tagged in a video of him making out with blond-haired Becky."

Ziggy hisses through bared teeth. "Fuck, how do you think you did on your exam after that?"

Her eyes glisten, and she swallows hard. "I don't know. Probably failed. I was trying not to cry the whole time or throw my desk across the room."

"If your parents pull your funding, I'll pay for it myself, okay?" Ziggy consoles. "You can retake the class. It's just money, not worth the stress."

She shakes her head. "You guys already pay for my text-books, my cell phone bill, and car payment. Never mind all the little things here and there. You just paid off my credit card—"

"It's fine," Lance says as he takes his wrist back from me and roots around in the shopping bag. "It's just money. We'll get more."

He pulls out two pre-made salads in plastic containers and sets one in front of her and me. My pinched lips tilt as I look it over, my appetite nonexistent. I'm not going to get away with denying food though, as Lance pops open the plastic container and mixes up my salad with the dressing and croutons before piercing leaves with the plastic fork and holding it in front of my mouth.

I take a bite and nearly expect my hunger to leap forward and command I fill myself, but it doesn't. Perhaps it's the fact

I've been consuming nothing but blood for the past few days, but the leaves taste strangely on my tongue and the crunch between my teeth has my stomach lurching. Still, I swallow the mouthful.

Stacey gently motions toward me. "Okay, but now there's another one of us to take care of? That's not fair for me to ask for more. Emry's taking summer classes, and he needs your help more than I do. You guys are taking risks every time you steal. I may as well just drop out and turn, so it's less strain on you."

"No, you won't," Lance says with a fatherly firmness. "She's only going to be with us for the next day or so, and it'd be a bigger waste to drop out when you're halfway through."

She hangs her head and heaves out a breath. "Fine."

"I'll eat Nate for you," Ziggy promises.

She gives him a sweet smile. "Thanks, Ziggy."

Ziggy asks me how I'm feeling once I've forced down half the salad, and I'm unsure what to tell him. I manage to keep it down, but with how long my stomach has been empty, it feels like rocks settling on the bottom of a lake of blood.

Lance wanders off to the club to hang out with a couple other of their familiars, and Stacey hangs around with us. A faint ache stretches my stomach, like it no longer recognizes food, and I wonder how much it shrunk from starving. My vague nausea has me still on the bed, as I fear any sudden movement will triple it and have me reeling with the need to puke. I'm not sure I'm strong enough to dart to the bathroom in time. I don't want Ziggy to have to clean me up *again*.

Lance returns to give me more blood while Ziggy tends to some club guests, and I remain tucked into bed most of the night with a cloud of weed surrounding us as I share a joint with Stacey.

Realizing I don't know much about Lance, I fish for a bit of info so I can think of a life other than my own. Lance claims there's not much interesting to know about him, but Stacey asks him what he means because his transformation story is *so sad*.

"Oh," I whisper, the taste of his blood still heavy on my tongue. "That's okay, you don't have to tell then."

"It's fine." He shrugs, his even, chronically calm face betraying no sign of haunting ghosts.

Lance's soft voice tucks me into 1979. He was twenty-three, alone at a London punk show after his friends bailed. He didn't mind not knowing anyone else there when he had some weed, good music, and a friendly atmosphere. But a boy in the far back corner—seventeen, he'd learn—did seem to mind his own invisibility in the crowd and kept looking at the makeshift bar like he was too nervous to ask for a drink despite appearing to long for one.

So Lance walked over and introduced himself, and though Wilder wouldn't—*couldn't*—drink, it was conversation he longed for more than anything. They talked, Wilder telling Lance his older brother died in the hospital last week, that he's new to the city and his brother was all he had. Lance and Wilder talked about music between loud songs. How Wilder loved so many of the same bands Lance did, and how Lance was working backstage gigs for bands at night and writing his own music by day, hoping for an opportunity for him and his guitar.

When the show ended, they swapped numbers and went their separate ways in the dark. Lance back home, to his loft room in his older punk friend's garage where he could smoke as much weed as he wanted and record softy lyrics and guitar, and Wilder . . . he wasn't really sure. But he called Lance the following evening and told him he had an extra ticket for Joy Division the next night. Wilder was so excited when Lance agreed, he promised to pick him up himself.

Lance stayed awake late that night, inspiration flowing

through his fingers to his guitar strings. He was up so late that he wrote the day off, smoked a big bowl, and crashed with the radio playing through his headphones.

And while he slept through the day—from the pieces he put together later, at least—his friend, living in the main house, drank himself into a stupor after his girlfriend broke up with him that morning, then decided during the late afternoon that he was going to drive to her house to plead.

His friend went to the garage, crawled behind the wheel with a bottle of liquor, and turned the car on. He passed out at the wheel with the garage door shut behind him, Lance fast asleep and unaware in the open loft right above the car.

Lance was already dead when he woke. His would-be ride to Joy Division was crouched in the loft with him, sobbing and apologizing, fanged teeth bared, and crimson eyes flooded with panic. Lance was too calm to feel horror, to feel terror or anxiety over how he was tied with belts and ropes to the loft's rail like he was some monster who needed to be preventatively restrained. Which, technically, *he was.*

Wilder explained he didn't know what else to do. He was surprised he even successfully turned Lance because he'd never met another vampire before. His brother, human, took care of him for years in secret, and had once restrained Wilder too when he found him unconscious after returning to the family cabin from canoeing at midnight. Wilder appeared suspiciously less dead than his massacred parents and sister, and his desperate denial had him clinging to horror comic book ideas about rising dead.

"The poor kid needed me," Lance admits. "Even when Wilder stopped calming me, I could *feel* how wrecked he was. Even if he hadn't passed his ability on to me, his grief was palpable. His brother was all he had. He helped Wilder hide. I was disoriented about what I was, but aside from the growing pains of being a newborn, I was more focused on getting myself situated so I could help this kid rather than focus on the fact my life was gone."

"That's really sweet," I tell him, my aches mentally dulled with new images for my mind to turn over.

He chuckles, his soft eyes holding mine. "I was relieved, to be honest. If he hadn't come to pick me up, heard the car running in the garage, and smelled the fumes, I would have died in my sleep anyway."

Stacey giggles. "And?" she says, like she's prodding him for more honesty.

Lance smirks and teasingly scowls at her. "*And* turns out I *fucking sucked* at guitar as a human. I was literally tone deaf and didn't know it. But with vampire hearing?" He lifts his hands and signs perfection with his fingers. "He saved me from the death of embarrassment I would've faced sharing my work. Now I can actually play without sounding like shit."

I can't help but giggle along with Stacey until my sore body has me cringing in pain and sparking tears in my eyes.

My weak body holds me to the bed, but as my stomach digests the salad, it gives me a tiny surge of energy that has me wanting to walk across the room to escape the confines of the bed despite knowing my muscles won't be able to handle it.

Regardless, after another round of ointment on my wounds, that's Ziggy's next plan. He pulls me out of bed onto my fawn legs and forces me to walk back and forth across the room with his assistance. I can't straighten my legs enough to fully stand, but with his hand around my biceps holding me up, I manage a handful of laps until my heart is spasming in my chest and my muscles are begging me to lie down.

I manage to finish the other half of my salad, scarfing it down with a sudden ravenous hunger that has tears welling in my eyes with the memory of how deeply it gripped me in the cage. Ziggy takes my fork from me to force incremental bites so I don't end up puking everything up. I take sips of cold water between the bites, fighting the urge to chug the bottle back with the glorious taste of it splashing over my tongue. I swear my mouth is still dry no matter how much I drink, and ask for Lance's blood—since Ziggy is tapped out still—to relieve it. With the fresh vampire blood flowing through me, I can feel my body strengthening bit by bit, and I wish I could IV drip it into my veins to keep the supply steady.

Ziggy hangs out in the club for a bit to feed before the night ends, and Lance tucks me into bed beside him, with Stacey on his other side. Emry returns and crashes on the couch, and the bed lowers with another body midway through the day as the scent of cigarettes and shea butter settles on the other side of Ziggy. I can't help my sleepy smile, especially when Lance and Ziggy's arms overlap me so they can hold one another too. The room feels so safe and warm with so much love in it.

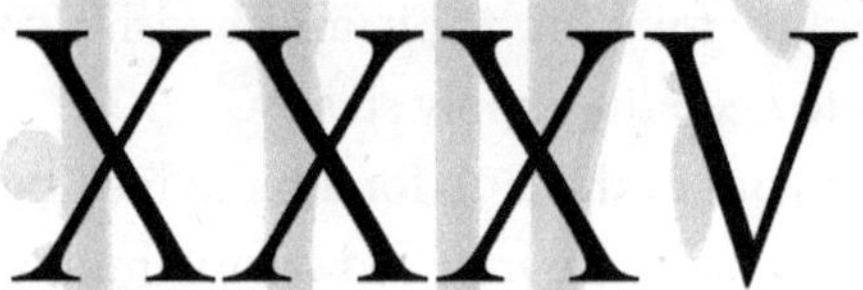

XXXV

The scent of the newest arrival wafts closer to me, her hot hand flopping against my arm as she hooks it over Ziggy's body. She brushes her hand back and forth along my forearm like she can tell from touch that I'm unfamiliar, her pointy nails summoning goosebumps as they gently glide along my bruised flesh. Her head pops up through the dim light leaking beneath the bedroom door, and she squints sleepily at me before offering a soft, welcoming smile before flopping back down next to Ziggy.

I wonder where their fourth familiar is, and if they will be as willing to have me taking from their vampires as these have been.

When I wake, it's just the unfamiliar girl remaining in bed with me. She lies on her side facing me, her body so comfortably close to mine it's like we're sisters. Her phone screen illuminates her pale face and silver piercings, a bit of mascara and eyeliner smudged around her eyes like it didn't completely wash off. She lifts her brown eyes to mine and tucks her bleach blond hair behind her ear as she smiles.

Her good evening is low, like she's worried about being too loud near me.

"Hey—" I cough against my dry throat, and she drops her phone and spins over to grab a plastic bottle of water off the nightstand. I notice the tiny smudge of black lipstick on the mouth, but don't care enough for it to stop me from chugging the remaining half of the bottle down like it's all that's left in the world. I gasp for breath and wet my lips. "Who are you?"

She chuckles and takes the empty bottle from me, setting it on the nightstand. "Maxine."

"Marianna."

Maxine's smile deepens. "I know." She glances toward the door. "Lance and Ziggy are somewhere around the club or clan rooms. Want me to find one of them?"

I shake my head against the pillow. "It's fine. Let them have a break from me."

A bit of sour guilt pools in my stomach knowing I've been sleeping between them, when they'd probably rather cuddle up against one another instead.

She playfully frowns and pushes out her bottom lip. "Don't feel like a burden. They like taking care of us. We all take care of each other."

"Still," I argue.

Lifting her thin hand, she combs her fingers through the hair at my temple and smiles. "I could help you tonight. It's my day off work."

My bladder nudges me for attention, and my limbs are so heavy I struggle to convince them to cooperate so I can lift myself off the mattress. With a sigh, I say, "Can you help me sit up?"

She happily obliges, and I get my feet under me on the cold concrete floor and use the nightstand and dresser for support as I make my way to the bathroom. I flick the dim light on, and Maxine closes the door for me. The sight of the graffitied tile shower across from me makes my heart flutter. It somehow looks so clean and dingy at the same time. The memory of it in my disorientation has my throat drying.

I immediately reach for the vanity countertop, which shifts under my weight like it's not fully attached to the wall. Self-care and beauty products rattle and roll on the countertop and onto the floor, and I heave out an exasperated breath, knowing I don't have the coordination to pick anything up.

"Just leave it," Maxine calls out. "This pigsty will get cleaned tomorrow on cleaning day. Sorry, it gets messy with six people here all the time."

I don't have the breath to respond, so I work my way to the toilet, which is somehow the cleanest thing in the bathroom. When I lower my boxers and sit on the cold seat, the pain from the pressure sores has me gasping for air and gripping the countertop with both hands.

The room rocks back and forth in what little of my vision remains. My groin burns when I pee, and the pain nearly disconnects me from consciousness as the room darkens. I manage to wrangle some air back, my breaths heavy and shallow as I force myself to stay awake.

With my bladder empty, the thought of having toilet paper touch my flesh has anxiety pulsing through me. I stare wide eyed and half-detached at the shower, the idea of relief from a warm stream on my aching body giving me the bit of perseverance I need to clumsily maneuver to my hands and knees and crawl into the shower a couple feet away.

I strip, leaning against the hard tile wall with the taps locked in my pin-point vision above my head. It takes all my strength to lift my arm to the closest tap, and the spurt of water from the shower head jolts me. Snagging the edge of the shower curtain between my toes, I close it halfway.

Shivers ripple through me as the water pelts my sore flesh. The smell of damp dirt and cold air moves in and out of me with my thin breaths. I have the passing thought I need to reach the hot water tap, but it's fleeting, and all I can do is think about how hard the tile is against my back and butt, and how badly I want to lie down and stretch out.

Somehow, I make it to my side, curled up since I can't fully extend my body in the small metal space. The early spring air has me shaking against the hard and smooth flat surface I lie on. It's pitch black again, and sweat sticks my greasy hair to my cheek, my hands too stiff and weak to push it away. I wish I had enough strength to pull my sherpa blanket over me.

Whispers circle me in the dark, and I ache to fall asleep, to escape everything for a little while. The cold, the exhaustion, the cage, the endless hunger and thirst . . .

"It's okay to let go and sleep," Marissa whispers.

A groan rolls out of me, and my eyes flit around the dark until they land on her sitting on the mattress in the dim light. Thick bars obscure my sight of her.

My chest aches with emotion, and I want to ask her to reach in and hold my hand. Instead, she vanishes with the jingle of keys, and I look up.

Denendrius squats at the cage door, a storm of apologies and explanations warbling in my ears as he pulls my stiff body from the cage. I'm too numb to feel anything about his return as he sets me in his lap and holds me tight. He presses his bloody wrist to my lips, but the flavor is wrong, and calm pulses through me.

My eyes flutter open.

Maxine's concerned face fills my vision as we sit on the bed, and in an instant, I fit the pieces of what happened together as my lips part from Ziggy's flesh. He holds me in a towel on his lap, his soothing voice filling my ears as I relax my weight into his body.

"I'm sorry," I whisper.

"There's nothing to be sorry for, love." He squeezes me tighter, the comfort of the pressure pushing tears from my eyes.

"I thought I was back in the cage," I explain.

"You're safe now," he assures me. "No matter what your mind tries to convince you."

The cage haunts my dreams, Marissa's voice vivid in the depths of my sleep. I wake through the day for blood to help scrub the lingering effects of it away. I feel a little stronger each time I drink from Lance and Ziggy. Physically, at least.

But when I wake again with them both gone, I can't bear to be alone in the dark of their room where my mind could so easily slip. I ache for a remedy, and with the weed used up—a familiar promising to bring back more later—spirits call me from the club bar. I crave the warm burn of alcohol to drown the emotions their blood can't wash away.

Despite being slow and unsteady, I manage to walk upright on my own. I drag myself from the room and down the hall of bedrooms, past a living room cluttered with mismatched couches, abandoned sweaters, scattered shoes, empty sodas and booze, and a pool of dried blood beside a flat-screen TV propped on top of an analog set with a cracked screen. I pass a makeshift kitchen and stumble toward the chest-thumping beat of drums spilling from the club beyond a heavy metal door that I only crack open wide enough to slip through. My head aches with the loud music when I enter the club, and the small smear of people moving around so swiftly is disorienting.

I keep an eye out for Lance or Ziggy and am thankful when I don't immediately spot them trying to intercept me. The ache in my body has me considering turning around a few times, but it would be a waste of effort to crawl back into bed. Besides, I'd rather be surrounded by strangers than alone with my thoughts.

I approach the bar, my gaze avoiding my reflection in the massive mirrors behind the shelves of booze, and fill the first clean glass that enters my sight—a wineglass—to the brim with straight whiskey.

As I wait for another surge of energy to move from the bar, I focus on the club guests around me. Handfuls of vampires and humans laugh and talk at tables, a handful more either standing around in the small open space to talk or move along to the music.

At the closest table, a bright human girl with blood-filled cheeks giggles as a paler man with maroon eyes and spikes in his lobes runs the back of his hand along her bare arm. I only overhear enough to know it's her first time here—the vampire fang tattoo on her wrist had immortal strangers curious on the subway—and that she's just met the vampires who've brought her.

She struggles to sit still in her chair, continuously looking at the maroon-eyed man like she wants to crawl into his lap until he asks her if she fantasizes about sex with vampires. The red of her cheeks only deepens as she timidly nods. Though when he proposes a trade—she can have her fantasy if he can drink from her—she's the first out of her chair with a subdued smile.

I can't help my intrusive gaze as I watch them stand and move across the club together. They pass the velvet sofa, where human Denendrius and I once sat and socialized with Ziggy, and slip into a room that—at a glance—appears furnished for such an exchange.

Remembering myself, I test a breath and step away from the bar with my whiskey, to a small but empty table in the back corner of the room.

I carefully lower myself with a heavy exhale onto the worn black upholstery of the metal chair and take a long swig. An artificial warmth burns down my throat and pools on the ice of my interior.

Staring at the gold liquid in my cup, I regret not sitting down with the entire bottle. I regret not having a different, more soothing gold to inject into this wasteland of a person I've become.

But most of all, I regret leaving Ziggy and Lance's bed when the chair across from me draws back and a man in his mid-twenties with curly black hair and piercing blue eyes sits down.

"You must belong to the king," he says, his smooth voice—fuck if I know or care where his accent is from—sounding both so friendly and untrustworthy.

"You must have mistaken me for someone who wants to have a conversation," I say limply as I lift the glass back to my lips for another long and burning gulp.

He smiles crookedly, a soft twinkle in his eye. "You must be. I've never smelled a mark like yours in my eternity . . . and your face is international news, Marianna."

"Are you just here to suck up my air, or do you have something to say? You're in my breathing space."

He chuckles and leans back in the chair, crossing his legs and wrinkling the black dress pants he wears. "You don't find it much easier to breathe now that you're out of the castle?"

I clutch the bowl of the wineglass in my hand. "Why would it be?"

He cocks a brow. "The king is a tyrant, you know? I understand Denendrius is no walk in the park, but I can't imagine being Viorel's pet would be any easier."

The thought of smashing my glass across his face flits through my mind, but I merely clench it tighter. I don't have the strength to effectively break it since the cage melted my muscles away.

"I wouldn't say he's a tyrant." I hope he catches the double meaning in my words. The warning, and the disagreement.

He purses his lips as he tilts his head to study me. "No? I mean, he *did* cleanse the castle, I heard. Nobody knows why most of those vampires were impaled and burned."

I glower in disdain. "They were upset about discovering Viorel was Huarsar, and didn't think me and my child deserved to live. They wanted to hurt Viorel and me. *Dethrone* him. Everyone who was executed was a betrayer."

"Yeah, I was around when Huarsar ruled . . . and I didn't like him either. It was better after we all thought he died. When there was no worldwide vampire warlord breathing down our necks." He chuckles, his blue eyes locking with mine in challenge. "How do you know they were *all* betrayers? Because *I know* who some of those people were, and their deaths are incomprehensible."

"A few of them were *actively* trying to breach the door and kill Viorel and me," I spit. "They stabbed a guard and clan members had to subdue Mitchell while other betrayers ran."

"Hmm. And what of the other fifty? What did they do?" He lifts his hand in a fake apology as I lean forward and glare daggers at him. "Sorry. What did they *think*, since most of them didn't *do* anything?"

I lean back and swallow. "Some of them *did* try to attack when we were all in the grand room. As for the rest, he never said, but something in their thoughts damned them."

"Like what?" he presses, saying the words like he's got me in some sort of checkmate.

I think about how Viorel ordered a clan member and his familiar to be killed after they went on vacation—for *thinking* he was a dolt, opposing my pregnancy, and disagreeing with his decision to let me live. A little twinge pricks me.

"It was in their thoughts," I reiterate. I hate how the uncertainty sneaks into my voice with the words. "Either way, they had plenty of time to leave the castle before it came to that. A good dozen left when his identity as Huarsar was uncovered. So yeah, their thoughts must have been impossible to ignore."

I tell myself it must have been enough to make them dangerous—especially if Adelia, who would have been in that room under scrutiny too, had thoughts Viorel judged loyal enough at the time for her to survive . . . but still later betray him.

He mashes his lips together and the corners tilt, a bit of sorrow clouding the blue of his gaze. "Yeah, well, I might have some unkind thoughts too if me and my thralls were made to stand packed in a room in silence beneath his heavy scrutiny for hours upon hours."

My lips twist against one another, and the discomfort of his words has my grip loosening on my glass. I don't miss his use of *thrall* either, that he's likely trying to distance himself from the implications of *blood slave* and *familiar* terminology, but I don't know what to do with that. I turn my head to stare across the club, my gaze unfocused on the crowd of vampires and humans entwined with the thumping music and their conversations.

I'm unsure what to say to him, and I don't mean to do it, but I think of how Denendrius was put in that cell in Sirmium to suffer for eternity, and how a contributing factor for that decision was Viorel hearing in Denendrius's thoughts how he wished he had killed his maker and taken his wife. A fleeting, desperate regret he *claims* he hardly considered despite Viorel believing it showed his character.

"Want to know what I think happened?" he whispers.

My heavy breaths whoosh in and out of me.

"I think he rounded everyone up in that room—made them stand shoulder to shoulder, packed into the room like cattle—and executed anyone who had even a morsel of aloofness about him. I believe most of the people he murdered were genuine followers, and he was testing how far he could push people before they disagreed with his antics. He held every single clan member hostage in that room and had guards blocking them from leaving. He created a self-fulfilling prophecy. Make over a thousand people stand in silence for hours with no known end. Don't give their human companions food, water, rest, or bathroom breaks, and of course, you're going to get a handful who are brave enough to disagree with the mistreatment. Kill everyone who complains —who even thinks that you're being a little unfair—and the rest will be a lot less inclined to complain in the future. Nobody wants to go through that ordeal once . . . and certainly not twice."

"You weren't there," I growl.

"My friend was. She saw nothing wrong with what happened either but told me all about it when she came to visit." There's pain in his pause. "I don't know if she survived . . . *what just happened there* . . . From what I hear, the castle is still locked down. None of the survivors are allowed to leave." He sighs, then laughs again. "But at least he didn't abandon them all *this time*, so perhaps his previous clan really was corrupted."

"Viorel has more life experience than every damned vampire in this club put together. Trust he had his reasons," I snap. "You don't know what those vampires were thinking. Maybe he had something worth risking his life for this time."

"He's still a tyrant," the man corrects gently. "And you're right. I don't know, but neither do you. He didn't disclose the exact reason for most of the executions . . . and nobody, not even his guards, would dare ask him."

I'm a tornado of half-coherent thoughts and feelings as I stare at him.

He sighs in dramatic defeat. "Ah, who am I kidding? I can't reason with Viorel's blood slave."

The whiskey has me too numbed to react as Ziggy appears and yanks the man from his seat by his jacket collar. "What the fuck did you say?"

The man smirks. "Was it the blood slave, or tyrant accusation?"

"You don't come in *my* fucking club and start spewing shit about the king," Ziggy snarls, his fistfuls of fabric shaking.

He's unbothered by Ziggy's grip on him. "Why? Worried your clan will be wiped off the map?"

My brow furrows at him, Ziggy's lack of immediate response making my eyes narrow. "What do you mean?"

He laughs in Ziggy's grip, casting him a smug glance before saying to me, "I'm sure your friend Ziggy here could recount years of yapping from his guests. *He knows what I'm talking about.* How sometimes entire clans vanish without a trace. Usually, they're vocal about their distaste for your master, or want to rule over this world themselves. I think Viorel fears a little healthy competition—"

Ziggy shoves him backward, flinging curses at him as he demands he leave and never return. A few other vampires help physically banish him. Then Ziggy returns to confiscate my booze and lecture me on drinking in my condition before he whisks me back to the bedroom.

I've devolved into tears by the time I fall into a heap on the end of his bed. "Ziggy, what if he's not completely wrong? What if *I am* a blood slave? What if Viorel is acting like a tyrant and I can't see it? What if I just don't want to see it because I need him to be my hero? Because I need somebody to go back to? A worthwhile life to fight for?"

Ziggy drops to his knee in front of me, his hands desperately scooping mine up as he fights to meet my watery eyes. "Marianna," he starts firmly, "you *are not* Viorel's blood slave. Blood slaves do not get upset over the idea of being their vampire's blood slave. They don't get scared they might be seeing them wrong. Do you understand?"

I sniffle and nod, tears running down my cheeks.

"Don't let that wanker get in your head. He wasn't there at

the castle when shit went down, but *you were*. You *are not* a blood slave. Trust your perception. You know Viorel better than *anyone else in the world.*"

My lip trembles. "But it's true what he did. That guy made it sound so much worse, but it happened. And Viorel didn't tell anyone what those vampires were thinking. I was happy when he did it, felt like he was protecting us, but what if I was misguided? What if he went too far?"

Ziggy's expression levels. "How many people were stuffed in that room?"

"Over a thousand vampires. I don't know how many humans."

He quirks a brow. "And how many did he execute?"

"Like fifty-four, and some of them genuinely tried to attack."

Sighing, he says, "That's not an impressive number, considering. That's barely a fraction of the vampires there. If he was on some massive cleanse for thought-crimes, there would have been *hundreds* executed."

Swallowing, I whisper, "The instigator, Mitchell, thought Viorel deserved to be dethroned for hiding the fact he was Huarsar. I know you only know vampire rule under Viorel, but what have you heard over the years? Are others on this side of the veil upset?"

"Yeah, I know a bit about Huarsar. He ruled for"—he blows out a noisy breath—"different lengths of time, depending on who you ask. But I don't think any living vampires remember a ruler before him, though there must have been one before he was made and took power. I haven't heard any other names, at least." Ziggy sighs. "Most people are understanding, from what I know. Huarsar falling shook the vampire world at the end of the fourth century. People were secure for thousands of years under his rule. Some still remember when Rome was becoming a hot spot for immortals as it expanded, and how he strategically moved there to keep brewing chaos under control.

People were comforted. So, when Denendrius tore the fucking place up and Huarsar couldn't even save his own fucking familiar from him?"

He shakes his head. "If Denendrius could split apart a power that had been unshaken for as long as they remembered, what did that mean? And then, when the opportunists took advantage after Denendrius's escape—thinking Huarsar was weak now—and tore the rest of it down? Shaken."

I bite my bottom lip, my mind reeling with new context for the bits of information I've been surviving off for months. Viorel's past as Huarsar is something I never brought up with him, despite my curiosity. I know it's one of his most painful wounds, and I didn't want to stick my fingers in there just to satisfy myself.

He continues, saying, "There was unrest. The oldest living vampire was presumed dead, and all that was left was a handful of vampire clans with leaders barely a fraction of his age scrapping to be that unifying force. The Argeşti clan—though I guess Denendrius fucking killed them too now—was the closest thing to a new power they had, and they were falling short spectacularly. Because how do you get ancient ass beings who are used to obeying a mythic power to respect what they view as essentially fledging vampires who are attempting to govern in more *modern* ways than they're used to?" He chuckles. "You don't. You get mass disorganization teetering close to world destruction. So the ancient vampires start looking for who amongst them is oldest, most experienced, and *fucking willing* to deal with patching the wound Huarsar's demise left."

I smile a bit through my tears, feeling a tad better with more perspective.

"So, the ancients are coming up short. They're finding old vampires—who mostly tell them to fuck off and leave them to their peace—but nobody even half the age of Huarsar. Until this small band of vampires brings a few of these searchers deep into the depths of the Norwegian fucking mountains to meet their clan leader after hearing their mission on a hunting trip in some cold ass village. He calls himself Viorel and asks them what the current state of the world is. They tell him *all.* They're scared without their dead mythic force from Sirmium. Clans are fucking shit up. Rome has fallen entirely, and nobody can come to a consensus on new laws and ethics. They want someone ancient and wise to clean up the mess and control things for them so they can enjoy their immortality.

"So Viorel shares just enough of his story to excite them, how he's born from a failed eugenics mission, how his maker wanted to rule the world in the very way these vampires fear, and that he was powerful enough to stop him. Huarsar could veil? Well, he can too. In fact, he has *multiple* abilities—unheard of. If they truly need him, he'll come out from where he's been resting for thousands of years, implement the same laws they were used to beneath Huarsar, and get everything back in order. Huarsar kept a clan safe and veiled in a fortress? Well, if that helps, he will too. He told them he'd build a beautiful castle—larger than Sirmium's fortress and *grander*—where the most deserving immortals can reside. All they must do is serve him and convince others to as well." Ziggy gives me a comforting smile. "Rambling aside, yes. Some have had that past pain resurface, some don't even understand what's going on—it's not like we have a government website to keep accurate records and intentions—but most are just happy he came back to take care of them again."

No wonder he set up in Romania then, if that's where he thought he was needed the most, with the unrest surrounding the Argeşti clan. I compare Ziggy's collected information and Denendrius's ramblings after finding out Viorel pinned the Argeşti clan deaths on him, plus everything else I know. If nobody but Denendrius escaped Sirmium with memory of Huarsar's face, I know that means he left all alone, especially if they believed he abandoned them during attack by crazy vampires and died. It means he wouldn't have trusted a single guard from Sirmium to accompany him.

How long did he tuck himself into some hard and snowy place away from the world to grieve? How long before he trusted enough to keep that small band of vampires around him there? If it was just over five-hundred years before he rebuilt in Romania, what are the chances he even planned on rejoining society? Was it only because they *needed* him? It makes perfect sense why he would eliminate the Argeşti clan now.

I walk through the logic of what it would be like to set up in the heart of instability, what the Argeşti clan must have felt— stepped on—to have this power built above them, cast them in shadow, and clean up what he interpreted as their contribution to societal mess. For this ancient to appear out of nowhere and tell the world he's the new king now. It would make sense if the Argeşti clan grew bitter over centuries, and why Viorel would have perceived a looming threat waiting to take advantage, just like in Sirmium.

If I were back home right now, I'd curl up near him and ask all my questions, try to get him to share some of that grief with me.

I steal one of my hands from Ziggy's hold to wipe my eyes. "I haven't heard it all like that. That makes sense, yeah. It's no secret that Viorel can be cruel, though. Should I be as okay with it as I usually have been? He *does* torture people. Horrifi- cally, most times. Orders violent executions and—"

Ziggy takes my hand back and gently squeezes them in reassurance. "Marianna, Viorel *must* be cruel. It's irrelevant if he *wants* to be. He can't apply modern ethics when only some human systems have taken them into consideration for the past handful of decades. Only a tiny number of vampires are modern. He must rule over the sorority girl vampires, as well as vampires from human cultures that practiced cannibalism, human sacrifice, child marriage, and slavery. One of those is far easier to keep in line than the others. He *must be* the most terrifying, cruel force in the vampire world, because that's the only thing keeping some of those fucks from doing the worst out in the open."

I think of that orphan eating vampire Adelia told us about and nod along, desperately wanting him to convince my anxiety away.

"Fear is the only way to keep vampires in line. Fear is universal. A concrete cell isn't uncomfortable for a vampire like it is a human. It's an *inconvenience* when you simply have to outlive your jailer or muster enough strength to bend the bars and escape. Unless your jailer is Viorel, *who's not dying anytime soon*, and you *know* that cell could come paired with unimaginable horror for a potentially infinite amount of time."

I blink tears from my eyes to clear them. "Viorel implied when he was talking about Denendrius that he prefers prisoners over executions because he said that death and thereafter is unpredictable, but that suffering in the dungeon is guaranteed..." I sob hiccups out of me. "Is that wrong? Should I think that's wrong?"

Ziggy frowns. "Love, death is hardly a punishment or deterrent for wankers who have already died once."

I can't help the embarrassed heat in my cheeks or my giggle at the honest absurdity. "Yeah, you're right."

He grins. "Of course I am. I haven't met Viorel personally, but I know this world. You can't rule it with mercy when some of these vampires would take over entire towns, breed humans like cattle, or expose vampires. They're always looking for a weakness they can exploit. Half the clans that spontaneously vanish also happen to be clans who have bounced around the idea that vampires shouldn't have to live in secrecy—that as top predators, we should own the world and do whatever we want with it, as the humans currently do. So of course they don't agree with Viorel, who makes secrecy our primary rule. Sure, we don't have a judicial system, but we have Viorel, who is older than all written fucking history. We know he will do literally whatever it takes to ensure he keeps power instead of someone worse. He scares the shit out of me, but the world would be a nightmare without him."

I nod, thinking of Sovetta's story and how his culture was wiped out by vampires using them as cattle. "I know. I'm just so scared of being like I was when I was Denendrius's blood slave. Fucking insane and delusional."

Rubbing the back of my hand, Ziggy gives them another squeeze and says, "I told you back then when Denendrius's mark was overpowering you, and I would tell you the same now. You're not a blood slave, and you're not becoming one. *I promise.*"

XXXVI

My emotions are a heavy, thick cloak as I curl back up in bed. I barely notice the new guy at the edge of the mattress, black-haired and dressed to match, focused on something in his hand.

I'm lost in my own unsettled thoughts about Viorel and his past until Ziggy's conversation with the human hooks my attention, and I look up to meet Ziggy's haunted eyes as they link with mine.

The last sentence of their muffled exchange settles in my mind, the gravity of the words making my brain recalibrate.

"Bone Decay released a surprise album. I got an extra copy for you, Ziggy."

I find myself taking the second CD case from the blanket beside him and turning it over in my hands like I need to be sure it's real. The paradoxical nature of Patricia's vision last year —that she saw me holding an unopened copy of Bone Decay's newest album while lying in Ziggy's bed—has my heart swelling in my throat. I let the CD fall from my shaky fingers, like I'm afraid picking it up is what made the vision real—and maybe dropping it will undo it.

My words come out in an airy breath. "I thought their CD wasn't coming out until summer?"

Sorrow shapes Ziggy's features as he drags himself to the bed. "I assumed it would be in summer, as that's when Rayonne booked her leave from the castle, and I know they would be infrequent."

Our heavy gazes meet again, and I ask, "Was Rayonne in Patricia's vision?"

Slowly, he shakes his head. "Logically, I believed she would be with you. Visions can be hard to analyze. A flash of a few moments doesn't always offer enough insight into the rest of the time surrounding it, so I filled in the blanks with what I thought to be true."

An anxious burn cascades over my brain, a squeezing in my skull that makes it hard to think straight. "I picked up the CD because I knew about the vision. How the fuck does that work? How could Patricia have a vision about what I do in the future *based on* me knowing about the vision? Like . . . *what?* That doesn't make sense. What does that mean?"

The unfamiliar guy releases a long breath, his voice soft as he says, "Visions are complicated and weird, and Patricia is only a little younger than Lance. Maybe you would have looked at the CD anyway."

I study him for a long moment, the way his soft green eyes look so sure.

"Ollie is right," Ziggy says, though the ache in his eyes doesn't make me feel better.

I have the horrible thought that *somehow* I caused this. That I created a prediction of me fulfilling it. The loop that sends my mind into makes the room tilt, and with my next breath, I double over in a sob.

"Oh shit—" Ziggy rushes to my side, and Ollie says he'll

give us some space as he leaves with the door thudding shut behind him. He laces his fingers through mine. "What's wrong, love?"

Squeezing his hand, I try to suck back tears with my breaths as I choke out, *"I wish you had marked me."*

His fingers press deeper between my knuckles, his silence so heavy as I cry, until he finally says, "I know. I'm sorry."

I gasp for breath against the razor pain in my chest, my voice strained as I say, *"I love my daughter, and Viorel, and Laurentius, but—"*

Things could have been so much easier had he marked me by force in the woods across from Carol's house that night we were attacked. I wouldn't have my daughter or the love of two men, but I wouldn't know any better to miss them, and they wouldn't be in pain right now missing me. I would be happy, probably in school by day and hanging out safe with Ziggy and Lance at night. I know they would have taken such good care of me.

"You'll see them again real soon," Ziggy murmurs, tucking a curtain of my hair behind my ear to see my face.

My head sways and I sniffle. "I don't believe that. *I just don't.*"

He gently pulls our hands apart and wraps his arm around me to pull me close. I sob into his shoulder—probably deafening him—and wrap my arm around his midsection.

"It's all my fault," he mumbles. "I was a bloody chicken. I should have held you down and forced you to drink from me anyway. I knew you couldn't make the choice yourself, but I felt awful about doing it forcefully because you would have fought me like a wild animal. Looking back, I shouldn't have even stopped the bike. I should have kept driving and brought you to Lance. He would have been able to emotionally handle you kicking and screaming at him, knowing he was doing the proper thing. That's my fault. I tried to pawn off the control on you, knowing you couldn't take it."

"You were worried about how marking me would affect Rayonne," I remind him with a sniffle. "We all still thought she was taking orders from Viorel's men. We didn't realize they were impersonators with no real connection."

He nods, but says, "I should have been a stricter master with her too, forcing her to quit that Agatha bullshit if she wanted to continue being my familiar until she was a vampire again. Should have convinced her better to let *me* turn her back. Maybe she'd still be alive."

I touch his leg. "You cared about what we wanted, even though you thought you knew best. You let us make our own choices."

He shrugs. "Well, look where my caring got us. One dead best friend, and another who is permanently marked and was locked in a castle until she was kidnapped by a psychopath again and kept in a cage. I could have prevented it all if I'd done the right thing. It would have been a hard thing, but it was the right thing . . . and I was a chicken. I was scared you two would be mad at me."

"Not one bit of this is your fault," I promise him as I wipe my eyes with the back of my hand.

"I should have shot Denendrius," Ziggy whispers. "I had a pistol on me, so I could have. He was fucking human."

"From what you knew, that would have meant serious trouble for you." I squeeze his midsection.

He sucks his teeth and sighs. "It would have been the right thing to do."

"It's not your job to make sure everyone is making the right choices for themselves." I wipe my eyes again and take a shuddery breath, realizing the slow growth of calm he's slipping into me.

His voice shakes. "I-I just want everyone to be safe and happy."

I swallow, my breath coming smoothly as it flows in and out

of me. I relax against him. "And that's the sweetest, Ziggy, but you're not omnipotent. When people aren't safe and happy, you can't take on that blame. You can calm us, but you can't always stop bad things from happening."

Ziggy kisses the top of my head. "Logically, I know, but . . ." He heaves out a breath. "I'm a fucking vampire, and still, I can only do so much."

I can't help my teary chuckle. "Hell, you sound like Viorel."

His chest jerks with a single beat of laughter. "What d'you mean?"

I sigh. "That's why he was so restrictive with me. Viorel was terrified something bad would happen and he wouldn't be able to stop it. He's going to be worse if I manage to get back. I know it. He's going to be a paranoid anxiety monster."

"Are you scared to go back?" he whispers.

"No, but . . ." I heave out a breath. "I know it's not going to be easy. What happened with me was literally his worst nightmare. I won't be shocked if he *actually* chains me to him this time."

Ziggy puts his hand on my knee, his thumb moving over my bruised flesh. "I wish I knew what to say."

I wipe leftover tears off my cheeks. "I'll be okay. I'd much rather be home with him—whatever that looks like—than be away. Once I'm a Darkling, things might be easier."

Once Denendrius turns me, I won't be so breakable, and hopefully that means Viorel will relax a bit.

"You're going to turn, then?" Ziggy asks.

With a hard nod, I say, "I'm fucking tired of being weak and human. I know I won't have the strength of most vampire men or older immortals, but at least I'll be able to fight back."

"Fuckin' right," Ziggy agrees, pulling me tight against him for an approving squeeze. "You're going to be one badass immortal. You're already showing traits of a proper vampire."

With a kink in my neck, I straighten off his shoulder and lean back to quirk my brow in question at him. "How?"

He gives me a toothy grin. "You're already agonizing over what ifs. It only gets worse as you get older."

"Trust me." I sigh, thinking of Viorel again. "I know."

He rubs tears from his eyes. "We should go out for a bit. I have to pick up Stacey anyway, so I'll bring you along and we'll stop for a treat. How about a bit of milkshake and pie? You could use some fresh air and some practice on those wobbly legs."

My mouth waters with the thought.

Ziggy lends me a thick hoodie and battle jacket, the denim heavy with so many silver spikes and rivets organized around the patches that it weighs on my weak shoulders. I ask him about my ouroboros bracelet, but he says I wasn't wearing it when they got me out of the cage, and they and Ollie never thought to look for anything specific when he dragged the cage through the doorway for them. With a frown, I realize it probably fell outside the cage or got lost in the blanket, since my wrists are skinnier now.

When I finally find a pair of boots I can walk in from the sizable collection, a tall and lanky girl with perfectly smooth tanned skin, and tidy gold and brown corkscrew curls wanders into the room. Her hazel eyes are deep with turmoil as she pauses halfway between the door and where I sit on the edge of the bed, waiting for Ziggy to get ready.

Ziggy turns around, dropping his wrinkled jeans back into the pile and pocketing the crinkled bills in his black buckle and chain decorated cargo pants.

"What?" he asks as he takes in the sight of her with slitted, suspicious eyes, a pinch of anxiety in his voice.

She smiles softly at me. "Hi, Marianna, I'm Patricia."

"Hey," I say, finally having a face to Ziggy's seer friend.

She wanders over and sits at my side on the bed. I stiffen

when she wraps her cold arms around me and pulls me into a tight hug, murmuring, "You'll be okay in the end, I promise."

My heart seizes as I stiffen.

"Oi, what did you see?" Ziggy demands, his tone matching the anxiety coursing through me. "Don't do this cryptic shit right now. Come on . . ."

I already know what she has to say. I've felt it all along. "Denendrius is coming back for me, right?"

"Yes, but I have no idea when," Patricia says as she pulls away. "Ziggy, Viorel will call you at some point tonight asking if you've heard from his men, or if they made it here yet. They aren't responding to any communication attempts."

Toxic dread burns through me, a sharp ache rolling from my center and down my legs. I know something bad has happened to the team he sent from the castle, but don't like the nauseating image of Mateo potentially being dead.

"For fuck's sake," Ziggy spits. "We're definitely getting out of here. I'm not fucking giving her back to Denendrius."

Patricia presses her palms together in front of her chest, pleading. "Ziggy, if you fight him—if you so much as argue with him—you will die."

"So I should hand her over? Why? So he can fucking hurt her? So he can keep her like a dog toy to hump and chew?"

"You will hand her over, because if you don't, Denendrius will kill the entire clan and all the club guests. He will torture you and Lance and make you watch and experience him torturing your familiars. Then, once you're dead, he will hunt down every surviving member of your family *like your daughter*. And in the end, he will still have her. Her future is set in stone. The only thing you can alter is the severity of everything between now and then."

The fact Patricia doesn't deny his worries makes my stomach feel like it's full of wriggling worms.

Ziggy stares at her, aghast. "Viorel told me to protect her with my life."

"Yes, well, it sounds like Viorel can be an emotional and short-sighted fool sometimes. He let Denendrius escape twice with his familiars. I don't think he's thought through his request of you," she says.

Ziggy's eyes widen, his hands coming up to cover his gaping mouth like the words fell from them. As he shakes his head and lowers them, he says, "*Patricia* . . . He is still our king. You watch your tongue before he has his men waltzing in here and goes Vlad the Impaler on us as he did his own clan last year."

She mashes her lips together and scowls at him.

Ziggy's breaths come quicker, the fear vivid in his eyes. "I'm serious, Patricia."

"This is coming from the anarchist pig-killer? Really? How very punk of you! Do you not make a snide comment each time the castle is brought up?" she snaps.

Frustration shapes Ziggy's face as he leans a bit toward her. "It's one thing when you're talking about pigs and human governments and not a supernatural entity who actually does a decent job of controlling the immortal world. Saying a hidden castle full of old vampires—without electricity and plumbing —is boring and restrictive is not the same as talking shit about the most powerful vampire who can smite you from across the world."

"You'll die because he asked you to?" Patricia challenges.

His lip curls back. "Marianna's my *friend*, so despite the king's orders, I'm still not going to hand her over. You can't just show me unfulfilled visions spanning years of our friendship and expect me to treat her like she's some stranger."

"Denendrius escaped prison twice, but somehow you're going to stop him from taking her?" Patricia crosses her arms.

Tears well in Ziggy's eyes and he exhales a shaky breath.

"Fuck off," he snarls as he twists away from her and storms into the bathroom, slamming the door behind him.

She gives me a pitying frown and drops her arms.

"I won't let him fight Denendrius," I promise her.

Patricia rests her hands on my biceps. "Thank you. It's not that we don't care about you—"

"I know. I'm not taking it personally. If he comes back for me before Viorel's men arrive, that's all there is to it."

"Still, I'm sorry," she murmurs.

I swallow a knot and nod.

"But you'll be okay, Marianna," she says carefully, subduing a cringe that makes it halfway across her face. "Everything will turn out fine, but I want you to understand you can't stop it. It's not your fault, no matter how it happens."

"What do you mean?" My voice sounds detached from my body.

Her eyes are level with mine. That all-knowing gaze of hers fills me with dread. "You and Denendrius are hurtling toward a dark place, and I need you to know there's nothing you could ever do or say—in the past or the future—to alter the inevitable collision. But you'll be okay, *I promise.*"

"Tell me," I demand.

She shakes her head. "I don't want to risk making the journey there any worse than it already is."

My heart hammers in my throat. "Then why are you being cryptic? Why bother saying anything?"

"Because that dark place is *looming*, but it hasn't fully taken shape yet. Hope creates comfort, and comfort can lead to carelessness. Alternatively, too much hopelessness kills. He's got a marker in his hand, and I've seen a lot of different timelines where he's smudged them black."

I gulp and nod.

I cannot become careless when it comes to this game with Denendrius.

Patricia's vision has done a number on what little strength I regained. I move slowly and need to hook my arm through Ziggy's to stay steady, but make it through the club and up the long, graffiti-covered concrete steps to the subway tunnel that conceals the club's hidden entrance.

The gravel is difficult to navigate, and the ache in my legs deepens as we move over it. It's still so nice to move around after being trapped in that cramped cage.

I pull the cool air deep into myself as we reach the road and move to the sidewalk, where Ziggy's car is parked a couple streets away. The block is spotty with life, more streetlamps overhead than the people they illuminate with their cold yellow glow. There's something calm about the night. Something simple and nostalgic, and I feel so warm next to Ziggy despite the early spring air and my impending doom.

Until a guy in his early twenties with shaggy black hair and an eyebrow piercing steps out from behind a parked truck ahead and stands in the middle of the sidewalk to face us.

"Fuck off, Ricky!" Ziggy bellows in frustration, already shaking beside me. "*Literally. Fuck. Off! I've had it tonight!*"

"You're not getting rid of me until I get Stephie back," Ricky says simply, crossing his arms. "You had no good reason to steal her from me."

Ziggy stiffens beside me, his back straight and his chest out and heaving with anger as he stares Ricky down. "I took your blood slave because you brought her into my club and proceeded to beat the piss out of her because she got a speck of blood on your white sneakers," Ziggy growls through grit teeth.

Ricky bares his teeth, fangs exposed. "She was *my* blood slave. I had every right to do with her as I pleased. You had no right to stop me."

"Some of us aren't pieces of shit, you know? We didn't all

become vampires like you and immediately leap on the fact we can create slaves. If I hadn't beaten the piss out of you and dragged you out, someone else would have."

"Just give her back, man. Seriously. I want her back."

Ziggy groans. "It's been three fucking years. Get over it already. Are you really going to waste your eternity harassing me over something like this? Don't you have anything better to do? Because I sure do."

"Where is she?" he demands.

"I'm not going to fucking tell you!" Ziggy hollers. "Somewhere off fucking happy, living her life! I don't know."

Ricky snickers. "Did she run away? See, that's what happens when you're so loosey-goosey with control."

Ziggy scoffs. "*Loosey-goosey?* Shut the fuck up! You're unbearable. She outgrew us, so we turned her, and she moved on with her life. Now *fuck* off."

"Fine." Ricky's eyes shift to me, the glint of a predator's gaze making me lean my weight closer to Ziggy. "Why don't I just take this one from you as a replacement?"

Ziggy spits on the ground between him and Ricky. "Piss right off. I will kill you."

Ricky tongues his bottom lip as he mulls me over. "Why, she special or something? She sure smells special; not like any marked human I've ever smelled, and I've been around a while." His eyes tighten on me. "Who's your master? Might he be a king looking for his kidnapped pet?"

Ziggy squares up. "Fucking watch it, Ricky. There's a lot of vacancy in his dungeon right now, I hear."

Ricky smirks, a chuckle bubbling past his twisted lips. "Yeah, I bet. But I'm not too worried. It seems like he has a hard time keeping occupants."

Ziggy *tsks* at him. "Only two prison breaks in two thousand years is impressive, Ricky, considering the rate this country has."

"Come on," Ricky challenges, lifting his fists in front of his face and widening his stance. "Fight me for her, since you seem to enjoy fighting over slaves so much."

Ziggy hooks his arm in mine and tries to navigate us around Ricky. He steps into our path, a smug smirk on his lips as he reaches out to grab me. Ziggy pulls me out of the way, slides in front of me, and plants his feet. His fists shake at his sides, his voice coming out with a warning. "I will punch your fangs into the back of your throat."

I press myself closer to Ziggy.

"Try it," he says, stepping closer and lifting his brows at Ziggy in challenge.

"Ricky, your ugly face is going to end up on a milk carton if you don't fuck off forever," Ziggy growls.

"Dumbass, they don't actually do that anymore—"

Ziggy swings, and they become a mess of punches and kicks as I stumble backward after Ricky's foot nearly swoops my legs out from beneath me. I watch with wide eyes as my heart drums in my chest. I can't help the half-scoff of excited disbelief as Ziggy beats the pulp out of him, blood spraying across the concrete as he switches between punching Ricky so hard he falls to the ground, to trying to stomp his head—that keeps moving out of his way—with his steel-toe boots.

I grin when Ziggy wrestles him onto his back on the ground and punches him in the head so many times that he can't recover fast enough and merely resorts to covering his bloody head with his forearms.

"Shoot him, Ziggy!" I suggest, since he slipped a revolver with wooden bullets into the interior pocket of his own battle jacket before we left.

Ricky's voice shoots up an octave. "Don't fucking shoot me!"

"I *should* shoot you! Right in the fucking heart!" Ziggy bellows. "Then you'd really piss off!"

With one frantic flail as he shoves Ziggy backward, he

manages to scramble out from under Ziggy and stagger to his feet. Ziggy grabs a fistful of his leather jacket, his bloodied grip slipping as Ricky yanks free and darts off.

"I just wanted a relaxing end to my fucked-up night, you fucking cunt!" Ziggy hollers after him.

I can't help my flat, pained laughter as Ziggy spits blood onto the concrete and slings his arm over my shoulder, muttering, "What an absolute fucking wanker."

"Sounds like he's a thorn in your side," I note.

Ziggy groans loudly. "I have to forcibly toss him out of the club at least once every six months. He keeps skulking around, hoping he'll be able to steal Stephie back. Next time, he's going in a grave where he belongs."

I wrap my arm around his back so I can keep up pace beside him as we continue walking. "It's sweet that you saved her from him."

He shrugs. "I guess. It didn't feel too great to do it. I had to tie her hands to the bedpost so I could get my blood down her throat. She was sobbing and screaming her head off and wouldn't stop punching and kicking me. I damn near had a panic attack and struggled to calm her. I was essentially attacking her, and she was fighting me off. She calmed down and was tearfully happy after she woke up with his mark stripped. But I didn't enjoy having to do that. It made me feel like a creep."

"Like you said," I start as I squeeze his side. "Sometimes the right thing to do is the hard thing to do. And I know, when the time comes soon, you'll do the right thing again."

He shakes his head and presses it against the side of mine, mumbling, "It won't be the right thing."

"It'll be the lesser of two evils."

"It's all evil." He shudders at my side. "Fuckin' all of it."

XXXVII

Ziggy helps me into the passenger seat of his lime green sports car. If it weren't for the heavy tint on the windows that are *barely* legal, I'd feel like I'm strapped to a giant bullseye. But with nobody able to see me clearly through the window, it's like I'm hidden behind a shield.

The Sisters of Mercy fill the car from Ziggy's expensive after-market stereo as we drive to Stacey's house. The low bass thrums through me, muffling the rhythm of my shuddering heart.

We park at a green house in the east of Lorimer's middle class, Stacey having an animated conversation in the doorway with someone inside—her leather-clothed back turned to us—that has Ziggy cursing under his breath.

"I'll be right back," he grumbles as he unbuckles and leaves, his swift steps bringing him across the wet sidewalk and to the door.

I crack the window, the loud argument only increasing in volume when Ziggy wedges himself inside. I only get bits and pieces, but Stacey failed her midterm thanks to the stress of finding out she was cheated on minutes before. And even though she still has a chance to pass the class, her parents are furious and are pulling their funding, convinced she's going to fail out completely. They sure aren't happy with Ziggy's presence in her life either, convinced he's why she switched her degree from Christian studies to doing STEM . . . which he enthusiastically accepts as fact.

Stacey and Ziggy continue to rant as they return.

"They're totally going to kick my ass out," she grumbles as she climbs behind his seat and plunks in the back.

"Then come live with us," Ziggy says breezily, as if it's the obvious solution.

She huffs. "Emry already does, and Maxine at least half the time. Where would I sleep full time?"

"We'll get bunk beds," Ziggy teases. "Nah, there's extra space somewhere. We'd fit you."

I melt into the heated seat and lean my head against the chilled window, my loud thoughts muffling Ziggy's and Stacey's conversation. I try to grasp the shape of their words so I can pull myself back to the conversation and participate, but I can't focus.

Ziggy nudges me, and I blink, dry eyes itchy, and realize we're parked in front of a diner, the colorful, retro style painting of a milkshake on the window filling my hazy gaze.

"Oh." My aching body weighs me down as I crack the door open, but I manage onto my feet before Ziggy can grip my arm.

My strength is a little triumph, but I doubt I'll have enough by the time Denendrius comes back for me.

I loop my arm through Ziggy's as we approach the diner. He sniffs at the air and stiffens as we walk in with the sound of bells. He shrugs off his concerns with a dismissive grunt and waves us over to a teal booth. Stacey sits on the other side of the pink table from Ziggy and me, with Ziggy next to the window. I slump against him to avoid the energy of keeping myself upright and unsupported.

A middle-aged woman rounds the long counter and comes to our table as Ziggy digs around in his wallet.

"I'm Mindy, I'll be serving you tonight." There's a tickled smile on her lips as she looks at the three of us. "How's everyone's night?"

"We're swell, thanks." Ziggy holds out a beaten loyalty card to her, but she doesn't make a move for it.

A little smirk plays on her lips. "We stopped using those a year after you stopped coming in. About . . . *fifteen* years ago?"

Ziggy's a deer caught in headlights, his hand frozen in the air, his brown eyes wide.

"Bringing these ones for milkshakes too?" she asks.

He nods, then chokes out, "I didn't think you'd remember me."

"You're not easy to forget, hun. You're loud. Tip well. It was always so calm when you came in, even with the place packed, but it never stuck beyond you leaving. You were a teenager last I saw you, right? Looking a little young for your early forties."

He bares his teeth like a guilty dog as he nods. "Yeah . . . it's all the . . ." He lowers his head in defeat and blows out a breath. "Yeah."

She chuckles, and I stiffen as she leans on the table, half her hand covering mine. I think it's accidental until she pats it as she draws it back.

"The others?" she asks.

His mouth opens and closes, and I realize she was checking my temperature.

"Dead?" she mouths.

He stares at her, swallowing before nodding. "In the best way."

The corner of her lip quirks. "These ones?"

He blinks at her.

"How long will they enjoy milkshakes?" She lifts a brow at him.

He gulps. "A while."

Her eyes shift between Stacey and me, a triumphant smile on her face as she asks, "What would you ladies like?"

"Chocolate with extra whipped cream and apple pie," Stacey orders, nervous eyes settling on Ziggy.

He gives her a consoling wave of his hand and a nod.

"Strawberry," I say, the confusion clear in my voice. "Apple pie too."

The waitress stares at Ziggy for a few beats until he finally lifts his head to look at her.

"I had my suspicions for years," she starts. "Never blabbed then, won't blab now."

He gives her a thankful smile and leans across me. "How do you—"

A coy smile shapes her lips, her voice coming out low. "You never ate, never drank . . . and sometimes your friends' sleeves rode up." She winks at him.

He grimaces. "Right."

She gives him a soft smile. "Milkshakes and pies coming up."

He heaves out a breath and relaxes in the booth. My gaze follows her to the jukebox, to her hands as she reaches toward the full bulletin board above it and removes a paper her body blocks the content of. But she looks me right in the eyes, and I catch the first four letters—*MARI*—and a portion of my photograph as she folds it up and tears it in half. Our gazes are locked as she rounds the counter and stuffs my missing poster in the trash.

I pick at my pie with a shaky grip on my fork—Ziggy watching carefully like he's considering feeding me—and tease my tongue with small sips of milkshake. My stomach churns and rolls after each swallow. Our relaxing outing for treats has all our muscles rigid as we trip through the night with stiff conversation.

A phone call from one of Viorel's men at the castle hits Ziggy's phone while Stacey and I take a bathroom trip, and he recounts—coded—when I return about how it's essentially what Patricia predicted. The confirmation has my milkshake curdling in my stomach, and I feel completely exposed in the brightly lit diner. I shrink tight against Ziggy's side as if someone will stroll past the large window and point me out. Or that Denendrius is behind the lost communication with Viorel's team of men and is ready to retrieve me.

Ziggy senses my building terror, my shortening breaths audible until he calms me down.

"Let's leave," he suggests, and we pile back in the car.

Ziggy's ringtone blares from his pants, and he takes a hand off the wheel to haphazardly lift himself off the seat so he can reach into the depths of his pocket for it. Pulling it out, he glances at the screen. From the backseat, I can see who is calling, and a cold shock rips through me.

He makes a shuddering noise as he pulls over so hard that a car honks as it narrowly avoids scraping against our side. I steady myself in the backseat as Stacey exclaims in shock, then I unbuckle and shift to the middle. He drops the phone when trying to flick it open with his thumb. It bounces off his lap and clatters by his feet.

The phone continues to ring, each sharp chime a knife in my flinching heart as Ziggy stares at the wheel with saucer-wide eyes and staggered, climbing breaths.

"You need to answer him," I choke out, steadying myself between his seat and Stacey's. "You have to."

He's rigid as he reaches between his legs to retrieve the phone from where it landed near the gas pedal.

We stare at the flashing incoming call until the screen dims.

The phone quiets for half a second, but my chest tightens as I wait for him to call again. Tears line my bottom lashes as his name flashes across the screen, and Ziggy flinches.

"Answer it," I urge.

He takes a deep breath and forcefully pushes it out as he wipes the hair out of his face and flicks the phone open. His hand shakes violently as he puts the phone against his ear. "H-hello." He clears his throat.

The sound of Denendrius's muffled voice sends my heart galloping like a prized racehorse.

"Y-yes, she's perfectly fine, Denendrius. W-we went for milkshakes, is all," Ziggy chokes out. He holds the phone away from his ear and extends it to me over his shoulder.

I lather on as much happiness as I can, taking the phone in my trembling hands and resting it against my ear.

"You're okay," I say, unable to hide the tremble in my voice. "I was so worried, Den."

His voice crackles on the line, the connection weak. The sound of him sends tears spiraling down my cheeks. "Hey there, sweetheart. I'm relieved to hear you're okay. Has Ziggy been good to you?"

I nod, my heart leaping at the thought that he could hurt him. "Yes. Yes, he has. H-he found me, and he's been making sure I'm safe. I asked him to take me out for something to eat. I needed a distraction. I was so worried about you."

"That's okay," he murmurs. "Just come back to Estrella de Sangre now, hm?"

My stomach roils. "Yes," I breathe. "We'll see you soon."

Ziggy mashes his lips together and violently shakes his head at me, his eyes swelling with tears.

"Love you, sweetheart," Denendrius whispers, the sound of a kiss coming through.

"I love you too." Numbness settles through me as I draw the phone away from my ear and hang up.

"You're not fucking going back," Ziggy pleads.

I hold the phone out to him, arm too weak to lift it for more than a few seconds. "I have to."

"No!" he shouts as he twists around to look at me better. "Absolutely fucking not. I'm hiding you somewhere."

My heavy gaze locks with his, and though numbness dries my tears, his overflow. Black streaks his cheeks.

"You have no choice," I argue. "He's at the club. If you don't go back, he will *kill* everyone there. Is that what you want?"

"*No!*" he spits. "Of fucking course not. But I can't just fucking hand you back over to him after he kept you in a bloody cage."

I close my eyes. "*You. Have. No. Choice.*" I pull in a long breath. "He will kill everyone, Ziggy. *Everyone.* And then he'll still find me."

He bites his quivering lip. "He'll hurt you."

"I know," I choke out. "But not as bad as he'll hurt you."

"Viorel ordered me to keep you safe at any cost."

I shake my head. "Viorel values my life over everyone else's, but my life isn't worth all of theirs, Ziggy. I'm not that important."

"You're my friend."

"And as my friend, I'm asking you to bring me back. I'm asking you not to fight this."

He looks out the window at the trickle of cars as they pass us beneath the glow of streetlamps, his eyes blurred with tears.

"I can't." He furiously wipes his eyes. "If he kills you, it'll be my fault. I can't just hand you over."

I wrap my arms around myself and lean forward against the side of his seat to rest my head on his shoulder. "Right now, Ziggy. He's sitting in the club with your entire clan. With *Lance.*

If I don't walk through that door soon, he'll torture every single one of them. I know him. He will make you watch Lance die, and all your familiars."

"Get out of the car, Stacey," Ziggy cries. "Get a cab and go home, please."

She gives me a long, mourning look, then puts her hand over his fist on his lap. "Okay," she whispers. "See you later."

He nods roughly as she opens the door during a break in traffic and steps out. When it slams shut, Ziggy releases a strangled breath and wipes the relentless stream of tears from his eyes.

"You're such a good friend," I whisper. "You did everything you could for me. I know it doesn't seem like it, but giving me back is helping me. I don't want to see my friends die. He's killed enough of my friends, do you understand?"

He closes his eyes again and sits back in his seat, a long sob rattling out of him.

A few tears dart down my cheeks, an ache working its way through the numbness in my chest. But the pain isn't for me, it's for Ziggy.

"I don't matter that much," I tell him. "I'm not worth more than all your lives."

"Don't say shit like that," he cries. "It doesn't help. You fucking matter to me."

I wipe my cheeks and sniffle. "Please bring me back."

"Fuck," he breathes, and he chokes on a sob he tries to subdue. "Fuck!"

I sit back as he places his trembling hands on the wheel and cranks the car into drive, his foot lead on the pedal. He curses at cars in his way, rolling his window down to call people driving the speed limit wankers and bloody arseholes. He cries quietly the whole time, soaking up rivers of tears down his cheek with the sleeve of his jean jacket as he white-knuckle grips the steering wheel with his other hand. When we come within a few blocks of the club, he collapses over the wheel at a red light and sobs into the leather until it turns green and honking cars have him lifting his head enough to see the road.

Should I be as upset as Ziggy about going back to Denendrius? A numb part of me knows there are far worse alternatives, but it doesn't make the weight of my choice any less suffocating.

"Should just kill you myself," he mutters, half sprawled over it as he creeps through the intersection and lazily turns a corner. "That's what a good friend would do."

"You'd still die. More horribly, too."

"May as well be dead." He turns a corner and parks behind another clan member's vehicle. "I'm not going to be able to live with myself after this."

"You don't mean that . . ." I lean forward and rest my hand on his back. "You love Lance and your familiars. Your clan. Your club. You know this is the best thing to do."

"Viorel's going to torture the fuck out of me and I'll deserve it."

"He'll understand," I assure him. "Viorel's quite logical and must know a group of Children of Stars stands no chance against Denendrius. He wouldn't expect you to trade your life and your clan's life for mine. I'm sure they were only desperate words."

We grip one another as we return to the club, the concrete steps seeming endless in our descent.

When we open the heavy doors to the club, we step into a weighted silence, so thick I struggle to breathe through it. The usual beat of music is missing, the hum of a machine the only sound echoing in the room. The sight of Denendrius waiting amongst a handful of people with terror-stricken eyes stops my lungs from functioning. There are so few people left in the club, only fifteen or twenty, including Lance, Patricia, Maxine, and Ollie. They're all rooted to chairs at tables like they were ordered to sit there and knew it would be unwise to flee, as the rest of the guests likely did upon his arrival.

"Here she is," Ziggy mumbles from my side as he stares across the faces of his clan and wipes his eyes.

Denendrius flashes across the room, his arms circling me as he lifts me off the floor, muscles so taut against mine it's like he wants us enmeshed. My body cries out, black pulsing in my vision from the pain.

"I thought I left you to die," he laments.

I gasp for breath in his grip until I'm seeing stars. He releases me on my weak legs and swiftly steadies me when I waver.

"I missed you," I cry, though it's grief that summons my tears. I knew this would happen, but that fact doesn't barricade the pain. "I'm so glad you're okay."

"I'm sorry," he whispers, holding my face in his cold hands. "I never meant to leave you there."

"I know," I force out. "I'm sorry for making you lock me in there."

With a soft touch, he tilts my head back and leans down to cover my lips with gentle kisses that scald my soul.

"I love you," he breathes.

Relentless tears cascade down my cheeks, and I wish with every part of my being that Mateo and his team would break through the door behind me *right now*.

But nobody can save me. I'm on my own.

With what little is left of me, I have to save myself.

"What's wrong?" Denendrius's eyes narrow on Ziggy beside me.

He chokes on a breath, the ache in his eyes contagious. It infects me. Overloads me. My weak fingers dig into the leather covering Denendrius's arm, the fresh growth of my nails digging into the material to stay on my feet.

Ziggy wipes his eyes, the tears quickly replaced. "I'm going to miss my friend, is all."

"Oh," Denendrius says flatly, though the look in his eyes as they flick over Ziggy is pitying.

As Denendrius makes a move forward to leave, Ziggy's hand shoots out and grabs my biceps. Denendrius stiffens and stares down at him, but he doesn't pry us apart.

"Can I have a hug goodbye?" The words rush out of him with a pained twinge, like he believes he'll never see me again.

Though there's no guarantee he ever will.

"Okay," Denendrius says, like the question was posed to him.

I let Ziggy pull me against his body, leaning my head on his shoulder and inhaling the comforting scent of weed and patchouli that wafts off him. I try to memorize the way his arms squeeze me, like he's trying to hold what's left of me together since he's placing me in rough hands.

"Miss you," he chokes out.

"I'll miss you too," I whisper. "Thank you."

He clears his throat and nods.

"You're a good friend, Ziggy," Denendrius says limply. "Thanks for taking care of my girl for me. I was hoping I could count on you."

Ziggy's arms unravel from me as I slowly pull away, knowing Denendrius will only let the hug go on for so long, and surprised he allowed it in the first place.

"You're welcome," Ziggy struggles to squeeze out.

"And thanks for the wine . . . and for fighting with us when Agatha tried to capture me." Denendrius gives him a smile that's so unemotional—but clearly meant to be friendly—that Ziggy hugs himself and flinches.

Ziggy gives him a quick nod. "Of course, mate. If you and Marianna ever need anything . . . you know where to find me."

His eyes dart to mine and back to Denendrius's before he returns a forced smile.

I shake my borrowed battle jacket off and return it to Ziggy —who hugs it—before Denendrius moves us forward to the door. Ziggy calls out to wait. We turn as he rushes through the club to the clan rooms at the back, and he returns with the pharmacy bag.

"She has wounds requiring tending," Ziggy explains as he gulps air like his immortal lungs are desperate for it.

Denendrius takes the bag, a frown pulling at the corners of his lips, and guilt thick in his russet gaze. "Thanks."

I look over my shoulder as we continue, my sorrow-wet gaze paralyzed on Ziggy's. Despite having no immortal ability like his, I can *feel* his desperation; the overpowering need he fights to fly forward and wrangle me from Denendrius's grip. I can only imagine the emotions he's feeling from me, and how it intensifies that urge.

Patricia appears at his side, fuzzy at the edge of my focus. She's an anchor keeping him in place, her hand appearing on his shoulder as he twitches.

She's a force that moves me forward, her visions of the future giving my steps some purchase on the tightrope I walk across.

The memory of her promise fills my head. *"You'll be okay, in the end..."*

The heavy club doors thud shut behind us.

XXXVIII

"I didn't realize you saw Ziggy as your friend," I say as I maneuver myself into the beige leather passenger seat of the unfamiliar black car.

Denendrius shrugs as he climbs behind the wheel. "It bothered me how he took to you, at first. But once I learned he married a man, wasn't romantically interested in you, and wanted to please us, I didn't mind so much."

"Us?" My brow furrows.

Denendrius sinks into the seat as his muscles loosen, and he smirks. "What? Is that jealousy? Can we not share friends?"

"It's confusing," I admit.

"The boy eagerly gifted me two bottles of wine when I was human, sweetheart. He was *desperately* trying to please me. A glass of wine is enough of a token of hospitality, but *two bottles to bring home*? It's over the top and practically trying to buy my friendship, but I appreciated it. It was fantastic wine."

Holy shit, he's just *generally* delusional. Did he not notice how uncomfortable Ziggy was around him? That he gave him the wine in hopes Denendrius wouldn't stamp him as *an enemy*? I suppose the baseline of people interacting with him is likely discomfort. He's probably blind to it by now.

"Where's Sergei? Is he alive?" I don't have to fake my concern. I'd much rather have Sergei around to help keep Denendrius in check and be his punching bag.

"He's alive, don't worry."

I gnaw on my lip. "Where is he?"

"We'll meet up with him soon," Denendrius promises, exhaustion creeping into his voice.

"What happened?" I press.

"That German clan—those Nazis—Sergei and I destroyed back when he was a newborn in the Second World War still have it out for us. You'd think they'd get over it after losing the war, but apparently their research was *super important*." He scowls at me, and for a split second I misread it, thinking he's upset with me, until he adds, "I wouldn't consider medical tests on bone-thin prisoners ground-breaking. Bunch of sadists. Anyway, they ambushed us as we neared Lorimer and nearly got us overseas."

I try to reconcile how Denendrius can be *Denendrius* and somehow still feel righteous enough to believe he's morally superior to a bunch of Nazi doctors. Especially when he kidnapped over three hundred vampires in his pursuit to find and test the cure.

"How did you guys escape?" I wonder. Though, if he can escape Viorel and the castle, I'm not sure any vampire clans have a chance of keeping him under lock and key either.

"They had us on a private plane and thought a daytime flight would help keep us contained, along with the chains." He chuckles. "Unfortunately for them, Huarsar tortured me with sunlight for enough decades that I learned exactly how long it would take me to reach various stages of *burned* under different thirst conditions. My arms and legs were useless, and one Nazi thought they were strategically placing us between them and the plane walls, so we'd have less room to fight free. Until I head-butted a window and sent everyone into a panic when sunlight spilled in. I fed on the nearest vampire to heal myself and get out of the chains."

I blow out a long breath, recalling the story he told me from Sirmium. How the dungeon guards kept and tortured him in a sunlight room with moving slats for decades, and how Viorel ordered them to stop when he showed signs of developing a resistance.

He snickers to himself. "Gave Sergei serious war flashbacks from when the Germans shot his Yak-9 down, but he used the distraction to shoulder a few more windows as we depressurized, despite all his furious yelling at me. I took more men down before the plane crashed into the ocean—they couldn't see very well, what with their retinas being burned out, so that wasn't too difficult—and we just used it for cover down there until sunset."

"Damn." I stare at him in shock for a long moment. "I'm really glad you're both okay," I lie. I wish he had died in a ball of flames before hitting the water.

He sighs as he comes to a stop at a light and lazily flicks his left signal on. "I miss having sunlight resistance, to be honest, but I don't particularly want to go through all the pain of regaining it. I'd have to suffer for *centuries*. I could get a lot more done during the day when I needed to, even if it drained me ten times faster."

Yeah, like *pick out teenage girls to abduct* who would usually be home safe after dark.

I unclench my jaw to say, "Viorel told me about how his maker was born with the ability to harness multiple abilities, that he often passed down sets of them to his offspring. Eventually, he created Darklings from a collection of them. Maybe sun-walking is an ability that slipped through unnoticed."

Alaire and Edmond had a level of sun-resistance too, though I remember they wore gloves to help. I still can't help but wonder how they became able to do that. Did they keep records about it, as they did about the vampire children they tested the cure on?

"Makes sense if it's gone mostly unnoticed," Denendrius says as he honks at someone going a few notches below the speed limit in front of us. "It took *years* of forced exposure before any resistance set in, and by then it was so obvious what was happening that Huarsar ordered them to remove the slats and wall them in. That sun torture was forbidden. Jokes on him though, I merely continued to expose myself for centuries after I escaped until I could handle full days with some extra blood." He purses his lips in thought. "I'm surprised he didn't take advantage of that discovery, though I guess the agony of making sun-walkers for his usage would conflict with loyalists."

I can't agree. I'm sure there would be numerous Darklings willing to undergo sunlight exposure for him if he asked, but the very idea of making sun-walkers seems unlike him. He believes vampires are *"thieves in the night"*, and I doubt he'd want vampires interfering with the natural balance of the world and risk consuming or trying to rule it like his maker planned, if they had an advantage during the day too.

But I just nod in agreement and study the slow trickle of traffic around us before saying, "Did you have trouble getting back to the club?"

I hope he'll volunteer information about Mateo and the other men sent to retrieve me. Perhaps gloat or complain about how he dealt with them. Because if he *didn't* deal with them himself, that leaves so many potentials that I can't bear to think about.

"No," he says. "Once I got on dry land, I couldn't spot anyone trailing me. I beelined for the club, hoping I'd find you there."

I know I can't ask directly, as Denendrius would turn around and slice Ziggy up if he was aware we had contact with Viorel, so I say, "Nobody got in your way at all? I'm just so nervous knowing people are after us."

He shakes his head. "Nobody, thankfully."

I study him, looking for signs that he's lying, but it's useless. Even if he did something to Mateo and his team, experience has taught me he's too good at lying for me to uncover it without him willingly telling me.

Giving up on trying to peel back the layers of his composure to find the truth, I let my body go slack in the seat.

Denendrius grabs takeout for me and checks us into a cheap motel, guiding my wobbly steps to the bed, where I collapse in a heap of defeat on the scratchy maroon comforter. The wooden furniture and the thick, striped wallpaper—pale blue and beige—make me feel like I've been transported to the eighties. The stale smell of cigarettes permeates the air. I ache for Ziggy's bed, for the soft, cold sheets and the safe shield of his and Lance's bodies. Instead, I get Denendrius's as he begins to carefully strip me, like he's worried about taking off a layer of skin with the fabric.

"Denendrius—" My breath hitches.

"Not tonight," he assures me as he lifts my heavy legs off the bed one at a time to slide my underwear off. "I just need to see the damage."

I study his face as he parts my legs, straining against the grimaces trying to take hold of my features as his featherlight touch moves over my rashes and sores. Guilt pinches his lips and furrows his brows as he draws his hand away and heaves out a breath.

He frowns at the faded bruises on my torso from where he beat me, and sighs. "I'm sorry, sweetheart. Really, I am."

I force myself to say, "It's okay, Den. I deserved it for shooting you and trying to leave."

Solemn, his head swings back and forth. "You're marked . . . I should have been gentler. More understanding. I was angry you tried to go, but mostly scared that you nearly managed."

Nibbling my lip, I work up the courage to finally ask, "Can you tend to my wounds? I can't see them properly." I don't want him to touch me, but it's better than infection if I can't treat them properly.

He nods, though his eyes narrow. "Who's been tending to them?"

Panic has my breath like a stone in my throat, and my lips part dumbly.

"Ziggy?" His expression is stoic, no fury in his eyes.

I gulp. "He didn't actually touch me, just used Q-tips."

His lips press into a firm line as he grabs the bag and roots through it. He doesn't bother with the Q-tips, though he scrubs his hands first. My muscles stretch taut at his touch, and I hate to admit that his cold hands stroking my stinging wounds are more soothing than the cotton. My eyes burn as he tends to me, my lungs ballooned with breath, anxiety stretching my ribs apart. I can't help the pained whimpers when he touches the worst sores. I only manage a thin breath through my tight throat as he presses his frigid, ointment-covered fingers to the wounds to ease them.

"I'm sorry . . ." The ache in his strained voice sounds raw. "I never meant for you to be in there so long."

"I know." I breathe through the pain of my agitated wounds.

I want to be furious he locked me in the dog cage at all, but the relief of being free and my overall hopelessness smothers any chance of flames igniting. Perhaps I should be screaming at him, blaming him for everything I went through, but I did plenty of that while I was in there. Plus, it doesn't help to know that he never meant to keep me there for more than a couple of hours, and that while I was trapped there, he was being kidnapped by Nazis.

"You must have been so scared." His eyes search mine. "So hungry and tired."

I nod, a few tears breaking loose from the inner corners of my eyes. He wipes them away with his clean hand, then stares across the room as he slides his hand down my thigh to rest on my knee.

"You should eat," he says.

He dresses me like I'm his doll, tucking my limbs into the fabric and ensuring everything is in place. He brings me my food—Chinese—and comes to my side to stroke my hair as we sit in silence. I eat slowly, the mere fact I'm with Denendrius and not with Mateo on the way back to the castle tightening my stomach. Yet I lean into Denendrius's soft hands, letting him think I'm desperate for his comfort when, really, I barely have the strength to sit upright.

My food is long cold by the time he moves, and I've barely made a dent in it. I continue to eat, only pausing for him to rest my sore body against the pillows he's stacked along the wooden headboard, in the nest of blankets he made for me. He secures the window with an extra blanket and his knife, then wanders from one side of the motel room to another like he's trying to find something to do.

He must give up, as he sighs and plunks down in the drawn back desk chair

Denendrius stares blankly at the carpet, his elbows on his thighs and his hands limp between his knees as he sits slumped in the chair.

I pick at my food, moving the rice and meat around as I cut my attention between his unchanging, flat expression, and the meal that travels down my throat like stones with each bite.

He sighs and pulls his phone from his jean's pocket, unlocking it before he types and scrolls while scrutinizing whatever is on screen. After a few minutes, he straightens back in the chair and brings the phone to his ear.

I scrutinize the grains of rice in my takeout dish, thinking he's calling Sergei, until he says, "Good afternoon, I saw your hours but want to book an appointment after hours for a substantial tip—No, I understand, but my girl has that sunlight allergy, solar urticaria, so she can't come during business hours without it causing unneeded stress, which sort of defeats the purpose of booking an appointment . . ."

My brow furrows as he pauses to listen to the faint voice coming through the phone.

The corner of his lip lifts in a ghost of a smile that's so far from meeting his eyes. "Yes, thanks. I appreciate the exception . . . A manicure and pedicure, trim and style, and facial . . . Yes, nine-thirty tomorrow night works. We'll see you then."

I put my fork down and study his vacant expression as he ends the call and slips the cellphone into the pocket of his leather jacket.

"What's that for?" I whisper.

His heavy eyes meet mine, and he half-shrugs. "Some pampering. You deserve it after everything you've been through."

For being trapped in a dog cage for a fucking week?

I swallow a knot. "Oh . . . Thanks, Den."

He nods once, his eyes focusing back on the carpet, though there's so much distance in his gaze.

"What's wrong?" I ask, voice wavering. I push my meal aside, his impending answer making me lose my appetite.

"I can't stop thinking about you stuck down there with him for nearly a year . . ." He shakes his head. "Him raping you. Everything else he might have done to you."

I gnaw on my cheek, my heart rattling in my chest.

Part of me wants to set him straight, assure him Viorel did nothing of the sort to me. But even if he took it as me trying to console him, though he could interpret it as me defending Viorel too, he wouldn't believe me. Especially since Viorel promised him he'd hurt me despite never planning on following through with his threats.

"And I keep thinking about you trapped in that cage. Alone in the dark, freezing and terrified. Waiting for me and not knowing why I wasn't coming back. Huarsar's guards would lock me in a metal box periodically . . . I know what it's like. The sensory deprivation and hallucinations. The cold from being so thirsty. Not being able to move properly, and wondering how long it'll be before you're released . . ." He exhales a shuddering breath. "I hate myself for putting you through that."

Yet he likely kept other girls in there too?

"You didn't mean for me to be in there so long." At least I have one bit of truth to console him with. "I'm not mad at you, Den."

I'm too broken to hold something as heavy as anger when I have other boulders of emotions weighing on me.

"I should have known Sergei wouldn't be able to control me when he turned me back," Denendrius mutters. "We wouldn't have been captured had I not lost control and drawn so much attention to myself . . . but I was unbearably thirsty and couldn't think straight. I forgot how fast news can travel in the modern world. It's partly my fault we were in that hell."

Partly. I don't miss the share of blame, and I know he's allotted the other half to me. But I don't dare take responsibility for the tip I sent Alaire and Edmond. The tip that their failsafe system ensured Viorel's men would receive in case of their deaths.

Yet I do my part in taking responsibility for this situation so things can pan out how I want, and say, "None of it would have happened if I wasn't so stubborn in the beginning. If I would have let you explain everything after I accused you of stalking me rather than freaking out."

He's nodding—though only slightly—before I'm even done

with my sentence. Then he shrugs. "I'm partly to blame there too. I don't know how I expected any other reaction." He shakes his head and forces out a breath. "It never crossed my mind that you wouldn't remember me while I was waiting for you—watching you—all those years. I knew you had gone through abuse. I knew you had a short fuse and were deeply unhappy and had a hair-trigger temper. I knew you were ready for the worst to happen, that you never trusted anyone and were waiting for someone to give you an excuse to unleash your anger on them."

His words grip me as I stare unblinking at his thought-filled eyes, waiting to hear more. Waiting for him to finally see things beyond the delusion that's been clouding his vision and judgment for so long.

"I suppose I thought everything would be different once we met again. I was convinced my arrival would . . . *set you free from it all.* I thought you'd recognize me immediately and light up with that brightness, that innocence you used to have, knowing my return meant the end of your suffering. I thought you'd introduce me to your friends, make up some lie about how we knew each other so well, and be giddy with excitement for the rest of the day, knowing you wouldn't have to spend another godforsaken day in a foster home."

"But I didn't remember you," I say, numbness coating me. How was I supposed to know he wrote a script he expected me to follow?

"At first, I thought you were faking it. Maybe you were furious with me for taking so long to return and pretended to forget me just to make me suffer. Then I saw how much you liked me on our dates, and I knew that couldn't be completely true. Near the end of our first, I thought you might have remembered—how you kept looking at me like you knew something but weren't sure if you were right." He exhales a frustrated sigh and closes his eyes. "I knew you so well. Felt so close to you that I couldn't see things from your perspective. But of course you'd interpret me keeping an eye on you as stalking. You saw me as a threat, like you did every other man. And if you couldn't remember me . . . why wouldn't you?"

When he pauses for a long moment to think, I'm not sure what else to add but say, "I was the first human you marked. Could you even tell my anger from your own?"

He lets out a twisted, ironic chuckle. "No, I couldn't. I knew blood marking would link your emotions to me, but there was never a moment where I could separate your feelings from mine. Your fear, your fury . . . It echoed mine. And I've always been moments away from succumbing to the hurricane of my own."

"Rayonne said we were probably in a negative feedback loop, feeding off one another's anger."

His lip twitches in disdain at the sound of her name, but he says, "It's probably true. When you were angry, fighting me, I felt like I was going to implode. There were so many times I just wanted to strangle you to death to rid myself of the anger."

Denendrius rises from the chair and returns to the bed, desperate eyes seeking mine as he crawls across the mattress to me. He maneuvers his body between me and the stack of pillow, circling me with his legs and arms as he pulls me against his chest. I rest my head on his shoulder.

"Scratch *partly* my fault. This is entirely my fault. None of this would have happened if I'd kept you all those years ago. You wouldn't have grown up capable of such anger—feeling so much pain—had I not given you back to Vianna and Kenneth. Your homesickness made me uneasy; I was depriving you of the perfect adoptive parents I would have been so lucky to have as a child. But you would have overcome your homesickness, and after I turned you, it wouldn't have mattered, because you would have remembered who your real parents were. Huarsar wouldn't have had a chance to lie to you about it." He holds me tighter. "If you had really remembered me and were mad I took so long to return to you, you would have had the right to be angry. I don't know why I waited so long. I shouldn't have. I should have come back for you on your twelfth birthday instead of your seventeenth, but I convinced myself it wasn't the right time yet, when in reality, I could have saved you from so much if I'd just given you my love when you could have benefited from it the most."

I swallow a knot, my gut tightening with discomfort at the mere idea of him trying to date and marry me so young. "So, you're not mad at me?"

He nuzzles his cheek into my head. "No, not anymore. I had plenty of time to think about things. I thought I'd return to find you dead in that cage. But I think the fates had things happen the way they did for a reason. Had I not been turned human, we wouldn't have had a chance to see one another beyond our squabble. It gave us a second chance, and we were doing well in Bellevue until the cure's side effects became too much. If I had planned my return to immortality better, we would still be there, just as happy as we were."

I merely nod in agreement, despite disagreeing with everything.

"I promised you a fresh start when I escaped, and I mean it. I want to let go of all that anger. I'm just happy to have you in my arms again."

"Me too," I whisper.

Still, I wonder how he believes a clean slate is remotely possible when I know of the skeletons he keeps in his closet. Hell, I tore the door right off its hinges, and I have to face their presence every day. Does he really think there is anything capable of cleaning it out? Anything strong enough to remove the rot from the walls and floorboards after how long they've been decaying there? Does he expect me to ignore it? Never speak about it? Because he knows I know about the countless girls he raped. He knows I saw those tapes —and that I had him help me destroy them before he could remember what they were. He must know that I know I'm not the first girl he tried to replace Mariana with; I found evidence of at least two before me. I wouldn't be surprised if there were many more.

Is he not mad about it? Not even enough to bring it up, to make an excuse, or gauge my thoughts on it all? Or does he assign jealousy to the reason I destroyed them, as he did when I found out they existed? Maybe, because he sees no wrong in what he did, he can't fathom how I'd really feel about it.

"I love you so much," he murmurs.

My voice is vacant when I say, "I love you too."

"I missed you, sweetheart . . ." He scoops my hand up in his and turns it over to expose my wrist, his thumb pressing into my vein. "Trade with me."

I willingly accept his offer, knowing his blood is more healing than the ointments spread on my flesh, and more potent than Ziggy's and Lance's blood.

Since the salon is in a strip mall off a busy street, we park in the alley behind it before meeting a tall girl with a neon pink pixie cut at the locked door.

"Hey, Anthony and Maria, I'm Tallie," she says as she ushers us in and shuts the door behind us, locking it while explaining it's so anybody who may think they're open from their lights doesn't walk in.

"Thanks for this," Denendrius says as he fishes his wallet out of his pocket. He pulls out a handful of fifties and folds them in half before unsnapping the chest pocket of his leather jacket and tucking them inside—like they're a prize he wants her to know she'll get once she's done a satisfactory job.

"What would you like to start with?" Tallie asks as she motions to the empty salon.

To the left, four hairdressing chairs face a counter lined with a long mirror. To the right, two pedicure chairs sit beneath shelves of nail polish, beside tables and closed cupboards.

"Hair," I decide as Denendrius parks himself on a nearby chair in the waiting room.

Tallie waves him over. "You can come sit near your girlie if you want since there's nobody else here."

He obliges and sits in the hairdressing chair next to the one she directs me to.

She turns it so I face myself in the mirror. The bags under my eyes make me look like I haven't slept in a week, and the bruising on my face is fading and yellowing now. If she has thoughts about them, she doesn't say a word.

"So, what are we doing to your hair tonight?" she asks as she runs her fingers through the long strands of my sandy hair.

"Just a trim," I start, pinching a small section of the bottom between my middle and index finger to show a couple of centimeters.

She nods in agreement. "Your hair is so beautiful and shiny."

"Thanks." Viorel's blood has helped with that.

"When was the last time you had a cut?"

My eye twitches at the memory. I was ten years old and was put into a new foster home. My foster parents' fifteen-year-old biological daughter was sick of sharing her room with placements—and honestly, I couldn't blame her and was uncomfortable sharing with her too—and decided to get back at them by cutting my hair while I slept. They were good enough to punish her, and they promptly took me to the salon to have it fixed. Thankfully, I woke up after the first snip.

"Ten years old," is all I say.

After washing my hair and nearly putting me to sleep with

a head massage, she leads me back to the chair. Thin tendrils of water escape the towel wrapped around my soaked strands. They dart beneath the plastic cape, and I shiver as they curl down my spine.

When she grabs the scissors, my heart spasms. "Please, *please* be careful. Don't cut it too short." I show her how little I want trimmed with my fingers again, searching Denendrius's calculative eyes in the mirror for any sign he's upset.

"No worries. We'll just clean it up."

"No more than this," I insist, remembering how upset Denendrius was when I teased him about cutting my hair as a disguise when he was human. He nearly came unhinged at the mere idea, and I don't want to know if a haircut is enough for him to discard or hurt me. He'd likely postpone turning me until it grew back out, at minimum.

A friendly smile spreads across Denendrius's lips as he says, "Trim her hair like your life depends on it."

When he laughs, she joins in on the humor with a chuckle and grin. But her life *does* depend on it. I know he'll kill her the moment her scissors snip too far.

"Oh, I usually do!" She laughs. "Hair is so special to us girlies, right?"

I merely nod.

She takes a small section of my hair between her fingers and holds it up for me to see. "How's that? We really don't need to take much off, just even some areas out."

I glance at Denendrius, and he gives me an encouraging smile and a wink.

"Yeah, that's good," I tell her, but hold my breath when she makes that first cut.

Denendrius tells me I can relax as she trims my hair, as if it's me who cares so much about it being perfect. I love my long hair too, but if he weren't in this equation, I wouldn't think twice about her holding those scissors.

When she's done trimming my hair with no incident, she asks, "Would you like some layers?"

I nod. "Yeah please—"

"What's that?" Denendrius interjects.

I swallow a knot. "It won't affect the overall length of my hair, just make it look less blunt across the bottom."

"Oh." He relaxes in his chair. "That would look better."

I give her a go-ahead nod, and she puts the scissors back to my hair.

She dries my hair after, the hot air occasionally wafting across my face making me crinkle my nose. Leaving my hair straight, we move on to a face mask before she gives me a manicure and pedicure. I keep my toenails bare of color and pick a soft blue I know Denendrius will approve of for my fingernails.

Denendrius dicks around with the hairdressing tools to occupy himself while Tallie tends to me. He studies the various bottles of hair care products but doesn't use any when he pulls his hair out of its elastic to brush it before tying it back again. He's most keen on the hair dryer though, cranking it to its highest setting before relaxing back in the chair with his eyes closed as he wafts the heat across his face and torso.

When my pampering is done, I feel no different emotionally than when I arrived. Though my face and hair feel softer, and my nails show no sign that my fingers were curled around metal bars just days ago, my core is just as heavy and aching.

XXXIX

I lean my head against the cool window, staring up at the streetlights as they dart past overhead. Exhaustion bumps me and throws my consciousness off balance. The pampering did a decent job of relaxing me, but somehow used up what little energy I had available.

Soft rock plays gently from the speaker near my knee, the warmth of the heated seat like a hug. I let the dash of yellow lights against the dark sky lull me to sleep, the smoothness of the car over the pavement rocking me. Wishing I could sleep forever, I let myself be stolen from this painful reality. I dream of late-night drives with my gang family . . . when somehow, things were so much simpler than they are now.

"We're here, sweetheart." Denendrius's voice reaches into dreamland and drags me out with a start.

It drags me right back to that dog cage, drowning me in disorientation and horror, because I know the sight before me can't possibly be real. I know the car cannot be parked in front of the apartment. The last time I was here, Denendrius was human, and I was his blood slave. We fled into the night under the shield of a shared delusion that led us to Bellevue.

An inhuman wail strangles me, and I can't feel the car around me anymore, just cold metal. It feels like I'm falling, so I reach for something to hang onto, and Denendrius's chilly hand slips into mine.

"It's okay, sweetheart," he murmurs.

My breaths are tangled. It's not real. It can't be real.

Pain explodes in my chest. Was none of it real? Ziggy rescuing me, talking to Viorel, our days together until Denendrius took me back?

"It's not real?" I choke out.

Denendrius turns my face to his, worry bleeding from his black eyes as they frantically dance over me. "Hey there . . . Hey, you're okay."

"This isn't real."

He nods. "You're here with me, Marianna," he promises. "This is real. You're real. I'm real."

"Why are we here?" I plead, waiting for the apartment to dissolve in front of me and show me nothing but the darkness of that cold dirt room again.

Denendrius swallows. "I needed to come back here once more before we left."

"Why?" My chest heaves, the feel of the car still so far away.

"Hold on—" Denendrius opens his door and vanishes, and I gasp as the passenger door opens beside me. "Come feel the ground."

My fingers are fuzzy with panic, the skin on my face numb with it. My breaths climb, my heart rate stuttering as he unbuckles my seatbelt and helps me out of the car. Cool air pushes against me, and I drag it deep into my lungs.

"You feel that?" Denendrius asks evenly. "How about the ground?"

I shift my weight between my feet until I can hear the

crunch of dirt between the soles of my boots and the parking lot. He takes my hand and rests it on the top of the cold car.

"Feel the smooth metal?" he asks.

I slide my fingers down the curve of the car, feeling the dirt residue against the pads of my fingers.

"This is real," he promises me.

"This is real," I repeat, a tear darting from my eye.

"You *are not* waking up in that cage again," he promises, his tone firm. "You are here, with me, at the apartment."

I nod and inhale the cool air. "We're at the apartment. The apartment's real," I tell myself.

Somehow, it doesn't quite feel real. Looking up at its old brown exterior, it feels like something left behind in my memories, in my nightmares.

He laces his fingers through mine and guides me along to the glass front door. It looks exactly how I remember it, smells hauntingly preserved as he opens the door and guides me to the old, carpeted stairs.

Stairs I fled down so many times, for so many reasons.

We make it up to the apartment, where everything started. Where all my nightmares spiraled out of control, and life as I knew it—as much as I hated it—ended.

I hold my breath, unsure of what to expect as Denendrius unlocks the door. When it swings open, I flinch. I don't know why.

It's unchanged, as if the place has been holding its breath since we left. I hug myself, the air heavy and cold like it's harboring the death we left behind. Like it's been lonely, waiting for us to return. I enter and step onto the white carpet, and Denendrius closes and locks the door.

Slowly, I let my eyes wander across the apartment. The eighties-style kitchen with its old brown wooden cabinets and outdated fridge is to my right, the hall up a few steps to my left. The dining room, still with its small metal table and chairs, no longer has the blow-up mattress Derek once had between it and the wall.

I step out of my boots and carefully move forward, turning toward the small living room across from the tiny dining area. I swallow a lump at the familiar sight. The black leather couch sits across from the wooden entertainment stand, just in front of the dusty corner where Denendrius's packed boxes remain. Beside it, the empty ladder bookshelves lean against the wall.

Someone is moving heavy boxes around in the secret room —the narrow second bedroom between the hall and living room, which Denendrius sealed off at some point and Rayonne and I discovered while he was human. I assume it's Sergei in there, but I don't care enough to ask.

"Are you okay?" Denendrius murmurs, and I look over my shoulder to see Denendrius and Sergei watching me.

"I don't know." I exhale and shudder, my knees weak.

There's something sickly comforting about this place. It must be the familiarity. So many things happened here. And somehow, as strange as it is, those things were still so much simpler than they are now.

"How is everything still here?" I hug myself tighter and turn back to face them.

Denendrius grunts. "There are perks to renting from slum-lords. I hypnotized him but also paid two years of rent in advance to leave me alone, and a few thousand to not ask questions or talk to the cops about me."

"You're not worried about Viorel's men looking for us here?" I ask him, drawing in another shaky breath.

Denendrius grunts dismissively. "No, we're hiding in plain sight. They'd have to assume I'd be an idiot to come here."

Sergei laughs. "You *are* an idiot for coming here."

A smirk breaks across Denendrius's face as he turns to look at Sergei, his own laughter coming from somewhere deep inside him. There's something about it—about the genuine sound of it—that makes my core ache with a hot sensation like sharp lightning down my legs.

Denendrius looks around at the apartment with a bit more wonder than I can manage, and sighs. "A lot happened in the handful of years I lived here."

I can't help but wonder how many people—young girls, in particular—he killed here. How many girls spent their last moments trapped in the confines of these walls? How many weren't lucky enough to escape?

Am I the only girl he's brought here who has ever left alive?

Denendrius sits on the couch and sniffs. "Is that what I smelled like human? Weird. Different from the first time I was human. I wonder why."

Sergei grunts. "Diet changes and different hygiene practices, for one. That's not even considering potential changes with the cure."

"Yeah, probably."

Sergei's chuckling as he says, "You probably stank like olive oil, wine, and fish back then."

"Shut up." Denendrius laughs, the sound too bright and genuine to be his own. "Oh, did you hear anything about the girl next door? I went a little nuts when I was human and tried to feed on her."

Pursing his lips, Sergei crosses his arms and says, "No. Should I look into it for you?"

Denendrius's smile doesn't even waver. "Nah, it doesn't really matter."

My heart hammers, sweat beading on the nape of my neck when I dare ask, "What about Allison, the girl you unburied in the lot across the street? Do you know if she was found like you wanted?"

Denendrius's annoyed scowl is instant, but he only looks at the balcony past me, the long, slatted blinds blocking his view from that exact lot.

I don't miss the way Sergei tilts his head at Denendrius as his brows shoot up. "Like you *wanted*?"

"Yeah, I looked it up, and they took her," Denendrius grumbles at him. His head sways back and forth in disbelief. "I thought I was being haunted by *lemures*, so I unburied her, hoping to fix the problem. But I was just having flashbacks, and the cure was screwing with my head."

Sergei laughs at him, and I don't quite understand, though Denendrius rolls his eyes and says, "Yeah, yeah, I *know*."

"What are we doing here?" I don't mean for the words to sound like a plea, but they do.

"We're spending the day, and I will organize to have everything moved to Italy tomorrow night," Sergei says, continuing to smile.

My eyes flit to Denendrius's, who is back to smiling at me, his eyes shimmering black like obsidian. They are far too bright to belong to someone who narrowly escaped being imprisoned by Nazis while his girl was dying in a dog kennel.

There's only one reason he could look so calm.

"This is it, then? We're going to Italy?" I'm too emotionally ragged for the excitement and relief I believe should blossom in me.

The corner of Denendrius's lip quirks. "Yes, sweetheart. A couple quick stops, and we're leaving Lorimer."

My heavy heart thuds in my chest, and I heave out a breath. "I can't wait." With a trembling hand, I tuck my hair behind my ear. "How long until you turn me?"

His eyes soften on me as he stands. "*Soon*. I've had my thirst tested plenty, and I think I'm ready."

My heart soars but clogs my throat and I cough at the feel of it fluttering there.

"Let's go to bed." He winks at me, the action like a poison arrow through my center, and my heart twists in a plummet to my gut.

Will he expect intimacy, knowing the state of my body? I glance at the bag of drug store supplies he brought and left on the kitchen counter, knowing I'm going to have to strip for him soon regardless.

Slowly, I follow Denendrius to the bedroom. Like the rest of the apartment, it's unchanged. The same bedding we slept in remains. It doesn't look like anyone slept there while we were gone.

As always, I crawl onto the left side. Tears sting my eyes when I rest my head on the pillow. I have Denendrius's, and somehow, after all these months, I swear it still smells like that human man. I turn my face into the pillow, a shaky breath expelled against the cold fabric before I inhale the memory of him again.

The ignorance—the blood slavery—was nearly bliss. He was a lot less frightening when his mark had me convinced his human self was somehow a different man.

Denendrius sits down on the mattress beside me. "What's wrong?" he coos, running his hand down my back.

"I don't know," I say, watching him deep in thought in the closet mirrors.

But it's *everything* that's wrong.

I roll over as Denendrius nestles into bed beside me, pulling the blanket over us. "I love you," he whispers as his fingertips slide the hair away from the side of my face.

I turn my head to stare at him, his onyx eyes inches from mine. They're softer than I've seen them in weeks. We hold each other's gaze for too many seconds, neither of us blinking, like we're waiting for the moment to shift—or snap and unravel. I reach my hand behind his head and pull the tie from his hair.

Does he ever regret turning back?

"Close your eyes," I whisper.

Smiling, he does. He looks so disarmingly sweet with the blissful curve of his lips.

I run my weak fingers through his soft hair, careful not to touch his cold skin while imagining it's warm. He exhales and relaxes under the blanket while I pretend he's still human for a minute—pretend he never turned back and nothing ever went wrong. Maybe it would be easier if we were still delusionally in love in Bellevue.

Tears well in my eyes and drip onto the pillow.

I'd still have my daughter if we were there, and there's a good chance the future would have changed since Ziggy told me. Would I be happy right now, holding my baby girl instead of being oceans apart from her? Sure, Denendrius and I would have likely had to move a lot to evade capture, but we would have been delusionally happy.

I'd still have a life, instead of lying in an apartment I fought so hard to escape from.

I could have had a relatively normal human life. Or at least *think* I did.

A part of me, the part I don't like to admit was really me, is homesick for it. For the laughs and smiles Denendrius and I shared in our insanity, for the simple dreams we had. He wasn't perfect—he still had a lot of issues beyond the side effects of the cure—but it felt like we deserved those versions of each other. He was like the man who asked me on our first date, who brought me to a nice restaurant and rented a whole boat for me. When he was human, Denendrius was that sweet—though *not quite right*—man I genuinely liked before I had the *audacity* to say no to him. And as long as I continued to say yes, to be his perfect partner, he stayed that way.

When he was human . . . when he couldn't remember that he liked to strangle girls to death or rape them for fun.

Should I be ashamed of myself for missing a tiny—dead— piece of him even though all the rest of him has ruined me? I suppose it's the feelings left over from his blood mark. Although the entire thing was an illusion . . . it *felt* real. And like Viorel said: in some ways, it really was.

I know Denendrius will turn me soon, and that we're so close to going to Italy now, but I can't feel the full relief of that yet, especially when I'll still have to find a way to make it out of that villa alive before I can go home. It makes the past, despite how I don't truly want to go back, seem easier.

"I'm so happy right now. I haven't been this happy since I was human," Denendrius murmurs. "Since the second time I was human," he clarifies.

The back of my throat burns and tightens as my eyes sting with more tears. I release a shaky breath. "If I ask you something, can you be honest with me? Completely?"

His brow furrows, his lips relaxed until he whispers, "Okay."

"Do you regret it?" Tears flood my eyes, my heart in my throat. "Do you regret turning back into a vampire?"

His lids lift, a wet sheen over his obsidian eyes as they hold mine. I see his deep swallow, and he releases a cold and shallow breath against my face. "I don't know," he admits. "I love being a vampire—having a human body is such a tiny part of my life —but I regret how I chose to turn back. I regretted it the most in Romania."

"Why?" I whisper, unable to stop myself from reaching out and tucking a loose curl behind his ear.

He makes a strangled noise when he tries to speak, then clears his throat. "Aeliana, mostly. We would still have her had things worked out in Bellevue. She wouldn't be lost to Huarsar. She'd be in your arms where she belongs, with me at your side. If I had to choose us like this now, or us with Aeliana and me sick and human, I think I'd choose the latter. Both options hurt, but at least in one, we have our family."

I bite my bottom lip. For a moment, his words make me see

the world as he does. I have to accept that Viorel is the villain in Denendrius's story, even if he isn't in mine. To Denendrius, Viorel is the man he was dropped in front of as a newborn vampire—broken, terrified, and claiming he needed help. Even if I want to believe Viorel imprisoned him for a good reason, not knowing for sure still hurts.

I wish I had known Denendrius in Rome, so I could know with certainty whether he deserved Viorel's wrath as a newborn vampire. I wish I could look into the past and know if he was already too far gone . . . already *wrong enough* to be written off.

I don't want this stinging thorn in my side, this little bit of poison in my heart, that might always wonder if part of my pain and suffering is indirectly a result of Viorel's decision.

Denendrius didn't deserve all of what happened to him . . . *but neither have I.*

I wonder if there's a timeline—like the one where Ziggy and I are the best of friends, with me as his familiar—where everything is okay for Denendrius and me. Is there a version of our lives where we're fated to be together instead of being the death of one another? One where Viorel helps Denendrius instead of shoving him in a cell to be abused? A timeline where the parts of Denendrius that were simply not quite right began to straighten out the farther he got from his trauma as a human under his father's thumb? Is it possible—was there ever a time —when Denendrius could have unlearned what his father taught him as a boy, and what the world reinforced in him as a man? Or was he simply broken too early to ever see the world differently?

I hope there's a timeline where we're both happy—together or apart. I just hope there's a timeline that doesn't hurt like this one.

Is there a timeline where he doesn't have all this pain that he's held inside him as he's traveled through time, passing bloody chunks to every girl he could get his hands on like he could somehow empty himself of them?

All of the harm he's passed along will be for nothing, because in *this timeline*, when I put him down, he will still be full of everything that was torn up inside him.

Tears flood my eyes and blur the sight of him.

Denendrius.

A man who was born to die. A man with a death prolonged for nearly two-thousand years.

He's a tragedy, really. We both are.

Two tragedies whose lives have crashed and twisted irreparably together.

Denendrius moves his lips to mine, a desperate kiss coming before he says, "I love you, Marianna, with all that's left of my heart."

But I know there's nothing left of it. There hasn't been *for a long time.*

My words come out on a sharp breath. "I love you."

"We'll be okay, you and I," he whispers, thumb running down my cheek and over my bottom lip.

Perhaps in another timeline.

But not this one. *Never in this one.*

XL

I wake to Denendrius softly stroking my cheek and murmuring for me to get up. The sight of the apartment bedroom has me flinching, but I recover enough to steady my legs beneath me. In the hall, the bloodstain from Denendrius turning back remains faded on the carpet in front of the bathroom.

Rubbing sleep from my eyes, I flick the bathroom light on. My joints lock me in place.

Marissa stands in the middle of the bathroom. Her usually greasy strands of dark brown hair are softer, and she wears low-rise jeans and a pink tank top that touches the waistline of them. My sharp breaths bring the scent of artificial strawberries into me before the abrupt stench of dirt and ammonia has my stomach spasming with the memory of the dirt basement.

My lips twitch to form her name, but she's already gone.

I stand there for a few moments more—waiting for my heart to calm but realizing it never really will—before going to the bathroom.

Denendrius and Sergei are coordinating something in

Russian when I come out. I hug myself as I move to Denen-drius's side, my skin prickling when he rests his hand between my shoulder blades to acknowledge my presence.

The sight of Marissa is burned into my brain, and my eyes dart around the apartment like I might see her again. I swear I catch a glimpse of someone moving on the couch in the reflec-tion of the black TV screen, but I wrench my eyes away before the figure has a chance to fully develop.

My voice comes out mousy when Sergei turns his attention to his phone and paces down the hall. "What now, Den?"

"We're going to part ways with Sergei for a bit and find another motel to stay in." He slings his arm over my shoulders, and I wince at the weight pressing against my weakened muscles. Noticing, he lets his arm slide down my back and grips my waist.

Soon, Sergei gives me a gentle goodbye squeeze before Denendrius and I return to the car. I watch the apartment building in the side mirror until Denendrius turns a corner and it's out of sight. Will I ever see it again? Will it still be standing in a few decades? Will it remain a vessel for his ghosts, for the girl that was once me?

We pick up the Mustang where Denendrius abandoned it a couple weeks ago—to flee from Nazis on foot—in the deep south of Lorimer, behind one of the many dilapidated and long-foreclosed properties found on that rough side of the city. I'm amazed the car hasn't been stripped for parts. I still can't wrap my head around why driving this flashing neon sign is so important to him that he's willing to risk his safety, but I suppose it's only one more of his odd obsessions.

On the way out of South Lorimer, I can't help but scan the dark, spotty lighting that outlines the unkempt streets, searching for the rickety house where I spent my formative years with my mother. Yet nothing looks familiar. I've avoided this part of town since I was removed from it and permanently placed in foster care at nine. So much has changed in this cold neighborhood over the years—crime has thickened, residents have thinned—that I might not recognize the house even if Denendrius parked right in front of it.

If I'm honest, I can't quite remember what the outside looked like, anyway. Certainly not the street we lived on. But that bedroom my mother kept me locked in all those years . . . Now *that* I have memorized.

"I burned it down," Denendrius says.

I turn my face away from the window to stare at him, the tip of my nose cold from resting on the chilled glass.

The intensity with which I studied the old stacks of wood and splitting roofs must have given me away. "Why?"

His revelation doesn't make me feel anything. That place has always existed strangely in the world—in *my* world. It was always more a part of me than this city. I suppose only leaving it a handful of times made it feel disconnected from the ground it sat on. Even though I always assumed it would be a tagged pile of rubble by now, those walls have been iron inside me. The place he burned down wasn't the same one I lived in. Its structure in my psyche is weaker than it once was, but I still visit it often enough that it's impossible to reconcile the idea that it could really be gone.

"After I called the police and they took you and your mother out of there, I kept going back. I'd sit in your bedroom and torture myself with the smells. So many men had been in there . . . I couldn't even bring myself to sit on the edge of the bed. It *stank*. For the first few months, I told myself I was going back so I could collect those scents and know who to track down and kill. Yet even after I killed all those men, I kept returning and driving myself mad with regret over giving you back. So, I set it on fire."

I'm not sure what to say, but I know what he wants to hear. "Thanks for burning it down. And for what you did." I lace my fingers through his when he shifts his hand to my lap. "Don't beat yourself up, okay? It's the past. We have a bright future ahead of us."

He may have burned it down, but as we drive to find another motel with vacancy, I'm back in that bedroom. It's been a long time since I was Denendrius's blood slave—and since I was with Viorel—that I dreamed of it. I think Viorel tried to guard my dreams. I never directly asked after that first time he changed it, and he never went out of his way to admit it. But he's not here now, and even though I'm not trapped in the confines of my dreams this time, the memories are vivid.

The stench returns. The sweat. The cigarettes and smoky meth scents. I can practically taste the air like a film on my tongue.

I grip desperately to Denendrius's hand to ground myself, and I part my lips for whatever first thought might leave my tongue to help distract me, but his phone rings.

We roll to a stop at a red light, barely out of South Lorimer now, the bright color reflecting off the black of the Mustang's hood. He slips his phone out of his pocket, and I glimpse Sergei's name as he answers it.

The strain in Sergei's Russian, like he doesn't want to utter whatever he's saying but must, has me tensing.

Denendrius races into the desolate parking lot of a low-quality motel across the street and slams the brakes. The seatbelt locks across my torso as I'm thrown forward.

"They what?" Denendrius grinds out as he yanks his hand from mine to curl it in a fist on his lap. *"What does that mean* if customs seized my samples? Why would they do that?"

My eyes fly wide. The fucking Italian border seized his sperm samples?

A subtle gasping sound escapes Denendrius's lips as he opens them to pull in a short breath. "Did they seize and dispose of Marianna's too?"

Muffled, I recognize Sergei's hard Russian *"no."*

Denendrius tears his leather jacket off, leaving it crumpled in the seat as he scrambles out of the car like the metal is going to collapse and crush him. He slams the door so hard the frame shakes. I sink into my seat when he hollers and paces in front of the hood, talking with his hands as he argues until he stills. He walks backward as he lowers the phone, his forearm pressed onto the top of his head as his wide eyes lock on mine through the windshield.

My chest lifts with heavy breaths, a sickening mix of terror and relief wetting the nape of my neck and palms. This is Viorel's doing, I know it. Somehow, he intervened. Why else would Denendrius's samples get seized and disposed of, but not mine?

Though I'm relieved I won't have to share anymore biological children with Denendrius, dread pools in my gut as I brace for the violent fallout and hope it's not directed at me.

He hangs his head, and I wait for the eruption. I can feel how it builds in the air like there's no metal or glass between us, the strangling thickness of it. Still, when he throws his head back and bellows at the top of his lungs with his hands spread out at his hips, I full-body flinch in the seat. He screams Latin like he's cursing the gods before he takes a few heaving breaths while stumbling back toward the car. He folds forward at the waist and collapses over the hood with his head on his crossed arms.

Slowly, I unbuckle and carefully open the door, taking a step into the parking lot and white-knuckle gripping the frame of the door while using it as a shield.

"Denendrius . . ." I know I have to take command of the situation before he spirals with it.

He doesn't respond, though with the way his shoulders move with his heaving breaths, I'm not sure he can.

I slip around the car door, each step toward him sending a shockwave of terror through me. "What happened?" I ask, wanting to be absolutely sure his samples are gone, but that mine are safe.

When he snaps up, I stumble backward into the car door and catch myself on the side mirror.

"Huarsar," he snarls, a wet sheen over his tormented eyes. His voice breaks as he continues. "I don't know how they knew, but the Italian government seized and destroyed my samples—made sure to tell our fertility clinic such—and yours were reshipped *somewhere*. The fertility clinic doesn't know what happened to them." His shoulders fall and he shakes his head in disbelief. "He must have figured out what I meant about ensuring we would still have our family . . . *I just had to open my mouth . . .*"

Tears well in my eyes and spill over, but they're not from grief this time. My knees wobble with relief. *I don't have to have another one of his babies.* And Viorel made sure to relocate mine? He must have sent them somewhere safe, where Denendrius couldn't get access to them.

Denendrius hangs his head again.

I let the tears barrel down my cheeks as I reach a trembling hand out. "Den—"

But he's *gone.*

I'm alone in the dimly lit lot with the damp air whooshing in and out of me. He left with such swiftness he might have been an illusion. Panic nestles into my gut like a sharp blade, and I hug myself as I glance around the empty street slick with melting snow, and the dark buildings.

I'm so alone . . . Trapped with myself. An invisible hand locks around my throat. Dread clings to me, and I realize I don't trust my mind. I know I should be more afraid of vampires tracking us—of someone lurking in the shadows, watching as I stand exposed in this desolate parking lot—but the threat of my own mind unraveling feels far more imminent.

"Denendrius?" I choke out. I'm sure he's so far from earshot by now, but still I whisper, "C-can you come back? I'm scared."

I grip myself tighter, pressing my body into the open door and side mirror as my wide gaze flits around the lot. Adrenaline builds in my veins and is the sole reason I move.

With so much free space in the parking lot, he managed to park between the lines enough that I can justify turning the car off. I slip into his leather jacket and shove the keys into a pocket, finding his wallet when I do. My eyes dart around the perimeter of the parking lot as I open his wallet, then drop to assess its contents. His fake identification and mine stare up at me, the leather thick with cash. There are a few worn gift cards he must have taken off victims, but not a single credit card.

Swallowing, I assess the dingy, severely outdated strip of motel rooms at the end of the parking lot, the neon light on the sign overhead advertising their vacancy. Figures. I can practically smell the musty, stale smoke of the rooms from here. Drawing in a cool breath, I make my way toward the office, the bells upon entering making me flinch beneath the fluorescent lights as I swing the heavy door open.

An older lady sits behind the peeling, old wood of the counter as she reads a yellow-page book while smoking, her true age distorted by the habit.

"I want a room," I tell her.

Her eyes remain on her book. "Sixty bucks. We're cash only."

I fish a few bills from Denendrius's wallet and drop them on the counter. She barely glances at them—doesn't even look at me—before settling her eyes back on her book as she reaches beneath the counter for a key. She drops it on the counter and shifts back in her metal folding chair.

Snatching the keys, I take long strides to the door in case she gains enough attention to ask for identification. There are only a dozen rooms, and I find mine in moments. Shoving the worn key in the lock, I search the parking lot for Denendrius before I gulp and unlock the door.

The stale stench of shitty weed, musty carpet, and the faint whiff of ammonia makes me crinkle my nose as I enter and flick the light on. Not trusting the worn maroon carpet, I keep my shoes on and snatch the TV remote.

I crave sound. People talking. Music.

Crawling onto the duvet, I shove the idea of bedbugs to the back of my mind as I search for something to watch. There are fewer options than the other motels we've stayed in so far, and I only recognize the names of cartoons and shows I know I dislike. I pick a cartoon and crank the volume so it's louder than my paranoid thoughts. The bright colors wash over me.

I don't care that my shoes wet the end of the blanket when I pull my knees up to my chest and hug them. Pressure builds in my head from impending tears, and I do my best to stop my sharp breaths from quickening. Even on the blanket and mattress, my bottom is sore. But the pain reminds me I'm *here.*

Focusing on the show is impossible. My eyes flick between the screen and the door a couple of meters away, but nothing more than a mess of colors and sounds registers.

Adrenaline has me twitching, anticipation making my heart flutter at the base of my throat as I wait for Denendrius to come back. Every sound has me tense and listening for the turn of the knob and the request to unlock the door. My only thoughts about running are from knowing I'm too scared to try again.

Denendrius got what he wanted, because right now, my fear of leaving him is stronger than my homesickness for Romania.

So I wait on the bed, watching the door and desperately

waiting like his good girl. One episode turns into another. The longer he's gone, the harder it is to resist pulling back the curtain and watching the street for signs of him.

I hate what he's turned me into. I used to be so tough. Too mean and cocky sometimes, sure, but I could hold my own. I was like a pit bull when he came back into my life, and now I'm a shrieking fucking kitten. I'm pathetic, because I know the moment he returns, I'm going to relax. Even if he's furious and ranting, I'll at least have the relief that he's here, and I'm not alone. I'd much rather have him here on top of me than be alone, because—

My heart free falls into my stomach, and I gasp for breath and squeeze my eyes closed so tightly it hurts. Hot tears cascade down my cheeks.

Because . . .

Because at least if he were here, he'd be able to tell me if something really moved in the shadows of the dark bathroom to my left.

My sobs are sudden, and I cry so hard I can't hear the giggling cartoon children on TV anymore. The bed feels like it's tilting, like it's trying to roll me off it, and I collapse on my side and hug myself tighter. When I hold my breath to stifle my cries, I can't hear the TV anymore.

My legs scream at me to stretch out, but I keep them tight against my body. I don't want to risk the cold metal bars against my feet.

I shiver, and my teeth chatter. When I pull Denendrius's leather jacket closer, my hands brush the sherpa blanket. I yank them away. My fingers tingle and go numb.

Why is it so cold?

A soft hand fills mine, Marissa's familiar voice whispery warm in my ear. *"It's okay, Marianna. You're safe. I promise. You can open your eyes."*

Her presence pulls a miserable groan out of me, and I

clench my jaw. *She can't be here.* I don't want her to leave me alone, but I know what it means if she's here. I try to tell myself it can't be . . . but I know there's a chance I might not be awake in the motel or cage at all. It's highly probable that my organs have failed and I'm on the cusp of death in a coma. Even if Denendrius returns, there's no guarantee any of this is real.

I can't feel the mattress beneath me. My body aches like I'm on hard metal. Each sharp, staggered breath pulls in scents so similar to that basement. I feel crazy—in denial—trying to convince myself I'm not there.

"Open your eyes," she whispers.

I'm much too scared to do that. Partly because I might open them to dark captivity, but also because if the motel is real, she might go away, and I'll still be all alone.

"Please don't leave me alone," I beg her, my mouth thick with saliva and salty tears that have run past my lips.

I'm unsure how much time passes with my hand clenching hers, but I focus solely on the feel of her warm skin against mine and her quiet breaths until a hesitant knock on the door —so soft it might not be real—yanks me out of my hellish void by my feet. I scramble to the motel door without making the conscious decision to move, yanking it open and throwing myself against him.

I hate myself for my instinctual response to his presence, for how I press my body into his and lock my arms around his center like I need us melded together. But his solid body is real. The acrid scent of iron—blood—on his breath and clothes is *real.* My breaths settle with the feel of his heavy ones beneath my head.

"You left me alone," I squeeze out. "I was scared without you."

If the admission didn't benefit me, I wouldn't dare utter it aloud.

He tries to subtly step away from me as he enters and shuts the door, but I'm as stuck to him as the scent of his latest victim.

"I'm sorry," he whispers, and the pain in his voice is a sharp blade as he chokes out, *"Do you still love me, even though I can't give you babies?"*

I squeeze him tighter, like I need to convince my body he's real. *This is real.* And though I hate him . . . *God, do I fucking hate him . . .* there's something in his words—something in the agony behind them—that sends a wave of nauseating grief across my skin, raising goosebumps on my arms. My chest hurts so badly that a sob cuts through me, and tears flood my eyes.

"I'm sorry," he cries, his tone begging. "I'm sorry, Marianna. Do you still love me?"

Sobs wrack my body so hard that I can't even force the lie out to make him feel better. I fight to regain control of my breaths and emotions. If he really believes my act, the fact I hold him as I do should be evidence enough. He should have no logical reason to believe I don't. Something about that makes me hurt for him.

"I really love you," I squeeze out as I furiously wipe tears from my cheeks with the heels of my hands. "We'll adopt a baby. Just like we had planned. Even when I was fighting you when you were first a vampire, I never had an issue with you not being able to have biological children." My breaths find a steady rhythm as relief fills his eyes, but then I blurt, "I'm not Marianne."

Though his stiff hands grip me, he's gentle as he peels me off him and pushes me an arm's length away. I loathe myself for how my hands automatically reach for him, but the darkness seeping into his eyes . . . suspicion tightening his gaze as he stares at me with rigid uncertainty . . . has me dropping them to my sides.

My next set of words slices my tongue on the way out. But I need him to believe that I love him no matter what. I need him to *drown* in the delusion of *us*. Sink so deep that all he finds are ways to justify any possible slip-ups I might have while I'm playing pretend.

"Marianne deserved whatever you did to her," I force out, despite the pain of each syllable. "I found that letter from the 1930s when I was exploring your hidden room. I read how she agreed to marry you, then left you with the ring and the letter to run off with her childhood friend the moment he became interested in her, all because you couldn't give her biological children."

His shoulders lower as he hangs onto my words, the suspicion vacating his gaze and making space for pain.

"What an *evil bitch*," I say while shaking my head in disbelief, but the words feel like turning a knife against myself. "She said she loved you."

Low, he says, "I killed her. She *suffered*."

I don't let the horror at his words make it to my face. Instead, I pretend to accept them, accept *him*, as I step closer and say, "She deserved it."

He merely nods, staring at me in partial awe, like he's amazed I can see things from his point of view.

My stomach clenches when I reach him and rest my hand on his stomach. "I would never hurt you like that, Denendrius. We were both adopted, so we know what it feels like. We'll find some babies and make sure they have no chance of growing up with parents who harm or reject them."

"Yeah?" he chokes out. "You don't think I'm less of a man?"

"Of course not. I love you no matter what."

His cold hand comes up to lift my chin, his eyes softening with relief as they lock with mine. "I love you so much, Marianna. I knew everything would work out for us one way or another."

"I love you too, Den." I bite my lip, tears welling in my eyes again at the pain of being so close to him. At the pain of this conversation. I find a way to use them to my benefit, saying, "I've really always loved you. Since the beginning. But you were right, I was scared. I was absolutely terrified of being in love. I'd never been loved properly before you, and I didn't know what to do. I thought if I cut you out of my life, I could deal with the pain of losing you sooner rather than later. I hated myself back then and swore you would eventually start to hate me too. But now I just want to be with you no matter what. Even if we can't have the family we want so badly, I want *you*."

"I know," he says. "That's why I've always fought so hard for you. It's why I'll always fight to the death for you."

I close my eyes as he leans down and crashes his lips against mine.

He murmurs against my lips, "We are woven into the fabric of the universe, sweetheart. Nothing can separate our threads. Nothing in life. Nothing in death."

Tears trickle from the corners of my eyes. The words would be much more romantic coming from someone as poetic as Viorel, rather than a monster like Denendrius who has done nothing but tangle and tear the threads of that fabric so he can stitch them into something that fits him comfortably.

Still, I try to mimic the depth of his love. *"Venus and Mars have nothing on us."*

He smiles against my lips and pulls me tight against him as he kisses me. He walks me backward to the bed and sprawls me out—my neck grateful for the relief after being craned back—and holds my head in his hands as he deepens our kiss and shoves my knees apart to stand at the bedside between my thighs. I let my thin tears drip from my eyes, the ache in my chest making it impossible to hold them back.

Gently pulling away, I throw out a carefully considered line and hook as I grip his cheeks in my shaky palms. "Maybe this is fate, right? You always talk about the fates. Maybe there's a greater reason this has happened. It hurts that we can't have our own biological children, but this means we'll get to save some babies by adopting them. Like we should have been saved. And this means we can raise as many children as we want over the years, and they'll all be equal to one another. We'll never have to worry about them feeling less than their older biological siblings."

He bites that hook, swallows it so deep I can see it in the intensity of his eyes and the frantic nod of his head. "*Yes,* you're right." His brow lifts with his pause. "I didn't realize you're beginning to accept the existence of the gods."

"With everything that has happened, us continuously being brought back together in spite of it all is proof enough."

In reality, this awfulness is only evidence there's no balance in the universe at all. No gods. Or, if there are, they're not worthy of worship.

He crawls against my side, pressing his body against mine and draping his leg over me as he squeezes me in his arms. His desperate need for comfort is palpable, so I hook my arms around his middle and lean my head against his chest.

"I'm *so lucky* you're mine." He heaves a cold breath against me. "Nobody has ever come close to understanding me like you do."

It's probably true, but it's not the positive thing he believes it is.

XLI

We lie there for a while longer until Denendrius dips out of the motel room to retrieve our belongings.

I notice the motel phone on the nightstand for the first time, and a fist squeezes my heart. I know the number Ziggy used to call the satellite phone at the castle, and it didn't even cross my mind to dial it. Though I tell myself it would have been stupid to try anyway since he's going to turn me into a vampire in a few days, and with my luck he would have returned mid-call, it's clear I'm not completely free of that cage despite not physically being there. But that was the point, right? Denendrius knew exactly what he was doing when he locked me in there.

When he returns, we have a shower before he tends to my wounds . . . which somehow develops into me blowing him since I'm still healing.

Dressed in soft pajamas with my hair damp and hanging, I curl back up on the duvet as Denendrius slips a pair of black silk boxers on. His own hair hangs wet below his collarbones.

"Can I ask you something, and you promise not to get upset?" I bite my cheek as I study his face.

The corner of his lip twitches back as his brows draw together. "Why would I get upset?"

I swallow. "Do you still believe in spirits?"

His face smooths, now unreadable as he slowly lifts a comb from my backpack. His eyes remain locked on mine.

My heart jerks, and I leap to add more explanation. "The spirits you thought were in the apartment. *Lemures.* Do you still believe in them?"

He combs his hair. "You're asking if I believe in ghosts?"

I rub my palm on the scratchy blanket and pull in a long breath. "Yeah, I guess."

Tucking loose strands of hair behind his ear, he looks across the room and his eyes fixate on the desk as he continues combing, like there's something more interesting there. "Do you believe in ghosts?"

My lips twist as I study him, the way he's withdrawing from the conversation like he wants to avoid it.

"Maybe." My voice comes out quiet, unsure enough that I could easily change my answer if I've somehow upset him.

He tucks the comb back into the backpack before sitting on the bed. He leans back, pressing his palms into the bed and stretching out beside me, rocking his leg a bit. "Do you think you've seen spirits?"

I press my top teeth into my bottom lip and rub them back and forth as I carefully consider my answer. "When I was in the cage, I thought I did."

He nods along as his leg rocks, his gaze remaining fixed on the desk. "Sometimes, when you're in isolation like that, it happens."

Impatience trickles through me, shaded with anxiety that makes my palms sweat and my mouth cottony. I wish he'd stop dancing around the question when I'm trying to have a serious conversation with him. "Seeing ghosts, or thinking you do?"

He purses his lips.

"Denendrius..." I sigh.

Finally facing me, he's fully composed, yet there's distance in his eyes. "What?"

"I'm serious. Did you see spirits in the apartment?"

His eyes search my face before connecting with mine. "Yes."

The knot in my throat loosens, and I manage to swallow.

"While I was imprisoned too," he adds, before he looks back across the room in thought.

I untangle my hands and wrap my arms around myself. "I saw things when I was in the cage."

He releases a noisy breath as he scoots up and sprawls out with his head on the pillow, mine near his waist. "You were sensory deprived and dying. I don't doubt you were hallucinating."

I tilt my head to look up at him. "I think I saw spirits too, though..."

He gives me a weak smile with no happiness in it.

I wait for him to ask me what I saw, but he doesn't.

I clear my throat, my impending words tightening it like my body knows they shouldn't be let out. "I saw..." I take a deep breath. "While in there, I saw a girl."

His eyes jump to mine, unblinking and unemotional as he stares at me like he's waiting to hear more.

"You, uh—" I clear my throat again and pull my hands in front of my stomach, twisting my fingers as I rest my eyes on them so I don't have to see him. "I-I-I know it wasn't real now, but you came back when I was in there. She was in the cage with me, and you let her out. You um ... Well, you took her to the bed and uh—" I cough. "You strangled her after."

My heart beats in the silence. I can feel Denendrius's eyes

on me, and I wait for him to say something about the girl or what he did, but he merely watches me in silence.

I scratch my face, a sudden itch in my jaw that moves to the back of my head. "She stayed around after, talking to me while I was stuck in there."

"Did she?"

I bite down on my bottom lip and nod.

"And you think she's some spirit or something?"

My shrug comes out more like a shudder that cascades all the way down my spine.

"Hm." He pets the top of my head, his touch making my heart miss a beat. "Maybe she was."

I look up and meet his eyes, trying to see his thoughts through them. The fact he doesn't deny killing anyone in the house or try to explain away the specific instance and make sure I understand it's not true, makes my body feel heavier on the bed.

"You think so?" I ask. Could I get him to admit it aloud? Admit that he kept girls in a cage there to rape them? That he killed them?

He purses his lips in thought. "Yeah, I've seen spirits at the old house before. It's an old house."

I don't let him get away with brushing away the reason for them. Houses don't get haunted by themselves. "And at the apartment? You said you saw a spirit there. A girl. Then you unburied Allison across the street later."

His gaze moves over my face. "Yeah, I saw her at the apartment."

"I saw a girl named Marissa," I whisper, studying his reaction. I wait for the look of confusion, or for him to tell me there are lots of girls named Marissa, so the odds he's killed at least one are quite high.

Denendrius stares at me for a long moment before blinking.

It's my turn to avoid his eyes. I focus on the TV past my feet, a silent commercial giving me a place to rest my gaze.

"Hm." I feel him shift onto his elbow, his legs parallel alongside my body. "She talked to you?"

My nod is mechanical.

"Well . . ." He makes a noise like he's tickled by the situation and scoots down on the bed so I can't escape eye contact. He takes my hand off the blanket and laces his fingers through mine. "What'd she say?"

I fight against the urge to pull my hand away, knowing he'll see it as withdrawing from him over the topic. "She comforted me. Kept me company. I couldn't tell when I was hallucinating half the time, and she'd tell me when things weren't real."

"That's very sweet of her." Denendrius strokes my hand with his thumb. "Have you seen her since?"

My hand trembles in his, my eyes burning with tears that I choke back. Panic clogs my throat, so I merely nod.

"I see them too sometimes."

Them.

Us. Marissa's word stumbles around in my head again, heavy with meaning.

"What'd she look like?" he asks, voice dripping with curiosity.

"Same as when she died." I wait for him to tell me that information doesn't help him. That he wouldn't know what she looked like when she died, because why would he?

"Hm." He subdues his smile, but bright delight shines in his eyes.

"She said she died in 2005, when she was seventeen."

I can't read Denendrius's expression when he casually climbs off the bed and roots through the backpack.

I wrack my brain, trying to remember if she was on one of his tapes. There were so many names that I can't remember. My stomach sours with guilt over the idea of them being forgotten.

"Did you—" I grapple with how to phrase it. "Was there a tape of her?"

He stops rooting and stares blankly at me. "You should know. You saw them when you tricked me into destroying them in your fit of jealousy."

I gulp, and don't dare correct him on my reasoning for destroying them. "I don't remember."

He pulls my bristled brush from the bag. "Were you nice to her?"

The question makes me double take. My brows stitch together. "Yes, why wouldn't I be?"

He lightly taps the back of the comb against his palm. "You get jealous when it comes to my past flings."

Flings. His words send ice water down my spine and my arms prickle with goosebumps. Is that how it is, then? The girls with similar names and features to mine get used as girlfriends, and the ones who merely fit his type are used for sex? I suppose it was obvious from the outside, but the fact he recognizes that too . . .

"I wasn't mean to her," I assure him, my voice mousy. "I'm sorry I was jealous."

I feel trapped in this conversation, like I opened the door for some gentle inquiries, and he shoved me in and locked it to twist it into an interrogation.

He sighs and lowers his hands. "It's okay. I understand, Marianna. When you love someone, you don't want to think of them being with anyone else, even if it's in the past. But I've been around *a long time*, so you have to come to terms with the fact I haven't been celibate my whole life."

I gulp and offer him a rapid nod. "I know."

His smile is soft as he returns to the bed and props himself on his elbow beside me. He takes a chunk of my hair and strokes the brush through the strands. "I'm not mad about the tapes being destroyed. It shows me that you love me so much you can't bear to have evidence of me and other girls around."

"You seemed really upset when I showed you them."

A nervous chuckle bubbles out of him. "I didn't remember doing anything of the sort before, so it was shocking. I went from only killing as a gladiator, to vampirism giving me the freedom to do whatever I want."

My heart sinks into my stomach. It wasn't guilt he felt? He wasn't sick seeing his acts? He was just . . . shocked? Was it the possibility of getting in trouble that shook him?

"Sometimes, we have to act at great lengths so people understand how we feel. Sometimes words aren't enough."

"Yeah," I agree, though I'm not completely sure what he means.

He pauses brushing my hair. "I know you don't want to hear about Marianne, but hear me out before you get jealous. You'll feel better."

My heart pounds, and I want to stick my fingers in my ears. I don't want to hear about Marianne, but not for the reasons he thinks.

"I was so jealous—so furious—that she wanted to be with her childhood best friend instead of me." He shakes his head. "We'd spent months together, were engaged, and she was willing to throw it all away for some boy who never returned her affections her whole life. He only wanted her when *I* loved her."

I gnaw on my cheek and grip a fistful of the blanket.

"I waited weeks for her to come home, and when she did, I fashioned a noose. I slipped one end over her head and tied the other to my mustang's saddle horn. Her lover . . . I bound him to the fence and showed him how I was a better lover to her than him. Then, I galloped through the pen and dragged her until her neck snapped. He screamed the whole time, begging me to stop because he loved her." He scoffs. "I loved her too."

My heart pounds furiously, her face entering my mind from the black-and-white photo of her and Denendrius on a porch swing. She was so happy, and my chest aches that she was able to see through Denendrius's mask just enough to know she was better off with her childhood friend, even if she says it was because Den couldn't give her children. It's just a shame he didn't show his true colors before that. Maybe she wouldn't have thought him sweet enough to deserve a letter explanation. Though, I suppose she wouldn't have been able to run farther nor fast enough to escape his brutal jealousy.

His story only makes me feel shakier with sick dread, and I don't understand why he thinks it would provide me comfort or reassurance to hear my fiancé recount how he killed his ex-fiancée after she left him. I scramble to come up with a suitable reaction for him, so all I ask is, "What did you do to him?"

"I let him live. It didn't make sense to kill him when they'd seek one another out in death. I wanted them apart, not together."

"That makes sense," I whisper, though it sounds absolutely insane.

He holds my hand. "I know it might be hard to understand that type of jealousy when you've only dated me, but I understand it, Marianna."

"Okay," I whisper. "Thanks for understanding."

I roll over per his request, and he brushes the rest of my hair before he draws the blanket back and pats the mattress. "Are you still mad at me for sleeping with Sarah? Especially now she's gone on TV and told everyone?"

Sarah. Of course he noticed the *Crime Nightly* special. A shudder ripples through me when I recall crying on the bathroom floor at school about how Denendrius was going to kidnap me and take me to Italy, and how she came in to talk to me. She told me then, and I probably wouldn't have given one last shot at trying to escape if it wasn't for her safety being on the line too.

I force my dry tongue to work. "Yes. That's partly why I ran from school that day Agatha captured us. Sarah told me, and I was hurt. I thought you didn't love me," I whisper as I maneuver to the cool sheet, holding his soft gaze to study his expression. I decide that answer is safer than denial. If I deny it, he might think my lack of jealousy means I don't actually care. Though, jealousy isn't the right emotion if he were to call the situation what it truly is. He abused her.

"That makes sense." He sighs and shifts to his hands and knees, pulling the blanket down as he crawls over it to get to the sheet. "I suppose it was overkill. I was furious you kissed CJ, but I see now you were merely testing how much I cared about you, wanted me to fight for you, and I failed. Killing him was enough to equalize the situation."

I'm speechless, my throat stark dry as I crawl under the blanket.

"If it makes you feel any better, I didn't enjoy it. She isn't pretty, and if she wasn't your enemy, I would never have done it. She was coming onto me the whole night, and I was disgusted . . . but anger is a lot stronger than disgust. I only wanted to make you hurt like I did. If it makes you feel any better, I put a pillow over her head and thought of you."

My stomach practically inverts itself.

That does not make me feel better.

"I don't want to hear about that," I squeak, desperate for him to change the subject.

"You're right . . . you're right. I won't bring her up again. I'm sorry for making you think of us together." He sighs and strokes my cheek with the back of his hand before a mischievous smile curls his lips. "We have one quick stop tomorrow night that will make you feel much better. Then, we're leaving all this behind us and starting fresh."

I draw my brows together, but say, "Okay." I don't think I want to ask him more questions tonight.

He kisses the tip of my nose and settles beside me. "Sleep."

"I'm not sure I can," I admit. The added horror of his words tonight doesn't help. "I'm scared I'll dream of being in the cage."

He kisses the flesh behind my ear. "It's better to dream of being trapped and wake up with the relief of knowing you're not anymore, than the opposite."

Denendrius must know from experience.

"I'll hold you all night," he whispers as he wraps his body around mine. "If you have a nightmare, I'll wake you."

"Thank you." I wish I were with Ziggy and Lance to keep me grounded if I can't be with Viorel and Laurentius yet, but at least being with Denendrius is better than being alone. The pain of being near him isn't as excruciating as the insanity waiting to creep up on me when I'm unprotected.

"I love you, Marianna. Forever."

"Forever," I agree.

When exhaustion pulls me under, I drown in my fears again. My dark dream is cold at the edges, with bars pressing into my skin. I'm too weak to cry out, to move a single muscle.

Marissa's voice comforts me, whispering my name in the dark like a light for me to follow. When my lids lift, she sits on the edge of the bed, the green digital numbers of the clock illuminating her skin with a green tinge.

She reaches out and grasps my hand. "You're out now," she whispers with teary eyes and a shaky smile.

I can't feel her warm fingers on my hand this time. When Denendrius rouses behind me, her gaze darts to him, and a tear dashes down her cheek. She's gone when I blink.

XLII

Denendrius checks in with Sergei as we settle back in the Mustang. The stars are extra twinkly tonight, something comforting about the cool air like it's the cold side of a pillow.

"I'll need to learn Russian once I'm a vampire," I tease as he hangs up the phone and sets it in the cup holder.

He playfully clicks his tongue as his head sways, like he's not fond of the idea but knows it's inevitable.

"And Latin," I add, in case, deep down, I've annoyed him with the realization that he'll have a harder time talking out in the open secretly around me.

Denendrius's eyes sparkle as they meet mine. "I'll teach you."

I heave out a long breath, my limbs suddenly weak from the stark reality this is really happening. *I'm going to be a vampire, and it's going to really fucking hurt.* "How many hours until you're turning me?"

He chuckles and gives me a look like I'm the sweetest thing he's ever laid eyes on. "Soon . . . *soon.*" He turns the car on and shifts to drive. "One quick stop, and we're leaving Lorimer for good."

"And then getting on the plane?" The words rush out of me, the impatient excitement bordering panic.

I'm practically shaking with giddiness in my seat. He grips my hand in my lap as he drives out of the parking lot like he needs to keep me tethered in my seat so I don't bounce away.

"Hmm." He winks at me and grins, the genuine calm of his smile only making me more optimistic.

"Yes?"

He gently squeezes my hand. "Mm, well, one more *very important* stop in America, but then Sergei will fly us home."

A frown descends on my lips so fast his eyes widen a bit and his grin turns toothy. Thankfully, his mood remains. "It's worth it. Trust me, sweetheart."

My disappointment and frustration are too thick to cover up. "Why didn't we do that already? We've just been hanging around Lorimer. We could have left sooner."

He shakes his head. "I've been waiting for your surprise to get here. It should have arrived this afternoon."

My brow furrows, the idea of Denendrius planning *a surprise* for me, making me pick at my nails in thought. I have no idea what to suspect, knowing it could be anything from diamond jewelry to some sick trick. I become so preoccupied with what he might have planned that I don't take final inventory of the surrounding sights before I never see them again.

My surprise comes like a fist in my gut when familiar streets lure my attention. When I recognize Sarah's house—the same white, two-story house I once spied on to see if her cop-father was home or not—my heart free falls into my stomach.

Voice betraying me, I quiver as I say, "Denendrius, what are we doing here?"

He parks in front of the house and takes my hand, pressing

a soft kiss to the back of it. "Sarah's family took a little vacation. Now that they're back, I'm going to kill her."

My mouth hangs agape. Reality twists, the edges sharp like a night terror, my body heavy in the seat I grip like I'm worried everything is spinning as uncontrollably as it seems.

He pouts at me. "You don't have to pretend, sweetheart. It's okay to be jealous and hurt that I cheated on you with her. That was too far, I know. I'm going to make things right. You can see with your own eyes how she means nothing to me, and we won't have any more baggage weighing us down when we go to Italy."

I'm an ice statue as he kisses my clammy cheek before exiting the car and beckoning for me to follow.

Adrenaline surges through me. I throw the passenger door open and scramble out after him, my words whipping the air like a brewing storm. "You can't fucking kill Sarah, Den!"

When he faces me with squared shoulders and a threat in his eyes, I back up over the sidewalk and nearly slip on a patch of muddy slush. His steps bring him toward me.

"I don't know what you're trying to prove, but you can either come with me and watch, or wait in the car," he growls.

"You can't hurt her."

"Get back in the car!" His fingers curl into shaky fists at his sides.

I back up and trip over the remnants of a melting snowbank and land on my ass on the dirty sidewalk. Fumbling, mud kicks up around me as I try to stand. Denendrius closes the space between us and takes a fistful of my sweater to pull me up.

"I told her I'd kill her if she told, and she went on TV. She's upset I want you and not her, just like she was at her party, and she's going out of her way to stir up trouble." He shoves me in the car's direction, and I land on my hands and knees, the cold ground sending a painful shiver through me.

Twisting, I spot Sarah in the upstairs window, her palms

pressed against the glass and her rapid breath steaming it as she stares wide eyed down at me. She shouts something, and Camille and Daina appear on each of her sides.

The sight of them knocks the breath out of me, and for a moment I forget I'm sprawled out on the ground and that Denendrius is yelling at me to get back in the car as he stalks toward the house.

Nearly a year later, and my two best friends are with Sarah? Emotion chokes me. They must have become friends after I disappeared.

Sarah's father's voice claws my attention away from them. "Stop and get your hands up!" he bellows at Denendrius as the front door swings open.

He stands in his doorway wearing plain clothes, his handgun raised in warning. My three friends scramble down the stairs behind him, staring at me past his stance as I pull myself to my feet.

There's no reality where Denendrius leaves without killing all three of my friends.

"Don't! Please!" I shriek. I scramble for a bargaining chip, something juicy enough to capture his attention, but come up short and resort to the only thing I've ever thought of that has worked in the past. "Why do you care so much about her when you have me? I don't care about baggage! I just don't want you two in the same room together!"

Sarah's father holds his ground. "I said stop—"

A gunshot has Denendrius reeling in shock as he reaches the front steps, gripping his throat as crimson sprays across the lawn. But the angle of the splatter is wrong, and I know before seeing the alarm on her father's face that he didn't take the shot. My eyes flit to the house next door, the only direction the shot could have come from.

A man with a blond buzz cut stands in the open doorway of the neighbor's house, the porch light enough to illuminate his onyx eyes. As Denendrius crosses the few meters between us and grabs my arm, another shot cuts through the air. He yanks me down onto the sidewalk as it clips the top of the car.

But it came from directly across the street, and with another crack, the man at the neighbor's house is hitting the ground with a hole between his eyes and blood spray across the siding. Denendrius crawls into the car through the passenger side as Sarah's father screams at her to stay inside with *"Doug"* as he darts across the yard to his cruiser in the driveway.

In the open second-story window of the house across the street, a black-haired man with dark skin points a rifle toward us.

"Get in!" Denendrius bellows.

I'm not about to take the risk of hoping one of the shooters is on Viorel's side, so I crawl into the passenger seat as another blond-haired man appears in the neighbor's doorway. He reappears beside a beige car in the driveway and climbs in.

Denendrius hits the gas before I have the passenger door shut, and Sarah's father nearly clips the Mustang's trunk as he reverses the cruiser out of the driveway

"What the fuck is going on?" I holler as I slam the door and duck in my seat. "Was that other shooter from across the street a vampire too?"

"I couldn't hear his heartbeat as he shot at me from the window, so probably," he snaps.

Sirens blare behind us, the spin of lights so close they blind me in the mirrors. "I take it you don't know who they are?"

He yanks the wheel to the right, and I fall into the center console as the car swings around a corner, narrowly missing another turning toward us.

"Whoever they are, they clearly don't like me," Denendrius retorts.

Fucking clearly.

"Your throat's okay?" I check.

He nods and swerves around another car. "Healed."

A shot shatters the window behind Denendrius. I duck in the passenger seat as a black car pulls up alongside Denendrius, its passenger window rolled down. As I brace myself, Denendrius hits the brakes to misalign our cars. The car behind us swerves and blares their horn as Denendrius slams on the gas and pulls a hard left, nearly clipping a sign as we're launched over a sidewalk and into a parking lot. He speeds through it, and I grunt as we drive over the sidewalk on the other side and hit the road.

"Second shooter is a Darkling," he tells me before muttering something in Latin as another police cruiser appears from a road on the left and slices through the street across from us, slowing to spin around and follow us with Sarah's father.

"You have a plan, right?" I nearly hit my forehead on the glove compartment when he slams on the brakes. He throws the car in reverse and launches us backward. When he cranks the wheel, my stomach roils as he twists the car in the direction we came.

I climb back into the passenger seat and put my belt on before I get launched through the windshield.

"We need to get out of Lorimer," he says through grit teeth.

I check the fuel gauge. He only has three quarters of a tank, and with the way he's driving, plus the countless detours the police will undoubtedly force us to take, I'm not convinced we'll be able to make it since we're nearing the center of the city.

Cars bail out of his way as we rip forward through the street, climbing up on sidewalks or nearly hitting other vehicles searching for safety.

"Sorry for the abrupt change," he grumbles. "I could hear police barricades ahead."

Denendrius swerves and weaves between cars, flying through red lights as we rip down the street. The flash of police lights pulses against dark building windows and nearby vehicles as the noise builds with more officers joining the chase.

"Choppers," Denendrius mutters a few moments before the Mustang is engulfed in a beam of light.

I switch the radio on as he sighs in annoyance while pulling a donut in the intersection to avoid police cars from ahead and left—a speeding civilian car headed straight for us from the right.

I grunt in pain as the Mustang's tires jump onto the sidewalk to avoid the cruisers who were behind us, struggling to keep upright in the seat as he dodges cars to get situated on the road again.

A long stretch opens ahead of us thanks to cars having already moved out of the way from our initial pass through. The Mustang's climbing speed presses me against the seat. The street is clear for blocks ahead as we're a bullet down it, a couple civilian cars and police cruisers swiftly recalibrating on nearby streets with clear plans to attempt interception. The gap between us and them swiftly grows, the speedometer needle pushing 140 miles per hour.

The voices of a man and woman comment over the radio, speculating about our sudden appearance in Lorimer after months of silence, and attributing "Charles's" return to possible outrage over Sarah's appearance on *Crime Nightly.*

I can't help but wonder too if half the reason we came back to America is that Denendrius never had a chance to kill Sarah before being forcibly turned human. He's not one to leave victims alive, though, those victims are never usually blond and blue eyed either.

I'm stone as my name rumbles through the speakers. They mention my presence in the car, how police are taking greater care to handle the situation more safely, while giving viewers a brief overview of *my case.* It sounds like they're talking about someone else when they mention how seventeen-year-old

Marianna Cortez—who would have just turned eighteen on March 18th—was last seen fleeing from West James High, where she attended tenth grade.

"Marianna has been known by Lorimer Police from a young age, though with her past involvement in local gangs and narcotics, they're surprised to find her on the other end of things and have no evidence that what they are treating as a kidnapping, has anything to do with her tumultuous past," the woman says.

The man's voice chimes in with, *"Though, with her case moving from local to international with the suspect's status and the two having been located in Romania, there are theories circulating that she has merely been swept into a professional stream of crime. With her status as a foster child, and with the disappearance of her schoolteacher and foster mother, some speculate the man she's with could belong to an international criminal organization and she's merely run away."*

"Theories, nonetheless," the woman reminds him. *"Though with the unmarked cars that have seemed to join the chase with clear professional skills, plus his own remarkable ability to evade the police so smoothly thus far, it's clear we've only skimmed the surface of the situation. Officials are currently trying to handle the civilian cars in pursuit as well, but it's possible they are mercenaries or government officials, potentially foreign—"*

My throat tightens.

Denendrius grunts and jams the radio button to silence it, glancing at me sideways. "Sorry, sweetheart. I doubt they'll have anything helpful to say. I'm able to hear enough from nearby police radios, anyway."

"Thanks," I whisper.

"You okay?"

"I just want to go to *fucking* Italy." My head is heavy with exhaustion as I sway it.

"Yeah, I didn't think others would be waiting for Sarah to

return and for me to respond to her stupid little show. I suppose that was pretty predictable . . . Oops."

I push a long breath past my lips. At least Sarah's still alive.

"Just lose them, please." I grip the passenger door handle.

His lip draws back with a sly smirk as he winks at me. "I will, sweetheart. I promise. This isn't my first rodeo."

I settle my gaze back on the road. A couple of blocks separate us from an army of police cars down the hill. Flashing lights swarm nearby intersections and streets in an effort to corner us.

The black car that fired at us nears the line of police between us and them, while the beige car veers down a side road that will cut ahead and put them in front of us.

"Think they're working for Viorel?" I ask, though my gut is heavy with doubt.

As if the universe is answering my question, the black car pulls up near a cruiser, whose back tire explodes with a shot that has it swerving out of control and colliding with two other cruisers in a storm of crushed metal and broken glass. Just as it speeds through the gap it forced, the beige car flies into the intersection ahead of it, and a hailstorm of bullets from an automatic weapon targets the black car. Tire rubber scatters across the road behind it as it comes to a stop, the beige car continuing through the intersection instead of chasing us. The remaining cruisers split, now pursuing the beige car too. The vampire in the black car flees across the street—gun in hand—like a track star before disappearing into the shadows.

Then I notice the handful of civilian cars on different streets through the flash of buildings, working toward us with speed and skill that makes them stick out from regular citizens.

"Oh fuck." My heart spasms in my chest, my nails digging into the leather of the handle.

It's open fucking season on Denendrius now, isn't it?

"Sweetheart, I'm going to keep the car steady as best I can, and I need you to crawl into the back and reach the trunk," Denendrius says evenly. "You can flip the backseat down to access it. I need the gray metal toolbox back there."

I give him a long stare until I realize he's not fucking kidding, and gulp as I unbuckle, steadying myself against the passenger door as he darts through a small gap between an SUV and truck.

"Careful, there's glass," he warns, as if I can't see it scattered over the backseat.

I shift onto my knees and perch on the center console, reaching a shoe out to brush shards as best I can off half the black leather.

"What's in the toolbox?" I climb into the backseat, searching for a lever or pull and finding it on the side. The seat comes down with a rough yank, and I clamber onto it, squinting into the dark of the trunk.

"Grenades."

My eyes widen as I reach into the trunk, my hand searching the dark for metal. "You've been fucking casually driving around with those grenades this whole time?"

"Yeah," Denendrius verifies, like it's a silly question. "I wasn't about to put them back in storage with all that's going on. Just"—the car swerves, and I grunt as my body bumps against the car wall—"be careful when you grab it. Try not to jostle it around too much."

He's worried about *me* jostling the fucking toolbox around?

Scowling and cursing under my breath, I sprawl out on my belly, swaying a bit as Denendrius steers roughly to the left. The screech of nearby tires and crunching metal has me mashing my lips together and reaching around quicker.

His clipped shout has me stiffening. "Brace yourself!"

I don't have enough time to move while the rear end of Mustang veers sideways to the right as he fishtails. Thankfully, being halfway into the trunk means there's nowhere for me to go except follow the force pulling me against the side of the upright rear seat. A sharp gasp escapes me as my body scrapes against the hard carpet when we come to a rough stop.

"You okay?" Denendrius asks as I slide a few inches deeper into the trunk with the car launching forward.

"Yeah, I'm fine. What the fuck was that?" I gulp back some steadying breaths and wiggle forward, fingers scraping over the rough carpet in search of metal.

"A man in a lifted truck tried to be a hero and run me off the road."

The Mustang swerves, and rapid fire hammering against metal nearby has me covering my head.

"Hurry up," Denendrius demands. "That was meant for us. There's more Darklings in an SUV too close for comfort."

I scoot deeper, only my feet left on the backseat as I search the end of the trunk. My heart skips as my palm slides across smooth metal. "Got it!"

His words rush out of him. "Slide it up to me, but stay back there."

I strain while I pull the heavy, rectangular metal box toward me as I wiggle back, shifting on my side to push the old toolbox down to my feet, where it's in his reach.

He glances at it and gives my legs a gentle smack. "Pull them into the trunk."

I don't question him as I crawl back into the dark trunk, the tires smooth on the road below me. Denendrius's speed steadies, and I hold my breath at the sound of the toolbox creaking open, the mechanical hum of his window rolling down, and the metal pin popping out of the grenade a moment before the Mustang launches forward. My entire body tenses, breath held and heart hammering.

The suddenness of an explosion has my eyes widening in the dark, my heart so loud I can hear it above shattering glass, squealing tires, horns, and metal slamming into metal.

I hear his window roll back up and I say, "Did you get them?"

He snickers. "Oh yeah! Tossed it through their window as they pulled up beside me with their gun aimed. I doubt they're dead, but they'll be sitting the rest of this race out."

I heave out a breath. "Cool. Can I—" I'm launched against the top of the trunk as he runs something over, my shoulders aching from dual impact when I come back down. I groan with the pulsing pain and force the rest of my request through grit teeth. *"Can I come back?"*

He makes an agreeing noise as the car swerves side to side, the racket of sirens intensifying behind us. "The ramp to the freeway is coming up, and we're nearly out of gas."

XLIII

We fly down the freeway. The police have backed off to reassess the situation since Denendrius whipped a grenade out of the Mustang, though the chopper overhead follows relentlessly. From the news report on the radio, they're putting half their efforts toward the vehicles pursuing us since Denendrius didn't take such drastic measures until they closed in on us. Plus, they're purposefully interfering with the police.

At this late-night hour, the larger gaps between the cars on the freeway that connect West Lorimer to the city center attached to the north side allow the space between us and law enforcement to widen. Denendrius pushes the Mustang to its limits while weaving between cars.

Despite being on the freeway, we're still *so far* from escaping the city. It's unlikely we'll be able to remain on it and take an exit ramp to the highway. With the chopper keeping tabs on us, Denendrius suspects they already figured out by our previous constant attempts to get on major roads or ones connecting to them, that we're likely trying to leave the city.

Denendrius scrutinizes cars as we zig-zag and weave between them, his eyes narrowing on a red Corvette a few cars ahead. He follows it with careful precision as he reaches beneath his seat and produces my Beretta—the gun I've had since my gang days and haven't seen since Bellevue—and grips it in his free hand.

"Stuff anything important from the console and glove compartment into the backpack."

My eyes widen, and I unzip the backpack in front of my feet, then quickly pop open the glove compartment. "We're abandoning the Mustang?"

His lip curls in disdain as he frowns, his grip tightening on the gun. "We don't have a choice."

"Fuck, I'm sorry, Den. I know how much this car means to you." I stuff paperwork, the hunting knife, and a box of ammunition I've never seen before but is compatible with my gun in the bag.

"You *don't* know," he whispers as his frown deepens. He shoots me a pained twitch of a smile. "But thanks, sweetheart."

I rifle through the center console before he makes me carefully unwrap a red, cylindrical incendiary grenade and a pineapple grenade from scraps of canvas cloth—as the rest are wrapped in the toolbox—and slips them into the interior pockets of his leather jacket. Then, he tells me to put the backpack on and grab the toolbox.

"We're taking that Corvette. As soon as I get out of the Mustang, grab the keys from the ignition, and race to the passenger side."

As we near a series of overpasses, Denendrius pulls into the lane alongside the Corvette, inching ahead. In the same moment we barrel beneath the first overpass, Denendrius hits the gas to bring us past the sports car. He cranks the wheel and slams on the brakes to force the driver to a squealing and violent stop to avoid colliding with us or the thick concrete pier to the driver's left.

As Denendrius shoves the door open, I hug the heavy metal box with one arm while twisting the keys out of the ignition and pocketing them to free both hands for the grenades. My legs wobble as I clamber over the center console to exit through the Mustang's driver's side. Denendrius stares the driver down through the window and hollers at him to unlock the door. It's clear windows are no shield against hypnotism, as the car unlocks while I reach the passenger side.

The shriek of sirens creeps closer as I pin the toolbox between my chest and the side of the car to free my hand to grab the door handle. As I get it open, Denendrius yanks a middle-aged driver from behind the wheel and dispatches a bullet into his skull that leaves him limp and leaking crimson onto the asphalt.

"Get in!" he hollers at me.

I collapse into the passenger seat, fumbling with the toolbox and the bulky backpack, making it impossible to sit properly and close the door behind me. Denendrius's scowling face fills my vision as he grips a backpack strap and drags me like a crumpled doll deeper into the vehicle. He shows no care in how he pushes me against the seat and console to reach over me to slam the passenger door.

"Sorry, sweetheart, but we have to go." He rests his arm on the toolbox, giving me a chance to release it, untangle myself, and straighten in the seat. I shove the backpack in the small space between my legs on the floor.

We glide down the freeway, the Corvette's breakneck speed and thin midnight traffic widening the gap between us and law enforcement with each minute we tear through. We collect choppers on our way toward the exit.

The closer we reach it, the signs for our exit flashing by, the deeper Denendrius's scowl chisels into his face.

Denendrius flashes past the off ramp, and I sigh. I can't hear the roadblock, can't see it so far below at the end of the twisting road, but I still *know*.

"Are we fucked?" I lean my head back against the seat, my body aching with exhaustion.

His voice is too quiet, too even, when he says, "I won't let us burn to death."

"But we're not getting out of the city tonight, are we?" I'm unsure how to feel about this likely reality. On the one hand, I want to be rescued and brought home, but I don't quite see it happening *this way*.

His head rocks to the side like he's going to shake it, but he instead stares straight ahead and swallows hard. "I'll make sure we get out of this."

My eyes ache as I stare out the passenger window, propping my elbow on the edge. The chopper's yellow beam locks on the car, relentless. Can they see me through the tinted windows? Are the guards at the castle reporting this to Viorel?

The silence is so thick it chokes me, my breaths deliberate, mechanical. I'm not sure how long I stare out in a daze before Denendrius's snarl and a heavy *thud* on the wheel jar me upright.

"We have company," he grinds out.

My gaze jerks to the side mirror, my heart fluttering in a panic at the base of my throat before slamming into my ribs.

Six motorcycles roar out of the trees alongside the road, flooding the freeway, the gap between us closing in seconds.

"Den . . . they're all on bikes." My voice barely rises above a whisper.

He glances at the rearview mirror, lips pursing. *"Yep."*

My throat tightens. Bikes must mean they have no intention of taking him prisoner.

Perhaps I should feel hopeful, think that rescue is imminent . . .

But honestly, at this point, I'm not willing to take any chances when my vampirism is only a few days away.

"Get down!" he barks as two bikes with an additional rider aim long-barreled guns toward us.

I slide into the footwell as the Corvette veers violently, Denendrius weaving to make us harder to hit. Gunfire erupts behind us. The deafening crack of bullets ricocheting off metal fills the air, and then—*clink*—*crack*. The car lurches, the rear left sinking as shredded rubber slaps against the asphalt.

"Oh fuck." My breath snags in my throat.

Denendrius's jaw clenches, the leather of the steering wheel complaining under his tightening grip.

The roar of bikes nearly overpowers the sound of the metal rim scraping against the freeway. The line of bikes tightens around the Corvette, two pulling up alongside us as the damaged tire forces our speed down.

My breath catches as the gunman on the back of the motor-cycle along Denendrius's side aims at us. I cover my head as the Corvette jerks violently to the left toward the motorcycle.

"*Don't try it,*" Denendrius snarls at the rider.

The bike to the left revs in a taunt. Bullets slam into the Corvette's side, and Denendrius yanks the wheel right. I squeeze my eyes closed as the front left tire pops, Denendrius's seething and incoherent words a fist on my heart as the Corvette jerks with the loss of speed and fishtails. My eyes pop wide as Denendrius stomps the brake and throws the car into park with such force the gearshift cracks.

He flashes toward me, his hand snatching my wrist. Pain flares as his fangs tear into my vein. He gulps me up, the power of my blood contorting his face instantly. His other hand darts to his jacket, palming a grenade. I'm dizzy with panic as leather-clad bodies dismount from bikes and rush the Corvette, an elbow slamming into the driver's window, a gloved hand darting in with the explosion of glass.

Denendrius shoves me back against the passenger door as he twists away with the grenade in hand—its pin missing, the lever already released on the red incendiary. I count the seconds—three swift beats pass—as the biker finds the button to unlock the door. Then, the biker at the window releases a guttural grunt and swiftly staggers backward with the collision of the grenade—so hard and fast I didn't even see Denendrius throw it.

Barely a second passes before he's engulfed in flames, his leather clothing melting as he bats at his body and shrieks. He's a blurry mess of roaring fire until he disappears from sight for a mere moment before a bullet from one of their own appears in his forehead and brings him to a hard stop—sprawled out on his back, yards away—in my vision.

A crack cuts through the silence, my balance tilting with my ringing ears as Denendrius slackens in the driver's seat, a bullet hole between his brows. A trail of blood leaks over his wide eyes, the blood vessels broken, angry veins spider webbing beneath his eyes from my blood.

My heart stops, the sight pulverizing my lungs. I'm frozen. My lips twitch together uselessly as my gaze darts between his comatose body and the surrounding vampires, who stare in shock at their bonfire of a friend.

All I know is the bullet needs out of his skull so he can heal and wake . . . but how the fuck do I do that *now*? We don't have time for it to heal around his brain either . . .

"Remember, they're watching!" a rider shouts at his crew as he points to the chopper with his gun.

I gape, realizing he shot his own man to prevent the world from witnessing a vampire attempt to escape their own burning body with inhuman speed.

Denendrius sputters and gasps, jerking upright as the bullet wound mends as if he was never shot. He looks around to orient himself while whipping blood off his brow.

Relief weakens me, and I let my full weight relax in the footwell. I don't want to know what might have happened if he had been shot without my blood to turbo speed his healing.

"How the fuck is he conscious?" one of the rider's bellows, a stroke of panicked disbelief in his voice.

I spot two riders through the back window, turning to face one another from their bikes. Long hair flows from beneath the helmet of one, her slender body tense as she shakes her head at the man next to her. He nods in agreement—I think—and they tear off in the direction they came.

Denendrius cackles, and I feel a slight twinge of relief now that he's awake and there are three fewer vampires for him to subdue.

Mere seconds have passed when Denendrius's gaze locks with mine as his hand dashes from the other interior pocket of his jacket and hides beneath the driver's seat. He twists awkwardly with his back to me while uttering, "Piggyback."

I fight disorientation and cold nausea to scramble to him, sitting on the center console and circling his neck with my arms as I lift my legs to his sides. He hooks his left arm around my thigh and holds me tight to him as the rider who broke the window turns back toward us, flipping his helmet visor up, his black eyes trained on Denendrius's face.

"Be careful," the rider warns. I don't miss the dull fear of his stare—likely from the monstrous show of my blood's power on Denendrius's face.

"You think I care about exposure?" Denendrius's bark of laughter has the vampire's expression twisting with fury.

Denendrius lifts his legs from the footwell and knees the door open into the Darkling as he pulls the handle. He staggers back with a grunt from the unexpected force before flashing forward to attempt seizing Denendrius's legs, another black-haired Darkling man appearing in the door beside him with the glint of a large, hooked hunting knife. He slams it into the center of Denendrius's chest—the other Darkling warning him not to slice my arms—as he writhes in the seat to free himself. Yet as soon as the blade withdraws from his flesh, the wound heals so rapidly through his sliced shirt I couldn't even visually process it.

I squeeze him with what little strength I have—ensuring my arms protect his throat—as a cool gust of wind circles me with the passenger door opening. Cold arms hook against my pits to try tugging me loose.

"Don't you want to go home? Let go of him," a man demands, Denendrius roaring with fury and grip tightening painfully on my thigh in response as he kicks at the vampires so hard they gasp for breath despite their relentlessness.

Fuck, *he has no idea how horribly I do*, but there's not a single shred of me that trusts their intentions.

My ribs ache as he continues to pull. The gasping, full-body shudders and jerks from Denendrius as he fights to push the vampires off him and escape the blade that repeatedly slams into his chest only agitate the bruising of my body. Every wound knits shut as fast as the blade opens them.

"Hold still!" the Darkling stabbing Denendrius bellows. "There's no winning now. Since a bullet won't do it, I'll just cut your fucking heart out!"

I cry out as the vampire gives me a rough tug, Denendrius's responding grip on my thigh so hard I feel his fingers through my muscles to my bone. I bury my face against Denendrius's shoulder blade, his movement shaking me.

The world spins. A cacophony of sounds and sensations has my eyes burning with tears. Glass crunches under fumbling boots outside the door. The roaring and acrid stench of flames from the vampire's burning body fills me with every sharp breath.

Bursts of Denendrius's blood linger in the air, staining everything crimson with each strike. My pants and arms sit just inches from the blood-slick weapon, and I flinch with every strike. The wheel, dashboard, window, and leather seats are all spattered in red. His grunts are guttural, raw. Each snarl vibrates through me, his jarring movements slamming me against his hard body.

Sirens wail in the distance. Chopper blades beat the air overhead. A gun reloads feet away.

A sob rises from deep within me, and I tremble against Denendrius. Weakness seeps through every part of me. I fight with everything I have not to give in to the vampire's pull.

"Don't hurt her!" the vampire with the blade snaps between furious breaths. "We won't be able to collect that fucking reward money if you do!"

Arms unravel from me. He must know separating me from Denendrius is futile.

Another Darkling appears in the passenger doorway, ordering the stabber to help the vampire fighting for control over Denendrius's legs as he cocks a revolver and aims it at Denendrius's heart. He ignores the order by scrambling onto Denendrius's lap in the seat, his blade slamming into the center of Denendrius's chest. The vampire's brow furrows, face scrunching in frustration as he shifts the blade around in Denendrius's chest cavity as he continues to thrash.

"Jesus fuck this bastard heals fast! He's practically healing around the blade each time I move it!" the stabber roars. He draws the knife out and gets Denendrius in the sternum as he moves beneath his aim. *"You need to fucking die! I don't care if I have to slice you up for the rest of the night!"*

The sound of metal scraping against metal beneath the driver's seat has me flinching and gripping Denendrius tighter. He yanks his arm out from beneath the seat and punches his fist into the man's abdomen as his hand comes up with the bloodied blade.

His eyes widen and he makes a high-pitched, strangled

sound, half-shrieking *"grenade!"* as he vanishes from sight and reappears a handful of yards away, in sync with rapid-fire gunshots ringing through the stunned silence of the vampires. With the back of his beige leather jacket riddled with bloody bullet holes, he crumples into a gasping heap.

Denendrius's grip on my arm and thigh tightens as the world blurs around me, the wet thud of an explosion and collective, horrified gasps stretching further away as Denendrius moves from the car. My vision straightens with the pulse of bullets. Denendrius grunts in pain and stumbles against the side of a bike as his leg buckles. I grip him tighter as he swings us onto the motorcycle seat and revs the engine with his blood-slick hands.

My heart stops at the sight in front of us, my eyes widening.

Ahead on the asphalt, the vampire moans between quiet, pleading sobs. Blood and bits of flesh and bone are scattered around him. The fingers of one hand twitch against the crimson road, the other lodged in what's left of his lower abdomen like he gripped the grenade as it went off. It's probably the only reason any of his heart remains in his chest—why he's still alive.

A couple guns lift in our direction, but Denendrius peels away, swinging us back the way we came, like he's intentionally putting me between the vampires and him. Still, a single bullet echoes past us as we tear away, like a last-ditch effort to snag the rear tire.

XLIV

The gang of vampires chased us for hours, starting from where we fled on the freeway and continuing as Denendrius avoided numerous police blockades with off-road shortcuts to get us back on city roads since the outer-city highway remained an unfeasible escape.

It took every morsel of strength available in my body to grip his torso and remain upright against him in the motorcycle seat as he sped through streets and made dangerous maneuvers that likely would have killed even more experienced human riders without immortal reflexes and strength.

Though the police continued to give us space, the racket of sirens persisted in the distance, the choppers' frantic searchlights trying to keep tabs on us while it did its best to follow us through the alternation of shadows and streetlights.

We outpaced the bikes long enough that our swap to a white Charger when we ran out of gas—and inevitably them as well—gave us confidence that they wouldn't be able to catch up before sunrise.

Sunrise.

"What are we going to do?" The fear in my voice weakens the demand. "We don't have time to get out of the city before the sun comes up now."

Denendrius flies down a quiet residential road, far enough ahead of police—with most about six blocks behind us—that they haven't had a chance to predict our movement to lay blockades and spike strips again.

"We'll have to hide out until sunset."

The words hit me like a punch. My frantic gaze darts over the middle-class family homes, each one a beacon of normalcy waiting to lose a draw. A ball of lead drops into my stomach. We're going to ruin someone's life today. "Oh."

Denendrius's sharp onyx eyes—no longer monstrous since his body burned through the power of my blood—scan the homes as we speed past. My heart thuds as he yanks the wheel, the Charger veering over the sidewalk and plowing into a yard covered in melting snow. The tires skid, sending us sliding to a halt just feet from the front window of a nineties-style, two-story house with beige paneling. Sirens swell closer, slicing through the cool air.

I scramble out of the car with Denendrius and join his side as he kicks the front door in. He pulls me inside and forces it shut behind us. The racket sends multiple sets of feet scrambling across the floor upstairs and down the hall, likely jarring everyone from sleep if the sirens didn't wake them first.

We stand in the entryway off the living room, the stairs immediately to our right.

"Do what I say and nobody will get hurt," Denendrius bellows as a middle-aged bald man slides out of his room in a black housecoat, a brunette woman in pink flannel pajamas behind him.

More voices carry from down the hall upstairs, concerned

and high-pitched inquiries about what that noise was and who is here.

"Stay in your rooms," the dad warns from the top of the stairs.

"Nails and blankets!" Denendrius barks as he sets the metal toolbox on the floor. "Cover the windows. No gaps. Get your kids helping. You've got minutes."

"I-I have nails in the garage," he stammers, pointing to a door at the bottom of the stairs to our right.

"Get them," Denendrius commands, and the dad flies down the stairs, nearly tripping in his slippers.

Sirens blare down the road as Denendrius and their father disappear into the garage, gaining volume as they approach the house. I half expect a handful of police officers to burst in after us, but the lights merely flash red and blue against the house and through the gaps in the blinds as they congregate outside. I suppose they don't want to risk it after losing sight of us. We've had vital minutes here to prepare. For all they know, Denendrius has rigged a grenade in the doorway or is waiting around a corner with one.

His wife stares at me from the top of the stairs, two teenage girls and a boy appearing behind her in the hallway. Their wide eyes lock on me as I breathe in the faint citrus of their once peaceful home. Part of me wants to mumble an apology, but I'm too numb for any real empathy.

"That's the girl from the news," a long-haired brunette— likely only a year younger than me—says as she exchanges a look with her tween brother, who wide-eyed stares toward the garage door like he knows of the monster who followed behind his father.

"Get blankets!" I shout, my voice sharp with hysteria. "All of you, *now!*"

They disperse like scared mice as Denendrius appears from the garage with their dad, a bucket of random, loose nails, and two hammers. Denendrius scoops a fistful and takes a hammer, demanding someone toss him down a handful of blankets before he sends their dad up to help them.

He pushes the ball of the hammer against the side of their dad's head as he takes his first step up the stairs. "Try anything, and your children will regret it. Do you understand? Don't even look at the police. Don't signal or call out to them. Just cover the windows *quickly* and return downstairs."

Their father nods and races up the steps. Denendrius joins me, his jaw set, his eyes scanning the room as if calculating every second we have left.

There are only three windows for us to cover on the main floor. There's a large one in the living room with heavy curtains we simply nail to the wall and use a blanket to cover the gaps around the bar, one over the kitchen sink, and another in a little office on the other side of the stairs next to a windowless bathroom.

We're done before they are, so Denendrius stalks upstairs and receives a terrified squeal of, *"Fuck, Dad, it's him!"* as hammering is interrupted.

"I didn't tell you to stop!" Denendrius bellows, his voice snatching a sob from one of the teen girls as the hammering resumes.

Once the upstairs windows are secured, Denendrius tells them to wait. I stand at the bottom of the stairs on unsteady legs, watching as he moves from room to room, opening closets and rifling through drawers. Then he calls the family down. Their steps are hesitant, muffled by the carpet, as they cling to one another like a lifeline. They bunch together as they creep down the stairs, one girl grabbing her mother while the other grips her dad.

Denendrius slings his arm over my shoulders and steers me to the living room. He settles me into a fancy leather recliner before ordering the family to sit still on the couch. Denendrius snatches the remote from the entertainment stand, standing in front of the TV as he flips through channels until he finds the news. The screen cuts between the aerial view of the house, a wide perimeter of flashing lights, with police going door to door in the neighborhood to evacuate residents. They show the Corvette tires getting blown out and the gang of riders dismounting from their bikes before the video cuts out with the news anchor's explanation of temporary technical difficulties on scene.

The erasure of our freeway fight has an ember of hope warming the cold cave of my chest. It lets me know Viorel's men are still in control of the media and government. Why else would the feed cut when it became clear an immortal battle was about to break out?

"What do you want with us?" the dad asks Denendrius with a trembling voice.

"Shh . . ." Denendrius's eyes narrow on the TV.

"Are you going to hurt us?" the oldest girl asks, her sister, maybe fourteen, pressed tightly against her side.

"Depends," Denendrius mutters, squinting at the screen before his gaze shifts to the picture window across from us.

"On what?" the dad asks.

"If you do what I want." Denendrius's brow furrows, and without another word, he strides over to the two large book-shelves flanking it. "Right now, that's shutting up."

The dad's knuckles whiten as he grips his knees, his jaw twitching as he watches Denendrius shove the fully loaded shelves, one at a time, across the floor as if they weigh nothing. His lips part, but no words come. His Adam's apple bobs in a hard swallow as if choking down the urge to protest. He hugs his wife tighter to his side, his son on his right, eyes flicking to me like I have any sort of control over the situation. I draw my legs onto the chair and hug my knees.

A voice comes through a megaphone outside, and everyone

—myself included—jerks in surprise. Everyone except Denendrius, as if he knew it was coming.

"This is Lieutenant Bradley with the Lorimer Police Department. We are here to ensure everyone's safety. Please communicate with us so we can resolve this situation peacefully," the voice crackles in the air.

Denendrius's sharp eyes scan the room until they land on the home phone sitting on a side table just inside the kitchen behind me. Silently, he comes and sits on the arm of the recliner, stroking my hair as his gaze locks on the front door.

After a minute, the youngest boy whispers, "Shouldn't we say something?"

The crackle of the megaphone cuts through the air, each sharp and deliberate word making me flinch. "This is the Lorimer Police Department. We have not heard from you and it's important to communicate to resolve this situation safely. Please respond so we know everyone is safe. Your cooperation is essential."

The corner of Denendrius's lip twitches, and he gives in to a smile. "Do you have names?"

"Mikey," the boy stammers, glancing nervously at his youngest sister beside him.

Tears streak her cheeks, and she trembles as she chokes out, "Maddie."

"M-Mira," the oldest adds, her voice barely above a whisper.

An airy chuckle escapes Denendrius. "Mikey, Maddie, Mira. *Fun.*"

"I-I'm Andy," their dad says quickly, his voice shaking. "This is my wife, Lynn."

Denendrius leans forward, his voice dipping into a low growl. "All right, now *shut up.* You're hostages. Do I need to take my gun out for you to get it?"

All their eyes drop to the floor.

The lieutenant on the megaphone continues with firm patience. "Charles, this is the Lorimer Police Department. We know you're in there with Marianna and the home's occupants, and we need to speak with you immediately to ensure the safety of everyone involved. It is in your best interest to communicate with us. We are here to help you, but we need your cooperation. Please come forward and speak with us now."

Denendrius merely smiles and continues stroking his hand through my hair. He delivers a soft kiss between the strands before chuckling. "Do they expect me to go outside? Shout through a wall?"

After another few minutes, the house phone rings behind us.

"About time," Denendrius mumbles as he stands. He plucks the phone off the dock and answers it, finding his spot next to me.

"Hello," Denendrius greets, clipped.

The volume is cranked, the lieutenant's voice audible from where I sit, barely a foot away from Denendrius. "Hello, this is Lieutenant Bradley with the Lorimer Police Department. Who am I speaking with?"

"*You* call me Charles." Denendrius stares at the front wall like he knows exactly where the lieutenant is standing.

"Good morning, Charles," his voice crackles through the phone. "Thank you for answering. I'm here to help ensure everyone's safety, including yours and the young woman, Marianna, you're with. Can we talk about how we can resolve this situation peacefully?"

Denendrius shakes his head in disbelief. "Peacefully," he snarls, wrapping his arm around my shoulders as he leans back against the recliner. "That's a big ask, *considering.*"

I stay frozen under his arm, my stomach knotting tighter with every word he spits into the phone. His fingers drum lightly, impatiently, against my shoulder—a steady beat that feels like a ticking clock. Sooner or later, I know he's going to say the wrong thing.

"Could you elaborate, Charles? Is there another factor preventing us from solving this peacefully? I'd like to have an open discussion with you."

"Yeah, I'd say so," Denendrius snaps. "You're going to have to move mountains for me if you want this resolved *peacefully*."

"Okay, Charles. We're prepared to listen to what you have to say, but first, can you verify that Marianna and the home's occupants are safe? Is anyone injured?"

"Yeah, they're fine," he snaps. "I haven't hurt them . . ." He turns his gaze to Andy and mouths, *"Yet."*

There's a crackle as his voice comes through again. "That's great to hear that they're safe and unharmed. Unfortunately, all the windows are covered. Would you be willing to give us visual confirmation of their safety before we proceed?"

My heart hammers at his request, and the plastic phone strains under Denendrius's tightening grip. "No," he utters carefully. "I won't be uncovering the windows. That is non-negotiable, understand?"

"I understand you don't want to negotiate on uncovering the windows, Charles. Would you be willing to let each of them confirm their safety?"

Denendrius exhales a breath of disbelief as he scowls and shakes his head. I don't miss their careful wording either.

"Yeah, fine," Denendrius says coolly as he pulls the phone away from his ear and puts it on speaker. "They'll tell you their names, so you can hear how they're fine, and nothing else."

"Okay, I appreciate that, Charles. I'm listening now."

He holds the phone out to them, and they each take careful turns lifting their shaky voices to verify their identities to the lieutenant.

"Does that suffice?" Denendrius asks, holding the phone on his lap.

I lean my full weight against his side, hoping my warm presence helps him keep himself under control.

"Thanks for letting us hear from the residents," the lieutenant says. "I noticed I didn't hear from Marianna, though. Can I?"

Denendrius licks his lips as they twitch back in fury. "Marianna is fine," he snarls, his fingers digging into my biceps as he holds me firmly to him. His jaw tightens, the faint click of his teeth audible as he grinds them. "You don't need to talk to her. She's safe now. She's happy. I'm taking good care of her."

I swallow against a knot and stroke my hand across his chest as I nuzzle my forehead against his side like a plea for peace. My comfort doesn't loosen the muscles in his arms though, or fix how he sits rigidly, like his joints and muscles are forged from steel.

"I understand that, Charles, and I'm not questioning her safety with you. But Marianna is important to a lot of people. Just a quick hello from her could put a lot of minds at ease since we haven't heard from her in a year."

"It's okay," I whisper to Denendrius, my voice low enough that I hope the phone doesn't pick it up until he gives the okay. "I'll just say a quick hello."

Denendrius tilts his head side to side, considering. His voice softens slightly as he looks down at me. "Okay."

Sweat immediately covers my palms, my heart thumping so hard it feels like it's bulging against the base of my throat. I wet my dry lips and clear my throat, forcing out words I pray sound calm. "Hello, Lieutenant Bradley. It's Marianna."

"Hi, Marianna. How are you doing?"

I look up at Denendrius, and he nods.

"I'm doing okay. D—Charles has been keeping me safe."

"Are you hurt at all?" the lieutenant asks.

Denendrius lifts the phone to his mouth, his fingers tightening around it like he might crush the plastic. Through grit teeth, he growls, "I haven't hurt her. If anyone has hurt her, it's the department. You've all stressed her out and frightened her, chasing us through the street like that."

"We didn't mean for anyone to get hurt," the lieutenant says gently. "Did she get hurt while we were in pursuit, Charles?"

"No, I'm fine," I cut in quickly, hoping to defuse the tension. "Just stressed out, like he said. Really stressed out."

It's not a lie.

"I'm really glad to hear you're safe, Marianna. Charles, thank you for letting her speak," the lieutenant says, his tone warm and measured. "Are you hurt, Charles? One of our officers stated you suffered a bullet wound to the throat."

"He's mistaken," Denendrius claims. "Whizzed by but didn't touch me."

"Okay, Charles. That's good to hear. Are there any weapons I should be aware of to ensure everyone is safe?" Lieutenant Bradley asks.

Denendrius grunts. "I don't have any grenades left. But to save us both some breath from questions, the toolbox your chopper likely saw me run in with is full of ammunition for the Beretta I have and contains a hunting knife. Marianna's backpack just has benign essentials and clothes. Understand me, Lieutenant, I really don't want to use weapons. I'm not here to hurt this family. I required somewhere safe for Marianna and me."

"Thank you for the transparency, Charles. I appreciate it. Let's talk about how we can work together to make this less stressful for everyone, especially for her. We're here to help you too."

Denendrius purses his lips as he taps the top of the phone against his chin in thought. "I've got a few *demands*. The other vehicles trying to interfere, never mind the gang that attacked us on motorcycles . . . They clearly weren't with the government, with the way they were pursued by police as well. What information did you gather about them?"

There's a crackle on the line again and a short pause. "I know about the vehicles in question, Charles. Would it be okay with you if I took a moment and looked into that?"

"Go on then," Denendrius says, shaking his head as he rolls his eyes.

The oldest girl, Mira, pipes up from the couch, her fearful gaze flicking from Denendrius to the floor. "Can I go to the bathroom? I haven't gone since last night."

Denendrius turns his stiff head to stare at her. "Empty your pockets. Do you have a cellphone?"

Wobbly, she stands and runs her hands over the hips of her fairy-themed pajama pants. "I-I don't have pockets."

His eyes narrow and he licks his lips. "Come here."

Mira stumbles toward him, trembling, her every step appearing weighted with dread. As she halts in front of him, Denendrius passes the phone to me without looking, his sharp focus pinned on her. My blood pressure skyrockets—tightness a band around my skull—when his hands land on her waist and he feels around her body for signs of disobedience. She shakes like a leaf beneath his palms, a whimper leaving her as he moves his hand across her back. My stomach churns, and I grip the phone so tightly it creaks, my fingers itching to pull her away. He's probably just trying to make me jealous, to make sure I still love him.

My hand snaps out to clasp the back of his jacket before I lose my chance to prove myself. Not to pull him away, but as a weak protest. "Den—"

Denendrius straightens and stares down into her wide eyes. "You wear a bra to bed?"

Her bottom lip trembles, and she flinches against his breath on her face. "S-sometimes."

"Hm." His lips purse as his gaze shifts to Maddie. "Do you wear a bra to bed?"

Maddie shakes her head swiftly, her face pale.

It's my turn to tremble when Andy opens his mouth, his fists tightening on his knees. "Why do you care about my daughter's undergarments?"

Denendrius stands abruptly, the movement so sudden Mira stumbles backward to avoid him knocking her over.

"I care about why your daughter took the time to put a bra on this morning when she was supposed to be helping secure the windows," he snarls. "And why she thought she could sneak a cellphone into the bathroom."

Andy's mouth opens and closes. His chest heaves as he wrestles with his words before spitting out, "Just give it to him."

Mira's trembling hands move to her chest. Slowly, she fishes out a slim black flip phone from her bra, the baggy fabric of her shirt concealing it perfectly until now. Tears well in her eyes as she holds it out to Denendrius. *But I-I really do need to pee.*

He takes the phone and slides it into his pocket. "You've got thirty seconds."

She makes a strangled noise and spins around, darting across the living room to the bathroom.

With a delicate touch, Denendrius grabs my chin and plants a kiss on my lips like he's letting me know I passed his test.

"Who else has a cellphone?" he demands.

Mikey shakes his head quickly, and Maddie mumbles, "It's charging on my nightstand." Their parents echo her, saying their phones are charging upstairs too.

"Time's almost up, Mira," Denendrius calls as he sits back down on the recliner arm. He takes the phone back from me and lifts it to his lips. "I'm waiting."

A voice crackles on the line again. "Thanks for being patient, Charles. I'm still gathering information. We haven't had time to make official reports, so it's going to take a bit longer while we check in with other officers involved in the situation."

Denendrius exhales a long breath. "Yeah, fine."

The lieutenant's tone shifts, curiosity edging his words. "I heard some noise over the phone while I was doing that for you, Charles. Did anything happen?"

"Mira decided to try bringing a cellphone to the bathroom without me knowing—" He turns his head toward the hall behind him. "Time's up, Mira!"

"I'm coming!" she half-shouts, panic thick in her voice as the bathroom door swings open. She darts across the room and collapses next to her sister, face streaked with tears as she shakes.

"I'm sorry to hear they aren't being as compliant as you need. Am I still on speaker? I'll make sure they understand how important their cooperation is."

"Tell them," Denendrius says, impatience clinging to each word.

"Hi everyone. It's important you all cooperate as well, okay? I understand you want to help resolve this situation, but it's better if we're all transparent with one another and work together. Can I get confirmation from you all, one at a time?"

They each take turns telling the lieutenant they understand, and I can't help but think it's just another way for him to verify they're all still alive.

"Thank you." There's a clicking noise over the line that makes me flinch, and Denendrius wraps his arm around me and presses a kiss to the top of my head. "So, Charles, I understand you came from Romania recently but were in America earlier last year. Where are you from, originally?"

"Europe," Denendrius says simply.

Curiosity lingers on Lieutenant's words. "Where about? I detect a faint accent but can't quite pin it down."

"The Mediterranean."

"There are a lot of beautiful countries there . . . Do you travel to America frequently for work?"

The annoyance is plain in Denendrius's flat expression. "I travel a lot, Lieutenant Bradley. Are we on a date, or . . .?"

Lieutenant Bradley doesn't break from his professionalism despite failing to pry information from Denendrius. "Okay, Charles, I apologize. We'll stay focused. Can I open a deeper conversation with you while we wait for the information you requested to be gathered?"

"What?" There's feigned cluelessness in Denendrius's voice, like he couldn't possibly know what else they might be wondering about.

I simply hope they don't prod him with the wrong questions.

"You must know you're wanted internationally for some fairly serious crimes, right? Terrorism, most recently. I know there was another young woman with you that the Romanian government is searching for. We noticed she's not with you and Marianna right now. Can you give me some insight into that?"

Wrong questions . . . *like that.*

Denendrius shakes his head. "I didn't kidnap her," he snaps. "He may have said I did, but I didn't."

"Okay," Lieutenant Bradley says. "I hear that. Are you willing to tell us where she is, and if she's safe?"

The two sisters share a look I don't understand until Mira strokes her fingers through her sister's long brown hair—the same color and only a little shorter than her own—and then looks at me.

"He'd just love to know about her, wouldn't he?" Denendrius snarls into the phone. "I'm not saying a word about her. Maybe she's dead. Maybe she's alive. He doesn't need to know."

I try to push her realization out of my head. That the three of us, and Adelia—who they must have seen on TV if they recognized me and Denendrius—are all brunettes. The two girls—with their ages, soft-brown eyes, and slim builds—have the same characteristics as the girls on Denendrius's tapes. The fact Sarah is blond likely doesn't help them feel any safer if they saw the *Crime Nightly* episode too, knowing that he's willing to break his preferences if it serves a purpose.

There's another crackle, and the faint whisper of another voice I can't make out. Denendrius's eyes narrow as he catches it too.

"Okay, Charles. Now, I don't want to put words in your mouth, so I apologize if I'm interpreting wrong, but it sounds like you care about this girl. You've mentioned a man who seems to be someone you have concerns about. I'm not sure who he is. Can you clarify?"

Denendrius's head swings side to side as he exhales a chuckle. "*You* may not know who he is, but your superiors do."

"My superiors? Do you know which ones specifically? I'm not trying to be clueless, understand, I'm simply trying to follow what you're saying so we can move closer to a peaceful resolution."

I struggle to get a full breath in. Would Denendrius out Viorel to the world? Would he *really* say anything that might expose vampires in hopes of provoking him, or was he bullshitting when he told that vampire on the freeway he didn't care?

"I don't know who specifically," Denendrius admits. "He's pulling strings from somewhere high in the government. He's the reason you care so much about me." He sounds incredulous when he says, "I didn't kill that Romanian political family. He's framing me."

"I hear you, Charles, but I just want to clarify a point. We're where we are right now because of your arrival at a police officer's house this past evening—the home of a girl who has spoken against you on TV for crimes she says you committed against her—with a girl who has been considered missing for a year. We have no jurisdiction outside of Lorimer."

Denendrius turns his head to the TV as a black SUV pulls up to join the collection of police cars and undercover vehicles on the sidewalk across the street. The sun shines weakly, the fact it's so close making my heart clench with a mix of fear and loss. All they have to do is put a hole in the window and we could get hurt.

"Is that the FBI?" he demands.

"You're watching the broadcast?" Lieutenant Bradley says, though there's no surprise in his relentlessly calm and even tone.

"Sure am." Denendrius stands and tucks one arm between his biceps and chest as he holds the phone up at chest level. "I'm assuming that's you on the sidewalk with all that equipment?"

After a few long moments, Lieutenant Bradley looks up at the camera capturing an aerial view and gives his hand a single stroke through the air as a wave.

"So you can see me," he notes, "but I still don't have a clear visual inside. Charles, would you be willing to open the front window a bit so we can make visual contact with you?"

Denendrius's free hand drops to a fist at his side, and I squeeze my eyes closed as my heart thumps in my temples.

"I'm not uncovering the windows or opening doors." There's a dangerous edge to his voice. "Is that the FBI, and have you gathered any information about the persons trying to *kill me and my fiancée yet?*"

I exhale a deep breath and open my eyes, glancing at the quiet but quivering hostages and the TV. A man and woman in black suits exit the SUV and group with a large collection of police officers.

"My officers are still gathering information for you, but they should have something soon. And I can confirm it's the FBI, Charles, but you need to understand that Marianna's case became federal when she crossed state lines. You both were briefly sighted in Bellevue, Washington."

Denendrius paces back and forth, the three teens clumping closer together and flinching with each of his steps. "They've trained you quite well, you know that? Using my name constantly to try to create rapport, phrasing my situation with Marianna as if I don't know you all believe I kidnapped her. You're bordering on condescension, Lieutenant. She's not in danger! I'm the one protecting her."

"I hear your perspective," Lieutenant Bradley says. "You're concerned about those vehicles who were pursuing you aggressively, and this man you say is framing you for crimes to garner international interest. Is it safe to assume you believe these two things are related?"

Denendrius laughs. "It's safe to assume it's a possibility," he says, tone patronizing.

"Okay," Lieutenant Bradley starts. "We'll make an effort to ensure they don't interfere with us right now."

Denendrius nods along, then says, "Limit the news broadcast. He's probably having someone feed him information. Cut the aerial view so he—or anyone else trying to interfere—can't dispatch a team to attack me while I'm trapped here. Have your officers search the trunks of parked cars in the area to see if any men are hiding. I was ambushed at that officer's house—they were hiding in neighboring homes—so do with that information what you will."

The line crackles. "I can see what I can do to address your requests, Charles, but I need some cooperation from you as well. I'll have someone ensure the media pulls back, but would you be willing to uncover *just* this front window? We want to prioritize the well-being of everyone, and being able to see inside would—"

Denendrius screams something furious and unintelligible —probably not even English—into the phone before whipping it across the room. It shatters against the front door as the family collectively gasps and yelps. The teenage girls sob, and Denendrius twists to them.

"Shut up!" he bellows, so loud his body practically shakes the words out of him. The police outside likely heard, even without an active call.

I scramble off the recliner to him, completely unsure if he'll react violently to my desperate attempt to calm him down as I wrap my arms around his midsection and rest my head on his chest. I'll take a slap if there's a chance I can settle him, so the police won't be as quick to send SWAT inside and inevitably burn us to death when they breach the doors or windows.

My head lifts and falls under his heavy breaths, and I force my own steady breaths against him in hopes he'll adopt them.

"I'm sorry, sweetheart," he murmurs to me before he releases a heavy exhale that whooshes against my head.

"If I tell them not to ask again, they'll probably listen. They're worried about me. They don't understand you're trying to keep me safe," I whisper, unable to hide the shake in my voice.

I look up through my lashes at him and he nods, then directs a question to the hostages. "Is there another house phone?"

Releasing Denendrius, I turn to face them too as Andy answers, "T-there's one in the office down the hall."

Denendrius smiles. "They'll call back. Let's fetch it."

Andy gingerly rises to his feet as Denendrius pulls the gun from the back of his pants where it was hidden beneath his jacket and hands it to me while motioning to the hostages. "Don't try anything."

I sit back down on the recliner, gun tight in my hand, knowing I would use it. I don't care how innocent and scared they are if they try to open the window or do anything that might jeopardize me getting home. All they have to do is listen to Denendrius. If I can do it, so can they. They don't even comprehend how much more terrified of him they should be.

"Are you okay?" their mother, Lynn, asks me as she leans forward.

I offer a clipped nod.

Mikey's leg twitches like he's thinking of getting up, and my hand tightens on the gun's grip. He looks between the gun and the hall behind me like he wants to convince me to turn on Denendrius or use the fact we're practically the same size to disarm me and shoot Denendrius himself.

"He'll kill you," I warn.

"You have the gun, though," he whispers.

I stare deep into his eyes and shift closer, making sure he knows how serious I am. *"He doesn't need it."*

Lynn's heavy gaze mulls me over, the questions clear in her eyes as she scrutinizes my arms and face. "You look hungry," she states carefully, the pity in her eyes making me grit my teeth.

I know I've lost weight from being in the cage. Looking much thinner than my missing poster must have enormous implications for everyone.

Before I can respond, Denendrius returns with the phone. It rings, and he hands it to me. My twitching fingers take it, and I answer the call and immediately put it on speaker.

"Hello?" I say before they've had a chance.

The pause is a few moments longer than I expect, and I wonder if they were anticipating Denendrius picking up and getting me has thrown them off.

"This is Lieutenant Bradley again. Am I speaking to Marianna?" he asks evenly, no sign of the concern I suspect he feels.

"Yes."

"Okay, Marianna. Is everyone okay? I apologize for trying to negotiate the removal of the window coverings after Charles stated it was non-negotiable. That's my mistake."

My heart pounds. "Don't bring the window coverings up again, please. Seriously. They can't come down under any circumstance, and you're just going to make him angry by asking again."

There's a pause that makes me bite the inside of my cheek. Denendrius glances at the front door, and I know he can hear them on the other side.

"I understand I made him angry, Marianna. It wasn't my intention. I'm simply focused on ensuring everyone remains safe and unharmed. Is everyone unharmed? I noticed Denendrius didn't answer the phone. I want to make sure he's safe as well."

"He's fine," I assure him. "The only thing harmed was a phone. Just please don't bring up the windows again. They need to stay covered."

"The window coverings sound important to you, Marianna. Can you help me understand the importance of them being covered?"

I glance at Denendrius, whose only guidance is a flat expression. "It's for our safety. You're asking us to jeopardize our safety by opening them."

"I respect your need to keep the windows covered, Marianna. Understanding more about this could help us ensure we respect your needs better. Could you clarify why this is critical for your safety?" Bradley asks.

"Uh . . ." I look up at Denendrius for direction, trying to read his expression until he gives me a slow shake of his head and mouths for me to change the subject.

I must take too long to answer, or perhaps they know I'm looking for guidance from Denendrius and want to jump to my rescue, as Lieutenant Bradley says, "That's okay, Marianna. I'll make sure the team understands how important the windows remaining covered is. Since visual confirmation isn't possible, can we do a quick check-in? I'd appreciate it if everyone could tell us how they're feeling today, or if there's anything specific anyone needs. Just as a standard, could we start by hearing from Charles? It helps us make sure everyone is all right."

I gulp and pass the phone to him.

"Hey there," Denendrius says, his tone as smooth as butter, like he didn't erupt mere minutes ago and smash the phone.

"Hello, Charles," Lieutenant Bradley greets. "Thanks for speaking with me again. I apologize for mentioning the window coverings. I respect that it's something you won't negotiate."

"Appreciated."

Denendrius allows the hostages to state that they're still alive, and there's a quick back and forth about basic needs— Lieutenant Bradley convinces Denendrius to let the rest of the hostages have a quick bathroom break—before everyone is seated again.

Lieutenant Bradley continues with, "As we go ahead with checking-in, Charles, I'm bringing in Special Agent Marshall because he has considerable experience in resolving situations like this without anyone getting hurt. He's here to help us navigate through this smoothly. Is that okay?"

Denendrius scowls. "Yeah," he says evenly. "That's fine."

A deeper, more gruff voice chimes in. "Good morning, Charles. I've been briefed about your situation, and I want to assure you that my primary concern is everyone's safety, including yours. How are you feeling?"

Denendrius stares blankly at the front door between us and the agent. He takes a deep breath. "I'm fine."

"That's good to hear." There's a clicking before Agent Marshall continues with, "So, Charles, pardon my bluntness, but let's scrap the bullshit, all right? You're smart enough to know exactly what's happening here, so let's stop wasting time and focus on the current issue at hand. You know our main, overarching goal is to recover Marianna, and we know you'll do everything in your power to prevent that. Am I right?"

Denendrius merely laughs, his grin stretching wide. "Hm. Sure, let's test this new angle and see how it works for you."

I can hear the smirk in Agent Marshall's next words. "That also means you're going to do *everything* to ensure she's safe, right?"

Denendrius's grin slowly morphs into an annoyed glower. "Obviously."

"That's great to hear, because right now I think the biggest threat to Marianna's safety is the numerous persons who are targeting you two. It's no wonder you want the windows covered. Me and my superiors want them handled as much as you do. Their actions were reckless and caused the injuries and deaths of civilians and multiple police officers. You understand how important it is that they're taking care of, right?"

Denendrius's eyes narrow as he chews on the agent's words. "I think I do."

My heart pounds. Maybe I'm being too hopeful, but what if Viorel knows exactly what's happening—and is working through Agent Marshall, even if the agent doesn't know it himself? It would make sense that Viorel wants any rogue vampires dealt with, for the exact reasons Agent Marshall has stated. Despite knowing how dangerous Denendrius is to me, the more immediate threats are those who aren't working in Viorel's favor to retrieve me.

"Fantastic, Charles. I think it's in both our best interests to work together to get them off our backs. I've ordered for the media feed to be completely cut. It's a little delayed if you look at the TV, but they've finished live recording and will soon stop broadcasting all videos of our current location. We don't want anyone—who doesn't already know, unfortunately—finding out where you two are."

Denendrius nods firmly as he says, "Good. I need to know what you know about the groups that were after us now."

Agent Marshall grunts, his proceeding sigh sounding like theatre. "Unfortunately, the police weren't able to gather any significantly useful intel. I was hoping you could help us help you."

Pondering, Denendrius purses his lips. "Are you sure you have the *ability* to neutralize these people?"

"I'm sure. Any information you give me will be passed along to those more than capable."

Denendrius's eyes narrow, and his lip twitches, like he suspects he's helping Viorel despite how it'll benefit him as well. "Fine. I hope you're either recording or have a pen and paper handy. Also, I expect updates."

"Affirmative on all points, Charles. I'm ready."

Denendrius, with his practically perfect memory and quick mind, unloads a plethora of information he gathered on our attackers during the chase. From intricate car details and plate numbers to wildly specific facts about each antagonizing body we dealt with. He divulges their methods, the implications of them, and carefully—so that anyone who wouldn't understand what he means would think nothing of it—emphasizes that all our attackers were "*Dark*-eyed." Agent Marshall must only be partially in the loop, as he asks for more specific eye color descriptions, until Denendrius insists there's no other way to describe them, and his superiors will understand.

Viorel's men—or any bounty hunters working with them— will have more than enough information now to hunt them down and take them out. Any nearby vampires who might be holed up will also be more aware of the danger in coming after us once we escape.

"That's gold, Charles. Thanks. Sit tight, and we'll handle the rest," Agent Marshall says.

XLV

Denendrius sighs and ends the call, his hard gaze raking over the hostages. As if on cue, my stomach grumbles, an agitated, demanding beast filling the tense silence of the room. Eyes flit to me, and Denendrius slowly turns and ponders me. I wrap my arms around my stomach and wind them tight like I can squeeze the hunger out.

Lynn clears her throat. "Charles, it's lunchtime. I could cook."

He twists, studying her for a long moment, that she squirms beneath before he says, "Okay. Let's all go on an adventure to the kitchen."

Denendrius holds his hand out to me as the others rise, and I slip my fingers between his and stand. We move to a large honey-wood table in the kitchen, Denendrius pulling a chair out for me with his free hand. I lower onto the tied-on red cushion and Mira takes a seat beside me, her sister taking one beside her, then her brother and father.

"What would you like me to make?" she asks Denendrius as she stands in front of the stove awaiting instruction.

"Ask my fiancée."

A line appears between her brows and disappears as fast as it came. She jerks her gaze to me. "What are you hungry for, honey?"

I shrug. "What do you have?"

"M-maybe we could ask them to bring something," Mikey suggests, daring eyes settling on Denendrius.

"Why would we do that?" Denendrius inquires as he sits beside me—loudly shifting the chair closer to me on the tile— as his gaze tightens on him.

The boy bites at his lip, and his voice wavers as he says, "I've seen it on TV. Usually they offer to bring food, and you could ask for anything you want. Fancy steaks, seafood . . ."

Denendrius's back straightens as he mulls him over. "We'd have to open the door. You don't see the issue with that?"

Mikey stares intently at the table. "I guess, yeah. Sorry."

Denendrius smirks, but the humor doesn't make it to his eyes. "Your mother will cook, but I appreciate your efforts to get a fancy meal on the department's dime." His smirk vanishes as his eyes dart back to Lynn. "She asked you what you have."

Lynn wets her dry lips, a swallow working its way down her throat before she pulls in a steadying breath and rattles off a list.

"Chicken Alfredo sounds good," I decide.

Mira leans a smidge closer and whispers, "It's my favorite. Mom cooks the best."

Denendrius stares at Mira, his sharp gaze cutting the space between her and me wider as she shifts closer to her sister.

Lynn moves to the fridge and pulls ingredients into her arms, her grip shaky as she shifts to the counter and prepares. I feel a sliver of guilt as I watch her weak hands, though I know she's more interested in cooking for her children than me. I'm merely a good excuse to feed them under Denendrius's control, and I suppose she believes if she pleases me, it'll please him. She's not wrong.

"Stop," Denendrius demands, rising to his feet, the suddenness of his voice turning her to stone.

"What's wrong?" She carefully rotates with a capped jar of chopped garlic.

I gnaw at my lip, my heart juddering with each step he takes across the kitchen toward her.

"You can't cook with that." Each word is clipped as he points to the jar in her hand.

She lowers it to the counter and takes a giant step back as he reaches her side. "Why not?"

"It'll make my fiancée violently sick," he tells her before *tsking*. "You don't want to make her sick, do you?"

"I'm so sorry," she pleads, the ache of fear in her voice. "Is there anything else she can't have?"

"Just garlic," he verifies.

She nods and moves back toward preparation, taking a jar from the spice rack in front of her, gaze flitting between the cutting board and Denendrius. As soon as she flips the lid open, Denendrius's hand constricts her wrist. She exclaims and pulls beneath his grip as several protests surround the table.

"Are you stupid?" he snarls.

Tears well in her eyes. *"I don't understand."*

With his other hand, he pries the spice jar out of her grip and assesses the label.

"It's a mix my aunt makes," she explains, frozen in his hold.

"There's garlic in it," he tells her as he sets the jar on the counter and closes it, only the words *Chicken Blend* scrawled in black ink over a half-torn label.

"I'm so sorry." A tear darts down her cheek. "I didn't know, I swear. I'm not trying to hurt your fiancée."

He sighs and releases her. "Show me the other spices you want to use."

She wipes her tear away and reaches a quaking hand to the spice rack, carefully selecting spices for Denendrius to approve. Though he gives her some space to move, he hovers around the counters, eyes trained on her hands as she prepares lunch like she's going to try sneakily poisoning me.

A touch on my wrist jars me, and I remember myself with a heavy blink before shifting to Mira.

"What're those?" She points at the collection of circular scars on my wrists.

I yank my hand off the table and into my lap, shaking my head.

After a few beats of silence, she says, "I'm seventeen too."

"I'm eighteen." It's strange to say aloud. The fact I'm a whole year older than I thought is so weird. Never mind how I should be turning nineteen next month if I weren't going to be a vampire.

"I'm going to be eighteen in six months," she says.

She won't be. It's the only thought that bumps around my head. That, and I don't understand the purpose of this conversation.

"Right," her sister whispers, eyes trained on me. "Your birthday was a few weeks ago, wasn't it, Marianna?"

Goosebumps litter my arms. Something about the fact these strangers know so much about me makes my stomach roil. I suppose they don't know my real birthday, the one Viorel pulled out of my mother, is in May. How I'll be nineteen soon. I don't bother correcting them.

"Yeah," I exhale.

"Happy belated birthday," they say in unison.

"Thanks." My tired gaze shifts to Denendrius to assess his possible reaction to the girls interacting with me.

His flat expression is unreadable as he stands as close to the stove as possible without being directly in front of the pan full of chicken. There's distance in his eyes as he stares across the room at no one in particular.

"I had a math quiz today," Mira mumbles, the chair creaking as she adjusts.

"At least you have a good excuse for why you missed it," I tease dryly.

Somehow, she smiles. But it's a shaky, frail thing as it passes over her chapped lips and comes nowhere near reaching her timid and terrified brown eyes.

"*Yeah,*" she breathes. "Maybe my friends will give me the answers before I take it."

A stone of emotion lodges in my throat as my eyes trail away from her. Have I accidentally given her hope? I know she won't survive this, but is it kindness to let her believe she will?

I stare narrowly at the wood grain pattern of the tabletop, a twinge of sharp jealousy passing through my center. I'd give anything to be worrying about a math quiz right now. Anything to be in school like every other normal teenager. Slowly, I expel a longing breath and slouch deeper in my chair. I'd give anything for school to be my sole stress right now. Stinging tears well in my eyes, but I don't let them free.

Exhaustion pulses through me. My limbs grow heavier with each beat my heart trudges through. I pull the chair closer to the table and cross my arms on top to lean my head on them. Though I know I won't sleep, I close my eyes.

"Are you okay?" Mira whispers, her voice only inches from my head.

"*Just tired.*" The room feels like it's rocking around me.

My ears prick at Denendrius's even steps crossing the room. His cold hand moves across the back of my head. "You could sleep on the couch, sweetheart. I'll bring lunch to you."

I rock my head back and forth on my arms. "No, I won't be able to sleep," I admit. How could I? "I'm only resting my eyes."

The chair creaks under his weight beside me, and he continues stroking my hair. "Okay."

The smell of cooking chicken and spices fills the air, and I breathe it in and out, teasing my complaining stomach. Hunger gnaws little holes in me, making space for anxiety to worm in. The pain in my stomach expands through my body, pulling the memory of sore limbs and stone muscles back. I know it's been less than twenty-four hours since I last ate, but my frantic stomach tries to convince my brain we're back in the cage. *That I'm starving.* My stomach roars at me again, overpowering the sound of bubbling water and sizzling meat.

Tears well in my eyes and saliva thickens in my mouth.

"What's wrong?" Denendrius coos, his fingers tucking loose hair behind my ear.

I know saying *nothing* won't suffice for him. "I'm hungry. I don't like being hungry."

"I know, sweet girl." The back of his finger rubs the exposed part of my cheek. "It'll be ready soon."

"Fifteen minutes," Lynn says with the sound of the spoon hitting the side of the pot.

It feels like such a long time, and I fear my stomach will be so full of anxious holes by then that I won't be able to properly fill myself. Rubbing my eyes against my arm, I try to scrub the tears away before anyone can notice. Faintness creeps into me and dampens the sounds of the room. My head fills with lead, my weak arms protesting under the weight.

"Come to the bathroom with me," he murmurs.

I nod, and he hooks his arm around my midsection and helps me to my weak legs.

"If anyone tries anything," Denendrius starts as he walks me across the kitchen, "you'll eat lead instead of lunch."

The pain in my stomach is more concerning than leaving them alone. They won't be able to take a single breath without Denendrius hearing it.

They stay silent as Denendrius brings me to the bathroom and only half-shuts the door. He leans me against the counter as he bites into his wrist and offers it to me. I wrap my hands around his forearm as I greedily lap him up, the cold of his blood putting out the hungry burn that was raging out of control inside me. He strokes my arm as I drink, and when the bite heals beneath my lips, I lick what's left off his skin and draw in a shuddering breath. I yearn for the day I never have to take from him again.

"Better?" he asks as I lift my heavy eyes to his.

I nod, the hunger a mere whisper now. Vague strength flows through me, and though I don't feel well enough to run laps, I can stand on my own.

"I'll be in the kitchen," he tells me as he presses a soft kiss to my lips before pulling the door closed behind himself.

Alone in the bathroom, I steal a few extra minutes when I'm done on the toilet to wash my face with fancy face wash and scrub my teeth with a new toothbrush I find in the drawer. Finding a comb, I rinse the clean bristles before pulling it through my hair. I feel a bit more human when I return to my chair between Denendrius and Mira.

Though, when their mom puts a steaming plate of chicken and fettuccine Alfredo in front of me, I dig into my lunch like he's been starving me. There's barely enough time to breathe properly between the teeming bites I shove past my lips.

It barely dawns on me how everyone else picks at their food, the clink of forks sharp in the tense air, until she says, "Charles, are you not hungry?"

I lift my head, my eyes flicking from face to sullen face as I swallow a mouthful so large it nearly gets stuck.

"No," he says, shoving his plate in front of mine like he's offering me seconds.

"I can cook you something else if you prefer—"

"*No.*"

She drops her gaze to her plate.

I finish my plate first, the others hardly having made a dent in theirs as their eyes—so full of distress—shift back and forth from one another. Bodies are rigid in seats, hands loose and shaking on forks gripped so tight it's a wonder the metal doesn't bend.

Agent Marshall briefly checks in with us, satisfied to hear we're all eating and assuring Denendrius that they're working on resolving their mutual concerns before ending the call with the promise to check back in soon.

Denendrius hooks his arm around my waist and pulls me from my chair to his lap with ease. I can't help the rigidity in my weak limbs as he positions my legs on either side of his, so I'm centered on his lap before circling his arms around my midsection. I lean on the table with my forearms until he pulls my back firm against his chest. The glances we receive make my heart drum and palms sweat. Do they notice the anxiety taut in my muscles? How I breathe opposite to their pulsing breaths with how I hold my air?

"It's all right," Denendrius murmurs in my ear, my cue to relax against him.

I let my body go limp in his hold, accepting his comforting words of how this will all be over soon that come between the delivery of soft kisses in my hair.

"I'm still hungry," I squeeze out, his constricting arms making my heart lurch to the base of my throat.

His grip unravels, and I exhale too much accumulated breath while shifting forward to pull his rejected pasta to me. I eat slowly, Denendrius's hands snatching half my concentration as they move over my back, alternating between gentle strokes and firm massages. He straightens in his chair, his lap stiff beneath me.

My hand freezes on my fork as I stare forward between Lynn and her husband, their faces blurry. I can feel the warmth drain from my face. Denendrius's existence around my body occupies the entirety of my mind. His arm circles my midsection, his other hand stroking hair away from my neck and inching the shoulder of my shirt down to allow his lips access. His heavy breaths pulse against my skin.

Would he do it here? In front of everyone? Are they mere objects around us? Not people enough for him to grant me privacy?

"How's your lunch, Marianna?" Lynn's strained voice breaks me from my spell, and my vision straightens. She doesn't quite look at me, her scrutiny to the side where Denendrius is lost in his own world of warm flesh and soft kisses.

After a few tries, I manage to say, "It's delicious. I wish I had a mom to cook lunches like this."

It's such a stupid thing to say, and I don't know why it comes out. Perhaps it's the way she ponders me, with motherly concern wrinkling her forehead and frowning lips, or how the girls look at me like I'm one of them.

Reality startles my senses, and for too many moments, I swap perspectives with them. I see myself as they do—a regular teen girl, gripped on the lap of a human man who is as terrifying and dangerous as a human man can possibly be. Skinnier and weaker than she was the last time anyone saw her, a year ago.

She should be in school right now. So should they. A teenager studying anything but the behavior of her captor just to emotionally assist him through a hostage situation. She should be home with parents, safe, instead of unable to relate to the girl she used to be.

Something about the way they look at me makes me feel so much lonelier. Much less hopeful. The questions in their fearful eyes puncture me. Do they wonder what's going to happen to me too? Do they see us with the same end, only mine prolonged?

"I'm going to the bathroom," Denendrius murmurs in my ear, his hands shaping my fingers around the gun.

I settle back into my own desensitized reality, where things are so much worse than they perceive despite how they've numbed me.

My mouth is too full to respond, but I grip the gun like I mean business with one hand while shoveling food into my mouth with the other. After a long minute, I catch the glance that Mikey and his father share. Their action is too swift for me to react—my mouth too full of food to shout—as they scramble across the table and knock me backwards in my chair on the floor. Food lodges itself in my throat, and I choke. When their father pries the gun from my weak grip, he might as well be taking it from a toddler.

In a moment, Denendrius is tackling him, their father's grip on the gun—he didn't even have time to adjust it in his hand properly—as weak as mine compared to Denendrius's strength. Denendrius stomps on their father's chest to pin him to the floor, aiming the barrel at his face as he glares down at him with bared teeth and a murderous stare as he huffs in fury. His pants are unzipped, his belt undone and hanging in the loops.

I choke my food down as I scramble to my knees and stare up pleading at Denendrius. I cough until I get words out. "Please! Please don't shoot him! SWAT will come in if you shoot him."

Stifled cries circle the table behind me.

"You're lucky," Denendrius snarls at him. "You're *so* lucky she's right."

Denendrius grabs a fistful of their father's pajama shirt with his free hand and yanks him to his feet, shoving him against the table with such force that water glasses topple. Their father mumbles desperate apologies as he takes his seat, Mikey already returned to the chair next to him.

Shaking his head in disbelief, Denendrius tilts his head down to me and sighs. "Are you okay, sweetheart?"

I nod, and he helps me back to my chair and sits next to me, the Beretta aimed at their father. "I hope you learned your lesson."

Both father and son utter a swift, "We did, sir."

Denendrius grunts. "Good. I've killed people for a whole lot less. The only reason you're not lying on the floor with a head full of bullets is because it would inconvenience me."

They gulp and resume eating their lunch.

I dig back into my food, glancing down at Denendrius's undone pants and belt with a kink in my stomach.

He winks at me but sets the gun down to zip his pants and cinch his belt.

Agent Marshall calls back soon, and not a soul dares mention the catastrophe of lunch while they assure the agent they're still alive and unharmed. Denendrius and Agent Marshall briefly discuss their common enemy, Agent Marshall divulging that they tracked down three of the bikes—along with surveillance video of vehicle swaps when they ran out of fuel—as well as locate the beige car. He also mentions how special agents are actively questioning the residents of the homes that the two groups of initial attackers were hiding in.

With lunch done, Denendrius herds the family back to the couch. He sprawls out in the recliner with me curled up on his lap as he rotates through different news stations on TV. I close my eyes and bury my face in his neck so I don't have to see ourselves on the screen.

Nearly forty minutes of tense silence passes before Denendrius makes a tickled noise. My eyes pop open as he calls Agent Marshall back, the hint of a smile playing on his lips as he lifts the phone to his ear. As I snuggle close to hear, the line connects.

"Agent Marshall? I've been thinking about what you said."

"I'm all ears, Charles."

A soft smile shapes Denendrius's lips, his eyes full of amusement. "It's true I'll do anything and everything—as you stated—to keep Marianna safe. I realize I haven't been direct with my wishes, and I suppose you can contribute that to a lack of trust. We've established some trust now, some respect, haven't we? You seem to get me."

Agent Marshall is swift to answer, nothing but friendliness in his response. "Of course, Charles. What can I do for you?"

"Marianna and I could really use a safe exit from here. I want a sports car—without trackers or any other nonsense—with a full tank of gas and a couple jerry cans in the trunk. I want these choppers called off, and for you and the department to leave. Just let Marianna and me go. We only broke in here out of necessity. We were in danger, understand? I don't *want* to hurt this family or anyone else. I just want to get on with my life with my fiancée." He kisses my forehead.

There's a beat of silence that has me straightening on Denendrius's lap before Agent Marshall says, "I'm perplexed, Charles. I clocked you as a man who truly understands the reality of these situations. I wasn't wrong, was I? You know full well we have intentions of retrieving Marianna. We're not in the habit of allowing suspects to ride off into the sunset with missing teens. So, what do you really want? Because we both know I can't just let you drive away with her."

Denendrius nods along. "Oh, Agent Marshall, I totally respect that. But we really need that car within the next hour and a half, and here's the thing: I didn't kidnap Marianna. Sure, she *was* missing by your standards. But here she is, alive and well, and capable of clearing the air and putting you at ease."

He puts the speaker on and thrusts the phone into my hand.

My heart hammers in my temples, sweat collecting between my palm and the plastic, mind scrambling for something to say.

Except I realize nothing I say will convince them of anything. They'll interpret my words as coerced or fear driven. My tired eyes hold Denendrius's. He must know that too, so what's he playing?

"Go on," he insists with a soft smile.

Whatever his plan, this is a brilliant opportunity to prove myself to him and help cement my act as reality. Since we know anything I say will probably make it back to Viorel, this is the ultimate test of loyalty.

"Hi, Agent Marshall." My voice shakes, so I clear my throat.

His gruff voice answers with the care of a father, and I wonder if he is one. "Hey, Marianna. How are you holding up?"

I pull in a shaky breath, trying to push the feel of Denendrius's hand climbing up the back of my shirt to trace lines on my bare skin to the back of my slow mind. "I'd be better if Charles and I could leave, to be honest. I'm exhausted. Charles is doing everything he can to help me feel better, but there's only so much he can do when we're surrounded by police. I'm scared you'll come in and try to take me because you think he kidnapped me. That's not true. I'm not being held captive."

Agent Marshall sighs. "I'm hearing you, Marianna, but if that's true, why did you simply disappear? Many people are worried about you. Your social worker. Your friends. Camille, Daina, and Sarah are their names, right? I heard they've been sick with worry. Your foster mother, Carol Greene, and your history teacher, Derek Henderson, even spoke to police, but they too disappeared. Can you help me understand more?"

My throat thickens at the sound of my friends' names, tears stinging my eyes. I work through shaky breaths until I get one stable enough to speak. "I don't know what to tell you about Carol and my teacher, to be honest. We left Lorimer before they disappeared."

"But you're saying you left on your own accord, Marianna? Why didn't you tell anyone?"

My voice is too quiet, too weak. "Yes, and . . ." I pull in a trembling breath. "I don't really know. My friends are great, but life in Lorimer was shit. I was scared of aging out of foster care, I was failing grade ten again, and there was a gang on the street that wanted to hurt me. I guess I thought my friends would be better off without me, that it would be safer not to tell anyone where I was going in case people—gang members—were looking for me. I just wanted a new, normal life, and Charles did everything he could to give it to me. He's still trying. You're just making it hard right now."

"I'm sorry this is hard for you, Marianna. Can you confirm that you and Charles went to Bellevue, Washington, then?"

Denendrius gives me a nod of approval.

"Yes, we did," I say.

"Yet you both just came from Romania, correct?"

My lips part, and I look for help again.

"What's your point?" Denendrius inquires, guarded.

Agent Marshall says, "Simply trying to create a proper timeline for both our benefits, Charles. You were staying in quite a nice place there." He rattles off the address of the home we rented in Bellevue. "Is that correct?"

Denendrius chuckles. "You already know."

Agent Marshall shares his humor in a *you-caught-me* sort of way. "Just needed the confirmation." He returns to his seriousness. "How were things there, Marianna?"

I inhale deeply. "Practically how I wanted my life to be. You can prod for signs of distress, Agent Marshall, but all things considered, I'm okay. I need you to understand that I'm safe with Charles. I *want* to be with him. I want to leave here with him. Please, can we have what he asked for? No tricks please, he's too smart to fall for them. The family is okay, I promise. We didn't come in here to hurt anyone or steal anything. We were desperate. Everyone has been after us, and we're tired."

A sigh of sympathy comes through the phone. "Okay, guys.

Let me get started on fulfilling your requests, Charles, is that okay?"

Denendrius slips the phone from my shaky hand. "I appreciate that, Agent."

I stare at Denendrius beneath furrowed brows. "Do you really think they're going to meet your demands without any tricks?"

Denendrius chuckles and shakes his head.

XLVI

The next hour and a half passes with one brief check-in on our needs, and another to relay information to Denendrius—useless and performative information, really—about our pursuers.

Denendrius paces back and forth in the living room, the phone gripped in his hand and held near his face with the speaker on. "So not only do you not have any useful information about the people trying to kill me and my fiancée, there are still choppers overhead, and not a single officer has driven away. Where's my car?"

Agent Marshall is as calm as before. "I understand the frustration, Charles. I wish I had more helpful information too. You're worried about getting attacked leaving here, and so is law enforcement. As for not having the car yet, we need more time to cut through some tape. It's coming though, I just need a bit more patience. As for the choppers, I'll send them off now, and I'll start moving men out when your ride is on the way."

Denendrius mumbles several 'uh-huhs' as he wanders from the room to the garage. A loud click has darkness falling over us, and one girl squeals as I blink rapidly against the pitch-black. I jerk upright as Denendrius touches my shoulder.

He sits on the recliner arm, and we wait in silence—save for the crying and various hyperventilating breaths—for several minutes before Denendrius stands. His steps pad away from us. There's another click, and the room comes alight. The phone rings after a few seconds.

Denendrius is slow to pick it up, answering on the third ring. "What?"

"Hey, Charles. What happened? The power went off."

"I turned the breaker off," he admits breezily, like it's a fact they should already know.

"Can you explain your reasoning? I thought we were making progress."

"You haven't given me what I want yet, so I figured there's no point talking to you. When is my car coming?"

"I see how it is," Agent Marshall says. "Charles, why don't you tell me what you really want? We're both too smart to pretend you're not using the classic request for an escape car as either a diversion or a way to stall."

A dark laugh bubbles out of Denendrius. "Here's the thing, Agent Marshall. I know it's a cliche request, but *truly*, it's what I need. We both know what the alternative is, hm? Right, Agent Marshall? We both know how this ends if you want Marianna and I won't give her back. You know you can't negotiate anyone's freedom or my surrender. You cannot manipulate me, and you know it. I'm giving you an opportunity to end this peacefully. It's your job to practice harm reduction, correct? So, reduce harm. I have no need to hurt this family, but I do have a *desperate need* to leave with this girl whom I love with such ferocity that I would do *anything*. It's simple math. I'm sure you're smart enough to crunch the numbers." Denendrius pauses before adding, *"Bring me a car, and let us leave."*

There's a calculated pause before Agent Marshall says, "I hear you loud and clear, Charles. You're right. I will ensure they pick up the pace and meet your demands quickly."

Denendrius smirks. "See, Agent Marshall. You're a smart man."

He hangs up, but an hour later, there's still no notice of any sports car. Despite how having one right now would do us no good since the sun blazes on, you wouldn't know it by how Denendrius skulks around the house like a pissed off phantom. He turns the breaker off again, and we sit in the heavy, silent dark, wincing through attempts to contact us through the megaphone with the threat of SWAT at the back of my mind until Denendrius relents.

He's increasingly agitated when he reinstates the power and answers the phone, reiterating his previous points with more frustration. While the choppers have disbanded and a handful of cruisers sent on their way, Denendrius whispers to me that he can hear from their radios how they've merely hidden themselves a handful of blocks away, and how they have placed snipers on rooftops.

With three hours left until sunset, Agent Marshall calls again.

"Hey, Charles. I apologize for keeping you waiting. We have a car selected for you, straight from a dealership. An officer is fueling it up and getting some jerry cans per your request. It's rush hour, but they'll be here shortly—"

Denendrius paces back and forth, teeth grit and seething as he snarls into the phone. "I've had it, Agent. You accuse me of playing games by asking for an escape car, but you're no more honest. You think I don't know you've been stalling so officers can coordinate street placement to attempt capturing me when

I drive away? That you weren't using that extra time for seasoned snipers to arrive and take position?"

"Charles—"

"*No!*" Denendrius bellows into the phone. "That's it! That's enough! I gave you an opportunity to be smart, and you're treating me as if you can trick me! You can't trick me!" His chest heaves with heavy breaths. "I want an armored car now so the shots you've ordered don't land, and I want it driven right up to the door!"

"Charles," Agent Marshall starts evenly, "I get this is frustrating for you, but let's talk about this rationally—"

"Let's!" Denendrius hollers. "Would you rather have five hostages safe or one girl? Reduce the harm, Agent Marshall, because if I don't get what I want, I'm going to show you the lengths I'm capable of going to, to ensure Marianna is safe with me! I will hurt this family so badly that this mistake will be the *biggest failure of your career.* Hear me, agent. I may not have any grenades left, but I will do things to this family—to these teen girls—so horrific you've only ever read about them. I don't need this gun—"

I clamber to him, eyes wide, my heart seizing with panic. I plead with him to stop as the family cries and clutches one another on the couch. I try to reason with him, tell him he's going to trigger SWAT to breach the house. That there's only a couple hours left, and to *please please please just stop.* Agent Marshall tries to speak, but Denendrius bellows over him.

"I will take those girls and their little brother, and I will make their parents watch what I do to them! I'll slip my knife into their pretty bodies, and you will marvel at my creativity when you're collecting pieces of their battered, torn up bodies in black body bags!"

Agent Marshall's voice comes through stern. "Charles, I need you to stop what you're doing immediately."

"Which one should I start with?" Denendrius snarls into the phone, twisting to lock sights on Mira and Maddie.

Chaos erupts, Lynn and Andy scrambling in front of the girls and pleading with Denendrius to leave them alone. I grab his arm but am shaken off, my begging only adding to the racket—Agent Marshall's stern words drowned out—as Denendrius stalks toward the girls.

I scramble behind him, uselessly shouting with the rest of the family as he roughly shoves Andy and Lynn aside and pretends to ponder between the girls.

"Denendrius, stop!" I scream, hoping to invoke his fury by using his real name to distract him.

But there's no chance anyone heard me, as Denendrius snatches a fistful of brown hair while laughing and sing-shouting, *"Pretty Mira!"*

She's screaming and writhing as Denendrius drags her shaking body toward the stairs, my frantic steps and begging, high-pitched words as panicked as her family's.

Denendrius holds both Mira and the phone tightly as he drags her up the stairs while she fails to grip the banister, teasing Agent Marshall with, *"I better have my armored car by the time I'm done having fun with Mira! Otherwise, I'll be taking her sister for a ride instead!"*

He hangs up the phone and whips it into the living room over the banister, easily fighting her father off as he froths with anger behind him. The phone explodes against the living room floor, a piece of plastic narrowly missing me from where I fight for breath at the bottom step, my shaky limbs leaving me behind, my sobs making it harder for me to fill my lungs.

By the time I get upstairs, the entire family is in the master bedroom, and Denendrius is vulgarly teasing Andy and Lynn as he approaches their bed with a disheveled and tear-blind Mira, her sister so close Denendrius could grab her with his free hand and have them both. I stumble past their brother, who stands wide-eyed and helpless in the doorway as he watches.

But Denendrius drags Mira past the bed, instead tossing her into the open walk-in closet and standing aside with an evil fucking smirk as her family clambers in after her. He whips my Beretta out from the back of his jeans and aims it at them, screaming at them to get against the back wall or he'll blow their brains out.

I finally make it to him, drenched in sweat and tears, and heaving for breath. He yanks me hard against his body, his mouth assaulting mine as a groan rolls in his chest.

"*I love you,*" he purrs. "You know I love *you.*" He kisses me harder, his pants stiff against my stomach. "*Oh,* I love how much you love me. My pretty, jealous girl."

His eyes glimmer as he pulls away, smiling, to hand me the gun. He tells me to shoot anyone who dares move or open their mouth and then leaves the closet.

My heart pounds as he walks out of sight, and a few moments later, the lights go out again. I don't know how he expects me to shoot anyone in the dark, but at least the blackness ensures escaping the closet is an implausible option.

I gasp when Denendrius's hands appear on mine, and he puts his palm over my lips to demand my silence before slipping the gun from my hand. I don't even hear him leave the closet. My legs buckle beneath me, and I grab a bar covered in hangers and clothes to lower myself to the carpet.

A few beats later, and a gunshot rips through the air downstairs. The girls yelp behind me before stifling their cries. A single stair creaks, and I rake at the darkness, willing my eyes to catch what Denendrius is up to. I wait for his whispered words or cold touch, but none comes. My heart pounds in my ears.

Someone shouts something outside, too close to the house for comfort. Synced bangs shake the walls, coming from each side of the house. Splintering wood followed by loud commands crush the air from my lungs. A blast of light beyond the master bedroom door has stars cascading over my vision when I'm returned to the dark.

Fucking SWAT. Why the fuck would he provoke them?

My shallow breaths make me dizzy, and I try to follow the sound of feet moving through the house and their commands, but I'm too off kilter to figure it out. I try not to think about what will happen if SWAT gets me outside in the sun.

I choke on a breath as cold arms appear around my body and bring me to my feet.

"Trust me," he whispers, his lips brushing my ear as he crosses his arm over my chest and holds my back against the front of his body.

I release a strangled cry as the sharp edge of a knife presses into my throat. Denendrius places something heavy, segmented, and cold in my palm; my heart stops as he shapes my fingers around the lever of the grenade. With the way he's holding it with me, and the pressure of his fingers on mine, I can't tell if it's pinned or not. Still, I'm thankful he keeps his hand over mine, because my weak fingers would have us all dead.

My chest heaves, Denendrius's arm across it constricting. I press myself into him, trying to evade the cold metal against my throat and how each tense swallow grazes the blade.

Heavy boots storm up the stairs, thin beams of white light searching through the dark, swinging back and forth as SWAT agents clear each room.

I don't have to feign my fear—my gasping breaths and squeal—when the white light swoops across the room. My heart beats with each moment before they find us, and I don't fully believe that Denendrius wouldn't harm me again if it served him. Would he try to heal me himself?

The light sweeps across me, so bright I crane my neck

farther away from the blade and feel Denendrius's grip on me constrict my breath. With the beams of light, it's a blur of chaos before me as several SWAT officers in black gear position themselves in the doorway with guns aimed, each small adjustment of their bodies making my heart rattle.

Denendrius's tense order comes out low, his breath against the top of my head. "Tell your team to withdraw *now*. Withdraw, or I will slit her throat and detonate this grenade."

I can't see their faces past the blinding light, and I squint, trying to make out their expressions.

"Withdraw!" Denendrius roars, the blade teasing my flesh. "Return, and I'll have each of them dead before your boots are through the door."

"Withdraw," a man orders evenly from the doorway. "Everyone back out slowly. We're stepping back."

A chorus of teary confusion stirs up behind us as the team inches away, their flashlights dwindling until they're out of view. One girl breaks out into hysterical sobs, choking on a mouthful of confused words while she pleads to understand why they're not helping them.

"Wait—!" Andy calls, his voice brittle with disbelief and fear. "Why are you leaving? Wait! Come back!"

Denendrius's chest pushes against me in a breath as he loosens his grip and lowers his hand from my throat. I don't have to ask him if he hypnotized the lead officer to leave; I can't imagine they'd go so easily. Though maybe the grenade was enough for them to pull out.

The home's doors close. The confirmation that the team is gone only sends the girls deeper into hysterics, their cries so loud I nearly miss how their brother shares the same sorrow.

Denendrius smirks and lifts our hands, brushing the intact grenade pin against my fingers. "See, you're safe, sweetheart." I hear him slip it into the interior pocket of his leather jacket.

I collapse against Denendrius in relief, his arm winding tight around me as the knife clicks shut in his other hand.

"You're bleeding a little, sweetheart. I'm sorry," Denendrius coos as he tilts my head back. His breath beats against my throat, his tongue darting across what must be a nick since I can't feel it. As he pulls back, he murmurs, "Stay here. I'll flip the breaker back on and make sure the doors and windows are secure."

He slips into the dark, his movement silent through the house. My heart beats in my stomach, jolting when the lights return with a hum. Denendrius returns, Beretta in hand, as he stares at the hostages huddled back in the corner.

"What time is it?" I ask, itching to escape into the cool air of night. My body aches with exhaustion.

"A little over an hour until sunset," he assures me. "We're almost free."

"Then what?" Andy rises to his shaky feet.

Denendrius's arm lifts, the Baretta's barrel aimed straight at his head. "What valuables do you have?" he demands. "Do you keep cash?"

"I thought you didn't want to rob us?" Mikey grits out.

Denendrius shifts his aim to Mikey, and Lynn leans in front of him.

"No," Denendrius says, the corner of his lip jerking back in an amused smirk before rapidly fading. "But while I'm here . . ."

"If we show you, will you promise to leave the children alone?" Lynn asks, eyes puffy with tears.

"Well . . ." Denendrius muses with a flicker of a smile, the potential of agreement in his voice as he lowers the gun to his side. He coughs and clears his throat. "You can certainly show me where your valuables are. If you can entice me with something shinier than your daughters, then maybe . . ."

I can only imagine how raw his throat is with thirst for them. He likely has his first drink selected of the bunch.

"I'll go with you," Andy volunteers, his swallow visible, the sweat on his brow shimmering under the light as he takes a step forward.

He flicks his gaze between Andy and Lynn. "You too," he tells her.

Her husband helps her to her feet, her shaking legs threatening to give out as he wipes tears from her watery eyes. "I-I have gold jewelry ..."

Denendrius hands me the gun, then lifts his hand and wipes a few drops of blood from the nick on my throat with his thumb. He brings it to his lips and licks it off, his black eyes fading to such a slight maroon that I suspect I can only tell from being so close to him.

His gaze jerks to the teenagers. "You're all too out of bravery to try anything now, aren't you?"

They merely tremble and stare wide-eyed at him.

A dark smile spreads across his lips. "Come on, daylight is fading."

He walks backward from the closet, Lynn and Andy's weak steps carrying past me and into the bedroom.

I shift my attention to the teenagers, a pensive wrinkle between the brows of the girls. We study one another in silence, my ears trained on the conversation a few meters away. There's a grin in Denendrius's voice as he looks over their mother's jewelry, more humor than annoyance when he tells her what she claims is genuine gold is fake or plated. Her husband tries to defend them, which has Denendrius assuming he purchased the fakes for her. He calls out to me that there's a few pairs of nice diamond earrings he wants to show me later, and that we should pierce my ears so I can wear them.

"Where's your safe?" Denendrius demands.

"W-we don't have a safe," the mother stutters, and the silence that fills the room is so thick with deceit that even I can taste it.

"I bet you've got one of those mid-size fireproof ones," Denendrius says. "Easy to carry. Cheap lock."

Andy swallows. "The keys are in my nightstand."

Denendrius chuckles. "Of course they are."

"We keep it in the closet in the office downstairs," Lynn whispers.

"How surprising. You people need to switch things up a bit." He sighs and calls out to me, "We'll be back."

Mira stands, and I tighten my fingers on the grip as her eyes lock with mine. She hunches a bit, her hands up in surrender —or to tell me she means no harm—as she takes a few careful steps toward me.

"I'll shoot you if I need to," I warn her, my finger sliding against the side of the gun, ready to shift to the trigger.

"Are you okay?" she asks, her shaky voice coming low. "You're bleeding a bit."

"I'm fine," I snap, though my tone is brittle.

"Maybe we can help one another," she whispers, though she's still not quiet enough for Denendrius's sensitive ears. "I heard about you. I saw you on the news, and your friend talking about you and him on Crime Nightly. He must hurt you."

"I know what you're doing." I slowly shake my head in disapproval.

"There's five—*six*—of us—"

I tilt my head in warning. "Don't do this. You can't do this."

"Aren't you scared?" She blinks back tears. *"I'm so scared."*

I merely stare at her, too numb to feel anything. "I'm too tired to be scared of much anymore," I admit, my eyes tacky with sleep.

"Thirty minutes until sunset, sweetheart," Denendrius reassures me as he stuffs small bundles of bills into my backpack after removing them from a medium-sized, fireproof safe that he carried out of the office.

I curl into a tighter ball on the couch. The sisters hold one another on the recliner while Mikey sits on the bottom step of the stairs, face heavy with hopelessness. Lynn and Andy pace.

"What's at sunset?" Mira asks.

Denendrius merely stares at her for a long moment before continuing to dig through the safe. He snooped through the rest of the house—finding a few precariously hidden pieces of jewelry and heirlooms—before finally unlocking it to root through.

I listen to the faint chatter of radios outside, the hum of engines coming and going. Law enforcement must be scrambling to come up with a new plan now that Denendrius has threatened to blow everyone up.

"You're scared of the sun more than the police, aren't you?" Mira blurts, but relaxes against Maddie and the recliner.

A wicked smile shapes Denendrius's lips, and he looks up at her from the safe, dark eyes glittering.

She locks eyes with him, eyes so dark that—with a little contemplation in the right direction—it becomes clear how they're a little too black to simply be dark brown. How they're not quite human. They're the darkest red can get with satiated thirst.

"You're just hiding here, right?" she says, low. "You keep threatening us . . . but you haven't actually hurt anyone. You didn't hurt me . . ."

My heartbeat races out of control. I rub my thumb over the scars on my wrists and consider how she noticed, knowing how obvious they are on my neck too. Denendrius made a stink about garlic, and wouldn't eat lunch, but licked the blood from my throat. She would have felt his cold hands too.

"Don't those dangerous little theories scare you?" he teases.

Her lips part, the question on her tongue. But she doesn't

speak it. She closes her mouth and glances at me, searching for a cue.

I pull my gaze from hers, unsure what to offer. My ears perk as the noisy chopper that has been hovering above the house for the past hour retreats, though the crackle of Agent Marshall trying to coax Denendrius into speaking with the megaphone has me sighing.

She wets her lips, her heavy gaze searching his face before she ponders me again and relaxes a bit more. I see her thought process then, through her smoother breaths and the way her shoulders lower as she looks between Denendrius and me.

Something like . . . *If I've been missing for so long, and with a vampire, maybe she's not in as much danger as she thinks. Maybe the vampire is just desperate. Maybe he's just running from vampire hunters. The media has it all twisted, and she doesn't need to be as scared as she has been.*

"A-are you thirsty?" she asks him, something reasonable that could mean nothing more . . . unless he will expand and verify her suspicions.

"Are you offering?" His smile grows.

I stare at him, my heart racing with the desire to flee into the night. To get what I know comes next over with . . . the part where she finds out which parts of her theories are true when she's choking on her own blood with her family dead around her.

She splits glances between Denendrius and me, her family quiet in confusion as they observe like they're too paralyzed by uncertainty to interject.

"If I am, would it help? Make it easier for you to leave?" The anxiety spikes in her voice. "If I don't need to fight, it's safer, right?"

"You're right, Mira. It would help." Denendrius's voice comes smooth like honey as he stands and gently beckons her.

Like she's about to approach a wild animal, she gingerly

stands—shaking Maddie's protesting grip off—and moves to him.

Her father finally finds his nerve and snarls, "Don't you dare touch my little girl again, you fucking pervert. Mira, don't go near him."

But with the gun so clear in the front of Denendrius's waistband, and the grenade in the pocket of his leather jacket, Andy does nothing. He's rooted to the floor.

Her eyes flick to me, and she slowly lifts her hand a bit in front of herself. He swiftly snakes his hand around her wrist.

Denendrius tears into her vein, the family gasping in horror. I sigh and rest my eyes as he makes his rounds, draining them before they can scream. When the gulping between noisy, thirsty breaths subsides, I open my eyes. The sight of their bodies sprawled across the floor is as common of a sight to me now as any other. I can't even bring myself to waste the effort of scrutinizing their lifelessness.

"Come on, sweetheart," Denendrius says as he zips the backpack and approaches with it. "Any moment now, and we're out of here."

He helps me sit upright, holding the backpack out as I slip my arms into it. I fight the urge to lie back down, forcing myself to my feet as he grabs the toolbox and returns to hook his fingers through mine.

Denendrius guides me upstairs as the sound of heavy trucks settles out front, likely in preparation to enact another breach with explosive handling in mind. He brings me through one of the girls' rooms, my eyes refusing to hold any information about the dark space as we work our way past masses of furniture and the bed to the covered window.

A storm of automatic fire rains across the front yard. The hollering of panicked and confused law enforcement orders cutting through the sound. Denendrius practically giggles as he tears the window covering away and swiftly opens the window.

"What's happening?" I breathe as he guides me onto the roof and hooks his arm around my waist.

He snickers and whispers, "I lured SWAT into the house so I could hypnotize them to leave at my will and turn on one another at sunset for a diversion."

I don't have time to respond before the world blurs as Denendrius flees with me into the night.

XLVII

We keep to the shadows as we evade choppers, law enforcement having become privy to our escape so soon after. My heart hammers against Denendrius's back, my arms and legs wrapped around his torso as he stays ahead of sweeping chopper lights while we move through alleys and backyards.

Yet the search light is only half the danger when any vampire who knows my scent could pick up on it for miles and hunt us down, especially with the breeze sending my hair fluttering behind me.

The neighborhoods we slip through are plagued with police presence, sirens clamoring, chopper blades thrumming, and dogs barking all around us. The deployment of canines tells me they know we fled on foot.

My sore, heavy eyes burn with sleep-desperate tears, Denendrius's one-handed grip the only thing keeping me on his back.

I want to ask him where we're going, and what the plan is now. How long until I can lie down? I don't want to risk someone hearing me though, and his continued silence after hoisting me onto his back assures me it's a valid concern.

At some point I must lose consciousness, as I wake with his breath-filled chest pressing against mine and my head on his shoulder, one of his arms hooked beneath my bottom, and my arms loose around his neck. I lift my lids just enough for the blurry rear walls of alley-side buildings to register under dull yellow lights, a tagged dumpster sitting a few meters away.

Denendrius's voice tickles past my ear. "Hey, we're best friends. I need you to give us a ride and follow each of my instructions carefully."

A man's friendly voice responds, a van door sliding open before I'm jostled with Denendrius's movements. He lays me on my back on something scratchy and smelling of dirt, his body stretching out alongside mine. Enough awareness trickles into me for a glance around.

We're in the back of a van on the scratchy carpet between two clothing bars partially filled with hanging suits, blouses, and dresses in clear plastic slips or garment bags. Past them, I read the reversed words of the stickered window. *Pristine Pickup Dry Cleaners.*

The van rolls forward, my body so heavy with exhaustion I don't have the strength to keep my legs from jostling with the vehicle's movements.

My sleepy eyes shift to Denendrius's calm face as he gazes down at me in the dim alleyway light sneaking through the partially obstructed windows. His voice comes low. "You can sleep now, sweetheart. We're safe, I promise. I got us miles from the house, and there's no reason they'd expect us to be so far already. And as far as I can tell, there are no immortals following either. I made sure our trail was hard to follow. Right now, nobody can see us down here through the sticker-covered windows and tint. Especially not with these garments in the way. This man is going to drive us out of the city. If we get pulled over, I'll hypnotize whichever officer comes to the window. Okay? You can relax. We're free now, Marianna."

I release a heavy breath from deep within and let my eyes drift shut.

Soft kisses freckle my cheeks and nose. I stir, rubbing my sticky eyes as I force them open. The van has halted, and my back aches from where I've slept unmoving on the hard carpet. I groan and Denendrius chuckles, his soft expression one of peace.

"It's almost sunrise," he murmurs, planting a kiss between my furrowed brows. "We're *hours* away from Lorimer, in a motel parking lot across the road from a truck stop. I sent our chauffeur in to get us a room. We'll stay for one day, and tomorrow night I'll find a truck driver to continue our trip."

"Okay." I yawn. "Are we going to Italy now?"

He kisses the tip of my nose. "Remember, one last stop—I promise it won't bring any chaos—then we're off."

I sigh and wipe my hands over my sweaty face. "Then you'll turn me?"

"Yes, sweetheart." His eyes glitter with excitement.

My smile is weak, sleep clinging to my body. "I can't wait."

His soft eyes study my face, and the peace of them is comforting. Makes me feel a little less on edge.

When our chauffeur returns—a thick, graying man who looks like he spent his previous years as a blue-collar worker from the wear on his face—he parks the van in front of a motel room and Denendrius carries me inside with our belongings. Then he drives off.

Denendrius pulls back the maroon comforter of the room's only queen bed and sprawls me on the white sheet. He shrugs his leather jacket off and crawls over me, his fervent kisses too swift for me to keep up with. I let him victory-fuck me, my heavy eyes stealing glimpses of the motel room—the clean, beige walls, and heavy blackout curtains—between the moments he ensures our eye contact.

He tries to be gentle since I'm not fully healed yet, but I somehow fall back asleep before he's finished. I wake with the sound of the motel door closing.

"Denendrius?" I look around the empty room, my heart leaping when my eyes land on our chauffeur on the couch to my right.

He clears his throat, his voice husky as he says, "The sun set. He went across the street to speak with truckers."

"Oh."

"I'm Harvey, by the way." He doesn't smile, though there's nothing quite unfriendly about his expression either.

I sit up and shove the blankets off. "I thought you left."

"I booked two nights. I've been unhappy with things . . . overworked. I needed to take a drive and think. My family will understand."

Ah, *hypnotism.*

I wonder how hard it is to master hypnotizing humans. Will Denendrius teach me, or will I have to figure it out on my own?

I drag my aching body out of bed, take too long in the shower in an attempt to sort my mind out, then eat a bag of beef jerky Harvey bought while gassing up on the way here. I'm so exhausted that I fall back asleep until Denendrius scooping me into his arms wakes me.

He carries me across the parking lot to a fancy-looking purple semi-truck with a white trailer, greeting a driver in his thirties as he brings me behind the driver and passenger seat to a twin bed. A thin, camper-style door separates us from the driver and the windshield.

After turning the little TV on that's attached to the wall at the foot of the bed, he snuggles close and relaxes beside me.

Though he won't tell me where we're going, he's kind enough to update me periodically with how many hours are left of our trip. I try to take peeks past the divider during the night, but never glimpse any signs through the windshield.

I rotate between watching TV and sleeping, never leaving the truck. The trucker brings me food when he fetches some for himself, and there's a portable toilet in a broom-closet behind a mini-fridge.

Denendrius's cellphone buzzes off and on, and he takes gleeful calls in Russian. I try to sneak glances at his phone when texts come through, but he playfully chuckles and tilts the screen away from me. I ask him if it's related to our next stop, and he's grinning with denial before eventually relenting and admitting it is. I'm only slightly less concerned knowing Sergei might be helping with it.

The heated passenger seat of the Bentley makes it hard to keep my eyes open as we cruise down the highway. Denendrius stole the car a few hours ago at the end of our trip with the trucker. With his even speed to not draw attention to ourselves, I've glimpsed enough signs to know we're back in Washington state.

"What are we doing here?" I try to hide the concern in my voice as I rock my legs back and forth, feet planted on the dashboard.

"You'll see," he half-sings.

I shoot him a teasing scowl, and he answers with a squeeze to my knee. When he flips the radio to classic rock, I sigh and turn to the window, staring out until exhaustion starts dragging me under. I try to fight it, like it's some shadowy beast with talons hooked around my ankles, but it's a losing battle. Maybe my whole being just wants out of reality.

When I wake, thick trees of a forest line the dark of the road, and my heart seizes in my chest until a log cabin with an unfamiliar, beige car parked out front comes into view as we round a bend in the road.

I quirk a brow at the cabin, the gold glow of interior lights spilling through the windows and against the thick trunks of surrounding trees.

"What are we doing here?" I ask.

Denendrius simply laughs as he parks beside the car, the sound bright and so full of genuine happiness that it disarms me. "I'm not telling . . ."

"I'm nervous," I admit as I shiver against a cool gust of wind once Denendrius exits the car and rounds it to open my door for me.

He laces his fingers through mine as we walk toward the cabin. "Me too."

I gnaw at my cheek as Denendrius pushes the squealing cabin door open for me. The sight of Adelia darting from around a corner, wearing a long, silky lavender dress with a sunshine smile, has me jerking backward into him. She throws her arms around me, then jumps back and looks me up and down as her lips curve into a frown.

"You're skinnier," she notes, taking my hands in hers to lift my arms and look me over. "What happened? I hope you didn't think you needed to diet."

I shoot Denendrius a glance, but his smooth expression offers me no direction, so I merely give her a tight-lipped smile before asking, "What are you doing here?"

Her grin returns, and she yanks me along to a bedroom, where the first thing my eyes land on has my heart clawing its way up my throat.

A fucking wedding dress.

It hangs on the mannequin, its floor-length skirt of silky white chiffon cascading in soft, airy folds. A plunging neckline melts into a bodice of delicate lace—white, sheer, intricate. Ethereal sleeves drift from thick shoulder straps, trailing in long tendrils. It makes me think of Rome, though just enough to suggest a Grecian influence.

"Denendrius picked it," Adelia says. "Do you like it?"

It's breathtakingly beautiful . . . *but I hate how it's mine.*

I'm too numb to cry. To be furious.

"When do I wear it?" I ask, though considering the effort it would have taken to bring her here undetected, I fear when is *now.*

She bounces on her feet, naive glee in her eyes. "Tonight!"

"A surprise wedding." The words leave me flat, tasteless.

Adelia nods and grins with such brightness it's like she's never heard of an idea more romantic.

She motions toward a chair. "Sit! I have to do your hair and makeup. Denendrius is going to dress in the other room."

I lower my weak body into the wooden chair that must be from the dining table. "Denendrius won't want me wearing makeup."

She grunts, and I'm sure an eye roll is paired with the noise. "I know, he told me. I negotiated mascara and lip tint, though. I only get to be the maid of honor for my sister-in-law once, so it's unfair if I don't get to do anything."

She does my hair first, a mix of French braids along the side of my head, pulled back with the length of my hair flowing curled down the nape of my neck.

I can't help my soft smile when I look in the mirror. With my hair done, I look so beautiful and elegant. It makes me wish I had learned to do my hair growing up.

"Denendrius said he used to braid your hair when you were both human," I say.

She nods as she wipes a wet rag on my face to prep it for moisturizer. "He liked to, yes. He started doing it when I was a toddler. Mother wouldn't teach him, but the slaves did. When I was older and questioned him about it, since it was unusual for a man to be interested in hairdressing, he told me he wanted to do his wife's and daughters' hair."

"That's sweet," I admit.

She rubs moisturizer into my skin. "He's always been like that, doing what he likes even if it's against traditional norms. Mother thought it was sweet that he was so set on marrying for love. He was single a lot longer than they would have liked because of it. I remember Father being furious that Denendrius wanted to be in love with one of the girls Father picked before he'd consent to marrying. But Father's picks were never good enough."

"Did he ever tell you he wanted to marry a girl named Mariana when she grew up?"

"Yes, I remember him saying something about it," Adelia says breezily as she brushes mascara on my lashes. She must have no context for the true weight of my question. "I met her mother a couple times. I went to their butcher shop, wanting to sneak a peek at whoever he was talking about, but I never saw her. Marciana was sweet, though."

"Do you think I look like her?" I'm unable to help how I hang on to Denendrius's and Adelius's comparisons.

She shrugs, and I don't like the discomfort in her eyes. "You would pass for sisters, I suppose. I wouldn't look into that, though, if you're concerned. Denendrius has just always preferred a certain look in girls. Despite how little I knew her, you're not much like her in personality. She was soft-spoken and mild, while you're a fire. He loves that. He picked you to marry for a reason, so I wouldn't compare yourself to her."

Does he love that? Sure, he loved my strength when it came to how I'd cast it on others, but he'd beat me for giving him the same treatment. He's always been nicest when I'm passive and mild for him.

"We're going to Italy after the wedding, right?" I prod, looking for holes in plans between them.

"I think you guys are going to honeymoon at a resort here for a few days, as a last hurrah in America before leaving for a lifetime," she divulges as she slathers red tinted lip balm on my lips.

I hold my breath when a frustrated sigh threatens.

I'm a happy bride. This is my special day. I can't be annoyed.

She spins around from the dresser with a blue velvet box and cracks it open much too close to my face. I flinch back slightly in the chair until the sparkling white diamond stud earrings come into crystal-clear focus beneath my eyes.

"My ears aren't pierced—"

"I *know*," she interrupts, a slight lilt at the end of her words. She sets them in my lap, then grabs a small plastic package off the dresser and tears it open, revealing a sterilized piercing needle.

"Oh . . ." My lips part, my body stiffening as she approaches.

She hesitates, her swallow visible. "Denendrius gave me the impression you wanted them done while you were still human . . . If you wait until after, you'll just have to pierce them each time. This way, you'll heal around the jewelry."

I gulp. The sight of the needle makes me nauseous. It's not that it reminds me of my addiction so much, or even that I think it'll hurt. It's that something so spontaneous, albeit small, feels like an anvil slamming down on top of everything else.

I inhale so deeply that she offers a pitying smile, as if she thinks I'm scared of the pain, then edges closer as I let the breath out.

"Let's do it," I decide. The thought of having pierced ears has crossed my mind before, but I've never been in a position to act on it. At least this way it'll be done, and I won't have to wish I'd had the chance while I was still human. Having to pierce my ears each time I want to wear earrings for the next however-many millennia seems profoundly tedious.

She tells me she'll be so swift I won't even feel it, but I'm so numb I likely wouldn't even if she were human. And hey . . . at least with an immortal piercer, I can trust they'll be perfectly even.

Once the dress is hugging my body, Adelia releases me from the room. Sergei awaits just beyond the door, wearing a soft smile and a black suit.

"Are you walking me down the aisle?" I quirk a brow, forcing a friendly smile.

He holds his arm out for me to take as he winks. "Helping."

I link my arm through his as he guides me through the cabin and to the tree line where a black horse, no doubt a Mustang, waits bareback at the start of the worn path between trees decorated in white fairy lights. Sergei takes the lead from a man.

"Am I riding it?" I lift my shaky hand and stroke the smooth black coat, my heart thudding in my chest. The cool wind has goosebumps dotting my flesh.

"Yes. I'll help you up. You'll sit sideways, and grip onto his mane."

I'm stiff as Sergei lifts me by my hips and places me on the horse's back. I wind my fingers through its mane, feeling so tall above Sergei.

"We're right back to how things should be," Sergei proudly proclaims as we reach the start of the aisle lined with pale flowers that look hand-picked for a fairytale. "I had my doubts over the years, but he was right. You proved me wrong, and I'm grateful. He's so happy with you. This is where we would have been had he brought you home to me and had me raise you. Despite a few . . . *detours* . . . it all worked out in the end."

I use the reminder that I'll be a vampire in a few days to coax a smile to my lips. "Me too, Sergei."

A blinking red light past Sergei snatches my attention. I catch sight of a fancy camera—filming me from a man's outstretched hand—and wrench my gaze back to the aisle before my eyes can fully lock with the lens.

My legs feel hollow, and I'm thankful I don't have to use them. Without the horseback ride, I'm not convinced my own legs would let me walk down the aisle to Denendrius.

Especially not when he comes into view, standing beneath an arch covered in vines and roses with little lights around the trim.

My heart thumps around thorns in its muscles. Denendrius looks painfully handsome in his silk dress shirt and black dress pants, his long curls and waves tame around his shoulders. If he were wholly his kind half, the sickness coating my sweaty skin would be from excitement instead of dread. But his beauty isn't enough for me to forget what he really is. A pretty weapon, capable of unimaginable pain and destruction.

There's warmth in Denendrius's twinkling eyes as Sergei brings the horse to a halt. It scorches my soul and screams the truth: I'm walking to join hands with the devil. That his goal is to bind me to him and his hell.

Denendrius helps me down onto a sheet of white petals, and I notice a man—an officiate, for show, of course, since there are so many reasons our marriage can't be legal—standing with us beneath the arch for the first time.

His chilly hand softly scoops mine up, and though my legs are incapable of helping me run away, nothing stops my mind. I don't know how it happens, but I make it through vows, only half-aware that my smiling lips are moving.

Until it's time to exchange rings.

I straighten my hand as he gingerly slips the ring on my finger like I'm a glass doll. But I know if my hands were to stiffen or flinch, he'd break my bones to get that band down my finger.

The white oval diamond, flanked by smaller ones on a polished white gold band, sparkles beneath the light, holding all my attention until Adelia reaches around me and slips a gold band into my palm. I'm on autopilot as I push it down Denendrius's ring finger.

The officiate says something, and then Denendrius's lips are crushing mine. Adelia squeals in excitement behind me as a camera clicks. Someone—probably Sergei—claps.

"I love you," he declares in a rush as he pulls away. There's so much happiness in his voice it unwillingly infects me. "Marianna, *I love you so much.*"

"I love you, Denendrius," I breathe.

I grin. I grin so wide and warm there's no way it doesn't seem genuine. And it is, really, since he's just put all the money I could ever need to get away from him on my hand, and he's going to fly me only a few countries away from Romania.

A camera shutter has my heart skipping a beat. But then it soars, because I know the image has framed me as his beautiful, *undeniably in-love* wife.

The excitement bubbles in me, and I bite my bottom lip to stop a giggle from escaping. Denendrius's smile is heartbreakingly sweet, lost in his own delusion and overjoyed to believe that we share it.

It's a treat and a toothache. A reward for being exactly what he wants me to be and for everything I've been through. For surviving this long. He'll make me a vampire soon. I deserve it.

XLVIII

My adrenaline-fueled smile carries me through wedding photos and Adelia's bouquet toss. I'm jittery by the time we pull into a high-class resort hotel, the reality I'll be a vampire soon settling in. I suspect he plans on turning me before our honeymoon ends, or as soon as we reach Italy. For any other human and vampire couple, making me immortal on our wedding night would be a romantic conclusion. As nervous as I am, it's about damn time.

We breeze past the front desk; securing rooms was one of Sergei's wedding duties. Denendrius keeps me close at his side, tucked between him and Sergei—with Adelia in front of us— which only hides me so much, considering I'm wearing a wedding dress. At least it's not extravagant enough to draw too much attention.

Vanilla clings to the hotel air, an intentional aroma that matches the beige walls with gold embossed designs. Laughter and lounge music trickle from the packed restaurant. The muted chime of slot machines somewhere in the distance to my left snags Denendrius's attention. I wonder if he'll drag us to the casino before we leave for Rome.

Sergei and Adelia split from Denendrius and me as we reach an elevator. He booked rooms on the other side of the resort to give us privacy on our honeymoon.

I clutch Denendrius as the elevator ascends, the motion throwing off my balance and nearly collapsing my legs. The elevator dings and opens on the tenth floor, Denendrius adjusting the bag on his shoulder as we step into a low-lit hall with beige carpet and white walls.

As we near the room, Denendrius scoops me up in his arms, his gleaming smile one of triumph as he unlocks the door with the keycard and pushes it open. He lifts me slightly to flick on the light as we enter.

From my position in his arms, I spot a small table at the end of the half-kitchen in the closest left corner of the room. A small three-tier white wedding cake, with gold lace wrapped around the bottom of each layer and topped with red roses, waits in the center of the table. Next to it, a card embossed with gold reads *congratulations*. A bottle of red wine and two engraved glasses—his and hers—sit on either side of it.

As he shuts and locks the door, I notice the luxurious room. Bouquets of roses are placed strategically, visible no matter where I look. There's one on a side table next to a brown leather couch across from a flat screen TV on my right. In the bedroom behind the couch, red petals are scattered on the bed.

"Wow," I breathe, remembering to keep my show up. An enthusiastic wife would be elated. "That cake looks delicious. There are so many flowers too. It's clear you gave Sergei thoughtful instructions."

"Anything for you, sweetheart," Denendrius purrs.

He carries me to the bedroom, where a line of moonlight spills through a gap in the curtains covering the glass balcony doors beside the bed. My heart lodges between my collarbones as he gently lays me down on the white, petal-covered blanket and crawls after me. Adoration shines in his gaze as he looks me over.

"*Finally* . . ." He sighs. "My beautiful wife."

"Do you know what would be so romantic?" I murmur, pulling the most starry-eyed, dreamy expression I can.

His eyes glitter with excitement. "Hm?"

"If you turned me tonight . . ." I pull in a long breath, savoring the perfume of roses, a blissful smile spreading as I release my breath. "Wouldn't it be so romantic to turn me on our wedding night? I can't think of anything more binding than that. We could consummate our marriage by making love . . . and then by making me yours for eternity."

He bites his bottom lip, holding my gaze. "That would be romantic."

"Will you?" I whisper, tracing my fingers over his lips while wetting my own. "Please?"

His tongue glides across his bottom lip as I pull my hand away. He inhales deeply, eyes losing focus as his thoughts drift.

Delicately, I run the backs of my fingers down his cheek and jaw. A tickled sound escapes from the back of his throat, and he leans into my touch.

"Please," I whisper, turning my palm against the side of his face. "Please make me yours forever."

He closes his eyes and leans deeper into my touch, pulling in my scent with another long inhale as he covers my hand with his.

"Not tonight," he whispers.

My chest burns with disappointment, so acidic my mouth tastes like pennies. I choke out, "But it would be so romantic."

"I know, but not tonight." His soft smile continues as he nuzzles his cheek against my palm, like he doesn't want to acknowledge how important this is to me.

My eyes sting with tears. "But I want to be a vampire."

He kisses the heel of my hand. "And you will be."

"When?" The hurt is sharp in my voice.

"Soon," he murmurs.

"When we go to Italy in a few days, right?" I beg.

He only smiles, and thin tears escape from the corners of my eyes, tracing down my temples and into my hair.

"Why not tonight?" I sniffle.

Slowly, his lids lift, his black eyes still shiny with the delight of having a new wife. "Why does it have to be tonight? Plus, I've been thinking . . . You still have a couple of good human years left. Are you sure you want to waste them? When I turn you, we can have another celebration. I've already picked out the dress you'll die in."

My heart thuds so hard it aches, the soreness spreading across my chest and weakening my arms. "A couple more years? But you promised . . ." I blink back tears. "You promised a few more days. Besides, when you were last a vampire—the day I ran from school—you were going to take me to Italy and turn me . . ."

A tickled smile curls his lips. "That was because you were fighting me, remember? I told you I was planning to give you a few more years as a human, if everything had gone the way it was supposed to. I only planned to turn you then so you'd remember how silly you were for resisting. But now that everything is right between us, and you've worked so hard to make it up to me, I think you deserve those years."

I can barely breathe. "But *I want* to be a vampire with you now. I don't want those extra years anymore."

He runs his lips across mine and whispers, *"But I do."*

I tilt my head back to mis-align our lips and he kisses my throat. "But I'm still marked to Viorel, and I don't want to be anymore. *You promised.*"

"I know, but you're doing such a good job at fighting his mark—"

"But what if I slip again? It's exhausting fighting his influence every waking moment. What if I upset you because of him, and we fight again? I can be a better wife with his mark broken," I plead.

He pinches my chin gently between his fingers, lowering my head to graze my lips with a kiss. "It'll be easier to fight as more time passes."

Desperate, I try a different angle. "But I don't want to get older. I want to stay a teenager forever. I'm already eighteen, turning nineteen next month, and I want to stay young and beautiful for you. What if I'm never more beautiful than tonight, on our wedding night?"

The tip of his tongue flicks against my upper lip before he crushes his mouth to mine, pulling away just enough to drop more soul-crushing words. "You still look so young. Sixteen, if I didn't know any better. Even eighteen is hard to believe right now. You'll stay youthful for years, especially with Huarsar's blood working its magic. And I won't mind if you're twenty, or twenty-one either."

I wrap my arms around his neck, my breath shaky as I whisper, "But if I'm immortal, you could be so much rougher when we make love. I know you like being rough . . . I'd just heal if you hurt me."

Excitement flares in his eyes, burning so hot at the thought of hurting me that it sets my heart on fire, the pain in my chest intensifying. Yet, I think I've hooked him, because he closes his eyes, groaning as he bites his bottom lip.

"*Hmm.* You'd want me to be rough when you're immortal?"

"Yes," I squeak. "I'd do anything to make sure you're satisfied."

His breath grows heavier, cold and ragged against my face as he searches my eyes, the flicker of darkness in them making me tense. "Hmm. How would you make me happy, sweetheart?"

Body laden with dread, my stomach roils as the words he wants to hear work their way onto my tongue. "I wouldn't complain if you choked and hit me. I wouldn't really need air to live, anyway—"

He presses his hand over my mouth, and my eyes sting. "You're a good little negotiator." A tickled chuckle bubbles out of him, followed by a groan as he kisses me again. "I would love that . . . but it's not quite the same as when you're human, sweetheart."

Something sinister slips into the room with us, and I fear Denendrius now thinks *I'm welcoming it, that I want to share it with him.*

He must think I'm accepting of this part of him now, because as casually as we would have any other conversation, he says, "I love putting my hands around your warm throat because I can feel your frantic pulse in my palm, and your muscles tighten around me when your body is begging for air."

"But you wouldn't have to hold back," I counter, my body so heavy I'm not sure I could slip out from under him if I tried. "You could be as rough as you want."

Denendrius sits back slightly and with gentle care places his hand on my throat, his thumb pressing against my throbbing vein.

My lips fall apart, his hand stopping the flow of air to my lungs despite how he applies no pressure.

Our gazes lock, and as I study the lust in his eyes, a question slips from my lips before I can figure out where it came from.

"Have you ever had any immortal girlfriends?" I wonder, thinking of the *human* girls on his rape tapes and the relationships I found evidence of.

He gives me a sheepish smile. "What a question to ask on our wedding night . . ."

My cheeks burn. "I'm sorry, I know."

"I know why you're asking," he murmurs with a wink. "You want to be my first immortal love."

I take it and nod.

His head tilts as he fights a spreading smile. "I haven't had an immortal girlfriend before. I've never even kissed an immortal girl, and I definitely haven't made love to one. You'll be my first."

His answer sends a strange sensation through me, something smooth and quiet that eases the pain in my chest and dries my tears. It feels like . . . acceptance.

It feels like finality.

And suddenly, the idea of him turning me fades. It feels like pure delusion. A false belief I've shared with him once again.

It feels like . . .

Like he's known, deep down, that he doesn't really want to turn me. He doesn't want to lose my beating heart, my warm flesh, the powerful blood pulsing through my veins, or the ease with which he can control me.

My arms go limp, slipping from around his neck to thud at my sides. My breathing steadies, and reality crystallizes, a numbness—a bitter peace—nestling inside me and calming my heart.

Denendrius is going to kill me.

I suppose he has more reason to than he did Marianne and fifteenth-century Marianna. Honestly, it's a miracle I'm still alive, especially with his imprisonment being my fault. Though I suppose he's sunk more effort into me than any of them, and it'd be a waste to discard me without squeezing out everything he can.

Still, I'm going to die before I can make it home.

Maybe not today, or tomorrow, or even next year. But he will kill me, just like he has every other girl he's touched. Some part of him must know turning me is a mistake, even if he won't consciously admit it. After his initial struggle to control me when he came back into my life, he must have doubts about whether he could manage it once I'm immortal. He would be right to worry.

And maybe . . . maybe dying is better than being used as a fuck toy until I can escape, than playing this exhausting act while my daughter grows up without me, while Viorel is forced to experience this turmoil as I do.

"How do you know you'll still love me when I'm immortal?" I whisper.

"I know I will." He mashes his lips against mine, hiking up the skirt of my dress to touch between my limp legs.

I feel like a passenger in my limp body as he touches me. I'm numb to his fingers and his mouth on mine, my muscles putty and my tongue useless. I inhale and exhale, but it's out of my control.

I am fading. I am nearly gone.

"Are you playing dead for me?" he murmurs, a dark glint in his eyes as I watch his hand motion back and forth between my legs. But I can't really feel it. "Okay, silly girl."

I can't help the grunt that rolls out of the back of my throat as his fingers move faster.

"Dead girls don't make much noise," he teases.

It's this ring, I realize. It has altered the dynamic of our relationship the moment he slipped it on and made him comfortable enough to include me in his most abhorrent thoughts. It gave him permission to discard his mask.

This ring that I encouraged.

This ring. This death of me.

"I want you so badly right now," he whines.

I keep playing dead.

"But I've got to be patient for once." He groans and pulls his hand away before fixing my underwear and winking. "I've got more planned for this special night. We'll work up to it."

"Like what?" I whisper.

"You'll see . . ." He crawls off the bed. "But first, food."

XLIX

I push my salmon around my plate, letting the disappointment thicken my voice when I say, "I really thought tonight was the night. I was hoping this would be my last meal."

He smiles softly. "Drop it."

We descend into a stony silence, the room feeling empty despite us both sitting here. I stare at the glistening red in my third glass of wine. Four hundred dollars a pour, he told me. I've been nursing it so I don't seem ungrateful even though my body hasn't recovered enough to handle drinking. Though I'm already lightheaded, I can't tell if it's from the wine or the situation.

"When are we going to Italy?" I poke a piece of salmon with my fork, but it's flavorless when I bite into it.

He leans back in his chair, drawing my attention. "In a few days. I don't know when we'll be able to return to America again, so I want us to have a little fun here before we go."

I nod, my head wobbling. "Okay." I take another bite of my

fish despite my loss of appetite. I know if I stop eating, he's going to move to the next thing, and we'll be closer to the time when he splays me out on the bed.

He crosses his arms, and I gulp.

"Why are you doing that?" he demands.

"Doing what?" My voice sounds lifeless, heavy.

"Going cold on me," he snaps. "Sulking."

I swallow, my words quiet as they slip past my numb lips. "I'm not sulking."

His arms tighten across his chest as he leans forward slightly. "Yeah, you are. I'm not turning you tonight, sweetheart. Get over it before you let it ruin our wedding night."

"*Okay.*" I move a few pieces of fish around before he slides the plate out from under my fork.

"You're done," he says evenly, rising to take my half-finished plate to the counter.

I gnaw at my cheek and place my fork on the table. As he turns back around, my limp voice escapes with a low, "I love you, Den."

"Why do you need to be a vampire so bad, *right now*?" he demands as he towers over me from beside the table and stares down at me.

I crane my head back to meet his icy gaze. "I love you, and I'm desperate to be immortal with you."

"But why is it such a big deal to wait a couple more years?" he presses.

Twice now he hasn't said he loves me back. My throat dries, my heart thudding.

"I'm just getting impatient, is all. I want to remember you. I want to know about my past, since you insist Viorel lied about it."

He stares at me for what feels like forever, the dread rising inside me until I'm sweating in his shadow and glued to the chair.

"What are you thinking?" I plead. "I'm not trying to make you mad, don't you see? I'm trying to make you happy."

"I am happy." But his voice is monotone and emotionless, and there's nothing but a war in his detached gaze. "You're the one who's trying to make this night *unhappy*."

I drop my gaze from his and attempt a new angle. What would I do—what would I think—in this situation if his fantasy were real? If I'd been relieved to see him after those twelve years? If I loved him the way he believes I have all along?

Hugging myself, I whisper, "I'm sorry. I just . . ." I pull in a long breath. "I waited for this day for over a decade, Den. Dreamed about my wedding like every other young girl does, except *I knew* who I'd marry. I had a lot of time to dream while I was locked in that bedroom for years . . . being dosed by my mom and sold."

His wince at the reminder of my abuse keeps me going. I've tapped that near-dry well of guilt he has.

I clear my stress-dry throat. "I remember had a crush on you, Den. It got stronger and turned into love as I got older. Thinking of you coming back for me kept me going in that house. For years, before I forgot about *us*, the only thing that kept me from killing myself was you. Marrying you and knowing you would give me a new life as an immortal."

My tongue is heavy, so I pause and swallow hard. "I dreamed of a beautiful white dress, a horse walking me down the aisle, exchanging vows in nature. You got my dream perfect, short of a big audience. But at the end of that dream . . . you turned me. I imagined crimson staining the white lace of my dress, turning the diamonds into rubies. Waking up as an immortal, starting our new life as husband and wife."

A shuddery breath escapes me, and tears stream down my cheeks. *"So yeah, I'm sorry, but I'm disappointed."*

His gaze softens, and I think I've gotten through to him, but he murmurs, "That's the sweetest, Marianna, but I can't tonight. *I just can't.*"

It's my turn to stare as the dread in my limbs weighs on me so hard that it numbs me.

I can't think of anything else to untangle myself from these strings of fate he's manipulated. They're too constricting, and I won't be able to breathe against this pressure for another two years. I'm going to snap before they do. One of us is going to drive the other to *my death.*

I'm going to die.

I'm going to die.

It's no longer just a thought, a distant possibility.

It's a fact now, like seeing the cliff the sign around the bend warned you about before you turned with a heavy foot on the gas in slick rain. Sure, you're not dead—you haven't hit the rocks at the bottom—but your back tires just left the road . . . and *there's nothing that can put them back on the asphalt.*

My heart hammers with such ferocity that it fills my ears and temples. My hands shake with a flood of adrenaline, sweat coating my feverish body in an instant. It comes with a prickly panic that has my brain buzzing with static from a frequency that disrupts the coherency and alignment of my thoughts.

I don't know how I'm going to live past tonight. I can't comprehend how to cope enough to make it to tomorrow.

And the next day.

And the next day.

And the continued hell after that.

"You're never going to turn me." I don't feel myself say it, but the agony and brewing anger are clear in my voice. "Never."

My vision narrows, but what remains of it—the sight of Denendrius's back stiffening, his jaw tightening—is crystal clear.

He closes his eyes, his clenched teeth visible through his parted lips as a windstorm works its way in and out of him.

"You want me soft and full of warm blood. *Viorel's blood.* Blood that practically gets you high. You want me to be easy to control, easy to hurt if you need to." The sensation of the floor vanishes from beneath my feet, and I feel like I'm floating in my chair. Like I'm already a ghost. "I won't be as good of a fuck toy if you can't feel my heart spasming, if my lungs can't beg you for air."

"*No,*" he rebukes tersely.

My tongue knots, my words starting slowly with a slur before it straightens out. "You're scared I'll be a powerful immortal, like they predicted. Impossible to control. Is that it?"

A dry, airy laugh slips out of him, but his face remains cold, his gaze devoid of warmth. "*Yeah, right.*"

"H-how many times have you tried to replace Mariana?" I demand. "Did you turn any of them?"

His hands curl into fists at his sides. "*No. I've only ever truly loved you.*"

The fact he doesn't reveal how many sends an icy chill through me. How many replacements have there been over his lifetime?

"Did you marry any of them?" I ask, knowing he murdered at least one—Marianne—after she broke off their engagement.

His upper lip twitches.

"If you love me more than you ever loved them, then give me something you never gave them. The thought that I might not be your first wife makes me violently jealous," I beg, the ache in my voice raw.

The ice in his glare, in his tense demeanor, chases the warmth out of the room. Goosebumps dot my skin.

"I have," he says, his tone low and controlled. "I haven't killed you yet, when time and time again it would have been justified. You're still alive. That's how I love you more than them."

"Yet," I echo. "You're not going to turn me, so what will you do when I'm too old for you?"

"I'm not going to kill you," he growls.

"You've killed every lover you've had before," I whisper, the knot in my throat so tight I can't speak any louder. "Why should I believe anything will be different when I'm probably your fiftieth wife? I don't feel special on my special day anymore . . . just *jealous*."

Denendrius jams the heels of his hands into his forehead, a deep sound rumbling out of him, making my heart trip.

"*Shut up,*" he snarls as he backs away from me.

I stand and wobble, bracing myself with a hand on the table as the room rocks. "Tell me why you won't turn me? I love you so much. It's not fair."

His chest rises with a deep breath that he holds for several beats before slowly releasing it. The forced calm on his face when he lowers his hands sends another shock of adrenaline through me.

"You're *tipsy*, and this is just Huarsar talking," he says evenly as he takes careful steps toward me. "It's okay, Marianna. I understand. You've been fighting his mark all day. A day where you married his enemy. I suppose I should be proud you didn't devolve into blood-slave hysterics coming down the aisle."

I move backward instinctively, my lapsing balance causing my backside to collide with the table.

"It's okay," he says softly, hand lifting to push loose hair behind my ear and I shudder. "You are so special to me, Marianna. We're not going to let Huarsar ruin our special day."

A breathless squeak escapes me as he wraps his arms around me, pulling my trembling body against his.

"I'll pour you more wine, and we can sit in the Jacuzzi. I'll bring you a slice of wedding cake. Hm?"

His bare skin stings against mine, the heat from my fury

making the cold of him unbearable. I'd beg him to let go of me if I could drag in a proper breath.

My trembling intensifies as he strokes the back of my head and holds me tighter. With a sigh, he loosens his grip, leaning back to hook his finger beneath my jaw, lifting my face to his.

Tears obscure my sight of him. They're hot rivers down my clammy cheeks as he presses his rough mouth to mine.

"I'll show you how special you are to me," he murmurs against my lips before nipping at them and slipping his tongue between them.

My legs give out, but his arm around me keeps me upright. I fight the urge to push him away and run to the bathroom with the bottle of wine that I'll drown before giving myself the same ending.

His hand moves to the back of my head, his lips rougher, like he can force mine to respond.

But I'm too exhausted to pretend. There's nothing left in me for that, especially after today. I wanted my wedding to be with Viorel and Laurentius, for my white gown to be adorned with rubies and black diamonds. Every first—sex, relationships, children—has been tainted in some way. I just wanted one special milestone, and Denendrius has stolen another from me.

"*Sweetheart,*" he pleads softly, his airy chuckle against my lips like he thinks I'm toying with him.

I never want to kiss him again. I don't think I have it in me to, anyway. If it weren't for his grip on me, my weak legs wouldn't hold me up.

His arms tighten around me, his fingers tangling painfully in my hair. His lips still for a moment as his cold, shallow breath wafts a warning across my mouth.

But there's not a threat left that's capable of making my lips move anymore. He's already doing his worst by keeping me human, and now the worst he can do is keep me alive.

"Kiss me," he demands with a whisper.

"No," I breathe, my head spinning. The word slips out so much easier with the bitter wine loosening my tongue.

He exhales frustration through his teeth, the roots of my hair burning under the tension of his grip. *"You don't get to say no. You're my wife."*

"No." I say it again because it's been so long since I've let myself.

He snarls Latin, drawing his head back, our noses nearly touching as he stares into my eyes. "Giving into his mark won't make me turn you any faster to rid it."

Denendrius's lids fall closed as his lips move back to mine. It's another chance for me to comply with what he wants. But I just *can't.*

His hand comes up against my cheek—a light warning tap. I'm so numb I barely feel it.

"You'll hit me on our wedding night?" I slur.

"You'll *deny me* on our wedding night?" He twists his hand tighter in my hair, and I whimper as he pulls my head back so our eyes meet as he stares down at me. "Once we start making love, you'll find it much easier to fight his mark again."

My heart thrashes in my chest, the thought of him touching me one more time too unbearable to act through. I'd rather he break my neck right now.

Denendrius's grip loosens, his hands caressing my body as he unzips my dress, slipping one silk strap off my shoulder.

"I love you, Marianna." His eyes sparkle as his hand trails across my chest to the other strap. "The gods must favor me to give me such a beautiful girl."

I live like I'm already dying, as if there are too few breaths left in my lungs to waste a single one on a lie.

Lifting my eyes to his, I cry out with, "I can't do this anymore. I don't have anything left in me to pretend to love you."

He half-smirks like he thinks I'm fucking with him, exhaling a silent beat of laughter as he tries to slip the strap off. I pitifully shove my weak, heavy hands into his chest, the straps of my dress sliding back into place.

The room spins, and I hit the floor with a thud, landing on my stomach between him and the couch. Instinct takes over, and I grunt, shakily lifting myself onto my hands and knees, crawling toward the door—even though I know there's nowhere to run. The straps of my dress dig into my skin, holding me in place. I look over my shoulder.

Denendrius has stepped on the skirt of my dress. "Where are you going? It's too late to be a runaway bride, Marianna."

Before I can think of my next move, he flattens me against the carpet with his foot, yanking my dress off and kicking it aside like it's worthless. I roll over, staring up as he towers over me.

He's so much bigger than me, especially from down here, that I no longer believe being immortal would make an ounce of difference.

"You're acting like you'd rather have Huarsar and that priest rape you than your husband make love to you on your wedding night," he spits.

My nails dig into his suit as I climb his body, wobbling back onto my feet, our eyes locking. I don't know why I bother standing—it won't last long.

My tongue feels thick as I stumble backward and half-slur, "*Maybe.*"

His lip twitches as he bristles with anger. "This isn't going to make me turn you."

My words tumble out, tangled and flat. "You'll never turn me, like I'll never love you."

"You're *trying* to hurt me. You don't mean it." He shakes his head, the cold in his onyx eyes no match for the dark, frozen space that's already cracked open inside me. "It won't work,

Marianna. I know you don't prefer monsters like them to a man like me."

"You're not a man," I snarl. "You're a monster—"

It rears wildly in his eyes—*that monster*—as he flashes forward and takes a fistful of my hair at the nape of my neck with a vibrating hand. *"I'll show you a man."*

L

Denendrius throws me against the seat of the couch, the hard impact knocking the breath out of me despite the cushioning. Before I can fill my lungs again, his belt is gone from his waist and cinched tightly around my throat.

I gag and thrash as he drags me around the couch, kicking my heels into the rough carpet and clawing at the thick leather as he yanks me across the floor to the bedroom like a dog on a leash. He wrangles my writhing body onto the bed before tearing my strapless bra off. I'm too focused on trying to loosen the leather and cold buckle constricting my throat to fight against the exposure.

With one swift motion, he grabs the belt buckle pressing into my trachea and yanks it from my throat, leaving me gasping for breath in my underwear as he folds the leather in half. He climbs onto the bed after me.

I yelp as the first strike of leather stings my cheek, the pain fiery and sudden, triggering an onslaught of tears. He's relentless as he whips me, the burn of the leather searing into my skin as I beg him through gasping breaths to stop. The sound of the belt cracking against my welted flesh is deafening.

"I'm sorry," I rasp, on my back, trying to kick him away long enough to speak. "I'm sorry! I know you're a man. I didn't mean it like *that*—"

He whips my leg aside and growls, "Shut up!"

"*Please, Den*—" I cry out as the belt slices across my stomach like a punch. "*I'll be a good wife*—"

He wraps his hand around the base of my jaw, lifting my head off the bed as he leans over me. "*Shut up*," he snarls in my face. "*I don't want to hear your venomous voice anymore! All you do is hurt me!*"

He throws my head back down, rolling me over and mashing my face into the blanket.

My ragged screams are muffled as he belts my back, each strike setting my flesh on fire. He huffs for breath, hovering on his hands and knees above me, no doubt fueled by the rush of hurting me since he doesn't need to catch his breath.

He strokes his hand down my aching back, and a whimper slips out of me. I stiffen as his hand glides over my bottom, stopping between my legs to rub me through my underwear.

A shaky sob escapes into the blanket, my cheek pressed against the tear-soaked fabric.

"*I love you so much*," I choke out, desperate to claw back every word I dared utter, so I can fix things. The words scrape like glass against my tender throat as I add, "Show me how much you love me, then let's cuddle in front of the TV. We could watch a movie."

I should have fought harder against my wine-loose tongue and emotions. Should have waited until he was satisfied and fast asleep before slipping out of bed to give myself a ruby necklace to go with my gown. I could have tried to give him no other option but to turn me, or escape with death if he failed to. I had to open my stupid, impulsive mouth again.

After witnessing the horrific rapes and deaths of his victims on those tapes, and being in Tatiana's place when Viorel mistakenly shared her final moments with me through our dreams, I know what end is waiting for me if I don't bring him back to sanity.

Did I really think any of my words could make him turn me? Did I really believe he would want to rid Viorel's mark and unlock my love and memories of him over my soft and blood-filled body?

It's all he really cares about. *Blood and bodies.*

I quiver as he leans in close, his lips brushing my ear as he whispers, *"Oh, I'll show you . . . One more word, and I'll break your jaw."*

Cold, clammy fear grips me, my heart shredding itself against my ribcage as my body shivers like I'm lying in snow.

The sound of his zipper sends a wave of nausea through me, and I squeeze my eyes shut, biting down hard on my bottom lip.

"Look at me," he demands, rolling me onto my back and shifting between my terror-limp legs.

I can't bear to open my eyes until his cold hands circling loosely around my throat in a threat have them flying wide. The look in his eyes has a scream trying to claw its way out of me and has my nerves heavy and shrieking with dread like I've been thrust into a vivid nightmare.

Denendrius stares down at me with the coldest, flat black gaze I've ever seen. It's a detached, unfeeling look I didn't even see when he took me to the woods to kill me so many months ago.

It's a look that tells me I'm going to die *tonight.*

The realization must be clear on my face, because a stiff smile crosses his lips.

He grabs a fistful of my silk and lace underwear and tears them off as he, low, utters, "Want to *make* a movie?"

My chest aches as I let out the most shrill, strangled scream I've ever heard from my own lips. He smacks me in the head so hard the sound fizzles out with my vision.

"You better hope nobody heard that . . ." His voice is distant, muffled.

I blink rapidly, my sight returning just as he stuffs my panties into my mouth. I gag on the fabric, my fingers lifting to dislodge it, but he clamps his hand over my mouth. *"Pull them out, and I'll shove them down your throat."*

When he starts unbuttoning his dress shirt, I turn feral. Kicking, clawing, thrashing at him as he smiles and effortlessly shrugs it off. But when he tries to wrangle my legs apart while pulling his pants down, I manage to shove my heel into his jaw. His hand crushes my trachea, and he violently rattles me against the bed while snarling Latin in my face.

I sob and screech when he pins my writhing body down and forces himself on me. I gag against the silk in my mouth and his palm constricting my throat. He's violent and unforgiving, the pain slicing through my hollow heart only making it more unbearable.

I strain against his strength, refusing to completely submit even though I know my resistance excites him. My nails tear and break against his skin, and he lets me beat him with my fists until my knuckles are busted. But I don't do it for him. I do it for myself, so I can convince myself I tried. So I hate myself a little less.

He strikes me, berating me through grunts and groans, his face twisted with loathing. My endless stream of tears does nothing to hide his expression. The pain he inflicts numbs me to everything else. At some point, blood covers my thighs and the bedsheets, and when he moves my legs, sharp pain slices through me that disconnects me from consciousness until he rouses me. When he does, I can't feel my legs or toes, or move them.

Denendrius chokes me until I pass out, then rouses me to do it again. *And again.* So many times he must be taunting Death with my soul.

I'm limp as I stare blankly at him, waiting for it to be over. The tacky blood on my lips seals them together despite the small bundle of fabric. His eyes hold mine, a demon staring back at me. There's no man here, just the embodiment of malevolence, a weapon disguised by flesh.

He rolls me onto my stomach, his body crushing the air from my lungs as I lie slack beneath him. His labored breaths deafen me, and I don't even flinch when his belt appears around my throat. I try to breathe, but as he gradually tightens it, my breath is sharply cut short, and I can't pull more air in.

I try to pull the fabric from my mouth, desperate for air, but he clamps his hand over my lips again. Pressure builds in my head, and I strain for breath that won't come. My hands tear at the fabric headboard, buttons popping off under my nails. I jerk under him, muscles spasming uncontrollably.

Denendrius grunts in my ear.

I didn't think it was possible for him to tighten the belt, but he does.

I'm too numb to blink as I try to block out the sound of his staggered breath in my ear, my stomach in a tangled knot when he moans and exhales a shaky breath as he finally finishes. He gives the belt slack, and my face drops into the mattress as he climbs off me.

I don't move, waiting for whatever comes next. I don't know what to expect.

Denendrius rolls me onto my back and fishes the fabric out of my mouth with his hooked finger, tossing it on the floor with a sigh of satisfaction. He sits on the edge of the bed, his chest and arms smeared with bloody streaks from my hands. Crimson soaks the bedding and coats his abdomen and thighs.

Even if I wanted to speak now, I don't think I can. I can

barely manage half-breaths, each one wheezy like a whistle, like someone has a heavy boot on my throat.

He casually stands, stepping back into his boxers and pants, threading his belt back through the loops like he's not redressing next to the girl he savagely raped. He pushes loose hairs out of his face and crawls back onto the bed beside me, a pitying frown shaping his lips as his bloody hand caresses my battered cheek.

"You were the most beautiful bride," he croons. "And for a while, I was the happiest groom."

Another bout of tears wells in my eyes. Now, he'll either have to turn me, or let me die.

Slowly, he leans toward me, and I briefly believe he's going to kiss me. A flicker of hope ricochets from one shattered piece of my heart to another.

But Denendrius *spits in my face,* and I flinch.

The tears spill over my bottom lashes and dart toward my temples.

"Oh . . ." He pushes his bottom lip out as he roughly wipes a tear off my face, his finger drawing back with diluted blood. "You really love me, don't you?"

A breath rattles in my throat as I try—and fail—to form agreeing words. I just want him to choose my immortality, to think he's punished me enough, or maybe realize he loves me too much to let me die, like he did the first time he tried to kill me in the woods and changed his mind.

He smiles, the twist of his lips as frigid as the look persisting in his eyes. "It doesn't make a difference." He stands. "Plenty of girls have died loving me."

I don't know how I ever believed any differently. That *I* would be the one girl to survive this monster when I'm no more special than the hundreds before.

My pleas come out as gasps and rattles, because I'm still

stupid enough to try convincing him. Still desperate enough to live.

Denendrius turns his face away from me, then strolls out of the room. He returns after some rummaging with a curled lip and an open knife in his hand. A half-formed squeal rolls around between the rattles in my throat, and I stiffen when he straddles me again.

My eyes droop, but I hope he sees how sorry I am through the swelling of my face. I know that without Viorel's blood in me that I'd already be dead. I'd be spared the fear from the hard look in his eyes as he assesses my body like it's for target practice.

When his hand twitches, I catch a fistful of his shirt, my fingers locking onto the fabric.

He pries them off and throws my hand back onto the bed. *"Don't you dare touch me."* He points the knife in my face. "You are my biggest mistake. I wasted *twelve years on you.* I should've done this the day you didn't remember me. I've done so much for you, and you've been nothing but ungrateful. We can't blame Huarsar's mark when you've *always* been this way. You give your love, convince me I have it, then rip it away the moment you don't get your way. *Manipulative little—*" He cracks my mouth open and spits between my parted, bloody lips as I flinch. He laughs. "I should have tied you to my bed for a few weeks and killed you like the rest of them instead, hm? Made some home videos with you." His smile falls, and he bares his teeth before snarling, *"The gods tricked me, bringing me to another girl with your name, when you weren't worth being made a girlfriend or wife."*

It takes all my focus to stay awake, my eyes pleading with him.

He waggles the knife at me. "Twelve years. *Months in a dungeon . . ."*

Pain rolls through me, my eyes tipping back as he slowly

tucks the sharp blade into my abdomen. I choke on a trapped breath. He pulls the blade out, and the tip scrapes across my stomach before he pokes a fresh hole into me.

"Look at me as I give you one for each wasted year," he growls as he pulls the blade free. *"Look at me."*

I force my gaze back to his, eyes stinging with agony as his blade nestles into my flesh once more. The pain is so widespread I'm unsure where he's buried the blade this time.

Denendrius leans over as his hand draws back, his stray hair tickling my numb face as he moves his lips to my ear. *"I know you love me. You've always loved me. That's why I'm going to leave you to die here all alone. As much as I crave the taste of your last breath, you don't deserve to die with my company. If you're somehow still alive when I return, we'll simply have round two."*

I regret Viorel's blood, how potent it is to keep me alive through this. It's like an anchor holding me here. At what point am I no longer alive, but just an animated corpse? Surely my body should be too battered to host a soul by now.

Denendrius must read my thoughts on my face. "It's going to take you *so long to die,* Marianna. I'm taking great care to avoid your organs and arteries, so you bleed out slower."

When he pushes the knife back into me, his eyes locked on mine, I pray the pain will make me pass out. But I'm forced to stare wide-eyed at him as he continues to stab me.

After the twelfth, he lifts the knife between us. My glimmering blood coats the blade. Crimson tendrils run down his hand, disappearing beneath the sleeve of his silk dress shirt.

"One more, for all the months I spent in the dungeon . . ."

My eyes roll back as he pushes the knife through two of my lower ribs, no doubt because I did the same to him when Viorel let me torture him.

"Goodbye, Marianna," he murmurs, the corner of his lip twitching into an almost smile. He tugs the wedding ring off my finger, then stands and licks my blood off the blade before folding it and tucking it into his pocket with the ring.

Casually, he moves to the bathroom, and I watch—ruefully awake—as he scrubs his hands clean in the sink. He takes a rag, wipes the blood from his face, and checks himself in the mirror, ensuring none of it shows.

The fact he willingly wears my blood beneath his clothes, like he can make what he's done to me last longer, intensifies the agony in my body.

His name rests on my tongue, but I don't have the energy to push it past my lips.

I cling to the idea that he's just punishing me, that he'll change his mind at the last moment like he did last time and heal me. He's spent so much time on me, gone through so much, that he can't possibly throw it all away, right?

But the reality is that thirteen years is so little time in the grand-scheme of his long life.

As he leaves the bathroom, his eyes sweep over me like I'm not even here. I ache to call his name, to have him look at me again, to change his mind. But he walks out of the room. I hear him grab his keys, phone, and room card, then slip into his shoes. The door opens, and though the urge to scream thrashes inside me, I can barely draw breath.

There's no hesitation, no pause, before the hotel room door shuts behind him and auto-locks.

Denendrius leaves my life as violently as he came into it.

The moments creep by, each as silent and painful as the last. I wait for him to come back, to heal me, to tell me he loves me and doesn't want me to die. That this was just another lesson, like when he put me in the cage to give me a reason to fight harder against Viorel's mark.

But he doesn't.

I wait for someone—anyone—to find me and help me.

But no one does.

Staring through the bedroom doorway, I know there's no way I could make it across the hotel room to get help. So I lie here, bleeding from my hot and aching stomach for what feels like hours when it surely can't be.

How much longer will it take me to die, thanks to Viorel's blood?

I think of Patricia's vision, the memory of her voice soft in my ears as she said, *"You and Denendrius are hurtling toward a dark place, and I need you to know there's nothing you could ever do or say—in the past or the future—to alter the inevitable collision."*

Despite the suffocating agony, and the regret of my damning words, I know in my core she's right.

This is just what Denendrius does.

Still, what will happen if I'm still alive when Denendrius returns? Could he change his mind? Or will he just strangle me? I'm not sure I want to be alive to find out.

Patricia promised I'd be okay in the end, but now I'm not quite sure what that means.

My eyes shift to the balcony just a few feet away. I think I'm going to die—that maybe being okay in the end means *all this suffering is over*—but the thought of no one finding my body makes my heart race faster.

I just want someone to know.

If I could make it to the balcony, *someone would know.*

I think things could be okay if someone *knows*. If someone other than Denendrius scoops up my battered body and buries me. Closes my case file with the shutting of a silk-lined coffin lid.

I fight through the pain, breath held and jaw clenched, willing my body to obey. My legs are useless, so I grip the sheets with my busted hands and use my shoulders to scoot to the edge of the bed. My legs remain in the middle of the mattress as I get my shoulder to the edge. I beg them to move, to shift, but nothing happens.

There's only one way to reach the floor, and I'm grateful I'm low enough on the mattress that the nightstand isn't aligned with my head.

I inch myself over the edge, no way to brace for the fall, and let my body drop off the side of the bed. My head and torso hit the carpet first, and though I can't feel my legs, I hear how they land like dead weights.

Unconsciousness sneaks up on me, but I manage enough breaths to shake the blackness away despite how my vision narrows.

I slide my weak arm across the carpet, my twitching fingers a mere inch from the balcony curtains. Shifting my shoulders, I stain the white fabric as I grab a loose handful and move it aside. The curtain slides open smoothly, and I come face to face with the dark city. I shift another inch, smearing blood across the glass as I attempt to get enough grip to slide the door open.

Wiping my hands on the carpet, I clench my jaw against the shooting pain in my fingers and press my hand near the opening, sliding the door open a crack.

The success sends a weak pulse of adrenaline through me —likely the last my body can offer—and I reach across myself with my other weak hand, curling both around the door's edge and sliding it open as far as I can.

The cool air beckons me, the light curtain fluttering and catching on my back like an arm urging me forward.

I'm thankful Denendrius picked an expensive, well-maintained hotel. Otherwise, he might have found me dead and laughed at my pitiful failure to get the door open.

With a grunt, I roll onto my stomach and face the balcony. A sense of urgency grips me as darkness shudders at the edges of my vision. My heart pounds, and my groan rattles in my throat. Blood gushes between my stomach and the carpet as I grit my teeth and force myself onto my elbows.

A few more feet . . . I can do it.

I have to do it.

Agony weakens me as I army-crawl forward, dragging my body inch by inch. The metal track digs into my wounds, my ribs shifting unnaturally, making my eyelids flutter as I fight fainting. I can't see, can barely feel the hardness of the balcony as I pull myself toward it. The cold air breathes against my naked body, a fresh breath curling its way through the crevices in my compressed throat. A strangled, wet noise escapes with my exhale, and my vision sharpens and allows me a pinprick of sight.

The balcony bars are only a foot away . . .

My dead legs thud onto the balcony behind me, but my arms give out. I can't feel the rough surface against my bare skin as I heave against it. After the sharp pain from him twisting my legs, I'm almost grateful for the numbness below my belly button. With how much blood I've seen, if I could feel the pain throughout my whole body instead of just half, moving this far would have been impossible.

I made it onto the balcony, but it's not good enough.

When I try to push myself back onto my elbows, I can't.

Frustration tightens my stomach. I'd cry out if I could, but I barely have the strength for emotion.

I just need someone to see me. That's all. Then I'll let myself *go.*

So I roll onto my back and stretch my fingers toward the railing. Just a couple inches . . . *a couple inches* . . .

I strain as I shift my shoulders, the effort causing more warmth to bubble up and flood out of me.

My fingers curl around the bottom metal of the railing, and with the very last of my strength, I drag my upper body to it.

Relief washes over me as I reach my arm through and let it hang limply.

I watch as my hot blood runs down my forearm and fingers, red tendrils dripping from them. I imagine the *drip, drip, drip* as it hits the pool yard below, cold by the time it splatters on the concrete. Or maybe it hits the water, the droplets too few for anyone to notice. If I'm lucky, my blood will tap on someone's arm, and they'll look up and see a dying naked girl reaching through the banister.

I wait for a scream. *I pray for one.*

Closing my eyes, I feel alone in this moment, despite the loud excitement of memories being made below me. But I know my loneliness is not entirely true. Viorel shares my pain, far across the world, just as unable to shake this agony or save me as I am. The pain connects us with a lock fashioned by Death himself. Only he holds the key, waiting on the other side for me to finally cross over to take it.

What's Viorel thinking? What has *he* been thinking these past few hours as his mark forced him to experience Denendrius's wrath alongside me? Has he been pacing, waiting for it to stop, as I begged Denendrius to? Or was it so brutal that Denendrius immobilized him in bed too? Could Viorel cry out for Mateo, demanding he *find a way to help?* Does he sit there now, *waiting* as my blood *drip, drip, drips* in the night, for the pain to stop? Is he waiting for the heaviness of the lock that binds us to drop, just as I wait for my heavy, struggling heart to stop?

Can he feel how much I love him, how much I miss him, through this pain? Can he feel how sharp that emotional ache is alongside this physical one?

Blood pools around me, the streetlights and hotel lights dimmer than they were a moment ago. It's still bright enough for me to see the crimson spread from my body, inching closer to the edge of the balcony until it too drips over.

I think of putting a foot through the banister, making myself an easier target to spot, but my strength seeps away with my blood.

Look up and see me. Walk beneath the balcony and accept my crimson call. I just want someone to notice. I don't care that I'm naked and broken. I just want what happened to me tonight to be part of a memory other than my own and Denendrius's.

Black shudders at the edges of my vision, the night slowing to a quiet hum. I cling to the comfort that Viorel is with me. That I'm not experiencing my death alone.

The pain fades, and I can't feel the cold banister under my arm, the hard balcony beneath my body, or the sounds of vacationers below me. There is no light left to show how much of my blood has spilled. There's a bit of peace knowing only Viorel and I share my death, that Denendrius won't get the opportunity to come back and steal it from me. He thinks dying alone is a punishment, but I'd rather slip away, my soul last touched by Viorel, than by Denendrius as he stares into it while throttling it from my body.

Darkness. It's not so bad anymore. I can hardly recall what's beyond it, or why at the very thin edge of my consciousness, the last thing I hear before I fall over it is someone screaming.

DENENDRIVS

LI

I exchange several hundred-dollar bills for chips at the cashier and navigate to one of the high-stakes Roulette tables, the racket of gamblers swelling around me as I wind through them.

I nod briefly at the dealer as I sit down, her voice barely penetrating my thoughts as she welcomes me to place my bet. My strategy tonight is thoughtless—my mind on Marianna—as I place a single hundred-dollar chip on all black.

The wheel spins, the dealer's voice nearly lost in the noise. *"No more bets."*

Marianna's scent grips me, her blood embedded in my sinuses. The taste of it rolls around on my tongue. I hold my breath, taking periodic, shallow inhales to avoid drawing attention. I'd hate for the flavor of this room to spoil what's left of her on me.

For a moment, the spinning wheel draws my focus, and I watch the ball circle in the opposite direction as I replay the last few hours in my head.

I can still feel her flesh on mine, the way she moved against me, the feel of her hot breath pulsing against my chest or in my mouth. The strain of her muscles beneath that soft flesh sends a shiver of excitement down my spine. I swallow and straighten in my seat. She's so much stronger than she used to be. I've never had a human girl this strong—just another side effect of Huarsar's blood. One more thing I can't complain about.

My mind traces the determination on her pretty face as she fought me, the way her blood pulsed through her soft neck as she pushed against my body with everything she had.

The dealer's pale hand sweeps my chip away, and I blink and see how the ball settled on red, fourteen. I've missed the call. I place two more on black, and she spins the wheel again.

A few heavy breaths leave my lips before I rein them in, putting my attention back on the spinning wheel. The division of colors remains crisp, and I can tell by where the ball loses momentum that I've lost again, even before the dealer closes bets. If I could focus past the image of Marianna, I'd place my bets accordingly, as I usually would. But money has no value tonight. A few moments later, red betters collect their chips while I'm down two more.

I bet on black again.

Marianna claws back my attention. The sight of her wide mouth and the sound of her gasps and grunts are thick between me and the room. I let it repeat in my mind, just as precise and nearly as vivid as before.

There's no roulette wheel to focus on, just the memory of her slender body. I'm transfixed by the sight of crimson on her flesh, the slick feel of it between our limbs. I lick my bottom lip, the faint taste of her lingering there. My flesh remembers her warmth, how it seeped into me, reaching deep into my core as I laid myself upon her.

The crotch of my pants tightens, and I blink rapidly, trying to bat the image away. I cross my legs and shift in my chair.

Aching to return upstairs, I crave her legs tight around me

and her hot blood on my tongue. I bet she's still alive. Yet even if she's not, but still warm . . .

No. She doesn't deserve my presence—not after being so cruel to me.

But oh, how I want her again!

I can't go back before she's dead, but I don't know how long it'll take with *his* blood pumping through her.

I wish I could preserve her like this forever. So soft, so warm, *so sweet*. So human.

The dealer takes my chips again, and I'm on autopilot as I bet another two on black.

If only she could understand why I so desperately want to keep her *like this*. But even I know it's not possible. I wanted to turn her for years, but the more I loved her this way—experienced her like this—the less I wanted to give it up.

I've never made love to another immortal before, the thought skulking at the back of my mind that it might be too opposite to what I'm used to. Too much like the men who've pinned me in those foul dungeons. No detectable heartbeat, flesh as cold as my own, and immortal strength that's difficult to fight.

Perhaps it might be fine to love her as an immortal, but if she stays still for too long . . . Without her warmth, she might remind me of the girls who've overstayed their welcome in my bed. Once their hearts stop pumping, they only stay warm for a little while longer. It's only fun when they stiffen while still alive.

I fear she'll feel like a body past use, and I'll stop loving her. That's always when I stop loving them.

Well, it doesn't matter now. I run my hands over my thighs, wishing I could keep the blood under my dress pants on my skin forever.

In death, she'll remain close to how I love her—*forever*. And she'll still visit me, just as she is now.

This way, I know I'll love her forever. And though she loved to manipulate me with her love—take it away when she was upset, as I'm sure so many foster parents and her mother did—it still hurt, even knowing she didn't mean it. At least she died truly loving me, and I won't have to suffer through the slow decay that love always seems to bring.

This way, she'll love me forever.

The dealer announces my win and pushes my chips toward me. I immediately place two more on black.

It's not about the money. If I don't keep my hands busy, they'll end up back on her.

"You okay?" the man beside me asks with a laugh, but my thoughts muffle his words. *"I thought finally winning would get a reaction out of you."*

I fill my lungs, the scent of Marianna diluting the smell of the humans around me and the too-familiar stench of the casino. The vivid memory of her heart galloping beneath my palm as I choked her excites me far more than a few hundred dollars.

The man beside me laughs again, saying something to his friend about how I'm off in *La La Land.*

Another man slides into the chair on my other side, and I catch him staring at me for extended periods through the next three rounds. He coughs and sniffles—grating, interrupting my thoughts of Marianna—and leans away from me when I adjust my shirt.

I sense his scrutiny on my hands, and I suspect he's analyzing my bets until I tuck a loose strand of hair behind my ear and spot the blood caked under one of my nails.

When the next round ends—*I lose*—he mumbles to whoever he's with that he's moving to another table.

Another man appears beside me. I've lost count of how many rounds I've played, but my chips keep shifting between wins and losses. In my peripheral vision, I catch his shoulder brushing against mine, and I might react if I could feel it. He adds to the conversation, his smear of words lost to me until he looks at me and mutters something that carries his blood-tinged breath to me. I blink and focus on his face.

Sergei.

"What?" I mumble.

His low Russian mutter takes a moment to register. *"I can smell you across the fucking casino. You reek of sex, piss, and blood."*

"Hm." I place two chips on black, shifting my gaze to the wheel as it spins and the ball settles.

I lose.

Sergei grumbles, "Grab your chips."

"Why?" I utter, considering giving red a chance tonight.

He hooks his arm around mine, and I snatch my chips and shove them in my pocket as he gently hauls me to my feet like I'm a drunkard. I grunt in annoyance, but don't fight him as he pulls me toward a row of empty slot machines.

I fish my wallet out of my pocket, pulling out a few five-dollar bills before lowering myself onto the seat and feeding the machine. A sigh escapes me as I pull the lever. The reels spin. Rainbow lights blind me as music spills from the machine.

Sergei sits beside me, and we switch to low Russian, making sure no one can overhear.

"How long has she been dead?" Sergei demands with an exasperated exhale.

He feeds his machine a bill, yanking the lever hard enough that I'm surprised he doesn't tear it off. He crosses his arms, eyes on the spinning reels.

My machine settles, but Marianna's bleeding body is a screen in front of my eyes. I must lose, as there's no celebratory music. I feed the machine another bill, tracing over the memory of her heart galloping against my chest as I pressed her into the mattress. I feel her soft skin, taste her sweat on my tongue . . .

Sergei curses and reaches across me to pull the lever of my machine. The moment he pulls back, I try to pull it again.

"I already fucking—what's the matter with you?" he snarls. "Where's your mind?"

It remains upstairs with Marianna.

I exhale a shallow breath.

"How long?" he asks again.

I lick my teeth and lips. Her taste still lingers in my mouth.

"She's not dead yet," I whisper, inhaling deeply and catching a thousand different flavors—half of which sting my throat with thirst. I return to shallow breaths, letting the scent of her blood under my clothes fill my lungs.

He shakes his head, perhaps because of my words, or the settling reels on his screen.

"Put money in your machine," he grumbles.

I unfold another bill from my hand and blindly find the slot, my eyes fixated forward. I imagine her weakening breaths as she lies limp on the blood-stained sheets. Her mind must be clinging to me, just as mine clings to her. Is she begging for my return, wasting the last of her sweet breaths on my name? The thought sends a shiver through me.

"What the fuck happened?" he demands. "I thought your plan was to turn her. This is your goddamn wedding night."

"We fought. She was upset I wouldn't."

The anger from her lashing words has dulled, drawn out of me by her blood and writhing body.

Perhaps it drew everything out of me.

In my peripheral vision, Sergei scowls. "Why won't you?"

All the reasons she spat in my face! Though she twisted them up all wrong.

"What if I stop loving her when she's a vampire? I've never been in love with a vampire before." I jam another bill into the machine. The fruits on the digital reels are clearer now that Sergei has forced me into conversation. Yanking the lever, I watch them spin.

Sergei grits his teeth, balling his fist on his thigh. "Why would it make a difference? A girl is a girl." He shakes his head. "So you promise to turn her, and now she's getting antsy and frustrated with you for dragging your feet, and this is your solution?"

"You should have heard the way she spoke to me," I hiss. "She knows better."

Sergei stares at me. "She's still marked by Viorel. You should count yourself lucky his mark hasn't made her feral. Turn her so it's broken, so she has her memories back. Seize the life you want."

I sigh, straightening the sleeves of my shirt. "I can't. She has to die. She won't forgive me for this, and it'll be impossible to deal with her now."

Sergei's lip twitches, and for a moment, it looks like he wants to knock my head off my shoulders. "You are being impulsive. You are too numb to feel what you're doing. You love her too much to give up on her and let her die. This is the first girl you've ever marked, the mother of your child. *Go upstairs.* Pray her heart is still beating. What will you do without her?"

I try to think past her death and see nothing but darkness.

Sergei has a point. It took me centuries to find Marianna. I'll never find another girl who made me feel what she did. I'm too tired to look again, anyway.

"She might be so angry now that she ruins it, even if I try," I argue. "It'll only be more difficult to manage her with immortal strength."

"What if she's thankful you changed your mind? You said everything was good when you were human, so clearly she forgave you once already. She's already forgiven you for this most recent hiccup . . ." He smiles and shoves another bill in each of our machines. "Turn her, and after seeing the villa and all the beautiful things you bought her, she'll be happy. Find her a new baby, and that should even things out."

"What if she isn't happy?" I counter. "If she continues to fight me?"

Sergei turns and locks eyes with mine. "Then you've done all you can. You put the girl out of her misery."

A breathy chuckle slips out of me as I stand. *Of course . . .*

"I suppose I should check on her, then." If she's still breathing, she'll be elated to see me . . . but she may think my future threats flimsy now.

Sergei's expression falls, his eyes focusing on something behind me. He switches back to English. "Friend, I think someone beat you back to her."

I turn.

SWAT enters the room, five M4 Carbines pointed in my direction as they shout at me to get down on the ground.

Marianna.

Everything snaps back into focus, the sounds and sights crisp again as people scramble aside in a cacophony of alarm. SWAT stalks toward me, shouting commands for me to raise my hands and surrender.

I do neither. Instead, I twist and bolt, moving as fast as humanly plausible through the casino. I shove through the doors, guests scattering out of my way as I race toward the stairwell.

"Runner! Suspect heading toward the stairwell!" A SWAT officer shouts. *"In pursuit!"*

The image of Marianna lying in bed, naked and confused, as paramedics and police officers surround her, flashes through my mind. I know they're taking her away from me, and it makes me grit my teeth.

A worse thought tears through me.

Marianna, bloodless with fading warmth . . . her soft corpse being poked and prodded as they snap photos of her.

Rage blinds me, nearly has me spinning on my heels in the middle of the hall to bludgeon every officer with my bare hands —immortal truths be damned.

I'll tear them apart if they've touched her.

She's mine! What right do they have to take her from me?

Energy surges through me, fury heating me and driving me forward. I yank the stairwell door open, an officer behind me communicating my every move to the rest of the team as they pursue.

I dart up the concrete steps, boots thudding in pursuit. Though I ensure I remain faster than them, exactly as far ahead as I need to be, the cameras keep my speed in check.

They shout commands—headset helmets feeding updates directly into their ears—while demanding my surrender.

I reach the fifth floor—halfway to my sweet girl—and slow my pace, letting them think the endless breaths in my lungs are running low.

Their headsets crackle with updates. *"Two floors above us, slowing down."* I hear the thudding boots and racing hearts closing in.

With a twist of my heels, I'm already descending the stairs toward them, too fast for their comms to relay my sudden maneuver. I cover the distance in an instant, the landing separating us disappearing beneath my feet.

As the lead officer lifts his boot onto the top step, I grip the banister from the fourth step, using my momentum to swing myself forward. My foot slams into his chest with a force that sends him crashing back into the officer behind him. They don't have time to react—noise flooding their headsets—before I've ripped an M4 from the team lead's hand.

"Drop the weapon!" an officer shouts as he scrambles to his

feet, half out from beneath another officer who tries to untangle himself from the man who was on the step above him.

They don't have time to lift their guns as I calmly switch the rifle to burst fire. The fear in their eyes sharpens, knowing what's coming. It ignites me with excitement as I nestle the butt against my shoulder and squeeze the trigger. Three-round bursts explode through the stairwell, each pulse precise, tearing through the small space. The rapid shots vibrate through my chest like a heartbeat, and the deafening noise would be unbearable if I were human. My heart—slow, merely fast enough to stop the blood from stagnating in my veins— thuds an extra beat quicker with the thrill.

Blood splashes the walls. Each controlled burst finds its mark, shredding their throats and faces, sending them tumbling down the steps. The smears of crimson on the white paint make my throat burn, my mouth thick with venom. Marianna's lingering taste only amplifies my thirst.

I release the trigger between bursts, the rifle spitting in deadly rhythm until the magazine runs dry. Heat radiates from the rifle, the warm metal satisfying in my hand. I drop the gun with a thud and pluck another from an officer's death grip.

At the end of the line, one weak pulse begs for my attention.

His partner lies half over him, a human shield who took most of the bullets. The officer's blue eyes lock with mine.

"Please . . ." He lifts a weak, black-gloved hand toward me in a plea for mercy, coughing as blood sprays past his lips. "Please, Charles, I have a wife and a daughter—"

I squeeze the trigger, sending another controlled burst of rounds into him. A few bullets—just enough to kill—pierce past his body armor and find his throat.

"So do I." I lower the rifle, inhaling the acrid scent of gunpowder and blood, staring at their bodies through a thin, smoky haze.

More officers scramble toward the stairwell below, so I grab a fresh magazine from a dead officer as a replacement.

Gun in hand, I continue up the stairs. I can hear them communicating, their strategies sharpening as I approach the tenth floor. By the time I reach the next landing, I realize going through that door will earn me a bullet to the head. It'll be awkward for me—and the other vampires—when I wake up in a morgue after my brain heals around it.

Two officers are stationed on either side of the door, while another is angled across from it. Farther down the hall, a calm heartbeat taps against the floor.

A sniper.

A message from the security control room alerts them to how I'm standing right outside the door.

I focus beyond the officers, trying to locate the faint, dying beat of Marianna's heart past the dozen armed men littering the hall. Her rattling breath, paramedics at her side—something, anything that tells me she's still here.

But there's nothing.

No coroner, no signature sound of a body bag zipping shut. My teeth grind, fury bubbling in my chest. *Did they take her?*

I listen for anything that tells me Marianna is in reach . . . but hear nothing.

"Drop the weapon and put your hands up!" the officer directly on the other side of the wall commands.

I inch my hand toward the handle, hearing the subtle shift of armor and muscle from the three closest men as they stiffen. My grip tightens around the metal bar.

"Drop the weapon!" he barks again.

With careful intention, I crack the door millimeters, and the contained scents of the hall spill into the stairwell.

Marianna's scent lingers thick in the air. Her living blood hangs in the space between the officers' breaths, as if she passed by on a stretcher minutes ago. The sharp tang of antiseptic curls into it, the faint reek of latex gloves nearby.

They took her. Alive.

My sweet girl is still breathing, and she must be frantic, terrified, with only humans between her and whoever wants to snatch her up and return her to Huarsar.

The sound of soft boots on concrete rises from below. Five more men sneaking up the stairwell, silent as if they could surprise me.

I pull the door closed with a soft click and dart up the next set of stairs.

"He's on the move!" someone shouts from the other side of the door as I pass by the window.

The police prowling the eleventh floor keep me moving upward. I catch an order crackling through their radios: extra men to the hospital where they've taken Marianna. Lock down hotel exits.

They think I know she's not in the hotel anymore.

They're not wrong.

Boots thunder on the steps behind me as SWAT abandons the element of surprise. I grip the M4 Carbine tighter, pushing upward until I reach a floor free of law enforcement.

I yank the door open and dart down the hall, shoving through another stairwell. My steps echo against the concrete as I descend, flying past floors until I reach the second. Another team of armed men surges into the stairwell from the first floor.

Racing down the hall, I find a room that—based on memory—has a balcony. I kick the door in, the lock breaking under the force. The room is empty, its furniture undisturbed. I dash through to the balcony, sliding the glass door open and stepping into the night. In one fluid motion, I plant my hand on the metal railing and vault over it, landing on my feet in the yard below.

Without breaking stride, I sprint toward the fence, jump,

and grip the top. The metal presses into my palm as I swing myself over with ease.

I tear down the road, darting through alleyways and back-yards so I can ensure I arrive at the hospital before law enforcement does. When there are only a couple blocks between me and the towering medical building in the distance, I scan the road until my sight locks on to a little silver sedan as it stops at a red light, its driver—a teenage boy with a face so young and friendly—more useful than the vehicle.

I dart into traffic, ignoring the screech of brakes. The boy doesn't notice me approaching until I've yanked the door open. With the M4 pointed squarely at his face, I snarl, *"Move over."*

His lip trembles as the sour scent of fear fills the car. He scrambles into the passenger seat, shaking against the door.

I slide into the driver's seat, slam the door, and lock it with a click so he understands there's nowhere for him to go.

"Are you going to shoot me?" he squeaks, so pitifully spine-less I almost want to kill him just on principle.

"No." I slam my foot on the gas, tearing through the inter-section as the light turns green. The car jerks as I twist the wheel, sending us careening toward the hospital. "But the police will."

LII

I park in the shadows between two trucks in the hospital's main lot. The calm at the entrance and lack of law enforcement signal I got here first. I text Sergei before twisting to the trembling mess of a boy in the passenger seat.

His green eyes dart in every direction but mine.

"Look at me," I snarl.

They leap to mine, and I capture them in a gaze so heavy it's impossible for him to look away. I focus on the terror in them as they glaze over, spreading his scrambling thoughts to make space for my orders to root themselves.

"No more fear. You're a brave boy now, got it? You're a soldier worthy of the Roman legion's pride." I adjust the M4 Carbine in my grip, holding it up between us despite knowing he can't draw his eyes away from mine to look at it. Even so, it doesn't matter.

He swallows hard, but straightens in the seat, his jaw clenching and lifting slightly at my command. The fear in his eyes hardens. "Yes, sir."

"You're going to hide this gun in your sports bag and walk casually into the hospital as if it's not there. Locate the most crowded area you can within fifteen seconds—the cafeteria right now, from the sounds of it—and aim for every *chest* you see. Don't stand in one spot too long, and hit as many people of any age as you can until the police shoot you and you're physically incapable of pulling the trigger. Focus on quantity, not casualties. The more chaos, the better."

He gives me a hard, single nod. "Yes, sir."

"Good boy." I show him how to use the gun, pressing key tips into his brain as if he's always known them. I can't give him my aim, but he'll get the job done. I shove the rifle against his chest and guide his hands into place, noting how steady his fingers are now.

He unzips his high school–branded football duffel bag, dumps out cleats and shoulder pads, and lays the weapon inside. It barely fits. He zips it halfway, leaving the strap loose, ready to sling over his shoulder. To anyone watching, he's just a kid visiting family after practice.

"Now, go," I command.

I step out of the car as he does. While he meanders toward the main entrance as if he's going to visit his dying grandmother, I crouch and weave between vehicles until I can safely move alongside the hospital, toward the opposite side of the building where I suspect the operating rooms are. Where I'm certain my sweet Marianna will be by now.

The sound of SWAT vehicles approaching from each side of the hospital has me swiftly selecting a personnel door. With a hard kick to the metal frame, I break the lock and slip through the entrance. Echoes of gunfire and shrieks erupt in the distance, setting my nerves alight. A smirk almost touches my lips—if not for the weight of Marianna's life pressing down on me, pulling it away.

The operating room is easy to find with the scent of Marianna's blood lingering in the air like a breadcrumb trail, guiding me unerringly toward her as I revel in each faint, echoing burst of gunfire. It's far enough that the staff in nearby rooms can't hear, and thus react as if they aren't about to have their hands overwhelmed and bloody.

I glide down the sterile, white halls, the sharp, clean smell of antiseptic hanging in the air. I much prefer the thick plume of blood, carried by shifting bodies and the ventilation, rising from the boy's carnage downstairs across the hospital.

A single, precise shot neutralizes my distraction just as two armed police officers guarding the operating room door come into view. Recognition flashes in their eyes just as I feel the crunch of their snapping necks in my grip, their bodies crumpling to the floor. I swipe an officer's M4 Carbine as I step over them, pushing through the doors without a second glance.

There she lies, intubated and motionless on the table, her naked body exposed beneath the harsh overhead lights with my fury on display. The antiseptic stench has me wrinkling my nose, but it doesn't overpower the scent of her blood thick in the air. I stride toward her with deliberate steps, barely aware of the whimpering doctors and refusing to spare a glance at the one who faints with a crack of her skull against the hard floor in my peripheral vision.

Marianna's chest rises and falls weakly. Blood stains her torso, and my vision narrows as I take her in. My sweet girl, so vulnerable. Anger ripples through me and my fist tightens at my sides.

"Charles, please!" the surgeon pleads, his hand shaking as he clutches a scalpel glistening with Marianna's blood.

"I have to fix her," I say, taking another step closer to her.

The room erupts in panic. The surgeon steps between me and Marianna, his palms raised defensively. I stop just short of colliding with him, my reflexes keeping us both from crashing into her.

"Let us fix her for you," he pleads, fear splitting his voice. "*Please.* You can watch over us. We're in the middle of surgery. *Let us help her.*"

"I need to fix her—"

"How?" he interrupts, the firmness of the word making my back straighten. "Do you even realize what you've done?"

I pause and latch my gaze on his, hungry for the details from his lips.

"Charles, it's a miracle she's alive. But we can save her, if you let us. Please don't try to take her to some back-alley doctor. She'll die the moment you pull those wires. Her spine is fractured, pelvis and ribs broken. You shattered her femur. You broke her orbital bone, cracked her jaw, half-crushed her trachea. *You raped her.* Stabbed her thirteen times. I wish that were all. She's going to need *hours* of surgery. You'll be lucky if she wakes from the coma."

"I can fix that." I grab a fistful of his green scrubs and hurl him aside.

He crashes to the floor, the scalpel clattering beside where he landed on his back. "Don't touch her! You'll kill her!"

"*Please!*" a nurse gasps, backing away as I reach Marianna.

The skin of her bruised cheek is still warm, slick with blood beneath my fingers. I fight the urge to yank the tubing from her mouth and rip the IVs from her body—at least until my venom is pumping through her system.

I slip my hand beneath her neck, lifting her just enough to expose her throat. Bruising, dark and thick, marks the band where my belt was, the claiming mark of my fingers overlapping the edge of her jaw. Ignoring the chaos around me, I sink my fangs into her throat. The bruising does well to disguise them; it must look like a kiss. I resist the scorching urge to drink—if I do, I'll only pull my venom back out with her blood. I take each of her wrists and bite as deep as her veins accommodate.

Within moments, the frantic rhythm of her heart fills the

room. I hear the words *cardiac arrest* between medical commands, their panic palpable and cutting through my focus.

They don't understand. *This is a good thing.*

Hope swells in my chest, the feeling like being lost at sea with the dry, lifeless bodies of your shipmates around you. Like having not seen land in days, only to hear the distant cry of a bird and knowing you'll hit the shore to wet your tongue soon.

I scrutinize the shape of my fury on her body, waiting for a shift that signals she's begun to heal. She's fortunate, really. She may not have enjoyed my anger, but if not for it, her mind would be whole enough to experience the indescribable agony of healing and the transformation. Marianna's better off, and in a way, things are balanced now.

Her skin, soft beneath the layer of blood, should be healing. But there's no change. The bruises remain vivid, the wounds still open. Her body should be responding, *but nothing shifts.*

Her heartbeat spikes on the monitor, and I hold my breath.

It crashes. A long, screeching line crossing the screen, so sharp and straight I feel it in my soul. I'm frozen, unable to blink or close my parted lips as I wait for a peak or valley. None come.

The scent of Huarsar dissipates from her, his blood mark torn from her with her life.

It's a permanent death.

I know Huarsar felt the tear, and though it may have physically hurt him, her death feels like someone carved my heart out of my chest.

I gambled with the fates, and I lost.

"She's dead," the surgeon breathes in disbelief. He plants his hands on his thighs, trying to steady himself. "You killed her. We had her stable, and you just—"

Why are they upset? Marianna meant nothing to them! She was mine. She meant *everything* to me.

The frantic energy continues around me. Desperation

sharpens in the air, my breaths inexplicably even despite the chaos of my mind. A crash cart is pushed up alongside the table, a nurse above Marianna's body giving compressions before paddles have her body jolting violently. The hum of electricity in the air has me holding my breath.

I wait for those crisp mountains and valleys to appear on the screen, but they don't. I should know they won't. That flat line continues to screech across the screen, the sound so agonizing it'll echo in my ears for the rest of my days.

Another shock.

Somehow, the sound of her death grows more piercing, that line thicker.

The nurse giving compressions glances at me, eyes wide with terror and defeat. Like she's trying to assess if I can see how futile their attempts are too.

Movement behind the woman over Marianna briefly draws my attention as a young nurse dashes toward the far door. I lazily lift the M4, my strength enough to keep it steady against my forearm. The shot is effortless. It splits the back of her skull and sprawls her against the crimson streak on the blue wall before she folds over on the floor.

Why did I do this to my sweet girl?

I have a thousand reasons, and though most of them are justified, I can't quite match them to why I let my anger take me this far. There's no relief seeing her there. There's no feeling of finalization—of justness—like there was with my past girl-friends who betrayed me. I always felt better when they died. *Peaceful.*

So why does this make me feel worse?

Why does it feel as though I've angered the gods despite all Marianna has done to me? Like there's nothing she could possibly do to me to deserve death?

Why does it feel like my life ends here with hers? Like the

only thing left to do is cut out my own heart to shed the agony of it?

Mere moments have passed since she flatlined.

Her heart holds the charge, and I hear a faint shudder before a slow beat sounds through the room. Then another.

"She has a pulse!" the nurse above Marianna exclaims, her face so full of shock I know it's a miracle from the gods.

I pounce forward and shove her off Marianna. Their exclamations—their tangled, twisted cries and pleas—fill my ears as I tear the IV from Marianna's arm and pry the tubing from her throat.

The surgeon lunges for my arm, his bloodstained latex gloves sliding off my dress shirt, desperation in his eyes as if I'm stealing *his* wife. "Don't! You'll kill her again! She can't breathe on her own!"

I shrug him off and hoist Marianna's small body into my arms.

Nurses weep, one accepting her position on the hard floor as she wraps her arms around her head.

With the thud of boots down the hall, I dart from the operating room and snatch a thin blanket off a tall cart to cover her naked body from prying eyes. I'm swift enough to outrun them without giving myself away, slipping through side doors and rooms until I'm breathing the crisp air of night with Marianna secure in my arms.

A car screeches to a halt in front of me, Sergei in the driver's seat. I scramble into the backseat with Marianna, splaying her out across it as I jam one knee between her body and the back of the seat while kneeling with my other on the floor.

"She's dead," Sergei claims as he peels away.

I fill her lungs with my breath. "No, she's not!"

As Sergei takes a sharp corner, I brace Marianna's body, steadying her as she shifts so I can begin compressions to keep the venom moving through her veins.

"She no longer smells like Huarsar, Denendrius, and I would barely consider what she has a heartbeat."

I breathe into her, then say, "She's not dead."

The flutter of her heart grips me. It's like a dying bird flapping weakly with broken wings against the earth. I force another breath into her.

"You tried to turn her?" He hits the gas at a yellow light.

Another breath for her. "Yes. She flatlined."

Sergei heaves out a noisy breath. "My friend, she is not coming back. The transformation failed."

I press my lips to hers, her heart so quiet I can hardly hear it now. *I'd give her all my breaths, if I could.*

Her cracked ribs strain under my force, but the venom can heal them later. I just need her heart to work. "I'm going to force the venom through her body. I'll make her heart pump long enough for it to heal her, then it'll do the rest. She flatlined, but they managed to get a pulse back."

"That's *impossible* if your venom stopped her heart. You know that." With the disbelief thickening his words, he may as well call me a liar. "Their equipment must be faulty. How long did it last?"

My words are clipped. "A couple beats before I pulled her off the table."

I steal a fraction of a second to bite into my wrist and spill blood down her throat.

"Denendrius . . ." Sergei says carefully.

I breathe into her and continue to stimulate her heart. "Just drive," I snarl before pressing my lips to hers again.

"She's not alive, Denendrius. Her heart isn't truly beating. *You* are making it beat, not her brain. She will decay around her pumping heart so long as you move it."

More breath. I huff, fury shuddering through me as I compress her chest. "I just need to force the venom to her brain so it can heal it, then it's smooth sailing."

"I've never heard of something like this working."

"Me neither," I admit with a twang that ricochets through my center like an arrow. "But the gods will make it so. I just have to prove myself to them. I'll heal her, and they'll give her back."

"*Oh,* my friend," Sergei murmurs with a long sigh.

I continue with compressions as I fill her with my breaths, waiting for her to grip one and exhale it herself.

As Sergei parks at the motel, I swoop her into my arms and dart from the car.

LIII

Sergei holds the motel room door open as I carry Marianna's soft body inside. I reel at the sight of Adelia. Her tear-streaked face turns away from the television and to me as Sergei shuts the door.

The judgment is deafening in her wet eyes and twisted brows, her upper lip taut with disdain.

"Why is she here?" I snarl at Sergei, my gaze remaining hostage in hers.

He scoffs. "You expect me to fly her home and get you a motel at the same time?"

Her bottom lip trembles. *"You killed her,"* she cries, splitting her hands in accusation between the television and Marianna in my arms before she yanks them down to her sides. *"Why did you kill her?"*

I spin free, twisting to Sergei before backing toward the bed. "Take her home, *now.*"

"You killed my best friend!" She fills the room with her noisy

sobs, so loud it's like she wants her upset imbedded in my eardrums.

I whirl around.

"Shut up!" I bellow at her, fury working its way through my limbs like it wants to wear me as a second skin. Black swirls at the edges of my vision, my thoughts in such a flurry I can't tell them apart.

Adelia shrinks away from me, fresh tears stroking her cheeks. Her gaze darts back and forth across my face, but I don't know what she's searching for.

"You promised," she cries. "You promised you'd never hurt her. *How could you do what you did?* How could you?"

I grip Marianna tighter to my chest, her quiet heart begging for my action. "She's still alive," I argue as I rush onto the far bed near the bathroom and splay her out on the hospital blanket over the green and pink floral one to continue compressions. Her heart pumps with my will again, and I offer her a breath. "I bit her while she was still alive and left venom in her. She'll turn. The transformation just needs some help."

She trails her eyes back to the TV, her arms limp at her sides. Shaking her head, she blubbers, "I heard what happened between the officers at the hotel as we were leaving . . ." She hangs her head. "You raped her. Stabbed her."

"They got her heart pumping again," I interject. "Which means the venom *did something* before she flatlined. I just have to keep it moving."

"The transformation won't take," Adelia claims, tears dripping onto her shirt and leaving wet splotches. "The odds are already so low, and you left it with nothing to work with. She flatlined *frater*. It killed her already. We know there's no coming back from that."

"Her heart is beating." Can she not hear how it moves with my hands? I fill her lungs again. "We can't go by the rules when Huarsar's blood was already changing them."

She lifts her eyes, settling them on my timed compressions. "You think you're the first to try that? You might be able to force the venom through her veins, but it's not enough to do anything. *She's dead.* When was the last time she took a breath on her own?"

"Go home!" I demand.

"Come on," Sergei tells her.

She stands, her eyes remaining on the floor as she passes by me to leave. When she reaches for her bag, I shake my head. She won't need anything on the plane, and I have nothing to take care of Marianna with.

She's about to carry on without it, when I jolt at the realization that the medical staff stole Marianna's earrings. "Wait!"

Adelia turns to me, her eyes pinned to the floor as she sobs.

"My hands are busy," I explain. "Come put that other set of earrings Sergei texted me a picture of in her ears before she heals."

But she makes no effort to move, merely wipes her eyes with her fists and blubbers uselessly.

Sergei sighs and gives her shoulder a pat as he digs them out of the backpack. He moves to my side and puts the heart-shaped diamonds in her lobes.

I give him a relieved nod, my hands still working her chest. "That's better."

"Go bury her," Sergei tells me as he walks back to Adelia. "I'll meet you there."

"She's not dead," I insist, but the door opens and closes without a response.

Outside, Adelia whispers, *"I miss my brother, Sergei."*

I push them out of my mind and return all my attention to Marianna.

The sight of her body, brightly bearing all my anger, sends a rush through my veins and my mouth thickens with venom and the desire to taste her. Her scent rises like a plume in the air, and I breathe it deep into myself before pushing it back into her lungs.

Sinking my fangs into her slowed blood, I inject more venom into her over and over as I steal little tastes.

I move the venom through her system by force, my swift compressions matching the frantic beat needed to spread it. I keep going until dawn breaks and the air between us and the heavy curtain warms, refusing to give her heart repose despite the shifting of her cracked ribs beneath my palms. Either her body strengthens, or I tire.

But it works.

Slowly, like fog creeping across a field at dawn, her flesh begins to mend, her bones fusing back together. Some of her warmth evaporates into the air around us before dissipating. Her bruises fade and leave behind soft, though blood-depleted pale flesh. When her ribs harden beneath my force, and the dozens of fang marks dotting her skin seal, my body buzzes with triumph.

With one swift knock of her heart's own volition against my pressure, it resists pumping to my rhythm. I withdraw my hands and fall back on them against the mattress with a heavy exhale of disbelief.

It's strange that crimson has not overcome the cinnamon of her eyes, but I know there's nothing usual about Marianna. Her past as a vampire child has undoubtedly left fragments of vampire DNA throughout her system—enough that I could never hypnotize her—and paired with the effects of Huarsar's blood, there's no certainty to how the rest of her transformation could play out.

For one, CPR has never worked as it has with Marianna. She shouldn't have been capable of surviving my fury as long as she did either, and her dead heart was receptive to the electrical shocks she received on the operating table when it shouldn't have been. Were she any other human, the transformation failing as it appeared would have left the weak muscle of her heart destroyed.

But she's special. I know she'll wake soon.

My slow heart rattles a few extra times as I take her beauty in. She's whole again, the marks of my fury cleansed. I can sense her forgiveness in the calm air around us, and I stretch out at her side to wait.

Marianna stares up at me. I smile at her so she knows I'm happy. So she knows everything is okay now. That I love her.

"Oh—" I dig her wedding ring out of my pocket and slide it down her finger, some of the dried blood flaking away. Then, I lift her hand over her face so she can see how I've given it back. "Sorry I took it away, sweetheart."

I run my fingers through her hair—tangled and caked with blood—and I can't believe I considered tossing such a perfect creature away in a fit of anger. What on earth would I be doing right now had I returned to find her truly dead?

Need throbs through me, and I trail the tips of my fingers across her soft and healed flesh, dried blood collecting between them and the bit of warmth lingering on her body. My chest tightens at the feel of her, and I can't help but give in to my desire. I study her faded eyes as I love her, hoping to see a sign that the transformation has worked beyond healing. I push the knowledge away that if it were working under normal circumstances, this would be the part where I stare into her garnet eyes and await her consciousness.

When I roll off her, my entire being courses with delight. Now, the only thing wrong with her is the blood tangling her hair and staining her skin. I carry her into the small bathroom and position her head on my chest, her arms around my neck, and her thighs pressing into my hips. I stand with her as the tub fills, steam curling off the surface into translucent wisps, before I climb in and lower us both into the water.

The heat of the water dulls my cravings, though it cools too quickly and the memory of Marianna's human, unmarked scent lingers enough to tease me.

She looks so peaceful in her sleep, so sweet and beautiful, like Venus, as her head lifts and lowers with each of my heavy breaths. Her gentle face shows no signs that the tongue past those rosy lips could cause such pain.

I wipe the blood from her body, and it tints the water rose. I ignore the complimentary soap on the counter for fear of ridding her salty, flowery sweet smell prematurely. Likewise, I don't touch the shampoo despite her hair needing it. Instead, I carefully work through the strands with my fingers. Her wet hair clings to her skin, the color like wet sand under the sun, as if she really was born of the sea.

When we're in Italy, and her human scent has faded, I'll clean her once more to prepare her for the pretty black gown awaiting her there.

"You should see the jet tub waiting for us at the villa. I can't wait to fill it with bubbles for you," I whisper as I trail my fingers down her bare back, the rosy water rippling around us as the pads of my fingers track each ridge in her spine. "I had a heat lamp installed in the bathroom. A sauna too. I can't wait to try them out with you."

There's enough space for both of us in the jet tub, unlike how my legs are bent on the edges of this one.

"I'm sorry I didn't turn you sooner," I murmur, pressing a kiss to the top of her head. "You were right. I was afraid of how it might change you. But I'll love you any way I can, as long as you're here with me."

When her eyes burn red, nothing will part us. In hours, we'll be closer than any mark, any ring or vow could ever make us. She will be part of me, made from me. She will remember me and will love me as purely as she did when she was young. When we are the same—bloodthirsty and products of death— she will understand why I could not remain human for her, though the idea, unglamorous as it would have been, was romantic. I would do anything to slip back in time and meet her instead of darkness.

When the water cools, I pull the drain and hold her tight until it empties. I keep her cradled in my arms as I stand, turning the shower on for a quick rinse.

I throw a white towel over her back, droplets of water pattering on the tile, then the carpet, as I walk back to the bed. I lay her down, letting myself drip as I carefully wipe the water from her before tucking her naked body under the covers. When I'm done drying myself, I crawl unclothed with her beneath the covers.

My eyes won't close as I lie beside her. I do my best to push the hundreds of voices and sounds—the overwhelming discordance of scents—to the back of my mind and put all my attention on the taste of her still lips and the feel of her smooth flesh alongside mine.

Sleep evades me, my mind too full to make space for it. The day passes in a blur of restless thoughts, and I pause every so often to whisper to her and check her body for progress.

Marianna is as soft as each moment I touched her before. A desperate part of me wants to break a finger or glide my knife across her pristine flesh. If she were truly dead, she'd be stiff with death and the initial smells of decay would waft into me with each breath.

Yet she remains frozen in the moment her heart stopped responding to my touch. I don't know what it means.

My chest is tight with resistance, my muscles too stiff to make a move for either idea.

Do I fear harming her pretty skin, or do I fear what might happen if I test it?

I'm heavy when I step out of bed with the setting sun, quietly numb as I dress and root through the bag Adelia left. I find a brush to stroke Marianna's hair, and dress her in a pair of yoga pants and a blue tank top that hug her body nicely. When my hands move to my jeans to unzip them, I have to talk myself into pulling them away. I want to have her again, but the urgency of needing to depart is enough to keep my pants on.

I wrap my sleeping girl in the motel sheet and wait at the window for the right opening to leave.

LIV

The journey to Vermont is cursed, the gods showing me how displeased they are with my actions each step of the way.

When a man parks in the motel lot, I have him give me his car. The engine sounds healthy, though when I take Marianna from the motel room and buckle her sleeping body in the passenger seat, the car dies, and the engine won't turn over no matter how I beg it. There's nothing wrong beneath the hood.

The second car dies during the first night of driving, not even a jolt from a passerby enough for the battery. I take the stranger's truck instead after drinking him, and make it to another motel before sunrise. Marianna remains unchanging at my side as we sleep through the day, and I have irresistibly sweet dreams of her warm flesh and hot mouth that convince me to partake in her again.

After the sun setting wakes me, we continue on the road. I miss an exit, then another. Somehow, my thoughts are so twisted I forget the roads that have changed so little in decades. I have to pull over and step away from the vehicle, my mind clearing with the air. Something like that has never happened to me as an immortal, and it's a reminder from the gods of what they could do to me if they willed it.

I get back on track, speeding to make up for lost time. The stereo won't work, and something is wrong with the headlight on the passenger side. It flickers at incessant intervals, so I pull over and knock it out to rid myself of the annoyance and the risk of it acting like a beacon on the dark highway.

Hours later, sleep tugs at me. It slips from the shadows of night and wraps itself around my consciousness no matter how I bat at it. Its thick form weighs on me, numbs the sensation in my limbs, and I—wracked with confusion—scarcely have time to pull over into the trees alongside the road and turn the truck off before it forces me under. It's a dreamless, restless sort of unconsciousness, and I wake with a fiery ache in my flesh and sunrise teasing the horizon.

Swiftly, I take Marianna and clamber beneath the truck bed's cover for protection, checking her flesh over in the dark to ensure she hasn't burned. We lie there through the day, the hum of vehicles a mere thirty feet from us making me tense against the metal. I wait for someone to notice the truck—link it to my kill or declare it abandoned—and tow it away. An hour from sunrise, and the engine roars to life, the vehicle vibrating beneath us. Yet no human approached, and even immortals can't open noisy car doors without the creaking hinges giving them away.

When the scents in the air shift with the retreat of day, I climb out of the flatbed when there's a long break in traffic. The sky is a deep blue, just enough light left to give the tufts of gray clouds definition. I buckle Marianna in the passenger seat, noticing how the fuel has depleted with an irritated grunt as I settle behind the wheel.

I gamble with my speed on the highway, slowing at the first

crackle of distant speed traps, and not so fast to cause enough concern for other drivers to report me.

With one last night in a motel room to escape the sun, I check news updates online before giving my full attention to Marianna. Her flesh is still so soft against mine as I move over her, though considerably less warm. If, by some chance, it's true she's a corpse, she's the most beautiful one I've ever had. I consider the effect of Huarsar's blood as I stare at her serene face below me, her head against the pillow. Might she stay preserved like this forever? I plant a soft kiss on her lips. *If only I could be so lucky.*

I carry her into the bath with me after, the temperature not as hot as I'd like since I don't want to scald her perfect skin. I splay her on my chest, stroking my fingers through her hair and down her back as I whisper stories to her.

I don't bother with soap again before getting out—the soak more for the warmth—so it doesn't dampen the scent of her. Once I've dried and dressed her, I prop the pillows against the headboard and settle her between my legs, her back against my chest as I put the television on for us. A horror movie plays— one of her favorites—and I hold her hand on her lap while debating if sleep will find me tonight.

"I'm going to turn one of the villa rooms into a home theater," I murmur, stroking her bare shoulder with my free hand. "Do you like that idea?"

A smile crawls across my face. I know she does.

I lean my head back against the wall, deciding sleep and I might finally meet as the movie ends.

"Let's go to sleep." I kiss the top of her head before I shift the blanket and sheet—stinking like cigarettes and harsh deter- gent—from beneath us. I slip her yoga pants off so she's more comfortable, then my jeans, before easing us under the blanket.

"Love you, sweetheart," I murmur. The memory of her

sweet voice takes shape in my mind. The way she'd say, *"I love you too, Den."*

I hold her close, breathing her in as I shut my eyes and remember our wedding night. Though the end result isn't preferred, I can't help but trace my thoughts over what happened again and again until the memory has lulled me to sleep.

Immortal hands grip my wrists against the hard stone, a heaving chest pressed to my back, practically hammering my body harder against the floor. No matter how I writhe with my knees scraping at the stone to find purchase to push me from beneath him, I can't crawl free.

With one hard pull, I break his grip on my wrist. He roars with a furious grunt and grinds the side of my face into the rough stone before he clamps his hand around my wrist again.

My gasp wakes me, though the temperature of an immortal hand remaining on my wrist has me tossing myself backward as the sight of the motel room returns to me. Marianna's hand lies on the mattress where it fell off me.

Crawling out of bed, I steady my climbing breaths as I tuck my loose hair behind my ears and gaze down upon her.

How am I supposed to sleep at her side when her temperature is the same as mine? As theirs?

I feel better after sharing my love with her, then take her for a hot shower before crawling back into bed.

With her at my side, I fall back asleep and into another dream.

I stare past the decorative wrought iron bars of a balcony and my small, dangling legs at the street vendor parked in front of a yellow-painted building. My intense focus muffles the festive music and excitement winding through the streets. The hot, blood-filled bodies that walk past below call for my attention, but my unblinking eyes are locked on the colorfully decorated cart teeming with *pan dulce.*

My eyes snag the vendor's hands as he plucks a bright pink one up and hands it to a boy. Rage compresses my chest like a hug that's too tight as he takes a bite. I lick my lips while wishing I could know its flavor. Breadcrumbs fall against his blue shirt, and I squeeze the balcony bars in my grip. The metal warps in my palms.

The unfairness has my thoughts in a flurry. I want to leap down and snatch the treat from him, but I know it will taste like dirt in my venom-filled mouth.

It's so unfair.

The boy senses me watching and turns his face up, the deep brown of his eyes friendly as he smiles.

Despite all the noise, I hear him clearly as, through a bite, he says, *"Hola!"*

Then he waves, the *pan dulce* swinging side to side in his hand like a taunt.

Tears well in my eyes, something bubbling in my chest until it overflows into an ear-splitting shriek of frustration past my lips. Hands grip me from behind, dragging me from the balcony and into darkness.

A skull-splitting pain forces me awake, momentarily shoving the confusion of the dream aside.

I groan in pain as I touch my head, the squeezing agony too deep to create concern beyond puzzlement. I'm unharmed, but that reality doesn't stop the ache that I've only experienced in the dungeon under Huarsar's will. My narrow gaze scours the dim room, peeling back shadows to see if any Children of Stars are here utilizing the same ability on me. But it's midafternoon . . . and it's merely Marianna and me here.

I pull the blanket over my head and complain loudly into Marianna's hair. I imagine her rolling over. She'd ask me what's wrong.

"My head feels like it's in a scavenger's daughter," I grumble.

"I wish your blood was still good, so I could have some and feel better."

Screwing my eyes closed, I wait for the vivid memory to pass and mull over my dream. No . . . it couldn't be *my* dream. I've been to Mexican villages enough during festivals to know that's where dreamland took me, but I've never been a little immortal girl before . . .

I know Marianna visited me in my dreams. It's not uncommon for my girls to do such a thing, though they are always dead when they do, and they never shape the dream as if it's their own memory.

Could it be one of her memories? I don't quite understand how, and the pain makes it impossible for me to think straight to determine a conclusion.

Hours pass with the agony in my skull, and I realize the gods are merely demonstrating their power again, showing me how they can hurt me in their anger.

"Okay," I grind out. "I get it."

They must not believe me, as the pain doesn't stop until sunrise.

I take back to the road, a bullet in the night until the car shudders and the headlights flicker a plea across the highway before the car stalls. Roaring with anger, I bring the car to a halt and throw myself onto the shoulder of the highway to check beneath the hood.

As I lift it, the smell of cattle fills my nose, a heavy heart thudding from thirty feet away as the body it rests in breathes the scent of chewed grass toward me. I turn to take in the black bull at the barbed-wire fence. It watches me and shakes its horns as if to say hello.

Of course. The gods want more from me. I suppose they would since I haven't offered a single prayer since I was human.

I point across the ditch to the bull, black as night, just as he likes. "Is this what you want to not take her, Pluto? A sacrifice? Is this why you've halted me here?"

The bull speaks, his low bellow my answer from the god of the underworld.

I draw in a deep breath and nod. "You will have him, oh mighty god."

Searching the truck, I smirk when I find an emergency pack that includes candles and a lighter. "Is this why you crippled the last car?" I ask Pluto. "Did it not have these things I need?"

I shove the small yellow candles in the back pocket of my jeans and join the lighter with my switchblade in my right. Though I don't have what else is normally required for the ritual—wine and coins—I have more than enough cash in my pocket to offer him. Lifting Marianna from the passenger seat, I carry her over my shoulder, across the ditch, and jump the barbed fence.

The bull shakes his horns at me, but either he is friendly with his masters or Pluto has tamed him, as he doesn't resist my grip on his smooth horn.

"Come with me, sacred bull," I murmur, meeting his large black eye in the dark as I draw him deeper into the field under the thick blanket of night.

I move us to a patch of trees, a crescent moon of tangled branches and trampled grass that blocks both the farmer's property and the road. It stinks like cow, and from some of the remaining warmth in the soil, it must be a favorite place for their bodies to rest.

Gently, I release the bull and command he stay as I lower Marianna to the ground. I place her behind me, my powerful body between her and the bull, and kiss her softly.

I move to my hands and knees and press all three candles into the soft earth so they will remain standing for me to light. Swiftly, not leaving enough time for the bull to approach Marianna, I gather a collection of fist-sized stones to stack around the candles to create an altar. Then, I pull every bill from my wallet and place it on the stones, holding them in place with a smaller one.

Three thousand dollars . . . I hope it's enough to please.

The bull pulls his head back when I flick the lighter, though curiosity of the flame has him rooted as I light each candle.

In Latin, I invoke Pluto, apologizing for his absence in my heart and promising to offer many sacrifices in the future if he will hear me. I beg him to refuse Marianna's entrance to the underworld, explain the deep regret of what I have done, and promise—for certain this time—that I will never allow my fury to mark her soft body again.

I close my eyes. "As you took Proserpina to be your queen, only for her to be pulled from you so often, so too has death taken Marianna, my sweetest girl, from me. I stand here, not believing us equal in experience, but as a desperate soul pleading for a reunion with his love. You, who know the pain of separation and the joy of reunion, understand the depths of my anguish. Please, mighty Pluto, grant me the mercy you once sought for yourself. *Please allow my sweetheart to return to me.*"

Standing, I fetch the switchblade from my pocket and flip it open, the moonlight catching the silver as the blade clicks into place.

"In your honor, ruler of shadows and keeper of the dead, I offer this sacrifice. It is a token of my sincerity and devotion. Accept this bull, with a coat as dark as death, as a sign of my devotion to you and *my* plea for my lover's soul."

I grasp the bull by his horn and hold his head firm. With a deep and swift score of his thick throat, blood rains from the gash—a heavy drizzle that wets the soil. His eyes bulge as his big heart thrashes in his chest. Dozens of eyes peer with curiosity, a few heifers mooing and bleating in our direction.

Thirst strokes my throat—a more casual suggestion than demand—as I watch his glistening blood pool on the ground until his legs weaken and he falls to his belly. The crimson is beautiful, the moonlight shining off it like it does on the calm surface of a lake, though the earthy scent is far from appetizing. As his heart slows and empties him, I lower to my knees and whisper my prayers again until it ceases.

"Pluto, great and powerful, show me a sign of your favor. Let the spirits be at peace and grant me the return of my sweetheart," I plead.

I wait for something . . . *anything* to know Pluto has me in his favor. Marianna remains still behind me, the stars reflecting in her faraway gaze. Staring at the steady flames—there's no wind tonight—I wait to hear her rouse behind me. Perhaps she'll mumble my name or groan from the heaviness of such a long rest. Will she reach out and touch me? I can practically feel the shape of her hand on my back with the thought. Or will she sit and ask where we are?

At once, the candles extinguish. My back straightens. Gray curls of smoke lift straight, undisturbed, into the air. With no wind or earthly force to blow them out, I take Pluto's sign.

In Latin, I thank him, and his presence—his approval and pleasure at what I've done—is light in my heart.

Smiling, I twist around to Marianna, understanding it still may take some time for her to wake, but knowing my plea has been heard.

I do not know the inner workings of the gods or what it takes to return a soul, but Marianna's body waits, perfect and patient, for it. Perhaps I have not completely angered the fates. Had it not been for the path by which all this has happened, Marianna would not have Huarsar's blood to keep her body so pristine, and Pluto would not have a proper vessel to return it to. Have the gods used my turmoil to bring me back to them?

Perhaps they knew my fury was as inevitable as always, and laid the path of our strings accordingly.

That's it! She was always bound to wake, so long as I loved her.

My smile comes easily, and I feel the calm of night passing through me. I bury the cash deep into the soil for Pluto, then take Marianna into my arms. I slip past cows that wander close to assess my gift, and return to the car where I set Marianna back in the passenger seat and splay the hospital blanket—the scent of her human blood and body entwined in the threads— over her so she'll remain comfortable.

"We should make it to Vermont before sunrise," I tell her as I take back to the highway. "I know there are nothing but bad memories there for you in that house, but I promise we're only meeting Sergei there. Then we'll go home."

I glance at her, expecting a response for a moment before the sight of her sends my eyes back to the road.

"Sergei is expecting me there," I explain.

He always finds me there.

"Are you excited about Italy? I know you've been waiting so patiently. I'm sorry it's taken so long. You probably wish you had leaped off the ship with Adelia when she went." I smile softly to myself. Of course she's excited.

No car troubles plague me for the rest of the journey, and I enjoy the feel of sailing along the highway as I hold the wheel loosely with one hand and grip Marianna's in the other. I sit with my thoughts, fantasies spinning in my mind's eye. I tell her about them. About the children that will fill our villa with their laughter. How I'll show her all the places I have once seen. It'll be nice to return to Rome, to finish what I started.

Though the amphitheater is long decayed, and there is no hope for me to ever have my own school and train as I so dreamed about all those centuries ago, I have my Mariana. I have my sister, and a beautiful home that outdoes our father's.

I will have a happy family, and all these aches will pass, and the fury that lives in my bones where it has grown with my marrow will no longer creep out to control me.

For once, I will know what it means for everything to be all right. I've never known before.

LV

Sergei is yet to arrive at my old home in Vermont when I show up. I rest Marianna on the bed of the basement bedroom, and find her gold ouroboros bracelet on the ground between the cage's imprint in the dirt and the mattress. After slipping it back on her wrist—she's far more deserving of an expensive piece of jewelry like it than Tatiana ever was—I nod to myself. Everything is in place on her as it should be now.

The lingering stench of her entrapment in the dog cage sends a jolt of unease through me as I inhale deeply. It quickly drives me to grab the thing from where it rests in the hall, its lock broken open, and drag the metal frame to another part of the house in banishment.

I fall into routine as I grab my rusting shovel from a different, collapsing basement room, though the ease at which it usually finds my palm is replaced with rigid fingers and a numbness that worms its way through me like a parasite.

Though I know Marianna isn't dead and doesn't need a

grave, I bring the shovel to the bedroom where she lies. Standing in the corner opposite the bed, I stare at the dirt floor.

I dig. A few chunks of dirt dislodge before I stop, resting my hands on the worn metal handle, its tip buried in the ground. My chest heaves with quick breaths, as if the task is a burden of effort.

Glancing through the darkness at Marianna, my breath catches. For a moment, I see Marissa beside her, curled up at her side. But as quickly as she appears, she vanishes—yet the image lingers vividly in my mind.

"You kept her company," I acknowledge, returning my gaze to the impending task in hopes she'll sneak back to Marianna's side and talk to me. "Thank you."

There's no response, but the scent of her—the strawberry vanilla body wash she used the morning I grabbed her on her way to high school—lingers across the room near Marianna. Her heavy gaze moves over me, and I resist the urge to look over my shoulder to catch her sparkly brown eyes.

I keep digging, so focused on the task that I forget I'm merely going through all too familiar motions. Would Marianna prefer Marissa's company? I could leave her buried beneath the mattress, so they remain close. Or would Marianna be jealous, knowing Marissa was one of my past flings? I should move the mattress above Marianna's grave instead, to assure her she's my favorite.

No, Marianna is not so illogical. She's jealous, at times, with love, but not so illogical that she would prefer to be alone. The girls won't want to talk about our time together with her anyway, because whenever *I* get the chance to reminisce with one of them, they usually get so emotional.

I'll keep them buried in the same room together. Marianna has always wanted a good friend, and Marissa and her bonded while I was gone. At this point, it would be nothing but cruel to move Marissa to the woods with the others and separate them.

After a few minutes, I've carved a six-foot hole into the earth. I grip the shovel handle, staring into the dark, rigid space below . . . how lonely it looks. For the first time, I wish I had a silk-lined box. Somewhere soft and warm where I could tuck Marianna safely inside away from the worms and wild animals. I know I should give her the bare minimum of a proper burial—anoint her in oils and say the proper rites, give her a coin so she can cross the River Styx to the underworld— so she does not become a *lemure* like the rest of my girls. But if she makes it to Pluto, I'll never have a chance to interact with her again.

But then, with a lurch of panic, I reunite with reality.

"She's not dead, you know," I tell Marissa, the smell of her persisting. "I'm just so used to burying you girls it has become automatic. Marianna is still waiting by her body, and I know Pluto will use his godly power to let her return to it. She's not going to become one of you."

Still, I can't stop myself from digging.

"The hole is deep enough," Sergei says as he pokes his head into the room.

I answer him with a shovel full of dirt.

"Denendrius, I'm here now."

I throw another shovelful from the hole, this time toward him.

He sighs. "Are you digging to Hell, friend?"

"I don't want anyone or anything to find her." I cut into the earth again and toss dirt over my shoulder.

But of course, I'm not going to leave her here. She has a perfectly good body for Pluto to return her soul to.

I catch Sergei cocking his brow and crossing his arms from the corner of my eye. "I never hear your worries about the other eighty girls you have buried around here."

His guess is off by a large margin. Take a shovel and start digging anywhere around the property and into the woods, and chances are you'll find a grave. I *have* owned this place for nearly a century.

"Doesn't matter. She's going to wake up," I say. "The transformation is working. She healed."

I can't decipher the long look Sergei gives me, then the blanket over Marianna. As his foot shifts, I dart between him and the bed.

"May I see?" There's too much curiosity in his voice.

I grip the edges of the blanket and hold them tight to the mattress so he can't yank it away. "You know how I feel about you looking at them."

His lips purse. "Well, you say she's not dead. So this is different."

My rigid fingers uncover her arm a bit so he can see how perfect and unbruised her flesh is.

"Her skin is as pale as death, Denendrius." His lips form a hard line. "Colorless."

I scowl. "She lost a lot of blood. She'll be starved when she wakes, but she'll get some of her color back."

He reaches out to touch her, and my hand strikes forward and constricts his wrist. "No!" I throw his hand aside and pull her against me, pointing a warning finger in his face. Venom sprays past my grit teeth as I growl, *Do. Not. Touch. Her.*

"Okay—" He withdraws his hand. "Is she stiff? Let me see her face, at least. Her eyes."

I stare down at her and shake my head.

"Please, Denendrius. I want to believe she's alive as well." He frowns. "I cared about her too ..."

I squeeze my eyes shut as I grapple with his request, but convince myself it's okay. Slowly, I slip the blanket off her sweet face. "She's healed, see?"

"Her eyes should be red." He gives me a pitying look. "They are brown and lifeless. Hazy."

"She'll wake up," I insist. *How can he not see it?*

He studies my face. "Then why are you digging the girl a grave?"

I shrug and force out an exasperated breath.

"I'll leave you alone to grieve," Sergei says delicately as he stands.

I huff. "I don't need to grieve."

"To come to your senses then."

For a bit, I test the idea of her truly being dead, just so I can go through the motions and show myself how silly they are, since I know she's still alive.

Despite having buried countless humans, there's something deeply unnatural about this situation. I pull the blanket back from her face and give her a long kiss, an anchor on my chest when she doesn't spring to life and return my affection. I can't tell if it's frustration or disappointment. They so often feel the same.

I stare into her faded eyes again, studying the way she stares at me unblinking with full attention. Her eyes are so pretty I nearly wish I could take them with me . . . but that's not a habit I want to start. They're better left where they are; framed by her perfect face. I give her lips another kiss and exhale a breath from the deepest part of me as I slowly slide the blanket back over her face.

Perhaps it's the blanket that's the problem. I've never bothered using one before. The fact it's a hospital blanket doesn't help, either. Yet the thought of unraveling Marianna from hers and setting her body straight on the cold dirt for her skin and clothes to be sullied causes a strange feeling in my gut.

I carry her into the hole with me, a tightness in my chest like resistance as I set her on the ground. My chest heaves as I stare down at her.

"Hm." I grimace at the sight of her in the dirt. When I pull dirt onto her body, the soft tap against the blanket makes discomfort squirm inside me. It feels like I'm burying her alive.

I drop to my knees and swiftly brush the dirt off the blanket, whispering to her that I'm sorry for putting it on her. I begin to unwrap her face, then jerk the blanket back into place so she can't see she's in a grave. The thought of covering her back up and leaving her all alone sends a twinge through me and I frown. *She'd miss me so much . . .*

There's enough space beside her, so I lie down in the dirt and nuzzle my face against the side of her head, inhaling all that's left of her scent. I've missed her smell, the way it was before Huarsar sullied it with his mark. I hate how his scent merged with hers into something familiar, yet *wrong*. Closing my eyes, I wrap my arm around her torso, imagining her chest lifting under the weight of my arm. She doesn't mind the heaviness too much now.

My eyes fly open as the radio crackles. It shouldn't be on, but the static screeches through the room, disrupting my moment with Marianna. I grumble and stand, ready to leap out of the hole . . . but I can't leave her down there by herself.

"Don't worry, sweetheart," I whisper, unwrapping the blanket. "I'll get you out of here."

I leave the blanket behind and lift her into my arms, holding her tight as I climb out of the hole. Walking to the bed and past the radio, I shower her cheek in kisses as I step onto the mattress and set her down.

Meeting her eyes, a faint smile tugs at my lips as I murmur, "Much better than the cold grave, hm? You don't belong in there. That was silly." I rest her head on her pillow and stroke her hair out of her face. I imagine she would be quite cold down here still, so I draw the duvet up over her shoulder and close her eyes. "You can rest while we wait for Pluto to send you back."

The screech of the radio takes my attention again, and I scowl as I snatch it from the floor and flick the power button.

My brow furrows when it lights up, and I realize I merely switched it on. I flick the button back, but the noise continues.

"Modern garbage," I mutter as I flip it over and crack the battery compartment open. I pop the batteries out and drop them on the ground, but the crackling static continues.

A girl's voice crackles through, a quick burst that has me stiffening. *"I can't—"*

Gently, I smack the radio, but the noise continues, the voice cutting through the static a little more clearly. *"Hello?"*

Slowly, I turn to look at Marianna, who lies so still and quiet.

"Hello?" I whisper.

The popping and cracking of static continues in waves that shift from loud and ear-splitting to quiet and weak.

"He won't—"

Crackling.

I fidget with the knob, trying to find a stable frequency. I switch it on and try all the nearby stations, but none of them come through this time, so I flick it off and twist the knob again.

"Hide."

Pulling my hand away from the knob, I stare at the machine with no power source.

A surge of delight rockets through me, and I twitch with giddiness.

One of my girls is talking to me!

I bite my lip as I hold the radio, looking around like she might walk into the room instead. Maybe she's too scared. Often, they're scared.

"Hey there," I whisper. "It's okay."

"Don't—" The static crackles, and the voice comes through crystal clear. *"Help."*

I'm cold, the excitement draining from me as I grip the radio and scramble back onto the mattress next to Marianna.

"Sweetheart . . ." I pull the blanket away from her and softly lift her lids to meet her eyes. "I'm here, sweetheart."

Her mousy voice—so small and terrified—comes through the radio again with a screech of static that makes me grit my teeth. The needle moves across the radio, the frequency changing with a crackle.

"Emperor Huarsar."

I swallow a lump of fury. "You're safe," I assure her. "I've got you, Marianna. You're free from his mark. Huarsar can't hurt you now."

After I set the radio behind her and crawl beneath the duvet, I pull her limp body tight against mine and stroke her arm.

"He can't hurt you," I murmur in her ear, my body relaxing with the certainty that she can hear me now. "I'm sorry we fought, sweetheart. But I healed you. You can come back now . . . It's time to wake up."

"Where—"

"We're back in Vermont, sweetheart. I know you hate it here, but we're going right away. How about I take you home to Italy?"

"Can't—" Crackle. *"Rome."*

"Shh." I kiss her head and hold her tighter. "Huarsar won't find us there. I know it's close to Romania, but we'll be safe there, I promise. I'll give you a pretty dress when we arrive, okay? You'll love the villa—"

"The carriage."

My brow furrows. "Are you back in your body now, lost in the land of dreams? You could visit mine, sweetheart. We can talk better there."

"Denendrius."

My smile returns. "I'm here, sweetheart. I hear you."

"Don't leave—" Crackle. *"Help—"* The radio whines. *"Dead—"*

"Marianna . . ." I bite my bottom lip, holding my breath as I listen carefully.

"Please."

The sound of a horse snorting comes through, then the static stops with the radio dying.

The whisper of the forest returns to me in the new silence. Wind whistles through the trees, the sound of animals foraging and stalking through the trees so noisy now.

"Marianna," I murmur. "It's okay to wake up now."

I lie with her body pressed to mine, stroking her tender skin as the minutes stretch on. The ache of missing her grows unbearable until I unbutton my pants and indulge in her softness while I patiently watch for her life to return to her eyes.

Then I fall asleep with her, until thirty-three minutes later, when the sound of Sergei returning through the woods wakes me.

"You haven't buried her," Sergei notes as he returns to the room.

"I can't bury her at all. She's alive," I argue, stroking a hand down her arm. "I just heard her voice on the radio—"

He releases a frustrated sound. "Oh yes, and Jeanne fucking spoke to you in your dreams. The girls you'd bury at sea would return as sirens and serenade you. Marissa would sit and watch TV with you so long as you didn't look at her except in its reflection . . . You say they all come to you at some point."

"It's true," I snap as I sit upright and grab my boxers, putting them on beneath the blanket. "She spoke to me through the radio, *and* earlier she not only visited me in my dream, but she shaped it to show me a memory of when she was a child vampire."

"You are my friend, Denendrius, but you are fucking psychotic . . ." He heaves out a breath and runs his hand over his head. "They are hallucinations and dreams. Do you understand? You hallucinated and dreamed her."

I shake my head. "No, Sergei—"

"*She's fucking dead!*" Sergei screams at me. "She's dead, because you fucking killed her! Now bury her before I do!"

"She can't be dead," I spit as I stand and step off the bed. "I made a sacrifice to Pluto, and he'll make an exception for me. She can't be dead."

"And why not?" Sergei snarls. "You fucking raped and stabbed her. She bled out and fell into a coma! Marianna's dead because you made it so. No fucking god will send her soul back to you."

"*I love her!*" I bellow, the sound clawing up my throat and sending several small animals skittering away outside.

"Then *why*, Denendrius, *did you fucking kill her*?" Sergei says, his eyes full of fury and pity as he shakes his head at me.

I waver on my feet. "I—"

"Why, if you loved her so much?" He tilts his head.

My chest is tight like chains surround it. I can't breathe against them.

"Why, Denendrius?" he presses, pity pouring from his eyes as it twists his face.

My breath chokes me, and I slowly lower myself to my knees before I plummet to them against my will.

"Fucking feel something for once," Sergei snarls. "Remorse, sadness . . . just feel something."

I stare up at him, my hands limp in my lap.

"Feel something about *this*. You dressed her and cleaned her up, wrapped her in a blanket. I have never seen you do that. You're struggling to bury her when usually a shallow grave suffices. You are regretful, or guilty . . . you just need to feel it."

I screw my eyes shut and shake my head.

"You loved her," Sergei whispers, his voice coming to my level as his boots shift in the dirt. "You loved her for thirteen years. That's a long time for you, friend. You actually made it to *marriage* with this one."

I squeeze my eyes shut harder, not wanting to risk seeing the pity in his again. If Marianna would simply wake up, this conversation would end.

"You were the happiest I've ever seen you when you were with her. I watched you destroy yourself for decades years before her. Even with Marianne on her farm, you said you weren't this happy."

"She made me feel alive," I whisper.

"But you ruined it again, *da*? You destroyed that girl. You did worse than kill her. Why?"

I lean forward and plant my hands in the dirt, burrowing my nails in it. *"She made me so angry,"* I grind out, heat pulsing through me.

"You let your anger control you. I need you to feel something else for once. I need you to learn from this. Otherwise, at this point, you might consider ending it here with her."

My heavy, rapid breaths spray against the dirt. A tear works its way open in my center. "That's not a bad idea."

The grave is big enough for both of us. I could have him cut my heart out as I lay beside her.

He sighs. "You would really rather kill yourself than process your emotions?"

I tangled noise leaves me and I shift to my elbows. My skull burns, my eyes on fire. I gasp for breath.

Sergei scoots closer. "She's dead, Denendrius. You will have to come to terms that you will now have to spend the rest of your miserable fucking life without her. Can you imagine that?"

I grit my teeth, the tear splitting into a rift so painful that I inhale sharply against it and exhale a twisted cry. It's impossible to picture the future without her. My eyes burn so bad they water, and pressure builds in my skull.

"I don't know why," I cry, a sob rolling through my shoulders.

"She made me so angry, and hurting her made me feel so much better."

He shifts closer, inches between us now. "Did it, though? How does it make you feel now?"

"I want her to wake up," I cry. "I love her so much."

"Well," Sergei says, "dead girls don't wake up."

I grit my teeth and push back against that painful rift trying to open wider inside me. My chest heaves with breaths as I focus on forcing it shut. I squeeze my eyes closed and shake my head, refusing to let a single tear fall.

I shove it all away until my whole body is on fire and I can't bear Sergei being so close to me. Shifting upright, I slam my hand against his chest to get him away from me. In a squat, he loses his balance on impact and nearly falls backward into the grave.

"I will kill you!" I scream at him as I scramble to my feet.

I'll cut his head off if he pushes me to it!

"God, fuck!" Sergei hollers. "You are a fucking lost cause!"

A strangled laugh twists its way out of me. "Then why stick around?"

Sergei rights himself and sighs. "Because you need me. I fear what you'd do to the world if left alone in it."

Twisting around, I release a breath of disbelief. "I'm fine alone."

He laughs. "Oh really? Did you not spend your time between your last companions' death and finding me in a burning pile of rubble, hunting and killing vampires on your quest to find a cure for vampirism?"

I wave my hand dismissively at him. "That had nothing to do with being alone."

"I see." Sergei grunts. "Just bury your fucking wife and let's get out of here. Your sister is at home waiting for you."

My sister . . .

Turning, I give Marianna another long look. She's still so

beautiful. I can't fathom how he thinks she's dead when she looks so fresh.

Sergei gives me a rough pat on my shoulder, nausea and dread rocketing through me so viciously I twist away as he says, "She is waiting for a good explanation. Have fun."

An explanation won't matter when Marianna wakes up. Adelia will be so overjoyed to have her best friend back that she'll forgive me too.

Stepping back onto the mattress, I kneel over Marianna and meet her eyes as I run my fingers through her hair. "We're going home to Italy now, just like you wanted."

I imagine her smiling at me, telling me she's so excited, and a grin stretches across my face.

Until Sergei opens his mouth, and it falls. "Absolutely not. You're not bringing a fucking body on my plane."

"Hm." I give her a quick kiss, the feel of her mouth bringing my smile back. "I'm not. I'm bringing my wife home."

"I put all my morals and *everything* I stand for aside to be your friend, but I am not letting you taint my plane with a corpse. The things I overlook for you, Denendrius . . . The kidnappings, the *flings*, the murder and necrophilia—" He lifts his hand as my mouth opens to clarify. "Do not start another argument about the semantics of fucking dead bodies! It makes no difference if you stop before rigor mortis! It's all the same!"

I merely shake my head at him and scoff, silent so he can finish his tirade.

"I must draw the line somewhere, and I do not want my plane stinking like corpse. You know how hard the smell of death is to get out; you are emotionally attached to your morgue on wheels."

"The Mustang does not smell like corpse," I argue. Sure, the scent of many of my girls lingers, but *corpse* is quite dramatic, even for the trunk. "You act like I haul around bloated bodies."

He jabs a finger at me. "She's not coming—"

"I'm bringing her," I say, no room for negotiation in my hard tone. "If it's true she's dead, I'll bury her in the backyard so she's close to me. If I leave her here, I'll never see her."

Sergei stares at me. "No, you fucking won't."

I can't bite back the laugh that bubbles out of me. No, he's right. I'll tuck her into bed with me if she's still so soft and smells nice. I'll take advantage of all the time with her that Huarsar's blood grants me.

He relents with a groan. "Keep her in the duvet."

"Sergei, relax," I warn.

After wrapping her snug in the blanket so she's cozy, I cradle her in my arms with her head against my shoulder while Sergei and I traverse through the woods to the car, where I slide into the passenger seat and hold her on my lap.

"Ah yes, let's put the dead girl in the front seat," Sergei mutters as he climbs into the driver's seat. "They will pull us over."

"I'm not putting her in the trunk," I snarl. "She's going to wake up at some point. Would you want to wake up there? *You* could lie there if you prefer."

He lifts one hand in surrender while sliding the keys into the ignition with the other and turning the car on. Grunting, he backs up while saying, "But if she starts to stink . . ."

"She's not going in the trunk," I growl. "She smells fine."

He sets his jaw as he turns around on the dirt road and heads toward the highway.

"Music?" I ask, pulling the blanket away from the back of her head to free her hair so I can comb my fingers through the soft strands.

"Yeah, fine," Sergei grumbles as he fiddles with the seat to pull it forward a couple of inches.

"I wasn't talking to you," I utter as I kiss her forehead and switch the radio on, turning the knob to search for a station through the static.

"The trunk might not be so bad," Sergei says, throwing me a grin. "Probably less creepy back there."

"Shut up," I quip, and he laughs.

I scowl at the dashboard, unable to find anything on AM or FM but the irritating crackle and buzz of static. Heaving out a sigh, I mash the button to turn it off.

We speed down the road, and there's another two miles between us and the noisy truck ahead. The dark forest lines each side of the highway. I study the trees, the quick movements of wildlife between them, as I stroke Marianna's hair.

Sergei's tone is delicate as he says, "You understand it's likely Huarsar's blood postponing decomposition, *da?* She may have healed, but she didn't survive the transformation. We know how common that is . . . how bad the odds of survival are for Darklings. The severity of her injuries—the blood loss— didn't exactly help those odds either."

I lift my chin and inhale through my nose, my grip on her tightening.

"Okay," Sergei murmurs. "I'll let you figure it out for yourself, but I'll be there when you do."

Unfolding the blanket more, I lift her limp body and place her head on my shoulder and rest my cheek on top of it, my arms cradling her against my chest, her legs bent securely between my right one and the car door. Lifting her left hand, I spread her palm and fingers against my chest before stroking the back of her hand and forearm. Her flesh isn't warm as it was days ago, but her skin is so soft it's not worth caring about.

I lose myself in thoughts of the future as we fly down the highway. Reaching past the newborn vampire struggles, I imagine the villa full of warm, little smiling faces and toys. Their voices and giggles echoing through the long halls and tall rooms. Marianna's arms will be warm from the imprint of babies that I find for us. I know despite not being our blood, she will love them as much as I will, as much as she would have loved Aeliana had Huarsar not taken her from us.

Kissing the top of her head, I lift her head with a heavy inhale.

"I'm glad you're coming to live with us," I tell Sergei, a smile pulling at the corner of my lips. "It'll be good for our children to have an uncle." My smile grows. "I'm glad Marianna found Adelia . . . they'll have an aunt now, too."

"Mm." Sergei nods, his eyes trained on the road.

I pull in another breath and relax my head against the headrest. "You should aid me in finding Adelia a husband. Then they can find children, and ours will be cousins."

"*Da*, I could help you find someone for her."

I quirk a brow at him. "You should find yourself another wife too—one that you turn, so she doesn't die on you again—and get more children. The villa would be so lively with a family that size." My grin stretches at the thought. "Can you imagine it?"

Sergei shrugs, intensely focused on the highway ahead. "I don't feel the need for another wife right now."

I plant another kiss on the top of her head. "You know, I first told her we would turn our children when they were little, but we decided it'd be nice having grandchildren and adult children. Marianna and I could turn them in their late teens, and they could find husbands and wives and adopt children too. The villa is big enough for all of us. Then, perhaps your next children will play with my grandchildren."

He sets his jaw, his eyes glistening until he blinks.

"Did I upset you by bringing up your dead wife and your children?" I ask, fidgeting with the wedding ring on Marianna's finger.

"No, no," he claims. "It's not that."

I lift Marianna's hand off my chest and place her palm

against my cheek. Letting my lids slide shut, I focus on the feel of her flesh on mine as I inhale what's left of her scent and try to come to terms with the reality that I'm really returning to Rome after nearly two thousand years.

LVI

A red car waits on the runway, a human girl—who must be Adelia's familiar—behind the wheel, and Adelia in the passenger seat. Adelia steps from the car upon my approach, and I stretch my legs in the passenger seat with Marianna on my chest as she and her familiar move to the backseat. I keep my narrowed eyes trained on Marianna's face as Sergei crawls behind the wheel and drives us home.

I can't help my aversion to the surrounding sights. It feels intensely critical not to look at them. When Adelia reminisces about all the places she has begun to remember, I squeeze my eyes closed and rest my forehead against Marianna's.

"How does it feel to be home?" she asks me, an edge to her voice. "Everything is so different."

There's a hollowness in me, no emotion opting to fill it.

"I don't know," I admit.

Strange is not even an appropriate word.

Do I fear remembering; not that the memories aren't nearly as vivid as reality, anyway? What is it then, that has me hiding from simple buildings and roads, so tense in my seat it's as if I fear a horribly wicked sight?

I haven't seen Rome in years, and the lands of Italy on TV or magazines appear so unfamiliar when I've glimpsed them. I've avoided looking at what's left of my past, the ruins and historical documents—I despise museums—though the allure of fulfilling my wonders hasn't evaded me.

A few years ago, when the internet was becoming a wealth of knowledge, I had Sergei search for my name. I'd avoided any books pertaining to Roman history, but then, I wanted to know what the human world knew of me beyond my connection through their blood.

Was my name mentioned with the long-dead, great gladiators of Rome? Perhaps it wouldn't be as disappointing—so unfulfilling—if it were, and I was still loved. Perhaps my dreams—the training school I envisioned so clearly in my mind, the money accruing for it in my pocket—would carry no weight on me if I achieved something greater. What could be greater than immortal honor?

But I did not *exist*!

There were no records of my great battles, of the way the stands would scream for me as my swords sliced through the air and flesh. My hardships, my efforts, were part of nobody's memory but my own. It was like the night I died, thousands forgot my name. Forgot that they once loved me, cheered for me, wanted me.

I had been modestly popular in my days. Never had I been so loved before. For once, the public saw me for who I was. They didn't see my father's distaste, think about how I was just his brooding adoptive son, or care about the speculations that I had barbarian ancestors when *lanistas* practically salivated over my size and potential in the arena when I enrolled. The *lanistas* helped me control my fury, channel it and master it for fighting like it was Mars himself joining my side.

The public spoke of my dedication, the way I would return to my feet no matter the pain or blood coating me. No creature was too fearsome to fight, no opponent capable of making me waver.

They said I fought like Pluto had no interest in claiming my soul. In truth, it was because battle was all I lived for.

Until Marciana. Until her cinnamon eyes and sweet smile found me. Her daughter loved me so much, without even meeting me. From the seats—somewhere in the crowd that always appeared as a smear of adoration to me—she saw me for what I was.

Not for my wealth, for my family's rich lands and connections, or for the way many loved me. But for the simple thing she saw before her. My dedication with my blades, my passion. Marciana said she carried excitement for my battles as if she were the one fighting. My periodic injuries did not have her contemplating my career, my future worth to the public, or the money lost from pockets. She was concerned with my happiness, with how I might feel if I could no longer fight.

Yes, she was terribly young, merely six, and I could not yet imagine things with her as I would a woman. But if, by twelve, she was anything like her mother—so beautiful, so kind and happy despite all she lacked in riches—I would have been the luckiest man in the world.

I would have done anything to have Mariana as my wife and Marciana as my family. I would have padded Marianus's pocket in secret—feigned grand prosperity for his butcher shop and aligned other business opportunities for them—so my father could not turn an appealing dowry away. I would have married any girl to please him while I waited for Mariana to come of age, and prevented any child she might have attempted to bear so that Mariana would have the honor of birthing my first.

I would have gone as far as hiring dagger-men to reduce my

father to a corpse to strip. My grandfather was no longer alive—dead when my father was young, along with the rest of his legion on some battlefield—so I would become the *paterfamilias* and could marry whomever I pleased. Honestly, I considered it most days. The house would have been far more peaceful for my wife and our children, for my mother and all my siblings, if Father were no longer around. Under my control, I would have taken a taboo and progressive approach to their marriages. Who cared about more land or false allies, when one could have love? We would live by the gods' example and take whom our hearts desired.

But I did not have the shield that immortality gives me now. Had I been discovered and charged with patricide, it would have overshadowed my gladiatorial triumphs in my execution, and it would all be for naught.

I was not mentioned in any patrician records either, though neither was the rest of my family. Nary a business record, a certificate, or even the graffiti of my youth remained.

It felt intentional, like Huarsar ordered it to be done, though it was probably no more orchestrated than all the other greats whose names can never be spoken again in the human world. Still, that rationale did not remove the feel that the world no longer wanted me around. That I had no place in it.

I certainly didn't feel desired in it—especially not in that dark, vile dungeon beneath Huarsar's rule. Before the torture started, while they were searching for Marianus to give his testimony about turning and leaving me, I was convinced I would be released. That Marianus would be appalled by his mistake and seek to rectify it. I was intended to marry his daughter, after all, and she and Marciana cared about me.

But his lies damned me. I couldn't comprehend what I had done to deserve them.

As I clung to the passing years in agony, I waited for Marciana. I dreamed that Marianus had turned her into an immortal, and that she would seek me out and reveal the truth. Why wouldn't she? *She cared about me.*

Centuries later, I thought for a split second—through my starving, hazy gaze—that she had returned to me when a head of long brown hair approached my cell.

It was just Tatiana.

She was thirteen when she first came to my cell: beautiful, curious, and eager to hear my stories. She would sit beside my cell despite my condition. I had long since figured out hypnosis by then, observing the guards for centuries. I used the skill to ensure our meetings remained special and secret between us and the few guards who indulged her desire to visit in a quiet rebellion against Huarsar's rule.

Tatiana loved me and could no longer bear to see me suffer after a couple years. She knew her uncle Huarsar had the cure and spun her golden story around me—of us both being human and free, of how she'd bear my babies and be my perfect wife.

She fed me her blood the night I escaped. It gave me a strength similar to Marianna's marked blood, and I feigned weakness until the guards descended on me again. I tore them apart.

But she used me—ensnared me—only to painfully yank her hook out when we reached the Sava River. She couldn't get cure blood from Huarsar. She didn't even know where he kept it.

I laid my fury upon her as I did Marianna on our wedding night, just as I'd imagined doing to Marciana for centuries, for her refusal to set things right.

Tatiana succumbed to it, my hands around her pulsing throat. There was no brothel owner at the back of my mind then, no voice wielding consequences for a girl's death.

It felt as divine as I had always imagined. And I realized then that if the guards could do whatever they pleased to me for no deserved reason, then surely the gods would be fine with me enacting my own godly power. If anyone deserved to do as they wished, it was *me* after suffering so thoroughly.

I let out a breath against Marianna and shake the thoughts away. That's all ancient history, and all that matters now is my Marianna.

Still, it was nice, for a while, having Derek to speak with about my history, even with his fatherly sights on Marianna. He loved my stories, and it felt good to be seen for my achievements as a human, rather than my perceived transgressions as an immortal. I was happier than I could ever recall—my memories mostly blood, Sirmium, and turmoil—and certainly happier than I ever was as a vampire. He was desperate to hear everything for the simple purpose of knowledge, and because of that, I felt comfortable offering parts of myself I had once fretted over giving to Marianna. He didn't use my history like throwing knives, hidden and hoarded to be flung the moment he found an opening in my defenses—the way I feared Marianna would.

Marianna was wild when I returned to her life. I'd observed bits from afar and knew fury possessed her as it possessed me, but I convinced myself my presence would cast it out. And I had hoped her presence might banish mine as well. We were at such peace together when I first found her.

My anger slept when I found her in Enchanted Land. There was something about her eyes—it was the same quality Marciana's had possessed—that reminded me of the happiness and hope our first meeting had brought. I wanted to keep that feeling inside me, and I'd heard I might be able to experience it through my blood in her veins.

Before that, I had refused to mark another human. Even the ones I had intended to marry, so rarely did I even admit my immortality. I suppose I was not keen on giving so much of myself away. Despite the danger of a fragile target my blood would create, I did not love them enough to be so close to them.

I had never felt such simple, pure happiness after I marked her. The world lost a bit of its dark tinge when I saw it through her eyes—processed and transformed into wonder. It felt as if the gods had finally decided my centuries of turmoil were enough, and were doing their best to return me to the life I had been forced to leave behind.

So they placed a little girl there—five, so close in age to Mariana—who bore her name and stared at me with the same wonder and love, without ever having met me, that Marciana once described. Venus must have instructed Cupid to prick Marianna, as she took to me so quickly, walking away with me as if the gods had visited her in her dreams and told her to wander from her family and wait for me to find her.

It was perfect timing. Sergei was settled in a house I had purchased in Maine—I needed something to invest my money in—and was taking a leisurely approach to his immortality. He seemed awfully lonely and still spoke of his children so often that I thought he would be elated to raise Marianna for me. Our trip there was the most pure, carefree fun and joy I'd ever experienced. I wanted it to last forever.

Yet she began to ache for her adoptive parents, and my happiness waned with her homesickness. I wanted to keep her, but I couldn't deny how kind Vianna and Kenneth sounded from her recounting. I would have been blessed to be adopted by people like them. I couldn't bring myself to deprive her of the experience of a whole home. She wouldn't have had a mother to teach her if I'd left her with Sergei.

But knowing what I do now, I squeeze Marianna's body tighter and remind myself that the fates have done what they have for a reason beyond my comprehension.

I suppose I should have known none of that happiness was truly my own. Not a single flicker.

For years, when my anger returned twofold and I grew more antsy to have her back in my life, I thought it was merely because she was so far from me. I thought that the moment we were together again, that blissful, simple happiness would come pulsing back.

I didn't consider that her unhappiness, her fury, was feeding my own through the mark.

For our first few dates, something mimicking happiness shuddered at the edges of me. It was hope, relief, and just enough of a twinge of the real thing to convince me it was returning.

But when she said she never wanted to see me again?

It had been years since I'd felt such burning fury!

It was unbearable, and knowing what the fates had planned was the only thing that stopped me from driving to her foster home the moment I hung up that call and laying my fury upon her as I did on our wedding night.

Back then, I wasn't completely sure who I should direct my anger at. The gods? Myself, for not being a seer, for not being wise to their plans, for trusting the human world to care for her while I continued on before returning to her? The vampires who refused to give up their pursuit of me?

It didn't matter. Marianna bore the brunt of all my anger.

If I could go back . . .

I would swallow my fear of those throwing knives, take them as they came and try to understand the circumstances that shaped the hands that threw them, or find a better way to approach without getting hit. Then I would return to her foster home with flowers and an apology for scaring her, as so many other men had.

I would bring the tapes and the boxes full of memories and show her, *tell her everything*, instead of waiting for her to remember on her own or force the truth from me.

Perhaps she finally remembered and was confused by the

reality of her memories, but hated me for leaving her. That is the easiest—the least painful—explanation I tell myself. I can understand how she might have felt betrayed, or as if she'd been abandoned.

It's shameful to admit, even to myself, but I was scared. Scared she would believe me . . . that I'd jog her memory, and it still wouldn't matter. That she wouldn't be able to move past her hurt.

Or worse . . . *undoubtedly worse*. She remembered, and she wasn't mad because of my actions. She simply didn't want me. I feared the reality that even with the truth laid bare between us, even with her acceptance, she would still change her mind. If the gods had made her anything like Mariana—as I suspected they had—I would never be able to keep her interest with money. Though I knew she yearned for it, and feared not having enough of it, I didn't believe it could make her love.

What if she couldn't cope with my inability to give her biological children? As an adopted child, I worried she might long for a blood connection of her own. What if it was all too unusual for her?

I knew, even when she was a child, that she didn't fear the reality of vampires, but she was desperate for the mundane comforts of the human world. I would wake to the sound of the hotel TV, and it was always a struggle to get her off it. But sweets and new foods, promises of parks or adventures, would always stop her tears.

I understood the ache for normality she had, as so many days passed when I wished I could wake up back in Rome. I would have taken my family's dysfunction and all the mundane problems in my life if it meant I could have that hope back. In a way, perhaps that's why we bonded so well. I enjoyed watching her experience all the things she'd never had before, due to being a child vampire and her entrapment with her whore of a mother, Bonnie, whom she would tearfully talk about.

It would have been a waking nightmare if she had felt amicable toward me in her rejection. That would have meant I simply wasn't good enough for her. If she remembered me—if she smiled and laughed while we reminisced about our twelve days of adventure—then hugged me and said she missed me and still cared about me . . . *but didn't want me?* That would have been the most unbearable outcome. If she thought I was handsome and sweet, but *only if I were human.* She was happy knowing about the immortal world, but she didn't ever want to be a part of it. If she thought I was wonderful, but preferred a human husband who could give her biological children and a normal life. I know she would have had an upper-class life, with a nice home and a job she loved, a huge extended family to fill her heart.

Marianna was so beautiful, so smart, and so bold that rich men would have fought to make her their bride. I know that as soon as she turned eighteen—when she was forced to face the realities of adulthood and sink or swim—she wouldn't have ended up the way she feared: homeless and addicted to drugs. She was far too brave and bold. She faced my fury like it was a beast she could slay. I hated when she fought me, but the truth was, I couldn't fathom how she had the strength.

She could have thanked me for saving her from the overdose and finally returning to her life, yet still turned me away with kindness. I would have been her wake-up call—a reminder that she once wanted so much more from life. She would have graduated, probably gone to art school. Even as a child, she was a magnificent artist. She would have found a husband and had beautiful little children like Aeliana. She would have had the life she always wanted.

I know she would have, and I hate the truth that she would have been okay without me.

Then what of me? Because I would not have been okay without her!

It was only when I was given the cure that she finally accepted her love for me. When I was *human* and normal. But that wasn't what I truly wanted, because it wasn't humanity I longed for. It was Rome. But the cure isn't a time machine.

By the gods, I would have killed myself! I might have done it right then, too weak to even get up.

No, that's a lie. My fury would have overcome my pain, as it always has, and killed us. If I hadn't had the sense to drive home and pour cure blood down my throat in front of her—hoping she'd love me—I would have made her hate me before I killed us.

I loved Marianna so deeply it terrified me. I'd never felt something but anger so strongly before.

I loved her *so much.*

"Denendrius?" a soft, tentative voice says. "*Denendrius, are you okay?*"

There's a burning agony in my chest, so heavy and hot like a cannonball. It punches through me and the force is so crippling I can't breathe.

I can't breathe.

It's not that I need the air. It's the discomfort and the false agony seizing my lungs that brings the panic.

A deep, tangled sob escapes me when I finally manage a breath and my flesh, my limbs, and muscles are sharp with agony. It's like death by a thousand cuts, *though I cannot die and this should kill me.*

If it could just kill me!

"Denendrius?" she asks again. "*How can I help?*"

I want it to be Marianna. I want to lift my head off the quickly growing spot of tear-soaked fabric covering her body, and for it to be Marianna murmuring my name. But I know it isn't and never will be.

Because she can't breathe, so she will never say my name again.

Sobs wrack me, my whole body shaking in my seat as I grip her against my chest.

"She's dead," I wail. *"She's dead, and she's never coming back."* I gasp for breath, the pain so sharp and gripping I want to tear my clothes and flesh off and drown myself in the Tiber River. I fight to swallow my sobs down, to punch this feeling away so I don't have to deal with it, but there's nowhere to hide it. It pours out of me like a torrential flood that wrenches away any stable ground I could have used to bury this.

It's so catastrophic that it sweeps everything out of hiding.

"She's dead. I killed her," I cry. *"I don't know why I killed her. I loved her so much! I loved her, and I killed her."*

My heavy breaths pull in the strange, unfamiliar air of Rome, along with the acrid stench of gasoline that tells me the car has been idling for some time. I lift Marianna's body with me as I straighten, tipping my head just enough to peer over her shoulder through my tears. The villa stands before us, and it's so quiet . . . as noisy with heartbeats as it ever will be.

Because Marianna is never coming back.

There will never be a villa full of happiness and love, with a wife who loves me, and little children who will never have to understand how cruel a father could be.

It will never happen. The fates did not intend it for me.

They have brought me back to Rome to die with the same pain I tried to leave behind. It must be what the gods intended, that I never leave at all. For me to die where Marciana and Marianus dumped me—*worthless*, as if they'd never intended me to be their family—with not even enough care to grant me a proper burial so I could cross the River Styx. They cared so little, they would have made me a *lemure.*

"I loved her," I choke out. *"Why did I have to die? Why did all this have to happen to me? I was finally happy."*

A soft touch lands on my shoulder, but it's like a singeing coal and I yank out from under Sergei and cry out. "Don't touch me!" I plead, hunching over Marianna's body as sobs wrack me. *"Please don't touch me."*

"My friend," Sergei starts, the pity in his voice another twist in my chest. "I am *so sorry*."

My sobs are deafening, and sitting here under their pitying scrutiny is unbearably shameful. I hold Marianna tight to myself and shove the car door open with my weak arm. I don't know where I plan to run. It doesn't matter anyway, because I only get one foot on the ground before I collapse on the gravel as I try to stand.

I can't care anymore about how Sergei and Adelia see me crack apart with weakness. I can't get my feet back under me, can't even pull my arm from its protective hold around her body to slam the car door shut as some sort of false shield between them and me.

So I curl up on the ground, holding Marianna while sobbing, wishing the great Sol would drive his chariot across the sky early so I can burn.

I bury my face in Marianna's hair as I lie on my side with her body pulled against me, my arms so tight Sergei will have to kill me if he wants to pry her from me. I'll rot beside her. Really, I should run to the amphitheater and lie there with her in wait for sunrise. It would have been better if I died in battle. That day had brought a brutal fight, and if I hadn't won, I wouldn't have met Marciana later that day.

I would be dead right now, *but I would have lived.* I would have lived and died, with my only legacy being what I worked so hard for.

The radio crackles, so loud from the car it's like a jolt of electricity struck me.

"Hello?" she says, and I'm so shaken I can't move. But my tears continue, and I know Sergei was right. She's not really there. Marianna is not waiting to come back to me.

She's dead.

"He-Hello?"

I roll half on top of her, squeezing my eyes closed. *"Please stop,"* I cry, begging my mind to rid the hallucination. "Please stop talking to me."

"Help—"

"Denendrius..." Sergei says carefully, but there's an edge to his voice that has my distrust flaring. "I don't think your girl there is dead."

I shake my head. *"Please,"* I beg him. "Don't do that. Don't treat me like I'm a crazy person who needs to be handled carefully. I know she's dead. I know you're right that she's not coming back."

The sound of waves breaks through the static, and someone gasps for breath. *Like someone drowning.*

She speaks through the radio again, her plea coming with a gulp of breath. *"Help—"*

There's a static screech that has Sergei cursing and turning the car off. But the static continues, and a frantic cry leaks from the radio and fills the quiet air.

"What's wrong with the radio?" Adelia asks. "That sounded like Marianna."

The car engine roars to life, and Sergei—having not started it—slowly pulls his hands away from the wheel.

"What the fuck?" he breathes. Then, to me, he shouts, "Open her eyes."

I shake my head against her body, unable to bear looking into her void eyes again, knowing they will never be full of life.

"Open her eyes," he demands curtly.

Gritting my teeth, I turn my face away and lift my shaky hand to lift her lids for him.

"Shit!" Sergei's tense exclamation has my eyes flying wide and my teary stare dropping to Marianna's face.

A void, crimson gaze stares back. There's no life there, but

. . .

"Oh my god," Adelia's excitement has me staring up at her, confused, as she scrambles out of the car. "The transformation worked? How?"

She drops beside me, her excitement so at odds with my grief that I merely reel and stare at her in crippling confusion, trying to understand what the gods have done.

"What?" I breathe, shaking my head.

"When was the last time you checked on her?" Sergei adds as the car turns off, appearing at my feet with his arms crossed.

"What?" I echo, my wet face twisted in disbelief as I stare up at him, the moon blinding past his shoulder. "You've been trying to get me to accept she's dead. I just . . ."

Adelia touches Marianna's face with the back of her hand, and I jerk Marianna tighter against my chest. Is this some ploy to have me release her so they can snatch her for burial? So they can hide her somewhere I can't visit, somewhere more difficult for her spirit to follow and find *me*?

"She lost so much blood," Adelia says. "What if she's comatose with thirst and can't wake up?"

"I've never heard such a thing for newborns." Sergei grunts. "But I'd like to know why it seems she's talking through the fucking radio."

"It's her spirit." It's the only rational explanation. She's doing everything she can to stay with me, even through death. To assure me she's not angry with me, despite the grief of our physical separation.

"Shut up about ghosts," Sergei demands. "They're not real. She's got power of some kind."

"She was full of Viorel's blood," Adelia starts. "It was already affecting her ability to go in the sun and consume garlic. Maybe she was inheriting his immortality—"

"She was a child vampire," I snap. "The DNA in his blood was affecting the fragments of hers."

"That's not what Viorel says," she disagrees.

"He's a liar . . ." I shake my head and stare down at her again, trying to grapple with the whiplash of fighting the reality of her permanent death, accepting it, only for it all to be torn away so suddenly and returns with everything I had hoped for. "She's alive?"

"She's a vampire," Sergei corrects. "You lucky fucking bastard."

I laugh, a twisted and strangled sound that has more tears brewing in my eyes. "The gods . . ." I don't have the breath to explain as I stare down at her beautiful face and shower it with kisses.

The gods care about me. About my Marianna and me. They worked through us on our honeymoon to ensure I didn't deviate from our fate by refusing to turn her. *Of course they did.* They heard my hesitation—my worries about making her immortal—and cared enough to intervene. To help me. It wasn't my fault I nearly killed her. They made me take her to the edge of death so I'd have no choice but to turn her.

They let me suffer for days as her soul waited safely nearby, to force me to prove to myself that she mattered to me enough. That I could cope with her vampirism. That I could bear the thought of her as immortal—her strength, her coldness, the absence of her human warmth and scent—as the alternative to losing her. They weren't punishing me for the fury I laid on her body, but for my hesitation to fully take her as forever mine. I should have bitten her the moment she begged me to. *I promised*, then retreated. Breaking that vow was an affront to the gods. To the fate they had spun with such care for us.

I promise this now: *I will never retreat from our love again.*

Pluto put that bull in my path to remind me they are here for me, to see if I would put all my trust in them. They knew I needed to believe she was dead for a moment, so I could understand that her being immortal was the best way to love her for eternity instead of from a grave. In the flesh. Of course they would choose my admission to send her back to me. They don't want me to believe I killed her. They don't want me to suffer so deeply, just *understand.* They wanted to show me grief and regret without her so I would *never again* lose faith in the eternal story they threaded for us.

I tell him how thankful I am in Latin as I spread my kisses over Marianna's face, Adelia's tickled giggle making me grin and lift my face to hers. "You have your best friend back."

She grins, pressing her teeth into her bottom lip, then finds one of Marianna's hands beneath the duvet and takes it tightly in her own. "Mia!" she calls over her shoulder. Then to me, she says, "We'll give her human blood. Then, she'll wake up."

"Perfect, then she can explain why she's talking through the fucking radio," Sergei says.

I don't care about that, I just want to hear her voice say my name again and tell me she loves me. I lock my eyes on her pretty face, the sound of Mia's approach making my mouth salivate with thirst.

Mia kneels down next to Adelia, who moves her wristwatch aside to add another two puncture wounds to the collection.

The sight—the delicious scent—of her blood has me enthralled until the hands spinning on her wristwatch have confusion shoving my thirst to the back of my mind.

"She's fucking with electricity," Sergei declares. "She inherited one of the king's abilities from his blood, *da*? Could he do *that*?"

Adelia shrugs. "I don't know. There wasn't much electricity at the castle. He's more Child of Stars than Darkling, depending on how you look at it. Maybe so much of his blood and DNA swayed the venom in that favor. I mean, Darklings are basically just one lineage of super powerful Children of Stars with a stable collection of inherited abilities . . . We technically aren't two different species."

"So you think she's a Child of Stars?" Sergei asks. "That the transformation reverted to the old origins in Denendrius's venom?"

"How should I know? I may be ancient, but I don't know everything. I'm not even sure Viorel knows how it all works." Adelia pulls Mia's wrist away from Marianna.

Blood pools in Marianna's mouth, a slow trickle down the back of her throat that has me sighing with a twinge of disappointment that she did not simply spring to life.

I run my fingers over her soft flesh, her temperature like mine now. "It would explain why I was waiting for the change to happen. Why her eyes did not shift from brown so quick."

Does that mean, when she's well fed, I'll still get to enjoy the sweet cinnamon of her eyes? How lovely.

"So she can manipulate electricity," I murmur, running my fingers over her cold lips to collect the leftover blood on them. "That's a strange ability."

Yet potentially *very* useful.

I lick Mia's sweet blood off my fingers, and a fire ignites in my throat. Swallowing it down, I tell myself I don't have time to feed. *Not yet.* I need to focus on Marianna and figure out why it's taking so long for her to wake.

LVII

The room is cast in a deep red glow, illuminating the thick steam that's collected in the bathroom from the bubbling Jacuzzi water teeming with rose-scented bubbles. I clutch Marianna to my chest in it. The heat is glorious, and would give Marianna's pallid flesh third-degree burns if not for her immortality.

If only she would wake and enjoy it with me instead of how she lies limp with her head resting back against the seat of the tub.

I sigh as I comb conditioner through the strands of her hair with the same floral brand she preferred as a human.

Gentle—still so used to her being fragile—I brush the back of my fingers against her cheekbone as I stare into her starving, claret eyes. "The water is nice, isn't it?" A small smile curves my lips, and I lean forward and press them to hers. The ridges of fangs through her supple lips have me grinning wider. "Thirsty girl, you've let your fangs down now."

I press my thumb against her upper lip; a strange surge of excitement at the sight of her fang squeezes my heart.

Because I made her—this forever beautiful girl.

She's eternally mine.

I find I don't quite mind that her skin is now the same temperature as mine, when the feel of it remains unchanged. Her human scent has washed away, and though I wish I could bury my face in her hair and breathe it in, I'm just thankful I'll never have to know the smell of her decaying body. I know I'll grow accustomed to her new scent in time, but it's not the same. Perhaps I'll love it more when I've known her longer as an immortal than I did as a human.

As I press my teeth into my bottom lip in thought, I lift my arm from the soapy water and wipe the bubbles from my wrist. Her jaw opens under my guidance. I raise my wrist to her fangs, inhaling sharply at the sensation of them pushing into my vein. The sting of her venom is surprisingly strong. *I like it.* Just as I love the sight of my blood drizzling onto her wet tongue.

"Drink, sweetheart," I plead. "Taste me."

Her venom keeps the incisions from healing, and I let her mouth fill before drawing my wrist away and tilting her head back so it'll trickle down her throat.

Her throat . . .

My breath hitches, and though I hate how there's no frantic pulse to rest my gaze on, the curve of her neck is no less appealing. I glide my lips over it, my throat on fire with the memory of her hot blood splashing onto my tongue and burning down into my belly. I release a groan into her soft flesh, my fangs releasing in anticipation. Human or not, I bet she still tastes heavenly . . .

I bite into her with the same care as always, her thirsty body giving her flesh no more strength than she had when she was human.

Only this time—my slow heart skips a beat, a pang knifing

through my middle—there's nothing. Her veins are as dry as mine have been at the hands of my torturers. My breath catches, the silence of her body deafening. Whatever blood she left the hotel with, has been all but used up by the transformation. But in her? Truly, *nothing*.

"Breathe," I beg her. She may not need oxygen, but her body should still automate the process. I search her eyes for consciousness—I was conscious when Haursar's men bled me and locked me in that metal box despite my body not having the blood to move to my demands or breathe—but her crimson gaze is so far away. "It's been days, Marianna. The transformation should only be a handful of hours. This blood should have awoken you."

What more can I do if my own immortal blood isn't enough to wake her?

Panic twists in my gut, writhing into a beast that claws at my insides. My hands clamp down on her corpse-pale shoulders, shaking her limp body with reckless force. *"Wake up!"* I bellow, my voice echoing off the tiles.

She doesn't even flinch, only slumps against the tub as I release her. Her head lolls to the side as my blood leaks from the corners of her mouth.

I push myself away from her to the other side of the Jacuzzi and rake my hands through my wet hair, a sudden pressure on my chest. My breath comes in shallow bursts. What if she never wakes? What if there is no amount of blood capable of pleasing her comatose body? Could this be my fault? My venom, my blood—what if it wasn't enough to complete the transformation? What if I've failed her in the worst way possible, trapping her between life and death?

Or, what if her past as a child vampire returned human has corrupted her body in ways I cannot comprehend?

I cover my face with my hands. My breath pulses back at me, and I groan in agony.

A realization rushes forward. *"No."* I lower my hands and shake my head. "She'll wake up." I lift my eyes to hers, voice softer as I say, "You'll wake up. The gods could not be so cruel as to tease me with your life."

Leaning my head back, I stare up at the ceiling as I steady my breaths and ponder everything I know about Huarsar. I analyze every painful memory of him and a striking commonality sticks out to me. Never once have I seen him without his eyes bright with thirst, and his fangs waiting.

I straighten, bubbles and water rippling around me.

Power like Huarsar's would require vast amounts of blood to sustain . . .

"I know what you need," I assure her.

Leaping out of the Jacuzzi brings a flood of water onto the terracotta tiles. I twist to retrieve Marianna, so used to the worry of her drowning when I'd bathe with her unconscious human body.

"I'll be right back," I promise. "Enjoy the bath, sweetheart."

I hope that if she's conscious, the heat helps alleviate even a fraction of the thirst that must be tormenting her.

After a quick rinse in the glass shower, I swiftly dry and slip into a pair of boxers before finding Sergei downstairs and sending him off to the nearest hospital.

When I return to the bathroom, Marianna is as still as I left her.

I crouch beside the tub, brushing her hair back from her face, my fingers lingering on her soft cheek. "You're going to have a bigger appetite than me, aren't you?" My lip twitches with a frail smile as fantasies of us feeding together flicker through my mind—our mouths pressed to opposite sides of a hot, pulsing throat, competing for our fill.

I'll let her win every time.

With the water having lost its warmth, I hoist Marianna from the tub and rinse her body before carrying her into our attached bedroom. I lay her on the maroon duvet that covers the gilded four-poster bed.

I straighten her head so she can see the painting on the vaulted ceiling. The gods watch over us as I dry her, the detailed, passionate faces of Venus and Mars at the center of them all. I steal glances at it, seeing it for the first time today and pleased the artist was worth the cost.

I find the lacy black princess gown in the wardrobe, where I had Sergei place it so many months ago. It's reminiscent of the black gown I bought her at Enchanted Land—about as close as he could instruct the seamstress to make it, given it's meant for a woman to wear. After slipping her into black velvet panties, I pull the dress over her body.

The sight of her crushes my heart. *So beautiful.* I run my hands over her, cherishing the way the fabric hugs the curves and lines of her upper body. After a long kiss, I move on to fixing her hair, pinning it into braids at the crown of her head the way she loves so much. I straighten the diamond hearts in her lobes, the ring on her finger, and the bracelet on her wrist. Then I align her arms alongside her body and talk to her while I wait for Sergei's return.

The crunch of tires down the driveway has me holding my breath, the rapid beat of a heart in the truck leaving me both curious and tense.

"Please tell me you have the blood bags and the nurse wasn't your last resort," I say, my voice carrying evenly through the open bedroom door, down the hall, and downstairs to where Sergei opens the front door.

"She's a bonus," he replies, her heart racing—feet pounding, metal clanging—as she scrambles to keep up with Sergei's brisk strides.

Relief floods me as he enters, two large white coolers stacked in his arms, a black bag brimming with supplies dangling from one elbow. The nurse—a brunette in pink scrubs—stands behind him, her green eyes flicking wildly around the room as she clutches an IV stand.

"How much?" The words rush out of me as I step forward.

Sergei grins. "Sixty-two units. Snatched a few extra for ourselves since there was a blood drive the other day."

I lock eyes with the nurse, catching a faint, even focus in her shifting gaze—a sign Sergei has already prepped her for instruction. "Ready my wife," I order in Italian, gesturing toward Marianna with a lazy flick of my hand. "Go on."

The nurse nods and carries the IV stand to the bedside, her terror-filled eyes darting between Marianna's crimson stare, Sergei, and me.

Sergei sets the coolers down and hands the black bag to the nurse, who accepts it with a trembling hand. "I can't imagine she'll need every blood bag, Denendrius. She's a small girl, and that's the equivalent of six humans' worth of blood."

"She's starving," I argue as Adelia bounds into the room, eyes bright with teary excitement.

"Can I help?" She looks at the coolers, raising a brow at the nurse, who slips a needle into each of Marianna's inner elbows.

I wince at the memory of her heroin addiction.

I nod toward the bathroom. "Fill the Jacuzzi with body-temperature water to warm the blood bags. You're in charge of cycling it. There should be a thermometer in the black bag."

"Got it!" She finds the thermometer and bounds off to the bathroom.

I'm thankful Marianna's survival has eroded Adelia's anger at me.

Soon, two warm blood bags dangle from the IV stand, my mouth on fire at the sight of red trailing through the plastic tubing and into Marianna's veins. My fangs refuse to retreat no matter how I will them, and if Marianna didn't need the blood more than me to gain consciousness, I'd be on the floor sucking them back faster than her veins are . . . which is at a surprising frequency in itself.

After fifteen minutes, Marianna's body has already consumed six blood bags, which alarms the nurse, who is used to patients absorbing only one over the course of several hours.

My words are sharp against my dry throat. "She's a thirsty girl."

Yet she still doesn't wake.

After the nurse swaps two more blood bags, my thirst claws at me, barely contained. I busy myself prettying the room for Marianna, avoiding the sight of the blood coursing through the tubes. I arrange dozens of candles on every surface, lighting them carefully before flicking off the chandelier to keep the artificial light from piercing her fresh eyes when she finally wakes.

With midday approaching, I call a local florist and place an expensive order for every color of rose they have, along with vibrant bouquets in hues designed to make any girl swoon.

The sweet scent and vivid colors will calm her when she inevitably wakes, likely disoriented and panicked. With a single glance at the flickering candles and the hundreds of flowers, she'll know without a doubt that I still love her.

The first florist calls back, utterly lost, claiming there's no villa to be found. I send the nurse to stand in the garden and check, and predictably, there's no car on the road she claims to be driving up and down on. My patience thins as I cast off the incompetence and contact a different kent florist, who finds the villa without issue.

By the time the room smells like a florist's shop, Marianna has drained forty blood bags. I pace, restless.

"Why won't she wake up?" Adelia asks from where she sits beside Marianna on the bed.

"I don't know," I snap, my tone biting.

After four more bags with no change, I want to tear my hair out. My breaths come heavier, and I inspect the wooden floor beneath my feet, half-expecting to find wear from my pacing.

Sergei shoots me a tensely serious look I don't quite understand.

"What?" I snarl.

"Have you ever heard of such a thing like this happening?" There's a wary edge to his voice.

I freeze, my head tilting as I grind out, *"What do you think?"*

"I'm just wondering if—"

An abrupt silence crashes over the villa as the power cuts. The hum from the kitchen dies mid-whirr, the buzz of lights in every room gone in a blink. Even the faint static in the walls vanishes, leaving the air heavy and still.

My eyes shift to Marianna, the IV lines limp and drained.

The room plunges into darkness as dozens of candles snuff out, thin curls of smoke ascending from the blackened wicks.

I swallow hard, my muscles tight as I stand rigid. *"Sweetheart?"*

My slow heart lurches as the villa erupts in noise, the room flooding with light from flame and bulbs in an instant. A radio crackles with pop music from Adelia's room upstairs, and the television blasts the end of the Italian movie she started nearly two hours ago. Every bulb hums with electricity, the entire villa thrumming with energy.

I force my feet to carry me to her and scoop up her hand to hold in my lap. "Marianna?"

"Adelia . . ." Sergei begins carefully. "What abilities are you aware of Viorel having?"

Her trembling voice puts me on edge. "Pyrokinesis, telekinesis, veiling, mind reading—"

"Any that might impact her awareness?" I demand. "Her . . .

abilities . . . are clearly developing out of control. What if it's not the transformation affecting her consciousness?"

Adelia frowns, the tension in her brow deepening. She gives a helpless shrug.

I cut my gaze to the nurse. "Give her more blood," I order tersely in Italian.

The nurse jumps to her feet and dashes to the bathroom.

Sergei releases a hesitant grunt. "Is that a good idea, Denendrius? She's burning through blood bags."

"She's thirsty," I snarl.

"You're feeding her powers," he counters, arms crossed. "And they're consuming more than we can keep up with."

I jerk to my feet. "I'm feeding my wife!" I bellow at him, venom spraying past my lips. *"She's trying to wake up!"*

A voice comes through the static of the radio upstairs. *"Help—"*

The ache in my chest is a branding iron against my heart. My voice cracks as I utter, "She's trying to wake up . . ."

The audio from the TV becomes clipped as channels rotate.

"Viorel—" Pop music cuts through the sounds of her voice. *"Fantasy—"*

I'm frozen as I hold my breath and beg to hear her voice more.

The radio station changes, an Italian man talking about the weather until—

"Hello?" The sound of ocean waves fills the room upstairs through the frequency. Her voice comes as a whisper, so quiet I'm not fully convinced I'm not misinterpreting static. *"I'm scared."*

I heave out a breath and stumble back, sinking onto the edge of the bed as the nurse exchanges the empty bags for two fresh ones.

"I'm here with you," I whisper to her, linking my fingers

through hers again and cupping her soft face with my other hand. "You're safe."

Her voice comes crystal clear mere feet from me then, heavy and hopeless. *"Am I dead?"*

But her lips remain still, her vacant eyes fixed on the ceiling.

My lips twitch as I try to form words. "Am I losing my mind?"

"I heard her too," Adelia whispers.

"Me as well . . ." Sergei shifts away a bit. "Is Viorel telepathic—?"

The bed trembles, the gold-plated feet rattling against the hardwood and sending Adelia and me scrambling backward. The frame vibrates beneath Marianna, shifting sharply a few degrees. Marianna's arms roll inward, the tubes twisting and cutting off the flow of blood. We're speechless statues until the movement settles, the bed stopping slightly skewed and pulled a few inches away from the wall.

"Denendrius . . ." Sergei says, as if there's *anything* I can do about this.

I motion toward Marianna, my gaze pinning the trembling nurse. In Italian, I say, "Fix the IVs."

Jittery, she moves to Marianna's side, sitting cautiously on the edge of the bed. Her sweaty fear lingers, sharp against the floral scent filling the room. Her heartbeat pounds in my ears, frantic as she reaches across Marianna, gripping her right hand to flip her arm over and straighten it. She reaches for Marianna's left hand and—

The nurse collapses across her body.

I suck a sharp breath in.

Adelia moves forward like she believes the nurse has merely fainted from fear and plans to continue the adjustment herself.

"Don't," Sergei warns, and she stops dead in her tracks.

I close my eyes in defeat when the radio crackles upstairs, interrupting an English rock station.

"Hello?" Marianna asks, her voice louder than the static this time. *"Who are you?"*

My lids fly open at that, my brow furrowing as the nurse's voice cuts through the static. She frantically asks in Italian where she is—how she got there—which makes Sergei and me exchange a look.

Rock music pulses through the sound of waves, then parts for Marianna's desperate, tear-filled voice. *"I can't understand you. I don't speak Italian."*

An unnatural pain ricochets through my skull, and Adelia and Sergei must feel it too as he staggers backward as Adelia releases a surprised, *"Ow!"*

Adelia giggles, the bubbly sound making me slowly rotate to stare at her in disbelief. Clutching her head in her hand, she shrugs and says, "Well, a seer *did predict* that she would be a powerful vampire."

But the humor quickly vanishes from her face as the room seems to shudder. Furniture shakes, candles and vases toppling over and clattering—shattering—on the hardwood. The crystal chandelier tinkles as the light flickers erratically, then the bulbs burst, casting the room in shadow.

I flinch as a window shatters behind me, the heavy green curtain remaining in place between me and the sun. Yet despite the wind's gentle breath against the trees outside, a quiet, airy whistle sneaks into the room as the nurse's heart pounds like a war drum.

"Oh my god!" Adelia falls backward in a gasping heap of terror and scrambles back to press her body against the wall.

I throw my gaze back to Marianna.

The nurse's skin shifts and grays, pulling taut over her shriveling muscles and pressing against the shape of her bones like thin, shrunken leather. Her heart shudders and halts. A guttural groan squeezes from her widened mouth, as if the air is being slowly crushed from her lungs. Her skin cracks—thin and brittle—her body bloodless as bone splits through. The bed rattles as her mummified form rolls to the floor in a contorted mess of scarcely attached limbs.

Blood moves through the plastic tubing like liquid through a straw, both bags shriveling as they're sucked dry.

I must be dreaming.

"What the fuck." Breathless beside me, Sergei chokes out, "Denendrius, *we must kill her.*"

"I can't," I force out through strained breaths. "I love her."

Her voice comes through the radio again. "H-hello? Lady? Where'd you go?"

"What the fuck is Viorel?" Sergei chokes out in horror. "She fucking siphoned her entire life force. *Blood and all.*"

"I-I don't know." I swallow hard, my thoughts snapping back to Dr. Sampson's office, when he told us they found Huarsar's DNA in her blood. "A geneticist studied anomalies in Marianna's blood without our consent when she was under-going fertility treatments. The base DNA was only *partially Homo sapiens.* The other sequences were from the *Homo* genus … but essentially undiscovered."

"You could have shared that," Sergei snaps.

I shrug. "I didn't think it mattered. I handled it."

"What kind of human species allows for *this* sort of vampirism?" Sergei demands, as if anyone has the answer.

Adelia clears her throat, her voice tiny. "Who cares? How can we help her? She clearly has no idea what's going on."

I shove Adelia's presence to the back of my mind as Sergei points a finger at me. "You better hope she isn't angry at you when she wakes, because you helped Viorel make a powerful monster, Denendrius. And if she wakes looking for more than blood …"

Angry or not, *she's going to be impossible to control …*

I dart out of the room and head straight to the leather case Sergei hid in the false stone of a basement wall, clutching it tight as I return to the bedroom and scramble onto the bed with it. I take a vial of cure blood from the case.

"What are you doing?" Sergei demands.

"I can't kill her. I can't." I pop the cork from the vial. "But I can try making her human again."

"What's the point? You'll only have a handful of good years with her before she's older than you. Then what?" Sergei says.

With a steady hand, I lower her jaw to part her lips and pour the crimson into her mouth.

"It'll reset her," I counter. "Huarsar's mark was stripped from her when she died."

"But clearly not the effects of his blood if she's showing signs of abilities after you turned her," he warns.

The blood still struggles to make its way down her throat, so I take a few seconds to grab a needle from the medical kit and fill the syringe with a second vial of cure blood. "Perhaps this will wipe all signs of Huarsar from her body. If she's a fresh slate, I can mark her and try turning her again soon."

"You're fucking crazy," Sergei says.

"I love her," I snarl as I push the silver needle into her jugular, my strength—and her thirst-weakened body—enough that it pierces through without resistance. I ease the plunger down, emptying the cure into her.

I stare at her as I wait for it to work, for her *slow, slow* heart to push the cure through her veins and let it reach her core.

But the minutes are agonizing as I feel each one pass through me. I watch unblinking, unbreathing, for ten minutes without so much as a sign of change in her.

The cure should only take moments to start working . . .

"What have you done, Denendrius?" Sergei whispers beside me, his voice thick with hopelessness.

Slowly, like I know it won't make a difference, I empty another vial into the syringe and fill her veins with it.

"She's immune to the cure now," I acknowledge quietly—like I don't want her to hear—after another fifteen minutes with no change.

"Please, kill her," Sergei pleads again. "For your own sake, Denendrius. Cut off her fucking head."

Adelia squeaks in horror at Sergei's suggestion, darting back to the bedside as if ready to help me defend her.

How could I kill her now? *Marianna is my fate.* We're meant to be together, the entanglement of us done so by the gods. I love her, and I know once she wakes that no power in the world—even her own—can come between us.

"You fear for nothing," I tell him, smiling softly to myself as my gaze traces over her slumbering body. "This is meant to be. When she wakes, she'll remember everything. Marianna will remember how much I mean to her. She'll recall her past life as a child vampire. She'll know Huarsar was the villain of our love story, and she'll use her power to protect us."

Sergei stares at me like I'm a ghost. "It doesn't matter if she loves you, or if she knew you loved her, Denendrius. Or that turning her has removed Viorel's mark. You still left her to die in her anger. I'm sure you two will make up as always . . . but I still predict her fury when she first sees you upon waking."

"What do you suppose I do, then? Hm?" I dare to run my finger down the center of her torso and wait to see if a breath lifts her chest or stomach beneath my touch.

"Put her in the cell downstairs until she comes to her senses, before she tears the place apart," he demands, the desperation barely masked.

My hand curls into a fist on her stomach before I pull it away, pressing it into the mattress. Through gritted teeth, I snarl, "You want her to start immortality by waking up in a hard cell? Do you have any idea what that's like? If she doesn't wake up hating me, she's guaranteed to if she does so in a cell."

He motions with both his hands toward the nurse. "You want to deal with a newborn vampire capable of *this*?"

How can he not understand? My smile is shaky. "Think of the possibilities with this power. I'm sure that once she's awake, properly fed, and no longer terrified, she'll be able to control her abilities just as Huarsar does . . ." My smile steadies. "What if her power matches his? She'll be most upset with him. *He has our daughter.* We might actually have a chance to get her back. He won't expect her because he'll believe she's *dead*."

Sergei's shoulders lower, his hands limp at his sides as his glossy eyes study my face. His tone is heavy with despondence as he says, "Denendrius . . ."

I sigh and turn back to Marianna, elation and excitement flaring in my chest as I scoop her into my arms and press a hard kiss to my love . . .

To my fate.

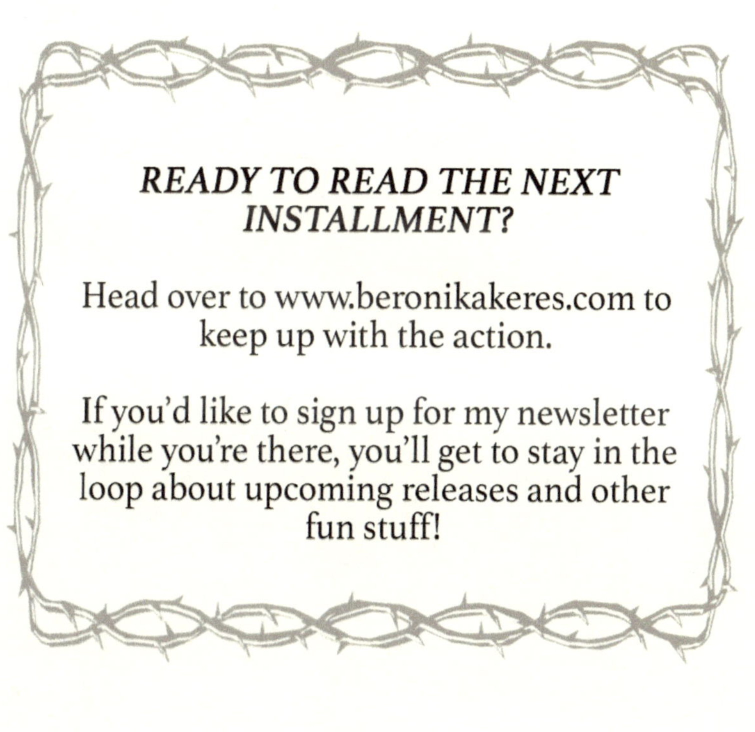

READY TO READ THE NEXT INSTALLMENT?

Head over to www.beronikakeres.com to keep up with the action.

If you'd like to sign up for my newsletter while you're there, you'll get to stay in the loop about upcoming releases and other fun stuff!

ABOUT THE AUTHOR

Beronika Keres is the Canadian author of the dark fantasy thriller series, Cracked Coffins. In the second grade, she decided she wanted to be an author and has spent her life honing her craft and pursuing her dream. She can often be found chasing plot bunnies and writing books.

When she's not writing, she enjoys spending time with her family or listening to some gothic rock, punk, or metal while working on her newest spike and patch-covered project.

To stay in the loop on future releases and exclusive content, visit www.beronikakeres.com and sign up for the newsletter. You can also connect with her on social media:

facebook.com/AuthorBeronikaKeres

instagram.com/beronikakeres

tiktok.com/@beronikakeres

bookbub.com/authors/beronika-keres

goodreads.com/BeronikaKeres